THE LEBANESE COLLECTION

Books by **David Cullen**

The Eye of Makarios
The Mesrine Conclusion
The Windsor Secret
Pick Up Sticks
Knock On My Door
The Baalbeck Decision
The Byblos Discovery
The Beirut Confession

Collections

The European Collection
The Eye of Makarios
The Mesrine Conclusion
The Windsor Secret
Bonus short story: *Shade*

The Lebanese Collection
The Baalbeck Decision
The Byblos Discovery
The Beirut Confession

DAVID CULLEN

THE LEBANESE COLLECTION

THE BAALBECK DECISION
THE BYBLOS DISCOVERY
THE BEIRUT CONFESSION

www.lulu.com/davidcullen
Facebook: DavidCullenBooks
Published by Culpro Books
an imprint of Cullen Productions

DAVID CULLEN

THE LEBANESE COLLECTION

THE BAALBECK DECISION

THE BYBLOS DISCOVERY

THE BEIRUT CONFESSION

The Lebanese Collection
First published 2015

A catalogue record of this book is available from the British Library.

These are works of fiction. Deceased historical characters have been used with respect. Fictional characters have been used with abandon.

ISBN: 978-0-9559911-8-9

www.lulu.com/davidcullen
Facebook: DavidCullenBooks
Published by Culpro Books
an imprint of Cullen Productions

Lebanon

The Baalbeck Decision   page   7
The Byblos Discovery   page 239
The Beirut Confession   page 499

A Glossary of Arabic and Hebrew Words and Phrases is on pages 729 to 733

THE BAALBECK DECISION

DAVID CULLEN

Culpro Books

There is probable cause to believe that the decision to assassinate former Prime Minister Rafik Hariri could not have been taken without the approval of top-ranked Syrian security officials and could not have been further organized without the collusion of their counterparts in the Lebanese security services.
- paragraph 124 of the Report of the International Independent Investigation Commission established pursuant to UN Security Council Resolution 1595 (2005)[the Mehlis Report]

Or could it...?

Clean feet leave no footprints
- Syrian proverb

Cast in order of appearance

Rafic Hariri [Abu Bahaa] – *Prime Minister of Lebanon 1992-98, 2000-2004.*
Basil Fleihan – *former Economy Minister of Lebanon.*
The Djinn – *a myth or reality?*
Marwan Mebarak – *a Captain of the Lebanese Army.*
A Corporal – *Lebanese Army.*
A Sergeant – *Lebanese Army.*
Colonel F – *Lebanese Army.*
Ghazi Kanaan [Abu Yo'roub] – *head of Syrian security in Lebanon 1982-2002, Syrian Interior Minister 2004-2005.*
An interrogator – *now dead.*
The Owner – *of many things, but not of what he wants.*
Al-Rajul [The Commander] – *a mercenary, an assassin.*
Samir Kassir - *professor, political commentator and journalist.*
George Hawi [Abu Anis] – *politician, former Secretary-General of the Lebanese Communist Party.*
Gebran Tueni – *newspaper editor and publisher, TV producer and host.*
Walid Eido [Abu Khaled] – *politician, former public prosecutor for North Lebanon.*
A member of the Syrian *mukhabarat.*
The Damascene – *a mercenary, an assassin.*
Maroun Khoury – *a Captain of the Lebanese Department of General Security.*
Yehya al-Arab [Abu Tarek] – *Head of Rafic Hariri's personal security.*
Jihad Merhi [Abu Samer] – *a Captain of the Lebanese Internal Security Force.*
Gisele Merhi – *wife of Jihad, formerly an agent of the Lebanese Department of General Security.*
Mama – *mother of Gisele.*
Deeb el-Gharib – *a Sergeant of the Lebanese Internal Security Force.*
Fadi Lattouf – *a Captain of the Civil Police of the Palestinian Security Force.*
A homosexual – *just doing business but went too far.*
Zahia Zalloum – *a Gatherer.*
Mohammed – *an earnest youth. Too earnest.*
Chadi – *friend of earnest Mohammed.*
Aboud – *an emissary, also* mukhabarat.
Karim The Butcher
Salin Namroud – *a young Palestinian.*
Kabalan Elb – *a young Palestinian.*

Elias Massoud – *a young Palestinian.*

Ahmad Adass – *a young Palestinian.*

Yazbek Nader – *a young Palestinian.*

Ibrahim - *a Lieutenant of the Civil Police of the Palestinian Security Force.*

Nada – *wife of Fadi Lattouf.*

Bassem el-Khazem - *a Sergeant of the Civil Police of the Palestinian Security Force.*

Selim Himo – *a Lieutenant of the Lebanese* Gendarmerie, *Bekaa Inquiry Brigade.*

A greasy man – *in charge of a warehouse in Beirut port.*

Major Ghanem – *Lebanese Internal Security Force.*

Mohamed Hassan – *an old refugee living in Bourj el-Barajneh.*

The young brother of Elias Massoud

FOREWORD
مقدمة واحدة

This book is a thriller, an adventure. It is not a book about 'the situation' in the Middle East, although politics play an integral part in the story. Where necessary I have included political narrative in order to assist in understanding the events.

There are many books written about the Middle East. To those wishing to understand more about the complexities of the situation in Lebanon in the late twentieth century, I can recommend Robert Fisk's *Pity The Nation* (Oxford University Press 1990/2001). For detailed insight, comment and facts on the events which form the backbone of *The Baalbeck Decision*, I recommend *Rafiq Hariri and the Fate of Lebanon* by Marwan Iskandar (Saqi Books 2006) and *Killing Mr Lebanon* by Nicholas Blanford (I.B. Tauris 2006).

Who killed Rafic Hariri? The answer to that question is unlikely ever to be known, scapegoats, tethered lambs and the suicided notwithstanding.

The Baalbeck Decision might be the answer.

Al-Haqiqa? Maybe. Murder is never what it seems.

Ma'ak,

David Cullen
ديفيد كولين

PROLOGUE
مقدمة اثنين

14 February 2005
5 Muharram 1426

Beirut, Lebanon

His socks were on fire.

Those who were first on the scene – those that were not killed or maimed, blinded or deafened in the one thousand kilogram TNT blast – said that the body of the large man lying in the road was unrecognisable. This was not true. They were simply in a state of disbelief – their minds unable to comprehend what their eyes surely saw.

Most of his blue suit had been blasted off, yet his undergarments were scorched but intact – death granting an important dignity to this Sunni Muslim. His hair – which had recently changed from his sixty year old 'salt and pepper' to pure silver, almost overnight – was gone, as were his eyebrows and moustache. His face was burnt yellow, his eyes swollen to slits.

He was lying on his back, but his arms were bent at the elbows and poking up into the air, his hands claw-like as if they were still gripping the steering wheel of his Mercedes S-600, which was ten metres back down Minet el-Hosn Street on the edge of the three metres deep crater outside the St George Hotel.

His left arm was on fire, yet the flames seemed gentle, almost reverential.

Someone started hitting the flames with an *abaya*, a cloak. With each whack, the body bounced, the last movements it would ever make. But at least the flames went out.

The area was black with smoke. Gunfire cracked rapidly, as if a manic battle was being waged. But there was no one to fire the guns. Most of those that would were dead. The gunfire was the seven hundred and fifty rounds of ammunition of the large man's bodyguards exploding in the flames.

Bodies were lying in the road. Parts of bodies were strewn over a wide area. Some pieces of human flesh were indeterminate, others – like the delicate woman's hand with carefully painted and manicured fingernails, rings still attached, one of the fingers still twitching, resting against the kerb – were obvious.

A boy, no more than a teenager, staggered out of the smoke, arms in front of him, two gaping holes where his eyes had been only seconds before.

Skeletons sat in the front of some of the cars of the shattered six vehicle convoy, their skin already burnt off by the intensity of the flames.

Other skeletons staggered out of the wrecked vehicles, hoping against hope that they could live. One, his clothes shredded to ribbons, called "Yasma, Yasma!", but his wife was in Geneva where he had left her the day before*.

There was blood, so much blood. Some of it cooking in the flames, smelling no different from the odours coming from the nearby *Spagheterria* restaurant.

And the large man's socks were on fire.

Across in Nejmeh Square, just a kilometre away, outside the Parliament building, The Djinn began to cry.

5 years earlier...

3 January 2000
26 Ramadan 1420

Dinnieh, Lebanon

It was a bright, sunny day, the sky an impressive blue for the time of year. But it was cold, so, so cold. The sun was fighting a losing battle against the snow on the ground up here in the mountains of northern Lebanon, and the forecast was for an overnight downfall of reinforcements for the crud.

Captain Marwan Mebarak sniffed at his own military analogy as he led his team of four back down the mountainside. He wished he could be pleased. No casualties and they had left five dead insurgents back in the caves. The clean-up team would remove the bodies for identification later, but it was unlikely their families would come forward to claim them for fear of retaliation.

It had started five days ago. The reports were that four members of the Syrian intelligence *mukhabarat* travelling in a car had been ambushed and killed by armed Sunni Islamists across the border up near Homs (Emesa). The Syrian security forces had begun a massive manhunt, leading – if the reports were to be believed – to a series of battles that had intensified as the days went on. In the end, eight hundred people had been arrested. It was, claimed *Al-Quds al-Arabi* (the Syrian branch of the Muslim Brotherhood), a huge over-reaction to what had been a simple local skirmish. It was even suggested that the original ambush had been staged by Syria to exaggerate the Sunni Islamist threat and show the United States that Syria was the only guarantor of stability in the region (in other words, to convince the US of the need for the permanent presence of Syrian forces in Lebanon, even if the Israeli army withdrew from the south).

Almost immediately, orders had been received at the Bahjat Ghanem North Region Army Command base in Tripoli. A group of up to three hundred Sunni militants known as *Takfir wal-Hijra* (Excommunication and Exodus), originally a splinter group of the Muslim Brotherhood, had established themselves in the Dinnieh mountains. They were to be routed.

Thirteen thousand Lebanese army troops, with tanks and artillery, had saturated

---

Basil Fleihan was to survive for sixty-four days before dying of 95% burns in the Percy Military Hospital, Clamart, Paris.

the area. Official figures would later claim that eleven soldiers and twenty-five rebels were killed in the fighting, with fifty-five rebels captured. The true figures, Captain Mebarak knew, were much more on both sides.

Mebarak turned to his men. They were walking down the mountainside behind him in approved anti-sniper wraggle-taggle formation, no straight lines, at least ten metres between each man, their tigerstripe commando camouflage uniform effective even in the snow. He nodded his approval.

"Is that it, *Naqeeb*?" asked the nearest man, an *'Areef Awwal* (Corporal First Class), slightly out of breath but not breaking stride. "Is that the end of them? Is it over?"

"I certainly hope so," replied Mebarak. Under his breath he said, "*Insha'Allah.*"

"I'm sorry, Captain? Did you say something?" The Corporal came level with him.

"No. *Maalesh.* It should be all over now. Time for a rest."

Only when he reached the temporary area command at the town of Aassoun thirty minutes later did he find out that he was wrong.

"*Naqeeb!* Captain!" A *Raqeeb* (Sergeant) stuck his head out of the communications truck as Mebarak approached.

"What?" Mebarak's boots crunched in the snow.

"The Colonel, sir. He has been trying to reach you!"

"Radio reception is never good up there, he knows that. What did he want?"

"He's on now, sir."

"Tell him mission completed. We did a good job. Needs to send the cleaners in now."

"Sir." The Sergeant disappeared back inside the truck.

As his team began to arrive back one by one, Mebarak went over to the nearest tree and unzipped his trousers.

"Sir?" It was the Sergeant again.

"For God's sake, man!" The Captain shouted over his shoulder. "Can't I have a piss in peace?"

"The Colonel wants you, sir. Urgent."

"One second. My old man takes precedence over that old man." Mebarak finished what he was doing, put himself away and zipped up his trousers.

There were two *Jundi 'Awwal* (Soldier First Class) in the truck, their green/brown US Woodland camouflage uniforms distinctly different from Mebarak's grey-green tigerstripe.

Mebarak took the proffered headphones and put them on. "*'Aqeed?*" he said into the microphone

"You on speaker?" asked Colonel F.

"No."

"Good. Just between us. There's some left in Kfar Habou."

"What?" Mebarak's mind flashed back to that morning's activities. About twenty gunmen had taken over the town of Kfar Habou, seven kilometres back down the mountainside on the road to Tripoli. Mebarak and his team, aided by army regulars, had been sent in. It had been bloody. Five gunmen were arrested and they had presumed the other fifteen were dead. Obviously they were not (sometimes you could not tell the gunmen from the locals – which was the rebels' intention).

"Lahoud* wants these Sunnis finished, and finished now," said the Colonel.

"Yes, sir."

"Do it."

5 January 2000
28 Ramadan 1420

Lebanese Broadcasting Corporation (LBC), Beirut

"The fighting in the al-Dinnieh region is over, the Guidance Department of the Army confirmed today. The fighting had been going on for nearly a week, with many rebels killed or captured. The army also sustained casualties. In the last major battle, in the town of Kfar Habou, four soldiers were killed and their commanding officer is reported missing."

10 January 2000
3 Shawal 1420

Aanjar, Bekaa Valley

The place on the western edge of the Bekaa Valley, just off the main Beirut to Damascus road and under five kilometres from the Syrian border, had been associated with power before.

It was founded as Haouch Moussa in the eighth century by Caliph al-Walid Ibn Abdel Malik who built himself a magnificent palace full of arches and colonnades, a mosque, Roman-style *hammam* (baths), a residential quarter and a souk with over sixty shops. The ruins can still be seen to this day.

Caliph al-Walid was the ruler of the Levant, and was based in Damascus prior to taking residence here in the Bekaa. He was of the Omayyads, the first great dynasty of the Arab Muslim empire. A warrior dynasty.

Haouch Moussa was chosen for its strategic importance, being near enough halfway between Damascus to the south-east, Beirut to the north-west and Sidon to the south-west.

Over twelve hundred years later, France built the town of Aanjar on malarial marshland immediately to the south of the ruins of the palace. It was built to house Armenian refugees from Alexandretta, a Syrian province which France had ceded to Turkey in 1939. The houses were built in an unaesthetic eastern European style, small and squat - but in compensation the French included the wide, tree-lined avenues they so love.

But even the warrior Caliph al-Walid would have been surprised, and possibly even a little intimidated, by the power that was to be wielded from Aanjar in the late

---

Until his election as President in 1998, Emile Lahoud was Chief of Staff of the Lebanese Army. Under the 1943 National Pact, and ratified by the 1990 Taef Accord, the President of Lebanon is always a Maronite Christian.

twentieth century. Because for nearly thirty years it was the base of the Syrian *mukhabarat* in Lebanon. And for twenty of those years it was the headquarters of the man who was dubbed the 'King of Lebanon', the man who effectively ruled the country as Syria's pro-consul. No political decisions were made in Lebanon without his agreement, even the election of the President. During the civil war, all militia leaders of whatever confession (sectarian persuasion) came under his influence. Through his web of agents and bureaucrats and politicians 'loyal to Syria', and backed by the Syrian military presence, and using his notorious charm and flattery, coupled with bribery and force, he gradually subdued the warring Lebanese militias. He manipulated the many-headed beast that is Lebanese politics, playing one side against the other, to ensure that Syria's interests always dominated. It was rumoured that he was as involved as anybody with the corruption that was rife in Lebanon after the civil war, receiving 'taxes' from the hashish growers in the Bekaa Valley and from the heroin and cocaine refiners in the remote reaches of Baalbeck and Hermel, not to mention the nightly plundering of fifty per cent of the takings from the Casino du Liban.

He was the head of Syrian intelligence in Lebanon: Abu Yo'roub, Brigadier General Ghazi Kanaan.

One and a half kilometres to the south of Aanjar, on an area of flat arable land, were several single-storey buildings, looking as they were meant to look: like a farm. But what was farmed there was not crops or animals: it was human blood.

The place was known as The Onion Factory, and it was Syria's main detention and interrogation centre in Lebanon. Local residents, working on their own farms, had long since learned to ignore the screams which could often be heard coming from the buildings. Hear nothing, see nothing, say nothing. For if they did not, the next screams they heard might be their own.

It was a cold Lebanese winter's night, but up above the sky was clear and riddled with an impossible number of stars. Light could be seen coming from behind one of the small shuttered windows of one of the buildings, but there was no sound. No screams.

For the man who now sat bound and naked on the metal chair in the centre of the large shed would never scream. Never. No matter what the provocation. No matter what was done to him.

His hands were taped behind him. His legs were taped to the chair legs, so that they were apart and his genitals were exposed. His feet were in a trough filled with rank, filthy liquid which might at one time have been water. His eyes were bound with an old rag. His tanned body was streaked with dirt and sweat. He stank of body odour, blood, piss and shit.

There were six other men in the room. Four were normal foot soldiers of the *mukhabarat*, dressed in their ubiquitous 'uniform' of black leather jackets, light cotton trousers and sandals. Another, the interrogator, had replaced his sandals with farm boots, and instead of his jacket he wore a long, rubber apron, streaked with the dried blood of hundreds of souls. He wore a face mask over his nose and mouth, and gardening goggles. In his hand he held the thirty centimetre long soldering iron which he had just removed from the subject's anus.

The sixth man was Ghazi Kanaan.

"I am a reasonable man," Kanaan gently removed the rag from the subject's eyes with his fingertips and dropped it on the floor. "Why will you not co-operate? All I want to know is your name."

The prisoner blinked his one good eye. The other was swollen shut.

"Is that too much to ask?" continued Kanaan. "Just your name. Then we can be friends. I can be a good friend, you know."

Still nothing. The one good eye stared at Kanaan.

"What were you doing there?"

Nothing.

"Were you seeking refuge? Or were you looking for someone? Who? You can talk to me, you know. I will not harm you. I just want to know. Then I can help you. Were you looking for someone? Perhaps I know where they are."

Nothing.

Then Kanaan said, "What would someone like you be doing at Ein Hilweh?"

This time there was a reaction. Slight, but a reaction nevertheless. The one good eye flickered. The swollen lips moved. A sound came out.

Kanaan smiled. "What was that, my friend? What did you say?"

The lips moved again. The mouth opened. And a bloody stump of tooth fell out onto the prisoner's chest.

"What did you say?" Kanaan ignored the red drool rolling down the prisoner's chin. He came closer, pretending concern, cocking his left ear. "Talk to me."

"Nahr."

"What?"

"Al-Bared."

"Did you say Nahr al-Bared?"

"Nahr."

Kanaan smiled. His ruse at naming the wrong Palestinian refugee camp where the prisoner had been arrested had worked, getting a reaction. "What were you doing there?"

"Don't know."

"What is your name?"

"Don't know."

"Please tell me then we can move on."

Suddenly the prisoner shook his head, nostrils flaring, snot spraying. His one good eye was wild. He started to shout. "Don't know, don't know, don't know! Sunni! Don't know! Kill! Kill!"

Kanaan stepped back. He looked at the interrogator. "Is he a lunatic?"

The interrogator pulled down his face mask. "Could be, sir. He has said nothing of sense." He bent down and put the soldering iron on the floor, picking up a welding torch.

Kanaan looked at the prisoner, who had now quietened down again. "Who are you?"

Nothing.

Kanaan nodded to the interrogator, who took a cigarette lighter from his pocket.

"I have lost interest," said Kanaan. "Disappear him." Then he turned and walked away, back outside to the black limousine that was waiting for him.

In the shed, there was a whoosh as the interrogator lit the end of the welding torch. The flame was instantly orange.

Outside, the car pulled away.

The interrogator walked forward, the noise and heat of the torch increasing as he came closer.

Suddenly the prisoner began to laugh. Not madly, not wildly, just humour-filled laughter, as if he had just shared a joke.

"You'll be laughing out of your arse in a minute, scumbag," sneered the interrogator. "It's wide enough."

The prisoner's good eye looked directly at his torturer. His cheeks moved, almost in a smile. He spoke, clearly and distinctly, with just a gentle hiss through the missing teeth. "Smokeless fire."

"What? What did you say?" Was that just a hint of worry in the interrogator's eyes?

"Smokeless fire," repeated the prisoner. "Born out of smokeless fire. You shouldn't have taped my hands, you should have knotted them. I would have been powerless then."

The interrogator's eyes widened, this time in genuine fear.

Moments later he was screaming.

PART ONE
الجزء الأول

FOUNDATION
الأساس

26 August 2004
8 Rajab 1425

Mediterranean Sea
15 miles off the southern coast of Cyprus 0:00

The yacht could not been seen at midnight.

The *Heliopolis* was a two hundred foot tri-deck, with a tonnage in excess of five hundred. Built by Oceanco Holland and registered in the Cayman Islands, amongst other things it had six state rooms, an integral swimming pool and games area, a skylounge taking up the complete upper deck, the expected 'mod cons' for an indulged and indulgent class of person, and superior quarters for a crew of five. And a helicopter pad aft. Discreetly hidden behind bulwarks on the top of the vessel were a range of aerials, antennae and satellite dishes for broadcasting, receiving – and listening.

It could have been a rich man's toy, which was the impression it wanted to give. In fact it was the home of the owner who, although he had seven passports which showed he was American, British, French, Israeli, Lebanese, Saudi and Syrian, lived on the yacht permanently. The last time his feet had touched 'dry land' was eight years ago.

The man in the wheelchair grimaced as he waited alone in the dark on the balcony of the upper deck. Eight years ago was the last time his feet would touch anything – because he no longer had any. Not since the incident. Eight years ago. When he had been blown up in his car.

Lucky to be alive, they said. The bomb had been attached too far forward underneath the Audi Sports Coupé. He had 'only' lost both legs at the knee, and his manhood had been irreversibly damaged. He had nearly bled out before someone had realised that one of the blackened bodies in the wreck of the car was still alive. But they had saved him.

And the irony of it all was that he was not the intended victim. He was collateral damage. He had owned the car for less than thirty minutes – a gift from the intended victim, the man he had gone to see, to challenge, to criticise, to ask why, *why*, he had agreed the 1996 April Accord with Israel ('The Grapes of Wrath Understanding') just nine days after the Qana massacre when Israeli artillery had killed one hundred and six people in the UN compound. The man who had visited him in hospital a week after the blast and given him a personal cheque for twenty million US dollars 'in compensation' and promised him anything he wished for to make his life easier.

He wished for a boat. And he had been given one.

But there was one thing he could not be given, not even by his billionaire benefactor: he wanted his wife back. But even Rafic Hariri could not raise people from the dead.

Lucky to be alive, they said. Alive with no wife, no legs and no manhood.

Alive to spend the rest of his days in mourning.

And in a wheelchair.

His reverie was interrupted by the lights on the helicopter pad suddenly bursting on. They must have received word in the control room that his guest was close by.

Only then did he hear the faint rapid percussion of the rotor blades, sounding like the distant retort of a machine gun. From the south-east two faint lights appeared in the black sky, but he had to strain to make out the silhouette of the Bell 206-B3 JetRanger.

With a well-practised flick of his left hand, he turned the wheelchair around and moved quickly back into the skylounge. Small LEDs in the floor illuminated his way over to the lift. The door was already open, and as he entered he said "Office", and the lift door closed silently.

He was sitting behind his desk when the visitor was shown in, the wheelchair invisible behind the vast slab of solid oak that was the desk top and the equally solid modesty board at the front. The floors were also uncovered oak, to accommodate the wheelchair, but two-metre high uplighting around the walls gave the impression that the room was more intimate and cosy than it was.

The man who was shown into the room was himself two metres tall. Upwards, he wore expensive trainers, faded blue jeans, and a black v-neck T-shirt under a leather jacket. On his head he wore a white *gutrah* (Arabic headdress) held in place by a black *ogal*. Underneath could be seen the outline of his *thagiyah* which held his hair in place. The *gutrah* covered his nose and mouth and was swept over his left shoulder; only his dark eyes were visible.

Al-Rajul said nothing as he stood in front of the desk and looked at the man sitting behind it.

The Owner nodded at the crew member by the door, who nodded back and then went out, closing the door behind him.

For a moment neither man spoke. Then The Owner said, *"Al-salaam 'aalaykum."* His voice was high, a little nasally, some might say effeminate.

Al-Rajul raised his black eyebrows. *"Marhaba."* In contrast to The Owner, his voice was low.

"Tfaddal?" The Owner held out his hand to a table on the right which was adorned with fruit and juices.

"Laa." Al-Rajul shook his head.

"Or something stronger perhaps?" The Owner pointed to a glass-fronted liquor cabinet.

"Laa. But thank you."

"Please sit down."

Al-Rajul sat in the plush leather armchair at one o'clock to the desk.

"It has taken me a long time to find you," said The Owner.

"As it should. I am found only when I want to be." The deep voice was not muffled by the *gutrah*.

"And you wanted to be?"

"I am found only when I want to be."

The Owner nodded thoughtfully. *"D'accord."* Their eyes touched for a few seconds. Then The Owner asked, "You know who I am?"

The eyes creased in a smile. "I have done my research. I know who you used to be."

It was The Owner's turn to smile, nodding again. *"Touché.* And how very true. For eight years I have been nobody."

"For eight years the world has thought you were as good as dead."

This time a bitter laugh burst from The Owner's lips. "As good as dead! How right the world is. Never, ever, underestimate the world, *rafee.*"

"I never have. Provided the world does not underestimate me."

The Owner leant forward and opened a silver box on the desk top. He turned it towards the visitor. "Do you indulge?"

"And take this down so that the cameras - which I am sure you have hidden here - can record my face? No."

The Owner turned the box back and took out a large cheroot. He lit it from a ornamental silver lighter. His voice was almost sad. "There are cameras, yes, you are right. But they are not on. Not for this conversation."

"Why?" asked Al-Rajul.

Instead of replying directly, The Owner asked "What do you know about Rafic Hariri?"

Rafic Bahaa el deen al-Hariri, the Prime Minister of Lebanon. A Sunni Muslim, as all Prime Ministers must be under the National Pact and the Taef Accord.

Born in Sidon, Lebanon, in 1944 to a modest family, he studied business administration and obtained a degree in accounting from the Arab University, Beirut, in the late 1960s. He went to Saudi Arabia, where he became a teacher and then a professional accountant, then started investing in business on his own account.

It was the time of the oil-boom, and Saudi was the place to be. In 1976 Hariri was in partnership with a Palestinian contractor. Hariri was already known and respected as a hard worker and a deeply religious man (he never failed to pay his zakat *(paying part of his income as a religious obligation)), and the partnership was given a contract by King Khaled to construct a new hotel and conference centre in Taef, the Saudi summer capital in the mountains. But there was one snag: the contract had to be completed from scratch within ten months.*

Hariri knew that the rest of his career depended on this single contract. The project was brought in a week ahead of schedule.

And Hariri was made for life.

He achieved the good graces of King Khaled and gained the support of Crown Prince Fahd (who himself became King in 1980). Hariri bought Oger, *a French construction firm on the verge of bankruptcy. From then on, it was used by the Saudi Royal Family to undertake all of their important construction work. In the five years between 1977 and 1982, the value of this work exceeded ten billion US dollars.*

Hariri wanted to give back to his community, to make his own personal zakat. *He developed major educational facilities in Lebanon, including the Hariri Foundation (originally the Islamic Institute for Culture and Higher Education).*

In 1982, Lebanon was into its seventh year of its fifteen year 'civil war'. After Israel withdrew from its occupation of Beirut in September, Hariri was asked by President Amine Gemayel to help restore the city. He secured aid from King Fahd and contributed twelve million dollars of his own money to clear up the streets of the destroyed city, to remove the rubble, get rid of the wild animals, help the displaced people, restore the water, re-open the roads – at the very minimum.

He became the envoy of the Saudi Royal Family, and gradually achieved international recognition for his humanitarian efforts.

Hariri was, first and foremost, a businessman and a philanthropist, but the complex tendrils of Lebanese politics were enveloping him. And once they envelope you, they will not let you go.

He was the Saudi's 'strong man' in the country. The Palestine Liberation Organisation had effectively collapsed and there was no Sunni leadership in the country to oppose and counteract the rising Shi'ite Amal militia.

Hariri was the force behind the Saudi-inspired Taef Conference in 1989; it is also strongly suggested that Hariri wrote the first draft of the Taef Accord, which brought the warring Lebanese factions together and put an end to the 'civil war'.

In 1992, with the support of the Saudis and under Syria's military 'occupation', Hariri became Prime Minister. In 1993, he oversaw the birth of Solidère (Société Libanaise pour le Développement et Reconstruction), the company that is rebuilding Beirut.

But six years is a long time in politics – especially Lebanese politics. Hariri had gotten along well with the Syrians, he had even been their friend, but he was opposed to the Syrian 'candidate' (choice) of Head of Army Emile Lahoud as President; Hariri supported the not-popular President Elias Hrawi, whose term in office he had been instrumental in extending by three years in 1995 through an amended constitution.

Through his opposition to Lahoud, Hariri had displeased the Old Guard of the Levant, those that really pulled the strings. And so the character-assassination of Hariri had commenced: the criticisms, the allegations of corruption (that everything Hariri did was first and foremost to line his own pockets), the true fact that the Lebanese public debt had increased nearly ten-fold in the time Hariri was in office – overlooking the fact that it might have increased more without him at the helm, ignoring that he was rebuilding the shattered country and dismissing the fact that he was trying to drag the most sectarian-divided country in the world out of civil war and into the twenty-first century.

Hariri wanted electoral reform and change in the administration of Lebanon. What he got from his vociferous opponents was constant, poisonous questioning and vilification.

In 1998, unable to extend Hrawi's term in office even more, Hariri watched as Emile Lahoud was duly elected President – and Hariri 'did not accept' the nomination to continue as Prime Minister.

But he remained active in Lebanese politics, and in 2000 – despite Lahoud being President, despite the continuing and constant smear campaign against him – he returned as Prime Minister. It would become an era of regeneration but tension, with the Prime Minister and President constantly in disagreement and often openly hostile.

"And it remains so to this day," concluded Al-Rajul.

The Owner was quiet, his round head nodding gently. Then he said, "Impressive. You are an educated man. That was almost unbiased." He finished his cheroot and spoke through the smoke. "You like Hariri?"

"I respect Hariri. I am not Sunni."

"What are you?"

The eyes stared. "I am nothing."

The Owner leant forward and stubbed the butt of the cheroot into a crystal ashtray. "We are all something, *mon ami.*"

"If you say so."

The Owner took another cheroot out of the box and lit it. He said, "Ten million US dollars."

There was no reaction in the visitor's eyes. "What about it?"

"That is what I want to give you. Half of it right here. Right now. Tonight. You can take it with you or I can have it transferred."

"For what?"

The Owner looked at the smouldering tip of his cheroot. Then he said, "For ten million dollars I want you to kill Rafic Hariri."

26 September 2004
11 Sha'ban 1425

Baalbeck, Lebanon 20:00

The four men were stiff when they climbed out of the Mitsubishi Pajero after the sixty kilometre journey from Beirut. The SUV had tinted windows with a one-way view, so they could see where they were going but they themselves could not be seen inside. Which was probably safer all round. Nobody could witness the collection of individuals being transported against their will.

Each had received a phone call that day, 'inviting' them on the trip. They were instructed where to be, at what time – and to come alone and tell no one. They had been picked up one by one from different locations in the city by two urbane, very polite but ultimately taciturn men in leather jackets, light trousers and sandals. Syrian *mukhabarat*. Each had been surprised when they saw their fellow travellers. But knowing how these things worked, they had said nothing to each other on the journey.

Three of the men knew each other well. The first to be picked up was Samir Kassir, the handsome, stubbled forty-four year old professor, political commentator and journalist. A Christian Orthodox, he was a strong and vocal advocate of the rights of Palestinians (his father was a Lebanese Palestinian) and of democracy in Lebanon and Syria.

The second to be picked up was George Hawi, the white-haired, moustached sixty-six year old politician and former secretary-general of the Lebanese Communist Party. Born into a Greek Orthodox Christian family, he was a professed atheist. That very month with Samir Kassir he had formed the Democratic Left Movement, a group of leftist intellectuals advocating social democracy for Lebanon and an end to Syrian hegemony.

The third man was Gebran Tueni, the smooth, dark-haired, moustached forty-seven year old Chief Editor and publisher of *An-Nahar* (The Day) newspaper and TV producer and host. A Greek Orthodox Christian, he was a long-time political critic of the Syrian presence in Lebanon.

The fourth man was different from the others. He was Walid Eido, the dapper, greying, balding, clean-shaven sixty-two year old former public prosecutor for north Lebanon who had been elected to parliament four years previously. A Sunni Muslim, he was a close friend of Prime Minister Rafic Hariri.

Now out of the vehicle, the men looked around, puzzled. They knew where they were, but why had they been brought here?

"This way please," said one of their escorts, indicating that they should follow him through the entrance to the temples. The other escort brought up the rear as they passed a long, black limousine that was parked as close to the gate as it could get without blocking the entrance.

Baalbeck, the Roman City of The Sun, is one of the major historical sites of Lebanon. The iconic image of the six pillars of the Temple of Jupiter, with or without the snow-capped Mount Lebanon range as a backdrop, is the country's second national symbol after the cedar tree. Little remains of the Temple of Jupiter except the six pillars, but the more intact outer courtyard and inner sacrificial courtyard hint at the majesty that was once this monument to Baal, the Phoenician warrior god of sun, thunder and lightning.

The later, smaller temples of Venus and Mercury (the latter erroneously known today as the Temple of Bacchus) have survived their two thousand years better, with the Temple of Mercury almost completely intact. It was towards this temple that the four men were now led.

It was sunset, and the site was closing for the day. The few straggling tourists heading for the exit paid no heed to the six men walking inwards. The late summer Lebanese evening was warm and all four men were in shirtsleeves, no jackets.

They reached the temple and began to walk up the steps towards the doorway with its friezes of corn sheaves, poppies, ivy and vine leaves. On the keystone above was a carving of an eagle carrying garlands of pomegranates and cedar cones in its beak, and with the thunderbolts of Jupiter and the caduceus of Mercury in its talons.

"Please, we wait here," said the escort as they reached the top. He stayed with the four men, the other escort was positioned down at the bottom of the steps.

The 'guests' turned around, surveying the ruins. At one o'clock in front of them was the small Temple of Venus. At eight o'clock behind them was the Temple of Jupiter. And immediately to their left was the sacrificial courtyard.

"Poignant, perhaps?" George Hawi was the first of them to speak.

"What is?" asked Gebran Tueni.

Samir Kassir gave an ironic laugh. "The sacrificial courtyard! Do you think, *mes amis*? Is it our turn?"

"They would not dare," said Walid Eido.

"You? No," agreed Kassir. "They would not dare to touch you, *akh*. But the rest of us..."

"Too symbolic," said Tueni.

"And too complicated," Hawi sighed. "For them."

They became aware of some shadowy figures approaching the steps down below from the way they had just come. Had whoever it was been waiting in that limo, watching them pass?

There were three figures. Two stayed at the bottom of the steps with the second escort, the third began to walk up on his own.

"My God..." said Hawi lowly as he saw who it was. "I don't believe it."

"Not your God," said Kassir. "You don't have one. And this is no God."

"But it is perhaps a devil," said Eido.

"A devil we have not seen for two years," said Tueni.

"No." There was anger in Hawi's voice as it grew louder. "Not *a* devil. *The* devil."

Part of the third step from the top had broken away sometime over the years to create a deeper, wider section of the fourth step. The figure stopped on this ledge and looked up at the four men.

"Messieurs. Massah el-khair," said Ghazi Kanaan.

The rule of Brigadier General Ghazi Kanaan as head of Syrian intelligence in Lebanon had lasted for twenty years. In 2002 he had been summoned back to Syria to become the overall head of Syria's political intelligence. Sold as a promotion, it was regarded by many – including Kanaan himself – as a demotion. Certainly in Damascus he was closer to the seat of power, but even here the old adage of 'keep your enemies closer still' applied. He was a powerful Alawite, and the powerful Alawite rulers of Syria did not want another powerful Alawite – who was regarded on a 'better the devil you know' basis by the US and its allies – potentially being groomed to take over should something sudden and unexpected happen to their new, young and still relatively fresh President.

And now here he was, in the penumbra of evening, in Baalbeck.

Kanaan climbed up the last three steps and nodded for the escort to leave them.

"Thank you for coming," he said to all four men.

Eyebrows were raised. As if they had any choice! The men said nothing, letting what they saw sink in. Kanaan was dressed in denim jeans and a loose white shirt, not the suave suit and tie that he had worn constantly when he ruled the country. He looked older, much older than the addition of the two years since he had last been seen in Lebanon. Something had taken its toll on him.

He began to walk around the men like a potential buyer at a slave auction. "Four thorns," he spoke as he walked. "Four out of the many, many thorns in my side, in the side of Syria. But the most vociferous."

"What are you doing here?" asked Eido, his body turning to face Kanaan.

"Come to that, what are *we* doing here?" asked Kassir.

Kanaan had done a complete circle around them. He stopped and after a moment sat down with a sigh on one of the fallen columns. "But even thorns have thorns. You are thorns in my side, I am a thorn in other people's sides."

"What the hell are you talking about?" snapped Hawi.

"Are you well?" asked Tueni. "You look... haggard."

"Haggard!" mocked Kanaan. "Haggard! In the name of Allah the most merciful, you would be haggard too! I nearly had to call off our meeting. Do you know what happened today? Today. In my own backyard." He raised his hands and ran them down either side of his face.

"No, we haven't seen the news," sneered Kassir. "We have been otherwise engaged during the last two and a half hours as guests of Syria."

"Today," said Kanaan, "in al-Zahera, Damascus, the Jews detonated a car bomb. They murdered Izz el-Deen Khalil, the Hamas Commander."

Hawi shrugged. "So? What is that to do with us?"

"To do with you, Abu Anis? Nothing. It is nothing to do with you. But," Kanaan began to shout, "it explains why I am looking fucking haggard!" He stopped, breathing hard. Then he said in a normal but still edgy voice, "Do you know what they want me to do, what Assad wants me to do?" He looked up at the four men, as if they had any idea of the answer. "He wants me to become Interior Minister. To counter and eradicate this threat in our own country. And we all know what happens if I cannot do that."

"And you have brought us here for what?" said Hawi. "Our sympathy?"

Kanaan narrowed his eyes. "Time was I would have sent you to The Onion Factory for a remark like that."

"Yes? And? What?" Now it was Hawi who was shouting. "Time was if I was a much younger man I would strangle you with my bare hands. You bring us here against our will - "

"You were asked to come."

"Bullshit. What for? A meeting of the Abu Yo'roub Appreciation Society? And why here, why Baalbeck? Such a beautiful place. But this is Hizbullah land. The Ain Bourdai training base is just down the road, and over there is the Sheik Abdallah barracks*. Is this supposed to intimidate us?"

"George, George," Kassir took Hawi by the arm, gripping and ungripping his elbow in warning. There were four armed *mukhabarat* at the bottom of the steps.

"I – I - ..." With a huge sigh Hawi said, "This man makes me so angry. Why can they not just leave us alone?"

"I know... I know." Kassir nodded in sympathy.

Suddenly Kanaan said, "I want your help. I have a decision to make."

In the hastening darkness, four sets of brows furrowed. The men were stunned for a moment. Then Eido said, "*You* want *our* help?"

"To decide, yes."

"What on earth is going on here?" asked Tueni. "What are you up to, Kanaan?"

Kanaan got up and again started the menacing walk around the men. Then he stopped, as if he had made up his mind about something. "Sit, sit," he invited calmly, indicating two other fallen columns at angles to the one he had been sitting on. Reluctantly, the men sat down, two on each. Kanaan resumed sitting on his column. "'*eeh!*" he called to the guards down below. One came quickly up the steps, hand inside his leather jacket.

All four of the guests tensed. Which one would be shot first?

The guard's hand came out of his jacket - with a candle. A lighter was produced from his trousers. He ran the flame over the bottom of the candle and then stuck it on the column between Kanaan and the men. He lit the wick, stayed to make sure it was alight, and then walked away back down the steps.

The light from the candle made it easier to see, but it also cast small sinister shadows over Kanaan's face.

"One month ago," explained Kanaan. "One month ago to this very day. There was a meeting in Damascus."

"Don't I know it!" snorted Eido.

He was interrupted by Kanaan's raised hand. "I was not present, but I have a transcript of it. So you know what happened, Abu Khaled?"

"I have been told," nodded Eido.

"By Abu Bahaa?"

"By his Head of Security."

"And what have you been told?"

Eido looked from one man to the other. "We all know that Hariri and Lahoud hate each other and that Lahoud wants an extension of his presidency, just like Hrawi got in ninety-five. Hariri opposes this, he wants a new President he can work with.

The storage facility for kidnapped hostages, including Westerners, during the civil war.

You – Syria – want Lahoud to stay in office, for so-called continuity in the region now that the US has imposed sanctions on you. President Assad called the Prime Minister to Damascus to inform him of Syria's decision and to ask him to - " he made air quotes with his fingers, " – clarify his position. He said to Hariri, 'This extension is going to happen or I will break Lebanon over your head.' And he threatened to 'get' him and his family. The next day, the Prime Minister agreed to the amendment of the constitution to allow the extension of Lahoud's presidency."

Kanaan leant forward with his elbows on his knees, resting his chin on his steepled fingers. "And do you think that really happened? That the President of Syria, a very honourable man, would use such threatening language?"

Eido did not reply.

"What about the rest of you?" Kanaan looked from one to the other. They remained silent also.

Kanaan sat upright, causing a draft which made the candle flicker. "There are plots hatching. Wheels within wheels, thorns in the side of thorns. Hariri is the lynch-pin in all of this. His fate is the future of the entire region, perhaps beyond. I have an involvement in the matter, and there is something I must decide."

"What are you saying?" asked Kassir.

"The people of Lebanon. Where are they?" Kanaan looked around theatrically and gave a huge shrug. Then he looked back at the men. "Why here they are." He held his arms wide, almost in an embrace. "There are four of them. The biggest thorns in Syria's side along with Rafic Hariri."

The men were staring in disbelief. Had the great dictator of Lebanon gone mad?

"There are two options," continued Kanaan. "There are people, not only from the West, that want Bashar al-Assad removed as President of Syria. But what is the alternative? The Alawites are a minority in the country yet they rule – because there is, no longer, any opposition, no viable alternative. There cannot be an alternative to the Alawites. But there can be an Alawite alternative to Assad."

"You," Hawi nodded as if it had all become clear.

"I did not say that. Syria cannot be invaded at this time, not by anyone, especially with what is happening in Iraq. Regime change must be more subtle. It must be seen to come from within, even if it doesn't. One idea is to destabilise Greater Syria." (Walid Eido flinched at the all-inclusive term for the area which included the land-mass of a non-existent Lebanon.) "To commit an act so outrageous, so unexpected, that the finger of blame will be pointed directly at Assad. That he will have to go or be got rid of by any means. With the reports of Assad's animosity towards him being exaggerated, even fabricated from scratch, one idea is to kill Hariri - "

"What!" Eido jumped up.

"Sit down, sit down." Kanaan flapped his hand. "To kill Hariri spectacularly, in public, in broad daylight and have the mark of Syria all over the atrocity."

"This is outrageous." Eido was attracting attention from the guards below. Hawi tugged his arm to make him sit down.

"After which other enemies of Syria will be removed one by one."

"Other enemies...?" Hawi let the question hang. They all knew who Kanaan was talking about.

"We are not Syria's enemies," said Kassir.

"But it is seen that way." Kanaan paused. Then he went on. "Assad will go, with direct evidence pointing at him and with certain video and audio tapes they have of him plotting Hariri's murder and authorising the removal of the other enemies."

"Who are *they*?" asked Tueni. He was not answered.

"It is wonderful what they can do with impersonators, body doubles and this new thing, CGI," said Kanaan. "Assad doesn't even know he is being set up." Before he could be interrupted yet again, he went on "But there is an alternative. Let the thorn linger, let it grow, turn septic. Now there is Resolution 1559*, and the world wants to interfere again in Lebanese affairs. If we allow Hariri to go on unhindered, if we encourage it, his very presence, his plans for Lebanon, together with UN interference, will quickly push Syria out of the country, Lahoud or no Lahoud. And Assad will still have to go, the UN will make sure of it. Either way Syria has a new president."

"And Kanaan is the winner," sneered Kassir.

"It is not to do with Kanaan. I have not said I will take over from Assad."

"But you have not said you will not," observed Hawi.

"That is up to others."

"Who's backing you, Kanaan?" persisted Tueni.

Kanaan's famous temper flashed. "That is not for you to ask!" He leant back away from the flame. His face was now completely in shadow. "But I have a decision to make. So, why have I brought you here?" Although the question was rhetorical, he still paused. "I want to warn you. I want to *ask* you. To lower your profile. Stop your attacks on Syria, mute them, tone them down. Let whatever is going to happen, happen. It will benefit Lebanon."

"Let you kill Hariri!" Eido was beside himself.

"I have not said Hariri will be killed. I have told you that is a decision to be made." He was quiet, his hard eyes on the men. He continued. "Stop making yourselves targets. Take the attention away from yourselves. Distance yourself. Then there will be no need for... final measures. Hariri has a lot of enemies, I know that there are others who are after him." He moved forward once more so that the flickering candlelight again painted his face. "To kill Hariri, to let Hariri be killed by somebody else, or to protect him...?" Kanaan licked his fingers and rubbed out the flame of the candle. In the darkness he said, "And that decision I have just made."

---

* *Adopted earlier that month, the UN Security Council Resolution demanded a withdrawal of Syrian troops from Lebanon, the disarming of Hizbullah and a free and fair Lebanese presidential election. Even in Lebanon, many thought it was an unwarranted intrusion in Lebanese affairs.*

27 September 2004
12 Sha'ban 1425

Old City, Damascus, Syria 19:00 - 22:30

The Damascene sat alone in an alcove in the steam room of the bathhouse, the *Hammam al-Selesa* near the Umayyad Mosque. He wore nothing but a towel around his waist and old flip-flops on his feet, so the scars and long-healed burns and gouges on his muscular body were visible, had anybody been around and had they cared to look. Which they weren't and they didn't.

His long hair was wet and stuck to his shoulders and down his back. His tanned face wore a day's stubble.

The room was dim. Grubby white tiles stretched halfway up the wall and then gave way to light blue paint, with damp patches here and there as if it was fresh plaster waiting to go off. Equally grubby light blue tiles formed the seating ledge in the alcove and spread out across the floor. He was glad the soles of his feet were covered.

The steam was more subtle than might have been expected, gradually creating cleansing heat and sweat from within the body rather than assailing the skin from outside. The place stank of the odours of men, even though he was the only one there.

He folded his arms and waited.

On cue five minutes later, the door opened and another towelled figure walked in. This body was older, the skin lax, showing the greyness of age.

"Peace be upon you," said the new arrival as he came over and sat down in the alcove.

The Damascene inclined his head, not saying what he wanted to say, not doing what he wanted to do – which was to reach out and rip this man's head from his body. But that would serve no purpose, not right now. Four years ago, maybe. But the time would come again.

"You are well?" asked Ghazi Kanaan.

"You are interested?" asked The Damascene.

"I like my prized weapons to remain in top condition," Kanaan patted The Damascene's right thigh, impressed at its solidity. "Good. You still train."

"You wanted something?"

Kanaan removed his hand. "I have been trying to contact you for the last month. You have been elusive."

"I have been around, here and there, back and forth. I do have a life outside of the jobs I do for you."

Kanaan sniffed condescendingly. "You have a life because I say you have a life, remember? Ah but you don't, do you? Remember? Not all of it."

The Damascene said nothing.

"As it transpires," Kanaan went on, "the timing now is perfect. I have been trying to contact you to prepare you for an assignment, but I did not know quite what that assignment was going to be. I do now." He rubbed his hands over his face as he began to sweat. "You like these places, these bathhouses?"

"Yes. They serve a purpose. They cleanse the body. And the soul."

"Is your soul clean?"

"As clean as yours, Abu Yo'roub."

Kanaan gave a gentle laugh. Then he said, "The usual terms? One hundred thousand US dollars?"

And I allow you to live, thought The Damascene. He said, "It all depends what for."

"Oh, does it now?" Kanaan did not notice the other man's fingers flex. "Perhaps this time I should ask you for a discount."

"Why should you ask for that?"

"This time it is different. A decision has been made."

The Damascene sat on his hands. "Abu Yo'roub, what are you talking about?"

The famed Kanaan anger and derision flashed in the older man's eyes. But he bit off his trenchant response as The Damascene turned full on to him and he could see the raw hole where the younger man's left ear had once been.

"It – it is of no concern," said Kanaan. "But this time it is not the usual request."

"So you don't want me to kill the President? So what is it? Do you want me to rob a bank?"

"Facetiousness does not suit you. There are plots afoot. Plots within plots, wheels within wheels, thorns in the side of thorns."

The Damascene frowned. Was Kanaan going mad?

"These are not your concern," continued Kanaan. "You must be your usual invisible self. You cannot be seen to do what I am about to ask, and certainly the request can never, ever be known to have come from me. No one would believe it anyway."

"You are speaking in riddles." A waft of garlic blew into Kanaan's face as The Damascene spoke lowly, mockingly. "Riddles within riddles." He turned away in disdain and stood up. As he did so, the towel fell away from his waist and he stood there stark naked. From the neck down, there was not a hair on his body.

It was not the first time Kanaan had seen him naked. He was impressed by, and very envious of, the physique - despite the scars. He stared as The Damascene bent and picked up his towel, putting it back around his waist.

"There are plots to kill Rafic Hariri," said Kanaan. "I have reliable intelligence to that effect. There is one in particular, from an unusual but unclarified source."

The Damascene swept his hair forward across the left side of his face. "I think Hariri's death would suit the purposes of Syria just fine."

"No, it would not."

"But it would suit your purposes."

Kanaan sighed. "In some respects, possibly. But that is not the road I am travelling. It suits my purpose that he stays alive. For now. Your job, my dear *Naqeeb*, is to prevent the assassination of Rafic Hariri."

It was dusk as The Damascene walked back through the Old City, but in the narrow, twisting lanes it was so dark it could have been midnight. The upper stories of the mainly two-storey buildings overhung the alleyways and forbade entry to the moonlight. Now and then there would be a group of illuminated shops, huddled together as if for safety from the darkness, or the mysterious entrance to a bazaar or souk.

But he did not mind the darkness, it did not bother him. He was dressed in a grey *burnus*, an all-in-one full-body cloak with hood, below which at the ankles showed the hem of his white cotton *dishdasha*. The hood was pulled up over his head and hid the top half of his face. His feet were sandaled. His footsteps were heavy on the cobbles. Perhaps the darkness was afraid of *him*.

His meetings with Ghazi Kanaan only happened two or three times a year, but he always left feeling angry. Kanaan was an arrogant, haughty, nasty individual who looked down on most people, not only the Lebanese. But what irritated The Damascene more than the machinations of the scheming Alawite was the fact that he owed Kanaan his life.

And he did remember, more than Kanaan realised. In fact, he remembered it all. Back to when he was a different man, back to when he was a normal human being. Back to when he was Captain Marwan Mebarak of the Lebanese Army Commando Unit...

It was supposed to be a simple mopping-up operation in Kfar Habou, back in January 2000 (Ramadan 1420). Even now he did not know what had gone wrong. Perhaps it was just tiredness. He and his team of four had been fighting in the town in the morning and they thought they had finished off the Sunni *Takfir wal-Hijra* rebels who had taken over the place. Then they had gone further up into the Dinnieh mountains to root out and kill five more. That should have been the end of their efforts for the day, but on returning to camp Mebarak and his team had been sent back to Kfar Habou – and that was when it had all gone wrong.

His team were killed with a frightening efficiency by a group who looked like – but obviously with hindsight were not – locals calling to them for help. They had gone over to the beckoning men who had suddenly produced pistols from their robes and despatched the soldiers to Allah for judgment.

Mebarak had been beaten, stripped to his undergarments and thrown into the back of an old van, which had sped off, presumably back down towards Tripoli.

The van exploded twenty minutes into the journey.

It was unlikely to be a roadside bomb; it could have been something they were carrying, or it could have been a rocket-propelled grenade launched by either the Lebanese or Syrian army. Whichever, Mebarak knew nothing until he woke up amongst the rats in a smelly back alley somewhere. Literally he knew nothing, not even who he was. How he had gotten there was a mystery. But, perversely, he recognised the area. He was near the Nahr al-Bared refugee camp. But that was Palestinian. Something in his shocked, addled mind said that he should be somewhere Sunni.

No sooner had he staggered out of the alley than hands were grabbing him again, a shit-smelling sack was rammed over his head, there was a thump and a little flash of light, and then he woke up in The Onion Factory. He did not know where he was at the time. He did not know who he was or even what he was. He just knew that he had a soldering iron up his anus and that the man who was defiling him was going to die.

He also knew the bastard Ghazi Kanaan the minute he saw him.

Before leaving, Kanaan had ordered that he be 'disappeared', which meant he would be taken to Syria and would never be heard of again. His restraints were not knotted, so he had broken through them easily, and he had killed the five Syrians in the building quickly, skilfully and with pleasure.

But he had not reckoned on Kanaan and his three bodyguards returning. He had heard the car drive away.

He was picking through the pockets of one of the dead *mukhabarat* – the one whose nose was now back in his brains, beyond his ears – when Kanaan had reappeared in the doorway. The car's headlights were on outside, and all that could be seen of Kanaan was an evil, malevolent silhouette.

"Well what have we here?" sneered Kanaan's voice. "Someone who refuses to go." With that, Kanaan raised the pistol in his hand and shot the captive in the head.

At that moment Captain Marwan Mebarak died.

And The Damascene was born.

Kanaan was everything everyone said about him, but he was also a pragmatist, a recogniser of talent. No one, in the twenty-plus years of Syrian 'assistance' in Lebanon, had ever overpowered and killed five armed *mukhabarat* in the same room, at the same time, with their bare hands. Kanaan was impressed. He was ecstatic when he realised he had not killed the captive but had merely blown away the flesh from the left side of his head, including his ear.

Mebarak was truly disappeared. A local man in Aanjar who bore a passing resemblance to him in stature, was taken and freshly slaughtered. His body, with its shot-away face, was taken up north and carefully positioned in the hills behind Kfar Habou where it would be found two weeks later after the wild animals had had their fill.

Captain Marwan Mebarak was given a funeral with full military honours. He had no wife or other family, which was fortunate because it saved Kanaan the expense of hiring a local gang to sort out the problem.

The Damascene knew nothing about this. He did not know who he was, his history or where he came from. But everything else he knew. The history of Lebanon and Syria, the language, the culture, politics both present and past, old songs, new songs, people who were famous or had been famous. From a guarded apartment in the new area of Damascus, he healed.

And soon he worked. Nasty jobs of elimination at Kanaan's request. He was told they were threats to the Syrian regime, but quickly he came to realise that they were threats to the Kanaan regime of plots and machinations. No one stood in Kanaan's way for long. And work was work.

When Kanaan was recalled to Damascus in 2002, The Damascene had to be moved out of the now un-guarded apartment. Now Kanaan was back in the centre of Syrian power, he could not be seen to have his own personal killer, kept like a pet to be unleashed at the will of his master. Kanaan had bought him a three-room apartment on the upper floor of a building in the Old City and he was given his freedom. He still undertook 'errands' for his old master, but now he was paid at

Middle Eastern going rates.

And what Kanaan guessed at, but did not know for sure, was that he began undertaking errands for other people as well, often mediating in local disputes between the tradesmen and residents of the Old City, sometimes even regularising the affairs of politically-linked businessmen in the new area. All for little stipends. Usually his presence was enough to settle matters (he was over two metres tall), sometimes a quiet word was necessary. Only rarely a broken bone. But he only killed for Kanaan.

Then, late in 2003, he remembered.

He did not suffer any shock, any sudden emotional wrench, any kick in the head by a mule. He just woke up one morning and remembered. Everything.

Anonymous telephone enquiries of the authorities in Beirut informed him of the fate of Captain Marwan Mebarak, a true hero of Lebanon. And it was then that he decided that, someday, he would kill Ghazi Kanaan.

The Damascene walked out of the shadows and passed Ahmad al-Nakhal's carpet shop and the next door barber's shop. He turned left, passing the antiques and souvenir shop on the right. A woman dressed in a black *jilbaab*, head covered by a black *khimar*, passed by but did not look at the tall, hooded figure.

Soon he was walking up the outside staircase to his upper level apartment.

The building was higher than its neighbours, so during daylight he could see out from his window with its rotting wooden frame over the domed rooftops, littered with satellite dishes and solar panels as if they had been haphazardly thrown down by Allah, to the ninth century magnificence of the Umayyad Mosque. Not that he ever went to the mosque. He did not believe. In anything.

Beyond the mosque was 'new' Damascus, with its already outdated high rises.

But now it was night, so all he could see (if he cared to look, which he didn't) was darkness punctuated by glows from skylights, bunched together like the lights in the alleys below. The mosque was an imposing, bulky shadow beyond which the more regular lights of new Damascus spread out like a nocturnal carpet of glitter.

A cooling, but not cool, breeze came through the wide-open window. It carried no sound. But as soon as he entered, the breeze told him he was not alone. He could smell another being in the apartment.

The Damascene left his old wooden front door open but he did not reach for the switch on the wall. There would be light in the room soon enough. He kicked off his sandals and removed his *burnus*, throwing it in the direction of a chair. The floorboards creaked as he walked towards his heavily and exotically cushioned double floor-mattress on the far side of the room.

He was halfway across the room when he saw the shadow entering from the washing area at the rear of the apartment. It was accompanied by a glow of diffused light, spreading out in a two metre circumference. A hand was shielding the flame, the source of the light.

The Damascene stopped.

The shadow and the light came towards him. He could smell jasmine.

The light moved to the right and downwards. It became stronger as the candle was placed on a wicker table next to the mattress. The being's back was towards him.

Then came the sound. A delicate *tinging*, singular and gentle at first, becoming stronger as the being moved one hand and then the other, expertly playing the silver metal zills.

She turned around, beginning the gentle shimmies of a *raqs baladi*, country dance. She was small, almost delicate, but he knew already that her body was hard and strong. She was dressed in her own variation of the dancing costume, different shades of red with gold accessories: beaded and coined headdress, small facial veil covering her nose and mouth, sleeveless top knotted between her breasts, a coined chiffon hip scarf above a sheer skirt. Her feet and abdomen were bare.

From above the veil, her heavily made-up eyes looked at him challengingly, seductively, as her belly undulated. She turned her back towards him and bent over at ninety degrees from the hips, fingers playing the zills, snake arms flowing in the air, her long black hair falling downwards, a black and gold hair clip reflecting the candle light.

The Damascene stared as she straightened up, made a hip circle turn, and then bent backwards again, her legs apart for balance, her delights visible beneath the diaphanous skirt. This sight he did care to look at.

Back up, with hip lifts and drops, then more shimmies as she came towards him with her musical arms open wide. He could smell her musk mixed in with the jasmine-based perfume.

She looked down and her eyes creased in pleasure as she saw that he had reacted to her beneath his *dishdasha*.

Still moving, she danced to within a centimetre of him. Then she stopped playing and her hennaed left hand came up to unclip her veil. Her breath was warm and pure as she said, "Master." Her fingers gave the lightest caress of his stubbled face then moved more firmly downwards through his still damp long black hair. Her hand stopped on his chest, the solidity of his nipple evident beneath the robe.

She looked down at her own chest. "Would you?" she asked. "You know I cannot untie knots."

He untied her top and then moved his hands to cup both of her small breasts, throwing the top to the floor. He said, "Or uncover anything that has been covered."

He bent down, crooked his right arm underneath her bottom and lifted her up. There was genuine warmth in his smile as he said, "My Djinn."

Her arms were around his neck as he carried her to the mattress and gently laid her on it. Then he laid himself on her.

Not so gently.

28 September 2004
13 Sha'ban 1425

Old City, Damascus, Syria 05:00

She was not there when he woke up. He knew she wouldn't be, she never was. That was why he had left the front door open, so she could leave. He was playing along with the little game. For real *djinn* cannot open closed doors. If she wanted to play at being a *djinni*, that was fine by him. She always gave him what he wanted, he could be tolerant.

Kanaan never mentioned her, but The Damascene knew she came from him. She turned up those two or three times a year after he met with Kanaan, a little sweetener against whatever distasteful job Kanaan had asked him to do. A reward. A payment in addition to the hundred thousand US.

And The Damascene had to admit that he enjoyed her visits. Her talents were plentiful. In his line of work, in his line of existence, there was no possibility of permanent relationships, so the assurance that she would appear before each assignment was welcome. And, of course, the wily bastard Kanaan knew that the unspoken promise of The Djinn's body would make him keener to accept whatever task he was given.

The Damascene wondered what The Djinn would do once he had killed Kanaan?

But that was for the future. Now he had the hardest job he had ever been given. Hurt, maim, kill – yes. But to *prevent* somebody being killed...

An interesting challenge. More so than Kanaan knew. For he hated Sunnis, and now he had to keep one alive.

The muezzin's call to *fajr* (dawn prayer) booming loudly from the twelve loudspeakers atop the Umayyad Mosque's minaret had awoken him, as it did every day. "*Hayya la-l-faleah - Hayya la-l-faleah.*" Hasten to real success.

He got up and strolled naked over to the window. The morning light was pushing in from the east. Morning of light, morning of joy.

Something *zizzed* past the hole that was his left ear. Morning of insects! Normally they did not bother him, he was not to their taste. But they must be able to detect the essence of The Djinn on him. He had been bitten during the night. He always was after she had been with him. He scratched the top of his right hand.

Damned *Hasharaat*.

The Jeep was waiting for him downstairs, as he knew it would be. Inside were two Syrian army conscripts, one driving, one sitting in the back. The Jeep was sideless and The Damascene threw his large holdall onto the empty back seat and climbed in next to the driver. No longer dressed in local clothing, he wore a loose white collarless shirt, blue denim jeans and desert boots. His head was unadorned, his long hair tied into a ponytail with a simple rubber band; it just about covered the hole in the side of his head.

Although the sun was rising, it was still dark in the alleys and the Jeep's full beams blasted light onto the closed and shuttered buildings as they drove away.

There was no Ghazi Kanaan, for Kanaan had given him his job, they had discussed the requirements at length, and now Kanaan would distance himself. They would not meet again until Kanaan had another job for him. The Damascene settled down in the front seat and permitted himself an inner smile. Or maybe this time they would not meet again until The Damascene had his hands around the bastard's throat...

Soon they crossed over the disused railway line and then turned onto the highway, heading west to Lebanon...

Bekaa Valley, Lebanon 06:30

There were no formalities at the border, the army vehicle simply swept through with hardly a reduction in speed, joining the narrower road on the Lebanese side. The sun was climbing higher in the sky, and presently the natural air-conditioning of the open-sided vehicle would not be able to cool them against the heat.

Soon they were passing Aanjar on the right. The soldiers were not aware of the slight tensing in The Damascene's arms.

They took the fork to the left, and as they started the dead straight eight kilometres between Barr Elias and Chtaura across the Bekaa Valley, The Damascene thought back to his meeting in the *hammam* yesterday evening...

"Are you acting on your own in this or are you acting for Syria?" The Damascene's dark eyes looked down at Kanaan, still sitting in the alcove.

"That is none of your business," Kanaan wiped the back of his hand across his sweat-streaked brow. "I am paying you to do a job."

"Syria wants to keep Hariri alive?"

"Some parts of it."

"Or is it Kanaan that wants to keep Hariri alive?"

Kanaan said nothing.

The Damascene stretched upwards, his muscles flexing. As he brought his arms back down, he again moved his hair to cover the hole in the left side of his head. "And how am I to prevent an assassination? The Prime Minister of Lebanon? Am I to become Hariri's head of security? Chief of the army? He has many foes."

"And many friends." Kanaan pushed himself up from the alcove seat. The Damascene still towered over him. "Which do you think are the more dangerous?"

"He has enemies within?"

"We all do."

"Enemies that want him dead?"

"I did not say that."

The Damascene raised his arms against the wall and began some vertical presses. Kanaan watched the scarred muscular back and the firm buttocks beneath the towel.

"And how long am I to prevent this assassination?" The Damascene spoke into the wall. "Forever?"

"Assassinations are never long-term, they are usually decided upon and... executed. I would wish to see you back within, say, six months."

You may never see me back, thought The Damascene. He said, "And after six months?"

"They can blow him to hell for all I care."

The Damascene straightened up and turned around. "What are you plotting, Kanaan?"

The Syrian smiled. "Me? Plotting? The Syrian Interior Minister-elect plotting?" The smile fell from his face. "Just remember who you work for."

The Damascene's stare was ice cold. "Oh, I know who I work for."

"Good."

Not you. "Massage?" He pulled open the old wooden door.

"What?"

"You going for a massage?"

"With that fat sadist Abdul? I don't think so."

"Too scared?" asked The Damascene.

"Too old," said Ghazi Kanaan.

Mount Lebanon 08:30

The pace of the Jeep slowed as the road climbed into the mountains after Chtaura, but soon they were passing through Bhamdoun and were on the downward run into Beirut. Just west of Jamhour they took a right off the main road onto a rough cinder track and pulled up in front of a new three-storey apartment block.

Without a word, The Damascene climbed out of the Jeep. He had hardly lifted his large holdall from the back before the vehicle sped off, dust and gravel flying from its back wheels.

The block had magnificent views out over Beirut, and in his pocket he had the keys to one of the two apartments on the top floor. His home for the next six months. Courtesy of Ghazi Kanaan. Or the Syrian taxpayer. Or both.

A blonde haired woman and three young children (a boy and twin girls) were coming out of the front door of the building, and the woman held the door open for him as he approached. She smiled in acknowledgement of his "*Shukran*" and then called to her children to hurry up because Mama and Baba were waiting.

The Damascene climbed the stairs. His shirt was wet against his back from the drive. He undid the buttons as he climbed. He needed a shower.

Opening the front door, he pulled his shirt off as he stepped inside the apartment. The chill of the air conditioning made him feel instantly welcome. His skin crinkled with the coolness.

The apartment was a duplex, spacious and well furnished. Tiled flooring, minimal but tasteful decoration, good quality appliances – even a flat screen Sony Bravia on the wall. He wondered what other uses the place was put to. A safe house? A luxurious holding facility? A love nest?

Throwing the holdall onto a leather couch, he walked over to the full-length sliding windows, pulled them open and stepped out onto the balcony, his naked torso once again enveloped by the heat of the day. He undid the rubber band and let his hair fall down either side of his face.

The views out over the city were indeed enviable. Far in the distance he could see the Mediterranean. He knew Beirut well and he narrowed his eyes and focused in on its heart, the downtown district, his eyes travelling from Martyr's Square (El Bourj) in the east, across the administrative hub in the Nejmeh and Serail districts. Then he looked further west, towards the Koreitem district.

Somewhere down there was the man at the centre of more than one target: Rafic Bahaa el deen al-Hariri. Rebuilder, saviour and Prime Minister of Lebanon. The man whom The Damascene's Syrian overlord had asked him to keep alive.

He threw back his head and laughed loudly.

In the name of everything he did not believe in, he had a job on his hands.

More than anyone knew.

One hour later, having showered, worked-out and showered again, The Damascene, naked and glistening with water (he preferred to dry naturally rather than to towel), lifted the holdall from the couch and put it on a nearby glass table. Inside the holdall were an assortment of clothes and various items which he might need during his assignment. He pulled out the clothes and threw them onto the couch. Then he pulled out something flat, square and metallic.

He looked at the item now in his hands: a Lebanese number plate, black numbers and lettering on a white background, with a white cedar tree on a blue background on the left. He had seen what he wanted on his way in, further back up in Jamhour, in the old repair shop near the Bejco dealership.

These false plates would fit perfectly.

29 September 2004
14 Sha'ban 1425

Koreitem, Beirut 08:00

It was known as Koreitem Palace, the term used in its colloquial sense, not regal. The man who had built it would never have regarded himself as royalty. He was Prime Minister. Lebanon did not have kings.

The mansion next to the Lebanese American University Campus in Tabbara Street was indeed palatial. It was not only the personal residence of Rafic Hariri and his family but it also served as his operational offices and housed his vast security team. It was set back behind the protective trio of high barbed-wire topped stone walls, canvas screens and hedges of dense pine trees. Security cameras, security men and security floodlights were everywhere, even in the streets outside. Men with sniffer dogs regularly patrolled the area.

The official offices of the Prime Minister of Lebanon are in the building known as the Grand Serail over on Serail Hill overlooking central Beirut, a few blocks from the Parliament Building on Nejmeh Square. Hariri had refurbished the sandstone building in Serail during his first term in office, adding the third floor to the original two and constructing luxurious and imposing offices.

Prime Minister Hariri would be at the Grand Serail during business hours, but billionaire entrepreneur Rafic Hariri operated out of Koreitem. He preferred, if he could, to keep the two elements of his life separate – but having been Prime Minister for ten out of the last twelve years that was impossible.

Hariri's aide, Lieutenant Colonel Wissam al-Hassan, had wanted that morning's visitor to schedule an appointment at the Grand Serail, that's what other Members of Parliament (Deputies) did. But Walid Eido had played the friend card. He had already had to wait three days since the meeting at Baalbeck, and that was three days too long. Now he sat on the opposite side of the breakfast table at Koreitem, watching Rafic Hariri eat his usual morning repast of *labneh*, toast, tomatoes and cucumbers (Hariri was trying to lose weight and to watch his blood pressure – damn doctors). A coffee pot sat on the table between the two men.

"Are you sure you won't have some, my dear friend?" Hariri gestured to his own plate. "Can I not tempt you?"

"You are most gracious, Abu Bahaa, but thank you." Eido shook his head. "The coffee will suffice."

"What would we do without it?" The big man smiled. "Coffee makes the wheels of commerce and the wheels of power turn. Only money is better." He wiped his mouth and put his cloth napkin on the table, a sign that he had finished eating. He poured his own coffee and refilled his friend's cup. His lips pursed under his moustache. "So what was he thinking?"

Eido shrugged. "With Kanaan, who knows? Of himself, of his own interest, most certainly."

"But to take the four of you to Baalbeck was an act of outrageous intimidation. He threatened you. He threatened us all. And he wanted to decide whether I should live or die!" The smile in Hariri's eyes was interspersed with flashes of anger. "How dare he! Who does he think he is?"

"We know who he is."

Hariri stared at his friend. Then he sat back in his chair and said, more quietly, "Yes, we do."

"I think he wants to use you to get rid of Assad."

"And then what? Take over himself?"

"Possibly."

"Or perhaps I should take over. Wouldn't that be a turn-up! Lebanon consuming Syria! Greater Lebanon!" Hariri's voice lowered. "Perhaps then I could break Syria over Assad's head..."

Eido looked around the room, concerned. "Be careful, Abu Bahaa."

Hariri raised his thick eyebrows. "Do not worry, Abu Khaled. My security is impenetrable. They are not listening."

"Are you sure?"

For the briefest of milliseconds there was a flicker in Hariri's eyes before he said, "Yes."

Eido sipped his coffee. "Kanaan said he would kill all of us if we told you of the meeting."

"I will assign some of my men to you."

"No, no! Please. You are most gracious, but no. Just please make sure no one knows of this conversation."

Hariri frowned. "But why should he be so threatening? The decision is that I be allowed to live, thanks be to Allah. So what is the problem? I profess I do not understand. Perhaps I should ask him, bring this out in the open. Maybe we could work together against Assad - "

"Please, Abu Bahaa!"

Hariri saw the pleading in his old friend's eyes. "No, no, you are right. I have given you my promise of silence and silent I will be."

"Thank you. Please."

Hariri looked pensive. "But what is Kanaan up to?"

"He said that he would arrange for you to be under his protection."

Hariri's laugh was loud and bitter. "As a wolf protects the lambs! First they threaten me and my family. Now they want to protect me. Do the Syrians really know what they want?"

"As always, Liban is being used in their own internal power struggles. Do not trust Kanaan, Abu Bahaa. Not for one second. He is plotting."

"Hmm..." Hariri picked up the coffee pot and looked from it to his cup. "In the name of the Prophet, peace be upon him, I am still hungry. These damn diets! Can I not tempt you to join me in a little *labneh*, my friend...? Or how about some *zaatar*...?"

Grand Serail, Beirut 11:30

The meeting in the Prime Minister's office at 11:30 that morning *had* been arranged through Lieutenant Colonel al-Hassan. It was a formal appointment, logged in the PM's diary, even though it was made in haste – and woe betide the visitor if he was late. Hariri was a stickler for punctuality. The meeting would last no longer than ten minutes.

In fact, the visitor had arrived early and for the last ten minutes had sat in the busy, bustling, noisy ante-room watching the phalanx of aides, assistants, secretaries and clerks go about their business. Busy, busy, busy, computers, telephones, faxes, personal callers. He was pleased his own office was less frenetic, he could not work in such a frantic atmosphere. Which probably explained why he was not Prime Minister, only head of a very small unit within the Department of General Security.

The appointment had been made through the offices of the General Director of General Security, Brigadier General Jamil Al Sayed. It was the Brigadier General who had ordered Maroun Khoury to report what he had discovered to the Prime Minister in person.

Khoury was slim and fit-looking for his age, mid-forties. He was bald on top, so he kept the hair at the sides and back cropped short, blending in with the trim, greying beard on his face. He wore a fawn suit and opened-necked white shirt, no tie.

At precisely 11:30, Lieutenant Colonel al-Hassan showed him into the Prime Minister's office, announced his name, and then left the room, closing the door firmly.

Rafic Hariri was looking out of one of the windows at the far side of the room, beyond his expansive desk. Khoury waited. He wondered whether to cough but then thought better of it.

After a few moments, Hariri turned. He was dressed in a grey suit, white shirt and colourful tie. It was Khoury's first meeting 'in the flesh' with the man dubbed Mister Lebanon, and he was impressed at his size. Not only his height and famed girth, but also by the size of his presence which filled the room without any words being spoken.

Hariri's frown gave way to a polite half smile as he acknowledged his visitor. "Mr Khoury."

"Prime Minister."

"Please." Hariri indicated an upright wooden chair in front of his desk. He did not offer his hand. "May I offer you some coffee?" He walked back over and sat behind the desk. "And perhaps something light to go with it?"

"Merci." Khoury shook his head and noted that Hariri actually looked disappointed at his refusal.

"The Brigadier General sent you?"

"He has asked me to report to you personally, sir. Something my department has discovered."

"And what department is that exactly?"

Khoury leant forward, hands clasped together between his knees. "We could best be described as information gatherers."

"Is that not Internal Security? Captain Eid?"

"We are... external security."

"And I have never heard of you?"

"Few have."

Hariri sniffed. "Including, it seems, the Prime Minister."

"Sir."

"So, what information have you gathered that Jamil Al Sayed sends you over here?"

Khoury sat back. "We keep watchful eyes and watchful ears on areas outside Lebanon's borders. Something has come to our attention - "

"How?"

"Please."

"Okay, I will not ask."

"Something has come to our attention concerning your security."

"A threat? Tell me something I don't know. From our friends in the east or in the south?"

"The east. But not a threat exactly. In fact, quite the reverse."

Hariri frowned again, this time in amusement. "The reverse of a threat?" He shook his head. "Hariri is confused."

"No more confused or bewildered than we were, sir. Kanaan is involved."

"Now why am I not surprised?"

"The information we have gathered is that Kanaan has sent his pet thug into Lebanon."

"His pet thug! Kanaan dares to send a pet thug after Hariri!"

"Well, no sir. That's the point. It seems he has been sent to protect you."

Inwardly, Hariri gave a nod of satisfaction. Walid Eido's information had been confirmed. Outwardly he was brash. "A thug to protect Hariri! I have the most sophisticated security team in the world, I am surrounded wherever I go, I travel in a convoy of six armour-plated vehicles - including an ambulance - with state of the art electronic jamming devices. And the Syrians dare to send one man to protect me!"

Khoury nodded in a show of sympathy. "How dare they indeed, sir. There is, however, another side to this situation. And that is why I am here, to apprise you of the whole position, so that you and your team are aware."

"What is it?"

"Is it Syria that is protecting you?" asked Khoury. "Or just Kanaan? Sending one man seems to indicate that Kanaan is acting alone. And we must ask ourselves this - "

"What?"

Khoury looked the Prime Minister in the eyes. "Who is it that he is protecting you from?"

South Beirut 11:40

At the exact moment that Maroun Khoury posed the question to the Prime Minister, the assassin known as Al-Rajul was in a very different part of the city from the plush, cosmopolitan downtown.

He was in the Hizbullah heartland of south Beirut. Here the city was palpably different. Restoration after 'the events' (the civil war) had not proceeded at the same pace as the rest of the city, and most buildings here carried the reminder of war, pockmarked with shell scars and myriad bullet holes. Some buildings still remained simply destroyed shells. He even saw a rusted old car still on its side as if it had taken root, in the same place as it was twenty years ago when people hid behind it from the sniper-fire. And died behind it.

The yellow and green Hizbullah flag was everywhere, in windows, draped between buildings, even painted onto walls, sometimes just abbreviated to the raised straight arm holding the machine gun. It was matched in quantity and locations by images of the Hizbullah leader, Sayyed Hassan Nasrallah.

Yet there was a sense of community about the area, a Shi'a people going about their business, confident in their leaders. Al-Rajul, who claimed to belong to no confession, was nodded at, even spoken to warmly, as he made his way along Annan Street.

Perhaps it was because of the white and black Palestinian *keffiyeh* he was wearing, a useful camouflage.

For he was heading into the Bourj el-Barajneh Palestinian refugee camp.

Antelias, north of Beirut 21:00

Frankly, Rafic Hariri had had enough for one day. Enough of Emile Lahoud, enough of Syria, enough of plots to kill him, enough of plots to save him, enough of running his beloved but constantly frustrating Lebanon – and enough of his damned diet. Tomorrow he had a meeting with President Jacques Chirac in Paris. Tonight he wanted to relax.

Late that evening, the Mercedes S-600 was seen driving quickly but stealthily out of the service entrance of the Koreitem Palace complex and turning into Madame Curie Street, heading west.

As always Hariri drove himself, but sitting next to him was his Head of Security Abu Tarek (Yehya al-Arab) and in the back were two more security men. The men were lucky. Tonight they would be dining with the Prime Minister.

Hariri did not like to dine alone. He usually ate with his family, or with friends, colleagues or allies, more often than not wheeling, dealing and sorting out problems. But today was different. He was drained and he was worried. He would not be his usual good company. He wanted to be alone, with just his trusted team around him.

Soon he was skirting St George's Bay and was on the coast road, the Debayeh Highway. Earlier an aide had telephoned 04 416 222 to make a reservation, and now Rafic Hariri was heading for one of his favourite places in Lebanon, if not the world.

The *Bourj al-Hamam* restaurant in Antelias.

The restaurant was busy but, as it was Wednesday, not over-crowded. Diners smiled when the big man who looked like the Prime Minister walked in with his three friends, and more than one client wondered to themselves if the likeness had ever been pointed out to the man. He had on an open-necked shirt, scruffy jacket and loafers, his hair was unkempt and he needed a shave, but smarten him up in a business suit and he could make a good living on the cabaret circuit as an impersonator of the PM.

One of the owners (a son of Fawzi, the founder), discreetly welcomed the party of four and guided them through the large main dining area, with its wood and cream-beige décor and the impressive back-lit faux-stained-glass windows with drawn scenes of old Lebanon (Hariri particularly liked the one of the ruins at Baalbeck with Mount Lebanon in the background). They were seated at a round table behind an ornate screen at the back of the restaurant.

Hariri did not need to see the menu. He ordered *kibbeh nayeh* (lamb kibbeh), *tabbouleh, hommous, plat légumes, makanek* (little sausages) and, to tease his guards, *cuisses de grenouilles* (frogs' legs). This would be followed by *farouj meshwi* (grilled chicken) with, of course, *frites,* and the meal would finish with fresh fruit. They would drink mineral water.

They chatted throughout the meal, the guards being respectful but not reverential. Sometimes laughter came from the table. They spoke of everything and anything – except Emile Lahoud, Syria, plots to kill, plots to save, the trials of running Lebanon.

And the big man's diet.

The person who had seen the Mercedes leave Koreitem Palace drew up outside the restaurant five minutes later. He had already watched the party enter from his position on the other side of the road, having followed the car from a safe distance all the way there. Now he parked the stolen Suzuki VL 1500 Intruder motorbike, studied the front of the restaurant for a moment, and then went inside. He had left it for the five minutes so as not to enter too close on Hariri's heels.

None of the other diners took any notice of the tall man in sandals, black slacks and loose white shirt, long hair tied in a loose ponytail so that his hair draped the sides of his face. He was greeted and shown to a small table set for two on the right near the front. He chose to sit facing inwards. The other place setting was removed and a menu was presented to him.

He ordered.

And waited.

Hariri and his team ate leisurely over the next two hours. But nature calls both the highest and lowliest of men, and as the fruit dessert was being eaten one of the men stood up.

The Damascene had wondered which one it would be. Had it been Hariri himself, it would have been the perfect introduction. But it was his Head of Security, Abu Tarek, who was the first to stand up behind the screen. No problem, that would do very nicely indeed.

Abu Tarek was a first class security chief, the best that money could buy (in this case, literally). But even he was unaware of the eyes watching him as he went round the back, or of the man who rose and followed him into the *toilette.*

Abu Tarek had cock in hand and was concentrating on his pissing when he heard the click of the main toilet door being locked behind him. He jerked his head to the right to see a tall man with long black hair standing with his back against the door, arms folded. Abu Tarek tried to do three things at once and succeeded in none of them: stop pissing on his shoes, put his cock away and reach for his gun in his shoulder holster.

"Careful, careful," The Damascene's hand was raised. "Don't panic, don't worry. Finish what you are doing."

Abu Tarek had popped himself back in without doing up his flies, and he had his hand inside his jacket.

"No need for your gun," continued the other man. "I just need to talk to you." The Damascene smiled as he pushed himself up from the door and walked towards the Herstal 9mm that was now pointing at him. "And no, this is not a *lootee* pick up. You are quite safe."

The gun did not move. Abu Tarek raised an eyebrow. Had he had his usual earpiece and throat-mike, his men would have been here already. But they had dressed casually for the evening which they had assessed as a low-risk situation. He had his cell phone in his breast pocket, one press on the hash key would send a signal–

Suddenly the gun was no longer in his hand. In a millisecond it had been taken, turned around and was now pointing at him.

The other man still smiled. "Now, do your flies up and you can have it back. A cold cock and a cocked gun is not a good combination."

For a moment Abu Tarek did not move. Then he reached down and zipped up his flies. He was surprised when the gun was held out to him, butt first. He nodded. He took the gun and held it loosely, pointing to the floor. "We have been expecting you."

"You have? Someone talked?"

"Of course."

"Despite the threats?"

"This is Lebanon."

"Of course." It was The Damascene's turn to nod. "We need to talk. I am sure you would not appreciate an approach through official channels."

"What makes you think I would appreciate any approach?"

"Hariri is in danger."

"Hariri has been in danger for the last fifteen years! Do you think we cannot cope?"

"Of course you can cope. The fact that Hariri is still alive proves you can cope, despite all the threats, despite all the attempts - "

"What attempts?"

"Oh come, come. Just because you deny them does not mean they never happened. Do you want me to list them? Shall I start with the most recent? That attack on the Italian embassy last week? It was nothing of the sort, was it? The target was Hariri."

"It was thwarted."

"Luck."

"Luck?" Abu Tarek's voice raised. "When you are protecting the Prime Minister of Lebanon, you do not rely on luck."

"Which is why you need me."

Abu Tarek shook his head. He turned and went over to the sinks, placing the gun on the unit top. He washed his hands, saying over his shoulder "Your arrogance is astounding. Rafic Hariri has the most skilled and sophisticated personal security team in the world. Kanaan sending his pet bitch to add to the protection is insulting."

"This time it is different."

"Different?" Abu Tarek dried his hands on a paper towel.

"This time the source of the threat is unusual and unknown."

"It is Syria. It always is Syria. It always will be Syria. You are murdering bastards." He threw the towel into a small bin on the floor and picked up his gun again.

"Not this time. And I am not Syrian."

Abu Tarek humphed in distain. "That is like saying that a dog does not assume the identity of its owner. Okay *chien*, your master is Syrian."

"And he is trying to protect *your* master. So perhaps that makes us both dogs."

The toilet door handle rattled as it was tried from outside. The Damascene thought it might be one of Abu Tarek's colleagues, but they would not leave Hariri's side – unless, of course, the big man wanted to piss. He was human, after all.

One more try of the door and then footsteps could be heard going away.

"Shoot me," said The Damascene suddenly.

Abu Tarek was taken aback. "What?"

"If I am a dog, shoot me, put me down." He held his arms away from his body, offering the target. Abu Tarek looked down at his gun on the unit top. He looked back up again to see the magazine of bullets being held in front of his face. He frowned – in frustration, annoyance, and admiration. Reluctantly he asked, "How on earth did you do that?"

"We need to talk."

Abu Tarek pursed his lips. Then he said "Maybe we do."

The handle rattled again and this time there was a knocking on the door. "Sir? Sir?" said a voice.

Abu Tarek coughed. "Yes, yes. In a moment."

"You are all right?" queried the voice.

"Of course I am. Can I not have a shit in peace!"

"Sir."

Abu Tarek looked at the other man as he reholstered his gun. "I am going to Faqra tomorrow evening. You know it?"

"Of course."

"Meet me there Friday. After sunrise prayer. You will be expected but no one will know your business."

"*Bien sûr.*" The Damascene unlocked the door. He turned the handle and pulled it open. "*Joumaa.* Oh, Abu Tarek Yahya?"

Abu Tarek turned as his bullet magazine was thrown towards him. He caught it in both hands.

"*Tusbih'ala al khayr.*"

Abu Tarek looked at the magazine in his hand. He nodded. "*Bon nuit.*"

From a safe distance outside, the Damascene watched as the Mercedes drove away. He was straddling the stolen Suzuki.

So, Abu Tarek regarded him as Kanaan's bitch, did he? Time was he would have killed over such an insult. But now he laughed. They had been in the right place for a male pissing contest!

But if they were using such metaphors, then Abu Tarek had made one mistake. Faqra was Hariri's mountain retreat, a good hour's drive from Beirut. They were to meet after sunrise prayer, which meant that The Damascene would have to travel there at night in darkness. And dogs and bitches didn't come out at night.

But wolves did.

He turned the key in the ignition and drove off.

30 September 2004
15 Sha'ban 1425

Bourj el-Barajneh, Beirut 20:00

It was Al-Rajul's second visit to the Palestinian refugee camp, and he knew he would never get used to the smell no matter how many times he visited.

It is not a 'camp' as most *anjabi* (foreigners) envisage, it is one square kilometre of basic brick constructions which pass as dwellings, packed so tight together that most paths between the buildings are less than half a metre wide (the one path in the whole of the camp that is nearly a metre wide is ironically called the Champs Elysées). There are no maps, no street signs. You have to know where you are going to find your way through the tight alleyways, over the broken water pipes, past the broken windows which might at any minute open into your face, through the sewage...

Posters or drawings of the smiling face of Yasser Arafat were everywhere, vying for space with posters of Fatah and Hamas.

The camp, and the others like it, was set up after *al-Naqba* – the catastrophe of 1948 when three hundred thousand Palestinians fled their homes in Palestine. It was built to deal with the 'temporary crisis' of the refugees. It was originally constructed to house ten thousand people, and the camp is forbidden to expand physically. By 2004, it was housing twenty thousand people in one square kilometre of hell.

And hell was the perfect recruiting ground for what Al-Rajul was planning.

1 October 2004
16 Sha'ban 1425

West Lebanon 05:30

The Damascene left well before dawn, driving down into Beirut, turning right at Hazmieh and soon reaching the coastal road. Traffic was lighter along the multi-lane highway at this hour than it was when he had followed Hariri to the restaurant two days before, but it was by no means sparse. There is always movement in Lebanon, people going places with things to do, either personally, professionally or politically.

This time he passed straight by Antelias and continued on to Nahr el Kalb (Dog River) where he took a right onto the main road which would eventually come out on the other side of Mount Lebanon at En Nabi Rchade on the western edge of the Bekaa Valley.

He turned off onto the secondary road at Faitroun and was grateful for the powerful motorbike between his legs. A normal car would have difficulty negotiating the climb into the mountains, he would have needed to have stolen a four-by-four.

It was getting light as he drove through Kfar Debiane, and by the time he reached Faqra the sun was shining into his eyes. Sunrise prayers would be well over.

Faqra, Lebanon 07:00

Hariri's eyrie was impressive, as The Damascene knew it would be. It sat at the top of the mountain, with the already snow-dusted ski slopes visible not too far away. It was a wide villa built of sand-coloured brick and stone, and with the ubiquitous orange tiled roof. It stretched over three stories, only two of which were visible from the rear as the building snuggled into the mountainside.

The Damascene turned off of the public road onto the much better private roadway leading upwards to the villa. He stopped at a metal barrier across the road and stared into the camera mounted on the barrier support. There were no buttons to push, no intercom to speak into.

Whoever was looking at him would have seen a swarthy man in jeans and black leather jacket with long dark hair tied simply at the back of his head. He wore no headgear, no crash helmet.

After ten seconds the barrier rose. He was expected.

He drove on, beginning to appreciate the size of the villa as he got nearer to it along the smooth, curving driveway quaintly populated at twenty-metre intervals by old-fashioned black urban streetlamps. The driveway stretched up the side of the villa through grassed lawns.

He pulled up in front of the small pine trees outside the covered main entranceway at the back. Because of its fit into the mountainside, it meant that the entrance to the building was on the middle floor. Several black important-yet-mysterious vehicles, mostly Mercedes, were parked nearby.

Two men came out of the villa. They were dressed in dark grey formal suits with white open-necked shirts – what passes for weekend casual in the world of security. Without saying a word, they gestured for The Damascene to raise his arms away from his body as he came towards them.

The body rub was professional. He was not carrying a gun (he would not have been so foolish – and it was not his preferred choice of weapon anyway) and his pockets revealed only money, a handkerchief and his apartment keys. They left the apartment keys in his pocket but took the motorbike keys out of his hand.

"*Yalla,*" said one, nodding for him to follow.

He was expertly sandwiched as they walked down a long corridor, one man slightly in front, one slightly behind, but with no body contact.

One or two people passed by, but they paid him no heed – they were used to visitors.

Up some opulently tiled stairs to the top floor of the building. They stopped outside a heavy wooden door and one of the men knocked. After a moment a voice from inside said, "*Shou?*"

The Damascene was motioned inside and the door was closed behind him.

Abu Tarek was standing with his back to a floor-to-ceiling window. Like the security men outside, he wore a suit and a white open-necked shirt. Behind him visibility was good, the Mediterranean a slash of blue in the distance beyond Jounieh.

"Ah, The Brigadier's henchman," he nodded. "The Interior Minister's envoy."

"Morning of light, Abu Tarek Yahya. And I think the expression you used two days ago was 'bitch'."

The Head of Security glared.

"Are we to continue our pissing contest?" asked The Damascene. "In which case, I will leave now. Or are we to talk like men? Your decision."

Abu Tarek stared for a few more seconds. Then, surprisingly, he smiled. "Of course. I apologise. You really must forgive me for the other day. I am not used to being accosted in the lavatory."

The Damascene bit off the witty retort that was on his lips.

"Please," continued Abu Tarek. "Sit down." He indicated a plush suite of furniture on one side of the room. There was a large coffee pot on a glass (possibly crystal) table, two bottles of Perrier, plates of figs and chocolates and a cigarette box.

The Damascene sat at one end of the large couch as Abu Tarek poured from the coffee pot. "You like Turkish?"

"Certainly."

"There is water also."

"No need."

Abu Tarek passed over a small, golden cup filled with the thick coffee. Taking his own, he sat at the other end of the couch. He took a sip and then said, "As you have probably seen on the news, the Prime Minister is in Paris. So, what do you think you can do that the entire security apparatus of the Prime Minister of Lebanon, both his official team and his private team, cannot?"

The Damascene also sipped from his cup. The coffee was exquisite. "There are two answers to that question. The first is: nothing."

Abu Tarek frowned and shook his head.

"You are right," continued The Damascene. "How many state security men does he have? Twenty? Thirty?"

"Forty."

"Plus his private team. So say fifty. And for the last fifteen years they have kept him safe. But think of the attempts there have been - " He raised the palm of his right hand as Abu Tarek opened his mouth to protest. "No, no, please. Do not treat me as a moron. We both know there have been many. You have foiled all of them. But his enemies have to get it right only once."

Abu Tarek's face was pensive. "Cigarette?" he asked.

"*Merci.*"

"A chocolate? Belgian."

"Perhaps. The second answer is: I can keep Hariri safe better than you can."

A laugh of scorn flew from Abu Tarek's lips along with his sip-full of coffee. "You *are* mad!" He leant forward, coughing. "I will have you thrown out."

"Why? That will look very good with your boss. Throwing out someone who only wants to protect his life."

Abu Tarek wiped his mouth on a handkerchief and straightened back up. "Your arrogance is astounding."

"I do not have arrogance," The Damascene's voice was low and controlled. "I have experience."

Abu Tarek looked at him disdainfully, nostrils flared. "What are you saying?"

"How many assassins do you have on your staff?"

Abu Tarek frowned. "None of course."

"Exactly. Your men are highly trained, highly experienced *security* men. They think protection and prevention. They are defensive, reactive. They have never been in the mind of a killer. They have never had to arrange a death, an assassination."

"Your point is?"

"I have."

The Damascene stopped to let those simple two words sink in. He took a chocolate from the dish. A Belgian chocolate filled with Turkish delight – eaten in Lebanon. He smiled inwardly. International. Why not?

He looked back at Abu Tarek.

"Care to tell me who?" asked the security man.

"No, I would not. I am an assassin. I think like an assassin, not like a security operative. I have the mind of an assassin. My controller in Syria - "

"You are Kanaan's bitch."

"Please. That is not necessary. I work for the Brigadier, yes. He has information of a specific threat to the Prime Minister. As you know, the Brigadier and the Prime Minister are old - "

"Adversaries."

" – friends. Brigadier Kanaan is not without affection for the Prime Minister."

Abu Tarek raised his eyebrows sardonically. "And what is this specific threat? From whom?"

"That we do not know. The Syrian intelligence apparatus have eyes and ears everywhere. They have been listening and they have heard something. And this time it is not a group from the opposing confessions, or a collection of extremists or dissidents. This time it is believed to be one man. One man has been sent to assassinate the Prime Minister."

"And Kanaan has sent his – you – to prevent it?"

"Not quite. I am to keep the Prime Minister alive. A difference. I am not chasing an assassin."

Abu Tarek stood up, shaking his head. "I cannot believe this." He walked over to the window and stared out. "Syria. Syria! The one country that has made more threats to the Prime Minister than all his other enemies put together. Syria now wants to save his life?"

"It would seem so."

He looked out over the view west. "Does President Assad know?"

He turned when his question went unanswered. The man on the couch was staring at him. "I do not know. I simply do as instructed."

"Only obeying orders?"

"If you like."

Abu Tarek came back over and picked up the coffee pot, testing it for weight. He raised his eyebrows in a query and held the pot out.

"Yes," nodded The Damascene.

Abu Tarek poured and then refilled his own cup. "So, what can you offer?"

"I offer you me. An assassin with an assassin's mind. I will not interfere. Like a security programme on a computer, I will be working in the background. I will be the firewall. You will not see me. I need just one stream of information from you: I need to know the Prime Minister's plans and whereabouts at all times. Day and night. Any last minute changes must be notified to me immediately. And only you should know of my existence." He swilled back his coffee in one.

Abu Tarek thought. Then he said, "And how do I notify you of these things if I will not see you?"

The Damascene stood up and put his hand into an inside pocket of his leather jacket. Abu Tarek tensed. The hand came back out, seemingly with nothing.

The Damascene opened his palm to show a tiny, flat object no bigger than two centimetres by one. It was a mobile phone SIM card. He offered it to Abu Tarek. "No one has that number except you and me. The number you are to contact me on is already in there. Get yourself a phone to put it in and leave it on. If you wish to take advantage of my offer, I will expect to hear from you within forty-eight hours. That is the one and only voice call you will ever make on that number. After that you will communicate with me by text message only. Twice a day, at sunrise and sunset, you will send me a message with Hariri's activities for the next twelve hours. I will never reply to you."

Abu Tarek took the SIM card, looking at it as if it was a poison chalice. "How long for?"

"I understand the threat is present. I will contact you – not on the telephone – when it is time to stop."

"And what if we don't wish to take advantage of your offer?"

"I have a job to do," The Damascene flicked a piece of hair which had fallen in front of his face. For the briefest of seconds, Abu Tarek glimpsed the hole in the left side of his head. "With or without your help, Abu Tarek Yahya, I will do it."

"I don't even know your name," said Abu Tarek.

"That does not matter," said The Damascene. "I no longer have one."

As the Suzuki VL 1500 Intruder roared off back down the mountainside, Abu Tarek entered a room on the ground floor of the villa. It was a smaller room, designed as an intimate study.

"What do you think?" he asked as he closed the door behind him.

The face of Rafic Hariri looked up from the large monitor on the desk. He had been watching the meeting on a live video feed in Paris. Abu Tarek could see an empty coffee cup and the skeletal vine of a bunch of eaten grapes on the desk next to the Prime Minister. He wondered if he had breakfasted yet – it was 06:00 in Paris.

Hariri smoothed his right eyebrow pensively. "Interesting. The Syrians wish to protect me?"

"Kanaan wishes to protect you. There is a difference." Abu Tarek spoke lowly but distinctly so that the link would carry his words clearly.

"Indeed." Hariri smoothed his other eyebrow. "Hmm..." He sniffed, then said "Trust in Allah, Abu Tarek – but tie your camel! There is no danger in having extra insurance. Let us see what happens."

"Yes, sir." The Head of Security moved his hand towards the mouse.

"And Abu Tarek?" Hariri moved closer, which made his face fill the entire screen.

"Sir?"

"Keep him close," instructed Rafic Hariri. "Then closer still."

Beirut 09:05

The Damascene reached the north-eastern edge of Beirut just after 09:00 and turned left at the Saloume roundabout, heading south and east for the further twenty minute drive to his apartment.

At that exact moment Marwan Hamade, Lebanon's Economy Minister and a friend and ally of Rafic Hariri, left his apartment overlooking the seafront corniche and climbed into his black Mercedes for the short drive south to Parliament in Nejmeh Square. He was accompanied by his driver Oussama Abdel Samad and his police escort Sergeant Ghazi Bou Karoum.

One hundred metres down the road, a parked Mercedes exploded as Hamade's car passed*.

Faqra, Lebanon 09:25

Up in Faqra, Abu Tarek was back on the webcam with Prime Minister Hariri immediately on hearing the news of the car bomb from security sources.

"Is he dead?" Hariri was grim-faced and looked ashen.

---

* *Due to driver Abdel Samad manoeuvring to avoid a speed bump, the blast hit the back of Hamade's car rather than the side. Sergeant Bou Karoum was killed and Abdel Samad was relatively unscathed. Marwan Hamade had all his ribs broken and one of his feet; his hands were burnt and he needed 450 stitches in his face and head.*

"We don't know," Abu Tarek was also solemn. "One person is dead, two are alive. We must pray to almighty Allah that he has been saved."

"Damn, damn, damn!" shouted Hariri. "This is it, you know. They've destroyed the new government. This is Lahoud's doing, I know it. Him and his allies."

"Be quiet, *zaim*, be quiet!" ordered Abu Tarek curtly. "These connections are not secure. You cannot say such things out loud, even on our own network."

Hariri sneered. "Damn each and every one of them."

Abu Tarek understood Hariri's anger. "You know we cannot accuse without proof. And that we will never have. Even now I am sure the streets are being cleaned, items taken away to be 'unfortunately lost' in official possession."

Hariri held his head with his right hand. "What am I to do? Why do the killings go on and on? It is like the events have never finished, except now only the generals are killed."

"I know, *zaim*, I know. Perhaps, dare I say, it might be prudent for you to remain away. Stay longer in Paris."

Hariri shook his head. "No. No, that I will not do. They will call me a coward. They will attempt to oust me from office while I am not there. I am meeting with Monsieur Chirac again in a few minutes to tell him what has happened. Then I will be on my way back. If they want Hariri out, they must do it in his presence."

"But you could be in danger."

"They dare not touch me!"

Abu Tarek did not let Hariri hear his sigh. He said, "Then we will take our usual precautions. You will travel nowhere except in the convoy. An immediate embargo will be placed on your calendar. Only you, me and al-Hassan will know exact details, Baba* to a lesser extent."

"Whatever," said Hariri. "As you wish."

"I will return to Koreitem immediately. We will issue a Press Release to say you are staying on in Paris and not announce your return until you are safely back in Koreitem. I will meet you at the airport later."

"*D'accord.*"

"And there is one other matter we now know the answer to."

"What is that?" Hariri popped a date into his mouth from an off-screen tray.

"What we spoke about earlier."

"*Naam.*"

"I will arrange it."

Mount Lebanon 09:40

The Damascene had just closed the front door of the apartment behind him when one of his two mobile phones rang, the Samsung D900 with the ringtone of the four-note opening of Shakira's *Suerte*. Only one person had this number. His brow creased in mild surprise at the speed of the response.

He put it to his ear as he went over to the window and looked out over Beirut. "*Oui?*"

---

* *Adnan Baba, Hariri's personal secretary for 28 years*

"All right," said Abu Tarek. "We will accept your offer. What have we got to lose?"

PART TWO
الجزء الثاني

CONSTRUCTION
البناء والتشييد

2 October 2004
17 Sha'ban 1425

Sin El Fil, Beirut 21:00

The Dubai Hall of the Metropolitan Palace Hotel, Habtoor's semi-circular five-star model of opulence and elegance, throbbed with the noise of the music, the cheering and the clapping. Especially the clapping.

The sixty or so guests stood either side of the dance floor clapping their hands in unison, like a modern version of a *sahjeh* dance. Some of the crowd whistled. In the centre of the floor Jacqui and Joe, the bride and groom, danced their first dance as a married couple. It was a slow love song but it was nearly drowned by the clapping.

After a minute they were joined by both sets of parents, dancing with their opposite partners. Then the clapping petered out as other couples began to wander onto the dance floor. Soon nearly everyone was dancing. The Dubai Hall was hot, heavy with the scent of food, tobacco and alcohol.

Suddenly the love song stopped and was instantly replaced by a pounding, thudding up-tempo number. The shouting and whistling started again as couples became individuals, dancing off on their own, each celebrating the wedding of this popular couple.

One man in particular was enjoying himself. He had long since removed his jacket and tie and had rolled up his shirt sleeves. Now he danced arms outstretched, stomping his feet, gyrating, occasionally dropping to his haunches and back up again (he would pay for that the next morning). He was happy to be at this gathering of family and friends, at the wedding of his brother-in-law.

But he was not as young as he was. After an admirable ten minutes of celebration he was relieved to see his wife Gisele beckoning from their table. She was standing next to Mama and one of the hotel staff. Gratefully, he made his way back through the dancing bodies.

"Jihad, look at the state of you!" scolded Mama as she looked at the saturated shirt clinging to his body. "You will kill yourself going on like that."

"Pah! How often do we have a wedding in the family?" he smiled at his mother-in-law. "I thought Joe would never get married. This is a great occasion." He looked at his wife. "And it will probably be years more before your sisters get married. We must enjoy these times when we have them." He grabbed a glass from the table and gulped down whatever it contained. Coke. "Mind you," he pulled out a chair, "I don't seem to be able to last as long as I used to," he exchanged a cheeky glance with his wife. "On the dance floor."

"Don't sit down, Jihad," Gisele touched his arm. "This gentleman has a message for you."

The smile dropped from Jihad's face and he groaned. No, not today. He looked at the smart, suited man.

"I am sorry to disturb you, sir, but there is a telephone call for you."

Jihad put his hands on his hips. He was not tall but he had stature, a presence. Many of his colleagues had come to fear that stance. "You are kidding me."

"Alas, no. The gentleman was most persistent. I explained that you were engaged, but he insisted. Short of hanging up on him there was nothing I could do but agree to inform you. Shall I tell him I have checked and that you are not available? He would not give his name."

There was no need for a name. Jihad knew who it was. That was why he had left his mobile at home.

"*Merde alors*" he mumbled, then said "No, no. I'd best take it. Where's the phone?"

"In the manager's office, sir. If you would care to come with me?"

Mama was making grumbling noises about work. Jihad looked at Gisele apologetically. "I won't be long. You know how it is."

Gisele nodded. She had been in the same business herself, so she knew.

He nodded at the hotel man. "*Yalla.*"

They walked around the edge of the hall to avoid the dancers and left by the main door. Outside the drop in sound volume was so sudden he thought he had gone deaf, until he heard the wheels of the trolley.

The two metres high wedding cake was being pushed along the corridor towards the doors. There were fireworks on it which would be lit just before it entered the hall. The ceremonial cutting sword was on the trolley next to it.

Jihad stopped and put up his hand. "Can you wait?" he said to the three white-coated catering staff. "Just for two minutes. I will be back."

They collectively shrugged and nodded.

Nodding his thanks and looking like thunder, Captain Jihad Merhi of the Lebanese Internal Security Force continued on towards the manager's office.

Left alone in the small but well appointed office, Merhi snatched up the telephone and said without preamble "Can't I be left in peace just for one day?"

"Sorry boss, I thought you'd want to know." Sergeant Deeb el-Gharib was used to his boss's 'little ways'. He had learnt over the years simply to ignore the implied criticisms or reprimands and go straight to the point.

"What is it?"

"Lattouf called you."

For a moment Merhi was quiet. Then he said, "Shit."

"I thought you'd want to know straight away."

"How to ruin a good fucking wedding."

"Yes, boss. Sorry."

Merhi sighed. "No, no, Deeb, you did right." He half-sat on the edge of the manager's desk, wondering why his forty-five year old legs felt stiff. "Did he say what he wanted?"

"As usual, no. He wants to meet."

"Balls."

"Yes, boss. Tomorrow morning at eleven. Usual place."

Merhi rubbed his left knee as he spoke. "Tomorrow? Sunday? Christ, that means

I'll miss mass again!"

"Then it's not all bad."

Merhi laughed. "Nothing a good penance won't sort out. Perhaps I should climb to the top of Harissa on my knees and kiss the Virgin's feet!"

"Even better, make Lattouf do it for you."

"Now there's an idea. But I think the gesture would be wasted on that fat Palestinian slob. Does he want me to call him?"

"I can do it."

"Okay, *merci*. Nothing else tonight, Deeb."

"I promise, boss. I had thought of leaving Lattouf but knowing how delicate these things are I thought you would want to know. I won't contact you again tonight, even if the earth opens up and swallows the whole of Mount Lebanon."

"Good. And not even then. I've got to get back, the cake is going in and the fireworks are about to go off."

Merhi put down the phone, not realising the prophetic accuracy of his last words.

3 October 2004
18 Sha'ban 1425

Verdun, Beirut 11:10

Merhi's description of Fadi Lattouf was two-thirds accurate at least. He was fat and he was Palestinian. Whether he was a slob was subjective. His wife would certainly agree that he was. His five children would say he was a cuddly Baba who always had time for them (when he was not asleep in his chair). His staff would not dare to comment publicly, although in private their opinions were split. Those miscreants he had locked up in his role as Captain of the Civil Police of the Palestinian Security Force in the Bourj el-Barajneh refugee camp would say, quite simply, that he was a bastard.

To Merhi's relief, his meetings with Lattouf were infrequent. Under laid down protocol, the Palestinian refugee camps in Lebanon are no-go areas for the Lebanese authorities. Lebanon is forbidden from interfering or intervening in the camps and from sending troops or other officials inside, including police. The camps have their own Palestinian police, colloquially called the Blue Police because of the colour of their uniforms.

Part of Jihad Merhi's duties was to be the liaison link between the Lebanese Internal Security Force and the Palestinian Police controlling the refugee camps in the Beirut area. His opposite number was Captain Fadi Lattouf.

They always met in the food court on the second floor of the Dunes Shopping Mall. It was one of the oldest shopping malls in Beirut, in the Verdun area over near the west coast and on the same block as the Holiday Inn Hotel. The location was Lattouf's choice: an easy drive from the Bourj in the south yet not too far out of his comfort zone for a quick return if necessary.

Naturally Lattouf did not wear his uniform when venturing north. This being a Sunday, to blend in with the other shoppers he was wearing rough blue denim jeans, for which he was about twenty years too old and fifty kilos too heavy, and a loose pink and blue checked shirt. But at two metres high and about the same around his waist, blend in was something Fadi Lattouf would never do, anywhere.

Merhi was ten minutes late (Sunday traffic up on Dunant Street), and Lattouf was already seated at a table in the food court, tray in front of him. The table looked like it had been hit by a litter bomb.

He saw Merhi coming towards him and raised his hand in greeting. "Morning of light, my dear Captain!" He half rose as they shook hands and then he gratefully plopped back down again, his backside consuming the chair beneath him.

"Morning of..." Merhi looked at the table. "A Big Mac and large fries, Fadi?"

The huge man looked bashful. "Well, you know how it is. A man gets hungry."

"Can I get you something else?"

"No, no."

"I'm having a coffee."

"Oh, well, in that case," Lattouf wiggled the cardboard cup which was dwarfed in his right hand. *"Merci ktir.* And perhaps a banana cupcake as well? Must have my fruit."

Merhi smiled and walked on. There was no queue at *Cup Cake* and he was back within minutes.

"Bless your hands," said Lattouf as the tray with two large coffees and three cupcakes (one banana, one chocolate, one carrot) was placed in front of him.

"The chocolate one's mine," said Merhi taking the cake and his coffee.

"Of course."

Merhi sat down. It must have been nearly a year since he had last seen the Palestinian and he looked bigger than ever. It was not helped by the fact that he was in those ridiculous clothes, and he was not wearing his captain's cap which he would do at formal meetings. He had a severe comb-over of the remaining strands of his black hair which served to emphasise rather than hide his bald dome. His beard was of the unshaven-look rather than the cultivated variety. There were flecks of grey – and flecks of Big Mac – in it.

"How is your dear Gisele?" Crumbs of banana cupcake were added to his beard as Lattouf spoke.

"Well, thank you. And Nada?"

Lattouf shrugged and nodded. "As ever."

"Number six not on the way yet?"

"Hah!" A large chunk of cake shot back out of Lattouf's mouth, landed with unerring accuracy in the half-used cartonette of tomato sauce, was retrieved and popped back in the mouth again. "I keep telling her that fertility is a blessing from Allah, but she is having none of it. She says five is enough. As far as she is concerned, in the bedroom we now have twelve months of Ramadan!"

Merhi could not help but smile. "Please wish Allah's blessings upon her." He tried to push thoughts of a naked and rampant Lattouf from his mind.

"Thank you. And blessings to Gisele too."

"Thank you."

There was a silence. Then Lattouf took a sip of coffee and said, "I have a body."

Merhi did not react. He broke his cupcake in half and then in half again and put a piece in his mouth. People died every day in the camps, of course, and it was an internal Palestinian job to bury or otherwise dispose of the bodies. The simple four-word sentence indicated something more, and he knew what it was. He blew on his coffee before tipping the cup to his lips.

"Or at least," continued Lattouf. "I have part of a body. The rodents have had the rest of it."

Merhi grimaced. Still he did not say anything.

Both men simultaneously swilled their coffees.

"Should I report it?" asked Lattouf.

"Does it need reporting?"

Lattouf shrugged.

"Male or female?" asked Merhi.

"We don't know."

"What?"

"The clothing of the young these days, even in the camps, they all dress the same!" Lattouf gave a false, almost nervous, half-laugh. "And most of it was ripped or removed."

"A sexual assault?"

"Who knows?"

Merhi was confused. "What do you mean? What are you saying?"

Lattouf gave a huge sigh. "We do not know if there was a sexual assault, we do not know for sure even what sex the body was, because... there is nothing there." He nodded downwards.

"It has been cut off? Defiled?"

"Eaten."

Merhi looked around the food court. It was beginning to fill up as it approached midday. He pushed his cake away. "That's the reason for the ripped and removed clothing. To hasten the feast. Somebody knew what he was doing."

"The entire epidermis has been gnawed. We do not know if there were any breasts, we do not know if there were any body hairs..."

"What about the head?"

"Destroyed. Caved in. Beaten to a pulp. We think that was the cause of death."

"You think? Time of death?"

Lattouf shrugged again. "Recently. There was no putrefaction. The rodents move fast but the maggots usually move faster. Within the last days."

"Could it have been an accident? A fall? Off of one of the buildings perhaps?"

Lattouf shook his head. "I do not know, my friend. I have seen such injuries before, thankfully infrequently. When I was stationed in Gaza. It has all the indications of death by trauma, by a blunt instrument to the head and face."

"With action taken to disguise, if not destroy, the identity of the victim."

Lattouf nodded.

"Anybody reported anyone missing?"

Lattouf looked almost aggrieved. "What do you think? This is the camp. Over-populated by one hundred per cent. Illegal by one hundred per cent. No one is going to report anyone missing, even to their own police force. In case of outside repercussions."

"Where is the body?"

"Somewhere cool. But not cool enough. It will be walking out by its own accord soon. Do you want to see it?"

Merhi looked at the Palestinian. "Why would I want to see it? It was obviously an accident. No need to report it to the ISF."

Lattouf nodded, grateful. "Good, I thought you would see it that way. I agree."

"Feel free to dispose of the remains."

"I will."

"Do you need any quicklime or acid?"

"No, we have our own."

"Okay then. Good."

"Just one thing, Abu Samer."

"What?"

Lattouf nodded at the table. "If you are not going to eat your cupcake, may I have it?"

6 October 2004
21 Sha'ban 1425

Bourj el-Barajneh, Beirut 19:00

Al-Rajul entered the camp at dusk. On his previous visit he had worn the full white *dishdasha*, which had been a mistake. It had ended up covered in blood and gore. Thankfully he had worn his street clothes underneath, so after the elimination he had simply removed it and thrown it away in a doorway (one of the poor wretches of the camp might be grateful for it, if they could get the stains out).

Tonight he wore khaki cargo pants, a loose off-white collarless shirt and the white and black Palestinian *keffiyeh* loosely wrapped around the lower half of his face.

He knew his way around the first third of the camp now and he needed to familiarise himself with the rest of it before the recruiting exercise could begin. He had the luxury of time because his employer had specified the date on which the contract was to be effected; not a day before, not a day after.

The camp was only one square kilometre but it seemed as large and complex as a major city. Lack of street names did not help (lack of streets did not help), and there was no set pattern, no grid system, no logic. Many alleyways resulted in a dead end, some turned back on themselves and led you back out exactly where you came in, others went on for a long distance and then just seemed to peter out as if they had lost the will to live – like many of the inhabitants of this hell on earth.

And the smell. The word vile would not describe it. It clung to you, got inside you, became you. Or you became it.

What had the Palestinians done to deserve this? The answer was: nothing. And yet the people retained their dignity, retained their pride. They knew that history was timeless and that their troubles, although nearly sixty years old now, were but a speck in the timeline. And they also knew that, very soon in timeline terms, they would get back their homeland. Allah would not forsake them.

Al-Rajul had been angry about what had happened on his previous visit. But it had been necessary. What had to be done, had to be done. In his line of work you did not dwell on causes, circumstances and results. You simply learnt from them and moved on.

It had been later than this, it had been dark. Many people had been indoors, eating with their families, listening to battery-operated radios or trying to watch old televisions when the intermittent power supply would let them. But some people were still out and about, upon their own business.

He did not carry a torch, that would have marked him out. He used the diffused light from the buildings to see by, until the intervals when the power was cut. He worked out that the power failed every twenty minutes for at least five minutes a time, so when he knew a cut was coming he would pause in a quiet doorway or sheltered alley and close his eyes. This was a trick he had been taught many years ago, so his eyes were more accustomed to the dark when the darkness came.

It was just before one of the power cuts when he was leaning on a wall with his eyes closed, listening to the far-away voices in the dwellings, that he heard a voice closer to him say, "*Salaam.*"

He opened his eyes. On the other side of the alley stood a youth of about sixteen. Like Al-Rajul he was dressed in a loose *dishdasha*, but with nothing on his head. He had a large mop of curly dark hair and a smooth face which was smiling. His eyes seemed very dark.

Al-Rajul nodded.

"Can you understand what I am saying?" asked the youth. His voice was low and smooth.

"I speak farsi."

"Really? That is good. We can communicate better."

"What are you doing here? You are not Palestinian."

The smile grew in intensity. "I work here."

Al-Rajul said nothing.

"You had your eyes closed. Are you tired?" The youth took two slow steps across the alley. "Did you want to sleep?"

Al-Rajul could now see that the youth's eyes were smeared with mascara. "No."

"Did you want to sleep with me?" The full lips pouted.

"No."

"I am very good. Look what I have." The *dishdasha* was raised, rucking upwards like a curtain in a theatre. The youth's penis was flaccid, but even in this state it must have been about eighteen centimetres long.

"Go away."

"You do not like me?"

"I am not that way inclined."

"I can turn round for you." The eyes were wide, the lips slightly open as he took two more paces forward. "You might like it. You might like me. Am I not beautiful? And I bet you are beautiful too."

It was at that moment that fate decided that the youth would die. Had he left his action two seconds later, the power would have been cut and he would not have been able to see. He reached up and pulled the *keffiyeh* away from Al-Rajul's face. He smiled at the last thing he ever saw and said, "Yes, you are."

Then the lights went out.

Al-Rajul was a professional. And like others in his business, he would not return to a scene of a hit just to gawp or to check that the victim was either still there or had been discovered or removed – he left that suicidal idiocy to amateurs or fiction writers. But he needed to know the geography of the camp, therefore he started that evening from as close as possible to where his scouting had been brought to an abrupt halt the previous week.

People were still out, shops (what there were of them) were still open, youths still played soccer in the occasional open space. And Al-Rajul wasn't paid any attention whatsoever.

It took four hours of walking, backwards and forwards, up alleys and down alleys, along streets, through derelict spaces. At the end, he knew every decorative mural, every political wall-painting, every Palestinian flag hanging limply from a window or attached to a wall, and every copy of the exact same picture of President Yasser Arafat.

And he also now knew intimately the Bourj el-Barajneh refugee camp.

So the recruitment exercise could begin.

He reached Annan Street and headed north, back into Beirut.

10 October 2004
25 Sha'ban 1425

Mount Lebanon 16:00

For ten days it had worked well. A text message twice a day had advised The Damascene of the Prime Minister's movements, mostly trips between Koreitem and parliament (three different routes being taken to and from, with Abu Tarek deciding at the last moment which route to take, not even telling Hariri in advance) and one visit to Faqra.

The Damascene would risk assess the location and routes, and each time the Hariri convoy drove past, the Suzuki VL 1500 Intruder and its rider would be somewhere in the background, observing.

But already he was beginning to wonder whether this was a waste of time. The convoy was impressive. The lead vehicle was a Toyota Land Cruiser carrying members of the national Internal Security Force. Then came a Mercedes S-500 with four of Hariri's private bodyguards. This was followed by Hariri himself, driving his armour-plated Mercedes S-600, and then another S-500 carrying Abu Tarek and three others. More private security personnel were in the fifth vehicle, another S-500, and then came a black Chevrolet ambulance containing paramedics and state-of-the-art medical equipment.

They drove in strict formation. The fourth vehicle, the one containing Abu Tarek, drove slightly to the right behind Hariri's car. The fifth vehicle slightly to the left, so covering both flanks in case of an attack. The ambulance kept back from the rest of the convoy by about thirty metres, so that it would miss any direct attack and be ready to deal with any consequences.

The personal bodyguards carried Heckler and Koch MP5 machine pistols, the other personnel carried M-16 rifles.

The three S-500s contained electronic jammers powerful enough to stop remote signals being sent to any bombs or other devices within a half kilometre radius of the convoy.

So, wondered The Damascene, what was the point of him being wherever Hariri was? The convoy was attack-proof. It could not be bombed because of the high-powered (and ironically Israeli-made) jammers, and there were so many security people around Hariri that any other direct assault would be suicidal for the attacker.

The only way to get to him would be from long-range sniping or close-up, body-to-body knife, gun or suicide bomb. And nobody would be allowed to get that close. Unless, of course, Rafic Hariri decided to go on another of his incognito night time sojourns when his appetite got the better of his diet. But that was now unlikely. Two weeks ago, maybe. But now, with the extension of the mandate of President Lahoud and Hariri's power in parliament weakening by its isolation, the pressure was on.

Hariri was too busy fighting for survival, for his plans for Lebanon, to go off on a jaunt.

So, by a process of elimination (The Damascene raised an eyebrow at his own words), the most successful way of killing Hariri would be by sniper fire – a most un-Middle Eastern way of doing things. But perhaps that was what was called for: the surprise element.

He would have to revise his way of working. There was no need for him to be there when the convoy drove past, that was far too late. He did not need to know routes, nothing was going to pass through the armour-plated Mercedes and its bullet-and-everything-else-proof windows. He needed to know departures and destinations. When Hariri would be out of the car.

He had seen Abu Tarek observe him in various places. Their eyes had locked but there had been no amateurish nods of recognition. He would need to contact the security man to tell him that he needed to know Hariri's calendar earlier than twelve hours in advance. He would also want to know of any last-minute changes, although these were not as important as they may seem – they were a good deterrent against planned sniping. But he had to cover every contingency. He had to cover the eventualities that the security team could not, instead of duplicating their impressive efforts.

He had to think at a tangent. To think like the assassin he usually was. Quite simply, he had to wake up each morning, check the Prime Minister's calendar and think *How can I kill Rafic Hariri today?*

Koreitem, Beirut 21:00

Winter in Beirut is December and January, when the temperatures plunge into the teens Celsius and thunderous rain falls in enough quantities to make up for its absence the rest of the year. In October the evenings are still warm. Pedestrians can still venture out without coats. But The Damascene was on his motorbike, so he wore his black leather jacket and denim jeans.

Temperatures might hold off until winter overpowers them, but nightfall holds off for no one. It had already been dark for two hours when The Damascene set off down the main Damascus to Beirut road into the city. It was a Sunday night and the traffic was heavy, but that did not matter with a bike.

Beirut was unusual in that, at that time, there were hardly any traffic lights in the whole of the city. Power cuts were so frequent that it was considered far more dangerous to have lights that went off without notice than it was to leave the traffic to fend for itself. In certain parts of the city, at certain times, gridlock was commonplace. In a car he would have gotten nowhere.

The Koreitem district was much quieter than downtown in the Nejmeh area. He passed Koreitem Palace and pulled up close to the mosque on Madame Curie Street.

The earlier text message from Abu Tarek had confirmed that Hariri was staying 'home' tonight. The Damascene was going to text Abu Tarek to demand an urgent meeting, so that he could explain his need for both more frequent and longer-term diary dates. Rather than give the Head of Security any pretext to delay, he would explain that he was outside and wanted to see him right now.

He turned and looked back at the palace as he took out the Samsung phone. The place was ablaze with floodlighting, as it always was at night, and there were two security men in the street with dogs. Inside there would be many more.

He was halfway through the text when he saw the main gate opening.

Two black 4x4s came through the gates, turned left onto Madame Curie Street, away from The Damascene, and then swiftly took a right into the back streets, heading south.

The Damascene's finger was poised above the keypad as he stared down the street. Had he just seen what he thought he had seen? Impossible, surely? But in his line of work he could trust no one - except himself. And he trusted what he had just seen.

Vehicles and visitors came and went at all hours at Koreitem Palace, that was the nature of it being not only a billionaire's residence but also the home of the Prime Minister. But there was only one person in the whole of the palace that would warrant a salute from one of the security men outside.

The Damascene turned around and roared the Suzuki back into life. He made a U-turn and sped off down the street in pursuit.

South Beirut 21:20 – 00:00

The two 4x4s were being driven determinedly but without excessive speed. It was easy to keep up with them, and to maintain a safe and inconspicuous distance.

The wind blew through The Damascene's long hair and made a hollow sound in the hole on the left side of his head.

As they headed further into south Beirut, banners and posters began to appear in the streets and on the houses. The green on yellow flag – the upstretched forearm with the hand holding the gun – and pictures of the bespectacled, bearded yet handsome face of Shi'a Cleric Sayyed Hassan Nasrallah, the Secretary-General of Hizbullah. Impressive and sending its message even in the shadowy illumination of the few street lights.

And The Damascene knew exactly where Rafic Hariri was going.

He found a discreet alley in which to park the Suzuki and took off his leather jacket and pulled his shirt out of his jeans. He had two days' rough stubble on his tanned face, which would help him blend in with the locals. His hair was longer than most, but that would not matter; he tied it back into the single ponytail.

To get too near the walled and gated compound would be foolish, it would be well-guarded and there would be security cameras around. But he needed to keep a watch on the place. He wandered the nearby streets, looking casual as if he knew the area well, but always with circumspect glances back towards the house. He found an old, run-down shisha café and ensconced himself inside with a Turkish coffee and a shisha of apple-flavoured tobacco. There were only two other locals inside, and after a few nods and muttered greetings they paid him no heed.

He could not see the compound directly from the café, but he could see the street and any vehicles that left through the gates.

After an hour he left the café to muttered wishes for a evening of peace, and wandered the streets in reverse formation to the way he had come, back to the bike. He put his leather jacket back on and, in case of any watchful eyes, spent twenty minutes crouched next to the bike pretending to inspect the wheels and engine.

After twenty-one minutes, he saw the gates to the compound opening and the two 4x4s drove swiftly out. A turn of the key and the Suzuki purred into life (the old repair shop up in Jamhour had done a good job). He moved off after them as it became Monday.

11 October 2004
26 Sha'ban 1425

Beirut 00:30

Why was Rafic Hariri, the Sunni Prime Minister of Lebanon, meeting with the leader of the Shi'a Hizbullah? A meeting so clandestine that the whole of Hariri's security apparatus had been stood down and replaced by two – what were they? Nissan Pathfinders? It hardly made sense. And who was the security in them? Hizbullah?

Secret meetings and changes of itinerary were anathema to an assassin. But had it not occurred to them that whilst Hariri was probably quite safe from personal threat, he could get mixed up in an attempt to take out the Israelis' number one target, Nasrallah? History would have a hard time explaining that one away.

But, reflected The Damascene as his hair blew backwards and the wind again echoed into the hole that had been his left ear, that was none of his business. What was his business was knowing Hariri's whereabouts at all times.

Abu Tarek had lied to him. Lying by omission. The text had said Hariri was home that evening. That much had been true, but it had said nothing about him going out again later.

Did the Hariri team want him to help? Or were they only co-operating to appease Ghazi Kanaan...?

The two 4x4s reached the Saeb Salam Avenue intersection, but instead of turning left onto the avenue towards Koreitem, they continued on into the centre of the city. The motorbike with dipped beam followed a quarter of a kilometre behind.

In the early hours of the morning, Beirut was now much quieter but by no means empty. They reached the intersection with General Fouad Chehab Avenue and continued on north, into the downtown area.

The two cars took a right into Emir Bechir Street and then they slowed almost to a crawl by the nearly completed Mohammed al-Amine Mosque on the south-west corner of Martyrs' Square.

The Damascene stopped outside St George's Maronite Cathedral further back and smiled. Hariri was financing the construction of the mosque. Had he made a detour to see how his project was coming along, how his money was being spent? If he had, he would be pleased. The mosque was magnificent.

After a few moments, the cars made a U-turn at the bottom of Martyrs' Square and came back down Emir Bechir Street, passing the motorcyclist on the other side of the road bending down looking at his engine.

The Damascene watched them go, on their way back to Koreitem.

Well, that had been an adventurous unplanned evening. There was an old expression: never let a day be wasted (for you never know when it will be your last). This had been a very productive day. He had found out that Rafic Hariri had a link with Sayyed Hassan Nasrallah and, perhaps more importantly for this assignment, he had learnt some of the geography of south Beirut. In his profession, knowledge of geography was paramount.

He climbed back onto the Suzuki and took the second right at Martyrs' Square into Damascus Street. It would be a direct ride back to the apartment. He had had enough for one evening, he told himself.

But in that he was wrong.

Mount Lebanon 01:30 – 08:30

The rough cinder track leading to his apartment block dipped deeply away from the Damascus road, so as he turned left onto it he was able to turn off the bike's engine so as not to wake his neighbours at this early hour. He cruised down and parked outside the front entrance. There was a parking area underneath the block but he always kept the bike outside in case he needed it quickly.

There had been no lights anywhere, in the buildings, in the street, for the last kilometre, so he knew they were having a power cut. That was why the modern apartment blocks had no elevators and were only three or so storeys high. And why they had no electronic entry systems – they relied on good old-fashioned keys.

He let himself into the block. It was pitch black inside. Using the light from one of his mobile phones, he walked silently up the stairs. There was not a sound in the building. The walls of each apartment had been built with brick and the front doors were of solid wood, so any nocturnal human noises were retained within.

He reached the top floor and turned his key in the lock. The door opened and closed soundlessly. He did not need the light from the mobile inside, night-time Beirut glistened beyond the full-length windows and cast a subtle penumbra in the apartment.

He walked over to the windows and opened them about twenty centimetres to let in some air. Then he pulled off his jacket and shirt and threw them on the leather couch, and undid the elastic band in his hair. Kicking off his trainers, he pulled down his jeans. He wore no underwear, no socks. He never had done. Not since Captain Marwan Mebarak had been stripped, tortured and murdered in Aanjar. He flicked the jeans onto the couch and enjoyed the feeling of being naked.

Cleanliness was important to him. He would shower before he slept.

Stretching his arms in the air, he breathed in and then stopped abruptly.

Perhaps he wouldn't be showering or sleeping.

Slowly he lowered his arms as he sniffed again.

Jasmine.

This was unusual, but most welcome. He smiled, waiting for the gentle sound of the zills.

But it did not come. All was quiet, and he wondered if he had been mistaken. Wishful thinking maybe. Then he felt the gossamer touch of an angel's hand against his back and he knew he had not been wrong.

He did not turn, he did not move, except for the involuntary appearance of goose-bumps as the hand travelled slowly, softly down his spine. It reached the small of his back, made one circular motion so that the fingers were pointing downwards, and then continued on over the crest of his buttocks.

The thumb and index finger were on one cheek, the third and fourth fingers on the other. The middle finger followed the natural ravine, moving down.

A voice whispered, "Master."

He controlled his heavy breathing. "That should be my job. My Djinn."

He reached round and gently took hold of her hand as he turned. She was wearing nothing except the small veil on her face and an ornate black clip in her hair. As always, he could smell her musk.

The eyes above the veil spoke without words. He reached down and took the veil in his big right hand. He thought of slipping it up and over her head and down her long black hair, but lust was not that subtle. He yanked the veil downwards and off.

She gave a little gasp. For a moment they both stood there in the shadows without moving, each completely naked. Her body matched The Damascene's for lack of hair. Then she raised the hand that had been caressing him to her lips and stared at him challengingly as she put the middle finger into her mouth.

"That," he said, "is rude."

She pouted and her low voice asked, "Do you want to be rude with me, Master?"

She got her answer over the next two hours.

He awoke at eight in the morning to sunshine and a breeze coming in through the open bedroom window. His hand moved across the wide bed, across the crumpled and in some places still damp sheet - but of course she was not there.

Like most men, he always slept well after sex. When he was with her, even more so. A smile creased his face as he thought of what they had done a few hours previously. How many ways were there to make love? And what she had done with, and into, the hole of his left ear was frankly obscene.

The answer to how had she gotten into the apartment was easy. This was a *mukhabarat* safe-house. Kanaan had obviously given her a key. But how she had arrived and left again was less evident. She might have parked in the area underneath the block. Or maybe she had a bike like him?

Whatever. Once again, The Damascene was grateful for the interlude. He needed it. In fact, he realised with just a slight feeling of surprise, he needed *her*. Which was interesting. That was almost an emotion. Only the living had emotions – and he was a dead man.

He got out of bed and went over to the open window. The breeze blew against his body, cooling. Now he would have that shower.

He scratched his left shoulder.

And once again he had been bitten by a mosquito when her scent was on him. Obviously he wasn't the only one who liked The Djinn!

Twenty minutes later, showered and drying naturally, wet hair falling down either side of his face, he walked naked out onto the balcony. Her odour had been washed away so the bugs would no longer be interested in him.

In his hand he carried the Samsung mobile. He switched it on and looked out over Beirut as he waited to connect to the service. The sun had just come over the top of the block, illuminating the panorama in front of him. It was another fine Mediterranean day. He could hear the children in the apartment next door but because of the design of the balconies he could not see them and, importantly, they could not see him.

It was a Monday, the start of a new business week. And the start of a new political week. He could guess what Hariri's itinerary would be today.

He had decided not to berate Abu Tarek about the lack of information. If they did not wish to tell him things and Hariri died as a result – well, that was up to them. But, as he had reasoned before, Hariri was perfectly safe on impromptu movements, unless he became collateral damage in other events – in which case there was nothing The Damascene could do about it anyway. It was the norm they had to worry about, the predictable, publicised known itinerary, not the unnorm.

The mobile throbbed in his hand. The expected text message, sent an hour earlier.

KOREITEM. SERAIL. PARLIAMENT. SERAIL. KOREITEM.

The exact routes would not be known until Abu Tarek made the last-minute decision. Hariri was safe.

For today.

Ras en Nabaa, Beirut 09:00

Captain Maroun Khoury of the Department of General Security did not wear a uniform. Indeed, he had never been issued with one. He would never appear in public, never need to make a show of his authority, either internally or externally. People in his line of work never did. In fact their existence was not even admitted.

And he did not like the designation of rank either. He was a team leader, the emphasis being on Team. His team were information gatherers and listeners, operating mostly outside Lebanon's borders. Anything and everything. Just in case. Protecting Lebanon from all threats.

He now sat with one of his Gatherers, Zahia Zalloum – colloquially known as ZiZi – a dark-haired Lebanese in her late twenties, one of the most trusted field agents of the DGS. For the fifth time they listened to the voice captured on the memory stick.

It was a man's voice, low, anxious but not distressed. "Get away. Get away from me, you bastard. Leave me alone. I'm not that way. Don't touch that - " There was a gap of twenty seconds during which the breathing became heavy as if some sort of physical exhaustion had occurred. Then it calmed and the voice said normally, "I didn't want that to happen. That was your fault. Look at my clothes! Well, to hell with you, the rats can have you."

Khoury looked up from the computer. "That is all?"

"That is all," nodded Zahia. "It doesn't last long, as you know."

"No... What do you think?"

Zahia shrugged. "The rats can have you? A sewer? Somebody pushed into a sewer?"

"Maybe. Nothing else? Nobody turned up in a sewer?"

"Not that we've heard."

Khoury stroked his beard. "No bodies turned up anywhere?"

"None that we know of. Could be early days though."

"Could be." Khoury was pensive. Then he said, "Okay. Let's monitor. Eyes and ears, ZiZi."

She nodded, smiling. "Eyes and ears, Chief."

16 October 2004
2 Ramadan 1425

Bourj el-Barajneh, Beirut 16:30 – 22:30

Al-Rajul had been watching for five days. Already he had chosen three young men in their late teens or early twenties. He needed two more.

He saw the next candidate kicking an old, semi-deflated football against a wall in the north-east of the camp. A typical dark-haired, olive-skinned young man with a wispy beard, dressed in jeans and a two-seasons-out-of-date Manchester United shirt. He had the agility of the young and his stamina was impressive: it was Ramadan, the sun had been up for many hours and the young man would not have had anything to eat or drink, including water, in that time. Yet his prowess with the ball was remarkable: he was on his twenty-eighth keepy-uppy and did not look like flagging.

Al-Rajul stepped casually out of the alleyway from where he had been watching. Today his head and face were uncovered, the Palestinian *keffiyeh* tied around his neck like a scarf and falling over his chest in front of his shirt. He walked as if he was going somewhere, nodding to the youth as he passed *"Ramadan Mubarak."*

"Ramadan Mubarak," mumbled the youth. Thirty-two, thirty-three.

Al-Rajul stopped as if he had just thought of something and turned back with a smile. "You are very good."

The youth concealed his irritation as he stopped at thirty-six, capturing the ball under his right foot. "Thank you, *ustaz.*"

Al-Rajul held in his laugh. Did he look that old? "Maybe you will play for Palestine one day, huh? In the World Cup."

The youth's snort was derisive but not impolite. *"Insha'Allah."*

"You must have had a good *Sahur*, to still have the energy to do that."

"I find it easy."

"Or do you cheat?"

"At football?"

"At fasting."

The youth frowned. "I am a good Muslim."

"Here," Al-Rajul rummaged in a back pocket of his cargo pants and pulled out a small, flat flask. He held it out. "Water. Even the Prophet, peace be upon him, would not mind if it meant Palestine winning the *Mondial!"*

"No, *ustaz*, no." The youth looked genuinely shocked as he shook his head.

"No?" Al-Rajul put the flask back. "Good. That is very good. How old are you?"

"What?"

"How old are you?"

"Nineteen."

"Nineteen. That is a good age. You live here?"

"Would I be here otherwise?"

Al-Rajul nodded. "A very good point. You have family?"

The youth bent down and picked up the old football. "Why all these questions?"

"I am sorry. Please excuse me." Al-Rajul turned and began to walk away.

"No, no. It is I who should be sorry. Please excuse my rudeness, *ustaz*."

Al-Rajul stopped again and turned back.

"I live with my mother and my sister," said the youth. "And two uncles."

"Your father?

"No. He is dead."

"I am sorry."

The youth shrugged.

Al-Rajul looked from side to side and then stepped nearer to the youth, close enough to smell his Ramadan breath. He spoke quietly. "I am on a mission. From Abu Ammar." He flicked his scarf. "You know him."

"*Meen*? No."

"Oh you do. He is your President."

The youth's eyebrows rose and frowned at the same time.

"Are you *Fatah*?" Al-Rajul looked from side to side again. "*Hamas*?"

Another shrug. "*Fatah*, I suppose."

"Good, good." Al-Rajul coughed and pulled away from the youth as two older men walked by. When they were out of earshot, he continued. "The President has asked me to recruit trustworthy *Fatah* men for a special mission."

"What is it?"

"I cannot tell you more at this time. The President has many reserves at his disposal to reward those he chooses. Should he chose you, I can guarantee that you, your mother and sister will be removed from this place."

"To where? Where is there to go?"

"Wherever you want to. Back to Palestine? It is only a matter of time now before the Zionists are routed. Or anywhere. Jordan, Syria, UAE? It will be your choice."

"And my uncles?"

"Of course."

The youth bounced the ball once off the ground. "What do I have to do?"

"Not here. Not now. Can you meet me tonight?"

"Maybe."

"After *Iftar*. Make an excuse to leave your family. Do not tell them or anyone of this conversation. Meet me at Annan Street at ten o'clock. Can you do that?"

From one of the dwellings, a baby began to cry.

"Can I not tell my mother?" asked the youth.

"Not at this time. But you will be the hero of the family on the day you tell them that you, and you alone, have managed to get them out of this place. That is your reward if the President chooses you. Can you meet me?"

"Yes."

"*Shoo 'es-mak*?"

"Mohammed."

"Same as me! We are both worthy of our name. Tonight. Annan Street. At ten. *Yaatik al-aafieh*." Al-Rajul turned and walked away, disappearing into the alleys. After a moment he heard the ball bouncing again in the distance.

He turned down a passage where the tangle of electricity wires between the buildings was hanging so low that he had to duck his head. He trod in something wet on the ground, grateful that he wore trainers not sandals.

The test had been set. Would the youth pass it? The other three he had already chosen had. A simple test of trustworthiness.

He passed by an elaborate mural and nodded in gratitude at the image of Abu Ammar: Mohammed Abdel Rahman Abdel Raouf Arafat al-Qudwa al-Husseini, popularly known as Yasser Arafat. The President of the Palestinian National Authority.

And bait for the youth.

Mohammed was unaware of the man tailing him.

He lived only three alleyways and two open sewers from where he had been playing with the ball. It was getting dark when he reached home. Conveniently for Al-Rajul the rooms Mohammed inhabited with his family were on the ground floor of a three-storey block.

Al-Rajul watched him enter through an old, broken wooden doorway. There was a window to the alley and Al-Rajul moved over to it like a wraith. He could hear women's voices talking to Mohammed. No other men. He moved away from the window and into the shadows.

Minutes later, as a call to *Maghrib* prayer came from somewhere distant, two men in their late thirties came along from the opposite direction, talking animatedly. They went in through the broken door. Uncles.

Al-Rajul glided back over to the open window and stayed there for twenty minutes.

The talk was inconsequential. If Mohammed was going to say anything, he would probably have blurted it out straightaway. At one point one of the uncles, to the derision of his brother, was announcing his ideas for a new commercial venture which would get the family at least into better accommodation, if not out of the camp altogether. The conversation became quite heated. An ideal moment for Mohammed to speak up about the *ustaz* who had approached him that afternoon, who had offered the whole family a way out of here. But he did not. He was a good boy.

The smells of cooking (not all of them pleasant) reminded Al-Rajul that he was hungry. He looked at his watch. Over three hours before his meeting with the youth.

He would not eat in the camp. He would go back out to Beirut, there were plenty of places there. He might even indulge in a shisha.

He pushed away from the wall, melted into shadow and silently disappeared.

Al-Rajul had been watching the Annan Street entrance to the camp since 21:30. It was a busy area and he could loiter unnoticed. He would have liked to have worn the *keffiyeh* on his head, but he needed to look exactly as he did this afternoon so that Mohammed would recognise him. Nevertheless, the Palestinians coming and going naturally thought he was one of their own. Except for the occasional greeting, he was left alone.

He saw Mohammed coming along at 21:55. Good, he was keen.

Because of the volume of other people, he did not notice for several seconds that Mohammed had someone with him.

"Merhaba, ustaz," greeted Mohammed. Al-Rajul smiled as they shook hands, his eyes pointedly travelling to the other person, a youth similar to Mohammed but plumper. "I hope you do not mind," said Mohammed in explanation. "This is my friend Chadi. I thought he might be able to help the President also."

Al-Rajul shook the outstretched hand. *"Al-salaam 'aalaykum."*

"'aalaykum al-salaam, ustaz," Chadi was respectful but perhaps just a little nervous.

"Mohammed has told you of our mission?"

"To help the President, yes."

"Good, let us walk."

The two youths came forward.

"No, no," Al-Rajul gestured behind them. "Back into the camp. It is quieter there. We can find somewhere to talk. Come. You like football, Chadi...?"

As they walked, Al-Rajul moved his *keffiyeh* up over his head and threw the end across the lower half of his face, across his shoulder.

They walked for five minutes. The lanes narrowed so that they could walk only two abreast, and Al-Rajul let them go in front of him.

Tonight it was dark in the camp, even without a power cut, but the residual light from the buildings and the growing moon gave them enough light to see by, providing they watched where they were walking.

They were chatting about the merits of the Reds versus the Blues (Chadi confessed to being a Chelsea supporter), when Al-Rajul gestured to a lane to the right. "Down here. I know it is a quiet place."

They walked down, avoiding a dripping waste outlet which was perilously close to a frayed electricity cable. "Mohammed has explained the rewards, Chadi?"

"Oh yes, *ustaz*," said Chadi over his shoulder "I would do anything to help my mother and father get out of here. And to help the President, of course."

"The President is looking for good men." Al-Rajul put his hand into his right pants pocket, caressing the small wooden object he always carried with him. It was a Holding Cross, a ten centimetre long piece of solid olive wood carved into the shape of a cross with the cross beam uneven to fit comfortably between a person's fingers. He had bought it a while ago now, in Beit Sahour, near Bethlehem in Palestine. "Men like you. To be chosen, a man has to be strong, courageous and trustworthy." He brought the cross out of his pocket, enveloped in the palm of his hand. "Which is, of course Mohammed, where you have failed."

He twitched his right hand so that the down beam of the cross flicked upwards from its place in his palm to poke out between his first and middle finger, the cross beam held within his fist. He rammed it across and to his left, hitting Mohammed in his head above and behind his right ear. The young man's skull broke on impact.

Chadi was aware only of the sound of a crack followed by his friend falling against the wall, as if he had tripped on an uneven piece of earth. Then his own throat was seized so that he could not cry out and the last thing he saw was the hand with the bulbous, rigid sixth finger hurtling towards his left eyebrow.

Chadi's skull fractured with the first blow, but Al-Rajul kept hitting him as he caught the body, dull thuds of splintering bone. By the time he had lowered the body to the ground, with a bizarre gentleness, Chadi's skull was gaping open and pink matter was flowing out like lava from a volcano and dropping onto the dry, dusty ground. His eyes were open and staring, his tongue hanging out.

Al-Rajul went over to Mohammed and felt for a pulse. He still had one, weak, but he was too far gone even to groan in pain. Al-Rajul thought of hitting him again but decided not to. The cosmetics would take care of him.

He stood up, looked about and listened. No change in the background sounds, faraway voices from the dwellings, the occasional shout, the intermittent static from a radio, the baby howling. There had been no noise during the killings, just the sound of fast-moving scuffling.

Chadi's gore was on Al-Rajul's shirt and pants. The pants he would have to live with, but the shirt might attract attention. It would be a snug fit, but he would take Mohammed's shirt. The youth would not be needing it now. Or ever again.

At that moment, the lights from the buildings went out. Power cut. Perfect timing.

Al-Rajul knelt down and began the cosmetics.

20 October 2004
6 Ramadan 1425

Mount Lebanon 08:00

The Damascene stood on the balcony, strong coffee in his right hand, Samsung mobile in his left. The text was as expected.

KOREITEM. SERAIL. KOREITEM.

It was 08:00. Already Hariri's security team and their dogs would have made the first sweep of the day, both inside and outside Koreitem Palace, looking for explosives or anything untoward. All the vehicles would have been searched and scanned with an explosives detector.

The six-vehicle convoy would leave for the Prime Minister's offices at the Grand Serail at 09:00. As always, Hariri would be driving himself in the armour-plated Mercedes S-600, the third car.

A similar sweep would have been made at the Grand Serail, and Hariri would not alight from his car until he was inside the complex in a secure area.

No one in this life was ever completely safe, but that was as safe as it got. There was no room for snipers.

Today The Damascene would continue with a little experiment had had been trying recently: attempting to guess which of the three routes from Koreitem to Downtown the convoy would take: the coastal route, the central route or the southern route. He had been unsuccessful so far, one correct guess out of five, just a normal average.

Abu Tarek would normally announce the route just as they were leaving. True randomness was the highest security. But if there was a pattern, even just a subconscious one, then that was a weakness.

The Damascene would study and analyse the frequency, patterns and timings of the routes chosen.

Because if he could work out a pattern, so could an assassin.

Central Beirut 09:20

That morning they took the southern route, through Sanayeh and turning left at Zoqaq el Blat. The Damascene had not expected it because it was the third time in succession that they had gone that way. Although that was good and would fool someone with ill-intent today, they needed to be careful. Too much use of one choice meant that it was unlikely to be used next time, which narrowed the guess down from three to two – or improved an assassin's choice from one in three to fifty-fifty.

But that was still too much choice for a lone sniper. Unless...

The Damascene pulled the Suzuki over to the side of the road in Syria Street, outside the Grand Theatre and looked back at the rebuilt centre of Beirut.

Unless there was a team.

Three routes. Three choices. Three strategically placed snipers.

He shook his head. No. That would still mean Hariri getting out of his car at some point along the route and within range of a sniper. That was something that just would not happen.

But then he had thought that Hariri having clandestine meetings with Sayyed Hassan Nasrallah was something that just would not happen.

It was a possibility to note, but not a concern.

A team would have to work some other way.

Mount Lebanon 18:00

In the perversely ironic way that fate operates, The Damascene was one of the last to find out about the momentous events of that day. He lunched in *l'Entrecôte* in Achrafieh, had other things to do, and then returned to the apartment in the early evening. He stripped and showered, grabbed a bottle of *Sohat* mineral water from the fridge, and then stood naked in front of the television, drying.

It was on every channel.

Rafic Hariri had resigned as Prime Minister of Lebanon.

His letter of resignation had been delivered to President Lahoud and Speaker Nabih Berri early that afternoon. Former Prime Minister Omar Karami had been asked to head a new government until the elections scheduled for mid-2005.

The Damascene did not care about politics. Any interest he had had in affairs of state had died when Captain Marwan Mebarak had been murdered. As he looked at the reports on the screen, he wondered how this affected his assignment – or if he now had an assignment at all.

Hariri was no longer Prime Minister, so the threat to his person would diminish accordingly. He was remaining as a Member of Parliament, and he would still be a thorn in the side of his opponents and his enemies, but the act of resigning had immediately downgraded his security risk from Code Black to Code Yellow.

Would there still be a threat to him?

Would he still require enhanced protection?

Those questions actually did not matter. The only question that needed answering was: was Hariri alive still of any use to Ghazi Kanaan?

He would telephone Kanaan, he had a direct line number to his office in Damascus. He would use the alternative mobile, the Motorola, but he would not call from the apartment. Calls made to the Syrian Interior Ministry were bound to be monitored, if not by the Lebanese then certainly by some other alien power, and he could be triangulated and located within just a few minutes. Not that he had done anything wrong, for the sake of Allah – he was helping to protect the Prime Minister (make that ex-Prime Minister). But he did not want any interest taken in him – and a call from the edges of Beirut to the Interior Minister's office in Damascus would at least spark curiosity.

He would travel further up the mountain, to Bhamdoun, about twenty minutes away. He might even take in a meal at the *Janna* restaurant with its magnificent views over the St Martin Valley. He would be on his own but he was sure a table for one would not be a problem.

Just for a moment he thought of The Djinn and what it would be like to have dinner with her, to get to know her – as a person, rather than his sexual reward – but then he dismissed such ideas. She might be a person. He was not. He was a dead man.

He dressed in a baggy white shirt over beige cargo pants, let his still-damp hair hang loose and went out.

Maybe his thoughts were still on The Djinn, that was why he missed it. Or if it did register, maybe his subconscious dismissed it as just another resident of the building, which indeed it was.

As The Damascene walked quickly down the stairs, the front door to the apartment directly under his opened, just a crack. Just enough for somebody to look out at the man going down the stairs.

Then it closed again.

Bhamdoun, Lebanon 21:00

He telephoned from the lobby of the Sheraton Hotel. He was in the seating area near Reception and looked no different from the others going about their business. Opposite him, a Jordanian had a laptop open on the coffee table.

It was unlikely that Kanaan would be in his office at 21:00, but this was a dedicated number and he was sure there would be a message for him.

It was answered on the sixth ring, a man's voice with a simple "'eeh?"

The Damascene identified himself by the name he was known as. He asked no other question.

After two beats, the voice said "You will be contacted" and the line went blank.

The Damascene closed his phone, stood up and left the hotel.

21 October 2004
7 Ramadan 1425

Mount Lebanon 00:30 – 15:00

He arrived back after midnight. The block was in darkness. He did not turn on the stairwell lights, preferring to use the light from his mobile phone.

The local cuisine at *Janna* had been superb and afterwards he had treated himself to a shisha while he watched the belly dancers and listened to the live music.

He had been told on the phone that he would be contacted. On his way back down the Damascus road he allowed himself to wonder if it would be his usual contact – The Djinn. Was the non-tactile entertainment in the restaurant the only form of belly dancing he would be experiencing tonight?

Immediately he opened his front door, he knew the answer. Tonight there was no subtle scent of jasmine, the apartment was awaft with the heady, full-on aroma of frankincense. Candles had been placed around the room, the walls seeming to move with the flickering. Background music was playing a distinct *raqs sharqi* beat.

She was standing in the middle of the floor, looking at him challengingly, defiantly. There was nothing on her head save for the ornate black hair clip. Her face was bare. A small, tasselled bra top covered her breasts. Below her navel was a golden, coined belt on top of black, diaphanous harem pants. Her feet were bare. In her hands she held a metre length of rope with a knot at each end.

Out through the windows, Beirut twinkled behind her.

The Damascene leant with his back against the front door, watching as her hips picked up the beat. The *raqs sharqi* dance was more defined than the *raqs baladi* country dance, and with each hip thrust she walked a step towards him. She played with the rope, first down her back, then between her breasts. Her eyes held his as she moved the rope down between her legs.

Then her hips began to shimmy then circle with the music. She came close to him. Reaching up, she placed the end of the rope that had been between her legs over his right shoulder.

She pushed his hair back and put her right hand over the hole that was his left ear, caressing it gently with her thumb.

The Damascene smiled. "Well, well. I did wonder."

She was pressed close against his body, her thighs astride his right knee. She moved against his leg. "You wondered what, Master?" Her right hand went around the back of his head and brought round the end of the rope.

"Whether it would be you that contacted me."

Her cardamom-scented breath was warm in his nostrils. "You want contact with me, Master?"

"Oh yes."

She pulled sharply on the rope, forcing his face down onto hers, tongues meeting, their lust irresistible.

The first time finished when he erupted inside her while she was bent forwards over the back of the leather couch. The second time was on the stairs. Only the third time was in the bedroom.

He awoke to light streaming in through the bedroom window, his body still sticky with the sweats of night time. His mouth and chin were crusty.

As always, she was not there. Pushing himself up onto his elbows, he looked at the bedside cabinet. The clock said 07:45. Had she left a message for him from Kanaan? A note?

There was nothing there.

Getting up, he stretched and ran his hands down his body, stopping at his balls to tug them comfortable. Walking over to the bedroom window, he stood with his hands on his butt, looking out over Beirut. Yet another sunny day. He scratched a mosquito bite on his left cheek, grateful that he usually slept on his front – otherwise the bite would have been too close for comfort!

Then he heard a sound.

Just one, a sharp *tink*.

He turned and ran silently over to the half-open bedroom door, pressing himself against the wall.

The sound came again. Another *tink*.

Silently he stepped out onto the landing and looked over.

Then he grinned. A moment later he was walking down the stairs, still completely nude.

He realised that he had never seen her in the daylight before, she had always come to him at night. She was in the kitchen preparing coffee – and she looked even more beautiful. She was wearing a white T-shirt with the English word PRINCESS in pink on the front. The shirt did not quite cover the cheeks of her bottom. Her long glossy black hair was bunched at the back and held by the black hair clip. Her face still bore the traces of last night's make-up.

"*Sabah el-khair*," he said warmly as he walked across the room.

Her gaze first went to his groin, then up the scarred, hairless body to his face. "*Bonjour*," she smiled.

"*Kifik?*"

"I am well, thank you. *Kifak?*"

"*Mnih.*"

He stood in front of her, and for a moment it was as if neither of them knew what to do. Then they both laughed.

"I have never seen you - " he began.

"With my clothes on?"

"In the morning. Or in daylight for that matter."

"I hope I do not disappoint you."

"Far from it."

"You want a message from me. I could not give it to you while you were asleep or... otherwise engaged. I have always been taught never to speak with my mouth full."

He nodded and just resisted the urge to lean forward and thwack her bottom.

Slowly she pressed the plunger on the cafetière, making even that act seem very sensual. He felt himself give a little reaction and, remembering his nakedness, hastily asked, "What is the message? Does he want me to carry on?"

"Yes. You are to carry on. Until you are told otherwise."

"I see. That is from Kanaan himself?"

"Who else?"

She began to pour the coffee into two mugs.

"And you?" he asked.

"Me?" She stared at him and shrugged, smiling cheekily. "My orders are the same as yours. To carry on with my mission."

He took a mug. "Good."

"So," she said, stretching out a hand and grabbing hold of his far from flaccid component. "Before I continue with my mission, can I ask you a question?"

"Of course." He felt the warm sensation as she started to rub him.

"Do you have *any* food in this place or just the packet of coffee?"

He received a text message at 08:00, while they were making love. He ignored it until he had finished at 08:05 and then studied the phone without speaking, just giving a little nod.

She left at 08:30. Her 'street clothes' were the PRINCESS T-shirt, tight blue denim jeans and black leather ankle boots. Her dancing clothes were in a brown Louis Vuitton bag which she carried on her shoulder. Her hair was down, with the clip at a jaunty angle on the right of her head. Had The Damascene been capable of expressing any feelings, he would have said she looked charming. And sexy. He thought these things, but he could not express them.

As she was leaving, he asked "Will I see you again?"

She stopped by the front door, which he was holding open. Because of her small frame, the Louis Vuitton bag looked enormous on her shoulder. "Is your mission completed?"

"No. You know I have been told to carry on."

"Well then," she said. "As I told you, I will carry on too. *A bientôt, chéri.*"

And with that she left. A little part of him, deep down inside, wanted to follow her, to see where she went, but he knew better. Those were the actions of a lovesick fool. She might even come from base in Syria, it was only an hour away by bike, which was what he suspected she used. He had to remind himself that she was the gift of the Brigadier, nothing more than Kanaan's whore. She would perform her duties whether she liked him or loathed him. Feelings were unnecessary and pointless.

He showered, dried naked on the balcony for ten minutes and then dressed, packing the things he needed for the day into his cargo pants pockets.

He went out at 09:30.

At midday, a white Opel car turned off the Damascus road and crunched down the slope, coming to a halt in front of the apartment block. The man who got out was on the tall side, slim but obviously fit, with short-cropped dark hair and the obligatory stubble. He was dressed in a black leather jacket, light shirt, light cotton trousers and sandals - the standard Syrian *mukhabarat* outfit.

He stood by the car and looked up at the building before going over to the front door. It was so quiet around here. Someone had chosen the safe house well.

The front door of the building would not open at his tug. There were six buttons on the wall in the same pattern as the apartments they serviced, with name plates next to them. Top left was 'Ibrahim', underneath that 'Ghorra', with 'Al Arab' on the ground floor. The three plates on the right were blank.

He pressed the top right button.

Nothing happened. He noticed that there was no remote entry system, no intercom, so the residents would have to come downstairs to let people in.

He gave it another minute and one more bell press.

Nothing.

Okay, he would wait. He was in no hurry. He leaned against the side of the car - not knowing that from above he was being watched...

Fifteen minutes later, the front door opened outwards and a boy about seven years old, dressed in the completely red kit of Liverpool Football Club, came out and walked over towards a cream Ford Explorer parked nearby.

The man caught the front door before it closed but then had to step back as an attractive tall blonde woman and twin girls of about five came through. He did not respond to the woman's nod of thanks, he just let them pass and then went inside.

Upstairs, the door to the top right apartment was of course closed. But to this one he had a key. He would berate the idiots at base for not giving him one to the block as well.

He knocked on the door.

No answer.

He took the key from his pocket and slipped it into the lock. The door opened soundlessly. Leaving the door ajar, he went inside. He stood looking about the place. This was impressive. There was money somewhere in this business.

He noticed two unwashed mugs on the kitchen draining board next to a third-full cafetière. The jug was cold to his touch. Pity, he could do with a coffee after the journey he had had. Was there a microwave? Where was the kettle? He might be in for a long wait.

He emptied the contents of the cafetière into the sink, turned on the tap and then frowned as the dregs had difficulty going down.

He was swirling them around with the index finger of his right hand when he felt a sharp prick like a wasp sting on the back of his neck.

"Shit!" He jumped and his left hand went upwards to his neck. There was nothing there, no sting had been left behind. "In the name of Allah!" he mumbled.

Out of the corner of his eye he saw something and turned. His hand was still holding his neck. He frowned and then smiled at the person standing there. "I'm sorry," he said. "Please excuse my language. Damn wasp!" He gave an apologetic laugh.

"Who are you?" asked the other person.

"Excuse me. I'm sorry. Yes, my name is Aboud," he rubbed his neck and took his hand down. "I am a friend of..." He gave the name The Damascene was known by.

"He has no friends."

"Well, actually, I'm a colleague – my goodness, what a view!" Aboud nodded towards the window.

The other person did not turn. "He has no colleagues."

"Well, we're in the same line of business - "

"You are an assassin?"

"No. Well - "

"You don't even know him, do you?"

"Of course I do."

"And you broke into his apartment?"

"I have a key. I need to see him."

"Why?"

"Why? Well..." Aboud frowned. Suddenly he did not feel well at all. His head was heavy. The room was moving like a wave. Was he having a stroke? "I... I..." Why did he need to see him? He couldn't remember...

He put his hand back up to his neck and rubbed it. "I'm not... Could you help me? I don't feel..." The room was now roaring in his ears, but it was going grey, fading...

The other person did not move.

Aboud staggered forward as his sight left him. Now the roaring seemed faraway.

As his legs buckled and his senses died, the last thing he was aware of was a smell.

Jasmine.

Sixty minutes later an old white Transit van pulled up downstairs and three men got out. From the back of the van they pulled three large suitcases.

The front door of the apartment building was on the latch and they went inside.

Ninety minutes later they came back out again with the suitcases which, by the way they were carrying them, seemed decidedly heavier than when they had gone in.

The front door clicked shut behind them.

They loaded the suitcases into the back of the van and drove off.

22 October 2004
17 Ramadan 1425

Ras en Nabaa, Beirut 08:30

Maroun Khoury and Zahia Zalloum sat together in front of the computer in Khoury's office in the DGS building, an unnecessary closeness as they were not looking at anything, just listening to the memory stick, but they had a history which both of them remembered with fondness. Their knees were touching but they pretended not to notice.

It was the same voice as before on the memory stick: male, but this time quite calm, conversational. "I need to trust. If I cannot trust them then they are no good to me."

Another voice asked, "Can you trust them?"

"Not the last one. The first three are good but the last one was bad."

"So what did you do?"

"They cannot linger."

"They?"

"He brought a friend. They both had to be disappeared."

Silence. Khoury asked, "Is that it?"

Zahia nodded. "Yes."

Khoury sat back, the action taking his knee away from hers, which he regretted. "Still no bodies?"

"We haven't heard of any."

"But potentially there are three."

"If we're interpreting it right."

Khoury nodded. "Okay. You are right to let me hear these, something is going on. Put a marker up with The Listeners just in case they hear anything that could be connected."

She stood up. "Eyes and ears, Chief."

Khoury gave a small laugh. "Eyes and ears, ZiZi."

As he watched her walk from the room it wasn't only her eyes and ears he was thinking of.

30 October 2004
16 Ramadan 1425

Bourj el-Barajneh, Beirut 13:00

Captain Fadi Lattouf of the Palestinian Security Force was in his blue police uniform, epauletted shirt open at the neck. His grey-black bush of chest hair poked upwards out of the shirt and joined the not so bushy neck hairs of his beard. He did not wear his Captain's hat when he was on business about the camp, too showy, too much of a target, too bloody hot. So his comb-over was stuck to his head with sweat.

He was sweating not through heat but because it was Ramadan. He had not had a thing to eat or drink since *Sahur* and would not do so until *Iftar* – unless his will, resolve and religious conviction wavered, as it often did in mid-afternoon. And the smell of raw meat in this butcher's shop made him want to retch.

He nodded in appreciation of the wrapped and bloody package that had been given to him as he entered. Nada would get two good meals out of it for the family.

Normally he would be accompanied by a sergeant when he ventured out into the camp, but when he had been told of the report that had been received he had decided that he needed to handle this personally, and alone.

"Where are they?" he asked.

Karim The Butcher nodded to his left. "Out the back."

"Show me." Lattouf put his package on the counter and followed.

Karim spoke as he led the way. "I thought somebody had left me a delivery, I couldn't tell at first."

"So they appeared today?"

"I don't know. I don't really use the back. My deliveries when I get them come through the front. And I am closed a lot during the Holy Month."

"So when was the last time you were out the back, before today?"

Karim shrugged. "Don't know. Ten days, maybe two weeks."

A small, dark corridor led to a back door padlocked on the inside. As soon as Karim removed the lock and opened the door, the stench hit Lattouf with such force that he staggered backwards. Quickly he put his right hand over his nose and mouth. "My God!"

Outside was a small yard only about ten metres square. Cables of various thicknesses hung between the surrounding buildings and liquid dripped from more than one cracked pipe. A small passageway hardly the width of a man (and certainly smaller than the width of Fadi Lattouf) led off from the right into another warren. There were a lot of flies.

On the ground to the left of the door was an object about the size of a large goat. A muslin sheet was draped over it, the sheet covered in pink, red, maroon and brown splotches which Lattouf realised must be old and new bloodstains.

"Did you cover it?" he mumbled from between his fingers.

"I thought it best," admitted Karim.

With an inward groan at his aching knees, Lattouf crouched down on his haunches.

"Okay..." he said quietly. This he did not want to do. He swapped his hands so that his left covered his nose and mouth. Reaching out with his right hand, his fingers touched the cloth. He baulked and withdrew his hand and then brought it forward again.

With a snap of his wrist he pulled off the cloth and threw it aside.

In the name of Allah the most merciful!

Lattouf fell backwards onto his arse, his booted heels kicking the ground, instinctively trying to move himself away. He could not believe what he was seeing.

There were indeed two of them, entwined like spoons – probably for ease of carrying. Their clothes were bloodied, ripped and gnawed. Some skin was left, but not all of it. One of them at least was male, a small half-eaten penis was poking out of what had once been the poor soul's undergarments.

And they had no faces, no front of skulls. Their heads looked like the husks of opened coconuts, crawling with maggots. They had probably been bloody, pulpy messes at one time, but the rodents must have thought *Eid* had come early. But at least the hair was partly intact, the shortness of it on each skull confirming that the other victim was probably male also.

And there was something else. Lodged between the two heads, slightly flattened. Lattouf leant his head forward without moving his body – yes, it was an eye. A solitary eye.

His hand covering his face had instinctively moved down and backwards as Lattouf had fallen. Now the stench entered him unhindered, up his nose, down his throat, into his very soul. He could taste rotting human.

Shakily, he stood up. He was a professional policeman, an investigator, a keeper of the peace. He knew that crime scenes should not be contaminated, even in the squalor of the Bourj el-Barajneh Palestinian Refugee Camp. But sometimes it just could not be helped.

He leant forward, both hands against the wall above him, and with an almighty roar vomited with the force of an elephant pissing after a night on the beer. Not once, not twice, but three times, the last one being just a dry retch. His spew splashed over his shoes and across the lower legs of his trousers.

He remained in that position for a minute, getting back his breath. Then he straightened, little flecks of vomit in his beard. He glared at Karim as if he was the murderer. "Inside."

They went in.

"Lock the door."

Karim did as ordered.

"In the name of Allah, the smell!" Lattouf muttered as they went back into the main room of the shop. Several flies had taken the opportunity to come in with them.

"In my trade you get used to it, Captain," said Karim.

"I'm talking about in here. Do you ever clean this place out?"

"I - "

"No, I am sorry, Karim," Lattouf held up an apologetic hand. "That was uncalled for. It's the shock. Just the shock." He supported himself against the counter. "You do not go back out there, you understand?"

"Yes, Captain."

"And say nothing to anybody. Have you spoken to anyone already?"

"No, Captain, I just waited here as I was told, after I went to the police. The shop has not been open."

"Good. And you did not touch the bodies?" Bizarre thoughts of Karim making pies flashed through his mind.

"I only covered them."

"Good. Some of my men will come by later. Let them do what they have to do. They will tell you when you can go back outside."

"What do I do until then?"

"You wait. Skin a sheep or something." He thought that that might not have been the most appropriate thing to say. "Don't let me down, Karim."

"I won't, Captain."

Lattouf turned to leave.

"Captain?"

Lattouf stopped in the doorway and looked back. Karim had the package in his hand. "Your meat."

Hesitantly Lattouf took it. "Thank you. Peace be upon you."

"And you, Captain."

Some hope, thought Lattouf as he made his way back out onto the Champs Elysées. His stomach was empty and he was ravenous. And he needed water, litres of it and quickly. He would have to break his fast. He would increase his *fitra* at *Eid* in recompense.

There was an *hadith* he had heard many years ago:

When Ramadan arrives,
Heaven's gates are opened,
hell's gates are closed,
and the demons are chained up.

So what had gone wrong in Ramadan 1425? Hell's gates were open and the demons were loose. What he had seen with the previous body and now these two was inhuman. Not of man.

Only, of course, it was.

What was going on?

Looking back to make sure he could not been seen from Karim's shop, for he did not want to cause offence, he drew his right arm back and threw his parcel of meat far into a dingy alley.

He was hungry, but perhaps the Lattouf family would become vegetarians for a while.

1 November 2004
18 Ramadan 1425

Jonblat, Beirut 09:30

Captain Jihad Merhi of the Lebanese Internal Security Force was reaching out for his cup of coffee when the telephone on his desk rang. With irritation he changed the trajectory of his hand.

He could do without interruptions. He was halfway through a report on the resurgence of the al-Murabitoun faction in Akkar in the north, a reappearance probably prompted by the shameful treatment of their fellow-Sunni Rafic Hariri whose act of resignation was a thrown-down gauntlet to his political enemies. Also three other thick files had appeared on his desk over the weekend, each of them demanding his immediate attention.

"Yes?"

"I've got Captain Lattouf of the PSF on the line, sir," said Sergeant Deeb el-Gharib from out in the General Office. "Asking for you."

Shit.

"Did he say what he wanted?"

"No, sir."

"Okay." There was a pause, a click, then Merhi said "Merhi."

"Morning of joy, dear Captain."

Merhi sighed inwardly. "Morning of light, my friend."

"How are you?"

"Busy." Hint. "But well. And you?"

"Allah still takes care of me. But I am troubled."

"You wish to meet?"

"That would be nice."

"Where and when?"

"Um, er... Tomorrow at sixteen hundred?" Lattouf was speaking loudly, distinctly, slowly, for the audience he knew was listening. "You choose the place."

Merhi nodded. That was good, Fadi. The Listeners would know he should be fasting, so it would be suspicious to name a restaurant. He had left it up to him. He thought for a moment. "Tomorrow I have to be in Saifi. Debbas Square, you know it?"

"I can find it."

"I'll see you then."

"Debbas Square at sixteen hundred. I'll be there. *Bukra*."

"*A demain*."

Merhi put down the phone, stood up and stretched. He came out from behind his desk and walked over to the window, looking out onto Bank of Lebanon Street.

Not all official telephones in Lebanon were monitored or bugged, but it was safe to assume that the important ones were. A Captain of the Internal Security Force was important enough to be on the radar of The Listeners, especially when he was talking to his Palestinian counterpart.

Their meeting would always be one day and two hours earlier than they agreed. So sixteen hundred tomorrow meant fourteen hundred today. It did not matter what location was named, they would always meet at the food court in the Dunes Shopping Mall.

Merhi stared down at the busy street below, wondering what the Palestinian wanted now. It had only been a month since their last meeting. Usually they might see each other maybe once or twice a year. He hoped Fadi wasn't going to invite him and Gisele to the Lattouf family's *Eid* celebrations, like he had done before. It was very kind of him, but for a Maronite Christian it was, well, uncomfortable.

But Lattouf had said he was troubled, so it must mean something had happened or was happening. Something that would need resolving, but without official Lebanese involvement. The camps were Palestinian territory.

He really didn't need this, he had enough on his plate already.

Merhi went back to his desk and re-found his place in the al-Murabitoun report. Would the Sunnis really cause unrest because Hariri had resigned?

He continued reading for a few minutes and then stretched out his hand and picked up his coffee.

It was stone cold.

Verdun, Beirut 14:00

The food court on the second floor of the Dunes Shopping Centre was less busy because it was Ramadan and because it was Monday, but the outlets were still open. The huge fat man had a quarter of the seating area to himself, dwarfing the table and chairs like an adult in a school first grade classroom – and dwarfing the small cup of coffee and solitary cup cake in front of him.

Walking towards him, Merhi could tell immediately that there was something wrong. Lattouf looked distinctly uncomfortable, almost nervous. He was dressed in the same ridiculous jeans and shirt as he had been the last time they met. Merhi was in his uniform shirt and pants, no jacket, the insignia on his shoulders ensuring that he would be given a wide berth wherever he went in the mall.

Lattouf stood up as he saw the Lebanese approaching. "Captain."

"Fadi." No traditional greeting from the Palestinian. No morning of light or evening of peace? They shook hands.

"Thank you for seeing me." Lattouf's grip was clammy.

Merhi pulled out a chair and sat down. "Are you okay, Fadi? You don't look well."

Lattouf looked around. "I hope I am not seen."

Merhi shrugged. "Who would see you? I'm going to get a coffee, do you want another? A cake?" He looked down at the uneaten cup cake on the table and then the penny dropped. "Ah."

"It is Ramadan," explained Lattouf. "I should not be..." He nodded at the coffee and cake. "That is why I hope I am not seen."

Merhi had never realised that he was so devout. "Okay, I won't tempt you." He stood up.

"But..." Lattouf grabbed his forearm. "I want to. I have not eaten since *Sahur*." Suddenly all resolve, as well as the tension, left him. "I will have a large coffee and another cup cake – make it fruit. *Shukran*."

The old familiar Fadi Lattouf was sitting there when Merhi returned with the coffees and a box of six cakes. He noticed that there was no trace of the original cake on the table, not a crumb. Or its case? "Assorted," he said as he sat down. "Help yourself, I only want one."

"Bless your hands."

Merhi let him devour two cakes – which took no time at all – before he asked, "You wanted to see me?"

Half of the third cake was in Lattouf's mouth. He nodded as he chewed and swallowed. Half the large cup of coffee was slurped down, even though it was scalding. He stifled a burp.

"My *fitra* will be a month's wages at this rate," he said, referring to the charitable donation given at the end of Ramadan to feed the poor.

"Which makes those very expensive cup cakes," commented Merhi. "What's up?"

Lattouf put down his polystyrene cup. He rubbed his right hand over his mouth and down his beard. "We have two more bodies."

"What? You are kidding me."

"I wish I was, my friend."

"Same as before?"

"Yes. Found together. Both male. Faces gone, probably done by the perpetrator. Brains gone – probably the rats. Or the maggots."

Merhi looked down at his one cake. "Same MO, same perp?"

"Must be."

"Enquiries?"

"All day yesterday. Nobody saw anything, nobody heard anything. No one reported missing – as yet. But you will understand that in the camp we cannot do house-to-house. We don't even know how many people live there."

"Too many."

"There you are right."

Merhi pushed his cake over to the Palestinian. "So what's going on?"

"I don't know. Two male adults, probably young but we cannot be sure. Plus the previous one, maybe male but we cannot be sure."

"Some sort of feud? Inter-gang rivalry?"

"Quite possibly. Except for one thing."

"The manner of death."

"Yes. It is unusual, no? The gangs, they stab, they shoot, they might even beat. But not like this. The victims must be dead long before he has finished with them. It is like he doesn't know when to stop. Or doesn't want to stop." The case was taken off the cake and thrown over his shoulder. The cake went the way of its brothers.

"You want to report it to me?" asked Merhi.

Lattouf shook his head and swallowed. "No, no. They were accidents."

"Of course they were."

"Already, we have disposed of them."

"Still okay for the quicklime?"

"Yes, thank you. This time they were disposed of *in situ*. It was an interesting place they were found. Plenty of drains."

Merhi did not want to know. He stood up. "Thank you for the information, Fadi."

Lattouf stood up to shake hands. "I will stay just for a moment. It would be a sin to waste that last cake."

"Of course. *A bientôt, mon ami.*"

"Peace be upon you, Abu Samer."

Merhi walked away, noticing the look of animal lust that Lattouf was giving to the *McDonald's* outlet.

He stepped onto the down escalator. He did not need this, not at this time. Lebanon was in a state of upheaval, with the resigned Prime Minister, the political uncertainty and next year's elections. He had much more important things to concern him than the Palestinians. But he was duty-bound to record and report this – *if* Lattouf had reported it to him, which thankfully he had not. Yet.

Hopefully this was the end of it. Just some inter-gang rivalry or vendetta within the camp, which would not spill out onto the streets of Beirut. Deaths of a people who were already nobody. Because if it was not internecine killing, there was only one realistic alternative.

He reached the bottom of the escalator and stepped off.

Was there a serial killer at work in the Bourj el-Barajneh Palestinian Refugee Camp?

6 November 2004
23 Ramadan 1425

Bourj el-Barajneh, Beirut 20:00

Laylat al-Qadr. The holiest night of the holiest month. The night during which God first began revealing the Qu'ran to the Prophet Mohammed through the angel Jibril.

One of God's mysteries is that no one knows exactly which night it is. It is believed to have occurred on one of the last odd-numbered nights of Ramadan. Sunni and Shi'a views differ on the range of dates, but there is one date which both denominations agree is a strong possibility: 23 Ramadan.

Al-Rajul had no faith but he was prepared to use others' beliefs to his own benefit. For *Laylat al-Qadr* is the Night of Power or Night of Destiny.

For the five young men he had chosen, it would be just that.

None of them were friends, he had made sure of that. For friendship between the young bred bravado, rivalry, cockiness and showmanship – four natures that were not required on what they had been told was a mission for their President. Each of them had passed the trustworthy test, unlike Mohammed and the unfortunate Chadi.

Al-Rajul sat in the grey Mitsubishi Express van just off Annan Street. The van was old and battered and fitted in with the area perfectly. No one would pay it any heed, nor notice the newer-looking number plates. Al-Rajul was wearing the Palestinian *keffiyeh,* thrown across the lower half of his face. People would think he was obviously a local. No one would pay him any heed just sitting there in the van – but if they did, one look from the hard, cold eyes would ensure they went on their way quickly.

He had a clear view of the entrance to the refugee camp. Night had fallen, *iftars* were well under way, some had even finished. He looked at his watch on his right wrist. He had told them to come to the camp entrance at ten minute intervals, where he would be waiting for them. Tonight they would be meeting each other for the first time, although they did not know it yet. Each one thought he was the sole selection for the mission for the President.

Which in a way he was.

The first one was two minutes early. Better to be prompt than to be tardy, but timing would be paramount for the mission.

Al-Rajul climbed out of the van and waved to the young man named Salin Namroud.

Salin saw him, smiled and waved back. He crossed the street.

"Evening of peace, *ustaz*."

"Evening of destiny, Salin," greeted Al-Rajul. "Thank you for coming. Would you mind sitting in my van? Others are coming."

"Others?"

"Yes. I will explain the President's instructions when you are all here. Come, come."

Salin went to get into the passenger seat.

"No, no," said Al-Rajul. "There is room in the back." He opened the back doors of the van. "Please."

Salin scrambled up. There was a bench down either side of the vehicle. He sat down as the man he knew as Mohammed closed the door behind him. There were no windows in the side of the van, but as it was a walk-thru design he could see out the front.

A similar scenario repeated itself four more times. Kabalan Elb, Elias Massoud, Ahmad Adass and Yazbek Nader. As each one was shown into the back of the van, they looked with surprise and a little suspicion at the others who were already in there, but no one said a word.

When they were all gathered – and the back door of the van was closed – Al-Rajul climbed into the front and turned to face them.

"The President already knows your names," he said without preamble, "and once this mission is completed he will take care of you and your families. He gives you his thanks. Now, I must tell you that I now have to take you all away from here. You will not return until the mission is completed." There were a turning of heads, frowns and quizzical looks. "Do any of you have a problem with that?"

No one spoke, although the general feeling of unease was tangible.

"Because if you do, say so now."

Still nothing was said, although there was a general fidgeting. Then Yazbek, the third one on the left, leant forward. "We are going away, *ustaz*? But where? Can we not inform our families, even if we don't tell them we are on a glorious mission for the President?"

"And what about our clothes, our things?" Elias Massoud, centre on the right.

"My mother will be worried," said Salin, nearest to the empty passenger seat.

"Relax," said Al-Rajul. "Your families will be informed. In the morning." He looked at Elias. "Do not worry about clothes. The Facility will have everything you need."

"The Facility?" frowned Kabalan.

"All in good time."

"We will miss *Eid*," Salin.

"Yes, you will."

"How long will we be gone?" Elias.

"Three months."

There was a collective gasp.

Al-Rajul gave them a frown. "You have been told of the rewards. They will be great. You are in a win-win situation. You are doing this for your future, for that of your families, for your President. Indeed probably for almighty Allah also. Do you think the rewards are just going to come to you, without you doing anything to earn them?"

They looked abashed. "No, *ustaz*," Yazbek spoke for them all.

"So, I'll say it again. If any of you have a problem or have changed your mind, say so now. Once I start the engine of this van, you will be under military discipline and under my command." He stared at each one of them individually. Heads were down but nothing was said.

Then a hand was half-raised. Al-Rajul's eyes stopped on the subject.

"I – I don't think... I don't think I can, *ustaz*," Salin's voice was almost a whisper. He was letting down his family, his President, even Allah. "My mother, she will be on her own."

"Didn't you tell me you have brothers?"

"Yes, but they are too young. I am the eldest. She needs me."

"You are sure? A little inconvenience now will bring untold rewards in the future. Can your brothers not manage for a few weeks?"

"I... I don't think so, *ustaz*. I... I am sorry."

Silence in the van. The other four young men did not look at Salin.

Then Al-Rajul said in a surprisingly gentle voice, "Okay. I understand. Do not worry." He opened the driver's door and climbed out, shutting the door behind him.

A moment later the back of the van opened. "*Yalla*, Salin. I will come with you. I will explain things to your mother."

Salin climbed out. "There really is no need, *ustaz*."

Al-Rajul closed the door. "Yes, there is." He put his hand in his pocket and pulled out a rolled-up wad of Lebanese pounds, letting Salin see it. "The President would like to thank her anyway. You are a very loyal son."

Salin was on the verge of tears. "Bless you, *ustaz*. Thank you, thank you."

The four young men left inside the vehicle watched through the front window in silence as the man they knew as Mohammed walked across the road with his arm around the other guy's shoulders and disappeared into the camp.

They were all loyal Palestinians and, although nervous, were keen to serve their President. And to reap the rewards. They would not have thought of moving from the vehicle. Which was just as well, because none of them realised that with no handle on the inside of the back door and the front doors double-locked they were, in fact, captive inside the van.

Mohammed was back in half an hour. The nights were now getting cooler, so naturally he had worn his leather jacket. The darker, shinier patches on his jacket – almost splashes – went unnoticed.

He unlocked the door and climbed into the driver's seat. "Are you all okay?" He looked over his shoulder.

There was a nodding consensus.

"Good. Right, you are now under the orders of the President of Palestine. *Your* President. And I am his representative and your commander. You will address me as such." He reached down onto the floor and brought up a six-pack of bottled water, passing it backwards. Ahmad grabbed it. It was followed by another bag of dates and other fruit.

"You are travelling," said Al-Rajul. "You are now exempt from fasting for the remainder of this Ramadan. You will need to retain your strength and your wits."

"Where are we going, *ustaz*? Sir? Commander?" asked Kabalan.

Al-Rajul started the engine and pulled out. Traffic was sparse.

"Paradise," he muttered under his breath. Out loud he said, "You will find out."

Kahale, Lebanon 23:30

The Maronite village of Kahale is in the mountains thirteen kilometres from Beirut, just a turning and a climb off the main Damascus road – an ease of access to the capital which made it ideal for Al-Rajul.

The sprawling two-storey homestead was in a wooded area to the south-east of the village, towards Aley. Set in a few cleared acres amongst the trees, it had at one time been an agricultural farm but had been abandoned during the events and left to fall into disrepair. It had been taken over (perhaps even bought, rural land titles post-events were fluid) in the mid-nineties by someone who had restored and renovated the place as a mountain retreat for himself and his family. It was quiet, it was secluded. The road to it was nothing more than a good quality track which did not go anywhere else.

But Fate had decided that the owner would never be able to use it. So the place in the mountains had been adapted once again, this time more for group or communal use rather than family living. It was hired to whoever could pay the not unsubstantial letting fees: businesses for training or conferences, governmental departments and agencies for whatever governmental departments and agencies did, even to individuals such as Lebanon's latest pop star who wanted a mountain retreat to write their next mega-selling album. It was flexible, it could be adapted to facilitate the hirer – hence its name: The Facility.

Al-Rajul had it on a three-month letting. He had not had to pay.

He was working for the owner.

They arrived in darkness. The building was just a hulking shadow in front of them. Before they were allowed out of the van, the man they knew as Mohammed and were now to call the Commander asked if any of them were carrying mobile phones. Kabalan and Yazbek were. The phones were taken off of them, with promises of state-of-the-art hi-tech models for all once the assignment was completed.

Leading them inside, the Commander showed them to their communal, but well-appointed, sleeping quarters on the ground floor. He indicated the table in the corner on which was water, juices, fruit and snacks, and pointed out the connected washroom facilities.

Then he locked them in for nine hours.

Each of the young men slept exceptionally well that night. The beds were the most comfortable things they had slept on in their lives, the mountain air was the crispest and cleanest they had ever breathed – and their drinks had been dosed with a mild soporific.

7 November 2004
24 Ramadan 1425

Kahale, Lebanon 08:00

When the Commander came back into the room at 08:00 the next morning, the recruits were waking naturally. They were told to pray if they wished, undertake their ablutions and be ready for a tour of the facilities in thirty minutes.

Al-Rajul was pleased that each one of them was ready when he returned. A promising start. He had chosen well. He was wearing the Palestinian *keffiyeh* but it was around his neck, not across his face. He also wore boots and military-style combat pants and shirt.

The recruits were impressed already by The Facility. Elias could not get over the fact that not only did the plumbing work but you could put your toilet paper down the *hammaemaet* and flush it away, you did not have to keep it in a separate bin for later disposal.

They were shown the ground floor. As well as their own sleeping quarters and washing facilities, there was a catering and dining area, a prayer room, a coffee and smoking lounge, a small gymnasium, a meeting room and further toilet facilities. The fridges and cupboards in the catering area were well-stocked. Meal times were 08:00, 13:00 and 19:00. Each would take turns cooking on a rota basis.

Upstairs was the Commander's quarters. They were forbidden to go there.

Outside was a small recreation area and a small swimming pool, which they could use when they wished.

"Now go and eat," instructed the Commander. "And be in the meeting room at ten. There are clocks on the walls. Be punctual."

At 10:00 the recruits were in the meeting room, seated in comfortable chairs in a line. The Commander was in a similar chair in front of them.

"While you were still in bed this morning," The Commander began with a smile, "your families were contacted. They have been told that you are working for the President and that you will be away for three months. Already they have been given a small token of the President's thanks."

The recruits looked at one another, pleased.

"Naturally they have not been told exactly what you will be doing – that is none of their business. It is between the President, yourselves and me."

Tentatively, Kabalan half-raised his hand. "What is it we will be doing? Sir."

"You will be told all in good time. It is of the utmost secrecy, that is why you have been taken into isolation. It would be dangerous for you and your families if anyone found out. The President has many enemies, even within our own society. For now, you will stay here. Regard this as a retreat. Pray, exercise, contemplate, swim, relax, then pray some more. I have pinned an exercise regime on the notice board. I expect you to do them daily. I will know if you have not. Look." He pointed behind them.

The young men turned and after a moment turned back again, their faces puzzled.

"You do not see it, do you? There is a camera in the wall – do not turn round again! You will be observed." Hints of consternation rippled across the faces. "The President needs you fit. The President needs you healthy – the kitchen is stocked with only the finest food." The Commander stood up and slowly walked behind the four chairs, touching each man on the shoulder. "I will be asking you to perform little errands. When I do, you will perform them quickly, accurately and without question." He reached the end of the line. "Is that understood?"

The faces turned towards him. Heads nodded. There were some mumbled *Yes, sirs.*

"What? I cannot hear you!"

"Yes, sir!" said the four voices together.

"Good. That is good. You will exercise, you will pray, you will keep yourselves in readiness." He sat back down in his chair. "You will not go upstairs, as I have told you. I will know if you do and you will be removed from the team. Your families will get not one *sou* reward. Also, you will not leave the grounds of The Facility unless you are on an errand for me. It would be dangerous for you even to attempt to do so." His face was hard, unyielding. No one was going to argue with him. "I shall not be here all the time. Can I trust you, Ahmad?"

The young man looked shocked at being singled out. He frowned, confused, and blurted "Of – of course. Of course, sir."

"Elias?"

"Yes, sir."

"Yazbek?"

"Of course."

"Kabalan?"

"Yes, sir."

The Commander nodded. "Don't make me regret choosing you. Once our task is complete, each one of you will be a hero of the Palestinian people. Your pictures will be hung across streets, on the sides of buildings. People will revere your names for years to come."

He looked from one face to the next. Young Palestinians, olive-skinned, wispy-bearded, aged before their time because of their plight. Hard – and yet with the naïveté of youth to believe every word of the bullshit he was expounding.

"My four recruits," he said.

Of which I need only one.

10 November 2004
27 Ramadan 1425

Mount Lebanon 08:00

The text that morning was not the usual terse statement of Hariri's locations. This time there was an actual message.

The Damascene stood on the balcony of the apartment, looking out over Beirut. There were clouds in the sky and the temperature was decreasing in preparation for the two-month winter ahead, but it was still warm enough for him to be naked, drying after his morning shower.

NEED TO MEET URGENT

Not unexpected after the political turmoil of these last three weeks following Hariri's resignation. Instead of slipping away into history as his opponents and enemies had hoped (but had known would never happen), Hariri was planning his comeback. He was determined that his Future Movement would win a landslide victory in the parliamentary elections in six months and he would again, naturally, be Prime Minister.

The Damascene's left thumb moved quickly.

Suggest

While waiting for the response, he began stretching: a pectoralis stretch against the side wall followed by a standing calf stretch, and then a severe standing hamstring stretch with his leg up on top of the glass balustrade. Then he went horizontal and face-down for ten full press-ups, ten diamond press-ups and, walking his feet backwards up the balustrade, ten planche press-ups.

His muscles were taut and hard. He had just returned to his feet and was performing an upper trapezius stretch (left hand over his head and touching his right ear rather than his right hand poking into the hole on the left side of his head) when the four-note text tone played.

He picked up the phone.

KOREITEM 1230

He slid the phone back down without replying, went back through the patio windows and walked upstairs for his second shower.

Koreitem, Beirut 12:40

Rafic Hariri's Head of Security, Abu Tarek, was seated behind his desk when The Damascene was shown into his office. Abu Tarek was dressed in grey suit pants, white shirt and subdued tie, his jacket hanging up nearby. In contrast, The Damascene was wearing trainers, jeans and a loose, collarless white shirt which hung down below his leather jacket. As always, his long black hair was tied back by a single rubber band, covering the sides of his face.

Abu Tarek's glance was disdainful. "You look like *mukhabarat*."

"Maybe I am."

Inwardly Abu Tarek winced. This man always got the better of him in verbal sparring. Really he shouldn't take him on. "Sit down, sit down. Coffee?"

The Damascene shook his head as he sat on the wooden chair in front of the desk. "*Merci*."

"So, how is my firewall working? You have been busy protecting Mr Hariri?" There was more than a hint of sarcasm in his voice.

"Is he dead?"

Their eyes locked. The Damascene could see Abu Tarek trying, and failing, to find a cutting response.

"And you are still supposedly protecting him, even though he is no longer in office?"

"I have been instructed to continue."

Abu Tarek nodded. He said, "Something else has happened. Do you know Ali Hajj?"

The Damascene nodded. It was his job to know everything about his clients. "The Major General. Head of Mr Hariri's official government security during his first term as Prime Minister during the nineties. Came back with him when he resumed office in 2000, but was soon sacked. Used to be police chief in the north-east Bekaa."

"Interior Minister Franjieh is promoting Ali Hajj to Director-General of the Internal Security Force. We have been informed that one his first tasks will be to reduce Mr Hariri's state close protection unit from its current forty officers down to eight."

The Damascene said nothing while he assimilated the news and considered the ramifications. After a moment, he said "A move calculated to leave Hariri more exposed?"

"What else? They are pretending that it is just normal procedure. President Lahoud has said that as he is now an *ex*-Prime Minister he is entitled only to eight official protection officers under Lebanese law."

"And is he?"

"Hariri is not an ex-Prime Minister. He is *the* Prime Minister of this country. Karami is just a fill-in until Hariri comes again. It is an insult."

"But perhaps not as dangerous as it may seem, or as they may want it," reflected The Damascene.

"What do you mean?"

"Hariri still has – what? How many men do you have? Over fifty?"

"Yes."

"Fifty men employed by you, by Hariri. Not by the state. Now you have one dedicated, loyal unit. Not two units with different employers and perhaps... different loyalties?"

Abu Tarek nodded, an eyebrow lifting in appreciation of the point.

"Replace them if you need to," advised The Damascene. "I know it will take a while, but there are literally hundreds of highly-trained private armies in the world from which you can recruit. Look at the western 'security firms' in Iraq."

Abu Tarek stroked his moustache. "I acknowledge what you say. Sound advice. And that is what I shall do. I shall recruit." He put both his hands flat in the desk top. "Starting right now. Join us."

"What?"

"Rather than this clandestine role. Come in. Join us. Help us from the inside."

"What are you saying? That I work for Hariri?"

"He will pay you magnificently."

"I already have an employer. And I have a job."

"It will be the same job. Who says you cannot work for two people doing the same job? Kanaan need never know."

"You want me to be the bitch of two masters?"

Abu Tarek grinned. "Or a whore, depending on which job title you prefer."

The Damascene raised his left hand and touched the side of his head.

"Think about it," continued Abu Tarek. "No need to respond right now. But can you take your jacket off?"

The Damascene frowned, pausing in the process of pulling his hair over his ear hole. "I'm sorry?"

"Your jacket. Can you take it off?"

"Why?"

Abu Tarek stood up. "Because it looks scruffy. Without it you will look much more presentable."

"Presentable?"

Abu Tarek looked at his watch as he slipped on his own suit jacket. "It is one o'clock. The Prime Minister is expecting us for lunch."

Rafic Hariri was famous for his Koreitem lunches, sometimes entertaining thirty or more people with whom he was wheeling, dealing, negotiating or compromising. So The Damascene was particularly impressed when that lunch turned out to be just the three of them: Hariri, Abu Tarek and himself.

The repast had been spectacular, an array of Lebanese dishes which more resembled one of the Gulf area's Friday brunches than a simple lunch meeting of three men.

Hariri had greeted him as if he already knew him and, in Hariri style, got straight down to business as they ate. The offer was one hundred thousand US dollars a month to be Assistant Head of Security to Abu Tarek.

The offer was refused, with grace. The Damascene acknowledged that he was a mercenary, but mercenaries abided by contracts, they did not change allegiances for the highest bidder. He explained that Hariri and Abu Tarek both knew that he worked for Ghazi Kanaan, the Syrian Interior Minister. He pointed out that if Kanaan's orders had been different, had Hariri been more useful to Kanaan dead, they would be facing an alternative scenario right now. Indeed, Hariri might not be facing anything at all.

Hariri had tried to keep his reaction in check, but The Damascene knew that the last remark had hit home. Hariri shrugged. "You only die when you die. Nobody dare kill me."

"We hope not," agreed The Damascene. "That is why I have been sent to add to your protection. But if I come in, if I work for you from the inside, that negates my effectiveness. I become just another security man – with all respect," he inclined his head at Abu Tarek. "I am not a security man, I am an assassin. I need to be on the outside, so I can see what an assassin sees, so I can think how your assassin thinks."

"My assassin," mumbled Hariri sadly.

"I cannot see what he sees if I am inside. I must be out there." The Damascene knew that some conciliation was required after the refusal. "But things can change now. You seem to accept the job that I am here to do. And the necessity for it?" He looked from Hariri to Abu Tarek, who both nodded. "There is no need for stealth, for me to be covert. My presence is acknowledged. Abu Tarek and I can contact more openly. Still by cell phone because that is the most secure – and use only the SIM I gave you. Just let me know your calendar as far in advance as possible, and notify me of any changes as soon as they occur, day or night. *Any* changes. Including meetings with Nasrallah."

Hariri sat back in his chair, lips pursed. He raised one bushy eyebrow and turned towards Abu Tarek. The Head of Security looked awkward, shrugging without comment.

"I see," said Hariri. "So you have indeed been doing your job."

"Of course."

Hariri wiped his mouth on his napkin. "As you wish." He put the napkin on the table. "Then I will let you two liaise." He smiled. "Perhaps it will be different when I win the election, eh?"

"Perhaps," said The Damascene.

Hariri stood up, closely followed by the other two. "May I have the pleasure to know to whom I have been talking?"

The Damascene wanted to say "Kanaan's bitch" but instead he replied, "Nobody, sir. You have been talking to nobody."

Hariri held out his hand. The Damascene shook it. "There is something I would like you to have," said Hariri. "Abu Tarek?"

Abu Tarek went over to a side table and took a small, bulky envelope from a drawer. He handed it to The Damascene. It felt like a three centimetre thick bundle of paper.

"Thank you for what you are doing," said Hariri. "Peace be upon you."

And he walked out of the room.

Ras en Nabaa, Beirut 14:00

In the offices of the Department of General Security, a Listener finished transcribing the lunch conversation from the already-burned disc onto a *Word* document, printed it off and took it down the corridor to his boss. Ten minutes later, his boss sent an e-mail to Captain Maroun Khoury of the External Security Unit.

11 November 2004
28 Ramadan 1425

Bourj el-Barajneh, Beirut 11:00

The slam against the wall was so fierce that the eyes of Karim The Butcher nearly popped out of his head. Yellow, phlegmy gob flew out from his open mouth and landed on his whiskery chin.

"But Captain!" he gasped to his assailant in a nasally whine. "I know nothing about it!"

"Do you take me for a fool?" Captain Fadi Lattouf had his huge left hand around the throat of the butcher. The middle and index fingers of his right hand were up the butcher's nostrils and were pulling outwards.

"It is a co-incidence. Somebody must have it in for me. I – I – I - " Karim tried to shake his head. "I know nothing about it!"

"Another body turns up outside your back door and you know nothing about it? What, is somebody leaving you extra supplies for the *Eid* celebrations?"

"I – I did report it to you."

Lattouf held the butcher against the wall and stared into his terrified eyes. He felt something warm and wet run from Karim's nose, down the backs of his fingers and settle on the back of his right hand. Then he said, "Yes, you did." He removed his fingers and wiped them on Karim's already stained and filthy shirt. A nostril hair and unpleasant attachment was lodged down one of Lattouf's fingernails. He flicked it off and wiped his fingers again. "But are you trying to bluff me?"

"No, Captain, no, no." Karim shook his head vigourously.

"So three bodies turn up in your back yard - "

"The yard is not mine, I don't own it."

Lattouf tapped him lightly on the face. "Three bodies turn up in your back yard and you profess to know nothing about them. The first two, happenstance maybe. But now the third, also with his head caved in? What are you doing, pushing brains as a special holiday delicacy?"

"Captain, please!"

"Take him," Lattouf nodded to the Lieutenant and Sergeant standing near the doorway. "Perhaps a night in the cells will jog his memory."

"No, please!" Feebly protesting, Karim was carted off. The Lieutenant and Sergeant, both of whom had seen the mess out back, looked only too pleased to be away from the place.

"Ibrahim!" called Lattouf. The Lieutenant turned back in the doorway.

"Sir?"

"Go easy on him."

"Sir."

Left on his own, Lattouf walked back down the corridor and stood in the open back doorway, surveying the mess. This one had been a splasher. And it had been recent, not many maggots yet or signs of rodent feasts. By the standards of the killer, this had been a quick job. The face had been obliterated, but everything else was very much intact. There had been no papers or any other identification on the body. Fingers were intact for printing but they would probably reveal nothing – they did not have the prints of all forty-thousand people in the camp!

Four bodies now. All of them would be recorded as accidents, but none of them were. Perhaps none of them should be recorded at all – maybe a little filing cabinet fire was called for.

He sighed. Was this what Palestinian life was worth nowadays?

He would get his officers to bring the saws, hosepipes, quicklime and sulphuric acid along. Again. Or should he show this one to the Lebanese? That would mean he would have to report it officially. The case would not be handed over to them – the camps were no-go areas for the Lubnans – but they would want to interfere.

If he washed another body – another human being – down the sewage channels, how many more would follow? This one might be the end of it.

Or four might only be the beginning.

What to do, what to do...?

There was an English word that Westerners often used. A noun, a verb, a pronoun, an adjective, a curse, a suggestion, a request, all encapsulated in one tiny word. What was it? Oh yes...

Fuck.

His scrotum itched. He put his right hand into his trouser pocket to have a discreet tug – and touched something hard.

Landline telephones were not permitted in the Palestinian refugee camps, but technology had outwitted this sanction. He pulled out his Samsung mobile telephone.

Lattouf nodded. He was being guided.

Allahu Akhbar.

He flipped up the phone and accessed his Contacts folder, the itching of his balls forgotten.

Jonblat, Beirut 11:30

Captain Jihad Merhi of the Lebanese Internal Security Force had just returned to his office after his morning meeting with his boss, Major Ghanem, when the telephone on his desk rang.

Let it ring or pick it up? The boss had been in a pig of a mood (when wasn't he?), lambasting him about his investigations into the re-emergence of al-Murabitoun, and Merhi was not in the mood for anything other than several cigarettes and at least a half bottle of whisky.

But he picked it up.

"Merhi."

"Lattouf."

Oh for God's sake.

"I need to see you tomorrow. At 12:30."

"But that is only... twenty-five hours away."

"Yes. I would see you today if I could." Which meant yesterday.

Oh shit.

"Okay. Er... the pigeon shooting range at Furn Ech Chebbak." It was the first thing that came into his head. It was immaterial, anyway.

"I'll be there." The line went dead.

Verdun, Beirut 12:30

Both policemen arrived in the food court of the Dunes Shopping Centre at the same time. Lattouf was not dressed in his ridiculous casual clothes like he had been before, but he had a black overcoat covering his uniform. Merhi was in uniform, this time with his jacket on.

They nodded and shook hands.

"You still...?" asked Merhi nodding at the food outlets.

"In some parts of the world, Ramadan is over," said Lattouf. "It is in mine."

"Cup cakes?"

"McDonald's. Big Mac meal. Three of them."

After a short delay, Merhi was back with a tray piled high. He put three Big Macs, three large fries and three large Cokes in front of the Palestinian. For himself he had a simple cheeseburger and an orange juice.

"Bless your hands," said Lattouf, ripping the top off the first box and commencing the demolition.

Merhi cracked the lid off his orange juice. "Another one, I take it?"

"Yes."

"Same as before?"

"Almost. Face gone, contents of skull pulverised. The rest reasonably intact. He was found early." Recollection of the graphic sight did not put Lattouf off his food.

"Another male then?"

"And dumped in the same place as the previous two."

"Interesting."

"Maybe. Or maybe it's just convenient. A small, unused area with just a narrow access. At the back of a butcher's shop."

"A butcher's?"

"We've taken him in for questioning."

"So it's solved then?"

The first Mac and fries were finished. The second lid was flipped up. "I don't think so. That would be too easy. And it doesn't explain the first one, which was found on the other side of the camp."

Merhi slowly ate his own burger. "So what are you going to do?"

Lattouf sighed. "Four bodies. With who knows how many more to come. What can I do?"

"You want to report it formally?"

"What happens if I do?"

Merhi made a face. "It's an unusual situation. You report it to me, I file a report. There'll be a shit-load of paperwork. Formally, we offer you whatever assistance we can – which will be very little if the bodies stay in the camp. We're not allowed in there, as you know."

"But I want you there."

Merhi stopped with the last piece of his burger halfway to his mouth. "Sorry?"

"Abu Samer, I trust you. I want you to come and have a look round. We are conducting our enquiries, but we get inured to the camp. People fear us but that does not mean they help us."

"You want me to conduct your enquiries for you?"

"No, no, not at all. That would be in breach of the rules."

"What you are asking is also in breach of the rules."

Lattouf stifled a burp (two and a half Big Macs down, half to go). "You don't know the camp. I just want you to have a little look over the crime scene. A fresh face. Assess it with your policeman's mind. See if there's anything we can consider."

"Fadi, it has been years since I was in the *Surêté*."

"But your training never leaves you, my friend."

Merhi was quiet as he finished his orange juice. He watched as the last of Lattouf's fries ended their very, very short existence. He said, "Report it to me formally."

Lattouf sat back in the small chair and shook his head. "No." He wiped his hand down his stubbly beard. "It becomes formal and you cannot enter the camp. But while it is not reported, there is nothing to stop my friend Abu Samer coming to visit me. I tell you what - " He leant forward again, eyes sparkling. "How about you and Gisele coming to celebrate *Eid* with me, Nada and the children? You enjoyed it last time. You and I can just disappear for an hour or two. Leave the women to it."

Merhi wanted to scream. He did not need this. He really did not need this. But if it meant the Palestinian not formally reporting the matter...

It could be a small price to pay.

13 November 2004
30 Ramadan 1425

Kahale, Lebanon 10:00

Elias and Kabalan were outside exercising in the crisp autumn sunshine when they saw the grey Mitsubishi Express van pulling in off the track. "He's back," said Elias.

"Thank Allah," said Kabalan. "I was beginning to think he had abandoned us."

"You have no faith," Elias grinned. "He is our Commander. And we are his men, capable of looking after ourselves."

"Maybe he was testing us."

"Maybe. But so what?"

The van pulled up and the man they knew as the Commander climbed out. He was frowning, his face grim.

The two young men picked up his aura instantly. Four days he had been gone, and something had obviously happened in that time. "Morning of joy, Commander," said Elias but without his smile.

"Morning, sir," Kabalan was a little nervous now that their leader had returned.

The Commander stopped in front of them and sighed. "I wish that it was, Elias. But thank you anyway."

"Sir? Has something happened?"

"Where are the others?"

"Inside in the gym, sir."

"Get them will you? All of you be in the meeting room in five minutes, and bring some coffee."

They were all there in four minutes, sitting in a row in the order that had become rote: Kabalan, Elias, Ahmad, Yazbek, the last two still in their work-out clothes. The Commander was in front of them with his coffee.

He said nothing at first, just looked from one young man to the next, holding their eyes with his. Already they knew better than to say anything. At the end on the left, Kabalan's leg shook a little, an unconscious nervousness which made him look as if he needed the toilet.

Then the Commander sighed. "I have some dreadful, dreadful news for you, my brave Palestinians."

There was general frowning and concerned looks.

"It is my unpleasant duty – my sad duty – to tell you that two days ago our President, Abu Ammar, passed into the hands of Allah."

There were gasps of shock, of disbelief. *What?*

"President Arafat is dead?" asked Elias hoarsely. Next to him, tears were welling in Ahmad's eyes.

"He died in hospital in Paris. May peace be upon him."

"How – how -?" Yazbek was shaking his head.

Al-Rajul knew the rumours that were now circulating about Arafat's death, the suggestions of poisoning or even AIDS that were being put out by his enemies, but he said, "You know he had been ill for a few weeks. They did everything for him they could, but Allah had decided he had served his purpose on earth."

The mood in the room was heavy. Ahmad was now openly crying. "We must pray for him. We must pray," he sobbed.

"And we will," said the Commander gently. "But first after that piece of dark news I must give you some good news. This does not alter our assignment. You are still working for the Palestinian National Authority, for the office of the late President - "

"Do we have a new President, sir?"

The Commander looked at Ahmad. "Not yet. There will be an election. Rawhi Fattuh is taking over on an interim basis, may Allah bless him. And he has said that all the President's ideals, his opinions, his strategies will live on, a fitting epitaph for a great man, a great Palestinian. And that includes us. We are needed, perhaps now more so than ever."

"Tell us what we are required to do, sir," sniffed Ahmad. "And we will do it. With pride. With honour." He looked at his colleagues who were each nodding earnestly.

Al-Rajul looked at them. You poor, misguided fools. He said, "Nothing has changed. You will be told in good time. But now we pray. Have you all performed *wudu*, your ablutions, today?" Heads nodded. "Then that will suffice for now."

The four recruits stood up and turned towards the window in an approximation of the *qibla*, facing the Kaaba in Mecca. Al-Rajul joined them, standing next to Yazbek. They raised their hands level to their ears and said the first *Takbeer*, "*Allahu Akbar*." Then Al-Rajul began the *salat al-Janazah*, the funeral prayer. "*Bismillah ir-Rahmaan ir-Raheem...*"

Al-Rajul's voice carried conviction even though he did not believe. But whether the President was with Allah or Shaitan, Al-Rajul was grateful to Mohammed Abdel Rahman Abdel Raouf Arafat al-Qudwa al-Husseini. He had served Al-Rajul's purpose well. Just the mention of his name and lies about his intentions had been enough to snare the recruits.

Now all he had to do was whittle them down.

14 November 2004
1 Shawwal 1425

Koreitem, Beirut 10:30

It was the first day of *Eid al-Fitr*, the Festival of Fast Breaking, the three day holiday marking the end of Ramadan. A time of prayer then celebration, of festive meals and occasional gift-giving. The time when good Muslims give their *fitra*, alms to feed the local poor, and some also pay their *zakat*, annual alms for the poor and needy based on a percentage of the giver's assets.

Rafic Hariri was at home in Koreitem with as many members of his family as could make it at this joyous time. It made The Damascene's job easy, but he also knew that he must not rest or assume. Complacency was the number one killer of important men throughout history. Denial of danger was the second. While Hariri lived, he was in danger – a statement as perverse as it was accurate.

Since his meeting with Hariri and Abu Tarek four days ago, The Damascene had received full and constant text information regarding Hariri's calendar, meetings, appointments, whereabouts – even details of another clandestine trip to see Hassan Nasrallah and Hizbullah a couple of days ago. It was not The Damascene's job to speculate on what they might be discussing.

Now as he approached Koreitem down Madame Curie Street on the appropriated Suzuki, he saw a small crowd of people outside the palace. As he got nearer he could hear shouts and chanting. Favourable chanting.

The Damascene pulled over just after Abd el Rahim Diab Street. In a way this was good. Hariri was effectively imprisoned in Koreitem by his supporters. On the other hand, anyone in this crowd could be an assassin with evil intent, using *Taqiyya* – concealing his true self, a concept which The Damascene had practised on many occasions.

Hariri was unlikely to make an appearance to the crowd, as he would know that to do so might whip-up emotions which could get out of hand. Even if he did attempt to do so, Abu Tarek and his men would stop him. But nevertheless a warning had to be given.

The Damascene pulled out his mobile phone. His left thumb moved fast.

Do not let abu bahaa appear outside not even at the window

It was two minutes before the reply came.

MATTERS ALREADY IN HAND. THANK YOU

Good. Not for nothing was Abu Tarek one of the world's top security men. Now The Damascene would park up and return to mingle with the crowd, practising his own form of *Taqiyya*. While joining in with the chanting and the cheering, he would be looking at faces and bodies, watching for anything suspicious, seeing if anybody was already in his vast mental archive. If there was an assassin in the crowd, he would find him.

An assassin other than himself, of course.

Bourj el-Barajneh, Beirut 16:30

"Eid Mubarak, Fadi," smiled Jihad Merhi as he entered *chez Lattouf*. "And to you, Nada." He bowed graciously to Lattouf's wife who was dressed in a black *jilbaab* with no head covering and was almost as fat as her husband.

"Eid Mubarak, Jihad," replied Fadi. "And to you, Gisele."

"Welcome to our home," said Nada as the two women embraced.

By the standards of the camp he policed, Lattouf's place was indeed a home. On the edge of the camp so as technically not to be part of it, it was a small two-storey house, part of a terrace of shops and service providers.

Fadi was dressed in his *Eid* finery of a lightly striped white shirt and grey slacks. No shoes worn in the house, of course. "Please, come in, come in."

Children appeared from everywhere as the Merhi's began to hand out small presents, then at a bark from their father they disappeared with their loot as quickly as they had come. Through the thin walls of the building, music could be heard from other celebrations taking place nearby.

"Bless your hands for the gifts," thanked Nada. "You are too kind."

"A drink?" suggested Fadi. "I have some very fine mango juice."

"That would be excellent, thank you," nodded Gisele. She had been well-briefed by her husband on his return home three nights ago with Lattouf's invitation ringing in his ears. She knew what this was all about and she understood: she herself had been a member of the Department of General Security some years ago. She always had to cover up the horrible-looking bullet scar on the left side of her neck, a souvenir from Paris in 1997. "Would you like some help in the kitchen, Nada?" she asked.

"Thank you, Gisele, you are most gracious."

"How long for dinner?" asked Lattouf as the women went off.

"One hour," his wife called over her shoulder.

"In the name of the Prophet, peace be upon him, I could have starved to death in that time! And poor Jihad here could have lost the use of his legs through hunger!"

Nada blew a raspberry and then the two women could be heard giggling and chatting in the kitchen.

Lattouf turned to Merhi. "You are well, my friend?"

"I am good, thank you Fadi." Underneath his North Face Galaxy parka jacket, Jihad was also dressed smart-casual in deference to the festivities: light blue shirt and black slacks with white socks. "No more, I take it?"

"No, thanks to Allah. Finish your juice and let us go, while the women do what women do."

"Will we have enough time?"

"An hour is plenty. The camp is very... compact. *Yalla*."

Within thirty seconds of entering the camp, Jihad Merhi was lost. So many alleys, so many dead ends, paths that went nowhere, hardly a straight thoroughfare in the place. The ground was hard and dusty, ripe for flooding when the rains came next month. Pipes dripped, cables sagged.

And the smell was... interesting. Much cooking was going on in the small dwellings and the odours were fighting street battles with the underlying sewer smell to provide a general fragrance that was cloying, almost intimate in the way it embraced you, yet not always unpleasant.

He wished he had worn his combat gear, not his fine clothes. But that was something he could not do. On no account could he be identified as a member of the Lebanese Internal Security Force.

Within five minutes they were passing a boarded-up shop front.

"That used to be the butcher's shop," explained Lattouf, his gut wobbling as he walked.

"Used to be?" asked Merhi.

"Sadly he is no longer with us." Lattouf was aware of Merhi looking at him. "My men were a bit too enthusiastic."

"But he was innocent?"

"Oh yes. But we had to take such drastic action to prove it. Allah will look after him."

Merhi shook his head as they turned first one corner then another.

"Down here." Lattouf could only just fit down the narrow alley between the buildings. Indeed, it was so small it didn't deserve the status of alley, it was just a gap. It led on to a small courtyard area.

Only one door led out into the yard, obviously the back of the butcher's shop. The other sides were blank walls with windows above. Even the political daubers did not come in here, but there were some brown splash marks over one wall.

"This was where the three of them were dumped," Lattouf pointed to the left.

"And nobody above saw anything, heard anything?"

"No. Selected use of senses is what keeps people alive in these places. You hear and see nothing if it does not concern you."

"You have cleaned the place up remarkably well."

"Thank you."

"Except the wall. How did you dispose of the bodies?"

"Stand back." Lattouf raised his foot and kicked in the door with one mighty blow. It shot inwards and stood trembling on its single hinge.

Merhi followed him in, and then almost wretched. The place stank like an uncleaned locked-up mortuary. Which, he supposed, it effectively was. Bodies were bodies, be they man or beast. All creatures – living or dead – stank.

"Here," Lattouf indicated a room to his right. In the half-light Merhi could see an old table against one wall. On the other side there was a wide, shallow gulley in the floor with a deep hole at one end leading down and, hopefully, out. A drain for the blood, and probably the butcher's latrine as well. There was a crystal dust residue on the floor along the edge of the gulley. "The quicklime is not always, er, quick," said Lattouf. "We had to encourage decomposition with knives and hacksaws. Thankfully the skulls were already shattered, otherwise they would not have fitted down the hole."

Merhi turned. He had an overwhelming desire to punch the fat Palestinian on the nose, but then he remembered that had Lattouf not done what he had done, the matter would have been reported formally and he would have been knee deep in something much worse than – what *was* that he was standing in? He looked at his shoes.

"The front of the shop is here," Lattouf beckoned him out. "Just a counter, a few hooks in the ceiling for the carcasses, and a small box where the old bastard used to keep his working money. It is empty now."

Merhi gave a cursory look round. "Yes, nothing of interest. How much was in the box?"

"A few thou – er, I don't know. It was empty when we closed the place up."

Well, I just hope you bought your snot-nosed brats an *Eid* present, thought Merhi. Or is it paying for tonight's meal?

They went back down the corridor and outside into the yard. Merhi looked at the brown splashes on the wall. "This was just the last one?"

"Yes, they weren't there for the first two."

"Blood on the ground?"

"A few stains only the first time, quite a lot for the last one."

Merhi went up to the wall and raised his hand horizontally and up, almost touching the top of the stain which was just over two metres high. "So he brought the first two here, killed the last one here. Allowing for an upward trajectory of about half a metre..." Slowly he brought his hand down and back towards himself. "The victim was about my height."

"Significance?"

"Probably none. But it's not like he was a child. Why didn't he fight back? I presume you checked his hands?"

Lattouf's face lit up. "I did! Young, signs of manual labour."

"But any cuts, grazes or bruises, as if he had been in a fight?"

"No."

"So why did he willingly allow himself to be led down this alley to his death? Why? Obviously he did not know he was in peril. Was he surprised? Was he with someone he thought he could trust?"

Lattouf shrugged. "Maybe he was brought here at gun point."

"Good point. Maybe." Merhi looked around. "But he was not shot. So the assailant would have had to put the gun away, or down, before... what? What were they killed with?"

"We don't know. Heads caved in, beaten to a pulp, but we don't know what with."

"Mr Evil, in the courtyard, with the lead piping. It's not gelling."

"Maybe there were two of them. Assailants. One covered him with the gun, while the other did the business."

"A possibility, granted. But somehow I don't think so. If there were two of them, why bother to squeeze down that little alley? Why not just bump and dump somewhere out there? This one wanted seclusion, to make sure he had enough time – or at least enough privacy – to obliterate the victim's identity. Why? Once somebody is dead, they're dead. To obliterate their identity is to stop us – you – from finding out who they were. From making a connection. From what? To whom?"

Merhi looked up at the buildings above. It was beginning to get dark but there were no lights on, which meant they were having a power cut.

"Fadi, I've seen enough. Let's go. What about where the first body was found? Anything for me to see there?"

Lattouf led the way back down the tight alley. "Nothing," he said. "And we've made a discovery. At least about the place, if not the victim."

"What's that?"

They came out of the alley.

"It is a place regularly used by *lootees*. Male prostitutes."

Merhi stopped, frowning. Then he said, "No. No, that's not what this is. No way." He began to walk on. "Someone setting out to kill *lootees* would want them to retain their identity, as a warning to others. These victims have had their very humanity obliterated, to prevent – or at least delay – identification. Let's say the first one was a *lootee* who stumbled across something. Or someone. But what? What, what, what?"

They were quiet as they walked back the way they had come. Suddenly lights popped on in the windows as the power came back on. Merhi didn't know whether it was an improvement, perhaps the place should remain in darkness.

As they turned out of the camp, Merhi said "Disregard the first one, concentrate on the other three. Three young men. They are somebody's sons, somebody's brothers. Maybe even somebody's husband or betrothed. Somebody must be missing them. Find a connection. It is there somewhere. And place a guard on that fucking alleyway."

"Bless your mind," said Fadi Lattouf.

17 November 2004
4 Shawwal 1425

Mount Lebanon 00:15 – 07:00

The three-day celebrations were over. Hariri remained safe.

The crowd outside Koreitem Palace had grown day by day, thousands of people showing their support. It had remained orderly, sometimes chanting, often with singing, sometimes quiet in contemplation, a solid mass in favour of one man and what he stood for. And The Damascene had scrutinised every one of them.

There were plenty of Syrian *mukhabarat* in the crowd, some disguised, some openly in their 'uniform' of leather jacket, light pants and sandals. There were Lebanese security agents too, obvious by their look of slight discomfiture. But none of the security services attempted any agitation or intimidation. They had let the crowd grow from an amorphous to a structured mass without interference.

Importantly, there were no assassins. The Damascene could tell, by looking at faces, by looking at mannerisms, by general demeanours. And with Hariri not even making an appearance, an assassin had been rendered useless anyway. The most someone with evil intent could hope for was a suicide bombing – and what did that ever achieve other than the unnecessary killing of collateral and the pointless loss of a trained killer?

As darkness fell on the third day of *Eid*, the crowd had begun to disperse, happy that their message had been heard not only here but at the Presidential Palace in Baabda and in Damascus too.

The Damascene had driven back to the apartment just after midnight, had eaten fruit, showered and had lain down on his bed upstairs. Sleep had come almost instantly, a recharging for some busy days ahead.

At 03:30 the front door of the apartment opened then closed noiselessly. A shadow glided in silence across the living area and up the stairs. It paused outside the half-open door of the bedroom, listened and then slid inside.

For a moment the shadow stayed in a corner of the room, watching the outline of the naked man on the bed, his breathing heavy and regular. Then it moved across to the foot of the bed, paused, then stepped up onto the mattress, one foot either side of the sleeping figure. Slowly it walked forward until its feet were level with the sleeper's upper stomach.

The sleeping man's breathing did not alter, but he suddenly said "You are not a real Djinn."

She said nothing, but he could feel her smile above him.

"Real Djinns cannot open doors." He opened his eyes. In the shadow of night he could see she was completely naked above him, her small, perfect, hairless body exuding a subtle warmth.

"I do not open doors... Master." Her voice was low, husky, sure in the inevitability of what was to happen. "Keys do. I just pushed it."

"Very clever."

As he raised himself up on his elbows, she knelt forwards, her knees on his shoulders. She weighed nothing, but he fell back onto the bed as was required.

"It has been three weeks," he said.

"I know," she replied.

She moved her hips forward and he kissed her on the lips.

She was gone when he awoke at 07:00, but the damp patches on the sheets and the inevitable mosquito bite, this time on his right hip, confirmed that he had not dreamed her visit, it had not been wishful thinking.

He lay back with his hands behind his head, his long hair splayed roughly over the pillow, a smile on his face. She seemed to have a thing about the hole where his left ear used to be. At one point during the night, she had whispered into it "Can you hear just as well out of this?"

"Yes, I can," he replied. "It is a burnt hole and the external ear is missing, but the drum inside works perfectly. Things are just sometimes faint and echoey on that side because I have nothing to catch the sound with and direct it inside."

"Fascinating." She moved her body. "Can you hear out of it now?"

He reached up and grabbed her left butt cheek. "How can I possibly with that covering it?"

She squealed as he pulled her down and they kissed, facial lips to facial lips, before making love for the third time.

Now The Damascene laughed out loud at the memory. He wondered if he could buy her off Kanaan, to have as his permanent muse? Money was no object.

He found himself hoping that her next visit was not going to be another three weeks away. The woman was bewitching – even if she was Kanaan's official whore.

Meantime, he had a lot of work to do.

Scratching the mosquito bite, he rolled out of bed.

18 November 2004
5 Shawwal 1425

Kahale, Lebanon 08:00 – 10:15

While the four young Palestinians ate breakfast, Al-Rajul examined their sleeping quarters. It was reasonably neat, reasonably tidy, showing that they were not used to such luxury and were treating it with the respect it deserved. Their removal from the camp and transport to Kahale had been quick purposefully, so that they had no chance to bring anything personal with them.

Nothing to identify them.

Each had taken clothing from the central wardrobe and had stored it in their individual unlockable lockers. Each locker had a *Koran* already in it. Two lockers now also had an item of fruit inside. That was it. Nothing else, nothing personal.

With one exception.

The third locker had a drawing tucked into the inside of the door. It was a pencil drawing of Yasser Arafat, a copy of the familiar, smiling sketch that adorned walls and hung from balconies and across streets in the camps.

Kabalan, Elias, Ahmad, Yazbek.

So, Ahmad then. He was a very good drawer. He had a talent. And he had been visibly and openly upset when he had been told of Arafat's death. So he had a soul as well.

Was that good?

Or bad?

After breakfast, the young men congregated in the communal area by the front door, as instructed. The Commander was waiting for them.

"I have been to see your families, again," his voice was friendly but retained the air of authority. "They send you the blessings of Allah."

The men looked pleased.

"Again I have given them money, to help them, to sustain them while you are away. I hope that is acceptable?"

"Of course, Commander," Kabalan.

"Yes, sir," Elias.

"Thank you," Ahmad.

"Bless your hands," Yazbek.

"I have told them what I am telling you now. Very soon I will be able to reveal to you the task that we are required to do, and you will understand why you will be revered as heroes for ever more. Until that time we have further training to undertake, and tasks to perform. Kabalan and Elias. You are fit, yes?"

"Yes, sir." Kabalan.

"Yes, sir," agreed Elias. "We have all been doing the exercise regime as instructed."

"Good. I have noticed. You are indeed fit. But I need strength as well as agility. I need you to concentrate on strength exercises. I have put up a new programme in the gym. Please start it as from today. You as well, Ahmad and Yazbek – but first I need you two to come with me. Kabalan and Elias, to the gym."

"Yes, sir."

Ten minutes later, the Commander, Ahmed and Yazbek were deep in the woods to the north-west, well away from the house. They were closer to the town of Kahale, and looking northwards up the mountain they could see the imposing three towers of Mar Antonios church at the top of the town. But they would not be bothered, the villagers never came down here, respecting the private property (and helped by the subtle, camouflaged but very effective electrified fence that ran round the whole perimeter).

Although it was the tenth hour of the day, it was dull in the woods. The sky formed a canopy held up by the tightly-packed trees, the sun was a single overhead light whose power was diffused as it came through the blue awning.

It was quiet.

"Okay." The Commander stopped in a small triangle formed by three pine trees. It was mossy under foot. He turned to face the two young men. "How is your orienteering?" He looked from one to the other. "Your sense of direction? Is it good?"

Yazbek grinned, knowing his next words would please the Commander. "I always know where I am, sir. I can always find my way to and from anywhere in the camp."

"You must forget about the camp."

The grin dropped from Yazbek's face.

"The next time you return will be simply to pick up your family and leave there for good." The Commander patted him on the shoulder. "When you have served your President and Allah."

Relief swept through Yazbek and the grin returned.

"Okay, your task is simple," said the Commander. "Get back to the house as quick as possible. Whoever gets there first will be rewarded."

The two recruits stood there, expecting more.

"That is it!" snapped their Commander. "What are you waiting for? Go!"

"Yes, sir!" Yazbek turned keenly on his heels and was off, followed by Ahmad.

The Commander took two strides forward and grabbed Ahmad's left arm in a tight grip, halting his run and pulling him backwards. "Wait, wait," he said softly as Yazbek disappeared back into the trees.

Ahmad winced and frowned a query at his Commander. His arm felt like it was in a vice. Although Yazbek was quickly out of sight, they could hear the twigs and undergrowth snapping under his feet as he ran.

The Commander unclipped the top of the holster on his belt and drew out a Walther P99. He pushed off the safety and pressed the gun into Ahmad's right hand.

"Kill him," ordered Al-Rajul. "If Yazbek makes it back to the house, you will not."

Bourj el-Barajneh, Beirut 10:15

Captain Fadi Lattouf eased the right cheek of his substantial arse off of his chair, braced himself and farted with the savagery, volume and force of an Airbus A380 at the point of take-off.

The walls of the offices of the security police were thin (the place was nothing more than a trailer, really) and his men were used to the Captain's internal propensities. However, knowledge before and after the fact did not help Sergeant Bassem el-Khazem who was halfway along the short corridor to the Captain's office to report as requested.

el-Khazem paused two paces away from the door-less doorway and waited for the inevitable. The aftershock came on cue (only a Cessna 172) and was emitted with a loud, satisfied sigh.

Embracing the inevitable, the Sergeant turned into the doorway and was immediately French-kissed by his boss's odour. Not for the first time in his long career in this hell-hole.

"Sir." He couldn't help but cough slightly.

"Bloody chickpeas," said Lattouf, a statement not an explanation. "Anything?"

el-Khazem shook his head. "People come, people go. And nobody wants to talk to the police, anyway. We have tried approaching gang members, but they just walk away when they see us coming."

"Should we pull some in?"

"Unwise, don't you think? And hardly worth it. If any of them had anything they wanted to say to us or bring to our attention, they would have done so."

"Huh. What about the posters?"

The posters had been Lattouf's idea. In the absence, and physical impossibility, of conducting door-to-door enquiries, he had ordered that posters be printed and put up on all walls and other available spaces in the vicinities of where the bodies were found. They had no pictures of the victims, of course. So the posters had contained a blunt and simple message:

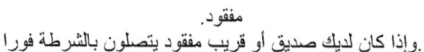

مفقود.
وإذا كان لديك صديق أو قريب مفقود يتصلون بالشرطة فورا.

Missing
If you have a friend or relative missing contact the police
immediately

"No response," said el-Khazem. "Some of them have been ripped down already."

"May Satan urinate on their mothers. What is wrong with these people?" Lattouf took a battered cigarette from a drawer of his battered desk and lit up with a battered match from a battered match box. If his wife Nada knew he had taken up smoking again (in fact, he had never quit – just lied), he would be battered too. "Okay," smoke oozed from his nostrils. "Widen the area. Get more copies done and put them up all over the camp."

"You think it will work?"

Lattouf snorted. "Do you want me to say yes and lie? But we have to try. Someone somewhere must care. Four young men are dead and no one is missing them? The camp is small, it is not like we are talking the whole of Beirut - " He stopped, staring at the Sergeant's face but not seeing him, the cigarette dangling out of the corner of his mouth. Something had occurred to him.

Slowly his brow creased. Surely not? It couldn't possibly be.

Could it?

Slowly his brow raised again. One thing his many years in policing had taught him: as well as the old investigator's adage of Suspect Everyone, Trust No One, there had to be added another truism: Discard Nothing.

He would have to run this by Jihad Merhi.

"Shall I do it then?" asked el-Khazem.

"What?" Lattouf was still with his thoughts.

"The posters? All over the camp?"

Again the Captain stared at him. Then he said, "That's what I said, didn't I? Shit - !" Two centimetres of ash had fallen off the end of the *seejaere* and onto his lap. He leant back in the chair, brushing down his groin as if it might combust at any moment.

Sergeant Bassem el-Khazem left him to it.

Halfway back down the corridor el-Khazem heard the sound of a Boeing 747 applying reverse thrust as it landed, and he was grateful he had left the room when he did.

Kahale, Lebanon 10:20

Ahmad ran through the trees, gasping, trying to catch breaths which just would not come. He had no time to think, no time to reason. The house was less than five minutes away at running speed. In five minutes he could end up dead, for he had no doubt that the Commander would fulfil his threat.

The moss was spongy under foot, in some places slippery. Twigs were broken where Yazbek had already run past but Ahmad still managed to get caught in the face by a wayward sapling, scratching his right cheek. He hoped he would not bleed, but he had no time to worry about that now.

Yazbek had a head start, therefore Ahmad had to run faster than him to catch him up. Could he do it? And if he did, could he pull the trigger? Kill a fellow human being?

He hopped past a boulder, the downhill trajectory taking him faster and faster. Yazbek did not know what was at stake, so he might not be running to his maximum. But where was he?

It was getting lighter up ahead as the wood thinned out. Two minutes to go – three at the most – until they reached the grounds and then the house.

Then Ahmad saw him. Up ahead, about twenty metres in front, Yazbek's head was bobbing up and down as he ran. Ahmad forced his heavy legs to go faster. Should he take a shot? *Could* he take a shot? He had used a gun before with the *Fatah* group he belonged to, but his experience was confined to firing in the air in celebration. He had never shot anyone or any thing.

He raised his right hand, tried squinting his eye to aim, cannoned into a tree, buckled at the left knee, but kept on running. He must do this. For Allah, for the President. For his life.

Then Yazbek disappeared.

Right on the edge of the wood, he vanished. One moment his head was bobbing, then he was gone. Out of sight.

What the...?

Ahmad kept his pace. He looked far ahead, over the open ground in front of the house, expecting to see Yazbek triumphantly running the last few hundred metres, but there was no one there.

He burst out of the wood – and nearly fell over Yazbek's body.

Ahmad forced himself to stop, his momentum taking him two metres past his prostrate colleague. Yazbek was face-down in the dirt, hardly moving.

"Yazbek?" Ahmad was puzzled. "Yazbek, you okay?"

Yazbek moaned and moved his right leg.

Ahmad looked back the way they had run to see if there was a rock or something his friend had fallen over. There was nothing. He must have slipped on the moss. Falling face down on the gravel, suddenly and unexpectedly, would knock the wind out of anybody.

Yazbek was still moaning. Ahmad knelt down and reached out with his left hand.

Yazbek began to move, to get up. But his moaning changed.

Into a laugh.

As he rose onto his knees, his right hand moved up. He was pointing a Walther P99 at Ahmad.

Jonblat, Beirut 10:30

"Merhi."

"Jihad, my old friend! It's Fadi Lattouf."

Bollocks.

"How are you, Fadi?"

"I am fine, fine. Good in fact. And you and the lovely Gisele?"

"Well, thank you. You have another?"

"Another? No. But I have a thought, an idea. I would like to run it past you."

Merhi hoped his sigh could not be heard down the phone line.

"Are you free on Saturday?" asked the Palestinian. Which meant he wanted to meet tomorrow, Friday.

Not even fighting against the inevitable, Merhi said "Gebran Garden, fourteen hundred?" Which meant the Dunes Shopping Mall at midday.

"I will be there."

Kahale, Lebanon 10:30

Instinctively Ahmad raised his gun. Both young Palestinians were in identical positions, on their knees facing each other three metres apart.

Yazbek's laughter stopped when he saw the Walther in Ahmad's hand, identical to the gun as he had been given by the Commander earlier, before breakfast. He frowned. "But I am to kill you."

There was surprise on Ahmad's face. "And I am to kill you."

One of the guns started to tremble lightly.

A finger tightened on the trigger of the other one.

"I – I do not understand," said Yazbek.

"Neither do I." Tears were welling in Ahmad's eyes.

The sound of the shot echoed through the wood, a sudden loud explosion cutting through nature's tranquillity. Birds flew out from the trees, wings beating hard and fast, taking them up and away from the human danger below.

Up in the house, Elias stopped his weight-lifting abruptly. Kabalan was still thumping on the treadmill at a fair speed.

"Did you hear that?" asked Elias.

"What?" Kabalan did not stop running.

Elias stood up from the bench. "That noise. Sounded like a shot."

Kabalan reached forward and lowered the speed on the treadmill. "A shot? I heard nothing."

"It was a shot, I'm sure of it."

Kabalan reduced the speed in quick stages to zero. He stepped off, sweat on his brow. Elias passed him a towel as he came over.

"Perhaps it was the locals hunting," suggested Kabalan as he wiped his brow.

"Perhaps," agreed Elias, walking over to the window. "But they have never hunted down here before in the two weeks we have been here."

Kabalan came over and put an arm around his colleague's shoulders as they both looked out over the grounds.

"I wonder where the other two and the Commander are?" mused Elias.

Ahmad's eyes were wide, staring at Yazbek. His hand gripped the gun with such force that his fingers would have had to be prised off of it if he was dead – which he was not.

Yazbek's eyes were equally as wide and staring. The gun and his hand still trembled, only now more strongly.

Both young men knelt there facing each other.

"Very good." The Commander walked out from the wood, nodding in satisfaction. "You have both passed."

Incredulity creased Ahmad's face. Yazbek still stared, unable to believe that he was still alive after Ahmad had shot him.

The Commander leant forward and took Yazbek's gun. Then he tugged at the warm gun in Ahmad's hand. "Ahmad?"

Ahmad looked up at him, in incomprehension.

"Ahmad, the gun."

Ahmad looked down at his own hand. Then his fingers quickly snapped away from the weapon and the Commander took it.

"Well done both of you," said the Commander. "Next time it might be live ammunition."

Snot dribbled down Yazbek's staring face. Ahmad let out a huge sigh and sat back on his haunches, then he immediately came back up again. His face creased.

"Come. Back to the house, both of you," ordered the Commander. "And say nothing of this to the others."

Ahmad began to cry as he stood up. Yazbek fumbled onto his feet like a newborn fawn.

The three of them began to walk.

"It upsets you to kill, Ahmad?" The Commander saw the tears on the young man's cheeks.

For a moment Ahmad did not reply. Then he said, "I – I am ashamed, sir."

"Ashamed? There is no shame in serving your President and your country."

"N – no, sir, it's not that. I – I've soiled myself." There was a dark and growing patch on the back of his trousers.

Al-Rajul tried not to laugh. "It is the sign of a man. It is not easy to kill another human being, not the first time. Defecation is allowed, indeed expected."

"Thank you, sir." Sniff.

"Sir?" said Yazbek who was walking two paces behind.

The Commander looked over his shoulder. "Yazbek?"

"I think I've shit myself too, sir."

Ras en Nabaa, Beirut 11:00

"Four will have to do. He did not want to come. Too scared," said the voice on the memory stick.

"So what did you do?" asked the other voice.

"Relieved him of his duties."

"Did you kill him?"

No response. "Did you kill him?" asked the other voice again.

Nothing, just heavy breathing.

"That's it?" asked Captain Maroun Khoury.

Standing in front of his desk, Zahia Zalloum shrugged. "For this time."

"So, another killing?"

"If our interpretations are correct."

He smiled. "I have every confidence in your interpretations, Zeez. So now we have four. Anything else? Where? Why?"

"Not yet."

"And no reports of bodies found?"

She shook her head.

Khoury reached for a cigarette. "And we don't know what this is all about. Might not be anything that needs our... intervention. You want to drop it?"

She sighed, not a little frustrated. "No. No. Something is happening, Moro. I just cannot figure out what yet. If a body would show up, just one, then we could progress. At the moment we just think there have been four killings."

"So in the meantime?"

"Eyes and ears."

"Listen and gather. L and G. It will break. It's just a matter of patience."

"Never my strongest point, as you know."

Through a mouthful of smoke, he said "You never did like preambles."

"I always believe in getting on with things."

They looked at each other, mischief and memories bouncing between them like pinballs. Out of the blue, she asked "Do you want to come round tonight?"

Khoury sat back in his chair. Oh yes, he would like nothing better. Sucking on a cigarette only gave so much pleasure. But he knew he would regret what he was about to say. "Perhaps not the best idea. Considering."

It was the answer she was expecting, and in some ways she was relieved. It had been her groin talking. You should never go back. "Yes, considering."

"Maybe when all this is over...?"

"Maybe."

She left the room, leaving Maroun Khoury thinking of the times when L and G meant something completely different between them other than listen and gather. Lick and gyrate.

19 November 2004
6 Shawwal 1425

Verdun, Beirut 12:00

Friday at midday is a busy time in the shopping malls of Beirut, and the food court on the second floor of the Dunes Mall was crowded. Nevertheless Fadi Lattouf had managed to secure an empty table for four, by a combination of glares, unfortunate personal habits and his sheer physical bulk.

When the man in uniform approached the fat Palestinian, people around him were glad that they had not sat any nearer. The onlookers expected a scene, anticipating that the Palestinian would at least be turfed out and might even be arrested, but they were surprised when the two men shook hands.

"Jihad, my friend!"

"Fadi, how are you?"

"I'm fine, fine. And you?"

Merhi looked down at the table. An open box from *Cup Cake* had two specimens still inside and a plethora of dead cake cases. One cake – a chocolate one – had been placed neatly in front of the empty seat opposite Lattouf. Next to it was a polystyrene cup of black coffee. Next to Lattouf's detritus were two polystyrene cups, one empty, one half full.

"Busy, but I'm good." Merhi sat down, picked up the cup and sipped the luke warm beverage.

"Thank you for seeing me again – oh, and Nada sends her thanks for the children's clothes. And I do too. It was very thoughtful of you and Gisele."

"It was our pleasure. I hope I got the teams right."

"Hmm! At their age, their allegiance is to colours, they don't care who the team is. Walid likes blue, so I gave him the Chelsea one. Yussef likes red, so he got Arsenal. The girls got the fancy Italian and Spanish ones."

Merhi smiled. Kids, the same the world over. How did they become so different when they grew up?

"So you don't have another victim then?" Merhi unwrapped his cup cake and bit.

"Thanks be to Allah, no. I had a thought, a theory, which I would like to run by you. You've said before you don't like talking detail on the phone because..." He waved his hand in circular motions in the air then pointed to his ear.

"Quite."

"I have put up posters in the camp. Firstly in the vicinity of the murders and now over the whole of the camp."

"Any results?"

"Sweet diddley."

Merhi wiped his mouth on a paper napkin. "Nothing at all?"

"Squat. Absolutely nothing. Zilch. Which set me thinking. Even if we discount the first one, we still have three men dead. And no one is missing them?"

"Or is it that no one wants to talk to the police? You do have, shall we say, a reputation?"

Lattouf wanted to look affronted, but he accepted the truth. "Maybe. Sometimes necessary measures in policing and crime control do not make us popular. You know that yourself."

"Granted."

"And we have spoken to the gangs, and also through official camp *Fatah* and *Hamas* channels. I am sure they will let us know if they hear anything or miss anybody." One of the remaining two cup cakes was unwrapped and popped into his mouth whole in one well-practised movement. It was followed by coffee lubricant.

"And you have a theory?" prompted Merhi.

"Mmm."

"Based on what?"

Lattouf put his huge right hand up to his mouth and stifled the burp down to the level of a minor earthquake rather than the Richter Scale busters he did at home. He received several glances from nearby tables. "Based on exactly that. Nothing. Based on the silence."

"And...?"

"The last murder was obviously done *in situ*. The first one we simply don't know about. But the middle two? We accept they weren't killed in the yard. They were brought there from somewhere else. But nobody in the camp knows anything or misses anyone? Well, supposing they didn't come from the camp?"

The skin on the back of Merhi's neck began to tingle. "What are you saying?"

"Supposing they were killed outside the camp? Somewhere else? Somewhere in Beirut? Or even further? And they were brought to the camp and dumped to put us off the scent. Or to put the blame on the camp when actually there is something else going on? When actually it is nothing to do with the Palestinians at all?"

At that moment Jihad Merhi hated Fadi Lattouf. He wanted to go round to his house, rip the shirts off his children and strangle them with them so that the fat slob's genes would die out and not pass on to future generations. Because, Merhi realised straight away, the bastard was right. It could be that way. It might not be, but it could be.

He spoke slowly. "Which would mean that... if it was nothing to do with the Palestinians... if it was not a Palestinian problem..."

Fadi Lattouf beamed through his beard of cup cake crumbs. "Then it is a Lebanese problem. Your problem."

Jonblat, Beirut 14:00

Damn Lattouf. Damn his wife, damn his children. Damn his parents who had the nerve to bring the bastard into the world in the first place. Damn the camps, damn the Palestinians. Damn the Dunes Shopping Mall, damn *Cup Cake*, damn you, damn me, damn the whole fucking world.

Jihad Merhi was grateful he was in his office alone, with the door closed. He had already snapped six pencils in half, had kicked over his waste bin, picked it up and then launched it with the venom of a pitcher throwing the last ball of a perfect game. He had smoked four cigarettes consecutively and now found himself with two alight at the same time between the fingers of his right hand. What the hell – he put them both in his mouth.

Opening his drawer, he pulled out his bottle of Johnnie Walker whisky and filled his mug to the brim.

He really did not need this. Really, really he did not need this. Major Ghanem, his boss, was already on his back about his interest in the resurgent al-Murabitoun (frankly Ghanem was telling him to leave it alone), the political situation was tense (the sooner next year's elections came round, the better), intermittent and spasmodic bombings were taking place (usually with a victim, either actual or intended) – and now this.

Lattouf might be wrong, of course – and Merhi hoped to God he was. But it was certainly a theory. Lattouf had played it well. Knowing the oaf as he did, Merhi was certain it was by luck rather than design.

Lattouf had never formally reported the murders. Which meant that Merhi could not now announce them without a shit-load of concern being expressed upon him from above. And Merhi could take no direct action on the theory that at least some of the murders had not taken place in the camp unless he had proof that the theory was correct. So he could not put out a formal bulletin or contact the *Police Judiciare* to put them on the alert. Which meant that the only course open to him was the time-honoured Lebanese tradition: contacts. Just as Lebanese business ran on contacts, favours made, favours called in, wheels oiled, with nothing on paper until the deal was already done, so could Lebanese justice. He knew people, people owed him favours. Time to call them in.

Stubbing out the conjoined twins of his cigarettes, he took a large mouthful of the whisky.

Opening another drawer, he took out a leather-bound indexed notebook and threw it on the desk in front of him. He picked up his telephone and then put it back down again. The Listeners.

This would be a cell phone job.

21 November 2004
8 Shawwal 1425

Kahale, Lebanon 23:00

The dormitory was in darkness. Outside, the moonlight was blocked from the earth by a picket line of cloud so any natural illumination was at a minimum. But the man who now silently entered the room had excellent night vision, so the lack of light coming through the open window was not a hindrance.

He stopped just inside the door. Four beds, three shapes. One bed was empty.

Three sets of heavy breathing, one light snore, one moan. The room had the musty, dank smell of humans asleep.

He moved across to the beds...

Elias was asleep and dreaming impure dreams when the hand was placed firmly over his mouth. He awoke with a start, eyes confused and still in a state of rapid movement. His natural instinctive reaction to fight off the predator was restricted by the body pressing on top of him.

"Elias? Elias!" whispered the voice. "Wake up. Wake up. It is me."

Still confusion, then slowly followed by recognition. "Mmm?" he said into the hand.

"Be quiet. Don't speak. Don't wake the others. I need you to do something. Do you understand me?"

Elias nodded.

"Good." The hand was removed from his mouth. "Ssh. Come with me." The Commander stood back as the young man swung his legs out over the side of the bed. Elias still looked a little bewildered, his senses adjusting after returning with such a sudden shock. He wore only his underpants.

"Get your clothes," instructed the Commander. "You can put them on outside. Come."

Elias grabbed his shirt, trousers and trainers from the chair next to his bed and followed the Commander out through the double doors. There were no lights on, the corridor was in dim shadow.

As Elias pulled on his clothes, the Commander asked, "Have you seen Kabalan?"

Elias frowned in the darkness and shook his head. "No, sir. At least, not since we went to bed."

"He did not wake you, tell you where he was going?"

"Where he was going?"

"He is missing. I looked in to check on you all, as I do every night, and his bed was empty. Do you think the others know anything?"

"I – I wouldn't think so, sir." He finished buttoning his shirt and flipped his feet into his trainers.

"Okay. Well, I want your help. I trust you more than the others."

"Yes, sir. Thank you, sir."

"I have searched The Facility, he is not inside. We must look for him outside. He could not have gotten far. The van is still out there so he has not taken it. *Yalla*." The Commander led the way down the corridor, Elias close behind. They reached the front hall and the Commander let the young man catch him up. "Has he said anything to you, Elias?" He was still speaking softly even though they were well away from the dormitory. "Has he been unhappy here? Does he want to leave?"

"I – I don't know, sir. He has not said anything. I know he has been anxious to find out exactly what it is we will be doing – but so have we all." Too late, he bit off the last remark. It might be unwise to let the Commander know of their concerns.

But he was relieved at the response.

"You all have every right to know. And you will very soon now. You are all good Palestinians. But I must be sure I can trust you. Most of you have proved this to me, but I have been worried about Kabalan."

"Has he done something wrong, sir?"

"No, no, just little things I have noticed. Nothing to worry you. But we must find him, he must be out there somewhere. Here – " The Commander grabbed a backpack from the floor near the main door. He rummaged inside and brought out a WiseLED Tactical flashlight. "Take this. We'll search the woods."

Three minutes walk from the house, they reached the edge of the woods. It was quiet, with eerie noises of unseen nocturnal creatures occasionally punctuating the silence. It was dark, but their flashlights were powerful, and here and there red or green eye reflections bounced back at them.

"Kabalan?" The Commander's voice was pitched, loud but not shouting. "Kabalan, are you out here?"

Nothing.

"It is good tactics to split up." The Commander sounded like he was giving a lesson. "I'll go to the north," he moved his flashlight to the right. "You go to the west."

"What shall I do if I find him, sir?"

"Tell him to come back! It is cold. It is no time to be out in the woods. I will meet you back here in half an hour, no later. If I find him, I will call you. *Yalla*."

The Commander moved quickly and within two seconds was consumed by the darkness of the woods.

Elias had to admit he was frightened. Shit-scared actually. The noise his feet made as he trod on the twigs and fallen branches below the trees seemed so loud they must have been able to hear him kilometres away, way up in the village. If Kabalan was out here, he would hear him too. Hopefully he would appear, grateful his colleague had come looking for him after he had gotten lost in the woods.

The powerful 1500 lumen of the flashlight helped ward off the monsters that must surely be lurking out here. At least in some ways. In other ways, the light was so strong that it made the areas it did not hit all the darker. Anything could be there. Watching him.

He had been walking for ten minutes when he came to a small clearing between three pine trees. He stopped suddenly.

What was that?

He had heard something. A sound. Not a twig cracking underfoot, not a rustling of night creatures, not even a feral cry. It was not an unfamiliar sound, but not one that you would associate with the woods and at night, and that made it disorientating.

There it was again!

It was... it was... a *creaking* sound. He jerked the flashlight over the ground and over the base of the two trees in front of him. He caught one pair of tiny red eyes, which quickly vanished, but otherwise there was nothing there.

"Kabalan?" he said in a whisper. "Kabalan, is that you?"

Nothing. Then it came again, a low creak, sounding like... like... *rope?*

As the thought entered his mind, something lightly thumped him on the back of his head. He nearly jumped out of his skin, dropping the flashlight. He dived to the ground, grabbing the light and turning, pointing it up into the branches next to him.

Kabalan was hanging from the tree.

Mount Lebanon 23:45

The Djinn sat in the corner of the living area in The Damascene's apartment, silent and still. She was fully clothed in jeans and T-shirt - and, she realised, tonight she would remain so. The Damascene had not come home. Hariri must be on one his night-time sojourns, probably into southern Beirut to see Hizbullah or maybe further south-east to see Druze leader Walid Jumblatt in his palace at Moukhtara. And where Hariri was, The Damascene would be somewhere nearby.

She rose to her feet, lithe and supple, not a sign of stiffness even though she had been in the same position for two hours. When he did eventually return, he would be too tired for her ministrations (although he would be too polite to refuse), but the new trick she had thought of to pleasure the side of his head would need his full attention and support. Pity, but never mind. It would keep until the next time.

Barefooted, she walked across to the front door and opened it with her toe. She clicked down the latch and closed the door behind her as she went out.

She did not have far to go.

Kahale, Lebanon 23:45

Kabalan's body was swinging, its back to the gawping Elias. The rope came up from around the neck and was attached to a branch about a metre above the head. The eerie creaking seemed to be louder now that Elias could pinpoint its cause and location.

Slowly the body swung clockwise. Elias did not want to see what he was about to see. He had heard that hanging made your face go purple, your tongue hang out and sometimes your eyes popped right out of their sockets.

He lowered the flashlight and put his head down as the feet turned towards him. No. No, he was not going to look up. He would not. He could not.

The feet stopped turning and floated in front of his face, swinging, daring him to look up.

Shaking, the flashlight made its way up the body. Elias felt sick, physically sick. He did not want to look up. He would call the Commander.

He tried to shout, but his mouth was dry. Nothing but a croak came out. In the name of Allah, he had to do it.

He looked up.

And at that moment he lost control of every bodily function.

Snot flowed from his nose, spit flew from his previously arid mouth as he gasped, he pissed and shat himself simultaneously.

Kabalan was grinning at him.

And he had a gun in his hand.

"K – K – ?" Elias could not even speak.

Kabalan raised the gun, pointing it at him.

Then there was a shout. The Commander's voice. "Elias, here!"

Something flew at him from his left. Somehow he managed to catch it, but in doing so he dropped the flashlight. He had caught a gun.

"Shoot him, shoot him!" screamed the Commander. "Now, now!"

Blindly, unthinking, Elias raised the gun and fired.

So did Kabalan.

The bangs and flashes lit up the forest like fireworks at a festival. There were ten reports in all, maybe five from each gun, maybe one had fired more than the other.

Then there was silence.

Then after a few moments there was light. The Commander had switched his flashlight back on.

Elias was sitting on the floor in a terrible state, his face creased in terror, his jeans damp, warm and smelly.

Up above, Kabalan also gaped, but he had retained control of his functions. Why was Elias not dead? The Commander's orders had been specific, he was to shoot him. He raised the gun again and pulled the trigger. The hammer came down on an empty barrel. He looked at the Commander, whose face was stone.

"Well done both of you," said the Commander without emotion. "You have both passed."

Kabalan wriggled. The rope under his arms was beginning to chafe. He did not understand what had happened but he wanted to get down.

"Go back to the house, Elias," ordered the Commander. "I am very pleased and therefore your President is very pleased. You have proven yourself. Clean yourself up and do not mention this to any of the others. Go, *yalla!*"

For a moment Elias was bemused, then he picked up his flashlight and scurried off without a word, leaving a faint odour in the night air.

The Commander looked up at Kabalan then walked around the dangling legs and stepped up onto a large, jutting root of the tree. Level with the young man, he pulled a knife from his waistband.

Kabalan was relieved as he felt the rope being cut. "Th – thank you, sir." The Commander supported his weight, holding his legs in his right arm, cutting with his left hand. "Was – was that a test?"

"Yes," replied the Commander.

But what he didn't mention was that, unlike the test he had set the other two recruits, and unlike the bullets in the gun he had thrown to Elias, the bullets in Kabalan's gun had been live.

And he had missed with every one.

"But," said the Commander. "I lied. You failed."

The rope had been cut from underneath Kabalan's arms but it was still wound tightly around his neck. Holding the young man's legs, the Commander jumped off the root and pulled hard downwards as he landed.

Kabalan's neck broke with a crack like a stepped-on twig.

22 November 2004
9 Shawwal 1425

Kahale, Lebanon 08:00 – 09:00

Elias was quiet at breakfast the next morning. Quiet and just a little bit concerned.

On returning to the house in the early hours, he had stripped off his soiled clothing and showered in the communal washrooms, not the dormitory *en suite*, so as not to wake the other two. He had wrapped his ruined clothes in two plastic bags and had gone back outside to bury them deeply in the rubbish bin.

Then he had returned inside and slipped into his bed. He would get fresh clothes from the wardrobe in the morning.

Overall he felt relief. He was still shaking from what had happened in the woods, but he was grateful it had only been a test – and one that he and Kabalan had passed. The Commander was pleased with them.

But the adrenaline in his body took its own time to assuage, and it had been over an hour before he could get back to sleep. Which meant that he knew Kabalan had not returned.

About forty minutes after getting into bed, he had heard the van start up outside and drive off. The Commander must have a task – a real task – for Kabalan, and they had gone off together.

Which was why his relief had turned to concern. Was Kabalan the Commander's favourite? Was he going to become a sergeant while the rest of them remained foot soldiers? That was so unfair. They had all done whatever was asked of them – exercised, cooked, cleaned, read, prayed. Why was Kabalan being singled out for preferential treatment? He had noticed the way the Commander sometimes looked at Kabalan. He was handsome, if you liked that sort of thing. Was there an ulterior motive in his preferential treatment...?

On waking up, Yazbek and Ahmad had commented on Kabalan's bed being empty, but Elias had claimed ignorance, telling them he had been asleep all night.

Then Yazbek had beckoned them over to the window, pointing out that the van was gone. What was going on?

With two minutes to spare before their daily gathering in the meeting room, the Mitsubishi Express van pulled in at the gate and drove up to the front of the house. Only the Commander got out, Kabalan was nowhere to be seen.

The Commander said nothing as he walked past them in the hallway. Like little chicks they followed him into the meeting room, taking their usual places. The chair on the end on the left was noticeably empty.

"Morning of light, my brave men," began the Commander.

Mornings of peace were wished back.

"You will notice that Kabalan is no longer with us."

"Where is he, sir? Has something happened?" asked a worried-looking Yazbek.

The Commander smiled. "Not at all. I told you I would tell you of your mission, your tasks, when the time was right. Well, Kabalan has his task and he has left us to fulfil it. Already his family are preparing to move out of the camp."

"Will he be coming back, sir?" Ahmad.

"No."

"And what about our tasks? Will we get them soon, sir?" Elias's concern had turned to enthusiasm. Perhaps he had been wrong. One of them had to be the first to be entrusted, it just happened to be Kabalan.

"Very soon," nodded the Commander. "When the time is right. There will be several tasks, including some where we will be working together."

The three young men looked pleased. Elias shook his fist in satisfaction. Soon they would be serving their President. Soon their families would be moving from the camp.

"One of the tasks will involve strength," continued the Commander. "So I want you to continue with your exercises. I have to go away for a while, but when I come back you will be closer to starting your first part of the mission." He looked keenly from one to the other. "My brave Palestinians."

None of them knew that, as he was saying those words, thirty kilometres away in a secluded part of the swamps at the Aammiq Wetlands in the Bekaa, a greater spotted eagle was pecking an eye from the remnants of the skull of Kabalan Elb.

Mount Lebanon 12:00

The Damascene returned to the apartment around midday. He had not slept in thirty hours and the first thing he did was to strip off his clothes and head for the shower.

As the water cascaded through his long hair and down over his body, he allowed himself a feeling of satisfaction. Hariri had been busy. It was remarkable how a man who had just had his sixtieth birthday could keep going at such a frenetic and constant pace. In the space of twenty-four hours he had not only been to see Hassan Nasrallah and Druze leader Walid Jumblatt, but he was also in liaison with some unlikely bedfellows from across the political spectrum such as the Christian Qornet Shehwan Gathering, the Democratic Forum, the Democratic Leftist Movement, exiled General Michel Aoun's Free Patriotic Front and even the banned Christian Lebanese Forces. There were rumours that they were organising a meeting soon – but this was really of no interest to The Damascene.

He was satisfied because all this coming and going, all the secretive, furtive and sometimes clandestine meetings, the whispered discussions in the bathrooms of Koreitem (with the taps running), the mobile telephone calls out in the gardens, all had proved that Hariri was almost impossible to assassinate.

His movements and whereabouts were too flexible for any snipers; his heavily-armoured motorcade with its state-of-the-art jamming devices would thwart any remote detonation of roadside bombs; a timer-bomb was out of the question as spot-on timed accuracy could never be guaranteed; and a close-range shooting or stabbing would always be prevented by the close-quarter protection of Abu Tarek and his excellent security team.

After ten minutes, The Damascene turned off the shower and stepped out. As the water dripped off his body, he walked downstairs to the open-plan living area, the place brightly lit by the weak November sun coming in through the floor to ceiling windows. He looked out over Beirut.

Hariri could be poisoned, of course (there were rumours that had happened to Arafat, just one of the many wild theories flying around about the Palestinian leader's death), but that just would not happen. Poisoning could be covered up as a natural death – they would call it a heart attack, quite believable for this ebullient, overweight, ageing man. Anyone who wanted Hariri dead would want it done in a spectacular fashion, as a message to the world.

And The Damascene knew how.

Now he needed sleep, to recharge himself. As he turned away from the window and back towards the stairs, something caught his eye. He made a detour towards the kitchen.

A small object was sitting on the otherwise empty breakfast counter that separated the kitchen from the living area. He picked it up, turning it over in his left hand.

It was light, hardly heavier than a circle of tin foil. It was a decorative golden coin – the sort that would adorn a belly dancer's outfit.

He smiled. She had been here and he had missed her – in more ways than one. It had been just five days – her visits were becoming more frequent.

He sniffed the coin. There was no odour. Pity.

He hoped she would visit again soon. He would welcome the relief of her body.

23 November 2004
10 Shawwal 1425

Damascus, Syria 19:00

Ghazi Kanaan, the recently-appointed Minister of the Interior of Syria, sat at his desk in his office overlooking the Barada River and absentmindedly tappy-tapped a pencil on the papers in front of him. It was a report on the interrogation of Kurdish detainees still in custody eight months after the football riots up in Al Qamishli. But his mind had wandered from the file, distracted by the fact that Kurds were majority Sunni – and there was another Sunni that was at the back of his mind.

Rafic Hariri. The thorn in his side was more popular than ever since his 'resignation', and his Future Movement was beginning to roll. Even at this stage, with six months to go until the Lebanese elections, the force was building for a political landslide. And that was not popular with some people, either in Damascus or Beirut.

Over a month ago, Kanaan had sent one of his foot soldiers to Beirut in response to his man's telephone call. The foot soldier had never returned. It was worrying but not surprising – anything could have happened. He could have been captured by one of the myriad Lebanese factions and either killed or held prisoner somewhere for future leverage. He could have simply deserted. Or Captain Mebarak might have done for him – Mebarak was, after all, first and foremost a killer.

Mebarak was faring well. Hariri was still alive. Kanaan now wondered whether he should call him off. He liked Hariri, had gotten along with him as well as he could have over the years, had even done some clandestine business deals with him, but the juggernaut of the Future Movement was not something Kanaan could now be associated with. His plans were slowly, slowly coming to fruition in Syria. His anonymous efforts at subtle destabilisation from within were beginning to crack the eggshell facade of the hierarchy. And soon, if everything went well, Syria might have a new leader.

And if everything did not go well...

Well, history would decide.

Should he call Mebarak in? He might very well need his pet mercenary for other internal elimination projects very soon. Or simply for protection.

Any outside source wanting to kill Hariri would have done so by now. Hariri was going to become Prime Minister again next May, a Prime Minister of a new, vibrant, independent Lebanon, no longer under Syria's protection.

Kanaan, on the other hand, would be under severe threat once those hierarchical cracks turned into fissures. It would be a matter of life or death.

Literally.

So what should he do about his man in Beirut?

1 December 2004
18 Shawwal 1425

Kahale, Lebanon 16:00 – 18:00

"Very good," Al-Rajul nodded his approval at the three young men prone on the ground in front of him. Each was face down, each holding a Russian SKS rifle with a bipod attached to the front of the stock. They had been firing empty at a target on the edge of the woods, about a hundred and fifty metres away. The target was a man's jacket, spread open and draped over a tree branch at about average head height. "Do you feel confident?"

There were mumbled agreements from the ground.

"Then next time you will use ammunition. Now, come on up. That is it for today. It is time for *Maghrib salat*. Go wash then pray. Then join me in the meeting room. I will pray on my own."

The three young men handed their rifles to their Commander one by one and headed off towards the house, chattering. Al-Rajul followed, rifles under his arm.

He knew that shooting Hariri was not what his employer had in mind, but sniper training was of benefit as a contingency. His employer had specified the date of Hariri's death. The manner, although important, was secondary. The date was unchangeable.

He could already hear the showers being run when he entered the house. He would not, of course, be praying (for what? To whom?), but he would shower and change in his own quarters upstairs.

Twenty minutes later, he was in the meeting room ahead of the recruits. He did not believe in God, he did not believe in Chance, but he did believe in Fate. The order of their entry into the room would determine the next selection – as natural a selection as there could be. Decided by Fate.

Ahmad was the first in, closely followed by the other two. They took their usual seats.

Al-Rajul was half-sitting against the edge of a table in front of them. He nodded. "How did it feel with the rifles this afternoon?"

"Good, sir. Good," said Ahmad.

"A little heavy, I have only used a pistol before," Elias hoped his conspiratorial glance at the Commander would be returned, but he was disappointed. "But I can get used to it."

"It was okay," said Yazbek. "I look forward to using ammunition next time."

"As you will, as you will," confirmed Al-Rajul. "Right," he pushed himself up off the desk. "The next stage of our mission is upon us. I will require one of you - "

"Me, sir!" Elias's hand shot up.

"I will decide." The look he gave Elias was hard. The hand went down quickly. "I will require one of you to assist me in a task. Ahmad, can you drive?"

"Yes, sir." Ahmad smiled.

"Yazbek?"

"Yes, sir!"

"Then Yazbek it is you."

Ahmad looked as sullen as Yazbek looked elated. Elias looked like he might cry.

"Your time will come," Al-Rajul reassured the unchosen. "Soon. For now, it is Yazbek. The three of you, go eat. Then Yazbek, join me out at the van an hour."

Mount Lebanon 19:00

It was dark by the time the van pulled away from The Facility. Its full beams pierced the blackness as it made its way up to the Beirut – Damascus road and turned right. The Commander was driving, an excited Yazbek was next to him.

As soon as they hit the main road, Yazbek asked "Where are we going, sir? What am I to do?"

"All in good time, Yazbek. All in good time," replied the Commander calmly. "Just relax and enjoy the ride."

Yazbek knew it would be pointless to push the matter, so he did as he was told – at least the enjoying the ride bit.

They drove past the town of Bhamdoun and upwards into the mountain. The main road was in good condition so the climb was not arduous. It was busy, as this road always was, no matter the time of day or time of year.

Up past Mdairej, the road peaked as it passed between the Barouk and Knisse mountains where they could already see snow. Then they began their descent into the Bekaa Valley. At Chtaura they turned left, into the foothills of Mount Sannine.

Towards Zahlé.

Zahlé, Lebanon 21:00

At night the red roofs of the town could not be seen, hidden beneath a hazy patina of diffused light. The lights became stronger and more distinct as they came closer to the town until the van's full beams were no longer necessary.

"Ever been here before?" asked the Commander as they turned left into the town.

"Me, sir? No," replied Yazbek, adding "I have never been further than Beirut."

The Commander's eyebrows rose but he made no comment. Then he said, "The city of wine and poetry."

"Really?"

"So they say. Personally I do not like poetry and of course I do not drink."

"Of course."

They drove north and found a place to park alongside the Berdaouni River at the bottom of the Wadi el-Aarayesh (Grape Vine Valley). Here innumerable restaurants stretched alongside the river, tree-shaded during the day, lit up by multicoloured lights stretched between the branches and across the road at night. Here the place was busy, each restaurant (known as casinos) vying for trade. An old woman was making bread outside one of the cafés. In a nearby casino a man dressed in traditional baggy trousers, shirt and waistcoat, fez on his head, poured thick and dark local coffee from an urn which he actually seemed to be wearing on his hip. Music played, voices were loud.

Nobody gave the parked van a second glance.

"Right," the Commander turned towards Yazbek. "Your job is to drive this van. You can do that?"

Yazbek's face shone brighter than all the lights in the Wadi. "Oh yes, sir! Where are we going?"

"*We* are not going anywhere. You are. I've got something to do."

"Sir?"

"Drive back the way we came. You remember it?"

"Y-yes. Just the main road. Am I to go back to The Facility? I don't understand. Have I disappointed you?"

"You will be doing exactly what I want you to do. You know el-Mdairej, up at the top? Near the snow. We passed by on the way."

"I – I think so."

"The bridge. The big bridge we came across."

Yazbek nodded. "Yes, yes of course."

"There is a rest area this side of the bridge. Meet me there in one hour."

"But how will you - ?"

"Do not question me! Do as I say." The Commander opened the van door and got out. "Come." He beckoned with his hand and the frowning Yazbek slid across into the driver's seat. "This is your task," the Commander's voice was more conciliatory. "Tomorrow you go and collect your family from the camp."

Yazbek nodded, conflicting emotions playing across his face.

"Do as I say," pressed the Commander. "Do not worry about me, I will be there in an hour. Now go. *Yalla!*"

He slammed the door as Yazbek started the engine, and stood back as the van jumpily pulled away from the kerb. He watched the van go as he began walking south.

Then he turned west and quickly disappeared into the back streets of the town.

It took just five minutes for him to find what he was looking for.

Yazbek was both excited and nervous. Nervous because he had never driven a manual vehicle before (he stalled three times on his way out of Zahlé and then drove the next five minutes just in second gear) and excited because he was at last serving his President and his country. He was one of the chosen ones. Tomorrow he and his family would be out of that wretched camp forever. He was, he thought, fulfilling his destiny.

And in that he was right. Every human being fulfils their destiny. It is only a pity that most of them never know what their destiny is...

Mount Lebanon 22:45

Yazbek needed the full hour the Commander had given him to get to the bridge at Mdairej. He lost count of the times he stalled the van on its climb up the mountain, even though he was on a main road. And it was an unfriendly darkness out there, up here at night in the cold. There was still some traffic coming towards him, but it was thin now, the oncoming full beams slicing through the windscreen like lasers. The van's own lights cast a dim jaundice into the darkness in reply.

Sixty minutes out of Zahlé he thought he recognised the rest area coming up. He leant forward, squinting into the night. Yes, this was it, he was sure. Although the bridge was the highest in the Middle East, he couldn't see it from road level, it was just black ahead. He turned in to his right and pulled up, leaving the engine running so that he could keep the heater on.

He turned off the headlights and then turned them back on again quickly. Too dark, *merci ktir*, he didn't want the monsters coming out! Just to be on the safe side, he flicked down the door lock.

Only one car came along in the next ten minutes, going down towards Chtaura, its headlights glaring at him, piercing into the van, and then going out instantly as the car passed.

Five minutes later he noticed some lights in his left wing mirror, coming up the mountain. They seemed to be approaching quickly, probably somebody in a rush to get back to Beirut before midnight. He averted his eyes as the lights filled the mirror, but then he was aware that there was light on the right side of the van as well. The vehicle had pulled in behind him.

Then the lights behind went out, and he was grateful but momentarily disorientated. There was a knock on the window and he jumped out of his skin. *Shit!* The Commander's face was staring through the glass, frowning as he tried the handle. Hastily, Yazbek opened the door.

"You are okay?" asked the Commander as Yazbek climbed out.

"Yes, sir, yes. I didn't know it was you."

"Why would you?"

Yazbek looked at the vehicle behind. It just seemed like a large shadow in the darkness, bigger than the van but with the word MITSUBISHI emblazoned across the grill.

"Our new transport," explained the Commander. "It will suit our mission just fine. Now we must ditch this one. Here," his hand went into his jacket pocket and produced a screwdriver. "You take the number plates off the Express. I'll do the Canter. We'll swap them over."

It was done within five minutes – a perfect replacement job on the Canter van, a not so perfect job on the Express because it didn't really matter.

"Are we leaving the Express here, sir?" asked Yazbek as he handed back the screwdriver.

"What do you think?" the Commander's reply was scornful. "Of course not. We must get rid of it." He looked at the watch on his right wrist. "Has it been busy along here?"

"Only one car going down in the last twenty minutes. Just you coming up."

The Commander looked behind him into the blackness. Then he said, "Right. We move and we move now. The van goes off the bridge. Get in."

"What!"

"Get in. Do as you are ordered. Crash it into the barrier, then get out and we'll push it over. Hurry."

"But I don't think - "

"In the name of Allah the Almighty! I will do it. Get out of the way. You follow to help me push it." The Commander climbed in and slammed the door. Immediately there was a crunching of gears and the Express van moved back out onto the road and onto the bridge. Yazbek ran after it. The Commander was angry with him, and rightly so. He would have to make it up to him. He did not want to fail in his mission at the last minute.

Halfway across the bridge, the van veered to the right and with a squeal of brakes rammed into the crash barrier. Both the barrier and the front of the van buckled. The van reversed back over the other side and shot forwards again, hitting the same part of the barrier, the Commander applying the brakes right at the last moment.

Again. And again.

At the fourth impact the barrier broke. There was still a metre of bridge left on the other side, and the van's wheels stopped with a few centimetres to spare before the edge.

Carefully, the Commander got out and stepped back over the barrier. "Come, Yazbek. Help me."

Yazbek had been staring open-mouthed from the other side of the road. "Sh – should we turn the lights off, sir?" He came over.

"Don't be stupid!" The Commander's left hand went into his jacket hip pocket. "Do you think someone who crashes pauses to turn off his lights before the fatal moment? Sometimes you Palestinians can be idiots."

Yazbek winced. That was uncalled for. And wasn't the Commander Palestinian also?

"Come, help me," ordered the Commander. "I can't do this on my own."

Looking sullen, Yazbek went to the back of the van, ready to push. Suddenly he did not like the Commander.

"Not there. Push from the front, by the door."

With a sniff of disrespect, Yazbek went round to the open driver's door.

"There is one more thing we need," said the Commander matter-of-factly, taking his hand out of his pocket. In his palm he held the hard chunk of olive wood, the Holding Cross. "The driver."

"The what - ?"

The cross slammed into Yazbek's forehead above his left eye. At the same time, Al-Rajul pushed him backwards into the van so that the blood would not splash out onto the road.

He hit him again and again, the hard wood hitting hard bone, hit, hit, hit, just like the van breaking the crash barrier, with the same cracking noises.

Yazbek died in silence and shock and in a state of hatred for his murderer, the man he had trusted. He was on his back across the front seats of the van.

Al-Rajul leant in and kept on hitting until his fist stopped hitting bone and moved into pulp and then liquid. Then he stopped, breathing heavily through his flared nostrils. He withdrew his dripping hand from inside Yazbek's head and wiped it first on the cadaver's shirt and then on its trousers, carefully cleaning the cross as well. The smell of brains was filling the cabin.

Al-Rajul pushed himself up off the body and out of the van. With two swift movements of his head, he looked around. There were still no lights in the distance.

No one was close. He leant back in and released the parking break. The gears were in neutral.

He kicked Yazbek's protruding feet into the van and slammed the driver's door. Then quickly he went round to the back. Bracing his feet, he leant against the van and pushed. One... two... three...

The van rolled forward.

And the front wheels tipped over the edge.

The van rocked, it beams nodding up and down in the darkness like searchlights.

Al-Rajul bent at the knees and grabbed the base of the van. Using its own rocking momentum and his own malevolent strength, he heaved. One – down... two – down... three – down... four – down... five – heave...! He let out a roar.

The van slid on its undercarriage off the edge of the bridge. The force of the wheels hitting the edge made it spin on the vertical as it went over.

Four seconds later a deep, loud *whump* shook the night as it hit the floor of the valley below. The lights were obliterated. Running to the edge and looking over, Al-Rajul could see nothing. There was no fire, no explosion. Good. Such things rarely happened in real accidents.

And this was a real accident.

He hastened back to the Mitsubishi Canter van, switched on the engine, turned on his beams and pulled back out onto the road. As he drove across the bridge, his lights illuminated the break in the crash barrier.

Wonder what had happened there? Bad workmanship? Or had somebody crashed? There was no sign of any vehicle. Maybe the accident had happened a long time ago and they had just not been bothered to repair it. Still, what did he care? It was nothing to do with him. He was just one of the farmers of the Bekaa Valley, taking his produce into the capital for sale...

2 December 2004
19 Shawwal 1425

Kahale, Lebanon 07:30

When Elias and Ahmad woke the next morning, they were surprised to see a white Mitsubishi Canter van parked outside. It had a separate cabin at the front and a large, half soft-sided cargo area at the back. It was the sort of van that the richer farmers would use for carrying produce to shops and markets (the poorer farmers would use smaller and more clapped-out vehicles). Was this a food delivery? The Express van was not out there, so the Commander must not be back.

But as they entered the dining room to get breakfast, the Commander was there waiting for them. As usual he wore his Palestinian *keffiyeh*, but tied around his neck as he had taken to wearing it recently, not on his head. For some reason it looked very bulky today.

"Morning of light, my brave Palestinians." He was in a good mood.

"Morning of peace, sir," smiled Elias.

"Morning of joy, Commander," nodded Ahmad.

"Before you eat I have something for you. Have you prayed?" They had. "Good. Do you like our new van?"

"It is ours, sir?" Elias.

"For our mission, yes. Yazbek helped me to get it last night. He has now fulfilled his task successfully and has left us. As promised, he will not be setting foot in the camp again."

Elias and Ahmad exchanged pleased glances, but they were also envious. They wished their turn would hurry up and come.

"I have also been in touch with the new President. He extends his congratulations to us, and especially thanks you two for your patience. As we are the only ones here, I can tell you now that you two have been singled out for more glorious, more trustworthy tasks than the other two. And your rewards, and the rewards for your families, will be that much larger."

"Indeed a morning of joy," nodded Ahmad. Elias was beaming.

"And he has sent you each a token of his appreciation." The Commander's hands moved to his neck and he took off one then two black-on-white *keffiyehs*, his own remaining underneath. He held them out. "For you. From the President. Wear them with honour and pride."

Elias and Ahmad accepted their gifts in subdued awe, not knowing what to say. For them? *From the President?* Smiling, glowing like little boys with their *Eid* presents, they put them on, giving each other approving looks.

"Today we will undertake more firearms training," announced the Commander. "And then more weight training. Soon the three of us will have a mission together, and I need you fit and strong. Now, go eat." He smiled dismissively.

Elias and Ahmad were pleased to the point of euphoria, and Al-Rajul knew that at that moment, and from then on, they would do anything for him.

He watched them filling their plates. He needed them physically fit and physically strong, but also mentally subservient. He did not want them thinking too much for themselves.

And apparently they hadn't.

Because neither of them had noticed that the cabin of the new van outside only sat two persons...

6 December 2004
23 Shawwal 1425

Jonblat, Beirut 10:00

"*Marhaba.* Captain Merhi?"

"*Naam.*"

"Jihad, *kifak?* It's Selim Himo, Bekaa Inquiry Brigade."

"Selim! *Mnih! Kifak?* It's been a long time."

"*Mnih, mnih.* That training course was too long ago now."

"How are you doing out there in the wilds?"

"It has its own problems, but it's a darn sight more peaceful than Beirut. And the *Gendarmerie* doesn't have the same problems as the ISF."

"Tell me about it. You made a good move."

"Jihad, I heard on the wire that you wanted to be informed if anything, er, unusual turned up."

"Ah."

"Well, I think I have something."

"Say no more."

"I understand."

"I'll call you back. You have a mobile?"

Himo read out a number.

"Okay, Selim. Ten minutes."'

Fifteen minutes later, Jihad Merhi was walking along Hamra Street with the Monday morning shoppers, smoking his third consecutive Cedars King Size and with a polycup of triple espresso in his left hand. His right hand held his mobile phone to his ear.

"Selim? Sorry about that, you know how it is."

"Only too well. Jihad, I have something that might interest you. Turned up on Friday, report was waiting on my desk when I came in this morning. Injuries consistent with your description."

Damn. "Where is it?"

"Still in place. Hasn't been moved."

"Can you leave it there for another day, so I can come see it?"

"*Bien sûr, pas de problème.*"

"I'll be bringing somebody with me. Just a... consultant."

"Fine, I'll ask no questions. And Jihad?"

"*Oui?*"

"Bring your *caoutchouc.*"

Verdun, Beirut 14:00

"What?! No way, no chance." Sesame seeds from either the quarter pounder with cheese or the Big Mac fell into the beard of Captain Fadi Lattouf of the Palestinian Security Force as he exclaimed, ate and shook his head at the same time. Special sauce lined his lips.

"Why not?" Jihad Merhi's intolerance was barely concealed. He knew this would be the big man's reaction, and he knew the game would have to be played out to its inevitable conclusion.

"It is not my case anymore."

"Says who? Yes it is, my friend."

"Now you have another body that proves it. My theory was correct," reasoned Lattouf.

Merhi sighed and pursed his lips. He looked at the plainly wrapped simple cheeseburger in front of him which had been waiting for him when he arrived. "You want this too?"

"You don't want it?"

"I am going home straight after this. Gisele is cooking one of her fish dishes. Don't want to spoil my appetite."

"You are a lucky, lucky man." Lattouf pulled the burger into his personal space (which was most of the table).

"We seem to have our first body outside of the camp, I grant you," agreed Merhi. "But how can we be certain unless you verify it? I haven't seen any of them, remember?"

"Send me a photo."

"That's not a chain of evidence or identification and you know it, not even in Palestinian law."

Lattouf shrugged.

"I am asking you as a colleague in law enforcement," persisted Merhi. "As a friend."

The last one hit home and a look of anguish briefly flashed across Lattouf's face. "Jihad, I have no jurisdiction outside of the camp, you know that. How would it look if a Palestinian policeman was involved in a Lebanese investigation?"

"The same way it looked when a Lebanese policeman was involved in a Palestinian investigation. I should not have been there, but I did it for you. As a friend."

"Yes, but that was - "

"Different? You were going to say that was different, weren't you?"

"I - "

"There's no difference. I'm not asking you to come in full uniform with sirens blazing. Just accompany me."

Lattouf slurped half of a supersize cup of coffee. "I could get in serious trouble. With the groups, you know."

"Let me run another theory by you, Fadi."

"Mm?"

"You contend that the murders are occurring outside the camp and the bodies are being brought to the camp and dumped - " Merhi stopped and watched the spectacle of Fadi Lattouf putting the entire cheeseburger into his mouth whole, folding it neatly at either side as it went into the cavern. Then he continued. "What if the murders are occurring inside the camp and your serial killer has now started to dump them outside? Have you thought of that? That puts the problem right back in your lap, my friend. And it also means that we would then have the right to liaise with you in whatever way we see fit, having been dragged into Palestinian affairs. And the groups certainly will not like that, will they?"

Lattouf stopped chewing, a small piece of bun poking from the left corner of his mouth.

"That," continued Merhi, "would be serious trouble with a capital S."

A puzzled frown creased Lattouf's brow as he started chewing again. He swallowed and said quietly, "How has it come to this?"

It was Merhi's turn to shrug. "Not your fault, not my fault. And we can possibly still keep a lid on this. Work it between us. Our masters would want that. No boat rocking. No," he made bunny ears with his fingers, "upsetting the delicate balance of Lebanese and Palestinian relations regarding the camps. Just come with me, Fadi."

Lattouf sighed. "When?"

"Tomorrow. Be downstairs here outside the car park at eight. The shops won't yet be open so it'll be quiet. I'll pick you up. And Fadi?"

"Yes?"

"Bring your *caoutchouc*."

7 December 2004
24 Shawwal 1425

Aammiq Wetlands, West Bekaa, Lebanon 11:00

The body was lying face down entangled in the reeds at the edge of the swamp, the water about twenty centimetres deep. It had been discovered by a Jordanian conservationist engaged in winter ecosystem studies, who had spotted what he thought was dumped rubbish and had gone to remove it, quickly stepping away and contacting the police when he realised it was – or had been – human.

"It has not been moved?" asked Jihad Merhi.

"Just turned over then quickly turned back again," replied Lieutenant Selim Himo of the Bekaa Inquiry Brigade. Himo was taller and younger than Merhi, having risen quickly through the ranks, a future star as yet uncorrupted by the pressures of future higher rank.

"Fadi - ?" Merhi turned. "Where the hell is he?" Lattouf was about ten metres back, still ploughing laboriously through the reeds. He had not brought any *caoutchouc* (there was not much call for waders in a Palestinian refugee camp in the Middle East) so had to borrow a pair – which of course were a few sizes too small, making him walk like an inexperienced cross-dresser in high heels. He wore an old black padded jacket, denim shirt frayed at the collar, and jeans. It was cool and damp down here in the wetlands, but up behind them the mountains were covered in snow. Merhi and Himo were in their uniforms, their waders of correctly-fitting sizes.

"I'm coming, I'm coming," mumbled Lattouf. "The things I do! These accursed rubbers are killing me. And I don't know what I'm doing here anyway."

"You are my expert witness," said Merhi sternly. "Come, witness."

Himo had asked no questions about the huge fat giant that accompanied Jihad Merhi, but obviously he knew he was Palestinian. Were they allowing them into the Lebanese police nowadays? Or was something else going on?

"Can we turn him?" asked Merhi as Lattouf reached them.

Himo nodded. "If you'll give me a hand. Best take off your jacket in case of accidents."

"Good idea."

Both men removed their jackets and gave them to Lattouf to hold. There were some mumblings about coming all this way to be a cloakroom attendant, but they ignored them. Rolling up their shirtsleeves, they crouched down. Merhi put his hands into the water this side of the body.

"No, no, reach across and pull him over towards us," advised Himo. "The swamp does not give up her possessions easily. It will be better if we tug rather than push. And there might be some other effect also."

They reached across and grabbed the body by its far side. The first tug achieved nothing, the second raised the body just a little before it fell back down again, making ripples. The damn cadaver seemed heavier than Fadi Lattouf. Merhi had a sudden empathy with the Palestinian's wife Nada. Five children conceived with that on top of you!

They put all their power and effort behind the third heave, both groaning to give themselves strength. With a sucking sound, the body rose and rolled with its back towards them.

Suddenly a shot of swamp water sprayed out from the head about a third of a metre into the air.

"Did that before," explained Himo breathlessly. "Suction where the hole is."

The body's own weight brought it over and it flopped onto the policemen's feet. Both stepped back rapidly.

"In the name of Jesus Christ!" Merhi straightened up quickly. Oh my good God.

Himo was grimacing.

Lattouf leant forward and looked. There was no face, the swamp life had seen to that. It was just the shell of a human head filled with murky water. The clothes on the body, still intact, were straight young person's wear: cargo pants and light shirt.

For the first time in his career, Merhi thought he was going to be sick. Thank God the swamp water was taming the smell of the corpse, but he expected it to hit his nostrils any minute.

Lattouf nodded and calmly straightened up. He seemed unaffected by the sight. "The others were worse," he said. "The waters have looked after this one."

"But it's the same?" Merhi swallowed back bile.

"Oh yes."

"There have been others?" queried Himo.

Lattouf's eyes shot to Merhi.

"We think we have a serial killer," explained Merhi. "Operating in... Beirut. This is the first outside."

"You want jurisdiction?"

"No, no. Do whatever checks and searches you think you need to do, but I doubt you'll find anything. This is the fourth young Pal... person... that we know of. None of them have had records, none reported missing. The murder would not have been committed here, this is just a dumping ground." He looked around, wondering: but why here? Probably thought the marsh would consume it, that it would never been found. But where was it brought from? He said, "If you could just give me a report, Selim, how long dead *et cetera*, that will be fine. We will eventually subsume it within the general enquiry."

"As you wish."

"Do you, er... want any help?" Merhi waved a hand at the body.

"No, no. I'll send some men for it."

"Perhaps you should just leave it here," suggested Lattouf. "A decomposing tourist attraction come the spring. Nobody will claim it, you'll only take it out to dispose of it later." He saw the look both men were giving him and closed his mouth. Suddenly there was a severe tickling in his nose at the same time as his stomach rumbled. He tried to breathe in, but the tickling only got worse with each small inhale. His face screwed up as if he was in excruciating agony, his mouth opened in a grimace. He threw his head back, making a growling *ahh* sound, rising in volume.

Then his head shot forward and he emitted a stentorian sneeze at the same time as a loud fart blasted from his rear. Birds flew into the air nearby.

"Bloody damp," mumbled Lattouf, still bent from the waist. Two more smaller farts popped out as he straightened up. "Sorry about that, gentlemen." The two policemen were staring into the swamp at his feet. He looked down and saw their two jackets resting on the water. Quickly he bent down and grabbed them, water running off them as he lifted them up. "They'll be fine," he said cheerfully. "Fine. It's just a little water." He held them out.

Slowly Merhi and Himo reached out and took back their jackets, nonplussed.

"Talking of this being a dumping ground, I think I need to," announced Lattouf. "Can we stop by your office on the way back? Or actually, I could do it here, couldn't I? It wouldn't make any difference. It is a bog, after all."

That, thought Merhi, would be something the swamp would never tame. In years to come, future ecologists would analyse Lattouf's dump and conclude that yes, earth had been colonised by creatures from another planet in the past. The poisoned marshes of Aammiq, where all life was extinct. "Not near the body," he said. "Go over there somewhere."

"You might want to give me a good clearance," advised the Palestinian. "I can sometimes be, er... vociferous."

"Too much information," Merhi held up his hand as he walked away with the bemused Salim Himo. "And don't cause a tsunami."

"My arse is always considerate of others," proclaimed its owner.

Merhi and Himo kept on walking. Twenty seconds after, they heard the three-tone trumpet blast, and while they were still walking and were at least fifty metres away, the swamp water around their feet actually rippled violently.

Chtaura, Lebanon 12:30

Back in his regional office, and with Captain Jihad Merhi and his idiot sidekick back on their way to Beirut, Lieutenant Salim Himo picked up the telephone. A future star as yet uncorrupted by the pressures of future higher rank he may be, but he also had the self-centred interest of all high-flyers.

He dialled a number.

Ras en Nabaa, Beirut 12:31

In his office in the Department of General Security, Captain Maroun Khoury answered his ringing telephone.

Five minutes later, with the call ended, he picked up the phone again and keyed a number. It took a few rings for the person to answer, then Khoury said "ZiZi. Some good news. We have a body..."

11 December 2004
28 Shawwal 1425

Jonblat, Beirut 11:45

Four days later and Jihad Merhi was a happy man.

He realised as he thought it that 'happy' was too strong a description. How could you be happy when you were a Captain of the Internal Security Force of Lebanon? That was not part of the job description, not one of the required competencies. Mildly contented, perhaps? Still too strong. *Pleased.* Yes, that would do.

Four days later and Jihad Merhi was pleased. Lieutenant Selim Himo of the Bekaa Inquiry Brigade had been good. Merhi was impressed. Himo would go far.

The report had been awaiting Merhi when he came in this morning. Copied to him 'as per ISF request', it reported the discovery of a body in the Aammiq Wetlands. Cause of death: unknown. No reason to suspect foul play. Probably an accident, it sometimes happens in the marshes. An unwary visitor gets stuck. No one else around. Dies of hypothermia, or possibly even a heart attack brought on by desperation to free himself from the cloying, sucking mud. Time of death: hard to say, probably no longer than two weeks. Identification: hindered by faunal digestion of face; local male, between 18 and 25. No fingerprints on file. Body to be disposed of in accordance with internal guidance.

So the case could be buried (Merhi winced at his own graveyard humour), which meant that the other deaths could still be kept quiet. Lattouf was off the hook.

And Merhi was off the hook too.

He looked at his watch. He best hurry. It was 11:45. Gisele was doing some shopping down on Hamra Street, and he had arranged to meet her at midday. She wanted his advice on some shoes she was thinking of buying (the advice being the one word: yes), then they were driving home together. It was Saturday and they had guests coming round for dinner, Gisele's brother Joe and his wife Jacqui, whose wedding they had been to two months ago. Gisele would prepare several of her sumptuous dishes, and as always Jihad would be the ebullient, perfect host.

As he waited for his computer to shut down he again gave mental thanks to Selim Himo for a job well done.

He did not realise that Himo was only doing as he had been told. The Lieutenant was, after all, a future star.

Jounieh, Lebanon 14:00

The shoes were, in fact, very nice. Red Jimmy Choo copies. They suited the elegant Gisele perfectly and, importantly from a male perspective, they had heels.

Gisele had also bought him a new shirt, which he would wear this evening, so it was a contented *Merhi à deux* that drove back along the coastal highway towards their apartment in Jounieh, twenty kilometres north of Beirut.

Gisele was driving the Toyota Land Cruiser (not in her new shoes) to give Jihad a chance to relax. This was the first day he had left work early in a long time (and a full day off for him was a thing of distant memory). Gisele knew he liked his brother-in-law immensely and he was looking forward to seeing him and his wife.

Over the south-bound carriageway to the left, the gently-waving Mediterranean formed a tranquil and timeless backdrop, a contrasting sedative to the frantic traffic on the highway. Lebanon's coastal road is always very busy, but on a Saturday even more so. Buses, coaches, lorries, vans, cars, old and new, gleaming and rusted, you name it.

So it was not until they had reached Kaslik and were close to the turnoff for home that Jihad realised they were being followed.

If Gisele noticed the sudden tension that filled her husband, she did not say anything. Merhi did not turn round, but his attention was now fully on the wing mirror. The tail was three cars back. He had been aware of the black Ford Explorer for some time, but it had not registered that it was any different to the rest of the Saturday traffic heading out from the capital – not until Gisele had pulled out to overtake a slow-moving Datsun. The two cars behind plus the Explorer had pulled out too, but then the Explorer had stayed out but had not overtaken the other two cars as would have been expected with its obvious extra power. After a few seconds it had pulled back in, so keeping the same formation, two cars in between the Explorer and the Merhis. A classic solo tail.

Merhi's subconscious had noticed the movement and swiftly brought it to the attention of his awareness, at the same time ordering a shot of adrenaline to kick him out of his reverie. His fist tightened on the end of his armrest, his eyes locked on the wing mirror.

They passed the statue of the Virgin Mary, *Notre Dame du Liban*, at Harissa, high up on the cliffs to their right, and then turned off the coastal highway towards Haret Sakhr.

Merhi watched. Car One continued on the highway. So did Car Two.

The Ford Explorer turned off.

Now there was nothing between them. The Explorer was three hundred metres back, but it was not hurrying to catch them. It was just following.

Calmly, he said "We have a tail."

Gisele looked in her rear-view mirror. There was neither shock nor surprise in her voice as she asked, "Want me to lose them?" She was well-experienced in surveillance and counter-surveillance techniques from her days in the field for the Department of General Security.

"No. Let's play it out, see what happens."

They drove on up into the coastal mountain, slowly because of the hairpin bends. The Explorer drove equally carefully.

"Obviously they want me to know," Jihad turned and looked back. "They're in plain sight."

"You want observation?"

"Yes please."

They continued up the mountain for two more minutes and then turned onto the track that led to their apartment block. Immediately they turned, Gisele pulled up sharply, wheels kicking up dust. Jihad turned around, kneeling on his seat.

A few moments later, the Ford Explorer carried on past. But Jihad observed the driver, their eyes meeting for a second as the driver looked towards them.

It was a woman.

He turned back round. Gisele had watched the Explorer pass in her rear-view mirror. "Well," she said, "we haven't had anything like that in a long time."

"No..." Jihad was thoughtful.

"Why would they be following you?"

"Don't know. Intriguing. Our address is not a secret, so it's not like they wanted to know where we live. They could have looked that up in records."

"So the only other reason for following, especially in plain sight - "

"Is to let us see them. A warning. To let us know they know."

"Know what?"

"Don't know."

Gisele put the car back into Drive and they moved the few hundred metres downhill to their cliffside apartment block. As she put on the parking brake, she asked "Jihad, what have you got yourself involved in now?"

16 December 2004
4 Dhu'l-Qa'dah 1425

Mount Lebanon 07:30

The Damascene looked at the still sleeping woman beside him. The Djinn. He reached out and lightly stroked the cashmere skin of her naked left buttock. Instinctively her bottom moved towards him, inviting or reminiscing. Maybe both.

He swung his legs around and got up off the bed. He always slept well after he had been with her, the natural physical release of his climaxes had a morphean quality giving him deep and dreamless rest, and he awoke refreshed and recharged.

Naked, and with his long hair falling either side of his face, he went downstairs to the living area and switched on the television, keeping the volume low.

It was on every channel, the slant given to it depending on the bias of the broadcaster.

Two days ago, the Bristol Declaration had been issued. It was the result of an extraordinary recent meeting at the Bristol Hotel, the first time since Lebanon's independence in 1943 that Maronites, Druze, Sunnis and many other sects and organisations (but not the Shi'ites) had formed a cross-communal political bloc. The Declaration was as direct as it was inflammatory, denouncing the amendment of the constitution and the extension of President Lahoud's term in office and demanding a fair and just law for an honest and free election and calling for the resignation of the Karami government and the installation of a new impartial government to supervise the upcoming elections in May.

Although Rafic Hariri had not attended the meeting (he had asked a friend to attend 'in a personal capacity'), he was immediately denounced as the instigator and ringleader, the government accusing him of whipping up sectarian dissent.

The Damascene flicked from channel to channel. The familiar faces kept popping onto the screen: Jumblatt, Nasrallah, Lahoud, Karami, Berri, Geagea, Aoun, Assad. And always, always Rafic Hariri.

As the Declaration had stated, Lebanon was indeed entering 'a very dangerous phase'.

But dangerous phase or placid phase, The Damascene was satisfied that Hariri was protected by Abu Tarek's excellent security team, augmented by his own risk analysis and presence if Hariri made an unfamiliar trip outside.

As he had figured out before, there was only one way Hariri could be killed. Today Hariri was ensconced in Koreitem, unless The Damascene received a text message to the contrary, and it would not happen there.

He walked over to the window. It was 07:30 but it was still dull and grey out there. He saw some lights still twinkling in downtown in the distance. The two-month winter had started on cue, and the last few days had been cold, wet and windy with more inclement weather predicted.

He was staring out the window, lost in his thoughts, when he saw a naked woman floating in the sky above Beirut.

At first he was perplexed. Was this an angel? Was he having a religious experience (the apartment was, after all, on the road to Damascus, so it would not be the first time it had happened on the highway)?

The woman was standing still and smiling at him, her long black hair pushed back over her shoulders not falling down her front, so she was fully exposed. He smiled back and she began to walk across the sky towards him.

He appreciated the hallucinatory effect of her reflection in the glass and his desire reacted as she came up behind him and ran her fingers down his spine so lightly that he wondered if she had in fact done it at all.

"*Bonjour.*" Her voice was morning-husky.

Without turning, he raised his right arm and she slipped underneath it, her arms trying to reach round his body but not connecting. She put her head against his hard right breast. She could smell his sweat and the natural scent from lower down. "Did you sleep well?" she asked.

"Of course."

"And I don't suppose you made any coffee?"

"Of course not."

She squeezed him. "Then I suppose if a Djinn wants some, she will have to make it herself."

"Of course."

She wriggled out from under his arm, and he admired the movement of her firm cheeks reflected in the glass as she walked back across Beirut to the kitchen area. "Is that all there is on TV?" she said, a comment rather than a question.

"Every channel," he said over his shoulder. "These are interesting times."

As rain started to pit-pat on the glass, he turned back to the window. There was a flash of lightning out at sea, heading towards land.

Storm clouds were gathering over Beirut.

PART THREE
الجزء الثالث

COMPLETION
الانتهاء

18 December 2004
6 Dhu'l-Qa'dah 1425

Hamra, Beirut 13:30

"Has anything unusual happened? You been followed or anything?" Although he wanted to keep his voice low, Jihad Merhi had to talk loudly into his mobile phone to be heard above the cries of the stallholders selling their wares and the honking horns of the cars. It was a cool day but that had not stopped the Saturday shoppers. Hamra Street was buzzing.

"Followed?" boomed the voice on the other end, tinny as it came out of the Samsung. "Nobody would dare follow Fadi Lattouf! My presence usually makes people flee. I repel, I do not attract."

"Could your phones be bugged?"

"Bugged! First they've got to work before they can be bugged! Thank Allah for mobiles. Why are you asking, my friend? Has something happened?"

"This day last week, Gisele and I were followed on our way home."

"Not nice."

"No."

"Did anything happen?"

"No, they followed us to the entrance to our block and then drove on. A woman."

"A woman! You haven't been...?"

"No, I certainly haven't. I think it was a warning."

"About what?"

"A good question. I have many ongoing cases, but it happened just four days after we went to Aammiq. I think it's connected."

"How? You have not reported the bodies, have you? Made it official?"

"No. Your four are still yours and the one in Aammiq has been reported as an accidental death. But the morning Lieutenant Himo's report lands on my desk, I get followed. Coincidence?"

"There are no such things."

"Exactly. Hey - !" Merhi slammed his hand down on the bonnet of a car which missed him by a centimetre as he stepped off the kerb. The driver's face glared but then changed into a raised palm of apology when he saw Merhi's uniform under his leather coat. He drove away quickly.

"Jihad, you okay?"

"Just some stupid driver."

"Where are you?"

"Hamra."

"Hamra! You couldn't pick me up some pickles from that stall on the square, could you?"

"No."

"Just two jars? I'll give you the money."

"Fadi, I'm serious. Be extra vigilant. If anything should happen or even seem just out of the ordinary, let me know straight away."

"If anyone dares to follow me in the camp, I will arrest them. See how they like a taste of Palestinian remand. You Lebanese are too soft."

Too soft! This coming from a man whose girth was the original template for bouncy-castles, thought Merhi.

"But yes, thank you Abu Samer," continued Lattouf. "I appreciate your warning. But why is this happening, if no one knows about our little... discoveries?"

"A very good question. One I don't yet know the answer to."

"And your phones are bugged?"

"Fadi, I am a Captain of the Internal Security Force. Of course my phones are bugged, as are everyone else's."

"I have one piece of advice for you, my friend."

"What's that?"

There was silence. For a moment, Merhi thought he had lost his signal but a quick look at the screen showed he was still connected. "Fadi?"

"Buy me three jars of pickles and I'll tell you."

"Fadi!"

"A small price to pay for advice which could save your life."

"Oh, you really are..." Merhi shook his head and stopped walking. As chance would have it he was at Hamra Square. "You're a blackmailer, do you know that? An extortionist."

"I've been called worse."

"Okay, okay. Two jars of pickles it is."

"Four."

"Three."

"Done."

"So what is this advice that I'm paying so dearly for?"

After a moment, Fadi Lattouf said "Always check under your car."

25 December 2004
13 Dhu'l-Qa'dah 1425

Kahale, Lebanon 09:30

Elias and Ahmad both felt proud and resolute as they walked outside. It was a grey, cold and damp day but they both had on new Timberland padded and waterproof jackets – the most expensive present either of them had ever been given in their lives. They tried to keep their faces serious, but their eyes gleamed – like children on Christmas morning.

"Right," the Commander came out two minutes later, carrying some bright red textile items in his hand. "Put these on so we will blend in." He threw one to Elias, one to Ahmad and kept one for himself.

Both young men caught the items and turned them over in their hands quizzically. Elias looked up and then burst into laughter. "A Santa Claus hat?" The Commander put his on, long and pointed with white fringing and a white bobble on the end. He adjusted it so that the long pointed bit fell down over his left shoulder.

Ahmad was giggling too. "But we are not Christian!"

"Since when has Christmas been a Christian festival?" asked the Commander. "Not for a long time. It marks the birth of the Prophet Jesus. You are perfectly entitled to celebrate. And anyway, as I said, we will fit in. Come." He nodded towards the van. "Elias, you will ride with me in the front. Ahmad, you go in the back."

Ahmad knew better than to query or argue. The back of the van was dirty and smelled of the fruit that used to be transported in it. But, he supposed, it could be worse. Imagine the putrid smell if this had been a butcher's van instead of a fruiterer's! "Where are we going, sir?" he asked as he undid the soft flap on the side.

"We're going to pick up some sugar," said Al-Rajul.

Mount Lebanon 09:45 – 11:00

The white Mitsubishi Canter van drove up to the Beirut to Damascus road and turned left for the downhill journey into the capital. Elias sat proudly in the passenger seat next to the Commander. Obviously he was the favourite, he thought. The taciturn Ahmad had been put into the back like livestock.

The road was less busy but by no means quiet. Shops and entertainment venues still opened in Beirut on Christmas Day and people would be out and about, having enjoyed their Christmas dinner yesterday evening. They passed through Jamhour and hung right, avoiding the Presidential Palace area at Baabda.

Christmas lights were in many shop windows, and in some areas downtown they would even be strung across the streets. Santa Claus hats just like the ones they were wearing were stretched across the headrests in many cars, and more than once they experienced the Lebanese phenomenon of a car going past blaring out Christmas songs to be followed under two minutes later by another car blaring out Muslim prayers. A friendly rivalry, in the spirit of peace...

They stayed on Damascus Street all the way into the city and up to the coast. They turned right at Trieste Street.

Into the port.

Marfa'a, Beirut 11:00

They drove quite a way in, along roads bordered by stored containers stacked on top of each other, past warehouses and sheds, and so many cranes. Elias was confused by the time they reached the warehouse they wanted, one of twelve in the general cargo area.

As the Commander stepped from the van, a fat bald-headed greasy man emerged from a wicket door in the warehouse and grunted. They exchanged nods.

The Commander banged on the side of the van as Elias got out. The flap moved and Ahmad climbed out, stepping straight into a puddle, looking a little dishevelled. Both young men came round to stand by their Commander. With their hats on the three of them looked like Santa Claus and his helpers.

Producing papers from an inside pocket, the Commander handed them to the greasy man who looked at them, looked up at the Commander, raised his eyebrows and then nodded, handing the papers back. The greasy man turned and, with another grunt, slid open the main doors to the warehouse. The Commander did not move to help him; everyone had their job, even in the port of Beirut.

The greasy man clicked on several light switches and the warehouse lit up like the Camille Chamoun Sports City stadium when the floodlights are turned on. Inside, the place was stacked almost to the ceiling with pallets of sugar imports from India.

"Yours are over here." The greasy man led the way in and to the left. He nodded at a block of fifty-kilogramme jute sacks, which looked no different from any of the others in the area. "You can back the van in if you want."

"*Shukran*. Ahmad."

Ahmad looked at the Commander and then quickly understood. Ignoring Elias's sulky frown, he dashed back outside and climbed into the front of the van. In no time, the van was reversing skilfully into the warehouse. It stopped exactly in the right position and Ahmad climbed back out.

"Those twenty sacks at the front are ours," said the Commander. He paused, waiting, and then said, "Well, go on then you two. Load them up."

Now they knew what the exercises had been for. It took the strength of the two of them to carry each of the sacks to the van and throw them in. Elias, as always confident and cock-sure, attempted one on his own, managing it but looking very pale afterwards.

It took them nearly half an hour to load the twenty sacks, and they both looked physically drained. Elias was ordered into the back – yes, he could rest on the sacks if he wanted to – and Ahmad was allowed to climb up into the front. The Commander shook hands with the greasy man, an envelope changed hands, and shortly they were making their way back along the wet quayside.

They stopped at the Customs office down near the Charles Helou Transport Station. The Commander climbed out, papers were handed over, examined, the side of the van was opened, the load visually inspected, the side of the van was closed, papers were stamped, and they were on their way back out of the port.

Kahale, Lebanon 13:15

Ahmad slept on the fifty minute drive back into the mountains, waking as they turned off the main road. They passed through the town and headed back downhill again towards The Facility.

They pulled up at the side of the main building, near the garages and outhouses. Getting out, the Commander pulled the Santa Claus hat from his head and threw it back onto his seat. "Dispose of that, Ahmad." He banged on the side of the van and lifted the flap.

Having slept on the sugar, Elias seemed more refreshed than Ahmad, and he jumped out, looking at the Commander for orders.

"Store the sacks in the garage," instructed the Commander. "And try to stack them neatly. After that, you can both rest. You have done well. Your families will deserve their extra reward."

"Thank you, sir," Ahmad came round.

As they both reached back inside the van, dragging the first sack over, Elias said chattily "I'm glad it's stopped raining, sir. We wouldn't want the sugar to get wet."

"No. We wouldn't," agreed Al-Rajul.

29 December 2004
17 Dhu'l-Qa'dah 1425

Mount Lebanon 10:00

The Damascene tied back his long hair with a rubber band into the simple ponytail, pulling the left side down to ensure it covered the hole of his left ear. He slipped into his leather jacket and grabbed the motorcycle keys from the breakfast bar. He had a 'touching base' meeting with Abu Tarek at Koreitem.

Yesterday the second meeting of what was being called the Bristol Gathering had taken place at the Bristol Hotel. Again, Hariri had not attended. His friend, Dr Ghattas Khoury, had gone in a personal capacity along with Basil Fleihan, Hariri's close advisor and former economy minister.

The only confession not on board this movement for change were the Shi'ites, and Hariri had continued his clandestine late night meetings with Sayyed Hassan Nasrallah whom he viewed as a potential Shi'te partner in the Arab cause.

Koreitem Palace was now campaign headquarters for the wave of change that would sweep through Lebanon once Hariri was re-elected next May. Today The Damascene would be refreshing his risk analysis with Abu Tarek and confirming his need for details of Hariri's itinerary whenever he left the palace.

He closed and locked the apartment front door behind him, his preconscious mind pleased that it was not raining today. Nothing worse than riding a bike in the rain – especially with the drivers of Beirut trying to kill first and ask questions later!

As he walked down the stairs he saw the door of the apartment directly beneath his closing quickly. Such was the strong and insulated construction of the building that he did not even know that there was anybody living down there.

As he passed by the door and continued on down, he smelt something. What was that? Seemed familiar.

Jasmine.

The smell of The Djinn.

He laughed. Now *that* was wishful thinking! Imagine him knocking on the door and ravaging the housewife because she was wearing jasmine perfume!

It had been nearly two weeks and his body wanted The Djinn again. He hoped she would visit again soon. He wondered what she did in the weeks between her visits? Probably some other jobs for Kanaan, on a similar line. Well, so be it, he was not a man of jealousy.

And, he rebuked himself, he must not let his desire get in the way of his task. The mission would be over soon and, although Kanaan did not know it, he would not be returning to Damascus. He wondered if he could persuade The Djinn to come with him on his future adventures...

He reached the front door and went out. Moments later the Suzuki was roaring up towards the main road.

30 December 2004
18 Dhu'l-Qa'dah 1425

Ras en Nabaa, Beirut 13:30

Captain Maroun Khoury ate falafel and bread for his lunch as he sat at the side of the desk of Zahia Zalloum. There were ten people in his team, but at that moment Zahia was the only one in the open-plan Listening Suite. But Khoury knew that others would be returning with their food soon, so he pushed to the back of his mind the thoughts he was having about ZiZi, the desktop and the pot of yoghurt in front of her.

"Why they keep the Watchers separate from us Listeners and Gatherers, I don't know," he was saying. "It would be so much better if we were one team. Bureaucracy and Lebanon are like inoperable conjoined twins."

"But still, they've paid off," Zahia tipped a spoonful of yoghurt into her mouth, fully aware that Khoury's powers of concentration were waning every second he sat next to her.

"Only because you had the bright idea to ask the question. Bravo you."

"Well, it didn't take us long to figure out who the fat guy shitting in the Aammiq Wetlands was. Palestinian... Merhi is the liaison for the camps... And let's face it, there are not many people who match the description given by Lieutenant Himo. Monsieur Lattouf. The Watchers had seen him and Merhi meeting quite frequently at the Dunes. Did you know they try to sidetrack them by arranging to meet twenty-six hours later than they actually meet and always name some stupid place? The Watchers worked it out long ago. But of course, they watch. We listen – and act. So they had no microphones. But they did have video. And," she reached into her drawer and pulled out a disc, "here it is."

Khoury nodded, impressed. "Have you viewed it yet?"

"No, I thought we might watch it together."

Khoury wanted to suggest "Tonight?" but instead he said "Come to my office."

They sat side by side, legs touching, looking at the computer screen. The picture clarity was pretty good for an indoor shot. It showed a public eating area, people moving about, carrying trays. Quite close to the camera was a massive back, obviously Lattouf. Merhi was facing him, his face clearly visible. There was an Americanised date on the top right corner of the screen: 12/06/2004.

There was sound but it was just general noise. Merhi was talking but they couldn't hear what was being said. "See what I mean?" said Zahia. "They watch. We listen and act. It's just as well I'm... good with lips." Khoury was aware of the glance she gave him. "Could you turn the sound off, Moro, so I can concentrate?"

He did as asked. Zahia leant forward, staring hard at the screen, one hand absentmindedly steadying herself on Khoury's thigh, the other on the mouse, clicking, starting and stopping the disc. "He's... he's giving him his own food for some reason. Something about not wanting to spoil his appetite. Okay... Ah, hold on, hold on... Yes! 'Our first body outside of the camp'." She stopped the disc. "So, the bodies have been in the camp, that's why nothing's been reported. Of course. Makes sense now." She clicked the mouse. "He's asking – arguing – saying he shouldn't have been there. The camp, presumably."

"No, he certainly shouldn't," said Khoury. "If Merhi was in the camp, that's grounds for castration in itself."

"He's asking... he's asking Lattouf to come with him. To Aammiq presumably. Oh! Hold on, hold on. Let's run that again." She stared at the screen, nodding. "'You... something... that the murders are occurring outside the camp... something... what – what if the murders are occurring inside the camp and your... something... killer has now started to...' Hump? Can't be... Dump? Dump them outside!" She leant back, still looking at the screen. "Blah, blah... They're talking about the groups, in the camp presumably... Looks like he's persuaded Lattouf to come with him... tells him to bring his *caoutchouc*. That's it." She pushed the mouse back to Khoury.

He stopped the disc, noting with disappointment that she had taken her hand from his leg. "So, our friend has been killing them like he said. Do you think he has been deliberately dumping them in the camp?"

She shook her head. "No. That doesn't fit. That's probably where he got them."

"But why? For pleasure? Is he just a serial killer after all?"

"Can't be. If he is, we're wasting our time. We can give it to the police. But that's not what this is about."

Khoury nodded. "I agree. It doesn't fit with what we know."

Zahia stood up. "I'm going to have to delve deeper. But I don't want Merhi and the idiot Lattouf stomping around all over this."

"What are you going to do?"

"Leave it to me."

"Okay."

"But, Moro," she leant forward on his desk, "we also have to figure out what's going on. Knowing what we know, why we started this in the first place."

"Why are young Palestinians being killed?"

"It's not for pleasure, there's a purpose." She pushed herself up. "And I'll find out what it is."

31 December 2004
19 Dhu'l-Qa'dah 1425

Kaslik, Lebanon 14:30

Gisele Merhi was preoccupied. She was getting a few last minute things in her favourite supermarket down in Kaslik and then had to dash home to prepare the food for their party tonight. They had about thirty family and friends coming round, as they did every new year, and Gisele was thankful that their apartment was big. The New Year's Eve weather was clement enough for any overspill out onto their double balcony with its views over the town below and the Mediterranean beyond. There might even be some fireworks from boats out at sea come midnight.

They had two extra guests this year: Captain Fadi Lattouf of the Palestinian Internal Security Force and his wife Nada. Gisele had baulked momentarily when Jihad had said he had invited them, but her husband had made a two-fold case: one, it was only right to invite them after she and Jihad had been to their *Eid* celebrations, and two, she could now get rid of the eyesore of the three large jars of pickles that had been glaring at her from her kitchen work surface for nearly two weeks. She only hoped the Lattoufs didn't bring their five fat kids with them.

She put the last item in her trolley (a tin of duck pâté, which was for her and Jihad, not for the party), and queued up at the till. She was thinking of her recipe for *sayoudeiah* as she unloaded her stuff onto the conveyor belt, and she took no notice of the person in front of her, a young woman dressed in jeans and brown leather coat with a brown *hijab* covering her head.

The woman in front paid for her two items, and Gisele's stuff had just started to move along the belt when the woman looked back at her and smiled. Gisele nodded back courteously. The woman said, "Tell your husband that they were accidents. Only accidents. He should leave them alone." Then she turned around and walked away.

What?

"Hey!" Gisele made to run after the woman, but her stuff was being beeped through and her trolley was in the way. She looked at the woman's departing back and then at the cashier. Quickly she threw her goods into the open bag in the trolley as they came through, threw notes at the startled cashier, and ran outside, pushing the trolley in front of her.

She came to a halt, looking right then left. This was a predominantly Maronite Christian location, but there were still enough *hijabs* about to stop her singling out anybody. She looked back and forth, frowning, angry, sighing.

Then from the side of the petrol station further along she saw a car pull out and ease its way onto the six-lane main road, driving off north.

It was a black Ford Explorer.

Jounieh, Lebanon 23:30

"So, we were right," said Fadi Lattouf. "They were accidents. There never was any need to report them."

Jihad Merhi's speech had the mellow timbre of an evening spent in the company of Johnnie Walker. "If they were accidents then your arse looks like the Mona Lisa."

"It has been said," agreed Lattouf.

They were on the balcony of the Merhi's apartment looking out over the blackness that was the Mediterranean, a diamante carapace of stars glinting overhead. In thirty minutes it would be 2005.

Lattouf cupped a cigarette in his hand, smoking surreptitiously in case Nada looked out. He had last seen her in the kitchen giving Gisele unwanted advice on how to prepare her fish correctly, but the cooking lesson might be over by now.

Merhi smoked his Cedars King Size openly. "Another warning," he mused.

"No, not a warning. Advice. It is better than a bomb under your car. And anyway," Lattouf reached out and picked up his pint glass of orange juice from its position balanced perilously on the guard rail. "It lets us off the hook." Half the pint disappeared.

Reluctantly, Merhi nodded. "But it's not right. It's not... justice, if you like."

Lattouf put his glass back on the rail. "Since when have you Lebanese let justice get in the way of convenience?"

Ouch.

"Us Lebanese?" Merhi prickled, but he knew Lattouf was right. He just didn't want to hear it, not from him. "What about you Palestinians? You never wanted to report the deaths formally."

"That is true. Perhaps, under the skin, we are not so different, the Lebanese and Palestinians."

"We are all human beings."

"Brothers."

Merhi took a pull on the cigarette. "Cousins. Maybe."

"If you cut me, do I not bleed? If you give me beans, do I not fart - ?" Lattouf's hand swung out – and knocked his glass over the edge.

Both men looked down over the rail into the darkness. They heard the glass smash three storeys below.

After a moment, Lattouf asked "What are you going to do?"

Merhi shrugged. "Clean it up in the morning."

"No, I mean about the bodies."

The music coming from inside emphasised the silence outside.

Merhi stared off into space. Then he said, "I don't know."

"We wanted to keep it quiet, now we can."

"We could keep it quiet when only the two of us knew. But now others know."

"And they want it kept quiet too."

"Yes, but why? If it's a serial killer at work, why would they want it covered up? It would not concern them. There's normally a word that goes before 'cover up'."

"What's that?"

"'Political'." Merhi took one final drag on his cigarette and launched the butt over the side to join the smashed glass of orange juice below. He turned to his friend.

"What have we stumbled into, Fadi?"

"And what happens," posed Lattouf, answering a question with a question, "if we find another one?"

4 January 2005
23 Dhu'l-Qa'dah 1425

Jbail (Byblos), Lebanon 08:30

Ahmad awoke with a start at the banging on the side of the van. Seconds later the flap was pulled up, flooding the cargo area with light and momentarily blinding him. It had still been dark when they had set off earlier.

"Ahmad, out," ordered the Commander. Elias was standing next to him. "Elias, in." Ahmad rolled out groggily, Elias climbed in reluctantly. The flap was secured back down.

"Come on Ahmad, get your wits about you, boy," urged the Commander. "Hurry, hurry. We're not supposed to stop on the highway unless it's an emergency." Seizing a lull in the traffic, the Commander hastened back round and climbed in behind the wheel. Ahmad climbed in and the driver's door and the passenger door closed almost in unison. "I told you we would stop halfway and let you swap over. Two hours in the back is enough for anyone." Checking his mirror, the Commander pulled back out into the traffic.

"Thank you, sir."

The Commander smiled and cast a glance at the young Palestinian. His attitude softened. "You are growing your beard like I told you to. It looks good."

Ahmad ran a hand down his whiskers. "Elias's is thicker than mine."

"That doesn't matter. You are obeying orders, that is the important thing. I am very pleased with both of you."

"You haven't told us why you don't want us to shave, sir."

"All in good time. Very soon now. Just concentrate on one task at a time."

Ahmad looked out of the window. He did not know where he was but he knew it was a long way from The Facility and a long way north of the familiarity of Beirut. The Commander seemed to be in a good mood, so he would ask. "What *are* we doing today, sir?"

"Today? I have just told Elias and I can tell you. Today we are going shopping in Tripoli."

Tripoli, Lebanon 10:00 – 16:00

The traffic was heavy and it took another ninety minutes for them to reach Lebanon's second largest city. The coastal highway came to a natural end at the north of the city, but they turned off at el-Bahsass and made their way along the beach front and up into el-Mina, the port area.

They parked in an unrestricted side street, all three of them flexing their legs as they got out. It was 10:00 and the shops would just be opening.

"What are we buying, sir?" asked Elias keenly, rubbing his butt.

"Well first," said the Commander, "we're buying *ftoor* – our breakfast. I fancy *mankoushe* if they have it – and some very strong coffee. Then we will hit the shops, just like the women do!" He slapped Elias on the back. "I want you to buy certain things. I will be there with you, but you will do the buying. You will like it. Today is a day for enjoying ourselves. But first, let us eat. Shopping is an arduous business, we will need our strength. *Yalla*."

They ate in *Brunch* coffee shop and then hit the City Complex, the American-style mall.

Two hours later they made their way back to the van, secured their purchases underneath the seats in the driver's cab and then drove up into the Old Town.

It took another three hours to complete their shopping, and then the Commander took them to the *Hallab* family patisserie on Riad el-Solh Street where he introduced Elias and Ahmad to the delights of *znoud el-sitt* (ladies' upper arms – in fact the house specialty, a cream-filled pastry looking like a large spring roll).

They left Tripoli at 16:00, heading south on the coastal highway. It had been a successful day, and they had purchased everything the Commander wanted, ten items in all: eight working mobile phones, one mid-range camcorder and a packet of blank videotapes.

Antelias, north of Beirut 18:00

They swapped places again at Byblos and then continued on south, but the Commander had warned them that they would be stopping again soon. Thirty kilometres later he turned left off the highway into Antelias.

He pulled in at the *Bourj al-Hamam* restaurant, its lights welcoming in the darkness.

"Get Ahmad out of the back," he instructed Elias, whose eyes were popping at the sight of the oasis in front of him. "It is dinner time."

When both young men were standing next to him, he said "This is a good restaurant. We have had a long and sticky day, but we are still presentable. They will serve us. We can bathe and pray when we get back."

They ate *kastaleta* (lamb chops with fries) plus *chich taouk* (grilled chicken skewers – with more fries), drank Coke, and finished with a dessert of fresh fruit and *achta bi assal* (cream with honey).

Three contented stomachs sat back and relaxed with their coffees. As the two young men chatted to each other about football, Al-Rajul looked from one to the other. He was very pleased with them. They had both suited his needs perfectly, he had chosen well. Had he had a gram of humanity, he would have regretted all the lies he had told them, the fact that he was using them purely for his own ends. But he hadn't and he didn't.

He stared at their faces as they exchanged friendly banter about a Portuguese football manager who was having great success in England. So young, so dedicated, so full of life.

It was almost a pity that, very soon, one of them would have to die.

9 January 2005
28 Dhu'l-Qa'dah 1425

Mount Lebanon 22:00 – 23:59

The Suzuki VL1500 Intruder roared up the Damascus road through Hazmieh. The cold wind pressed into The Damascene's face and blew his hair straight out behind him. It was a damp day.

It had been a boring day too, and The Damascene did not like boredom. Hariri had met with the head of Syrian intelligence in Lebanon, Rustom Ghazaleh, for lunch in Koreitem, but the meeting had ended in discord with Ghazaleh storming out. Ghazaleh had put forward proposals about the election law being drawn up by Interior Minister Suleiman Frangieh (grandson of the former President and an opponent of Hariri), but Hariri had refused them point blank – he did not want to include six pro-Syrians on his list of electoral candidates and he was not going to stop waging a nationwide electoral campaign and concentrate solely on Beirut.

Hariri now openly agreed to what he had known all along: the electoral odds were going to be stacked against him. There were people who did not want him winning and returning as Prime Minister. He decided it was time to declare openly his support of the Bristol Gathering.

The Damascene had watched and listened to all this from another room in Koreitem, at the invitation of Abu Tarek. All well and good, and he was flattered by the invitation, but this was nothing to do with him. He was completely disinterested in politics. The Damascene's job was the protection of Hariri, and whilst the events of the day heightened the danger to Hariri in this arena where death was the first, not the last, recourse of political disagreement, Hariri's claim that he would 'barricade himself inside Koreitem to fight the electoral battle' meant that The Damascene's job was easy to the point of superfluousness.

He needed to talk to Kanaan. But he supposed The Djinn was reporting back to her boss. He would ask her to give Kanaan a message next time she came.

He turned off the main road onto the track that led to the apartment block. His face was wet from the dull, constant dampness in the air, and water actually dripped from the end of his nose as he parked the bike by the main entrance.

It had been over three weeks now since The Djinn had last visited, so she would be with him again soon, any day now. And that pleased him.

It was not only his boredom that needed relieving.

Halfway up the stairs to the third floor, the lights went out. *Damned power cuts.* It was pitch black in the stairwell as he reached for his mobile, flipped it up and lit his way up to his front door.

As soon as he entered, he knew she was there. He could smell jasmine. Not just the wishful-thinking olfactory reminiscence he had had previously when he had walked past the apartment downstairs, but the distinct aroma mixed with just a hint of cardamom from her breath.

As he closed the front door, a hand touched his shoulder in the darkness. Nothing was said. The fingers reached up to his face, feeling the wetness from his journey.

He reached out – and touched skin. He moved his hand up and down - bare flesh, no cloth.

Her hand went round the back of his neck and tugged downwards. He obeyed and their lips touched, softly, tentatively, then strongly with obvious desire.

"You are wet," she said as they pulled apart, his left hand caressing her chest.

"Beirut. Winter." He shrugged.

"Let me dry you." She took his hand. There was enough moonlight coming in through the windows to give about one lux of illumination in the apartment. She led him up the stairs, but he resisted when she made for the bathroom.

"I have a better idea," he said, moving her hand down so that she touched him, and pulling her towards the bedroom. "Make me wetter still."

It was just before midnight and they both lay naked on top of the bed, crumpled sheets beneath them, little damp patches here and there. The Damascene was on his back, snoring lowly, firmly, constantly, the wonderful oblivion of a man who had been brought to climax three times in the last ninety minutes.

Beside him, The Djinn was awake and smiling, lying sideways on to him so that her legs were across the top of his thighs, a tigress who had captured her mate. She also was satisfied, if a little tender. He was as inventive a lover as she was, and two inventors with one common cause always made for good karma.

But – she had a job to do.

She lifted her legs off of his thighs and moved slowly, lightly, into an upright position, careful not to wake him. She reached up and undid her hair clip, gently shaking out her hair. Holding the hair clip in her left hand, she pushed the metal clasp back so that the small needle underneath was exposed. She flicked the body of the clip three times with the middle finger of her right hand.

Calmly leaning over, she injected one milligram of sodium thiopental into the top of his right thigh.

One minute later, she was shaking him gently and saying, "Captain. Captain Mebarak. Marwan. I need to talk to you..."

10 January 2005
29 Dhu'l-Qa'dah 1425

Mount Lebanon 07:00

He had a dull headache when he awoke the next morning, as he always did when she had been with him, but he would soon shake it off.

She was not there. Nowadays sometimes she stayed, sometimes she did not. But he was disappointed that he would have to shower on his own.

He let the hot water scald him everywhere except the left side of his head which he kept away from the spray until he had turned it fully to cold. Absentmindedly he scratched the top of his right thigh where he had been bitten by an insect – a small price to pay for the pleasure she gave him.

In between their second and third bout last night he had asked her to give a message to Kanaan, asking for further instructions regarding the continuance of his mission (he was careful not to tell her what it was, official Pleasure Givers did not have the required Need To Know level – and the last thing he wanted to do was to have to eliminate her!). Naturally she had agreed that his words would be passed on.

Downstairs, he watched the morning news in the nude while he drank his usual breakfast of two strong cups of coffee. Then he dressed and went out.

He had some shopping to do.

18 January 2005
7 Dhu'l-Hijja 1425

Kahale, Lebanon 12:00 – 15:00

By now, ten weeks into their 'training', the remaining two recruits were used to their Commander's comings and goings. Often he would be away days at a time, leaving them with a list of training to be undertaken or tasks to be performed. This time the list had been brief, the task simple: charge up the mobile phones and the camcorder.

Their task completed, Elias and Ahmad had spent the first hour of that morning playing football (one was Atletico Bethlehem, the other Real Gaza), then they had gone for a walk in the woods. They returned to The Facility in time for *dhuhr*, midday prayer. As they came out of the woods they saw the van parked around the side by the garages. The Commander had returned.

He was sitting on one of the sofas in the reception area, eating fruit. Today the *keffiyeh* was worn fully on his head, not just around his neck like a scarf. They had not seen him like that in quite a while. As they came in, he stood up, smiling. "Day of glory, my brave men. Who won?" He nodded at the football in Ahmad's hand.

"Bethlehem, sir," replied Elias with a mock-frown. "But I think he should have been sent off."

"Hah! Gaza are the filthiest players in the league!" countered Ahmad. "You well deserved to lose."

"Twenty – eighteen is almost a draw."

"Losers always say such things."

"Losers! Gaza are not losers. Just you wait till the second leg!"

"When you will be thrashed again."

The Commander let the banter continue until it almost came to fisticuffs, then he stopped them with a curt "*Khallas!* You are worse than the English. Go, wash and pray. Then eat. Join me in the meeting room at fourteen hundred." He looked them both long and hard in the face. Then he said intriguingly, "Gentlemen, our task begins."

Elias and Ahmad could not believe their eyes when they entered the meeting room on the stroke of 14:00. It looked like a movie studio! All but three of the chairs had been pushed back into one corner and on the opposite side of the room a piece of black fabric had been attached to the wall. About three metres in front of it, the camcorder stood on a tripod. The Commander stood next to it.

"Your training is over," he announced without preamble. "Our mission has been confirmed and we must enact it. We have the green light."

The faces of the young Palestinians lit up. "What is it, sir?" Elias looked like he was going to explode with pride. "Can you tell us now?"

The Commander looked at them thoughtfully. Then he nodded. "Yes, I can. Sit, sit." They sat on the three available chairs, Ahmad removing some black and white textiles from his seat and placing them on the floor.

"It was a discovery made by one of our intelligence operatives," lied Al-Rajul. "An undercover Israeli agent has been found in the Lebanese government. He has been there for a long time, influencing decisions, sowing poison against Palestine and Syria. He has probably been the cause of all the unrest in this country since the war. We have only recently found him because he has been so good, so deep under cover."

"Do the Lebanese know, sir?"

"No, Ahmad. If we told them they would probably not believe us. Or at the very least our man would be tipped the wink and he would high-tail it back to the occupied lands. It was reported to our late President, who recruited me to solve the problem. I, in turn, recruited you. Only those in the upper echelons of the Palestinian Authority who needed to know have been told about this traitor, and they have now sanctioned the solution. He is to be removed, publicly, as a warning to others."

Elias leant forward. "And we are to...?"

"We are to kill him."

Elias and Ahmad looked at each other.

"What did you think the training was for?" questioned the Commander. "Firearms, combat. Did you think we were going to rob a bank?"

"No, sir, no," Elias shook his head. "Of course not. It – it has just come as a bit of a shock, that is all. But don't get me wrong. I am pleased. At last we can serve our country."

"Did the others know?" asked Ahmad.

"No. Their tasks were minor. Their rewards have been minor. They are now back in Palestine, but they will not be living as you and your families will be living. You will be heroes. Your actions will influence they very future of Lebanon, freeing this country from the pernicious Israeli manipulation that they haven't even known has been there."

Elias's eyes had filled. "You honour us, sir. Truly."

"You honour yourselves. You are two strong, brave Palestinians. Your actions will go down in history."

"Thank you, sir, thank you." Elias looked at Ahmad, who nodded his agreement.

The Commander slapped his hands on his thighs and stood up. "Now, our first task. As I said, this is to be a public removal – so we must prepare the background. Ahmad, here."

Ahmad walked over with the Commander to a nearby table. The Commander picked up a thick white marker and gave it to him, then he picked up the card that was underneath it. "I know that you are good at drawing. Write this on the fabric." He nodded to the wall, passing the card over. "Big enough to fill it, as if it is a flag. Can you do it?"

Ahmad read what was on the card. He looked up. "You want me to write this?" He saw the look in the Commander's eyes and hastily said, "Of course, of course."

As Ahmad began to write, the Commander went over to Elias, bending down to pick up the textiles from the floor. "Put these on, Elias. You will do it first, then Ahmad will do it after. I will decide which is the best.

Elias took the proffered textiles, opening them out and holding them up. A plain black robe and a white turban. He frowned, then said "Shall I undress?"

"No, put them on over your clothes. They should fit, and you are both about the same size."

Elias did as he was told, the Commander helping him with the pre-formed turban.

Ahmad had finished writing on the fabric on the wall and he turned round, only just managing to stop himself laughing at his colleague.

The Commander studied what Ahmad had written, nodding his satisfaction. "Good, good. You truly have artistic talent, Ahmad. That could be your future," he lied again.

All three of them stared at the white writing on the black cloth.

لا إله إلا الله. هو محمد رسول الله. الله أكبر.

There is no God but Allah. Mohammed is the messenger of Allah. God is greatest.

19 January 2005
8 Dhu'l-Hijja 1425

Kahale, Lebanon 01:00 – 13:00

01:00 hours. In his room upstairs, Al-Rajul worked in the dim light given off by the screen of the laptop computer. He had watched the performances given by the two young Palestinians over and over, considering them not only from the point of view of the local news media – who would eventually receive the tape – but also from the international aspect.

He had made up his mind.

He watched his selection once more. The Palestinian sat in front of the flag with the holy words. He was dressed in the black robe and white turban, his bearded face serious as he read from the paper in his hand.

"To support our brother mujahidin in the land of the two holy mosques and to avenge their righteous martyrs who were killed by security forces of the Saudi regime in the land of the two holy mosques, we resolved, after relying on Almighty God, to carry out fair punishment against the agent of this regime and its cheap tool in Greater Syria, the sinner and maker of illegal money, the Israeli, through implementation of a resounding martyrdom operation. This confirms our promise to support and wage jihad, and will be the beginning of many martyrdom operations against the infidels, renegades and tyrants in Greater Syria."

Now Al-Rajul had to make a subtle amendment and then transfer the finished product back to tape. It was so tempting simply to burn it onto disc, but the fictitious *al-Nasr wa al-Jihad fi bilad al-Sham* group (Victory and Jihad in Greater Syria) – from whom the message would purport to come – would not be that sophisticated.

He picked up the microphone attached to the laptop and said two words into it. Then he selected the edit function on the program. Over and over, the two words he had recorded came out of the speakers, so he could tweak them into the slightly higher tone of the person on the screen, and time and match them precisely to the moving lips.

It took him twenty minutes.

Twenty minutes to exactly find and replace *the Israeli* with *Rafic Hariri*.

At 05:00 The Facility was still in darkness. It was fifteen minutes before *Fajr* prayer, which they usually missed anyway, and over a hundred minutes to sunrise prayer. The only sound that could be heard was muted snoring.

In the corridor, a figure walked quietly. His night vision was good and he did not need a torch. He certainly would not put the lights on.

He stopped at the closed door to the meeting room and looked cautiously behind him. Noiselessly he opened the door and went in.

They had tidied up the room before retiring last night. The flag had been taken down and would be disposed of later, the camcorder box was in a far corner next to the eight mobile phone boxes and the loose tripod.

He went over to them, bent down and selected what he wanted.

He had done what he wanted to do. He should not have, but he was pleased that he had. Nobody would know and he would have put some minds at rest.

At 05:15 he left the meeting room, softly closing the door behind him. He walked carefully back down the corridor. Suddenly there was a flash of lightning. Then another, and another.

He gasped, looking up at the overhead fluorescent light as if he had never seen it coming on before. There was no clap of thunder, but the shock as he looked back down sent a jolt through his system greater than any lightning strike.

The Commander was standing at the end of the corridor.

"What were you doing in there?" His voice was flat, emotionless.

Nervousness made Elias giggle. "N-nothing, sir. I – I couldn't sleep. I thought I would pray."

The Commander nodded as he came towards him. "That is good. That is good." Suddenly his right hand shot out and grabbed Elias around the throat. Spit flew from the young Palestinian's mouth as he was pushed back into the meeting room.

"I'll ask you one more time," growled the Commander. "What were you doing?"

"I was just praying - "

The Commander's left fist rammed into Elias's stomach. The young Palestinian doubled over and the force knocked him onto his knees and into the chairs.

"What were you doing?"

"I – I - "

The Commander's left foot swung back, but Elias's hands raised in defence and supplication. "No, sir, no, sir, please! I am sorry, I am sorry. I was just..." He sat up, sliding backwards out of reach. "I... I wanted to contact my family. Just to tell them I was okay. It has been a few weeks."

The Commander's eyes shot over to the pile of boxes in the corner then back to Elias. "Which one did you use?"

"Sir?"

"Which phone did you use? Show me."

Elias scurried over on his knees, pulling out a box from the middle of the pile. "Nokia," he laughed nervously. "My favourite."

"Give it to me."

Quickly Elias opened the box and held out the handset. The Commander moved forward and slapped it out of his hand onto the floor.

"Don't you realise," he said angrily, "our location can be detected if we turn these things on?" He raised his booted left foot and slammed it down, again and again, the phone splitting and breaking.

Elias stared at the phone, terrified of the fury on the Commander's face. He shook his head. "I'm sorry, sir, I'm sorry. I didn't think."

The Commander stood there, looking down at him, his anger palpable. There should have been scorn in his eyes, but there was nothing. They were blank. After a minute, he sighed. "Okay, get up. No harm done. We all make mistakes, that's why we're human."

Elias stood up, humble. The Commander put his arm around his shoulders, leading him out of the room. "Let's go eat."

As they were walking back down the corridor, the Commander said "Actually, you are right. It was wrong of me to keep you out of contact with your family for so long. They will indeed be worried, even though their rewards will be great. I think we should pop back to see them. Just for a quick visit, so that they know you are all right..."

When Ahmad awoke sixty minutes later, he was surprised that Elias was not in his bed. He was even more surprised when he realised he was on his own in The Facility and the van had gone.

During the morning, Ahmad bathed, prayed, ate, read the Koran, undertook a gentle exercise regime and bathed again.

It was just after midday, as he was on the verge of letting his concern upgrade to worry, when the van returned. He watched out of the window as it pulled up in front of the building. He expected the Commander and Elias to get out, probably triumphant after some morning task that he had not been privy to, but nothing happened. The van had stopped, he could see just one person inside it, but no one got out.

Ahmad frowned. Did they need help? Had they gone to pick up something?

Then there were three loud peremptory blasts of the van's horn.

Quickly, Ahmad ran outside. The Commander was looking out of the open driver's window. He did not look happy. "Ahmad, I need you to do something for me, immediately."

"Sir?"

A key flew through the air and landed on the gravel. "Go and check on the sugar. Count the number of sacks. Then join me in the meeting room in half an hour."

Ahmad bent down and picked up the key. "Now, sir?" He straightened up.

"Yes!" barked the Commander. "Now, now. Go!"

Ahmad scurried off towards the garages and outbuildings around the side – allowing Al-Rajul to get out of the van and walk into the main building unseen.

He was covered head to foot in blood.

Half an hour later in the meeting room. The Commander was freshly bathed and he was dressed in a long white *dishdasha*, his head unadorned, hair damp. Ahmad was surprised when he came in – he had never seen the Commander dressed like this before. He looked good. Very noble, very Arabic.

The Commander went straight to the point. "Ahmad, I have made a decision. I broke the news to Elias earlier. He has now left us and is with his family. They have been rewarded. They will never see that accursed camp again."

"That is good, sir."

"It is. So now it is just you. You will be the biggest hero of all my recruits. You have been chosen."

"For what, sir?"

The Commander stood in front of Ahmad and put both his hands on his shoulders. The young Palestinian looked up at his mentor. The Commander smiled. "You will kill the Israeli traitor."

Bourj el-Barajneh, Beirut 13:00 – 16:30

At the same moment that the Commander said the words to Ahmad, Sergeant Bassem el-Khazem of the Palestinian police hurriedly entered the office of his Captain, trying not to recoil. The stench in the room could be cut with a knife.

"Captain, there's some people you should see."

Captain Fadi Lattouf quickly closed his drawer containing his lunch box of *kibbeh*, tomatoes and cucumber, as if he had been caught doing something he shouldn't. "What? Can't it wait? I was going to have my lunch."

"I think you will want to see them."

"After lunch."

"It's about this." el-Khazem waved the crumpled, dirty piece of paper he had in his hand.

Lattouf frowned before recognising it as one of the 'Missing' posters they had put up, but it looked like somebody had been drawing on it in red. His eyebrows rose in interest. "They have some information?"

"Better. Or worse."

Lattouf heaved his massive frame out of the chair. "Shaitan's scrotum, Bassem, must you talk in riddles?"

"You will want to hear this for yourself."

Outside, an elderly man stood nervously against one of the walls. Next to him was a boy of about thirteen, sniffling, sobbing, eyes downcast.

Lattouf's booted feet clumped down the corridor. "Well?" he shouted. "You have something to tell me?" The subtleties of coercive interrogation had never been Lattouf's strong-point.

The old man cowered backwards, his arm protectively around the boy. "Th – they are dead, sir."

"What? Who?"

"All of them. All five of them. Please, I will show you."

"What are you talking about, man? What is your name?"

"M - my name is Mohamed Hassan."

"Where do you live?"

"The camp."

"Of course you live in the camp! I meant where?"

"I am the neighbour. Sir, they are all dead. Please, you must come."

As Mohamed Hassan waived his free hand expressively, Lattouf noticed it was marked with the same red ink that was on the poster el-Khazem was holding. "You an artist?" he asked.

Hassan was thrown. "What?"

"I said..." Lattouf stared at Hassan's hand, then slowly turned and looked back at the paper in el-Khazem's hand. The penny dropped, as did the colour from his face. "Where?"

"I will show you."

There are many specific and stringent requirements for a job with the Palestinian police, but a degree in criminology is not one of them. So Fadi Lattouf was unaware of the history of the world's most heinous murders, but he knew that what he was confronted with now would rank alongside some of the worst excesses ever perpetrated by human kind. He was so glad his stomach was empty, because if it hadn't been it would be now.

The room on the upper floor of the old breeze-block building would have stank normally anyway. Now it reeked of iron, urine and faeces – the unmistakeable perfume of death.

There was blood everywhere. Pooling on the floor and indiscriminately splashed up every wall and across the peeling ceiling, as if somebody had stood in the centre of the room and let fly with a paint spray gun. It was over the sparse furniture and was probably dripping through the floorboards to the dwelling underneath.

There were five of them. Each with their faces caved in. At least two of them had had their necks broken, the angle of their heads was hideous – probably a quick *en bloc* despatch with the facial abuse as a post mortem cosmetic. No other parts of their bodies had been defiled though, so Lattouf could tell there was one middle-aged woman, one middle-aged man, a younger man and two young women, one of them pre-pubescent. An entire family.

And no accident.

He watched transfixed as a piece of grey matter oozed out of the hole in the head of one of the young girls and spread across the floor as if it was trying to escape. He turned quickly.

"When did you find them?" he snapped at the old man standing in the doorway, still with his arm around the sobbing boy. Sergeant el-Khazem was next to them, trying not to look at the bodies.

"I –I didn't," said Mohamed.

"What?"

"He – he did." He nodded downwards at the boy.

"Your son found them?"

"He is not my son, sir."

Lattouf sighed loudly in irritation. "Then, in the name of the Prophet, peace be upon him, who the - ?"

"They are my family." The boy said it so quietly that Lattouf wondered if he had heard him at all.

"What did you say?"

The boy looked up, eyes bloodshot, red-rimmed and wet. "My father and mother. My sisters. My older brother."

"What?"

"My - "

"I heard you, I heard you." Lattouf looked back at the bodies, then at his sergeant, then back to the boy. "You found them? So you had been out?"

"I – I didn't know my brother was coming back. He has been away for a while. He never told me last night he was coming back - "

"Wait a minute, wait a minute. You spoke to your brother last night?"

"He telephoned me." The boy fished into his pocket and pulled out a battered old mobile phone and held it up.

"Where has he been, your brother?"

"I – I don't know."

"You don't know? Did your parents know?"

"No, none of us did. We saw your piece of paper a few weeks ago," he nodded at el-Khazem. "But we went to the groups. They said not to contact you."

Lattouf cursed under his breath. Who ran the camps anyway? Well, he knew the answer to that, and he knew it wasn't the PSF. "What did your brother say to you?" he asked.

The boy replied, and moments later Fadi Lattouf was running back down the stairs shouting into his mobile phone.

This time there was no subtlety, no oblique speaking, no meeting at the Dunes with a twenty-six hour time difference. There couldn't be any flashing blue lights, that would have been suicidal, but ninety minutes later the blue Toyota Land Cruiser sped into Annan Street and pulled to a halt next to the waiting figure of Fadi Lattouf.

Jihad Merhi had not had time to change out of his uniform, but being the middle of winter he did not look incongruous with his North Face Galaxy parka zipped up to the chin. "How many?" he asked without greeting as he got out of the car.

"Five." It was getting colder as night fell, and Lattouf was rubbing his hands together. "Five little accidents."

"Five! Where are they?"

"Some way in. You don't need to see them. Same as before. Only this time fresh. Done today. The bodies weren't cold."

They spoke as they walked into the camp.

"Five..." Merhi shook his head. "In the name of Jesus..."

"And all the other prophets. It was a family. An entire family. Or so the perpetrator thought."

Merhi looked up at the big Palestinian. "What do you mean?"

"He missed one," grinned Lattouf. "He thought he had taken them all, but one was not there."

"What are you saying, Fadi?"

"We have him. And he's talking. Come."

They had reached the police office. Lattouf led the way inside, past the front area and down the corridor past his own office to the small cell at the back.

Behind the bars, an old man was sitting with glum resignation on the bench against the wall. Next to him was a young teenager with a swathe of padding taped across his nose, eyes black. He wore a grubby white polo shirt and had an even grubbier towel around his waist, original colour indeterminate. He had no trousers on.

"What happened to him?" asked Merhi.

"Clumsy youth. Fell against the table in the interview room."

Merhi gave an 'Oh yeah?' grimace but said nothing.

"But he had some interesting information to report." Louder, Lattouf said "He is an upright citizen. A good Palestinian."

"Will he talk to me?"

"No need. He is a bit nasally at the moment, sounds like a fighter after fifteen rounds. But I've got it all down. Come to my office."

In the office, Lattouf indicated an old wooden cafeteria chair in front of his desk. It wobbled as Merhi sat on it.

"Coffee?" Lattouf held up a huge black flask. "Nada made it this morning, but it should still be warm."

It was the last thing Merhi wanted. "Yes. Thank you."

Lattouf poured some sludge into an old cracked cup which looked like it hadn't been washed since before the war. Merhi took it and hoped his show of gratitude wasn't too insincere.

Lattouf swilled from the flask and then wiped his mouth with the back of his hand. "They are – were – the Massoud family. Father, getting on a bit – well, he isn't anymore, but up until this morning he was. Mother ten years younger. Eldest son in his early twenties, a daughter in her late teens, another son in his early teens and a younger sister. The younger boy was out at school when... the visitor called."

"And he found the bodies?"

"Yes."

"Shit."

"Yes. And he did. That's why he's wearing the towel." Lattouf took another swig from the flask. Out of politeness, and much against his better judgement, Merhi raised the cup to his lips, pleasantly surprised to find that the coffee was not that bad. A knife and fork would have helped, though.

"He has an interesting story," continued Lattouf. "His brother went missing in early November. Went out one night, just did not come home."

"About a month after the bodies started to appear. Connection?"

Lattouf shrugged. "I would have said no. Until today, of course."

"Didn't his family report him as missing?"

Lattouf's look was pitiful. "This is the camp. What do you think? Young Palestinian males often go missing, perhaps lost in fighting, who knows? But yes, once my notices started to go up they decided to report him. But not to me, not to the police."

"Ah, I see."

"They were told to do nothing. Then early this morning, just before *Fajr*, the boy received a telephone call from his brother."

"I thought phones weren't allowed in the camp."

"On his mobile. He had found the phone a few months ago in Beirut."

"Found?"

"Found. He had changed the SIM but kept the handset. His parents didn't know he had it, but his brother did. His brother told him he was safe and had been selected for a mission instigated by our late President. They had been training up in the mountains. Now the mission was starting. He just wanted to let his family know he was safe and soon he would be getting them out of the camp."

Merhi curled his lip at the sick irony. Well, they were certainly now out of the camp. Then he said, "They?"

"What?"

"You said *they* had been training up in the mountains?"

"What of it?"

"Don't you see? *They*. Young Palestinian males, early twenties?"

Slowly Lattouf's mouth opened. "The bodies."

"Exactly. Until today all have been young local males." Merhi paused in thought, tapping his nails against the side of his cup, making a pleasant tinkling sound. The incongruity of the situation was not lost on him: here he was, in the squalor of the Bourj el-Barajneh refugee camp, drinking coffee out of a bone china cup, cracked and dirty though it may be.

Lattouf leant forward, elbows on his desk, chin resting on his hands. After a minute, he said "Baby seals."

Merhi was snapped out of his thoughts. "What?"

"What is it they do to baby seals? You know, when they bash their heads in."

"When they...?" For a moment Merhi didn't understand. Then he said, "Oh my God. Culling. They call it culling."

Lattouf sat back, pleased with himself. "There you have it."

Merhi was aghast. "But..."

"He has been culling young Palestinians," Lattouf was speaking in the tolerant tone of master to apprentice. It was good to get one up on the Lebanese, no matter how much he liked him. "Only the strong survive."

"Or only the chosen. He has been testing. Choosing. Whittling. One or more young Palestinians. For what? To do what?"

"Oh, that we know."

"We do?"

"Oh yes. The deceased, Elias Massoud, told his brother. There is an Israeli agent at work in Beirut. They are going to kill him."

20 January 2005
9 Dhu'l-Hijja 1425

Jounieh, Lebanon 00:45

Jihad Merhi arrived home after midnight – nothing unusual in that with the job he did – and Gisele was already in bed, tucked up warmly under the quilt. The Levantine winter would soon be ending, but for now it remained cold. She had left a dim bedside light on for him so that he could see and not crack a toe against the bottom of the bed, as he had done in the past (the Merhi's had been in the apartment only six years and, being a man, Jihad was still getting used to the geography of the furniture).

Having had a cigarette out on the balcony accompanied by a nightcap of a small Johnnie Walker, Jihad now slid into the bed. "Unbelievable," he was shaking his head. "Absolutely unbelievable. The idiot Lattouf actually worked it all out. Well, there's a first time for everything, I suppose." He stretched out and turned off the light. "The murders have been nothing more than a recruitment and selection process. Probably by one of the Palestinian groups. Who knows? They are always so damned extreme. Why kill their rejects? Why not just throw them back into the pond? Crazy. And what is it are they going to do? Kill an Israeli agent at work in Beirut. Lattouf presented it as if I would never have known that the Jews had agents working here! The Palestinians can kill them all, for all I care." He lay back, hands behind his head. "But that gets me out of it. The body up in Aammiq has already been recorded as an accident. Lattouf is now fully writing up the murders and reporting them to his superiors as a solved case – the why if not the who. And considering the nature of the operation, I doubt his superiors will even worry about reporting it to us. They'll let us hear it on the news if the killing ever happens!

"Still, that's good. Let Lattouf get the credit. Perhaps he'll leave me alone for a while. God knows, I've got enough to do..."

He looked at the shadow of his wife next to him. She was fast asleep, as she had been all along. His talking had not disturbed her. She had not heard a word he said.

But somebody else had.

21 January 2005
10 Dhu'l-Hijja 1425

Kahale, Lebanon 11:30

The Commander had his hands around Ahmad's throat. The young Palestinian's eyes were popping, staring at the face just centimetres in front of him, a booger wobbling on the end of his nose.

"You know what to do," snarled the Commander, his garlic breath wafting into Ahmad's face.

"But - "

"Do it! Or I will kill you."

For a minute the terror stayed in Ahmad's eyes, because he knew the Commander wasn't going to let go. Then all of a sudden the fear was gone and he relaxed. His mentor was right, he did know what to do.

His right hand shot out and grabbed the Commander by the balls. As the Commander shouted out, Ahmad pulled his own arms down and then thrust them upwards in an inverted V-shape, breaking the hold around his throat.

The Commander staggered backwards, half bent over. "You little bastard. I didn't teach you that!" There was a hint of admiration behind the anger in his eyes.

Ahmad was worried he had gone too far, but he was pleased with what he had done. "I knew a man of your skills would be waiting for the upward V," he said a little breathlessly, wiping his wrist across his nose. "It would not be enough to get you off me."

"So you decided to improvise?" The Commander straightened up.

"Yes."

The Commander stared, cold, and for a moment Ahmad thought he was going to lunge for him again. Then he smiled. "Excellent. You have learnt well. Good. As I explained, we are unlikely to be apprehended. There will be too much confusion. But it is worthwhile to have these skills, just in case." He rubbed his testicles. "Bravo."

Ahmad picked up a towel and wiped his face. "When will it be, sir?"

"Soon. I have an exact date. Problem is, until the day, until the hour, I will not know where the Israeli will be. That is why we must have a rehearsal, a trial run."

"When?"

The Commander undid the *keffiyeh* from around his neck and began to unbutton his shirt. "Today is Friday. We will have our trial run on Monday, so that we have the correct experience of the weekday traffic. I have prepared and tested the electrics but we must try them out in the real theatre. Later today I must leave. I will be back on Sunday. Enjoy yourself this weekend, and now no more exercise. You are at the peak of fitness. I don't want you overdoing it and injuring yourself."

"Thank you, sir." Ahmad was proud.

"Now," said the Commander. "Let us shower before we pray."

22 January 2005
11 Dhu'l-Hijja 1425

Mount Lebanon 23:50

It would have been funny if it was not so serious.

Since the tumultuous, abruptly-ended meeting two weeks ago between Hariri and the head of Syrian intelligence in Lebanon, Rustom Ghazaleh, the verbal attacks on Hariri had increased to the point where they were so incessant as to be ludicrous. The wildly-flying accusations were absurd – but absurdity did not decrease danger.

Abu Tarek had become aware of a plot to have both Hariri and Druze leader Walid Jumblatt arrested on fabricated charges. Jumblatt was to be accused of ordering the assassination of former Lebanese president Rene Mouawad, while Hariri was going to be charged with something equally as ludicrous.

Nothing had come of the plot to remove the two major opposition leaders, due in no small part to Nayla Mouawad* warning Jumblatt of the plot after she had been informed by Suleiman Frangieh, the Interior Minister.

But The Damascene had been called in immediately by Abu Tarek. He had considered the situation and concluded that his risk assessment remained the same: it was Hariri's movements that presented the security risk, not the bombastic words and fantasies of his enemies. But the alert status was increased from Black to Black Special.

The Damascene knew that no matter what they did, no matter how they stacked the electoral law against him, Hariri was going to triumph in May.

And there were those that did not want that.

She was there when The Damascene returned to the apartment just before midnight. They made love tenderly and roughly, slow and fast, with consideration and selfishness, but always with the skill and precision of experts in carnality.

At 02:00, The Damascene was bitten by a mosquito.

---

* The widow of Rene Mouawad and a leading member of the Qornet Shehwan group.

24 January 2005
13 Dhu'l-Hijja 1425

Beirut 11:00 – 14:00

The white Mitsubishi Canter van drove down the Beirut to Damascus road towards the Lebanese capital. Al-Rajul, the Commander, was driving, Ahmad next to him. It was an overcast but dry day. They were dressed in normal working men's clothes – jeans, shirts, old winter jackets – to match their cover story if they were stopped. They were farmers from the Bekaa, collecting orders from their customers. On the actual day of operation, when the sacks of sugar would be in the back, they would be wholesalers from Zahlé delivering the sugar to customers.

The journey had been timed so that they hit the Beirut traffic at 11:00, operational conditions for the trial run. They parked in the pay area on Weygand Street, opposite the Grand Café, stopping as near to the exit as space allowed.

"On the day you will be on your own," explained the Commander. "I will be using other transport. Park as near to this exit as you possibly can. It is imperative that when I tell you to move, you move. You understand?"

"Yes, sir." Ahmad's thoughts flashed back to the briefing last night when the Commander had explained exactly what would happen on The Day. Now they were having the practice run, and he had to admit to being nervous.

The Commander could sense it, and he put a reassuring hand on Ahmad's knee. "It will be all right, my brave man. That is why we are having this trial run, so that you will be prepared on the day. You just do what you have to do and leave the rest to me. Okay?"

"Yes, sir. Thank you, sir."

"And I promise you the camp will be a thing of the past." He removed his hand. "Now then, you have the three phones?"

Ahmad tapped his jacket pocket.

"Right. When I get out, move over into this seat and put them on the seat here beside you. You remember the meanings?"

Ahmad took the phones out of his pocket one by one. "Nokia – the northern route. N for north. Samsung – the southern route. S for south. LG – the western route. LG – *la gauche*, going left."

"Good. And the three places?"

"North – the St. George Hotel. South – the Four Points Sheraton Hotel. West – the Future TV building. At the precise moment the subject passes by, I press the red button." He nodded to a button which the Commander had installed near the parking brake, but not too near as to be accidentally touched. It looked like a domestic doorbell.

"Press it now."

"Now?"

"Yes, just to test it."

Ahmad reached forward and pressed the button. Immediately a buzzing sound came from inside the Commander's jacket. He reached in and turned it off.

"Excellent. Right, we'll try it out. When you get the signal from me, move and move fast. You must get to the location before the subject. When he passes by, you press the button. I will be waiting further along the route. Ten seconds later, he reaches me, I fire, he's dead. You are already driving away, I will vanish into the back streets. We meet back at The Facility. How will you know the subject?"

"He will be in a convoy, a Toyota, four black Mercedes plus a Chevrolet ambulance behind."

The Commander unlocked the door. "Today, of course, we have no subject. So just pretend. Stay where you are after you've pressed the button. I will be working in real time, so between thirty and forty seconds after you've pressed it, I will be with you." He stepped out then looked back as Ahmad shuffled over into the driver's seat.

Then the Commander did something unusual – he smiled. Then he said, "Go with God, my hero." He slammed the van door and walked off towards the Omari Grand Mosque.

Al-Rajul walked straight down Omari Grand Mosque Street and into Nejmeh Square (Star Square, Place de l'Etoile). A symbol of the destruction of the city during the war, it had been rebuilt by Rafic Hariri and Solidère into a crisp and impressive modern version of how it used to be, many of the streets pedestrianised and lined with up-market shops and restaurants. In the centre was the renovated clock tower, originally erected during the French mandate. To his right was the Parliament building.

He walked on, down Parliament Street. The pedestrianisation of the area did not worry him. On The Day, he would have his own means of transport.

Stopping at the end of the street by Kuwait Airways, he scanned the junction. Riad es Solh Square at eleven o'clock, Federal Express at one o'clock. Away back at four o'clock, the Grand Serail and the Prime Minister's offices. If the northern route wasn't chosen, on The Day this was where the southern and western routes would split.

He made up his mind which route to use for this rehearsal and walked on.

Ahmad wanted to pee. He sat in the driver's seat of the van, his right leg bouncing up and down. A copy of that day's *Al-Mustaqbal* newspaper was open across the steering wheel, something the Commander had told him to do so that he wouldn't look suspicious simply waiting in the van. The face of Rafic Hariri stared up at him from the paper.

It had been forty minutes, and he was wondering whether he should just nip into the back of the van and piss into a corner when one of the phones buzzed. He jumped, and just a little bit of pee-pee shot out into his underpants. He looked at the phones on the seat next to him.

It was the LG. The western route.

Ahmad pulled out into Weygand Street, turning left. They had gone over and over the routes last night, and a point the Commander had hammered home was that he was not to take the same route as the convoy would take. He did not want to be seen near them or following them. He just needed to *be* there at the right time. And he must not speed or draw any attention to himself.

He entered the Bab Idriss area, heading west and south. He hit Soleiman Franjieh Avenue, where the traffic was heavier but the street wider, and then took a right into Michel Chiha Street. A left, taking him past the Sierra Leone Consulate, then he stopped at the junction with Spears Street. He waited for a few cars to pass, then pulled out right. He parked where he could, just opposite the Future TV building, the Beirut Chamber of Commerce ahead on the right.

It would never have occurred to Ahmad that the paper the Commander had given him, *Al-Mustaqbal*, was owned by the former Lebanese Prime Minister Rafic Hariri, as was Future TV where he was parked. Why would it? He had no interest in Lebanese politics – he was on a mission to kill an Israeli agent, for the sake of Allah! And the Commander would be pleased with him, he was parked exactly where he should be.

Reaching forward, he pressed the red button.

And waited.

Half a minute later, he saw the Commander walking quickly from the direction of the Sanayeh Gardens. He was intent, not looking at the van. Had he seen him? Should Ahmad beep? No, no, don't be so foolish.

The Commander reached the van and it looked like he was going past, then his hand shot out, opened the door, and he climbed in. "Good. Go."

Ahmad pulled out and took the first left down Medhat Bacha Street, heading south.

Mount Lebanon 14:30 – 16:30

The Djinn opened the front door to The Damascene's apartment and let herself in. Real *djinn* could not open closed doors, but a door was never closed if you had a key.

She was dressed in a plain pink T-shirt, split-at-the-knee jeans which looked old and worn but cost a fortune in Ashrafieh, and Nike trainers. Her long black hair was down but, as always, the hair clip was in place at the back. She wore no make-up – there was no need, she knew he wouldn't be there. In her hands she carried a large cardboard box.

Her prey was spending more and more time away from the apartment now, spending more and more time concentrating on Hariri as the elections approached, which meant that she had to time her visits more and more carefully – both when he was there and when he was not.

She put the cardboard box down on the breakfast counter and then began her thrice-weekly search of the apartment – every drawer, every cupboard, inside and under every piece of furniture, every nook, every cranny. She never found anything, but she knew it had to be done – one day he might slip up.

She then checked on the eight strategically placed bugging devices inside the electricity sockets. All in order, not touched or tampered with. Unlike herself! She smiled naughtily as she went back to the kitchen and, after a struggle with the packaging, took out the contents of the cardboard box: a Krups filter coffee machine.

A present for the best lover she had ever had (and, in her job, she had had many). It was just a pity his coffee making skills did not match his bedroom skills. She always enjoyed a stiff coffee after a stiff... interrogation session.

She primed the machine and then filled it with water for its first coffee-less drip-through. She wanted it ready so that, after their next joining, she would have to wait only the few filtering minutes for her caffeine fix while he slept after she had questioned him.

As the water dripped through, she went over to the window and looked out over cloudy Beirut. She was glad to be back here after her many months of foreign assignments. The place had changed while she had been away: so much building, so much reconstruction, new projects starting everywhere. She hoped there were never any more wars or attacks from foreign enemies to harm this beautiful city – and her love of Beirut was why she was so pleased when she had been given her current mission, so she could come home. The mission would be coming to a head soon because these were dangerous times to be a public figure in Lebanon.

She turned as a louder-than-the-rest gurgle indicated that the water had run through the machine. Back into the kitchen, she poured the steaming water down the sink, dried the pot and put it back in place, leaving the machine sitting squarely on the breakfast bar so he would see it as soon as he came in and he would know she had been there. A little tease, a little promise.

As she walked towards the front door, she heard a tap-tapping at the window. She turned. It was starting to rain, one of the heavy Beirut winter showers. And she had only her T-shirt on, no coat.

It was just as well she didn't have to go outside.

She only lived in the apartment below.

Her apartment on the second floor was geographically identical to the one above it but naturally the furniture was different (it did not, for example, have the boy-toy of the massive wall-mounted widescreen television). It was more homey than the functional apartment above, but it still had that not-really-cared-for look of a rental. She was here only temporarily, for as long as the current job took.

Dressed in a white towelling robe, she was in the open-plan kitchen preparing her favourite pasta dish when she heard a single, solitary bump from the speaker sitting on the coffee table in the living area. She stopped stirring her sauce, straining to hear over the hum of the hob. There was nothing else, but she was professional enough to know that she hadn't imagined what she'd heard.

She moved the saucepan off the ring and stepped lightly across to the coffee table. The speaker was attached to a VHF audio receiver, the base hub for the listening devices hidden in the apartment upstairs. She knelt down next to the table, listening.

Nothing. No sound. Nobody moving about, not even the sound of a coffee machine being put on. But she had heard something, that lone bump. She fingered the clip in her hair. The sound of the apartment door opening would be too subtle for her to have heard above the cooker. If he had arrived home, she would be hearing other sounds like she usually did. Unless someone had come in and then immediately gone out again.

Quickly she rose to her feet and ran over to her front door, opening it cautiously. Nobody there, she went out into the stairwell – just in time to hear the front door of the block closing downstairs.

She took the stairs two at a time in her bare feet, her robe flapping open, reaching the bottom in no time. It was getting dark as she went outside into the rain.

But it was still light enough for her to see a van pulling up onto the main road and heading east.

27 January 2005
16 Dhu'l-Hijja 1425

Jounieh, Lebanon 06:15

Jihad Merhi climbed into his Toyota Land Cruiser, turned on the ignition and quickly put the heater on max. It was still cold, especially at this godforsaken hour of the morning. He needed to be in early, he had his bi-annual appraisal meeting with Major Ghanem later and he wanted to be prepared – the old bastard would take the opportunity to quiz him on the finer details of each and every case he had on hand, as he always did.

At least the traffic on the coastal highway would be lighter at this hour, and he should be in the office by 07:00. He turned on the Toyota's full beams and moved slowly up the track towards the mountainside road.

As he reached the road, a large shadow shot in front of him, blocking his way. Had he been going fast, he would have crashed right into it. He pulled up sharply, wheels crunching on the gravel of the track. *What the hell?* Quickly he reached for his gun.

The driver's door of the Ford Explorer opened at the same moment as Merhi leapt out of the Toyota, aiming the gun over the open door. "Hold it! Hold it right there!" he shouted.

The figure in the darkness stopped, arms raising into the air. "I am unarmed," said a female voice.

"Walk into the light," ordered Merhi.

Squinting against the full beams, she moved sideways. She was a local woman, probably late twenties, dressed in jeans and thick woollen jumper. There were no visible weapons.

Keeping her covered with the gun, Merhi stretched in and dimmed the beams. Then he stepped around his door and came towards her, gun still raised. "What do you want?"

Tentatively she lowered her arms a few centimetres. He said nothing to stop her so she put them down. "Captain Merhi," she said. "I'm Zahia Zalloum of the Department of General Security. Your wife was a trainer on an unarmed combat course I did a few years ago."

"Really? Wow. Impressed."

"Captain, we need to talk."

29 January 2005
18 Dhu'l-Hijja 1425

Mount Lebanon 01:00

It was an interesting situation.

Politically, it was an intense time for Rafic Hariri. The electoral law had been unveiled a few days earlier and, as expected, it was hedged against him. National constituencies were smaller. Beirut had been split into three electoral districts, which strengthened the Christian, Shi'ite and Armenian representation while weakening the Sunni. On the other hand, it was widely accepted that even this would not stop an overall opposition victory in May.

But from a security point of view – which was all The Damascene was interested in – things were locked-down tight. Hariri lived and worked in Koreitem. Any official trips outside (for example, to and from Parliament) were undertaken in the convoy of armour-plated vehicles with the electronic jamming devices to prevent roadside bomb detonation. Unofficial trips (for example, the trips into the south of the city to visit Hassan Nasrallah) were only ever arranged at the last minute and were now done in a single armour-plated vehicle – and usually had a man with long hair and a missing left ear riding on a motorbike a little way behind.

That day, Hariri had met with his two main political allies – his Protestant economic advisor Basil Fleihan and Dr Ghattas Koury, a Maronite Christian surgeon – and had reaffirmed his alliance with the Bristol Gathering. With gallows humour, he had asked Walid Jumblatt, the Druze leader, "Who will be assassinated first? You or me?"

Well, The Damascene knew who it wasn't going to be. He had a job to do, and he was on top of the situation. But he must never, ever, become complacent.

Now he turned in his bed – and kissed The Djinn full on the lips. It was something they actually rarely did.

When they broke after thirty seconds, she smiled. "That was nice."

"Of course it was. For me too."

Laughing, she punched his shoulder. "You arrogant male!"

He sniffed. "Just male. The arrogance comes with the territory, it's a given."

"Okay then, you male. Well, I'm a tiger and I'm going to claw you!" She threw her leg over him and rolled up onto his stomach. She meowed as her hands moved backwards up his glistening body, her nails giving him kitten scratches.

"Oh really?" He reached up and grabbed her face in his hands. "Tigers have to be tamed. And I know just how to do that." His left thumb was in her mouth and he tugged lightly sideways as he kicked upwards with his right leg.

Growling, her teeth closed over his thumb as she fell, her mouth sucking. He rolled over her. She feigned defiance, trying to push him off, her nails scratching down his back, one nail sharper than the rest. She let him push his hips between her legs, and she felt him pressing upwards.

"Tigers on top," she hissed into the hole in his head as she shoved back against him and deftly slipped out from underneath.

He flopped face down on the bed. And did not move.

He was fast asleep.

She had fallen off of the bed and was kneeling on the floor, breathless. A few moments later, she was shaking his shoulder, saying "Marwan? Captain Mebarak? I need to talk to you..."

30 January 2005
19 Dhu'l-Hijja 1425

Hamra, Beirut 10:45

The lid of the jar opened with a satisfying pop.

"You're not going to eat those walking along the road?" queried Jihad Merhi.

"Why not?" shrugged Fadi Lattouf. "It has been a long time since breakfast." He saw Merhi look at his watch. "I was up early. And anyway, that woman makes the finest *mekhallel* this side of Gaza. I'm glad you said to meet here so I could get these. Those jars you gave me at new year didn't last long." Juice trickled into his beard as he shoved two pickled cucumbers and something long, pink and shiny into his mouth.

They were walking along busy Hamra Street, Merhi with his leather coat open revealing his uniform, Lattouf with his old padded windcheater done up to the neck, concealing his uniform. Merhi carried a jar of pickles in each hand, looking after them while Lattouf gorged from a third jar.

"So ten bodies that we know of," salivated the Palestinian. "And your Department of General Security wants us to do nothing about it. Did this woman say anything about my culling theory?"

"She really didn't say anything. Said they were in the dark as much as we were – but they've been getting information from somewhere, they've been following leads of their own. They've only recently realised our, er, interest."

"How?" A large piece of pepper flopped over Lattouf's lips like a deformed tongue and then disappeared with a sucking slither.

"Don't know. They've been listening, of course, but I thought we'd been careful."

"Perhaps not careful enough."

"Perhaps. But it's worked out okay, as you say. We don't have the threat of an official murder investigation hanging over us."

Juice dripping through his fingers, Lattouf crunched down on a piece of cauliflower. "Do we have any threats hanging over us?"

They paused to cross over Omar Ben Abd el-Aziz Street. "No threats, just two requests," said Merhi. "One, back off. Two, let them know if any more turn up."

"They are expecting more?"

"Didn't say." There was a break in the traffic and they crossed the road.

"Well, at least we now know who we're dealing with on the official side. Why you Lebanese have to skulk around with your mysterious car-followings and secret warnings, I don't know." Lattouf took the last items from the jar, two more pieces of cauliflower and a gherkin.

Merhi gave an ironic nod, acknowledging the truth. "In Lebanon the balance is always... delicate. Right hands never want left hands to know what they are doing."

Lattouf huffed. "I think thumbs don't want index fingers to know what they are doing! I will never understand you, I have given up trying." Still walking, Lattouf swilled the remaining juice around the jar, raised the jar to his mouth and drank it down. Merhi looked on aghast.

Putting his hands out for his other two jars and giving Merhi the empty one, Lattouf said "But we should still keep looking under our cars, my friend. Sometimes thumbs can turn nasty."

1 February 2005
21 Dhu'l-Hijja 1425

Kahale, Lebanon 15:00

"You are in good shape." The Commander stood with a towel around his waist watching Ahmad finishing his shower.

The young Palestinian wiped his hands down his wet face as he came out. "Thank you, sir." He was unashamed of his nakedness. Everything that had happened in the last three months, especially the successful trial run into Beirut a week ago, had instilled confidence in him. He began to dry himself.

"But, as I said, don't overdo it," cautioned the Commander. "You are at your peak. The day of action is fast approaching. Everything is coming together well."

"When is it, sir? The day?"

"Two weeks. Just two more weeks." The Commander announced it matter-of-factly, no great fanfare.

Ahmad's face lit up. It was news he had been waiting to hear. "Two weeks," he repeated.

The Commander dropped his towel and walked naked out into the changing area where they had left their clean clothes. "You are happy about driving the van?" he asked over his shoulder.

Ahmad picked up the Commander's towel, feeling its wetness and warmth as he draped it over the towel rail. "Yes, sir," he called. "It was a good experience for me, in the city. I am confident."

"Good. Because on the day you will be driving it on your own."

There were a few seconds before Ahmad said from the doorway, "Sir?"

The Commander pulled his white *dishdasha* over his head and flicked his hair out at the back. He looked up at Ahmad standing there naked. He shrugged as if it had been obvious. "I cannot be with you, Ahmad. I will be watching for the Israeli and then getting myself into position. I was there on the rehearsal only to tell you what to do. I will have my own transport."

"That... that is logical, sir."

"You are confident in driving the van?"

"Yes... yes, of course I am, sir. I just didn't think."

"Nothing to worry about. We will go in together but we'll have two vehicles. We will split up. You will go and park. I will do what I have to do, and you will be waiting for me when I have killed the Jew."

"I – I am honoured, sir."

The Commander nodded. "You are the chosen one, Ahmad. Out of the four. It is an honour, but you have gained this by your own merits. You will be revered by our people. The new President will probably wish to meet you."

"I don't know what to say."

"There is nothing to say."

Ahmad was still absentmindedly drying his body.

"Just one thing," continued the Commander. Ahmad looked up. "Take off those few body hairs you have. We need to be clean for combat."

Ahmad looked down at himself. Yes, this was combat, wasn't it? He was serving his people. He was a soldier killing a Jew. He nodded. "Whatever you wish, sir."

11 February 2005
2 Muharram 1426

Mount Lebanon 20:30

Rafic Hariri's schedule was hectic. Too hectic for a sixty year old man, no matter what his status or ambitions. In the last twenty-four hours he had been in a constant process of liaison with various people and entities, including dinner at Koreitem with UN envoy Terje Roed Larsen (who was attempting a smooth implementation of UN Resolution 1559 whereby Syrian troops in Lebanon would withdraw to the Bekaa), meeting again with Hezbollah leader Sayyed Hassan Nasrallah (who successfully persuaded Hariri to include two pro-Syrian candidates on his electoral list), meeting with Maronite patriarch Cardinal Sfeir (to reassure him that he was not opposed to the government's plan for the smaller constituencies), and asking to meet the Christian opposition Qornet Shehwan gathering at Koreitem (to discuss a mutual position on the electoral law).

It was the response of the Qornet Shehwan that had given The Damascene the evening off. They did not want to meet at Koreitem as they were uncomfortable at showing too much of a united stance with Hariri at this time, so they had suggested that the MPs of Qornet Shehwan meet with Hariri in Parliament on Monday morning instead. So Hariri was 'relaxing' at Koreitem this evening – which meant that The Damascene could relax at home.

He stretched out on the leather sofa, watching a news programme on the TV. On the coffee table were a glass of apple juice and a box with a selection of baklava and ma'amoul. He wasn't really that interested in news or politics (which were the same thing on local television), he was a worker who obeyed the instructions of his masters – his masters being those who paid him. A true mercenary, created by circumstance, created by the murder of Captain Marwan Mebarak of the Lebanese Army. Created from hell.

There was a knock at his front door. He smiled. Perfect timing. How did she know he would be home tonight? Or was she taking a gamble? Muting the volume on the television, he rolled off the sofa and stood up. Why didn't she use her key? Perhaps she was knocking first, keeping up the *djinn*-can't-open-closed-doors legend.

He was dressed in just a black pouch. Should he put something on, or just surprise her?

Deciding on the surprise, he went over to the front door and opened it.

Ghazi Kanaan was standing there.

"You have been doing well," Kanaan sipped from his freshly-filtered coffee, sitting on the sofa.

"You have been keeping an eye on me?" The Damascene stood with his back to the window. The question was rhetorical, he knew the answer, of course. The Djinn.

He was now dressed in a white *dishdasha*, his hair tied back tightly. He liked to expose his lack of left ear to Kanaan, just to remind the bastard.

"No need. The fact that Hariri is alive is evidence."

The Damascene inclined his head.

"But I need you back," continued Kanaan. "That is why I am here."

"But these are dangerous times for Hariri. You don't want me to stay until the election?"

"These are even more dangerous times for Ghazi Kanaan. I believe I am under even greater threat. There are plots against me in Damascus."

"But surely the Interior Minister has his own security personnel? Talking of which...?"

"They are downstairs. They are being discreet, don't worry. We came in the one car. And yes, the *Interior Minister* has his own security personnel. But what if I was no longer Interior Minister?"

"You are being replaced?"

"Only a matter of time, I suspect."

The Damascene did not ask why. It was none of his business. "When do you want me back?"

"Now."

"Now?"

"You can come in the car."

"No." The Damascene shook his head. "I cannot simply disappear and abandon Hariri. His man Abu Tarek has been very co-operative. They know I come from Syria. How would it look if the man sent from Syria to protect Hariri was summarily withdrawn at this crucial time?"

"I am giving you an order."

"You do not give me orders. You give me instructions."

"I have paid you." The Damascene said nothing, so Kanaan went on. "I have rebuilt you. I have saved your life."

"After you took it from me in the first place." The Damascene's left hand clenched and unclenched, anxious to be let loose on Kanaan's throat.

There was silence while the two men stared at each other.

Kanaan was the first to look away. Sighing, he asked "When then?" When he received no reply, he said one word which The Damascene had never heard him use before nor would he ever hear again. He said, "Please."

The Damascene raised his eyebrows, nothing less than shocked. "It is that serious?"

Kanaan nodded. "Yes, it is. I will either be President in the next few months – or I will be dead."

The Damascene finished the glass of apple juice he had been holding in his hand. "Give me a few days. A few days to round things off with Abu Tarek. Then I'll return."

"A deal. Thank you."

The Damascene walked over and took a ma'amoul from the box. A piece of walnut fell out as he bit into it. He said casually, "I'm surprised you came here yourself."

Kanaan put the empty coffee cup down on he table. "If you want a job doing properly, you have to do it yourself. The last person I sent - "

At that precise moment the lights went out. Power cut.

"Wait." In the darkness, The Damascene went over to the kitchen area and opened a drawer. "There." The beam from a torch pierced the room.

The Damascene lit Kanaan's way to the front door, reaching in front of him to open it. "Will The Djinn be coming back to Damascus?" he asked as he stood back to let Kanaan pass, shining the torch out onto the stairwell.

"Who?"

"The Djinn. The girl."

Kanaan sounded perplexed. "What girl? A *djinn*?"

"The one you sent. The one that has been visiting me for a while now. In Damascus."

"What are you talking about? I have never sent a girl to visit you. Why should I do that? The one man I did send never returned." Kanaan walked towards the stairs, his tone saying that he did not wish to be bothered with this trivia.

"The girl. In Damascus. Followed me here. I sent you messages with her." The Damascene stiffened, his mind flying backwards over the months, thinking of her visits.

Then there was a sound. From below. Someone running rapidly down the stairwell. As if they had been listening and knew they were found out. And there was an upward breeze, carrying a faint scent of jasmine.

Kanaan was shaking his head. "I really don't know what the hell you are talking about - " He was cut off as The Damascene pushed him out of the way.

The Damascene took the stairs two, three at a time, the torchlight bouncing, but he was hampered by the flowing *dishdasha* and his bare feet. Reaching the bottom, he slammed through the outside doors.

It was dark outside. He looked from right to left, swinging the torch. Two men were standing smoking by a limousine, obviously Kanaan's retinue. No one else was about. He went towards them. "Did you see - ?"

Suddenly the area was bathed in light. There was a screeching of wheels as headlights came blazing up from the car park under the block, dazzling, blinding. The Damascene put his right arm up to shield his eyes, turning and pushing one of the men against the car, his left hand going under the man's jacket and pulling out his gun.

He turned, fumbling with the safety as the vehicle sped up the slope, kicking up dust and gravel. He fired off one shot and missed as the vehicle turned right towards Beirut.

Instinctively he wanted to leap onto his Suzuki and follow, but he knew that would be impossible wearing the *dishdasha*. And if he took it off he wouldn't get far riding the bike nude, not even in Beirut!

Passing the gun back, he looked towards the doorway as Kanaan came out. "What the hell was that all about?" demanded the Syrian.

For a moment, The Damascene said nothing. Then he said, "Nothing."

One of the men opened the car door. "A few days," said Kanaan, climbing in. "I will expect you back in Damascus."

"I'll be there," he lied.

The Damascene watched as the car drew away, up the slope, turning left for Syria.

A few days and he would be out of this forever, he thought. It would give him plenty of time to do what he had to do.

And maybe also to find a *djinn* driving a black Ford Explorer.

The lights went back on ten minutes later, by which time The Damascene was back standing by the window, staring out over Beirut.

What was she? Who was she? She had been with him for months and he had always assumed she was Kanaan's gift. Obviously not. Had she been spying on him? If so, for whom? Kanaan's enemies? Syria's enemies?

It did not really matter as the sum total of their time together had been based on sex. And, latterly, coffee machines. And, of course, damned mosquito bites.

Still, The Damascene did not like not knowing. He would complete the mission he had been paid for, then he would find out.

Al-Rajul also did not like not knowing. But now he knew a lot. From the outset his employer had decreed the date on which Rafic Hariri should die. And now, thanks to the Qornet Shehwan baulking at meeting Hariri in Koreitem, he knew the exact time Hariri would be at Parliament on the chosen day. He would not have to hang around. And, more importantly, he would not have to keep Ahmad hanging around either.

The young Palestinian had his destiny to fulfil.

12 February 2005
3 Muharram 1426

Koreitem 11:30

The Damascene was at Koreitem to tell Abu Tarek of his departure back to Syria when news of the arrests came through. At first he did not know what was going on. A secretary burst into Abu Tarek's office without apology and said something about the Beirut Society for Social Development and, after a curt "Excuse me", Abu Tarek dashed out, leaving The Damascene sitting there.

Not respectful, thought The Damascene. What was happening? Was Hariri under attack? If so, he should be involved.

He did not find out for thirty minutes, when Abu Tarek came back, by which time The Damascene was fuming. It was just as well his involvement was finishing.

"My profuse apologies for keeping you waiting," Abu Tarek sounded sincere. "Yet another attack."

"An attack?"

"Not that sort, not physical. It is one of Mr Hariri's charities. It supplies food packages to the needy during the Holy Month, including olive oil. As Ramadan was before the olive season, this year we left notes in the packages saying that the olive oil would be delivered as soon as the olives were picked, pressed and bottled, which we did recently. Now four workers from the charity have been arrested."

"Arrested? Why?"

"They are accused of giving the olive oil as a bribe in advance of the election."

The Damascene shook his head. Lebanese politics!

"It is nonsense, of course," continued Abu Tarek. "Foolishness. Mr Hariri is taking charge of the situation personally. So I regret, my dear sir, that I have to go."

The Damascene stood up. "Is he going anywhere?"

"No, he is overseeing things from here. It is likely to take some time to get the workers released."

"Then you do not need me."

"No. And thank you for everything you have done, all your advice. It has been appreciated."

The two men shook hands, looking into each other's eyes.

"*Afwan.* You are welcome," said The Damascene. Then he added, "*Fi aman Allah.*"

13 February 2005
4 Muharram 1426

Kahale, Lebanon 15:30

With a grunt, the Commander and Ahmad lifted the last fifty kilo sack of sugar into the back of the van in the garage. Both were slightly out of breath. "Well done, Ahmad. Thank you," said the Commander. "Now, you go and pray and rest. Ask for Allah's blessings for tomorrow."

"Yes, sir." A little sulkily, Ahmad went out. A few moments before he had been snappily reprimanded when he had asked the Commander if they really needed all this sugar as their cover as merchants. Wouldn't just a few sacks do?

The response had been sharp and terse. Twenty sacks were required to create the right image of successful tradesmen, and it was not his place to question the Commander's decisions.

Al-Rajul was pleased the little *contretemps* had arisen, otherwise he would have had to contrive another way of getting the young Palestinian to leave him alone in the garage. Now he went over to the door and bolted it from the inside.

From a cupboard at the back of the garage, he pulled out a taped cardboard box. Cutting the tape with a cardboard-cutter knife, he took out a reel of wire. Attached to the end of the wire was a button that looked like a domestic doorbell, identical to the one installed in the cab of the van.

It took him forty minutes to replace the one in the van with the new model, drilling holes so that the wire went underneath the van and came back in again in the back. When he had finished, there was no way of telling that the button had even been changed. Ahmad would never know.

Then he went back to the box and took out a smaller box from inside: a selection of detonators and initiators.

He chose what he needed and set to work.

Bourj el-Barajneh, Beirut 20:30

Captain Fadi Lattouf was the last to leave the police station that evening. A rare occurrence, but he'd had meetings with camp representatives of both *Fatah* and the resurgent *Hamas* that afternoon and he needed to make a record of both. Only in note form, nobody would ever read it, but it needed to be done. Also there was an unfinished pack of *khobz 'arabi* (Arabic bread) in his drawer that needed his attention.

It was 20:30 when he padlocked the door of the police station from the outside and began the ten minute walk back to *chez Lattouf*. The streets were quiet this

Sunday evening, only a few people populating the nearby café. He was tempted to stop for a shisha, but Nada was bound to smell it on him and that might spoil his chances for other activities this fine Sunday evening – for Nada had given him that look this morning, the one he received only about four times a year.

He waved at the café proprietor, shook his head at the come-inside hand signal, and helped himself to a newspaper somebody had left on the solitary table outside. That day's *Al-Mustaqbal*.

Soon he was home. The children were in bed, which was a good sign that he hadn't imagined this morning's promise, and a plate of rice and lamb was awaiting him. The plate stretched into three plates, then he sat back contented, his trousers undone to let his mammoth gut expand even more.

"Nada," he called sweetly, swallowing a burp. "How would you like to make a little Lattouf...?"

Mount Lebanon 22:30

She entered The Damascene's apartment with her gun in her hand, a Herstal 9mm. Careful, cautious. The place was in darkness, and she moved around in silence, like a ghost.

He was not there, she hadn't expected him to be.

Up in the bedroom, she noticed his large holdall on the floor. Some of his clothes were inside. He was getting ready to leave. She had heard the conversation with Ghazi Kanaan. He was to return to Syria.

She was angry because, now he knew she did not work for Kanaan, she could not go back with him and continue their regular... therapy sessions. Pity, but so be it.

But she was also angry at something else. Cold and emotionless he may be. Assassin he may be. The best lover she had ever had he may be. But none of that was an excuse for ignoring simple human decency. Politeness.

The bastard had never thanked her for the coffee machine!

Koreitem 23:59

Rafic Hariri's time was dominated that weekend by the olive oil arrests, then that evening he held counsel with friends and allies including Walid Jumblatt and Ghazi Aridi*.

It was close to midnight before Hariri went up to his private quarters on the seventh floor of the Palace. He was on his own. Nazek, his wife, was in Paris with their daughter Hind, and he was going to join them there on Friday to celebrate Hind's birthday. His three surviving sons, Bahaa, Saad and Fahd were grown men with their own businesses and families.

He made a telephone call to Saad in Saudi Arabia, but as usual it was constrained and stilted due to The Listeners. But it did not stop him telling his son that he loved him.

* *The Minister of Culture until he had resigned the previous September in protest at the extension of the term of President Lahoud.*

He was alone as it became Monday 14 February.

14 February 2005
5 Muharram 1426

Mount Lebanon 06:00

The Damascene was up early. He showered, exercised, showered again, drank his usual breakfast of two strong coffees (he liked the new machine), and dressed in jeans, black T-shirt and his leather jacket.

He wanted to wear his long hair down, but he knew today he must look nondescript, he must blend in, so he tied it back with an elastic band, making sure that the hair was tightly against the side of his head to cover the hole of the missing ear. Kanaan's legacy.

He filled his jacket pockets with what he had to take with him and left the apartment. Outside it was still dark, but it was dry and a fine day had been predicted.

The Suzuki started smoothly, and in a few moments he was up the slope and turning left onto the main road.

Kahale, Lebanon 07:00

"Morning of joy, my dear Ahmad." The Commander was already in the dining area when the young Palestinian came in.

Ahmad was dressed as he had been told: sandals, old jeans, shirt and old jacket, all provided for him by the Commander. He felt good, he felt confident. He had slept well, not knowing that his rest had been assisted by a small draft the Commander had slipped into his tea yesterday evening. "Morning of peace, sir."

"You are ready?"

"Oh, yes."

"These are your last hours here. Later you will be with your family and you will be out of the camp forever. Tomorrow afternoon I have arranged for you to meet with the President, at his request."

Ahmad's face shone. "Really, sir? I am honoured. My family will be proud."

"Your nation will be proud. You will be a hero, Ahmad." After a pause, Al-Rajul added "This is your day of destiny."

Koreitem, Beirut 07:10

Rafic Hariri was called by his personal secretary Adnan Baba at 07:10, though truth be told he was already awake. It had not been a good night. He was missing his wife, Nazek, and he looked forward to seeing her at the end of the week. Today was the start of the parliamentary discussion on the electoral law, which was expected to last three days. That and the fall-out from the olive oil arrests would take up his week until he flew to Paris on Friday. But firstly today was his meeting at Parliament with the Qornet Shehwan, after which he had twenty people coming for lunch at Koreitem.

While Hariri ate his usual breakfast of *labneh,* cucumbers, tomatoes and toast, Abu Tarek and his team began their first security sweep of the day.

Bourj el-Barajneh, Beirut 08:30

Fadi Lattouf decided to have a lie-in that morning. After his exertions with Nada last night (which in fact had lasted little over a minute), he was feeling benign, content and at peace with the world. Sergeant el-Khazem could open up the shop today. Fadi would have a leisurely breakfast and then stroll in about 11:00.

As he lay staring at the ceiling, his stomach rumbled. Five seconds later his fart shook the walls of the buildings within a ten block radius, like the sonic boom of the Israeli aircraft when they performed one of their regular intimidating flyovers of Beirut.

The mattress increased in height three-fold as he rolled out of the bed. His stomach was right. He needed to get rid of some of the rice and lamb before starting on his morning eggs with sumac (and probably some *zaatar* as well, he was feeling peckish – regular sex did that to a man).

He hoped one of the kids wasn't in the toilet. If they were, he would have to throw them out. His need was greater, not to mention the additional hole in the ozone layer that would be created if he didn't go and go now.

Kahale, Lebanon 09:00

"One final time," ordered the Commander. He was sitting in the driving seat of the Canter van, Ahmad next to him. The van was in front of The Facility, which they had now locked up. Al-Rajul would return later for the final cleaning of the place.

Patiently, Ahmad said "I wait in the car park until you ring. The phone determines the route."

"Say them."

"Nokia, north. Samsung, south. LG, west."

"Good. And the three places?"

"North, the St. George Hotel. South, the Four Points Sheraton. West, Future TV."

"The target?"

"The target will be in the third car of the convoy. I press the button to alert you at the exact moment the target's car passes by me. Not before, not after."

"Good." The Commander sat there for a while, saying nothing. Then he said, "It is time. I will be right behind you until we reach the city." He held out his hand. Ahmad was stunned for a few moments, and then he reached out and shook it. "Allah is with you," said the Commander.

Ahmad smiled. "May He be with you too, sir."

The Commander got out as Ahmad moved over into the driver's seat. The Commander slammed the door and banged on the side of the van. Ahmad raised his hand and then moved off.

Al-Rajul watched as the Mitsubishi Canter Van reached the end of the driveway, paused and then turned right. The van with the earnest but naïve young Palestinian aboard.

And one thousand kilos of TNT.

Bourj el-Barajneh, Beirut 09:10

The lamb took longer to shift than Lattouf expected. It must have been mutton, not lamb (he would have a word with Nada – his wonderful, sweet, sexy girl Nada – later), and his delicate gut had had difficulty digesting it. Some of it his gut had tried to push through as was, coming out the same as it went in, and that had caused a painful rectal breach birth which had stung his rectum like the tongue of a sand viper. It had taken him fifteen minutes on the toilet, and the neighbours certainly knew about it. Soon the sewage systems of Beirut, if not the whole of the Middle East, would know about it too.

Then he had washed and dressed, so it was gone 09:00 before he sat down for his breakfast. He was ravenous. His stomach was empty.

He began his first plate of eggs, casually reading yesterday's *Al-Mustaqbal* newspaper which he had picked up last night. It was an Hariri-owned publication and the front page was screaming about the arrest of four charity workers.

He was chewing *zaatar* and he had just taken a mouthful of coffee when his eyes reached the bottom of the page. What he read made him shoot forward in his chair, the contents of his mouth spilling out into his beard and down his shirt.

In the name of Allah!

"N – Nada!" he coughed, spluttered, shouted, his voice hoarse. "Nada! Where are you, woman? Nada, quickly! Pass me my phone!"

Jonblat, Beirut 09:20

Jihad Merhi was heading towards the office of his boss, Major Ghanem, when his mobile telephone buzzed in his trouser pocket. He kept walking down the corridor, wedging the pile of folders under his left arm, retrieving his mobile with his right hand. It was probably Gisele checking on the menu for next Saturday's visit of sister-in-law Violette and her husband Toni, she said she was going shopping down in Kaslik today. It was a bit early though.

He looked at his phone and his shoulders sank. Oh for God's sake! Why had he ever given him his mobile number?

He pressed the reject button. He would have to wait.

He reached the boss's door and knocked, making a mental note to add Fadi Lattouf to his blocked numbers list later.

Furn el Chebback, Beirut 10:15

Ahmad had driven carefully, as instructed, and the Monday morning traffic was heavy as always. The Commander had been behind him on the journey down from the mountains, occasionally coming up beside him to exchange okay signs and then dropping back again. They had entered the city through Hazmieh. Now the Canter van turned in to the parking area of City Furniture just beyond the Chevrolet Roundabout and the Commander pulled in behind it.

Neither Ahmad nor the Commander left their vehicles. This stop was planned, this was where they would split. The Commander stared at Ahmad's face in the wing mirror of the van. Ahmad smiled and nodded.

The Commander returned the nod, then he pulled away, out of the parking area and back into the traffic. Ahmad watched him go past the Abraj Centre and then disappear from view. The Commander would be heading west through Ain el Rommaneh, picking up the main Corniche el Mazraa and then heading north into town on Selim Salam Street. Ahmad would be staying on Damascus Street all the way in to Martyrs' Square.

He gave it five minutes and then pulled back out into the traffic. He was on his own now. Serving his President, serving his country.

Killing a Jew.

Jonblat, Beirut 10:20

The meeting with Major Ghanem had taken longer than expected (why couldn't he just leave this al-Murabitoun investigation to him and not interfere?), so it was a full hour before Jihad Merhi left his boss's office. The phone in his pocket had vibrated regularly throughout the meeting, sending at-any-other-time-not-unwelcome tremors through his groin, to the extent that his movements to get himself comfortable attracted curious looks from the Major. At one point, the Major had asked "Are you all right? Do you need to relieve yourself?", after which it was all Merhi could do to keep a straight face. Perhaps he did need to relieve himself, but not in the way the Major thought!

Now back in his own office, he took the phone from his pocket. Twenty missed calls. Oh Lattouf, you were going down big time for this!

Knowing that the fat slob would not leave him alone, he pressed the Call button. Might as well get it over with, see what he wanted. Three super size Big Macs and fries?

Connection made, the line rang.

And rang.

And rang.

Koreitem, Beirut 10:35

"I will be back at one," Rafic Hariri, seated behind the wheel of his Mercedes S-600, took his reading glasses from his secretary. He had left them on his desk and he would have been lost without them. "Thank you, Adnan." Next to him sat his friend and former Economy Minister Basil Fleihan who had returned from Geneva the night before to attend the parliamentary session.

The secretary stepped back from the car. *"Maa Salameh."*

There was a bip of a car horn and the convoy moved off.

It was a bright, sunny Beirut day.

South Beirut 10:40

You do not see Palestinian police cars speeding through the streets of Beirut with their blue lights flashing, horns blaring. It would cause untold political and protocol repercussions. It is simply not done. It does not happen.

Except that day.

Lattouf's vehicle was a dented, rusting light blue police Ford Transit van donated by the British to the Palestinian Authority ten years before, still with the pompous small metal plaque affixed above the Ford sign on the back door proclaiming *Provided under British aid*. It carried the distinctive red number plate of the Palestinian military.

He headed north up Hamid Franjieh Avenue at a speed that would have frightened Formula One drivers, cursing, gesticulating, eyes wild, leaning on his horn. Damned Lebanese drivers! Get out of the way, get out of the way!

This really could be a matter of life or death.

Nejmeh, Beirut 10:50

The convoy arrived in Nejmeh Square, the lead vehicle pulling up in the exact position so that the third car would stop right outside the entrance to Parliament. Rafic Hariri and Basil Fleihan got out and entered the building.

On the southern side of the square by Maarad Street, a man with long tied-back hair sat astride a Suzuki motorbike, watching. Abu Tarek gave him a small nod then followed Hariri into the building.

Jonblat, Beirut 11:15

Merhi had just opened *Word* on his computer when he heard the shouting from out in the General Office. Then scuffling. Not another football discussion that had got out of hand!

But no, the voices were getting louder. One was shouting, booming, the other authoritative but trying to placate. Only when they neared his door could he make out Sergeant Deeb el-Gharib saying "I don't care who you are, you can't just come barging in here!"

"Get your hands off me!" responded the booming voice. "Jihad! Abu Samer! Merhi! Are you - " The door to Merhi's office slammed open as it was given a mighty kick from outside, the frosted glass cracking with the force. " – in here?"

The mountain that was Fadi Lattouf was standing in the doorway, the arms of Deeb el-Gharib on his shoulders in a failed headlock, the hands of a Lieutenant around one of his thighs, the Lieutenant himself horizontal having been dragged along the corridor.

"What the hell?" Merhi joined in the shouting as he stood up. "Cease, all of you. In God's name what is going on? Let him go, let him go."

Reluctantly, el-Gharib took his arms away, bending down to support the Lieutenant who would have a nasty face-down one metre fall to the floor unless he was assisted. "I told him he couldn't just come barging in here," he mumbled.

Giving them an I-told-you-so look, Lattouf shook his shoulder and leg even though the Lebanese were already off. "You haven't been answering your phone," he explained reasonably.

Merhi closed the door as the Palestinian came in, giving a rueful look at the crack across the glass. "What is it now, Fadi?"

"Have you - ?"

He was interrupted by another commotion, this time from out in the street. Shouting, car horns blaring. Merhi went over and looked out. A Palestinian police van, blue lights still flashing, was blocking one half of the road and the other drivers were playing chicken trying to get round it. "You never came here in that!" Merhi growled angrily as he turned – to find Lattouf holding up a copy of *Al-Mustaqbal* newspaper.

"Have you seen this?" asked Lattouf.

Merhi frowned, shaking his head. "I have work to do, I haven't read today's papers."

"Not today's. Yesterday's."

Merhi shrugged.

"Look." Lattouf put the paper flat on the desk, pointing at the main story.

Merhi leant over. "The olive oil arrests. It is nothing. It will blow over."

"Yes, but look." Lattouf's thick index finger jabbed the bottom of the page.

Merhi read.

And tensed.

He read it again.

Slowly he straightened up. "Oh... my God... Oh my God. So that's what it's been about. And we haven't known."

"How could we? It could have been anything."

Merhi shook out a Cedars King Size cigarette from the pack on his desk, Lattouf's hand stretching out and taking one before it was even offered. They lit up and dragged.

"It was a recruitment exercise all right." Merhi bent back over and read the piece for the third time. Just twenty-five words.

> These unjustified arrests come just one month after the foiled attempt to have Mr Hariri arrested on the false charge of being an Israeli agent.

"An Israeli agent at work in Beirut is what the last victim's brother said he said," Lattouf swallowed smoke. He looked Merhi in the eyes. "They are going to kill Hariri."

Nejmeh, Beirut 11:25

Ahmad sat in the van in the parking area on Weygand Street, that day's *An Nahar* newspaper open across the steering wheel in front of him. Today he did not want to pee. He was not nervous, he had done this before – only this time it was for real. He was confident, he was proud.

He wondered how the Commander was feeling. It was the Commander that would be doing the actual killing, of course, Ahmad was just the point man, but it still felt good to be serving his country. And to be getting his family forever out of that accursed camp.

He was not wearing a watch, that was an order from the Commander. At first he had wondered why, but the Commander had explained that, consciously or not, he would keep looking at it and that would attract curiosity from anyone looking at him: a man sitting in a van constantly looking at his watch. Whereas a man sitting in a van reading a newspaper would attract no attention. There was a clock on the dashboard, and Ahmad found himself casting regular glances at it – so proving the Commander's caution.

He smiled to himself. Allah had blessed him the day he had been chosen by the Commander. The Commander had not let him down, ever. He was a true soldier, a true comrade.

He looked at the three muted phones on the seat next to him and wondered which one would buzz.

Horch, Beirut 11:45

The black Ford Explorer was stuck in traffic on Hamid Franjieh Avenue in the Horch district when her mobile rang. The traffic was going nowhere, so Zahia Zalloum had time to rummage in her bag and retrieve the Sony Ericsson. She looked at the screen. It was a number she had put into her Contacts only recently.

"Captain Merhi," she answered.

"Zahia!" Merhi was speaking loudly, a hint of triumph in his voice. "We've worked it out." There was a raised voice-off, then Merhi said "Okay, okay. Actually Fadi Lattouf worked it out."

"He has, has he?"

"The bodies. The Massoud boy. Remember he said his brother was going to kill an Israeli agent?"

"Yes."

"Have you seen the papers?" More mumbling off. "Yesterday's paper. *Al-Mustaqbal*."

"Captain, get to the point, please." The traffic had begun to move slowly.

"I never knew about it, you probably didn't too. Apparently last month there was a plot to arrest Hariri and charge him with being an Israeli agent – Hello? Hello? Zahia, are you still there?" He could hear car horns blaring and wheels screeching.

Then she was back on, screaming "We have to get to Hariri!"

"I'll get back-up."

"No, no! You never know who's in on it." She wrenched the steering wheel, bumping over the central reservation, going up the avenue on the wrong side, horn blasting. "He's at Parliament today, it was on the news. The electoral debate. Meet me at Nejmeh. Now!" She threw the phone onto the seat next to her.

Merde, thought Zahia. *Merde, merde, merde.* What she had seen, what she knew, made her certain.

It was going to be today.

Jonblat, Beirut 12:00

Merhi and Lattouf dashed from the State Security building – and stopped dead. Traffic was at a standstill, both ways. Caused not least by a Palestinian police van, blue lights still flashing, that was blocking half the road. Lattouf looked sheepish, but he shouted "Get in!"

"No, no!" Merhi grabbed hold of his arm. "Where the hell can we go?" He looked right, then left. Then he said, "We'll have to walk. *Yalla.* The exercise will do you good."

Nejmeh Square, Beirut 12:25

From his position at the south side of Nejmeh Square, The Damascene saw Rafic Hariri come out of the parliament building, walking down the steps with Ghattas Khoury. The two men stopped, discussing something for a few minutes. Then they shook hands and went separate ways.

Hariri and a bodyguard walked across the square, and just for a moment The Damascene thought he was coming towards him, but they detoured into the Café de l'Etoile, where some journalists had been waiting for an hour. But was there a recognition, an acknowledgement, in the eye contact Hariri had made with him?

A few minutes later Hariri came back outside and sat at a table with Nejib Friji, the Tunisian head of the UN Information Office. They had a deep discussion for five minutes and then both men returned inside the café. Moments later they were joined by Basil Fleihan and a Sunni MP called Samir Jisr.

Then The Damascene saw movement down a side street next to the parliament building. The convoy was getting ready to leave.

The Damascene stood up from his leaning position on the Suzuki, putting his hands in his jacket pockets.

The convoy rolled slowly out of the side street, across the cobble-stoned square to wait in front of the café.

The Damascene watched.

Serail, Beirut 12:50

As they passed the United Kingdom embassy on Army Street, Fadi Lattouf thought he was going to die. By the time they passed the Grand Serail building, he knew he was. He was a man of strength and intensely intellectual powers – his legs weren't meant for walking!

He got no sympathy from Jihad Merhi who, although he had started off at a pace to rival an Olympic walking champion, had now slowed to a normal, middle-aged walk, trying hard to hide the stitch in his side.

They turned left into Parliament Street. They could see the clock tower in the middle of the Etoile down at the bottom.

Nejmeh Square, Beirut 12:53

Rafic Hariri and Basil Fleihan walked out of the café, Fleihan getting into the front passenger seat of the third car, the Mercedes S-600. The security man who had driven the car over held the driver's door open for Hariri. The big man paused, looking back at the café. He smiled, waving at Nejib Friji and the reporters. Cameras clicked.

This time there was a distinct look towards The Damascene. Hariri nodded. The Damascene inclined his head.

Then the convoy was moving off, around the clock tower, past the Italian embassy and down Hussein el-Ahdab Street.

The northern route.

The Damascene took the three mobile telephones from his pocket and chose the Nokia.

Nejmeh, Beirut 12:53

Ahmad was waiting in the van round on Weygand Street, thinking of the Commander and how he adored and respected him. In Ahmad's opinion, the Commander was the one who was the true hero, not him. He wondered if they would ever get to be friends after this? Perhaps they could be a team, undertake other assignments together? It would be good to know more about the man. The story of how his left ear had been blown off to leave him with a hole in the side of his head must be fascinating. And those scars on his body -

One of the phones buzzed.

The adrenaline shot through Ahmad, jolting him like a slap round the face. It was the Nokia. N for north. The northern route.

He moved quickly without thought or fear. Sweeping the newspaper onto the floor, he started the engine, manoeuvred, and pulled out into Weygand Street.

There was a gap in the traffic, caused by several black limousines coming out of Hussein el-Ahdab Street to his right and performing a small dogleg by the municipality building and going down Foch Street, which gave him space to turn left for the straight run down to Fakhr ed-Dine Street.

Then north to the corniche and the St George Hotel.

Nejmeh, Beirut 12:54

Zahia had left the Ford Explorer down on Emir Bechir Street because of the traffic. She ran down Maarad Street, not caring that her running was attracting looks from the diners in the restaurants which lined either side of the road. She could see the clock tower in the middle of the Etoile down at the bottom.

She reached Nejmeh Square – just in time to see a Suzuki motorbike, ridden by a man with long hair tied in a ponytail, zooming off up Abd el-Hamid Karame Street on the other side of the *ronde place*.

"Hey!" she shouted, but she knew it was futile.

Two men standing next to the clock tower in the middle of the square turned, thinking she was shouting to them. Jihad Merhi and the giant Lattouf. Merhi raised his hand in greeting.

Lattouf frowned. "This is she?" he asked. "A mere girl?"

Ain el-Mreisseh, Beirut 12:56

Ahmad slowed to a crawl as he reached Minet el-Hosn Street, driving close to the kerb, allowing others to overtake him. He frowned as he saw a line of cars by the entrance to the St George Beach Club opposite the still war-gutted ruins of the St George Hotel. There was nowhere for him to park!

But the Commander had been most specific. He needed to be exact. The Commander would be a little way along the road with his sniper's rifle ready. So Ahmad did the only thing he could do – he double-parked.

Under two minutes later he saw the convoy approaching in his wing mirror, headed by a Toyota Land Cruiser. They were going very fast, the Commander would need to be a very good shot to get this right. He wondered what sort of a Jew warranted such an opulent cortege. Must be a rich man.

He watched the mirror as the convoy reached him. He leaned forward, finger hovering over the button. This would be like a computer game, shooting down the enemy! The Land Cruiser whooshed past, then the first Mercedes, then the second –

Ahmad pressed the button.

And changed Lebanese history.

Nejmeh, Beirut 12:56

The blast of the explosion was heard all over Beirut and up into the mountains. Kilometres away from the epicentre, buildings shook, windows rattled, glass fell out onto the streets, building and car alarms were set off. A pall of dense yellow and black smoke rose from the seafront like the eruption column of a volcano. Instantly it began rolling its evil shroud over the city.

Standing by the clock tower in the middle of Nejmeh Square, Jihad Merhi and Fadi Lattouf looked at each other, faces blank with shock.

Next to them Zahia Zalloum, The Djinn, began to cry.

Minet el-Hosn, Beirut 12:56

From his vantage point outside the Monroe Hotel at the top of Fakhr ed-Dine Street, the man known as The Damascene or the Commander – or simply as Al-Rajul, The Man – felt the rush from the blast and even a wave of heat. The cloud down at the site was so black as to be impenetrable. One thousand kilos of trinitrotoluene will do that.

He felt neither sadness nor elation. He had a job to do and he had completed it. In a matter of hours, when the already-obvious success of the assassination had been confirmed, another five million dollars would be added to his bank account on top of the five million deposit already there.

Now he must carry out the final cosmetics. Crossing the Ts, dotting the Is.

He gunned the Suzuki and roared off back towards downtown.

Downtown, Beirut 13:30 – 14:10

At 13:30, al-Jazeera news received a phone call at their offices near the United Nations building. Made from a mobile telephone, the caller said that the *al-Nasr wa al-Jihad fi Bilad al-Sham* group had carried out the bombing. The statement was broadcast at 14:00.

At 14:10 another phone call was made to al-Jazeera from a different mobile phone. It said that a tape could be found in a tree by the United Nations building.

The tape was retrieved and was broadcast three hours later. It showed a man in a plain black robe and a white turban sitting in front of a black flag on which were the words *There is no God but Allah. Mohammed is the messenger of Allah. God is greatest.*

The man read from a paper in his hand. "To support our brother mujahidin in the land of the two holy mosques..."

The cosmetics had been applied.

Damascus Street, Beirut 15:30

Now that it was over Al-Rajul, The Damascene, could properly relax for the first time in six months. After hiding the tape in the tree, he was enjoying a pasta meal at *La Piazza* restaurant, in the Sodeco area. Not only was it one of his favourite restaurants in Beirut, but it was on Damascus Street, the city end of the main road which led back up to his apartment.

Damascus Street. The Green Line of Beirut during the events of 1975 to 1990, the division between the Muslims to the west and the Christians to the east. Called the Green Line because of the foliage that grew in the uninhabited space. It was a fitting analogy for his two jobs: one to kill Hariri for ten million dollars, the other to protect Hariri for Kanaan. To protect Hariri from himself! It felt good to have deceived and ultimately thwarted Kanaan, far better than putting a gun into the bastard's mouth (although he still gave himself the option of doing that one day soon).

Now he would not be returning to Damascus. He had many options. Perhaps he would follow many of his fellow-Lebanese and head south-east to the UAE. Become The Emirati rather than The Damascene!

And what would be the consequences of his actions today? There might now be a sizeable shift in Lebanon and Lebanese politics – he did not really care. But he knew it would be ironic. Everyone would assume it was a political assassination, they would never guess it was personal.

He thought back to his meeting nearly six months ago with The Owner on board the yacht. The *Heliopolis* – the City of The Sun, the Roman name for Baalbeck. Once

Al-Rajul had made the decision, agreeing to carry out the assassination, The Owner had explained his requirements. He did not mind how it was done, but it had to be spectacular. But he was adamant on the date. He wanted to give his dead wife a fiftieth birthday present. She had died at forty-two, but she would have been fifty on 14 February 2005, Valentine's Day. The man The Owner considered responsible for her death was to die on this day.

And he had.

Al-Rajul signalled to the waiter for his check. He would leave a sizeable tip. He could afford it.

Mount Lebanon 16:30

Al-Rajul parked the Suzuki by the front door of the apartment block. There were no official limousines around, he had no visitors. Kanaan was probably too worried about what had happened in Beirut today, too busy with his colleagues in the Syrian government, to worry about his man in Beirut – his man who ultimately had failed in his mission to keep Hariri alive. But even if he did spare a thought for his puppet, the last place the Syrian Interior Minister was going to appear was in Beirut on the evening of 14 February 2005!

The stairwell lights were out – another power cut! – but the daylight had only just started to fade so he could see his way easily up the stairs. In the apartment, he retrieved his large holdall from the bedroom and began to pack his things into it. The only possessions of The Damascene, who would be no more. He had a Syrian passport in another name, and that would see him out of Lebanon and into wherever he decided to go.

By the time he had finished, the night had fallen quickly, as it does in the eastern Mediterranean. He flicked switches up and down but the power was still off.

Looking out of the window over Beirut, he saw lights twinkling in the areas that were still connected to the grid. It was a beautiful city, restored to its former splendour due in no small part to the efforts of Rafic Hariri and Solidère. But as from today it would be a changed city. Whatever the future held for it, Beirut – The Wells – would be forever etched in human history.

But not in his. He needed to leave.

He zipped up the holdall and threaded his right arm through the handles, hoisting it up onto his shoulder. Over at the door, he managed to get the keys in the lock at the third attempt in the dark. He had an amusing thought: what should he do with the keys? Put them back through the letter box? This was still a Syrian-owned property.

He pushed down the handle then suddenly stopped as he experienced two unexpected sensations at once.

One was a smell: jasmine. The other was the feel of cold steel pressed hard into the back of his neck.

He did not move, but his left hand fell away from the door handle to rest near the trouser pocket which contained the piece of solid olive wood, the Holding Cross.

"Turn," ordered the voice from behind.

Slowly he obeyed, his hand going into his pocket, his fingers circling the cross. He could see the small shadow in front of him, within striking distance.

As his hand came back out of his pocket, the lights went on. The gun was pointed straight into his face. Behind it, the black eyes of The Djinn were as cold as a she-wolf's.

They stared at each other.

Then she smiled. "Fancy a cup of coffee?"

In memory of
Rafic Bahaa el deen al-Hariri
1 November 1944 – 14 February 2005
15 Dhu'l-Q'adah 1363 – 5 Muharram 1426

I trust revered Lebanon and its good people to God Almighty
- Rafic Hariri
20 October 2004
6 Ramadan 1425

Also in memory of

Yehya al-Arab (Abu Tarek)
Basil Fleihan
Samir Kassir
George Hawi
Gebran Tueni
Walid Eido

and all the others

POSTSCRIPT
حاشية

The Syrian military presence in Lebanon – ended on 26 April 2005 after thirty years.

Ghazi Kanaan. On 12 October 2005, Ghazi Kanaan, still Syria's Interior Minister, telephoned *Voix du Liban* radio in Beirut to refute allegations made on New TV the previous evening that he had received bribes from Rafic Hariri during his time as head of Syrian intelligence in Lebanon. His phone call was a rambling monologue, a valediction in which he justified Syria's role in Lebanon. He ended it by saying "I believe this is the last statement I might make."

Just after 10:00, Kanaan was found dead in his office in the Interior Ministry in Damascus. He had been shot through the mouth by a .38 Smith & Wesson. The official verdict was suicide.

There was no regime change in Syria.

The Owner of the *Heliopolis* was last seen by his crew on the upper deck of his yacht just before midnight on 14 February 2005. His wheelchair was still there the next morning. The Owner was not. No trace of him has ever been found.

The Damascene disappeared without trace on the evening of 14 February 2005. His existence is not formally acknowledged.

The Djinn also disappeared without trace on the evening of 14 February 2005. DGS agent Zahia Zalloum is recorded as 'missing during operations' on or around the same date.

Jihad Merhi and **Fadi Lattouf** – will return in *The Byblos Discovery*.

THE BYBLOS DISCOVERY

DAVID CULLEN

Culpro Books

"Murder is often a way of preventing something worse from happening"
- Dr Frederic Wertham, 1895-1981
American psychiatrist

"I and Ali are the fathers of this nation... And from Ali's descendants are my grandsons al-Hasan and al-Husayn, who are the masters of the youths of Paradise, and from al-Husayn's descendants shall be nine... the ninth among them is their Qa'im and Mahdi"
- hadith quoted in the *Ikmal* of Al Saduq

GLOSSARY
قاموس المصطلحات

Byblos – Greek name of the Phoenician city Gebal, today known as Jbeil in Arabic. It is 37 kilometres north of Beirut, Lebanon. Founded around 5000 BC, it is the oldest continuously inhabited city in the world. 'Byblos' in Greek means papyrus; it is the derivation of the English word 'Bible'.

Houri – In Islam, houris are the companions of humans and djinn who enter paradise. They have great beauty and are noted for their white eyeballs and black pupils. They can be male and female. In European usage, houris are voluptuous, beautiful, alluring women.

Djinn – Origin of the English word 'genie'. In Arabic folklore and Islamic teachings, djinn, humans and angels make up the three sentient creations of God. Djinn can be good, evil, or neutrally benevolent. In modern usage it can also mean a seductive, beguiling female.

al-Mahdi – In Islam, the prophesied redeemer, the Guided One, who will rid the world of error, injustice and tyranny alongside Isa (Jesus).

ad-Dajjal – In Islam, the Great Deceiver.

A Glossary of Arabic Words and Phrases is on pages 729 to 733.

Cast in order of appearance

A dead man, walking.

Omar Arif – *Assistant First Secretary of the Permanent Mission of Iraq to the United Nations.*

Carla Chedid – *a member of the Lebanese Department of General Security.*

The Damascene – *a mercenary, an assassin.*

Love – *a* houri, *protector of The Secret.*

Paradise – *a* houri, *protector of The Secret.*

Brother Malek – *keeper of The Secret.*

Captain Maroun Khoury – *Lebanese Department of General Security.*

Abu Yussuf – *a private investigator based in Jbeil.*

Madame Gourhant – *a client of Abu Yussuf.*

Captain Jihad Merhi (Abu Samer) - *Lebanese Internal Security Force.*

Albert Gourhant – *distrusted husband of Madame Gourhant.*

Gisele Merhi - *wife of Jihad Merhi, formerly an agent of the Lebanese Department of General Security.*

Sergeant Deeb el-Gharib - *Lebanese Internal Security Force.*

Captain Fadi Lattouf – *chief of the Civil Police of the Palestinian Security Force in the Beirut refugee camps.*

Nada Lattouf – *wife of Fadi Lattouf (and with the patience of a saint)*

Acting Captain Selim Himo - *Lebanese Department of General Security.*

Lana Lattouf – *daughter of Fadi and Nada Lattouf.*

Wissam Lattouf – *youngest son of Fadi and Nada Lattouf.*

Major Ghanem - *Lebanese Internal Security Force.*

Three members of The Circle of Haouch Moussa

PROLOGUE
مقدمة اثنين

30 December 2006
9 Dhu'l-Hijja 1427

Al-Kazimiyah, north-east Baghdad, Iraq 06:00

He had not slept that night.

Those who are about to die never do. He had spent the last hours praying and eating. His last meal was chicken and rice with a cup of hot water and honey. He had then read verses from the Qur'an and snacked on Milky Way candy bars.

They came for him just before 06:00. He was already dressed in grey trousers, a white collarless shirt and his thick woollen overcoat, protection against the chill during his last moments. Absentmindedly he stuffed a couple of Milky Way bars into his coat pocket and then picked up his Qur'an as he turned to face the four hooded men. Their eyes were hard, mocking and yet, perhaps, just a little fearful.

Good, he thought. Let them be afraid. He wasn't.

He walked out through the cell door. He knew where he was going.

The irony of the time and place was not lost on him. It was the announced first day of *Eid ul-Adha*, the Festival of Sacrifice, when Muslims celebrated the willingness of Ibrahim to sacrifice his son as an act of obedience to God, a sacrifice which was changed on God's command to the sacrifice of a goat. Today, he thought, he would be the sacrificed goat. The scapegoat. No doubt afterwards they would slit his throat.

The place was Camp Banzai, previously military intelligence headquarters, now perversely renamed Camp Justice. He knew the gallows well, he had been there often.

There was pandemonium as he entered the room, masses of people were in there, all shouting and screaming in his direction. All Shi'a traitors, collaborators with the invaders. Sunnis would never behave this way, he told himself. "Down with the invaders," he shouted back. "Down with the invaders!"

He did not tarry. With his four hooded praetorian, he climbed the steps.

He noticed a mobile phone in someone's hand below.

Even the men on the gallows were now shouting, chanting "Muqtada, Muqtada, Muqtada!", mocking him with the name of the young Shi'a, the fourth son of Grand Ayatollah Mohammed Sadeq al-Sadr and son-in-law of Grand Ayatollah Mohammed Baqir al-Sadr, both of whom had been murdered by the old regime along with many other family members.

He sniffed in disdain. "Muqtada?" he sneered mockingly. "*Allahu Akbar!* The Muslim Ummah will be victorious and Palestine is Arab!"

"Go to hell!" screamed a voice.

"Is this the bravery of Arabs?" he asked.

The noose was placed around his head, the knot on the left side of his neck.

"Long live Mohammed Baqir Sadr!" screamed another voice. "Go to hell!"

"The hell that is Iraq?" he responded.

"Please, I am begging you not to!" shouted a sudden voice of reason. "The man is being executed."

He looked around but he could not see who had spoken. It was like a circus. A zoo. Animals, all of them. He began to recite the *shahada*, the Islamic creed. "*Allahu Akbar.* There is no God but Allah. Mohammed is the messenger of Allah. God is greatest. *Allahu Akbar.* There is no God but Allah. Mohammed is the messenger of Allah. God - "

The platform dropped.

Even above the noise, the cheering and the cursing, a loud crack was heard.

He was dead.

4 years later...

28 June 2010
16 Rajab 1431

Upper East Side, New York City, USA 17:30

Omar Arif, Assistant First Secretary of the Permanent Mission of Iraq to the United Nations, walked down the steps of the four-storey brownstone mission building at 14 East 79th Street, between Madison Avenue and Fifth, and turned right.

He walked at what he hoped looked like a leisurely pace. There were two reasons why he could not be seen to be rushing: one was the heat – it had reached 98 degrees Fahrenheit in Manhattan that day and anyone rushing would be sure to attract attention to themselves. And that was the second reason also – he must not attract attention to himself. Every fibre of his being was telling him to hurry, get a move on, run. But if anybody from the Mission – or, worse, anybody *watching* the Mission – saw him acting in any way out of the ordinary, questions would be asked. And the last thing he wanted was questions. He had too many answers.

He passed the five-storey townhouse at number 17, the home of New York Mayor Michael Bloomberg, and then turned right into Madison Avenue.

As it was, he was already doing something out of the ordinary – he was not going straight home to his apartment up on 92nd. But that could be explained, if anyone asked. He was enjoying a Monday evening out in The Big Apple. Nothing wrong with that, he was not a prisoner he was a diplomat (well, actually, he was nothing more than a middle-ranking civil servant, but he had diplomatic status).

He crossed Madison at 78th and a block further down turned left, heading for the 77th Street subway.

Midtown, New York City, USA 18:00

The lobby of the Grand Hyatt Hotel next to Grand Central Station on 42nd Street is opulent, big, busy and bustling. The constant background musak of the lobby's huge cascading waterfall means that if you talk intimately, quietly, to the person next to you you cannot be heard by those passing or even those sitting just a few feet away from you in the central area near the elevators. It is a perfect place for a clandestine lovers' tryst, a private business deal – or a meeting of spies.

Carla Chedid sat in one of the double settees, a polystyrene cup of not-at-all bad Café Americano from The Market, the foyer café, on the table in front of her. She was dressed in an already-short white cotton summer dress that had ridden up as she had sat down, and her olive thighs were now attracting surreptitious glances from two middle-aged businessmen sitting at ninety degrees to her. She smiled coyly as she tossed back her long black hair, at first pretending not to notice – then suddenly looking directly at her two admirers, challenging. Caught out, the men blustered, fumbled, looked away, spoke gibberish, one of them actually asking the other "Did you see The Mets last night?"

She grinned. Hell of a game, boys, hell of a game. But on a scale of one to ten you stood a cat's chance in hell with her. Her heart – and her body – belonged elsewhere. For you, she would not be dancing.

She reached forward for her coffee, took a sip and put the cup back down on the table. She noticed them looking again. Was it her fault the dress was low cut?

From her Guess purse she took out her HTC mobile phone to check the time.

He was late. He'd better show. He *would* show. She was his handler, and like every good handler she had enough on her agent to ensure strict obedience. The publication of just one of the photos she had of Omar Arif playing stick-the-tail-up-the-donkey with a firm-buttocked and astonishingly hung young man from Hell's Kitchen would be enough to end the Iraqi's diplomatic career and probably give him a free face-down swim in the Hudson River.

She finished her coffee and treated the businessmen to a slow, sensual lick of her lips (in your dreams, boys) before taking her make-up bag from her purse.

Just as she finished applying Mac's cherry electric lipgloss, she saw him on the escalator, rising up into the foyer from the 42nd Street entrance. When he came over, they would kiss for pretence's sake, just in case anyone was watching. After all, what could be more natural than two Middle Eastern UN diplomats meeting and hitting it off, strangers in a foreign land and all that? He was Iraqi, she was Lebanese, but as far as the Americans were concerned that was the same place!

But as he came towards her she could see that something was wrong. She stood up, something she would not normally do, smiling anyway. "*Habibi*, I thought you had forgotten." She spoke in English, her voice deep and accented.

"I – I am sorry I'm late." There was sweat on Arif's brow.

She took his hands and pulled him towards her, the action reminding him of their need to kiss. He pecked her on the cheek and pulled away. "We need to talk," he said lowly.

"Of course we do, Omar." She noticed the two businessmen exchanging raised eyebrows with each other and knew what they were thinking. *We need to talk* – the universal signal of a relationship end. Was the Arab jerk actually breaking up with the – what was she? Puerto Rican? And a perfect age. No longer a babe, not yet a cougar.

"No, we really need to talk." Arif said lowly, staring straight into her eyes.

"All right. Over dinner."

"Now."

She held in her irritation, flaring her nostrils. Somebody needed a good slap. But this was also worrying. What was vexing him so? "Okay..." She opened her purse, ostensibly checking that she had put away her make-up and telephone. She did not carry a gun on the streets of Gotham, but there was something else in her bag - a ten centimetre long piece of solid olive wood. It was carved into the shape of a cross with the cross beam uneven to fit comfortably between a person's fingers. A Holding Cross. She had been given it a few years ago. "We cannot talk here."

"Yes, we can." He did not say it in English, which made the two businessmen look up as they heard the sudden foreign language. But they would have no way of understanding Kurdish, one of the two official languages of Iraq for the last six years.

For a moment Carla did not move and did not speak. Slowly she sat down. "*Tayyib,*" she said in Arabic. "Okay. But speak Arabic, my Kurdish is not good." She grabbed Arif's arm as he went to sit down next to her. "But first you can get me another coffee."

He nodded and went to move off, but she held onto his arm. "And a pastry. The raspberry Danish. You know us Lebanese and our sweet teeth." She smiled without warmth.

As Arif went across to the café, the two businessmen stood up to go, obviously disconcerted by the lapse into the foreign – and to them hostile-sounding – tongue. She ignored them.

Five minutes later Arif returned with two poly-cups and two grease-proof bags. As he laid them on the table, Carla said "*Shou?* What?"

He sighed, sitting down next to her. "I have found out something terrible. Terrible. It is my own fault, I should not have been listening."

"What is it? You have weapons of mass destruction after all?"

"Please."

"*Aasif.* Sorry. But what is wrong with you?"

Leaving the grease-proof bag on the table, Arif leant forward and carefully tore it open to reveal an almond-encrusted *pain aux chocolat*. He touched the top of the cake with his index finger but did not pick it up. He looked over his shoulders, first one way then the other. There were many people about, but perhaps there was safety in numbers. He took a deep breath and said, "Sajida was right."

Grand Central Subway, New York City, USA 18:45

Passing by the shoeshine 'boys' outside Grand Central station, Arif used the subway entrance by the Park Avenue overpass. Earlier he had planned to take a short trip five blocks west to Times Square to check out the action after he had met with Carla, but now he did not feel in the mood so he made his way to the northbound platform. He would catch the express to 86th Street. Then it would be a six-block walk to his apartment on 92nd.

Carla was not happy with him. She had wanted proof of his accusation that Sajida was right – but he had none. How could you prove something like that? He had simply overheard the conversation. There would be nothing written down, no file on a computer somewhere, the knowledge was too sacrosanct, too precious, too unbelievable. Too holy? Only a handful of people alive would know it, those who were in on it, those who were waiting for the right time. It would be knowledge and word-of-mouth only. There would be no tangible record. It was too dangerous.

So, sorry Carla, there was no material proof. And the physical proof was elsewhere. You had asked him to report 'anything and everything' and he had. Job done. What you did with the information was up to you. Arabs should not be spying on Arabs anyway, they should be on the same side, especially when they were surrounded by The Great Satan.

The subway was throbbing with the evening rush hour, the northbound platform crowded with people going home. And it was so damn hot down here, mirroring the sweltering summer weather above. The Blue Jays were playing at The Yankees tonight, so the Line 4 express train would be extra full all the way to 161st Street. The Line 5 would not be much better. Perhaps he should change his plan and catch the Line 6 local?

There was a blast of stale but very welcome air and an anticipatory shuffling and moving forward as the 4 train approached. He would catch this, he decided. It was stifling down here, he needed to get out. He would have to stand but as it was the express it was only two stops.

Someone bumped into his left arm, and at first he thought it was a pathetic attempt at a pickpocketing. But he looked to his left to see a tall, stunning blonde woman smiling at him apologetically, mouthing "Excuse me!" above the din of the arriving train.

"No problem!" he mouthed back smiling and quickly turned as the train doors opened and the crowd moved forward.

On the train he stood shoulder to shoulder, back to back, front to front with his fellow travellers, hemmed in tightly, facing the doors as they closed. He noticed that the woman who had bumped into him had not got on, but was still standing on the platform smiling at him, her head tilted slightly to one side. Her gaze followed him as the train moved off, and it made him frown.

She was beautiful but she had the strangest, most disconcerting eyes. It might be a trick of the light refracted in the train's glass, but they looked like they had no colour. The irises were white, almost glowing, the pupils blacker than black...

Like a houri.

He stiffened, fear shooting through his body as the train re-entered the tunnel and he lost sight of her. *In the name of Allah!* There, Carla, there was your proof!

He thought of the bump into his arm...

Omar Arif was dead before the train reached its next stop at Lexington and 59th. But no one knew it. The body, eyes open but dull, remained held in the upright position by the crush of passengers. Only at 161st Street when the Yankee fans disembarked did the body fall, landing with its head on the platform, feet still in the car. People waited, looking, expecting the idiot to pick himself up. But he did not.

And never would.

Murray Hill, New York City, USA 22:00

Carla Chedid stood naked at the window of her thirtieth floor apartment on East 39th Street and looked north over the lights of Midtown. The room behind her was in darkness so there were no reflections to spoil her view of the Upper East Side way beyond. Nearby she could see the United Nations Building backing onto the East River. She knew that just to the west of it, although it could not be seen from her elevated angle, was United Nations Plaza. At number 866 was The Permanent Mission of Lebanon to the United Nations, where she had been stationed for the last five years.

For five years she had been the 'permanent representative' of the External Security Unit of the Lebanese Department of General Security at the United Nations, unbeknownst to Ambassador Salam or anyone else at the Mission, who thought she was an Assistant Counsellor. In fact she was a Gatherer – of information, facts, ideas, theories, thoughts, anything and everything that may or may not affect the security of Lebanon. And in the intriguing world of Lebanese politics, that meant watching your own kind as well as foreigners.

Five years... and she had not been home. Five years of effective exile. The things she had done for her country – she could write a book. Five years ago she had not been as quick as she could have been, she had been two minutes late in getting to Nejmeh Square in Beirut, one hundred and twenty seconds too late to stop a seismic event in the history of Lebanon. There had been reasons for it, but it was a mistake she would never make again. That was why she had been exiled and given yet another new name. She was too good an operative for the DGS to lose but the name Zahia Zalloum, code-name The Djinn, was now permanently linked to the darkness of 14 February 2005. So she had become Carla Chedid.

She stretched upwards, the muscles of her small, thirty-something body still taut, her gluteals hard. As she brought her arms down, she ran her fingers through her long black hair, massaging her own scalp. Then she leant forward, shaking her hair over her face then flicking it back. In the light from Manhattan outside, she walked away from the window and went over to the dresser, picking up her ornate black and gold hair clip and fastening it in her hair.

She looked at the man on the bed, lying naked and satisfied in the shadows. The man with the long hair now sticking with sweat to the sides of his face, hiding the hole of his missing left ear. In this light she could not see the scars on his body, but she knew where they were, every one of them. She had counted them often. She had licked them often.

"You think it is true?" asked the voice from the bed.

Carla shrugged. "As we both know, strange things happen in the Middle East. For example, who would have guessed the identity of Hariri's killer?"

"But this sounds ridiculous."

"Preposterous, I admit."

"You do not believe in a second coming?"

She smiled. "You being rude?"

"For once, no." He reached out and turned on a bedside light. He raised himself on his elbows, admiring her hairless body.

She came over and sat on the edge of the bed, in turn admiring his hairless body, caressing his right thigh. "Do we have *al-Mahdi*? Or *ad-Dajjal*? Indeed, do we have anybody? It is only hearsay." Her fingers reached his groin and stopped. "But one thing I do know, Marwan." She patted his thigh and stood back up. "The world is not ready for *Yawm al-Qiyamah**. Or Armageddon. This needs to be sorted, if it exists. And stopped. They need to know." She walked over and took her purse off the top of the dresser.

"What are you going to do?" he asked.

She shrugged. "If there is anything to it, it is too dangerous to commit electronically by whatever means, even voice." She rummaged inside the purse and brought out the Holding Cross. For a moment she was distracted, caressing the wood with her fingers, she looked over at the bed and said gently "I always carry you with me."

Then she said, "I am going back."

---

* Judgment Day

PART ONE
الجزء الأول

THE RETURN
عودة

30 June 2010
18 Rajab 1431

Coastal Highway, Lebanon 18:00

The ninety-one kilometre journey from Beirut to Tripoli is nominally timed at two hours. Maybe someone had done it once in that time – or maybe they had just made it up. When your journey includes extricating yourself from the car park at Rafic Hariri International Airport to the south of Beirut, the drive through the eastern periphery of the capital, the volume of traffic on the coastal highway and the crazy drivers, the trip between Lebanon's first and second cities is likely to use up more than three hours of your life.

The woman called Love was tired as she drove her black Jeep Wrangler Ultimate over the Nahr el Jaouz (River el Jaouz) and continued northwards on the highway. The journey from JFK Airport in New York had taken over thirteen hours; firstly American Airlines Flight 44 to Paris and then Middle East Airways Flight 206 to Beirut. Club Class helped, of course, but travelling was simply tiring no matter your seat pitch or how well (or not) you were treated.

She would have liked to have driven with her blonde hair blowing in the wind, but she had had to leave the Jeep's removable hard top on while it was parked for four days at the airport. The windows were down but it was still warm in the car. But she did not sweat. Never had done, never would do.

The traffic on the highway was thinning now she had passed the fishing port of El Batroun so she could increase her speed. Shortly she was passing Chekka, the Mediterranean Sea clearly visible again on her left after the highway's little inland detour.

Soon now she would be home, and she was glad. She had her job and she had done what had to be done.

But she wanted to be with Paradise again.

Tripoli, Lebanon 18:40 – 20:00

Tripoli is the most conservative, the most Middle Eastern, the most Islamic of Lebanon's cities. The Old City is dominated by the Ottoman-restored Castle of Saint Gilles which looks down upon the maze of souks, madrassas, khans and hammams below with the benevolence and protective instincts of a big brother.

Although she was not from these parts, Love felt at home here. She was religious but without favour – she regarded Sunni, Shi'a, Druze, Christianity and all the rest as merely sects of the one true deity, different rooms in the same father's house. The piety of Tripoli calmed and inspired her.

She parked the Jeep in its usual place in the Parking at Al-Nejmeh Square, unloaded her rucksack from the back and walked eastward down Khaled Chehab Street. The evening sun was lowering in the west but it was still bright and hot.

To her right was the Great Mosque with its mix of Western and Islamic architecture and the minaret which so obviously used to be a Christian bell tower during the building's previous incarnation as the twelfth-century Crusader church of St Mary of The Tower. To her left she passed the fourteenth-century madrassas of al-Khayriyat Hassan and al-Nasiriyat. Then she crossed over towards the entrance of Souk al-Sayaghin, the gold market.

The souk was narrow and shaded by a half-covered wooden ceiling. As in any market, there was hustle, there was bustle. Traders stood outside their shops beckoning in passers-by, offering that 'special price'; elsewhere voices seemed to be raised in the most terrible of arguments but in reality it was purchasers and sellers going through the usual haggling.

Instead of going down in to the souk, Love stopped at the entrance by the juice stand on her right. The owner of the stand smiled when he saw her, placed his right hand on his heart and gave a small half-bow. "*Salaam*," he said quietly, reverentially.

Love returned his smile. "*Salaam*. All is well?"

"'*eeh, madame*. It is."

She nodded and walked past him behind the juice stand.

Into the Hammam al-Nouri.

The now abandoned and derelict Hammam al-Nouri bathhouse was built in the fourteenth century. In its day it was the crown-jewel of all the hammams in Tripoli, noted for its smaller than usual dressing room and tepidarium and larger than usual hot water steam hall surrounded by private bathing alcoves. Multi-coloured marble was used on the floors, fountains and basins, and the bright decoration of the walls and ceilings can still be seen even though the place is in disrepair. Looking up from inside, the domes in the roof are perforated with green and blue glass roundels, giving the day-time illusion of a thousand stars in the heavens.

It was quiet inside, dim, but no longer damp as it would have been in the days when it was in use. Love trod softly, respecting the tranquillity of the place. She stopped in the middle of the steam hall and said softly "*Ahlan...?*", her voice magnified and echoed by the domes above.

She heard a noise. A shadowy figure appeared in the dressing room entrance way. Love turned towards the shadow but said nothing more as she placed her rucksack on the floor.

Suddenly the figure moved, running with an alarming speed, grabbing Love before she even had a chance to straighten up. Love felt herself being crushed, hands were in her hair, on her face...

Then lips were on hers, in affection not lust. Her face was covered in kisses.

After a mutual hug which lasted a lifetime, the other figure pulled away and Love looked at the mirror image of herself. Same body, same height, same blonde hair, same face, same white eyes with the so black pupils.

The other one said, "Sister, I have missed you so."

Love reached out and caressed the other face. "And I have missed you, my darling Paradise," she said to her identical twin.

"I have already filled the bath for you," smiled Paradise.

"Thank you, sister, that is much needed."

"And there is spiced lamb to eat. Or are you not hungry?"

"Oh yes, I am. I didn't eat on the planes."

"How did it go?" Paradise bent down, picked up the rucksack and handed it to Love.

"Fine. A successful conversion. Thank you." She took the bag.

"Just the one?"

"Just the one. A fool who was listening when he shouldn't have been. The one who was overheard has been dealt with by the disciples. It was in his favour that he reported the eaves-dropper himself, but now he is on two strikes. If he needs to be converted, they will call us again."

"My turn next time."

"Of course."

"Now you go and bathe, the food will keep until you are ready. You can tell me later how you did it."

They hugged, lingering on the final extra squeeze. "Oh I missed you so," said Love. "It is not right, we should not be apart. We are the same person, after all."

"And I missed you too much. But as we said before, America is hardly ready for one of us let alone two. We'd have been too noticeable."

"Hiding in plain sight?"

"There is that."

"Or we could have put the lenses in so that we did not stand out. We could have even forced ourselves to dress differently."

"Next time, yeh?"

"Next time – Oh! I have something for you." Love put the bag back down on the floor and crouched over it. Unzipping and rummaging, she pulled out a blue crescent-shaped object. "I have one too." With a deft flick of her left wrist the object opened to its proper shape and she handed it over. A New York Yankees baseball cap.

Paradise beamed. "Sister, thank you!" She flipped it onto her head.

Love put hers on. She stood back up, taking her sister's hands. "Now we're two All-American girls!" she laughed.

"Or," chuckled Paradise, "two All-American *houris*."

Love could hear the call to *salat al-Maghrib,* sunset prayer, from the mosques outside as she leant forward in the bath for her sister to reach over and wash her back.

The alcove was illuminated by candles, the flames casting shadows up the walls and into the domes above. There was no electricity in the place, meals were cooked on a portable gas stove in another room. And, of course, the water was cold. But the women had gone through much worse things during their training than not having hot water to bathe in. They had learned to like the effect it had on the skin, that moment when you eased yourself into the water and your whole epidermis corrugated. And it made your hair shiny too.

Love had told Paradise about New York: following the fool from the Mission, seeing him meet his girlfriend in the lobby of the hotel (it looked like he might be finishing with her – well, how right he had been!), the trip into the subway, the syringe under her false nail into his arm, his face at the end as he looked into her eyes from inside the subway car and had realised what had happened. It had been perfect, a sublime conversion.

"You are always so skilled," Paradise scooped water over her sister's back.

"And so are you, my dear."

"When I need to be, yes. But you... you make it an art form."

"The gods like art."

"Oh indeed they do."

Love stood up, the water rolling from her fair skin. Turning round, she held out both her arms and Paradise helped her climb out. As she dried herself on a thick cotton towel, Love asked "So we're happy that The Secret is safe?"

"We have ensured that it is so, as we are charged to do."

"Until *Yawm al-Qiyamah*, then the whole world will know. But should The Secret be moved? We normally do when there has been a breach."

"The thought had occurred to me," Paradise took the towel and began to dry her sister's back. "This was not a serious breach, our action was pre-emptive. The leak plugged before there was any spillage. But the final decision is not ours."

"We must ask Malek."

"Yes, we will visit the treasure of life in the morning."

1 July 2010
19 Rajab 1431

North Lebanon 05:30

They left early, just before the end of *salat al-Fajr*, dawn prayer. The shops in the souk were closed, the juice stand covered over. No one was about. The sun was just pushing in from the east, the night sky retreating rapidly before it. It was going to be another clear, hot day.

At al-Nejmeh Parking they unscrewed the hard top off the Jeep and left it occupying their usual space. It would be safe.

Then they were off, Paradise driving, Love next to her in charge of the backpacks containing water, fruit and chocolate. They were dressed identically in white cotton sleeveless vests, camouflage combat trousers and desert boots. In the back of the car were two khaki cotton shirts which they would put on later in deference to their destination. Each of them had tied their hair back into a simple ponytail. They wore no make-up – beauty never needed it.

They took the highway south-east out of Tripoli to Zgharta then turned due south onto the main road following the Nahr Jouiet. Soon the road began to rise, leaving the river behind, and they were climbing into Mount Lebanon, past olive groves and vineyards, forests of cedar, oak and pine trees, the land becoming more rugged, the vistas more spectacular. They stopped just south of the busy summer resort of Ehden, pulling over into a quiet area for their refreshment and relief.

As they leant against the Jeep, they looked out over the stunning Qadicha valley, the Maronite holy valley, below. The place was tranquil. They could see orchards of apples and mulberries, and farms, green arable land. From way down they could hear the sound of bells from one of the many monasteries and churches below.

While Paradise finished her second peach, Love felt into one of the front pockets of a backpack and brought out two small, flat plastic cases. "Here, we'd best put these in now. We don't want to frighten the holy men." She offered her palm with the two cases in it.

Her sister smiled, taking the case furthest from her. "What's the score?"

"I lead thirty-two to thirty."

Slowly, tentatively, Paradise opened the case. Then she grinned, opening it wide and holding it out. "Green!"

"Thirty-two thirty-one. You're closing." Love opened her own case, raising it up to her face and leaning forward slightly. With great care she put the brown contact lenses into her eyes.

Deir Qozhaya, Lebanon 08:30

They drove down into the valley past the village of Aarbet-Qozhaya, Ehden now well above them. Soon they could see the red roof of their destination: the ancient Monastery of Saint Anthony of Qozhaya.

Qozhaya is a word of Syriac origin, meaning 'the treasure of life'. To the six monks and two hermits who inhabited the vast monastery this meant Jesus Christ, to whom they had dedicated their lives. As well as the fifty-room monastery, there were two caves. One cave was used as a church. It had a man-made facade of pink stone with three arched bell towers, lower arches, windows and a doorway leading into the cave behind.

The other cave was less pious but nevertheless useful: previously it had been used to imprison the insane, in the hope that Saint Anthony would cure them miraculously. The chains used to constrain the inhabitants can still be seen on the walls.

Now with their shirts on and contact lenses in, Paradise and Love drove into the courtyard in front of the monastery. They were well-known here, they did not need an appointment.

They had come to see Brother Malek.

They were shown into their usual small meeting room on the third floor. Brother Malek would be with them shortly, they were informed. Whether the monks that lived here ever wondered why one of the long-stay pilgrims was regularly visited by two young women (and identical young women at that – apart from their eyes: one had green, one had brown) they did not know. There must have been curiosity, but the regular, handsome donation given to the monastery for Malek's board and lodging ensured no questions were voiced openly.

They had brought one of the backpacks in with them, leaving the other under the seat in the Jeep in a forlorn protection against the heat. Thankfully they had eaten their chocolate on route. The bag which Love now placed on the heavy pine table contained fruit, confectionery, fizzy drinks and other items, their usual little gift for the Brother.

They were standing by the window admiring the magnificent view across the valley to the Deir Qannoubine, the Qannoubine Monastery – the seat of the Maronite Patriarchs for four hundred years until 1800 (1215) - when a voice behind them said, *"Al-salaam 'aalaykum."*

The twins turned and said together *"'aalaykum al-salaam,"* both giving a little bow of the head.

They had not heard him enter, they never did. He always moved in silence, like a wraith. He was dressed in a black full-length cloak, a *burnus*, with the hood up. Poking below the hood, his beard was long, wispy and bushy, the natural black pigmentation fighting to an inevitable defeat against the grey of age.

His right hand indicated the bag on the table. "My gift?" His voice was deep.

"As always," said Love.

Malek opened the bag and peered in. He asked, "The situation has been resolved?"

"Yes," nodded Love. "In the manner specified. A permanent conversion."

"How exactly?"

Love held up her left index finger, saying nothing.

Malek nodded. "Then the leak is sealed. Once again, only the trustworthy know The Secret. The disciples."

"And half of those we have already permanently converted, as instructed and as necessary," said Paradise.

"God will be pleased. You have both proved worthy protectors of The Secret. Your commander has proven to be a good friend."

"When will it be time?" asked Love. "When will the world know The Secret?"

Malek looked back into the bag. His hand went in and brought out a box of Al Fakher two-apples flavour *ma'asel*, shisha tobacco.

"There is cherry in there too," said Love.

Malek spoke as if there had been no diversion. "The time is not yet right. We must keep a close eye on events. The Secret will be revealed when God says so. But I think it will not be long now." He picked up the bag, keeping the tobacco in his left hand.

"There is one other thing," said Paradise.

The hood turned towards her.

"We must consider whether The Secret needs to be moved."

"We always move The Secret when it has been compromised," said Love.

Malek remained silent for a while. Then he said, "But you told me you had resolved the situation."

"Yes," nodded Paradise, "but we must not become careless or complacent. It is not for my sister and I to decide – we are merely protectors – but we make the point with recommendation. Moving has served us well in the past."

The hood nodded. "As has your idea of keeping yourselves many miles from that which you are the protectors of." Malek knew that the twins had not yet let him down or failed in their duties. "That is a masterful stroke. If anyone ever finds out you are the protectors - "

"Which they will not," said Paradise.

Malek stopped. A full minute later he went on, "Then they will expect The Secret to be with you, not many miles away. If you are ever compromised that gives me time to ensure The Secret is safe. To alert the disciples." He put his hand into a pocket of his robes and brought out a Samsung mobile phone, holding it up. "However... I take your counsel well. Maybe it is time to move The Secret."

The women were nodding.

"Perhaps," suggested Malek, "to somewhere where the reception is better?"

The women smiled. "I think that is a good course," agreed Paradise. "Your decision is sound, as always." She had learnt in the past that it was best to let Malek believe the ideas came from him.

"Where will we go?"

Love walked back over to the window, admiring the Qadisha Valley for what she now knew would be the last time. "We have been here in Tripoli and The Valley for some time."

"We should move further south," Paradise was still standing by the table.

"We were thinking..." continued Love.

"Maybe Charbel," suggested Paradise.

Deir Qozhaya, Lebanon 10:30

From his small cell-like eyrie in a top far corner of the monastery, Brother Malek watched the two women drive off in their Jeep. They were good, he thought. Very, very good. His own personal *houris*. They were efficient – and lethal. Protectors of The Secret. And they would be of even more use in the future, once The Secret was revealed.

He turned away from the window. They were right, of course. It had always been accepted protocol that a breach, any breach, would necessitate a move. He had been here at Qozhaya for some time now, so that in itself was also reason for a move. Too much familiarity, too much routine, led to complacency.

They were going to try to secure a place for the pilgrim Brother Malek at Deir Mar Maron, the Monastery of Saint Maron and Saint Charbel, in the Jbeil District. That was logical, a Christian pilgrim would be expected to move from one sacred shrine to another. So he would need to prepare The Secret for transportation.

But not before a little indulgence...

Next to his small basic mattress on the floor was a dark blue carrying case, about forty centimetres square with brown reinforcements on each corner and a brown leather handle on the top. He went over and knelt down next to it, unhooking the clasps and opening the lid. Carefully he took out the pieces: the water jar, the body, the plate, the hose, the bowl, gently placing them on the floor. His *argileh*, his shisha pipe...

He already had charcoal and matches. Water he would get from the latrine downstairs. Then he would settle down and enjoy a two-apples smoke.

He assembled the pieces deftly and then sat back on his heels, nodding at the 70 centimetres high *argileh* in admiration. It was certainly a work of art, a one-off piece, a fitting climax to the career of the artist, the sculptor, the genius who had made it. The artisan who had so tragically died on the same day as he had completed it.

The artistry, the filigree, was beautiful and delicate. Stunning yet subtle multi-coloured shapes and patterns adorned the body and the bowl. The bowl was not glass but pure crystal. And the body, the plate and even the tongs were not base metal. They were pure twenty-four carat gold.

It was the most expensive *argileh* in the world.

Two hours later, after a satisfying and thoughtful smoke, Brother Malek used the residual water in the bowl of the *argileh* to wash his hands and face, wetting the floor of his cell as he did so. Packing the pipe away in its box, he pulled his mattress into the centre of the small room, covering the wetness. Standing at the end of the mattress with his hands raised, he said *"Allahu Akbar."* Then he bowed and began to recite *"Subhana rabbiyal adheem..."*. God is most great. Glory be to my Lord Almighty...

Kneeling on the mattress, the Christian Brother Malek continued with the Muslim *Dhuhr* prayer.

3 July 2010
21 Rajab 1431

Ras en Nabaa, Beirut 21:00

Captain Maroun Khoury of the Lebanese Department of General Security was a slim, fit-looking man whose looks belied the fact that he was in his fifties. Bald on top, he kept his hair at the back and sides cropped short, not quite shaved, blending in with the trim greying beard on his face. He was the Chief of the External Security Unit of the DGS, a unit whose existence was unknown even to senior members of the Lebanese parliament. After all, who would believe that Lebanon had, or needed, its own equivalent of the CIA or the SIS-MI6? He reported to no one except the Director General of General Security, currently Major General Wafic Jezzini.

Khoury's team was divided into sub-units of Gatherers, Listeners and Watchers. They gathered, listened and watched anything outside, or originating outside, Lebanon's borders that might affect the security of the country. A very wide brief, even for a country as small as Liban.

It had been a busy day as usual. The United Nations Special Tribunal for Lebanon – which was investigating the 2005 assassination of former Prime Minister Rafic Hariri – was due to report in the autumn and issue indictments, and Khoury's team were the only people in Lebanon who had seen the first draft (obtained by clandestine means, of course). There were powerful groups inside and outside the country that would not like what the Tribunal had to say. Also it was the fourth anniversary of the 2006 'summer war' between Israel and Hizbullah, and the usual annual threats of a repeat of the bombing of Lebanon were being issued. Khoury wondered wryly how anybody could get to sleep in Lebanon during the summer with the constant noise of sabre-rattling!

But one of the privileges of rank was that he could go home each night, unlike some of his field staff who could sometimes be away on assignment for months, if not years. Khoury lived in Ashrafieh, just a kilometre away from the DGS building. He longed to make the healthy walk across the park, up past the Lycée Franco-Libanais, across Elias Sarkis Avenue then through to his apartment just south of Abdul Wahab el Inglizi Street, but protocol forbade it. He had to go by car.

To him this was nonsense. He acknowledged his rank and the sensitivity of his position, but surely it was easier to put a bomb under a car than under a person? And he was skilled in self-protection and evasion techniques to thwart any threat to his person in the street. And anyway, few knew that his unit even existed.

It was an argument he had had with successive Directors General, but none of them would listen. The only concession he had been granted was that he could drive himself instead of being assigned an official driver and bodyguard.

So at 21:00 that Friday evening, Maroun Khoury drove his Mercedes M-Class SUV out through the entrance of the DGS building and headed home.

Ashrafieh, Beirut 22:00 – 23:59

At the last minute, Khoury decided to pop up to Spinney's in Mar Mitr for some weekend shopping, so it was another hour before he arrived back at the Ottoman-era building where he lived. The building and the tree-lined street were in darkness, which meant just one thing – another Beirut power cut!

Shopping bags in hand, he began to climb to his apartment on the fifth floor, one from the top, using his mobile phone to light his way. If he couldn't get fit by walking to and from work, Beirut's frequent power failures and the stairs would ensure he did not turn to flab!

The gated, see-through elevator in the middle of the winding staircase was stopped between the second and third floors. As he went past, he shone his phone inside to confirm no one was trapped – and it was also a handy excuse just to take a little rest.

He was breathing heavily, but not gasping, by the time he reached the fifth floor. Putting down his shopping as he stood outside the ornate wooden door of his apartment, he felt in his pocket for his keys. He sniffed. The cleaners must have washed the stairwell today, he could smell jasmine.

He was just offering the key to the lock, holding the phone in his left hand, when a voice from above said *"Massah el-khair,* Moro."

He froze, key in mid air, controlling his breathing, aware of his gun in the well of his left armpit under his jacket. For a moment he did nothing. Then he said to the door "Well, well..."

Slowly he turned, the light from his phone moving at the same speed as his gaze, across the landing, up the stairs to his right.

The first thing that came into view at the top of the stairs was a pair of pink trainers. Then knee-ripped blue jeans. The light progressed upwards over a plain pink T shirt, then shone on the long black hair with the ornate hair clip and then the smiling olive face.

Khoury relaxed. "If I'd known you were coming - "

"You'd have baked a cake?"

"I'd have met you at the airport." He turned the key in the lock and opened his door.

Slowly she began to walk down the stairs. "And spoil the element of surprise?"

He smiled. "You always were one for the dramatic. Here, come in." He bent down and picked up his shopping bags.

She reached him as he straightened and planted a kiss firmly on his lips.

The lights came on like fireworks exploding.

During all the years she had worked for him she had never been into his apartment, even during the brief but intense two-month period when they had been lovers. She was taken aback by how modern it was, totally in contrast to the antiquity of the building. She sat down on the wide cream leather couch. "Nice place."

"*Merci ktir.*" Without even asking, the first thing Khoury did was to prepare and activate the filter coffee machine. Only then did he begin to unpack his shopping. "You have eaten?"

"No."

"I have falafel, hummus, tabbouleh... All Spinney's best, except the tabbouleh which was from Monoprix yesterday."

"You are kind, thank you."

Khoury paused with his head inside one of the open-plan kitchen cupboards. He said, "I'm surprised they let you in the country. There are still those who would like to find out exactly what Zahia Zalloum knows about Hariri's killing."

"Zahia Zalloum is not here. Carla Chedid is. Zahia is missing during operations, has been for five years. Carla's papers are not false, I would not be flagged up at Immigration."

"True."

Khoury had finished unpacking and was busying himself with plates and food. Carla stood up and went over to the gurgling coffee machine. She found cups in the second cupboard she opened.

"Why are you here, ZiZi?" Khoury was pulling leaves from a romaine lettuce.

"CiCi."

"What?"

"Carla Chedid. CiCi."

"To me you will always be - "

"What will I always be, Moro?" She was up close to him, two cups of coffee in her hands. He could smell her perfume, mingled with her musk from the flight.

Putting the lettuce onto a plate, he picked up some tomatoes on the vine. He wanted to say she would always be a temptation, the best and most skilful lover he had ever had, but instead he said "My most skilled field operative."

"Would you like me to wash your tomatoes?" she asked innocently. She placed the coffees on the work surface, reached out and pulled two fruits off of the vine.

Khoury grinned, unable to come back with a witty retort – but oh how he remembered her washing techniques! She could do it with one hand. As she turned on the tap and ran the fruit under the water (indeed with one hand), he said "Tell me."

She shook the fruit, leant over him and placed them on top of the lettuce. "It's probably nothing and I am being over-cautious. But I didn't want to put it in writing or tell you over the phone, just in case The Listeners have listeners. It could be delicate. Can I wash your *khiyar*?" She stretched across.

"I'll wash my own cucumbers, *merci*." Khoury snatched the two small cucumbers out of her hand. "Why don't you - "

"Bathe," she said. "May I bathe? It was a long journey and I came straight here after dropping my bags at the hotel."

Their eyes met. Khoury could have sworn the cucumber in his right hand grew a little bit. "Of course," he smiled. "Sorry. I did not think. It is through there, down the hall. Next to the bedroom. I'll get you some towels - "

"No, no," her hand touched his arm. "Just tell me where they are, I'll find them. We'll talk over dinner. As I say, it might not be important or even real."

"Okay, as you wish," said Khoury, wondering whether he should offer to wash her back.

Or other parts.

"One of my UN contacts," Carla crunched down on a leaf of lettuce with tabbouleh balanced on top. "A gay Iraqi."

"Naughty boy." Khoury scooped hummus onto a piece of *khobz*, flat bread, and popped it into his mouth.

"He has never been very productive. But he overheard something at his Mission. He was very keen to report it to me."

"Keen?"

"As in keen to keep me happy so that I did not send his superiors certain, er, recreational photos I have of him."

"Zi – CiCi you are outrageous."

"I had a good teacher, Moro. Anyway, from what he'd overheard he claimed that Sajida was right."

Khoury stopped eating, frowning. "Sajida? Who, what or where is Sajida?"

Carla explained it to him.

Khoury nodded. "Oh Sajida, of course." He laughed, sipping from his glass of *arak*. "The rumour. The Great Secret. The Second Coming. The Messiah. Well, we are two thousand years on from the last one! *al-Mahdi*. Nobody believed Sajida, of course."

"Perhaps they did not want to believe."

"There was no proof."

"There still isn't. But you understand why I could not tell you except in person."

He nodded. "But what's it to do with us, with Lebanon?"

She sat back, wiping her mouth on a paper napkin. "Telling you this now makes me feel like it is all indeed stupid nonsense. Non-believers dispute that there was ever a Messiah in the first place, let alone a Second Coming." She sighed. "Was I foolish to return?"

He reached out and touched her hand. She did not pull away. "No, no you did right. And it is good to see you again after all these years."

"And you too."

"But what has it got to do with Lebanon?" he repeated.

She leant back in her chair, her hand naturally moving away from his. "Apparently The Great Secret is being kept here in Liban."

"Here?"

"On the basis that it would be the last place the searchers would look. Saudi definitely. Syria maybe. But little old Liban? Who would think it?"

"So we are near *Yawm al-Qiyamah*?"

"Who knows?"

"Can't fight Judgment Day."

"Who says?"

Khoury laughed out loud. "Shall we sit more comfortably?" He nodded over into the living area. "I have baklava if you would like some."

"My teeth are always sweet."

Five minutes later he came to join her on the couch with more coffee and a box of baklava. He sat close but not too close. "Where are you staying?" he asked.

"The Hotel Albergo."

"Just round the corner? Very nice. But I hope my departmental budget can take it! I have an idea. Stay here. No, no - " he held up his hands. "No hidden agenda, I promise. I have spare rooms, it makes sense. And this place is secure, nobody else knows you're back and we can keep it that way."

She was smiling, shaking her head. "You don't have to sell it, Moro. Or add riders. I'll stay here tonight and tomorrow we can decide what to do, if anything."

She popped a baklava into her mouth and for the first time in his life Maroun Khoury wished he was wrapped in layers of filo pastry and covered in a sugar sauce...

Beirut 23:59

In her assumption that The Listeners have listeners, Carla was right. In the complex, sectarian-driven world of Lebanese politics and government, distrust and intrigue between the factions is mandatory not optional. The Listeners have listeners, The Watchers have watchers. Spies spy on spies, narks nark on narks. It is a given. Known and accepted.

As the Chief of the External Security Unit, Maroun Khoury was not blind to the obvious. At least once a week he swept his apartment for hidden devices, using the officially-issued Super Sweep 2000 professional bug finder.

Listening devices can be hidden in anything: power sockets, lights, telephones, picture frames, pens, calculators, absolutely anything – even walls. A major benefit of the Super Sweep 2000 is that it will not only sweep for listening devices but, if left in a room, it will continuously monitor, detecting any devices that may be brought into the room even before they are hidden. So with his weekly sweep and the machine's constant monitoring, Khoury was happy that his apartment was clean.

But he was wrong.

It was a question that had been asked through the ages: who guards the guards? The Super Sweep could detect any listening device, concealed or brought into the room. But it could not detect itself and the special adaptation that had been made to it prior to issue: the tiny listening device concealed deep within it.

And so at 23:59 that night, someone listened and transcribed and then picked up the telephone...

4 July 2010
22 Rajab 1431

Deir Qozhaya, Lebanon 09:00

The Jeep Wrangler Ultimate, with the hard top on, was waiting in the courtyard when Brother Malek and one of the monks came out of the monastery. Although it was already thirty degrees, even up here in the valley in the mountains, Malek was wearing the *burnus* with hood up. He said a few words to the monk, embraced him, and then walked towards the Jeep. He carried a small backpack and the small dark blue *argileh* case.

Love was waiting by the open back door of the vehicle, and Malek experienced just a little shock when he looked into her eyes. It had been a long time since he had seen either of the *houri* without their lenses in.

Silently he climbed into the Jeep, throwing his bag onto the seat next to him and placing the *argileh* case gently next to it.

Love made sure the hem of Malek's *burnus* was tucked in, slammed the door and climbed into the front next to her sister. The car moved off.

"Everything is arranged?" Malek threw back the hood and scratched his head, shaking his unruly bush of hair. He was grateful that the air conditioning was on.

"Yes," Love half-turned in her seat. "They are expecting the pilgrim Brother Malek to arrive today, scheduled to be staying for at least three months."

"And The Secret will be safe there?"

Paradise looked at him from the rear-view mirror. "We are satisfied."

Malek looked back. After a moment he said, "Then I am too."

"We have made financial arrangements," continued Love. "A donation. But they have asked if you would like to work as well while you are there."

"Work?"

"The Monastery has much land. They grow fruit and vegetables and produce wine and jams, to sell locally and to the visitors. They ask all lodgers to help out."

Malek sniffed. "I may be too busy praying."

"As you wish," Love turned back.

"But then again, I would wish to fit in. Maybe I can do a little work somewhere quiet and unobtrusive. I don't wish to be involved with the hoards of pilgrims and tourists. Couldn't I stay in the hermitage? That would be an ideal place for The Secret."

"It has not been used as a hermitage for fifty years," Paradise was concentrating on the less than perfect road leading back up to Ehden. "It is now a shrine to Saint Charbel."

Malek nodded. After a moment, he said "Lebanon's patron saint by acclamation. I wonder what Saint Maron thinks about that, it is his monastery after all."

"I would think the saints are above petty human-style squabbles," said Love.

"Indeed..." Malek looked out the window at the valley disappearing below. "Where will you be?"

"We will be down in Jbeil," answered Paradise.

"Old Byblos! We are going where the crowds are now."

"It is better than being alone," explained Love. "Too conspicuous."

"But in Jbeil you are within easy reach of me at the monastery in Annaya," nodded Malek, understanding. "Good. Do you have anything for me?"

Love leant forward and rummaged in the bag between her legs. She passed a silver tube over her shoulder.

Malek took the cap off the end and slid the *Romeo & Julietta Churchill* cigar into his palm. He looked up to see Love dangling a lighter over her shoulder, which he accepted. "Should I open a window?"

"Try it," said Paradise. "But you may get too hot. Do not worry, the smoke does not affect us."

Malek lit up carefully, starting with quick, sharp puffs and then a long sensuous draw. Reluctantly he had to exhale. "I was contacted by the disciples," he announced.

Love turned in her seat, her white and black eyes intense. Paradise's identical eyes looked at him via the mirror.

Malek said, "I think more conversions might be necessary."

Ashrafieh, Beirut 19:00

As it was a Sunday, Maroun Khoury allowed himself the luxury of leaving the office earlier than he normally would. He did, after all, have an incentive back in his apartment.

Much to his disappointment, CiCi had slept in one of his spare bedrooms last night. It was expected but, like any man, he lived in hope. Their time had passed, but the passion, the lust, the abandon of their two-month affair never left his mind even though it was many years ago now. He wondered if he would ever see her belly-dance again? Well, she was staying in his apartment, so it would be now or never.

They had discussed the matter of The Second Coming over their breakfast croissants and *labneh*, Khoury being a little distracted by the fact that Carla wore her pink T-shirt – and nothing else, as a surreptitious glance confirmed.

The Sajida statement and the inferred prophesy had surfaced now and again over the years, but nothing had ever come of it, and Khoury had thought that it had at last been consigned to history, filed under Lies and Misdirection. He did not believe it, never had.

It was not that he was non-religious – he was as good a Maronite as the next man – but religion had nothing to do with this. If Sajida was right all along then the world was looking at *ad-Dajjal* not *al-Mahdi*.

As discussed with Carla, he had set The Listeners and The Watchers in motion, and he had contacted the latest unit of the DGS, The Readers. This unit was not under his command (yet) but they would be looking at all e-mail and text activity flowing into and out of Lebanon and looking for trigger words and phrases.

Carla had agreed that she would not be taking an active role in the investigation. There were still too many people in Lebanon and adjacent countries who would very much like a conversation with her about her knowledge of the Hariri assassination five years ago. She would be returning to New York tomorrow morning.

Which meant, reflected Khoury sadly, that he had one last night with her. He must make the most of it.

"CiCi? Carla?"

The apartment was silent and still.

"ZiZi? Zahia?"

Nothing. He felt the reassuring bump under his left arm but he did not draw his gun. She had not said she was going out. But then again she had not said she was staying in. But where did she have to go to? He probably knew better than she did the identities and the quantity of people who wanted to talk to her, and that worried him – until he saw the note on the coffee table.

> *Moro,*
> *Have gone to pick up my*
> *stuff from the hotel.*
> *C xxx*

What an over-reactive idiot he was, he chided himself. And he liked the last three letters of her note. Did it bode well for the coming night?

He would take her out to dinner – his favourite local restaurant, which he considered one of the best in Beirut, was Abd el Wahab up on the same street as her hotel. Then he would suggest an early night, as she had an early flight tomorrow.

And who knows? Maybe she would dance for him. For old times' sake...?

There was a knock on the door. Good, she was back.

He went across and opened the door, smiling.

And then stood back, his eyes wide...

Ain el-Mreisseh, Beirut 19:15

The memorial statue to Rafic Hariri is larger than life.

The stunningly accurate suited figure of Lebanon's assassinated former Prime Minister stands with hands in pockets in a special garden overlooking the site of his murder outside the St George Hotel, his wise-owl face seeming to say "I knew it would happen."

The small woman in a headscarf and dark glasses had been there for five minutes. She was not the only one pausing to reflect, to pay respect, but she knew she should not linger. For her, it could be dangerous.

The taxi that had brought her from the Hotel Albergo was still waiting. With a nod, she climbed back in. "*Yalla*. Back to Ashrafieh Street, *s'il vous plait*."

Ashrafieh, Beirut 20:00

Carla got out of the taxi two streets away from Khoury's apartment. Old habits never die, they just harden. She enjoyed the feeling of the Mediterranean sun on the left side of her face as she walked northwards, wondering when, if ever, she would be back in her homeland again. She loved this Land of The Cedars, but there were people in it who did not love her. So tomorrow she would return to her exile. But tonight she would enjoy her last evening, she would take Moro out for dinner and then suggest an early night. She had already checked in online for the first leg of the journey to Paris, so the rush in the morning would be reduced. Who knew? They might even get some sleep.

Then again, they might not.

She skipped lightly up the stairs to the fifth floor, her thirty-something legs firm and untiring. She had a spare key that she had found concealed in a lampshade in the hallway (old habits never die...). He might not be back yet, in which case she would destroy the note she had left for him and then get herself ready for the evening.

She went into the apartment and immediately knew something was wrong. It was still. Too still. And there was a smell.

Of body, of faeces... of death.

Her left hand went to her hair and pulled out the hair clip, in one smooth motion pushing the metal clasp back so that the needle underneath was exposed. The micro-syringe was not loaded but she could easily kill someone with the needle alone.

"Maroun? Moro?" she called quietly, trying to keep her voice normal in case she had got this all wrong. Which she knew she hadn't.

There was no reply. It was quiet. So, so quiet. Keeping her back to the wall, she moved swiftly over to the window, glancing out at the small Juliet balcony. As she turned back she saw his feet sticking out from behind the couch. *Oh God, Moro.*

But she did not rush over. His assailant might still be here, and she would make the perfect target bending over him.

Carefully, her movements as silent as a djinn, she explored the apartment: the kitchen, the bathroom, his bedroom (she noticed there was an open bottle of Ksara red wine on his bedside table), her bedroom, the third bedroom. In cupboards, under beds, behind furniture.

She was alone.

Grim-faced, she went back into the lounge, quickly kneeling by the side of Maroun. He looked up at her, smiling. But she knew he could not see. And the ligature so tight around his neck that in some places it had broken the skin and sunk inside him, told her that the smile was a rictus grin.

Captain Maroun Khoury, Chief of the External Security Unit of the Lebanese Department of General Security, was dead. Slaughtered like an animal. His hands were at his sides but his fingers were bent like claws, a reaction to his final excruciating moments. On his shirted chest was a sheet of paper.

A single tear rolled out of Carla's left eye. Was this to do with her? Had she returned to Lebanon and brought death in her wake? In his position, Maroun would have lots of enemies, lots of people who wanted him dead, both foreign foes and, sadly, internal foes. Anybody could have done this.

But she knew she was kidding herself.

She reached out and lifted the piece of paper off his chest. She already knew what it was.

She was looking at her online check-in boarding pass for her flight tomorrow. It was a message to her.

She stayed kneeling on the floor next to the body for ten minutes, just in case his soul had yet to leave. Then she sat back on her heels, angry, sad but resilient. She had shed her tear for Maroun. Now she needed to dust the place and then leave and leave quick.

But one thing was for certain.

She would now be staying on in Lebanon.

PART TWO
الجزء الثاني

THE DISCOVERY
اكتشاف

5 July 2010
23 Rajab 1431

Jbeil, Lebanon 09:00

For the oldest continuously inhabited city in the world, Jbeil has some surprisingly modern suburbs, commercial districts of glass-fronted office buildings in which twenty-first century life continues apace. But this evidence of the latest inhabitants of the city is ignored by the thousands of tourists who come each year to see the old town, the Byblos of history, with its fishing port and sheltered old harbour, stone buildings with red-tiled roofs, the many Roman and pre-Roman ruins, the Crusader castle, the church of Saint John the Baptist with its Byzantine origins, and the souks.

Dating from the Ottoman era, the souks are a maze of intersecting alleyways, sometimes no more than two metres wide, with old stone buildings and covered arcades. Nowadays the Byblos souks are mostly geared towards their tourist visitors, with souvenir shops, modern boutiques, cafés and restaurants, but in some parts traditional trade still exists: a baker, a spice emporium, a gold merchant, a bookshop.

And, in the souk furthest away from the modern travellers, up near the Roman road and backing onto the cemetery, a *Muhaqqiq Khass* – a Private Investigator.

Abu Yussuf was originally from Palestine, but with his medium complexion, medium height, medium weight and medium age, thinning dark hair and neatly trimmed moustache, he could pass as a native of any country in the Levant. His non-descript appearance served him well in his current profession.

He was sitting behind his desk observing the sobbing, grim-faced woman sitting opposite. "Madame Gourhant, I am a busy man," he lied. He was anxious to get back to his game of solitaire, and he cast a glance at the pile of playing cards he had hastily scooped into his drawer. Okay, the woman could represent some well-needed money – especially if he stretched the job out and asked for daily retainers – but it was summer, it was hot and, really, could he be bothered?

The small, ineffective fan in the corner of the room clanked from side to side. What little coolness it produced did nothing for the humans but it seemed to provide a welcome updraft for the flies. There were at least three gliding about the room.

"He has done it before," sniffed Madame Gourhant, gathering herself together after a five minute weeping indulgence. "But back then I was young and things were different in Liban. We had our place and we did what we were told. Now we are liberated and we have rights."

By 'we' Abu Yussuf presumed she meant woman-kind. If so, perhaps not as many rights as you imagine, he thought. But he kept his reflections to himself. "And what would you like me to do?" he asked.

With a mighty sniff, Madame Gourhant pulled herself up from her slouch, tears ceasing. "I want you to find evidence. Evidence that I can use in a divorce."

"You do not have any evidence already, to support your allegations?"

"I have the evidence of a wife's feelings, her intuition. But it is not evidence that will stand up in a divorce hearing."

"No, that is correct. You know that divorce in Lebanon is... complex, shall we say? Were you married here before a religious court? Or were you married abroad?"

"I was married here. In church."

"You are a Maronite?"

"Yes."

"In which case, there is no concept of divorce, as you must know. You will be petitioning to have the marriage annulled. How long have you been married?"

"Thirty years."

Abu Yussuf's eyebrows rose. Then you were on a hiding to nothing, dear lady. Nullity meant proving vices that existed at the time of the marriage. "May I ask, madame, how old you are?"

She did not bridle at the question. "I am fifty-two."

"And your husband?"

"Eighty-two."

His only reaction was a slight cough, but he could feel his cheeks rising in mirth. Quickly, he pulled a cigarette from the packet on the desk and busied himself lighting up. He turned the packet to face the lady, eyebrows raised. She shook her head.

This could be the perfect summer job for him, he thought. Would a man of eighty-two really be committing adultery? Technically it was possible, physically also to a lesser extent. But there was great truth in the saying that when you reached a certain age you'd rather have a cup of tea than be bothered with the effort of having sex!

So, the lady wanted evidence her husband was sipping from another cup. If he was, Abu Yussuf would prove it. But whether the lady would be given the evidence was another matter. It would be useless to her without the historical evidence also. It might be more useful if he sold it to the husband, turn a double profit.

He pretended to have given it much thought, eventually nodding."It is something I could take on. I charge two hundred and fifty thousand pounds a day, plus the same amount on hand-over of the evidence."

"What is that in dollars?"

Abu Yussuf took his new pirated Apple iPhone from beneath the playing cards in the drawer, found the calculator application after three attempts and tapped in some figures. He announced "One hundred and sixty-six dollars."

Madame Gourhant nodded. "That is acceptable."

"I do, of course, have other cases. Naturally I will charge you only for days worked." Both lies were said with a straight face.

"Of course. You would like a payment in advance?"

"Two days, if you would be so kind madame. And do you have a photograph? Of your husband?"

"I do." She rummaged in her bag and passed over a folded A4 sheet of paper with the tips of her fingers, as if she was pleased to get rid of it.

As she was counting out cash onto the desk, Abu Yussuf opened the paper and smiled at the printed photograph of a fat, bald, lugubrious old man. Eighty-two? He looked ninety-two! Was he worn out by the copious amounts of illicit sex? Or simply by being married for thirty years to this *sahira*?

This, thought Abu Yussuf, *muhaqqiq khass extraordinaire*, was going to be easy.

Ashrafieh, Beirut 09:30 – 12:30

Carla sat on the edge of the bed in her opulent room on the fourth floor of the Hotel Albergo gently rubbing her temples with her fingertips.

She had not slept well, but was it any wonder? Her erstwhile lover, her friend, her boss was dead. Murdered. And she could not report it. She was *persona non grata* in Lebanon, in fact she was probably *persona* on several hit lists, and so her return, even under a different name, must be kept *sub rosa*. Maroun would have to wait for his body to be found by someone else.

That was bad for the body and its potential decomposition, but good for her. She could start investigating a murder which no one knew had happened yet. No one except the murderer, of course.

Was it anything to do with her? No, no one knew she was in the country. Mortal threat was part of the job description of the Chief of the External Security Unit. It might be connected to a case the unit was involved in, or a past case, or someone with a vendetta against the ESU or even against

Maroun personally (Lebanese memories have no time constraint). Or perhaps one of the factions had decided, simply, that the ESU needed a new Chief. Murder was the weapon of expediency in the world of 'intelligence'.

But the manner of the murder was unusual. Car bombing was the preferred and accepted method of removal, or shooting if necessary. Garrotting to the point of near decapitation was unusually brutal. Indicating, perhaps, a personal nature to the crime.

For the thousandth time she wondered if she was doing the right thing. Should she just go, flee back to her exile in New York, pretend to be as surprised as anybody at the eventual announcement of a new ESU Chief? (The announcement, when it came, would not give any explanations as to why, it would just say that Captain Walid Ibrahim or whoever was assuming the duties of Unit Chief from that day. Maroun would not be mentioned. No one ever received any thanks for a job well done – even if they had been murdered in the line of duty.)

She looked at her watch. She was far too late to get her Middle East Airlines 10:25 to New York via Paris now. She could always rebook, of course, the next flight was at two in the morning – but who was she kidding? She owed it to Moro to find out why he had been killed.

Subconsciously her hand went up to her hairclip.

And she owed it to him to exact revenge.

But she would need help. To whom could she turn without endangering herself?

Her thoughts were interrupted by a knock on the door and the announcement "Housekeeping."

She went over and looked through the security peephole. The maid was there, pale blue uniform with white hat and pinafore, with her trolley of towels and maid-paraphernalia behind her.

"*Un moment, s'il vous plait!*" called Carla. This was perfect timing, she needed to get out of this room despite the opulence of its oriental rugs, inlaid wooden furniture and crystal chandelier. She would go to the rooftop pool, relax in the sun, maybe have a swim (did they rent costumes? If not, she would send out for one). And she would think.

Grabbing her key card, she threw her Guess handbag onto her shoulder. "*Bonjour,*" she said as she opened the door.

"*Bonjour, madame,*" greeted the maid. She was holding an armful of clean towels.

"It's all yours."

"*Merci.*" The maid stepped back to let Carla leave and then went inside, leaving the room door open.

Carla walked down the thickly-carpeted corridor towards the lift, still thinking about the murder of Maroun Khoury and what she was going to do now.

Where did she even begin?

Carla enjoyed her morning on the roof, sometimes swimming, sometimes just floating in the pool, sometimes sitting on a lounger in the sun and enjoying the views northward over east Beirut to the shimmering Mediterranean beyond.

The swimsuit that had been purchased for her from a nearby boutique suited her perfectly, a one-piece costume, black with a gold pattern and mesh sides, complementing her long black hair and tanned olive body.

At midday she slipped on a white cotton robe (compliments of the hotel) and declined the offer to eat at the poolside. She was not hungry and she needed to begin her investigations while – and she grimaced as she had the thought – the body was still warm.

She had thought all morning about who could help her. There was one person, just one person out of the two million plus in Beirut, who might be able to. If he was willing.

Down on the fourth floor, she padded along to her room, bipped her key card and went in, kicking the door closed behind her. She had already extended her stay by one night so she had no need to worry about checking-out times –

Her head was wrenched backwards as a rope was whipped around her neck.

Instinctively Carla's hands went up, grabbing the ligature, trying to get her fingers under it. She felt one of her false nails ping off. The rope was was tight, so, so tight.

The person behind crossed their arms and pulled.

Carla's mouth opened but no air could come out. Or go in. She was being shaken from side to side like a rag doll.

Giving up on the rope, she reached up and behind, grabbing hair, pulling. Pulling, pulling, pulling. She was winding the hair round and round in her hands as she pulled. But the pressure on her neck increased. Popping sounds started in her ears.

Then she let her legs go from beneath her, dropping to the floor on her rear, pulling the assailant down with her by the hair so that she would not simply drop and hang herself.

The attacker's chin banged painfully on the top of Carla's head, but she heard the hollow clunk as lower teeth bashed into top teeth. There was a grunt from above. The rope loosened. Quickly Carla rolled to the left, grabbing the now uncrossed hands which were still holding the rope but were now in front of her. Mouth open, gasping for air, she pulled the assailant off balance, onto one knee. Let's get a look at you...

She was staring into the face of the maid.

The maid's hat had been knocked off and long blonde hair cascaded down over her face. Blood was trickling from her mouth. Behind the hair, glowing white eyes stared at Carla, sending a shiver through her body. A *houri*?

Carla yanked at the rope. The maid yanked back. For a few seconds they went back and forth. Then unexpectedly the maid shoved Carla backwards. Carla staggered for a few steps and then fell over, back onto her backside. But the shove had given her distance. As the maid stood up, ready to come forward, Carla reached up and pulled out the clip from her hair, flicking it open, exposing the needle. "Okay *habibi*, you want some?" she panted, grinning. Her robe had fallen open to reveal the swimsuit underneath.

The maid stopped, breathing heavily, nostrils flared, the bizarre eyes staring unblinkingly, the bloody mouth expressionless. The rope dangled from her right hand.

"Who are you?" Carla had the needle protruding between the index and second fingers of her left hand. Tentatively she moved forward, giving little threatening thrusts. "What do you want?"

The maid backed away, looking at her curiously, her head slightly tilted to one side. "Your eyes," she said. "Are you one of us?"

Carla frowned. "My eyes are not like yours."

"But they are black. They are beautiful. Opposite."

The maid reached the door, feeling behind for the handle. She said, "You will be converted. *al-Mahdi* wants your soul."

"*What?* What are you talking about?"

"You will not stop The Second Coming." The maid pulled down on the handle.

"Oh, I won't won't I?"

"*Allahu Akbar.*" In a flash the door was open and she was gone.

Carla dashed over, the needle still held out in front of her. She looked left then right along the small corridor. No one.

She ran to the lift and stairwell, looking over the stairs, listening for footfall.

Nothing.

For a minute she stayed there, listening, aware. A couple came out of a room further down. Quickly she closed the robe, exchanging nods with the couple as she went back to her room. She locked and chained the door, leaning against it, breathing heavily.

She flexed her jaw, rubbing the joint below each ear with her right hand and simultaneously reforming the hair clip with her left. Tentatively she ran her fingers over her neck. She could feel the welt.

Was this what had happened to Moro? If so then she knew she was completely responsible for his death. They had tried to get her too.

In the name of God.

She went over and knelt down by the side of the bed, like a child about to pray. Then, not for the first time in Beirut, the woman previously known as Zahia Zalloum, and sometimes as The Djinn, began to cry.

Jbeil, Lebanon 16:00

The slap hurt Paradise's face like the simultaneous sting of a hundred bees. The force of the blow knocked her head five centimetres to the side but she stood her ground, accepting her punishment.

"You stupid bitch," said Love, anger in her eyes. "We do not fail in conversions, do you hear me? Never!"

She raised her hand again and Paradise screwed up her eyes but did not move away. They were in their new accommodation, a disused and boarded up shop behind the old Mayadoun Bookshop on Rue St John just inside the northern medieval ramparts of the old town.

"I... I am sorry, sister," Paradise lowered her head in shame. "I did not expect her to have such skills of resistance. And you should have seen her eyes. They were so, so black. But I have no excuse. Please punish me more."

"Oh no," Love shook her head, putting her fingers under her sister's chin and lifting her head back up. "You would like that too much. If the controller finds out you have failed, we will be recalled."

"But our job here is not done."

"We can be replaced. There are others."

"What about Malek?" sniffed Paradise.

"He must not find out, never. Otherwise we will be done for."

"But it is not your fault, I am the one who failed."

"We are the same person. Two halves of one whole. What is visited upon one is also visited upon the other."

Suddenly Love whipped her hand back sharply across her sister's face, again knocking her head to the side. This time Paradise staggered one step backwards, reaching out and grabbing Love's arms to steady herself. She looked across into eyes as white as hers. "Do it again," she whispered. "I am not sufficiently chastised."

"No. My refusal is your punishment."

Disappointed, Paradise lowered her eyes. "Yes *uhktee*."

"We are agreed?" asked Love. "We say nothing about this?"

"Yes *uhktee*. But what about the woman?"

"We will revisit her. She sounds intriguing. The eyes of a *djinni*. She will be a good conversion."

Paradise smiled. "That is good. That is right."

The hardness left Love as she reached out and caressed her sister's chin. "I have started your lip bleeding again."

"It is my punishment. I deserve to bleed."

"No," said Love. "No, you don't. I will look after you as you always look after me. Here, let me wipe it."

She pulled Paradise's face towards her, leant forward and with soft laps of her tongue began to lick the blood from her sister's lip.

6 July 2010
24 Rajab 1431

Jonblat, Beirut 09:00

Captain Jihad Merhi of the Lebanese Internal Security Force was pissed off. A state, he reflected, that he seemed to be in permanently nowadays.

Today was the funeral of Grand Ayatollah Mohammed Hussein Fadlallah[*], who had died on Sunday, and dignitaries from around the Middle East were attending. Such was the great man's standing that a day of national mourning had been declared in Lebanon, which meant that banks and public offices were closed. But as the ISF was not a public office in that sense, Merhi was not only at work but also his unit was expected to provide 'discreet security' at the internment at the Al-Hassanein Mosque in the suburb of Haret Hureik later (non-discreet security would be provided by other entities).

After years of staff cuts, Merhi really did not have the manpower to provide a 'for appearance's sake' presence. His officers could be better used assisting with the enquiries into the clashes between UNIFIL (the United Nations Interim Force in Lebanon) and a number of residents down south last week (there was an allegation that a French battalion had destroyed acres of tobacco plantations, for reasons unknown), but his objections had been overruled, as usual, by his boss Major Ghanem.

On top of this, and to add to his pissed-offery, Ghanem had told him to prepare a risk assessment for the joint visit of Saudi King Abdullah and Syrian President Bashar al-Assad at the end of the month, including detailed security arrangements for their discussions with President Michel Suleiman at the Presidential Palace at Baabda.

So the small, slim, powerful, currently chain-smoking, often whisky-drinking, fifty-one year old Merhi was not happy.

And the last thing he wanted was a telephone call.

His mobile phone rang at 09:03.

Merhi was intent on his computer screen and at first he did not hear it. It

---

[*] *The Shi'a cleric, described by some as the 'Spiritual Mentor' of Hizbullah.*

took a few moments for his mind to register that there was a ringing coming from somewhere. He frowned at the phone on his desk but then realised that the sound was coming from behind him, from his uniform jacket draped across the back of his chair.

Cursing, he turned in his seat, fumbling into an inside pocket. It was probably his wife Gisele wanting him to pick something up on the way home tonight. Couldn't she just have texted?

The phone stopped ringing as he pulled it out.

1 MISSED CALL

Damn and buggery. Well, the light of his life could ring back, or he would ring her later when he was less busy (using this criteria, that would be about next Easter).

Leaving the phone on his desk, he turned back to his screen.

The phone rang again.

UNKNOWN

Merhi picked it up and stared at the screen. So it was not Gisele. Not many people were privileged to know the mobile number of a Captain of the Internal Security Force, and those that did were all 'plumbed in' to the phone's memory. The Caller ID would show. This lack of name meant Stranger. If it was a spam phone call, someone selling something, he would castrate them and serve them their testicles dipped in chocolate on ice cream topped with a strawberry sauce.

The phone stopped ringing.

Good, better all round perhaps.

He had just typed in his estimate of the number of armoured vehicles needed for the journey from Baabda to the Prime Minister's Office at the Grand Serail when the phone rang for the third time.

He snatched it up in irritation, this time pressing the green key. "Who the fuck is this?"

There was silence at the other end.

"Hello?" shouted Merhi.

A deep voice said, "Captain Merhi?"

He couldn't tell whether it was male or female. "Who is this?"

"Is this Captain Merhi?"

"Who are you?"

"Jihad Merhi?"

"How did you get this number?"

There was a pause. Then: "You gave it to me."

"Who is this?"

"It is best if I do not say."

"If you're pissing me about - "

"Five years."

"What?"

"Five years ago. You gave me your number."

Merhi fell silent, feeling the fingers of history creeping up his spine. "Five years...?" he said quietly.

"Yes. I would like to meet you again."

"Five years was a long time ago."

"Yes, it was. Can we meet?"

"Is it about what happened?"

"No."

"Then...?"

"Can we meet?"

"Why?"

"I... I need your help."

Merhi's mind was racing, tumbling back five years to a turbulent time in Lebanese history. "Are you - ?"

"Please do not say it! Do not say my name!"

"But..."

"Please. Can we meet? It is a matter of life or death. Mine."

Merhi was quiet again. Then he said slowly, "Okay."

"I know you will be busy today, with what is happening. Do you remember your little code you had with your Palestinian friend?"

"My little code?"

"When you arranged meetings?"

"Oh. Yes."

"So on that basis can we meet on Thursday? At 13:00?"

Merhi was working it out... The named time less twenty-six hours... Tomorrow at 11:00. "Yes."

"You name the place."

He plucked something. "Outside the *Voix du Liban* building in Ashrafieh?" It did not matter, the place would always be the same and it was not there.

"Yes. Thank you. *Merci ktir.*"

"Are you all right?"

"I hope so."

"Can you tell me what this is about?" There was no response. "Hello? Hello...?"

Jbeil, Lebanon 10:00

Private investigator Abu Yussuf yawned and looked at the time on his iPhone.

It had been a long ten minutes since he had sat down at this table outside the coffee house in Rue Cheralam, near the small but popular Ahiram Hotel on the northern coast road. His subject, eighty-two year old Monsieur Albert Gourhant, suspected adulterer and sex fiend, was in the barber shop opposite.

Abu Yussuf signalled for a second espresso and took a long draw on his cigarette, idly running his fingers across the phone's touch screen. His first full day on the job of following the old man and he was bored already – admittedly a boredom assuaged by the quarter million Lebanese pounds a day his client was paying him.

He wondered for how long he could prolong his nice little summer earner. How long did it take to confirm an eighty-two year old's infidelity or fidelity? Actually possibly a long time if he was, say, a once a month man, which was quite possible due to Monsieur Gourhant's age. A younger man would just take a few days, a week at the most.

A *muhaqqiq khass* less scrupulous than himself might drag this out for months and just sit in his office and do nothing and lie about his investigations. But not Abu Yussuf. He would let it take a month at the most and, to prove to his client that her quarter million a day was money well spent, he would give her a schedule of her husband's movements, hour by hour, location by location. The fact that he would also try to sell the schedule to Monsieur Gourhant was just good business practice.

The screen on his phone suddenly changed and he quickly pulled his fingers away, aware that he had pressed down too hard and had opened an application. He frowned in curiosity, then smiled with the pleasure of a skinflint when he realised he had hitched a ride on someone else's WiFi.

It was the GPS application, one he had not been in before. This was good, it gave him something to play with. A visit to a Lebanese barber's shop was always more a social event than a business transaction, especially on an unexpected public holiday such as this, so the subject would be in there for at least an hour, chatting, philosophising, sorting out the problems of the world.

Abu Yussuf watched as the number of satellites found above were counted out on his phone. Ten and rising! Was nowhere private anymore?

He looked over at the barber shop window. Well, there was no privacy for you Monsieur Albert Gourhant. Your wife was watching you.

Grinning, he opened Google Maps and began to play.

Ashrafieh, Beirut 11:30

Paradise smiled as Love held out the two contact lens cases. They were sitting in their Jeep outside the Hotel Albergo. As always, Abdel el Wahab el Inglizi Street was busy and crowded with traffic, but they had simply double-parked. Taxis did that.

Paradise chose the case nearest to her and slowly opened it. Her face lit up. "Green! I win again."

"Thirty-two thirty-two," nodded Love. "We are equal. As we should be." She opened the other case, leant forward and put in the brown contact lenses. Then she looked at her sister, blinking. "All right?"

"Yes. You still look beautiful. Even with human eyes." Paradise had not put in her contacts. She did not need to, she was staying in the car.

"If I need you, you'll know." Love bent across, kissed her sister on the cheek and then got out of the car. Her blonde hair was tied up and she was dressed in a smart dark grey two-piece suit and open-necked white blouse, a look which hinted at corporate uniform.

She walked through the tall, ornate gates of the hotel, past the small garden area and up the marble steps into the opulent foyer. Over at Reception, she said "Taxi for Room 431."

The male clerk tappy-tapped on a keyboard and looked at a screen below the level of the counter. He nodded and picked up the telephone. "I will let her know you're here."

Love waited, watching the clerk intently. Already he had confirmed that her prey was still at the hotel. Now she just wanted to know whether she was in. The clerk would not have the chance to tell the prey that there was an unrequested taxi waiting downstairs, he would be asleep before the words left his mouth. "She has asked me to help with her luggage." Love stretched out, touching his arm.

The clerk raised a sardonic eyebrow. "We have porters to do that – hey, are you all right?"

The taxi driver had suddenly pulled her hand back and grabbed the side of her head, screwing up her face. "*Kakhbah!*" she gasped, her brown eyes glaring at the clerk. "No!" she looked back towards the entrance. "No, no, no!"

Turning away from the Reception counter, she ran back out.

Carla Chedid was not stupid. After yesterday's attack on her at the hotel it was obviously too dangerous for her to spend another night there. At first she had thought of going back to Maroun's apartment, but that was a non-starter, people might be knocking at the door wondering why the Chief of the External Security Unit had not reported in. And even if they weren't, poor Maroun would be well and truly over-ripe by now. So she had checked in to the Sofitel Le Gabriel on Avenue de l'Indépendance, a few blocks away.

But she was curious. Curious as to the murdering maid at the Albergo. That the maid had killed Maroun was beyond doubt: she had tried to kill Carla in exactly the same way. But how did she know about Carla? And why, anyway, would she try to kill her if this was a hit against the ESU Chief?

The two answers were obvious. She knew about Carla because she, or someone, had been listening. Despite Maroun's precautions, despite his conviction that his apartment was clean, it wasn't. Carla well accepted that the ESU was only one group of many Listeners operating in the maelstrom of Lebanese politics.

As to the second question, there was no need to kill Carla because of Maroun's murder: she had not been there at the time, she had not seen anything. So, she was being targeted 'in her own right', as it were. Why? Because of something The Listeners had heard. What? What knowledge did she possess that would get her murdered? What knowledge had she passed to Maroun that had necessitated his elimination? Well, there was only one thing, wasn't there?

The knowledge that Sajida was right.

Although Carla had not stayed at the Albergo overnight, she had not checked out. Dressed in her ripped-knee jeans and pink T shirt, she was returning now to pick up her small suitcase and pay her far-from-small bill. She knew she needed to be careful. Yesterday's attack had been in the middle of the day. She would watch the staff carefully, although obviously the tall, blonde female assassin was not an employee. But she might try the same cover twice. She might be waiting.

Abdel el Wahab el Inglizi Street is naturally narrow, as are many of the old streets of Ashrafieh. Cars were parked on either side and the traffic was heavy and moving at a slow pace thanks to a Jeep that had double-parked outside the Albergo.

It was as she was standing on the kerb opposite the hotel, waiting to cross the road, that her eyes passed over the Jeep and then went back again with a jolt.

Her face hardened, fists clenching. Well, well, well...

Ripping the hairclip from her head, she dashed out between the slow-moving cars to a cacophony of horns and shouts. A woman driving a beige Ford Explorer with three children inside called her a son of a donkey.

In the Jeep, Paradise looked up to see what all the shouting was about.

Carla saw the startling white eyes as she reached the open window of the Jeep. Her left hand lunged outwards and grabbed the woman by the throat.

Paradise clawed at the small but vicious hand on her throat, eyes looking at the needle that was coming towards her. Her air was instantly restricted, already her chest was tight.

The needle stopped, almost touching her left eye. Paradise could smell jasmine. The woman leant in the open window and put her lips close to Paradise's left ear. "Houris are supposed to protect djinn," she snarled. "Not kill them." Pulling at her throat, she banged Paradise's head against the seat headrest. "Next time the needle goes in."

She let go of the throat, drew her hand back and landed a hard punch to Paradise's left temple.

Paradise was gasping for air and falling sideways at the same time, dizzy, hurting.

The next thing Paradise was aware of was the passenger door opening, and she knew she had to fight back. A hand touched her head, and she flailed out hoping to make contact. Then she heard a voice say, "Sister! Sister! What happened? Are you all right?" She could see Love holding the left side of her own head.

Paradise grasped her sister's hand. "It was her," she croaked. "She's here." She felt the hand pull away sharply.

Love ran around to the other side of the Jeep, looking up and down the street. There were cars everywhere, people going about their business. A woman driving a beige Ford Explorer with three children inside suggested that her mother had made love to a camel. But there was no one running, no one hurrying away.

The prey had disappeared.

Coastal Highway, Lebanon 13:00

"You are all right, sister?" asked Love as she drove the Jeep northwards over the Nahr Ibrahim (River Ibrahim), her hand touching her own left temple.

"Just a slight ache, probably nothing you can feel," said Paradise reaching out and turning up the air conditioning. "But it is so hot with the roof on. Sometimes I wish we could sweat."

"We'll soon be home," consoled Love. She pulled out to overtake a slow-moving Mitsubishi van. The coastal road was as busy as always, perhaps even more so on this unexpected public holiday.

Love had shaken her hair back down in Beirut after she had gently pushed her stunned sister across into the passenger seat, belted her in and then climbed into the driver's seat. As she had driven eastward out of the city she had managed to remove one of her contact lenses but then she had hit the highway and needed both hands for driving, so one lens remained in, making a peculiar sight.

In a while, as they were passing the town of Halat, Love said, "I am sorry."

"What for?"

"For what happened. For you getting hurt."

"You got hurt too, sister. You feel what I feel."

"This woman," Love shook her head in frustration. "I should have converted her in New York."

Paradise touched Love's arm. "But how were you to know?"

"I wish I had seen her eyes then."

"Well, you didn't. You thought she was just Convert Arif's girlfriend. And our instructions are not to make any unnecessary conversions, only the selected ones who deserve it. Only those who know The Secret."

"And now we find out she is a Lebanese agent! We know she knows The Secret. Therefore she qualifies. She is being clever, elusive. She will not be converted easily."

"And..." Paradise looked at her sister, wondering how she would take what she was about to say. "She let me live."

Love eased the car to the right, ready to turn off the highway. She sighed. "Yes, she did... She did. Why did she do that?"

"I do not know. There is something about her..."

"I know what you mean. What is it, do you think? Why is it we feel unsure about her? In the past, we have converted many. But this one...? Do we feel... a kinship?"

Paradise frowned, shrugging. "She is not one of us, we would know. But yet, we do feel, don't we..? She said some-thing about *djinn*."

Love raised a cautionary finger. "Not a word about this to Malek tomorrow."

"Of course not."

They had reached Jbeil, passing the town clock and bearing left onto Boulevard al-Mina.

"But I failed today," admitted Love. "Just as you did yesterday." She pulled into the parking area just beyond the Seven Seas Restaurant, found a space and turned off the engine. "So," she continued, "you must punish me like I punished you." One brown and one white eye turned to her sister. "Only worse."

7 July 2010
25 Rajab 1431

Verdun, Beirut 11:00

Captain Jihad Merhi of the Internal Security Force stood at the edge of the Food Court on the second floor of The Dunes Shopping Mall, his mind awash with memories. It had been over five years since he had last been here. Five years since those dreadful events, when he had almost – almost – prevented the most horrendous Lebanese political assassination of recent times.

He sighed. Not pleasant memories.

Meeting at The Mall was the idea of his counterpart who was in charge of policing at the Beirut Palestinian refugee camps. The Mall was one of the oldest shopping complexes in Beirut, and the Verdun area over near the west coast and on the same block as the Holiday Inn Hotel was an easy drive from the Palestinian's base in the Bourj el-Barajneh refugee camp in the south of the city near the airport.

When Merhi met officially with his counterpart, it was in Merhi's own offices in Jonblat. The Food Court of The Dunes Shopping Mall had been used for unofficial meetings when they did not want to be monitored, overheard or even seen. There was a period when they met here frequently, but such a circumstance had not arisen for those full five years.

But now somebody else wanted to meet him here and it seemed like the last five years had never happened. Over there was *McDonald's, DipnCrunch,* and the *Frizzy Center*. The *Haagen Dazs* booth was still in the middle. All as he remembered. Was *Doodle Doo* over in the corner new?

The Food Court was not yet busy. Even if it was, Merhi's uniform white shirt and blue trousers, and all the accoutrements around his waistband including his gun, would have ensured him a quick passage along any queues.

He went over to *Cup Cake* for a double chocolate special and a coffee. There was one person ahead of him, a youth probably going to a bargain early showing at the Cine Empire opposite.

Merhi could tell it was early. The food odours had not yet encroached, he could still smell the cleaner's polish. Jasmine.

"Captain Merhi."

Inwardly he jumped and his right hand just gave the slightest twitch towards his gun. The low voice came from behind but he had not heard anyone approach.

He turned, looked and recognised.

"Well, well. Agent - "

Her soft finger went to his lips. "Please. Do not say it."

Merhi's eyebrows rose, then he nodded in acceptance. The finger was removed. "May I get you something?" He indicated the kiosk.

"An espresso please."

"Anything to eat?"

"*Merci.*" She shook her head.

"Do you mind if I do? It has been a long time since I have been here."

"Please."

As they sat at a table in a far corner of the court, she with her tiny polycup containing an even tinier amount of espresso, he with his black Americano and double chocolate cup cake, she said "My name is Carla Chedid."

Merhi slowly peeled the case from his cake. "Is it?" he said. "Not - "

"If you think I am anyone else, you are mistaken. That person has been exiled from Lebanon. For what happened."

"I see." He broke off a piece of cake and put it in his mouth.

For a moment there was silence between them. Merhi looked at the small, black-haired, black-eyed, olive-skinned, exotic creature opposite in her knee-ripped blue jeans and pink T shirt, and wondered what on earth she wanted with him. Their time was in the past.

She drank her espresso in one and said, "I need your help."

Merhi nodded, in understanding not in agreement. "With what?"

"You are the only person I can trust."

"I say again, with what? Is this an ESU matter? Or a personal matter?"

"Possibly both." Carla looked around the Food Court, satisfying herself that there were no Listeners or Watchers about. Then she asked, "Do you know Sajida?"

Merhi frowned. "Sajida? Didn't she appear at the *Casino du Liban* recently?"

Carla couldn't help but smile. "No, really. Do you know who Sajida is?"

Merhi shrugged and held his palms open.

"In which case," said Carla, "it is perhaps better that I do not tell you what this is about."

"Hold on, hold on," Merhi leant forward, putting down the piece of cake he was about to pop into his mouth. "You want me to help you? You come back to Lebanon after five years, you come back into my life after five years, you ask me to help you and you won't tell me what it is about?"

"Bluntly, yes."

Merhi sat back. "Is this conversation over?"

"I hope not. Let me explain to you. If you knew Sajida, if you knew what I was talking about, then I would explain everything. But as you do not, I am protecting you by not telling you."

Merhi raised an eyebrow. He popped the final piece of cake into his mouth.

Carla went on. "Have you heard of Captain Maroun Khoury?"

"No. What district is he in?"

"He is – was – my boss at the ESU."

"Was?"

"I went to him with what I know and the next day he was killed."

"As a direct result of what you told him?"

"I am almost certain. That is one of the first things I want to find out. If my suspicions are confirmed then I must take action to avenge him - and protect myself. And to stop what is going to happen."

"What is going to happen?"

"I will tell you when I need to. When I can be sure you will be safe."

Merhi pulled out a packet of Cedars King Size cigarettes from his shirt breast pocket, offering them to Carla with an inquiring look. She shook her head.

He took his time lighting up. Then, looking at the glowing tip of his *seejaere*, he asked "What would you want of me?"

She looked relieved. "Thank you. *Merci ktir.*" She reached across and touched his arm, sending a mild tingle through his bicep. Taking her hand away slowly, she asked "Firstly, do you have access to street CCTV?"

Again Merhi shrugged. "For sure."

"If I gave you a street and a time, could you arrange for me to look at it?"

Another shrug, used as a silent confirmation.

"If it proves what I think it will prove," said Carla. "Then I will need to take action. And I may need the help of your intelligence resources."

"Well, one step at a time, eh?" He took a long drag on the cigarette.

"Yes. Okay. May I buy you a coffee?" She nodded at his empty cup.

He looked at it, considered, shook his head. "*Merci.* Give me a day, time and street and I will see what I can do about the CCTV. You will need to come to my office to view it."

"No problem. There is, though, just one other thing."

Merhi blew smoke. "What is that?"

Carla pouted. "I need somewhere to stay."

Jbeil District, Lebanon 14:30

Although it is designated a primary road, the route from Jbeil to Annaya is bumpy, especially if you have a sore bottom.

Love fidgeted uncomfortably in the passenger seat of the Jeep. She had asked to be punished for failing in her conversion yesterday, but perhaps Paradise had been just a little too rough last night. A little too keen.

Love was glad her sister was driving, the stinging in her currently mottled-purple cheeks would have distracted her. Full concentration was needed for this drive high up into the mountains, the road meandering, curving, often bending back against itself as it made the ascent.

They passed through the villages of Hboub, Kfar Qouas, Breij, and stopped just the other side of Ras Osta. It was the beginning of high summer, the sun was intense, but it still felt cooler up here; they were glad they had worn long-sleeved tops.

Love smiled as she rummaged in a holdall and brought out the two contact lens cases, offering them to Paradise on the palm of her hand.

Paradise smiled and pulled the Jeep over, stopping close to the edge. Looking at the cases, she put a finger to her lips, thinking. She stretched over towards the case furthest away, then at the last moment pulled her fingers back and touched the one nearest to her. "This one."

Love let her take the case and then slowly opened the one she was left with, raising the lid away from her so that her sister would enjoy the exquisite anticipation until the very last moment. She looked and then let the case flop open in her hand. She had her own lenses, the brown ones.

"Yes!" Paradise gave a little air-punch of triumph. "I picked right. Three wins in a row! Thirty-three thirty-two."

Love nodded. "Congratulations, *habibi*. It is your time. You are on a roll."

Paradise was self-deprecating. "It is nothing. Just our little game." She leant forward, balancing one of the lenses on her index finger and pulling her eyelid open with her other hand.

"Yes, but Allah is favouring you," insisted Love. "That is good for the next conversion."

Paradise came back up, one green eye one white eye. "You think there will be more?"

Love shrugged. "We still have this djinn to deal with. And who knows? Malek might have others. He said the time is close now. The re-birth cannot be disrupted."

"No," said Paradise. "It cannot. The world has waited too long."

They both finished putting in their lenses. Shortly the Jeep was moving off again with the two identical women inside, separated only by the colour of their eyes.

They drove higher, to 1350 metres above sea level.

To the Deir Mar Maron.

The Monastery of Saint Maron.

Annaya, Lebanon 15:45

The orange-roofed monastery of Saint Maron is Lebanon's most visited pilgrimage site. It is where Youssef Antoun Makhlouf, Lebanon's revered Saint Charbel, lived and died. So popular is the saint that the monastery is often incorrectly referred to as the Deir Mar Charbel by the tens of thousands of people who come each year, an error uncorrected by Charbel's followers who give service in the new church housing the saint's tomb, or in the bookshop, the restaurant or the monastery shop.

Although it was midweek, the parking area was busy. The two tall blonde women in camouflage combat trousers, desert boots, white vests under black hooded tops, hairs in simple ponytails, attracted some glances from the devout visitors, but they were looks of the *oh-look-twins-aren't-they-sweet?* variety. They avoided the new church and walked eastwards to the monastery itself.

Love had her mobile phone to her ear. "We are here," she announced. "Yes... *oui, d'accord.*" She pressed the End icon and put the phone into a thigh pocket. "He will meet us outside," she said to her sister. "They are not keen on having young women in the monastery – even if we are novitiates, which is what he told them." She smiled. "Sister Paradise."

"Sister Love," Paradise nodded. "It suits you."

"Perhaps we should take the cloth when he comes again."

"I think our rewards will be much greater than that, dear one. Much greater."

"Not long now and we will find out. Ah, there he is."

The tall, hooded figure had come out of the main monastery door and was walking towards them. Sandaled feet poked out from beneath the full-length *burnus*.

"*Salaam, oh Malek,*" greeted the twins in unison.

Brother Malek raised his right hand in a gesture of blessing. "*Salaam.*"

"The place is to your satisfaction?" asked Paradise.

Malek's face was hardly visible beneath the cowl. His grey-black beard moved up and down as he spoke. "Come, walk with me."

He turned back and the twins caught up and went either side of him. Like bodyguards. They walked casually along the side wall of the monastery, shaded from the midday sun.

"It will suffice," he said in his curious way of talking without acknowledging any pause in the conversation. "I have my own cell well away from others, befitting for a monk with hermit inclinations. And they have asked me if I would like to work, as you said they would." Suddenly he was gruff. "Of course I do not wish to work!"

Paradise and Love exchanged glances.

"But," Malek went on, calmer. "I must fit in. So I have asked for something where I do not have contact with others, just like a hermit would. Tomorrow I start work harvesting vegetables. Physical work. It will be good for... my soul."

"Your soul is mighty," said Love softly.

"Mighty," agreed Paradise.

"The conversions," Malek went on as if they had not spoken. "They were successful?"

"Your collection of spirits has increased," confirmed Love, hoping he had not noticed the very slight pause before she answered.

"Good. That is good. The Secret remains safe. God is pleased. Do you have anything for me?"

They had reached the end of the monastery and Malek paused, looking at the holdall on Love's shoulder.

"Of course," she said, turning her back so that Paradise could get into the bag.

Paradise brought out a paper bag and gave it to Malek. He did not look inside it.

The three of them turned and began to walk back the way they had come. They were silent, walking in the tree-lined shade, respectful of the tranquillity.

When they reached the main door of the monastery, Malek held up his hand. He said "I have been in contact with the disciples. I have some news. It is close now, very close. After all this time."

"*Allahu Akbar*," said Paradise softly.

"The preparations are made. We have a date for The Second Coming. Satan is running with his spiked tail between his legs. In eight weeks. Just eight weeks and The Secret will be revealed. The world will be saved from itself."

"*Ma Sha' Allah!*" Love was genuine in her surprise. "You must tell us what you want us to do."

"I will, I will," the voice from beneath the cowl was benign. "You will be with me, my sisters. My right and left hands."

"You are too good to us, Malek," said Paradise.

Malek looked into the top of the bag they had given him. "Now it is time for prayer," he said. "Go in peace, sisters, I will call you. Soon the world will be at our feet."

"*Insh'allah*," agreed Love. Both women knelt down as Malek held out the backs of his hands. They kissed the hairs above his knuckles.

As Paradise looked up she could just see his eyes in the shadow of the hood. They were bright, anticipatory, almost excited.

Without further word, Brother Malek turned and went back into the monastery.

The twins rose and turned to each other. "*Yalla,*" said Love, taking her sister's hand. "Time to go."

Back at the Jeep, Paradise said "We did right not telling him about the djinn. Wouldn't want to spoil his excitement, would we?"

"No," agreed Love. "What *al-Mahdi* does not know - "

"*ad-Dajjal* does not grieve over."

They climbed into the Jeep and soon were heading back down the mountain.

As Brother Malek mounted the stairs to his cell on the third floor of the monastery, faint singing was coming from another part of the building, a joyous Maronite holy song. But he did not hear it. All he could hear was the *azan*, the Islamic call to prayer, recited by the muezzin in his head. It was time for '*Asr salat*, afternoon prayer.

In the bag was strawberry-flavoured *ma'asel*. He would wash, pray, and then enjoy a leisurely *argileh* before his evening meal. He would not join the other pilgrims in the refectory, his meal would be brought to him.

After all, he was a monk with hermit inclinations.

Jounieh, Lebanon 18:00

"How could you do this?" Gisele Merhi spoke lowly, her tone on the cusp between not-at-all-pleased and outright anger. "You know Samer and Sary are due home for the summer soon."

"It will only be for a few days," reasoned her husband. "And what was I supposed to do? Refuse a colleague in distress?"

They were standing in the kitchen of their mountainside apartment, high above the town. The summer evening sun was streaming in across the Mediterranean beyond the coast. Jihad still wore his uniform shirt but he had swapped his trousers for an old pair of jeans.

"And it's not as if you don't know her," he reasoned, cigarette propped in the side of his mouth, glass of whisky in hand. "She was one of your students once."

At one time, Gisele had been a member of the Lebanese security service – that was how she and Jihad had met – and she knew that her husband was right. You do not leave a colleague in the field in harm's way. But now she was a wife and a mother – and a Lebanese wife and mother at that – she knew she had to make a fuss, it was part of the job description.

"So?" she asked. "Are we to accommodate all the students I have ever taught if they come knocking?"

"Actually," Jihad took a long swill of his Johnnie Walker. "Yes. If necessary. You know that, Gigi. It's how we work in our job."

With one downward stroke of her kitchen knife, Gisele cut the head off a sea bass on the chopping board in front of her. Jihad winced and subconsciously moved his groin backwards.

She slit open the fish's belly and began to gut it. "Well, as long as you are sure it will only be for a few days," she was giving in, playing the indignation through. "What if she is here when the boys arrive?"

"Then we will have a full house. It is not like we do not have the space."

"And what will we tell Mama and Baba? And Joe and Jacqui will be arriving soon from Dubai."

"We tell them the truth! Sort of... she is an old friend, not been back home for many years. Last minute decision to come back. You know."

Gisele turned, holding a handful of fish entrails. She nodded. The scene had been played out. She was satisfied. She said, "I've heard of bringing your work home with you, but you, dear husband, take it to extremes!"

She smiled and bipped him on the nose with her index finger, leaving a round fingerprint of fish blood above his right nostril.

Jounieh, Lebanon 19:45

"I'm truly grateful, Gisele, thank you. Thank you both." Carla spooned fish and rice onto her plate. "And this *sayadieh* looks delicious." The three of them were sitting at the table in the dining area.

"It is her special way," said Jihad. "She removes the fish head before cooking."

Gisele nodded thanks to her husband as he poured white wine. "*Beyti beytak*, Carla. You are welcome here. And you won't tell us what it is about? Who this Sajida is?"

"Not until I need to. Not until I have to. You are my gracious hosts. I need to ensure your safety. If I establish that Maroun was not killed because of what I told him, then I will tell you. But I have a strong suspicion that he was." Carla took a mouthful of fish. "I need to see that CCTV, then I will know for sure. This *is* delicious, Gisele."

"I will call for it tomorrow," Jihad also ate as he spoke. "It should be with me pretty quick. Will you be safe coming to my office?"

"Nobody knows me in Internal Security – except you. As long as you can get me through the doors."

"I will meet you and escort you in personally. The team might wonder who you are but no one will ask. And if they did, I would tell them the truth. You are a liaison from the ESU. Keep it as simple and as truthful as possible. In falsehood lies confusion."

"One of Gisele's lessons," smiled Carla.

"Er... yes. *Sahtik*. Cheers." Jihad swilled down some wine

Gisele grinned at her husband's forced acknowledgement.

"There is one thing though," said Carla, touching Gisele on the arm. "I had to check out of the Hotel Albergo by telephone. To preserve my cover I had to ask them to ship my case back home to New York. The only clothes I have are these ones I'm wearing. Gisele, you don't fancy going shopping with me in the morning, do you?"

Gisele's grin became wider and Jihad inwardly groaned as dollar signs rolled before his eyes like the loaded drums on a casino slot machine.

8 July 2010
26 Rajab 1431

Jbeil, Lebanon 11:45

Private investigator Abu Yussuf drove his old, battered, rusting, burnt orange, over thirty years old, apple-of-his-eye Datsun Bluebird south out of Jbeil down the coastal road. He was following a tivoli blue Citroen C4 Picasso driven by its owner, the sexual animal and octogenarian Monsieur Albert Gourhant.

The sun was over the coastal cliffs to Abu Yussuf's immediate left and was beaming straight into the Bluebird, which meant he had to drive with the car's sunshade down and his *Ray-Bans* on. He drove one-handed, his left arm hanging out the open window, cigarette between his fingers, warm air blowing into his face.

Yesterday had been a quiet day. Sex God Albert had stayed at home - or he had been confined indoors. Today he had been let out – or he had escaped. It would be interesting to see where he was going. South to Beirut?

Soon the Citroen slowed as a modern five-storey building came into view on the right. The Hotel Victory Byblos, its name emblazoned in large green letters on the roof. Albert kindly indicated he was turning.

Throwing his cigarette away, Abu Yussuf brought his left arm back into the car, turned in after Albert and parked three spaces away from him.

Well now. A just-out-of-town hotel in the middle of the day? It had 'tryst' written all over it.

Was Madame Gourhant, his esteemed and very generous client, right after all?

Picking up his iPhone from the passenger seat, Abu Yussuf got out and followed Albert Gourhant into the hotel.

Annaya, Lebanon 12:30

Brother Malek was not happy.

Because of his publicised hermit inclinations, he had been given work in a secluded corner of ground near the monastery. Pulling up potatoes. He could see others at work further away, but no one was near him. No one was helping him. It was his responsibility to bring in several sacks of *batatis* before vespers, the daily Christian evening prayer.

He would do it, but he was not young any more. All the bending was making his mortal bones ache already. And it was so hot under the hooded cloak. He felt dirty, sweaty, unclean.

He needed to work because he needed to fit in, but he did not like it. He was Malek – the King. The King of Kings. He had come to save the earth – not work on it.

But, like a good hermit, he kept his head down and got on with his task. But he was not happy.

And an unhappy Brother Malek was not good for any one.

Jbeil, Lebanon 12:45

Well it was a tryst of sorts, but not the kind that would interest Madame Gourhant. Monsieur Albert Gourhant was in the Health Center of the hotel having a massage!

As Abu Yussuf sat in a low chair in a corner of the Health Food Bar trying to pretend he was enjoying the carrot juice he had ordered, he wondered how Madame would interpret this. She would probably say he was toning himself for his slut tart, his fast-becoming-imaginary bit on the side. In reality it seemed that Monsieur Albert was simply an old man going about his business, looking after himself. Getting out of the house.

Abu Yussuf smiled. And who could blame poor Albert for wanting to get out of the house!

He was only three days into his investigation and he had given himself a month. Just in case. But already he was reaching a conclusion of innocence regarding the unfortunate Albert. The next twenty-eight days would drag, and although his boredom was assuaged by thoughts of the daily fee he was earning, he would need to find something to fight off the *ennui* of the waiting-and-watching times. He wished he had his playing cards with him.

Or perhaps he should read a book. He had read one once. At least he thought he had, couldn't remember.

He played with his iPhone, many of the apps unavailable because he was not online. He went to reach for his cigarettes in his pocket and then thought better of it, looking guiltily around the Health Center. Instead he took another very small sip of his juice.

Five minutes later, Monsieur Gourhant came out from somewhere in the back, accompanied by a local girl in a white uniform dress with 'Victory Byblos Health Center' in green on her left breast. Gourhant shook her hand, slipping her the expected few notes tip, and went over to the main counter to settle his account.

Abu Yussuf casually stood up, pretended to take a final long swig from his juice, left a low-denomination note on the table, and followed Gourhant out. Now, which way would he go? Back to town? Down to Beirut?

Gourhant stopped by the elevator in the lobby, pressing the Call button. Abu Yussuf stopped, surprised, and pretended to read something on a notice board about beach facilities. Well now, he wondered, what was this?

The elevator door pinged open. Gourhant went to get in but then stepped back with a nod to let three people out.

Abu Yussuf walked over behind Gourhant and followed him into the small elevator, just the two of them. As the doors closed, Gourhant asked over his shoulder "Floor?"

"Top," said Abu Yussuf, watching closely to see what other button Gourhant pressed.

"The same," said Gourhant, pressing just the one button and then staring straight ahead at the doors, as people in elevators do.

The elevator was slow but there were only four floors. As it juddered and then stopped at its destination, Gourhant stepped back to let his fellow traveller out first.

Abu Yussuf was expecting a floor of rooms but instead he stepped out into a bright, spacious area with a magnificent view through a semi-circular glass doorway out onto a terrace and the Mediterranean beyond.

He was in the rooftop restaurant and lunch was being served.

Jonblat, Beirut 13:30

Jihad Merhi sat at his desk, cigarette between his fingers, Johnnie Walker in his mug, looking at the latest pile of *ilishael* that had been dumped upon him by Major Ghanem. Apparently the Israelis had released photographs and maps purporting to show Hizbullah training sites in the south, together with details of arms and rocket locations below the Litani river. The Jews were threatening a pre-emptive strike against the training sites. Problem was these 'training sites' were in fact villages and the alleged weapons depots were in fact schools and hospitals. Although Ghanem had acknowledged that this was a matter for the Lebanese army, Merhi had been asked 'to comment'.

Merhi had one two-word comment, the second word being 'off'. He had enough to do.

His mobile was in his right hand, and as he listened to it ringing at the other end his eyes travelled over to the closed door of his office with the cracked pane of glass that had not been repaired in five years.

"Hello, light of my life. I hope you've spent all our money for the month on something frivolous which you don't need," he said, still listening to the ring tone. He took a swig of whisky, avoiding burning his forehead with the cigarette in the same hand with the deftness of a hardened smoker.

Eventually Gisele answered and he put the mug and cigarette down as if she could see him. "Hi, Gigi. Had a good time? Great. Tell your cousin everything's okay. Tomorrow at 16:30." Which meant today at 14:30, in one hour's time. "Yes. Okay. I'll see you tonight. Yes, I love you too. Bye, bye, bye."

Jbeil, Lebanon 14:15

Sometimes life just gives you an unexpected bonus, reflected Abu Yussuf, stifling a burp. A little reward for being a good boy.

It had been a surprisingly sumptuous Italian meal in the rooftop restaurant of the Victory Byblos Hotel. It was too hot to sit outside on the terrace, but he was given a good table for one just inside the semi-circular glass doorway, facing inwards. And facing Albert Gourhant three tables away.

He had not dined alone, he had been accompanied by a bottle of imported Barolo wine and then by two limoncello liqueurs and two double espressos. And best of all, he wouldn't have to pay for it. The delightful and rather-beautiful-the-more-alcohol-you-drank Madame Gourhant would see it on her bill.

Albert Gourhant had also dined with just liquid company. Now, as Gourhant put down his coffee cup and wiped his mouth, Abu Yussuf counted out a sizeable amount of US dollars and put them on top of the check in the plastic cover.

He watched Gourhant pay by card, and then he rose, deliberately ahead of his subject. The small bar was near the elevator, and he stopped to exchange small-talk with the barmaid until he was sure Gourhant was leaving. He was waiting at the elevator when Gourhant got there.

Abu Yussuf entered the elevator first then nodded in faux mild surprise when he saw Gourhant, acknowledging their previous encounter. He pressed the button for the ground floor. Gourhant did not reach across for an alternative.

When the elevator thumped to a stop at its destination, Abu Yussuf stepped back and Gourhant left first with a nod of *"Merci."*

Feeling a food and alcohol induced pleasantness, Abu Yussuf followed Gourhant outside and watched him climb into his Citroen, start the engine and move off.

Up at the main road, Gourhant signalled left.

Starting the Bluebird's engine, Abu Yussuf had the first pangs of guilt about drinking the alcohol. But he was on a case, he reasoned, under cover. Allah would understand.

Jerkily he drove off, also turning left at the main road. Going back to Jbeil. Back home.

Nothing discovered today.

Jonblat, Beirut 14:30 – 18:00

"No shopping bags?" asked Jihad Merhi as he walked Carla Chedid up the stairs to the ISF offices on the second floor of the State Security building.

"Gisele has taken them home," her deep voice echoed up the stairwell. "We could only just get them all into the car." She gave him an impish sideways look.

Merhi raised an eyebrow, knowing she was teasing him. The Merhi's car was a Toyota Land Cruiser, an ex-official issue on which he had got a good deal. To fill that with shopping bags of girlie things was... she *was* kidding, wasn't she?

Carla laughed. "Do not worry, Captain, I am playing with you."

That comment set his mind off on completely different thoughts, and as he stood back holding the door open for her he cast a quick downward glance at her small, fit body. She was dressed in all black, tight T shirt above jeans which she must have been poured into, black Reebok trainers. Across her body she carried a dark grey Barbour wax cotton messenger bag. Her hair was down and held back with a black and gold hairclip.

They walked down the corridor past the General Office.

"I'll be busy for about half an hour, Sergeant," called Merhi through the doorway.

"Okay boss," el-Gharib was busy on a computer, carefully tapping something out on the keyboard, and did not look up.

As he closed his own office door, Merhi offered "Coffee?"

"No, I'm fine, thanks."

"Cigarette?" He indicated the packet on his desk.

"*Merci.*" She shook her head.

"Please, sit down." Merhi indicated a wooden chair in front of the desk, taking a cigarette from the packet and putting it in his mouth. Carla sat.

"So my darling wife has gone back?" He lit up, feeling instantly more relaxed as the nicotine hit.

Carla took off her bag and draped it over the chair back. "She said you would bring me home."

"Did she now?" Merhi looked at his watch. He went behind the desk and sat down, switching to business. "I thought of asking The Watchers but I didn't want them asking questions, so I went to the Traffic Division first on the off chance. They've sent over two discs." He held up a brown envelope. "I asked for the intersection of Ashrafieh Street facing north and Abdul

Wahab Street facing south, between 14:00 and 16:00. I don't know what we've got, I haven't had time to look at them yet."

"I can look at them on my own. If you are busy. Looking through two times two hours of CCTV might take some time."

"Could you? I do have one or two other things that need my attention."

"Just put me somewhere where I won't get in the way."

Merhi nodded back to the General Office. "Most of the team are out, I'll find you a desk out there."

Carla looked quizzically at the cracked glass in the office door as he held it open for her. "History," he mumbled, following her out. "The last time we met actually." In the General Office he called across to the Sergeant. "Deeb, this lady is from the ESU. Which desk is best for her to use?"

"The Lieutenant's," el-Gharib said without looking away from his screen. "He won't be back today."

"*D'accord.* That's this one," Merhi gestured to a nearby desk, handing over the envelope containing the discs. "Let me know if you need me. The Sergeant will show you where the coffee is. If you can call it that."

"Thank you, Captain," Carla said loudly then, as he turned away, she reached out and touched his arm. She smiled sweetly and said softly, "You won't forget to take me home, will you?"

She dismissed the disc looking north from Ashrafieh Street after five minutes. It was blurred and occluded (it looked like a bird had done its business right on the camera lens), and anyway Maroun's apartment building was too far down the street.

If she did not get better from the second disc, she was going to be thwarted before she even started.

The computer hummed, thought about it, did what computers do, and then the picture came up on the screen.

The view was in colour, which was encouraging, better than the other disc, clearer but not clear, and she could distinctly see Moro's block a few buildings down on the left. The top of the screen told her that the date was 040710, the time was 14:00:00, and the time interval was 10SEC - so viewed as a movie it would be jumpy.

She did a quick calculation in her head. Two hours with a picture every ten seconds viewed as continuous...

6 frames per minute x 60

= 360 frames per hour

= 720 frames for the 2 hours.

Viewed at 1 frame per second

= 12 minutes to view it all.

Not bad, but she didn't want to miss anything. She would slow it to half speed, one frame every two seconds. It would still take only twenty-four minutes.

As she suspected, because of the long time interval, movement was fuzzy and jerky. She could just make out humans; passing vehicles were just smudges.

At 14:30:11 a pink fuzz came out of the building, turning left and appearing in just three frames. That was herself, going to the Hotel Albergo to pick up the taxi to take her to see Hariri's memorial.

She continued watching.

At 15:00:52 a dark smudge in the road slowed and metamorphosed into a car. It found an empty place further along the street and a fuzz got out. The fuzz came back down the street towards the camera. She could see a bald head. It was Moro.

Oh Moro, Moro, Moro...

She watched, wrapped up in her thoughts.

Then a pink fuzz entered the picture again coming from Ashrafieh Street. Carla frowned and looked at the time on the screen. 15:58:26. It was her, returning.

At precisely 16:00:00 on the screen, the disc stopped and the computer politely asked *Play again?*

What? Carla sat back in the chair. Had she missed something? Had something been cut out, edited? She looked at her watch. *Non*, her calculations had been correct. It had been twenty-five minutes since she started watching the disc.

She had seen no one else leave the building except herself, no one else enter except herself and Moro. What did this mean? Had the assassin been there before 14:00, lying in wait? Carla had been there on her own, but she had not been attacked. Moro had been.

If it was the same assassin who attacked her the next day, why hadn't she done her then in Moro's apartment. Why had she been left for a day? It did not make sense.

Unless it was not the same assassin.

Sighing, she stood up. "Excuse me, Sergeant. The Captain said you would show me where the coffee is?"

"Over there, *madame*." Eyes still fixed on his screen, Sergeant el-Gharib waved a hand to a far corner of the room.

"*Ah oui, merci.* Would you like one?"

"*Merci.* You can use the white mug."

Carla went over to a low filing cabinet upon which was a tray with an encrusted spoon, an old kettle and a Nescafé jar containing hardened granules. Not quite the freshly-ground she was used to, but it would have to do. Next to the tray were five mugs. She assumed the dirty one with brown liquid stripes was the 'white' one.

Back at the desk with a thick, hot brew which tasted nothing like coffee, just a beverage, she clicked on the play icon then immediately clicked the pause button. She would go through this frame by frame until she was one hundred per cent satisfied.

She looked back down the glass-walled corridor to the closed office door. Captain Jihad Merhi might be late home tonight.

Now she viewed the disc in real time, one frame every ten seconds, using the pause button when she needed to. She stopped after the first hour of disc for more coffee. Disappointingly, the slower viewing confirmed that in that first hour no one had come out of the building except herself, no one had gone in except Moro.

So either the assassin was invisible or moved at lightning speed or, as she had suspected, had arrived in the building before 14:00. Which meant that Moro had been the sole target that day, not her. The assassin was waiting for him to come home. Again the question: why had she been left until the next day when she had been in the apartment on her own and 'available' for assassination?

She topped up her mug for the third time and then embarked on the second hour.

Forty minutes later she almost missed it. She had the mug with the last mouthful of her fourth coffee tipped to her lips when the frame for **15:33:30** came on. A bit screen-drunk by now, she glanced casually at the monitor, looked away then quickly looked back again, banging down the mug, leaning forward.

There was a shadow coming out of the building. It looked like one of those photographs of ghosts that regularly appear online and sometimes in the newspapers.

She went back to the frame before. Nothing. She advanced to the frame after. Nothing. One shadow on one frame. Whoever it was must have been moving rapidly to have been captured on just one frame, out of the building and away in nineteen seconds.

There was no vehicle smudge so the person must have left on foot. Therefore in order not to be caught on the next frame, they must have come towards the camera and disappeared underneath it. North to Abdul Wahab el-Inglizi Street.

Carla nodded. That was do-able. But did whoever it was know about the CCTV camera or was it just luck? Did they move at that speed anyway? Or could it be that the camera could not pick them up because of some other reason?

Could she zoom in on this frame? she wondered. Did they have picture-enhancing software on the ISF system?

She opened her mouth to call across to Sergeant el-Gharib, who looked like he was packing up for the day, but then she thought better of it. No need to spark any curiosity. She would play with the software herself.

There was a zoom facility, that was easily found, but after a few moments looking she realised that there was nothing that would enhance the picture. So be it. She clicked on the magnifying glass icon and dragged it to the shadow on the screen.

No good, it just seemed like the enlarged shadow that it was, the zoom didn't really help at all. But she had her own natural internal picture-enhancing software! She squinted her eyes real tight and concentrated, staring at the screen...

And there she was.

Still fuzzy but the features were distinct enough when you knew what you were looking for. Female. Tall. Long blonde hair. It was the person, the creature, that had attacked her at the hotel the following day. The one she had allowed to live when she had seen her outside the hotel because she was not one hundred per cent sure she was Maroun's killer.

The *houri*.

Beirut, Lebanon 18:45

"I knew it but I had to confirm it," said Carla above the blast of the full-max air conditioning. They were in Merhi's new official-issue decuma grey Toyota Land Cruiser V8, the upgrade to his old LC5 model which Gisele now had. It was top-of-the-range, as befits a Captain of the Internal Security Force, and, just like most cars, had many features which its owner would never use. This one had built-in sat-nav which had never even been turned on.

"So you can now tell me what this is all about?" he asked. They were driving east on General Fouad Chehab Avenue, heading for the coastal highway which would take them north to *chez Merhi* in Jounieh. This was their first chance to speak since leaving the State Security building. Although the likelihood of Merhi's telephone being tapped was great, it was less likely that his office generally was bugged. But Carla had not wanted to take any chances, and she had shaken her head and made eyes when she had returned to his office and he had asked the question.

"*Non*. But I can confirm that the same person killed Maroun Khoury as tried to kill me. So it is all connected to the reason I came back."

"You have a positive ID?"

"Oh yes."

"Then I can run him through the system, see if we've got anything."

Carla shook her head. "The picture is too blurred, too vague. But I know it is the same person. And it is not a 'he'."

"It's a she?" Merhi drew on his cigarette

Carla gave a deep breath, almost a sigh, as she looked at the ABN Amro Building passing on her right, with the name Tufenkjian Frères announcing the famous jewellers underneath. "Maybe," she said.

"Sorry?" Merhi frowned.

"Nothing, nothing. A 'she', yes. Perhaps if I make up a composite you can run that through the system?"

"*Oui. A demain.*"

"*A demain,*" she agreed. She settled back into the leather seat. "That is enough work for one day. I think Gisele may have a surprise for you when you get in."

"Really?"

"But you're not to say I said anything. Something we bought today."

"Something I can eat?"

She laughed. "Well, not directly! But you might want to eat what it encloses. It is a little gift, from me to her. An outfit."

"An outfit?"

"How long has it been since you enjoyed a *raqs sharqi* belly dance?"

As they crossed the Beirut River, the Toyota Land Cruiser V8 accelerated heavily. Merhi smiled. And it was not even his birthday!

Jbeil, Lebanon 20:00

"For a moment I thought something was wrong," said Paradise as she pressed the End icon on her mobile phone. The twins were walking back to their accommodation in Rue St John, each carrying a *shawarma*, a small carton of *fattoush* salad and a can of Coca-Cola, which they had purchased in one of the fast-food outlets in the souks. Love's *shawarma* was chicken, Paradise's a mix of lamb and goat. Love had already started to nibble hers.

As usual they were attracting glances, which they acknowledged with gentle smiles when eye contact was made. They were wearing their lenses (it was now thirty-four thirty-four).

"Another conversion?" asked Love.

"No, he wants some mint tobacco."

"Mint?" Love took her sister's Coke so that she could tuck the phone back into her cargo pants. "That's unusual. He only asks for that when he is distressed or something big is about to happen. Like when we left the Promised Land."

Paradise took back her drink. "Well, The Second Coming *is* upon us."

"But it is still weeks away. He must be stressed. We must see if there is anything else he needs."

"He just wants the tobacco. If he had wanted anything else he would have asked for it. We'll take it to him tomorrow."

They walked on, past the wax museum on their right, the Church of Saint John the Baptist visible on their left. Paradise took a sliver of goat from her wrap and put it in her mouth.

"I'm glad it was not another conversion," mused Love. "He does not realise how much they take out of us. We put our soul into taking their souls. That's why we can only do one a day."

"It is not his problem," reasoned Paradise. "We have been sent to protect The Secret and convert *kafirs*, until the glorious day - which will soon now be upon us after all these years. He is not interested in our weakness. Only in our strength."

"And talking of conversions," Love took a full bite of her *shawarma* and spoke as she chewed. "We still have this djinn to deal with. Or should we just leave it?"

"No," Paradise sounded stern. "Malek has issued conversion instructions, therefore we must obey them."

"She might be gone by now."

"You think so? *Djinn* do not run away."

Both of them touched the left side of their heads remembering their last encounter.

"You are right," agreed Love. "But how will we find her?"

Paradise stopped, her sister turning to look at her. "Don't forget, we have a disciple who can help us with these things. It may be time to awaken him."

Love smiled. "Yes, I had forgotten."

They walked on, the evening sun shining on their pale faces as they headed west.

After a minute, Love said *"Sabah a Allah."*

"Indeed," agreed Paradise. "God is good."

They turned left into Rue St John.

9 July 2010
27 Rajab 1431

Jounieh, Lebanon 07:00

"*Sabah el-khair mes amis*," greeted Carla as she entered the kitchen. "Good morning." She suppressed a grin as the Merhis pulled away from each other, Jihad flustered, over-compensating by fiddling with plates and cutlery. They had been in a romantic embrace, so obviously the outfit she had bought Gisele had worked last night!

"*Bonjour* Za – Carla," smiled Gisele (oh yes, she had the look). "Sorry, can't get used to your new name."

Carla was dressed in a just-long-enough loose white T-shirt – and nothing else. "I hope very soon it won't matter." She held up a piece of A4 paper. "I have done this. It is a good likeness."

Jihad took it, trying not to stare at the T shirt and what was beneath it, as Gisele asked, "Coffee?"

"Please."

"And help yourself to whatever we have. There's *labneh* in the fridge, some meats. Cheese. There's lemon cake. Or we have Jihad's good, healthy, traditional Lebanese breakfast – donuts!"

"Just the coffee for now, Gigi, thank you." As Gisele turned away to pour, Carla asked Jihad "What do you think?"

He was nodding positively. "Very good. You are a talented artist. Look, Geeg." He held up the drawing. The lifelike face of a young woman with long light hair stared out into the room. She was pretty but there was something disconcerting about her.

Gisele handed Carla her coffee. "What is wrong with the eyes?" she asked.

"Nothing. That's how they are."

"Sorry?"

"Her eyes are white."

"Well, shouldn't be hard to find her then," Jihad bit into his traditional Lebanese breakfast, jam oozing out over his fingers. "Might not even have to run the picture, just the description. She is blonde?"

"Yes."

"A blonde haired, white-eyed female assassin. Not too many of them in the world." He licked his fingers. "We could have a quick result. You want me to make it official now?"

"*Non.* Let us identify her first, then we will decide what we will do." Both Jihad and Gisele noted the 'we' but they did not say anything. "I will have my shower now, if that is all right? Then, Captain, could you give me a lift into Beirut? There are places I would like to visit."

"If you're quick."

"I will be. Like a djinn!" She smiled as she span away, taking her coffee with her.

Jihad watched her go, the T shirt gripped in the crevice between her gluteals. "Nice..." he was aware that Gisele was looking at him. "Weather today."

The slap around the back of his head nearly knocked his traditional Lebanese breakfast back out of his mouth.

Jbeil, Lebanon 14:00

Was Albert Gourhant addicted to going in different directions? wondered Abu Yussuf, the best private investigator in Jbeil (in fact, the only private investigator in Jbeil). On Tuesday the alleged adulterer had gone north up Rue Cheralam to the barber's shop. Yesterday, Thursday, he had gone south for his massage and meal at the Victory Byblos Hotel. Today he was going east.

Was he a compass-obsessive?

Abu Yussuf drove his Datsun Bluebird in his usual manner, one-handed, left arm hanging out the open window, cigarette between his fingers. He was dressed in a short-sleeved, open-necked white shirt, light brown slacks and loafers. A co-ordinating jacket was on the back seat in case he needed it, which he might do. It looked like Albert was heading into the mountains.

Was this to be the big reveal? Was this where his lover lived? Or at least, one of his lovers. Madame Gourhant had alleged that her husband was both prolific and serial.

Frankly, Abu Yussuf was surprised Albert had been allowed out today. With excursions from the house on Tuesday and Thursday, he had thought an every-other-day pattern was emerging. But he had been wrong. Just shows one never knew what to expect in this game.

And talking of game, to make sure he did not get bored if he had to wait outside somewhere while Albert sated his lust with one of his harem, today he had brought along his playing cards. He could play solitaire or maybe challenge himself to a game of poker (although he regarded solo poker akin to solo sex: an end result was achieved but you knew the outcome beforehand. It was better when at least one other person was involved). Or he could practise some card tricks he had been learning recently, to impress his cousin's children. He was becoming quite adept at making a card pop up out of his breast pocket.

And, of course, he had his iPhone.

Through a cloud of cigarette smoke, he looked at the blue Citroen C4 Picasso a little way ahead. So, where were you going, dear Albert? It looked like today might be a longer journey...

The road became bumpy as it climbed up into the mountains, with some sharp curves that made Abu Yussuf drive with both hands on the wheel, cigarette now lodged in the corner of his mouth. He followed the Citroen, up through Hboub, Kfar Qouas, Breij, Ras Osta...

Annaya, Lebanon 15:00 - 17:00

The Deir Mar Maron.

Being a Muslim, Abu Yussuf had never been here before but he was aware of the significance this place had for Lebanon's Christians. Wasn't one of their prophets or saints or something buried here?

He pulled in at the opposite end of the parking area, well away from Gourhant's Citroen which had parked up near the monastery. He watched as Gourhant got out of the car and went through a door to the left of the large statue of a bearded, hooded figure.

Throwing his cigarette onto the ground and discreetly treading on it as he got out, Abu Yussuf put on his jacket. Not only was it cooler up here, but a jacket was a sign of respect.

There were many people about, evidenced by the number of vehicles, parked either facing the mountains or looking out over the stunning view towards the coast. Abu Yussuf hoped he did not stand out, did not have *I am a Muslim* written in large letters on his forehead. He surveyed the other people, who were paying him no attention whatsoever. No, they looked just like him. One woman was even wearing a *hijab*. He would blend in, as a good *muhaqqiq khass* should.

He walked casually, like the other visitors. This was a place of pilgrimage, reflection and prayer – a sort of local Christian *hajj* – it was not a place for rushing. A few children were running around, ignoring their parents admonishments to be careful. He smiled. God bless them, whatever their creed.

The statue was impressive. Modern yet traditional. Its right hand was raised in a blessing, the left hand carried a holy book – the Christian bible. Two people were kneeling in front of it, praying.

Behind the statue was a raised, bricked area topped with grass and flowers. A wooden sign announced in English and Spanish:

The first tomb of Saint Charbel
In which he was buried on Christmas Day 1898
Few months later lights appeared upon it

Abu Yussuf looked at the door to the left. It was busy, people going in and out. A sign said it was the Tomb Church and Museum.

He went in, still wary that alarms might go off, detecting a Muslim in a Christian holy place. But there was nothing except an air of calm. He followed the general flow downstairs to the museum.

Like the statue outside, the museum was modern yet traditional in style. Behind wooden-framed glass enclosures were liturgical vestments, some heavily stained with secretions, utensils used by the saint, cloths which wiped his face, letters from believers worldwide, and even a wax tableau depicting the saint's family.

To the left of the entrance was a small kiosk-style shop. And one of the two people behind the counter, selling small items, accepting donations, and giving out relics, was Monsieur Albert Gourhant.

This could be a long wait, thought Abu Yussuf as he applied the parking brake. He had just moved his car so that it faced outwards and he could enjoy the views.

How long would Albert Gourhant be here? Probably until the museum closed in the evening. That could be four or five hours yet. Should he just give up for the day and return to Jbeil?

It was tempting, but he had resolved to give the distrusting Madame G a timetable of Monsieur's movements, so he would stick it out. It was highly unlikely Albert Gourhant was conducting an affair in the church! But he would be thorough. It was possible the old man could have a little respite stop somewhere back down the mountain on his way home. Possible but unlikely.

Abu Yussuf had placed his playing cards and telephone on the passenger seat next to him in the car. If this wait was as long as he expected it to be, before the evening was through he would be adept at all the games on the phone and well-rehearsed in the card tricks to show his cousin's children.

He picked up the phone, pleasantly surprised that he could get a signal on it up here, and accessed the apps. Casually glancing in his rear-view mirror, he saw a Jeep pull into the parking place he had just vacated facing the mountains. Two identical blonde-haired young women got out and walked off towards the monastery.

Twins, thought Abu Yussuf. How sweet.

Brother Malek stank.

Even if the twins had not had ultra-sensitive noses, they would have whiffed him anyway. The *burnus* seemed limp and clinging. And his mood was black.

Paradise and Love were wary as they walked either side of him along the shaded side of the monastery.

"This was not a good choice," he growled lowly. "I know I need to fit in but this physical work is too much. I have come to save the world. And look at the state of me. You have it?" He scratched his beard.

Love took a brown bag out of her rucksack. Malek took it without thanks.

"Hurt yourself," said Paradise.

Malek stopped walking. Without forward movement, his stench became even stronger. "*Maa?*"

"Hurt yourself. Say you have pulled a muscle, hurt your back or something. You are only working to fit in. It's not like we have not paid the monastery well for your stay. They will not quibble if you just spend your days in prayer and contemplation. You have tried to work but you have hurt yourself."

For quite a while Malek was silent. The women exchanged glances.

Then he said, "The twenty-second day of Ramadan."

The twins waited but he did not elaborate. Paradise gave a gentle nod of encouragement. "Yes, brother?"

For a moment, nothing. Then the hood moved from one to the other of them. "Fitting, don't you think? The Second Coming during the Holy Month. Satan has been vanquished, even now he is retreating. The first of September is the day, my sisters. Prepare yourselves for triumph."

Love breathed in through flared nostrils. "*Allahu Akbar. Sabah a Allah,*" she said softly, euphorically, grasping her sister on the forearm. Paradise patted her hand.

"Yes, it is a good idea. My back aches, so I will not be lying." Seamlessly Malek returned to the previous conversation. "But I must wash now and wash these robes as well. It will soon be time for '*Asr salat.*" He reached out and touched each woman on the shoulder. His mood had changed dramatically. "You have pleased me, my sisters. My right and left hands. My dexter and sinister. I bless you."

The twins went to turn back towards the monastery entrance, but were stopped by Malek's non-movement. "There is one thing I would like you to do for me, right now," he said.

Paradise put her arms by her side, a gesture of readiness. "Anything, oh Malek, you know that."

"I have left a sack of potatoes out in the field. Retrieve it. Fill it until it just closes and then leave it at the end of the monastery wall over there. I will say that is where my back gave up and I could carry it no further. One of the Christians will move it later. The earth will be changed on the twenty-second day of Ramadan. Rejoice."

Brother Malek nodded towards the nearby field, then, reaching into the hood and scratching his beard with both hands, he turned and walked quickly back towards the monastery entrance, head bowed, not wishing to be seen.

Like a hermit.

Abu Yussuf was bored. He had been in the car an hour and a half now. All the games he could access on his iPhone had been played, the card rising out of his top pocket had been rehearsed to perfection, two packets of cigarettes had been smoked as could be witnessed by the pile of butts beneath the car door. And he could be here a few more hours yet.

He climbed out of the Bluebird, stretching his legs and flexing his back. This was the worst part of surveillance, the waiting. In many cases, waiting was rewarded by the culprit eventually revealing himself, getting found out in the sin. But he doubted that Albert Gourhant had ever done anything naughty in his life. He was a volunteer at the monastery, for goodness sake. His wife was just a suspicious, jealous harridan.

But she was paying the piper. He needed to move, but he couldn't go far from the museum. Sod's Law said that the minute he turned his back, Albert would slip out and be away, beyond pursuit.

The idea of puncturing one of the old man's tyres flashed into his mind but was immediately thrown out like the unwelcome thug it was. That was not a nice thing to do – and anyway he could be stuck up here all night if he did that.

He needed a drink and perhaps a bite to eat. This time he had brought his phone and his cards to stave off boredom but he hadn't given a thought to his physical needs. Next time he would bring food and drink as well. Might even treat himself to a little picnic hamper.

There must be a café or some sort of restaurant facility around here somewhere. He would have a little look around, always keeping one eye on the front of the museum...

It took Paradise and Love thirty minutes to find the abandoned sack of potatoes, fill it up to its required level, tie it and haul it back to the rear wall of the monastery. They did not sweat (never had, never would), but their hands and white vests were grubby, and Love had a black smear across her nose as they stood by the dumped sack, trying to brush off the earth from their cargo pants.

They did not voice any complaints, they had been sent to protect The

Secret and obeying Malek was part of that protection, but they had worked up an appetite and Love joked that a quick conversion of two of the huge potatoes via a microwave oven would be good for the cause!

Paradise gently wiped her sister's nose with a tissue as she laughed at the conversion suggestion. "Come *habibi*. Let us return to Jbeil. He will not want to see us again today. I will ring him and tell him we have done as he asked."

They moved off towards the front of the monastery.

Brother Malek felt human again – which, as he considered himself divine, was not really as good as it sounded, but at least he felt better than he had before. A full fifteen minute shower had washed away the grime and sweat of his toil, but he did not feel completely clean. His beard still itched. It had been a long time since its last trim and it had grown into the long, straggly Maronite style of old. It was time to take it down to modern levels, maybe even take it off and let it grow back evenly during his final weeks here.

He did not have washing facilities in his cell upstairs, he had to use one of the monks' two communal washrooms on the ground floor, just like the others. He had chosen the smaller of the two and had wedged the door closed with a bible. So he had time. First scissors, then razor.

Wispy grey and black hairs fell into the sink as he began to snip...

That was better.

Abu Yussuf had found a small refreshment kiosk in the park area and he was now on his second bottle of orangina and third packet of Oreos. In his pocket he had a wedge of cake. He needed the sugar.

He had had to lose sight of the museum while he found the refreshment kiosk but as he came back into the parking area he was relieved to see Gourhant's Citroen was still there.

He walked slowly. Now that the immediate pangs of thirst and hunger had been sated, he could eat and drink his remaining items leisurely.

The late afternoon sun was still warm on his face as he walked down the side of the monastery. He could hear singing from somewhere inside. Must be some Christian song; it sounded melodious.

Way down the other end of the building he saw two figures turn the corner, coming his way. One of them was on the telephone. Idly, without much thought to what he was looking at, he glanced in at an open window in the monastery wall.

And he stopped dead in his tracks.

Brother Malek, wet hair pushed straight back, beard removed, lines of foam still on his face, was speaking on his mobile phone and looking straight out of the window. He stopped talking abruptly when he saw the man outside staring at him, open-mouthed.

Their eyes locked. Malek's were dark and malicious. Abu Yussuf's were wide, incredulous, like an *arnab* caught in the headlights.

Still with his phone to his ear, Malek said "I have been seen." The person on the other end spoke, then Malek said "Yes, him. Deal with it."

Abu Yussuf could not believe what he was seeing. At first he thought his mind was playing tricks, the effects of a malevolent sugar-rush. In a microsecond he blinked, shook his head, then blinked again. *No, it was impossible.*

Then he became aware of people running to his right. Glued to the spot, he turned his head. It was those two young women he had seen parking earlier, the identical twins.

He looked back at the window. The man was still there, staring at him blankly.

The women reached him. One stopped two metres away on his right, the other moved around to his other side. What would they think when they looked in the window? "Look," he said breathlessly, a tremble in his voice. "Look!" His fingers shook as he pointed.

But they ignored him. From the other side of the window an accented voice said, "Convert him."

Abu Yussuf frowned. Convert? He was a good Shi'ite, he did not want to be converted. He would never be Christian.

Then something happened that made him doubt his sanity. The two women brought their hands up to their faces and then leant forward. *In the name of Allah, they were taking out their eyes!*

The two heads snapped back up. Bile rose in Abu Yussuf's throat as he gasped at the white eyeballs and black pupils focused on him, the heads inclined to one side, curious.

The woman on the right moved. But so did Abu Yussuf. Instinctively, without thought, he threw his bottle of orangina at the approaching woman. It cracked onto her brow but weirdly there were two gasps, one from her, one from the woman behind him. Both women leant forward, holding their heads.

What on earth...? Had the bottle bounced off one onto the other?

Abu Yussuf ran. He did not understand but he knew he needed to get out of there. Something mad was happening. Something evil.

Up ahead, people were still going in and out of the museum. He would be safe in a crowd.

Still running, he risked a look back. Both women were on their haunches, still holding their heads. It looked like one of them was bleeding – but he would not stop to find out!

He ran past Albert Gourhant's Citroen but it did not even register with him. Back at his Datsun Bluebird he fumbled with the keys, got them into the lock at the second attempt, got in, slammed the door and quickly locked it.

The engine started on the first turn. Breathlessly, he engaged the gears – and jerked forward. Just in time he slammed his foot on the brake before he took off over the mountainside.

He found reverse and turned in his seat – to see the two women running round the corner up by the museum.

Rubber smoke from the tyres and cinders from the track flew into the air as the Bluebird shot forward and away.

Coastal Highway, Lebanon 17:30

Three times Abu Yussuf nearly drove off the mountainside on his way down. Once one of his back wheels actually went off the edge on a hairpin bend, but the speed of the car kept his momentum forward, saving him. He prayed to almighty Allah that he would see a Jeep Wrangler Ultimate somersaulting down the ridge behind him - but his prayers went unanswered.

They were in pursuit, but he knew if he could reach the highway the Bluebird had enough power to at least match the Jeep, if not outrun it, despite the Bluebird's age.

He still could not believe what he had seen up at the monastery. He needed to tell someone. Someone he could trust. Someone who could help him.

He reached the coastal highway, speeding onto the south-bound carriage to a cacophony of blaring horns from the other drivers. It was busy as always, but at this time of day the north-bound side was busier. Was that a consolation or a hindrance?

Half a kilometre behind, he saw a black Jeep also careen into the traffic flow, immediately pulling out into the far left lane. The chase was on.

He needed to do something, just in case he didn't make it to his destination. He looked at the playing cards and his iPhone on the seat beside him. He had an idea.

Keeping his eyes on the road and keeping his left hand on the wheel, he fumbled in the glove compartment for his pen...

Beirut 18:10 – 19:30

He kept them at bay all the way down the highway, just about matching the pursuers for speed, the Jeep only gaining on him by about three cars on the forty kilometre journey.

The background of irate horns continued all the way down into the capital – once he even took someone's wing-mirror off. Many drivers were on mobile phones, but were any of them reporting him? Unlikely knowing the drivers of Lebanon, they'd be too afraid their own sins would find them out! Where were the police when you needed them? Where?

The sheer volume of traffic made him slow down as he entered Beirut, but what slowed him would also slow his followers. He would stay on the highway for as long as possible and then use the major boulevards through the city. The last thing he wanted to do was to get caught in traffic in the narrow side streets.

The Dora Highway became Charles Helou Avenue. The traffic was maintaining a strong pace. He couldn't see the Jeep in his rear-view mirror but he knew it could not have gotten any nearer to him.

He would be looking to turn south, probably along George Haddad Street.

But he never got that far.

As he approached the entrance to the Port of Beirut on his right, the Bluebird stuttered. It caught its speed back then stuttered again.

What the hell?

He looked at the dashboard.

No, he did not believe it. He had not been aware of any warning lights. Perhaps the car did not have any – he had never run out of fuel before.

Now he needed to get off the avenue quickly. If he stopped here they would get him in no time. He wrenched the wheel to the right taking the road that led down into the port. The Bluebird stuttered, slowed, stuttered, slowed. Soon he would be running on fumes only.

Another right took him onto the narrow road running underneath Charles Helou Avenue. Slowly and more slowly he rolled along it, taking another right into Berberi Street.

At the junction with Pasteur Street, the car stopped. He swore, turning the key, knowing it was futile. Clunk, shudder, clunk. Grabbing his phone, he jumped out of the car, looking back down the road, the busy avenue above him.

There was no Jeep. Had they missed him turning off? If so, they would have gone speeding off into Gemmayzeh and then into the downtown district and they would have lost him. Perhaps running out of fuel had been the best thing that could have happened!

He had lifted the phone in his hand, ready to make a call, when he heard the sound of a vehicle coming down the same way as he had. He shouldn't worry, he told himself, it could be anybody. Casually he looked back.

And saw the Jeep.

He took off at a run, hearing the engine accelerate behind. He crossed Pasteur Street. He couldn't hope to outrun a car, he needed to get somewhere where they couldn't follow... Ah, he knew!

He ran left down a narrow street into the Rmeil District. He heard the Jeep turn after him, but he knew it would have to go slowly to avoid people and parked vehicles.

His breath began to go. What he would do for a cigarette right now!

He turned right into Gouraud Street by the post office. If he remembered correctly, there was a police station a little way down. But he wasn't heading for that.

He crossed over the street and raced up onto the Saint Nicholas Stairs.

Also known as Daraj el-Fen, the Artists' Stairs, it is a street of stairs connecting Gourand Street with Sursock Street. One hundred and twenty-five stairs divided into twenty-three flights and stretching for half a kilometre, it is lined either side by apartment blocks and houses, and twice a year is used for art exhibitions.

After two flights of stairs, Abu Yussuf had to stop, leaning on a waste bin, catching his breath. His legs were beginning to shake. There were people about but no one was paying him any heed. Still with his phone in his hand, he tapped his jacket pocket for his cigarettes then remembered that he had smoked them all up at Annaya.

Warily he looked up and down the stairs. Well, the Jeep certainly couldn't climb up here. Looking back, it seemed quiet down on Gouraud Street this Friday evening.

Except for the tall, blonde young woman coming up towards him.

Adrenaline shot through him as he straightened up, injecting power into his weak legs to keep on climbing but making him drop the phone. It smashed onto the ground, the back flying off and both parts spinning off in different directions.

He made it up one more flight and stopped, looking back. Now he was afraid.

The woman seemed to be in no hurry as she walked up the stairs. Her white eyes were looking at him curiously, dispassionately. But surely she couldn't kill him here, with people about?

He looked upwards to see if there was anyone who could help him. Surely there was somebody...?

But what he saw made the tension leave his body and he knew it was all over.

The other twin was walking down the stairs towards him. He was cut off, one coming down, one coming up.

He began to pray. *"Ash-hadu alla ilaha illaha illa llah. Ash-hadu anna Muhammadan-rasulu llah..."* I testify that there is no deity except God. I testify that Mohammed is the Messenger of God...

The women met on the stairs next to him, embracing each other, laughing. For a moment it seemed like they did not know he was there. Then the four white eyes turned to him, the two faces smiling. One of them patted him on the shoulder and then, linking arms and still laughing, they walked down the stairs, not looking back.

Abu Yussuf shook his head, bewildered. He couldn't believe it. No knives, no guns? Had this just been a warning all along?

He had an urgent desire to pee, but that would have to wait. This was a respite, a let off. Allah was protecting him. *Allahu Akbar.*

He needed to find a taxi and fast.

Back down on Gouraud Street he found a service taxi, identified by its red licence plate. Beirut's service taxis pick up and carry more than one passenger, but a generous *pourboire* for the driver as he got into the decrepit old vehicle ensured that Abu Yussuf would travel alone.

He did not give his exact destination, just told the driver to head south towards the airport area. He would direct him further later.

Five minutes into the journey he began to feel ill.

By the time they reached Annan Street, Abu Yussuf's chest was heavy and a thick red fog was swirling over his eyes. Sweat was beaded on his brow. His mouth felt dry and tasted foul, and he just managed to say *"Hon"* to the taxi driver before his tongue ballooned up.

The driver was mumbling, swearing. He did not like to come down this far south. This was on the edge of the hell-hole that was the Bourj el-Barajneh Palestinian refugee camp, and this was not a place anyone wanted to be unless they had to, even on a light, warm summer's evening.

The taxi pulled over and Abu Yussuf dropped a bundle of notes over the front seat, which shut the driver up for ten seconds. He opened the taxi door, tried to step out but found himself sprawled on the ground. He had alighted at a terrace of shops and service providers, but the place he wanted was... What was it? He couldn't remember... Oh yes, the small two-storey house...

He got up, reeling like a drunk. The buildings were swimming in the thick red fog. He saw the door he wanted. Wondering why it was getting dark so early, he staggered over, raised his hand to knock, and missed the door completely.

He hit it on the third attempt, slapping it pathetically. Summoning up his last gram of strength, he struck the door harder. Harder, harder, harder...

A pain ripped through his stomach and he fell backwards, bent in half.

Then a voice boomed from down the road and a large shadow was running towards him. No, he thought, no. Not the women again. Hadn't they killed him already?

Another pain, making his bowels move violently, and he fell to the ground, rolling in agony, gripping his stomach. His tongue was so swollen he was unable to breathe through his mouth. Snot was shooting in and out of his nose as he tried to inhale.

The shadow reached him. "Chadi?" said a voice. "Chadi? Chadi!"

Abu Yussuf opened his eyes but he couldn't see the figure kneeling next to him. But he knew the voice and his cheeks twitched in a smile. He tried to say something but all he could manage was a grunt. So he moved his left arm.

The kneeling figure gasped in bewilderment as a playing card rose out of the breast pocket of Abu Yussuf's jacket.

The door behind opened to reveal a fat Palestinian woman dressed in a black *jilbaab* with no head covering, a small child of about three looking out from around her legs. "Who is it, husband?" she asked.

The kneeling figure looked up, shaking his head, perplexed, unbelieving. "Nada. This... this is my cousin. Chadi. The one from Jbeil... And he's dead," said Captain Fadi Lattouf of the Civil Police of the Palestinian Security Force.

PART THREE
الجزء الثالث

THE TAKING
أخذ

10 July 2010
28 Rajab 1431

Jonblat, Beirut 09:00

Jihad Merhi did not like attending the office on a Saturday, but he acknowledged that being a Captain of the Lebanese Internal Security Force was a 24-7 job and sometimes needs must. And, he had to admit, there was the advantage that the office was quieter – unlike the street outside which was the lead-in to the Hamra shopping district and was already crowded and noisy. Out there, somewhere, Gisele and Carla were once again preparing to donate inordinately large sums of money to the poor shopkeepers of Beirut.

Yesterday had been one of those frustrating days when he was constantly busy but had seemed not to get anything done. In Parliament, the March 14th coalition of parties was preparing to re-present Walid Jumblatt's bill on Palestinian rights* - nothing to particularly worry the ISF except that Prime Minister Saad Hariri had called for national unity on the conferring of civil rights to Palestinian refugees, and a call for national unity often gave ideas to people with ill-intent.

And yesterday had also been the annual Miss Lebanon contest and, as always, certain sections of society objected to such things. If the mood took them, they might have wanted to express their complaints in a tangible way - but thankfully the event had taken place without incident.

So he had been unable to proceed with Carla's drawing of her assailant and the alleged assassin of the DGS captain. She had been understanding when she came in late last night (she had been out all day, she did not say where, he did not ask) and he had promised to clear the decks this Saturday morning and get down to it.

When he came in he had placed his mug of so-called coffee on top of the notepad on his desk. Picking up the mug while his computer was booting up, he found a note underneath. It was in Sergeant el-Gharib's handwriting.

Lt Himo rang 18:00

---

* *The bill would allow many of the 425,000 Palestinian refugees living in Lebanon (mostly in the country's 12 refugee camps) to obtain work permits for professions from which they were currently barred under Lebanese law, for example doctors, dentists, lawyers, engineers, and accountants. It had not been passed when first presented the previous month.*

Merhi's eyebrows raised. Lieutenant Himo? Selim Himo? Good heavens, he had not spoken to him since he knew not when. Himo was in the Bekaa Inquiry Brigade of the *Gendarmerie* and had helped him out with the serial killings investigation five years ago.

The raised eyebrows reformed into a frown. Five years again...

Well, Himo would have to wait. Carla was his priority today.

Out in the General Office it took him fifteen minutes to scan Carla's drawing into the system (el-Gharib would normally do it but he was off duty). He filed it under 'Unknown female' and forwarded it to himself.

Back at his desk, he opened the national database (it was now much more user-friendly than in the past; it had been updated last year when the government had decreed that religious affiliations need no longer be shown on national identity cards). Then he brought up the scanned drawing, linked it into the database, inserted 'Female' and 'Under 50' filters, and pressed Search.

Faces shot onto and off the screen, and he turned away, reaching for his cigarettes.

He had time to go outside and make another so-called coffee and then return to enjoy it with a leisurely Cedars King Size while staring out the window at the traffic on Bank of Lebanon Street before the screen stopped its maniacal face churning.

NO MATCH FOUND

Well, no surprise there. Most of the assassins operating in the country were not Lebanese, and this one was no exception. He would try the national criminal database.

This search was quicker.

NO MATCH FOUND

Now his task became more difficult. He wished he could look at the databases of other countries, especially Lebanon's neighbours. He had heard rumour that the Israelis had a universal hacker that, with the right input, could search any system anywhere in the world, by-passing all firewalls and other security features. The Jews might have shared it with their allies but Lebanon would never get it. Which meant that he might have to make verbal, written or electronic requests of other countries. Which meant his enquiries would have to become official. He would need to run that by Carla first –

His mobile phone rang.

As he stretched out for it, the landline telephone on his desk rang as well. My, wasn't he popular all of a sudden!

Assuming that the mobile would be Gisele seeking his agreement to spend money, he picked up the landline.

"Merhi, excuse me just one second." He pressed the reject button on his mobile to shut it up. "Yes, hello."

"Jihad, I wondered if you would be in. It's Selim Himo."

"Selim, *kifak?* They left me a message that you rang. How are things in the Bekaa?"

"I'm fine thanks, as I hope you are."

"I'm good, *merci*. Busy, of course, as always, but good."

"Jihad, I'm in town. I wonder if we could meet? There's something I really need your help on."

Shit, thought Merhi. This was not needed, not right now with the work he had on – not to mention the Carla business. But he owed Himo, owed him big for the help he had given him five years ago. "For you, any time. When would you like to meet?"

"Can we make it Monday morning, at your office?"

"If you are happy with that, yes." They both understood Merhi's oblique reference to The Listeners. "Around nine?"

"Perfect. Enjoy the rest of your weekend. *A lundi.*"

As he put the phone down, Merhi wondered whether he should return Gisele's phone call. She hadn't called back, she had probably bought whatever it was she was going to buy, taking his non–answer of the phone as tacit agreement. Deciding to meet the challenge to his bank account head on, he reached for his mobile – just as it rang again.

He answered without looking at the screen. "Hi."

"Morning of light, Jihad my dear friend!"

Merhi nearly dropped the phone in shock. In the name of Jesus Christ, the Almighty in Heaven above! The voice, the shout, was unmistakeable. He felt his strength draining away.

"Fadi Lattouf, how are you?"

"I am well, my friend, well. And you and the charming Gisele?"

"*Shukran*, we are good. And Nada and your family? How's the little one?"

"Everyone is well, thank you. Little Wissam looks more like his father each day!"

Feeling nothing but sympathy for the poor child, Merhi asked "Number seven not on the way yet?"

"Pah! Chance would be a fine thing. Nada thinks that abstinence will bring us nearer to Allah. I told her Allah will be seeing us soon enough and in the meantime we should honour Him by doing what comes naturally, but she was having none of it."

Well she certainly had some of it three years and forty weeks ago, thought Merhi. He said, "I wish you well in your continued quest, my friend."

"Thank you, thank you. Jihad, I need to say something to you that I thought I would never have to say again."

"What is that?"

There was a pause, then Fadi Lattouf said "Jihad, I have a body."

Sodeco, Beirut 14:00

Gisele Merhi smiled at the waiter as she handed back her menu, then she turned to her husband and said, "Fadi Lattouf. I cannot believe it. After all this time."

"As if I do not have enough on." Jihad pointedly did not look at Carla, sitting next to his wife opposite.

They were in *La Piazza* restaurant. It was one of Jihad's favourite eateries and he had surprised the women by offering to take them here when he had met them up at Hamra. He was in need of the familiar – and good food. Carla had never been in the restaurant before, but she had heard of it from a close friend. She was amazed at the setting. They were inside but were sitting in an Italian town square; on the walls around them were murals of houses, some even with laundry hanging out to dry. It was quaint, charming and, unusually for a restaurant with such a strong theme, Jihad had assured her that the food was excellent.

"It is Ramadan soon," continued Gisele.

Jihad dragged on his cigarette and pulled a face. "What of it?"

"What comes at the end of Ramadan?"

The pulled face dropped as he realized. "*Eid*. Oh no, not again." They had gone through a three-year phase of being invited to the Lattouf's to celebrate *Eid* and, in return, having to invite the Lattouf's to Jounieh for the New Year's celebrations. It had started during the events of five years ago but had then dropped away during Madame Lattouf's sixth pregnancy. Jihad did not want to resurrect the tradition.

"Was he that Palestinian you were with?" asked Carla. "The huge one. In Nejmeh Square."

"The same. The giant. He is supposedly in charge of the refugee camps in the Beirut area, but we all know who really runs them. I think even Fadi now accepts that he and his men are nothing more than window dressing. We used to meet officially twice a year, but even that has gone now, when we realized the meetings were pointless."

"What does he want?" wondered Gisele.

"I'll find out tomorrow." He had not mentioned those ominous four words: *I have a body*.

An appetizer of garlic dough balls was delivered to the table, together with other bread and separate olive oil. As they began to eat, Jihad asked

Carla, "So do you want me to make official enquiries?"

"She is not local, we could have guessed that." Carla dipped bread into oil and took a small bite. "Which means she has been brought in from abroad. Just to kill Maroun?"

"That would be very extravagant."

"To kill me?"

"Still extravagant. With respect."

"No, no, you are right. And she has failed with me. Perhaps she has gone. Quickly in, quickly out." A small dribble of olive oil ran down her chin. She caught it with her little finger and smoothed it back upwards into her mouth, dabbing the residue with her napkin.

"Or perhaps Maroun and you are just sidelines," suggested Gisele. "Think broadly." Once a trainer always a trainer. "Maybe you are not her main purpose. She was just conveniently here to deal with you while doing something else."

Knowing what she knew, it was a conclusion Carla had also come to. "Yes, I agree. And that means she is still here. So," she rubbed crumbs from her fingers over her plate, looking at Jihad, "can you make enquiries without specifying a reason?"

"There is another route I can take. I can be vague," he nodded.

"Then please do so."

Meantime, she thought, I shall enlist help of my own.

11 July 2010
29 Rajab 1431

Jounieh, Lebanon 02:30

The night was warm, the stars shimmering in the cloudless sky. It was a new moon so natural light was sparse, but the coastal highway way down below was well-lit by traffic despite the hour. Beyond the road, way out to sea, a boat bobbed, small lights fore and aft.

Jihad and Gisele were in bed and asleep, at least one of them snoring for Lebanon as Carla had glided soundlessly past their bedroom door. Now she was outside on the balcony and for a moment she closed her eyes and lifted her face, absorbing the air and warmth, as if she was being recharged by the stillness of the dark. She was completely naked.

Then a light shone from her left hand as her cell phone trembled. Right on time. She lifted the phone to her ear.

"*Bon soir*," she smiled, speaking low, looking out westwards into the night...

Verdun, Beirut 11:30

Captain Fadi Lattouf of the Civil Police of the Palestinian Security Force was two metres tall and seemed to measure the same around his stomach. How he had not spontaneously combusted - or simply burst - in any one of his fifty years was a mystery to many people.

Jihad Merhi could see the Palestinian in the Food Court of the Dunes Shopping Mall as he came up the escalator. Lattouf's backside was so big that it consumed the chair beneath him and gave the impression he was squatting on thin air. He still had the severe comb-over of the remaining strands of his hair, which served to emphasise rather than hide his bald dome, but they were greyer than the last time the two men had met. His beard was greyer too, still of the unshaven-look rather than the cultivated variety.

Lattouf was dressed – *oh my goodness*. He had on the same clothes as he did when they used to meet here five years ago! Rough blue denim jeans, for which he was about twenty-five years too old and fifty kilos too heavy, and a loose pink and blue checked shirt. He used to wear them to blend in with the other shoppers. He failed then and he failed now. Giants did not blend, giant Palestinian policemen even less so.

The state of the table in front of him looked like McDonald's would have to send out for some more burger wrappers before the lunch-time rush began.

Merhi decided to go straight up to *Cup Cakes*. When he was a few metres away, a voice from behind boomed out "*Ay, ay!*" making cups rattle on trays, and he looked back to see a beaming Fadi Lattouf with his right hand in the air. Merhi half-raised his hand and gestured with his head towards the counter. Lattouf nodded (was the Pope a Catholic? Was the President of Lebanon a Christian?).

A few minutes later Merhi was placing a tray down onto the now empty table, the floor beneath littered with the McDonald's wrappers.

"Morning of joy, my dear, dear friend!" Lattouf stood up and Merhi knew what was coming. Lattouf grabbed him and planted five kisses on his cheeks. "Mwah, mwah, mwah, mwah, mmmmmmWAH! It has been a long time. It is good to see you."

Merhi thought that three ribs were broken. "And you, Fadi. You're looking well."

"Pah! Nada has me on a diet," Lattouf tapped his gut which looked bigger than ever. "I am wasting away, look at me!"

"Then you won't want these cakes," Merhi gestured to the tray on which sat ten cup cakes, two supersize coffees and one double espresso.

"It would be rude to reject your hospitality," reasoned Lattouf. "Bless your hands." He sat down, once again making the chair below disappear.

Merhi sat down also. "One of the chocolate ones are mine." He took the espresso off the tray and helped himself to a cake, pushing the tray and its remaining contents towards Lattouf.

"Of course," smiled the Palestinian. "You Lebanese and your sweet teeth!" He picked up one of the coffees, steam rising from the polycup as he took off the lid. Much more quietly he said, "To you, my friend."

Merhi gestured with his espresso cup. He had to admit, it was good to see the fat, stupid, ebullient bastard again. Perhaps another *Eid* celebration with him wouldn't be so bad after all. "And to you, Fadi."

Half the contents of the polycup had vanished when Lattouf put it back on the table. Sweeping two cakes up in his hand and peeling off the cases, he said "Jihad, you find me a sad, sad man."

"Oh? Why?"

"I have had a death in the family."

"I am sorry to hear that."

Lattouf shrugged. "*Shukran.* He was my cousin. I could not say we were close, but a family death is a family death."

"Of course."

The two cakes were placed in his mouth, one on each side. "He lived up in Jbeil. Moved up there in 2006 after his wife and son were killed by the Jews when they bombed Beirut."

Merhi did not say anything. The constant, regular destruction of Lebanon on an any-excuse basis by the Israelis was a source of hatred for all Lebanese.

Lattouf picked up two more cakes and began to peel them. "His *kunya* was Abu Yussuf, but his name was Chadi."

Merhi quickly rammed the remains of his cup cake into his mouth. How did Lattouf manage to do this, to bring out such a range of emotions in him? The flare-up of anger at the reminder of the Jews had been replaced by the urge to burst out laughing. Chadi? Chadi and Fadi Lattouf? Sounded like a vaudeville comedy act! Quickly he sipped his espresso then reached across and took another cake from the tray.

"My – my condolences," he coughed, stifling the giggles, reaching in his jacket pocket for his cigarettes.

"Thank you, my friend, thank you." Lattouf reached across and touched his arm, mistaking his watering eyes for an expression of sorrow.

Both men ate cake.

"You said you had a body?" Merhi prompted.

Lattouf frowned. "Yes. My cousin."

"Oh, sorry, sorry! I didn't realise he was the... erm..." Merhi looked around, cigarette in his hand. "Do they still allow you to smoke in here?"

"I am sure nobody is going to argue with you." Lattouf nodded at Merhi's uniform.

"No, I suppose not." He slid the packet of Cedars King Size across the table. "I'm sorry, Fadi, perhaps you had better start from the beginning." He lit up.

Lattouf's eyes were full of sadness – as he looked at the cigarettes. "I had better not. She will smell it on me." He pushed the packet back.

"You could say the smoke got on you from me."

The packet was grabbed back and a cigarette removed. Merhi passed over his lighter.

As he inhaled smoke, Lattouf said "There's not much to tell. Two nights ago I was coming home from work. Around seven-thirty. I was walking down the street towards my house and I saw a *service* pulling up. Someone fell out of it, got up and started banging on my door. I realised it was my cousin. As I got to him he fell back onto the floor, clutching his gut. He was trying to say something to me but he couldn't. Then he died. Right there in the street."

"Did you call the emergency services?"

"Why? He was dead."

"The street is under Lebanese jurisdiction. You should have reported it."

"The street might be. My house isn't."

"Ah, I see. A Palestinian problem then. So why have you called me?"

Lattouf sucked a full two centimetres from the cigarette then stubbed it out in one of the cup cake wrappers. "Chadi was in his forties, no illnesses that the family knew of."

"Death happens, my friend. Sometimes very abruptly."

"As I was washing the body prior to burial last night I noticed something on his left shoulder. A distinct puncture mark. Fresh."

Oh heavens, here we go, thought Merhi.

"I think my cousin was murdered," said Fadi Lattouf.

Annaya, Lebanon 11:35

The Monastery Church of Saint Maron was quiet, deserted except for the three people sitting near the first wall alcove on the right, beneath the two pictures of Saint Maron with the vase of flowers underneath. Visitors rarely came to this 1840s church, even on a Sunday, most preferring the new, round Saint Charbel Church on the other side of the monastery.

Brother Malek was dressed in his full black *burnus*, hood up, only his stubbled chin visible. Because of the heat he wore nothing underneath. But no one would know that.

Paradise and Love knelt on the pew in front, facing him, their green and brown eyes (thirty-five thirty-six in Love's favour) looking at the chin moving as he talked.

"If necessary we will convert the world. I have done it in the past, I will do it again." Although his voice was deep and low, every word was distinct. "Soon now we will no longer have to keep the secret, we will reveal it to the world. Those disciples left behind are now preparing for the second coming. The way is being cleared. It feels like they have been waiting millennia, but they will be rewarded for their patience."

"What can we do?" asked Paradise.

"You are already doing plenty," his voice softened as he reached out and patted their arms. "Follow me, my daughters. Keep the faith."

"Should The Secret be moved?" asked Love. "There was a breach."

The hood turned in her direction. "Was The Secret compromised? Did you not deal with it?"

"Of course we did, Brother," said Paradise. "As always it is your decision. But we would be failing if we did not bring it to your attention."

There was silence. The twins could detect the change in mood, the change in aura, coming from the cowled figure. Eventually he said, "You have somewhere in mind?"

Love looked at her sister. "We were thinking somewhere near the triumphal road. To prepare for the journey come the time. Beyond Baabda. Jamhour perhaps, maybe even Bhamdoun."

Again silence, this time for quite a while. Then: "No. The Secret has moved enough. The time is so close now we will not move again until we begin our journey. The breach was an accident. A *kafir* passing, a chance happenstance. He has been converted and I will not be using that washroom again. I am satisfied The Secret has not been compromised."

Paradise nodded. "Your decisions are always infallible. But take this." She nodded to Love who put her hand into a front pocket of the rucksack on the pew next to her and brought out a tiny object, no more than two centimetres long by one centi-metre wide. She placed it in Malek's outstretched palm. "We have the number," continued Paradise. "Naturally no one else does."

Malek closed his palm over the new SIM card.

"We did not bring any more *ma'asel* because you did not request any." Love now had her hand in the main part of the rucksack. "But we thought you might like these." She passed over a folded yellow and green *Spinney's* carrier bag.

Malek felt it without looking inside. The hood moved up and down, nodding. He tucked the bag under his arm and stood up.

Before the twins could rise he had placed a hand on each of their heads. "The Secret is safe. All conversions have been achieved. I will let you know further details of The Second Coming once the disciples have prepared the way. Our route will be strewn with palms..." He took his hands off their heads. "And the bodies of the unbelievers."

Silently he walked back down the church. He stopped by the door, the hood turning back towards the women. He spoke no louder but his voice carried. "You have pleased me, my daughters. Soon now I will please you."

The door creaked open and the hooded monk glided out.

Paradise and Love were left looking at the shaft of bright sunlight piercing through the half-open door.

"Did you feel it?" asked Paradise.

"Yes," said Love, touching the top of her head. "He almost burnt our scalps."

Verdun, Beirut 11:45

"And you want me to investigate it?" asked Jihad Merhi disbelievingly. "A man dies in Beirut, you drag him into Palestinian jurisdiction and now you want the Lebanese authorities to investigate it because you think it might be suspicious? You can't have it both ways, my friend. You should have reported it in the first place."

"And have strangers' hands over my cousin's body? Maybe cutting him up? And anyway, I did not know he had been murdered - "

"You still don't."

"I think I do. But I need you to confirm it." Lattouf finished the second cup of coffee and stifled a burp down to sonic boom proportions.

"You want another?" Merhi could not believe he had just asked that.

"I will get them." Lattouf fumbled for money in his jeans pocket.

"No, no, I will."

"Okay then. *Merci ktir.*"

When Merhi returned with one large and one medium Americano plus a four-pack of chocolate chip cookies, he asked "In what way can I possibly help you? Your cousin is dead, you have buried the body, what can I do?"

"Bless your hands." Lattouf pulled the lid off his coffee like a man in the final stages of dehydration, slurping it, mixing it with air like a fine wine, confirming Merhi's opinion that he had an asbestos oesophagus. Lattouf shook his head. "You are wrong, my friend. I did not say my cousin was buried. I was preparing him for burial when I found the puncture mark. So I didn't bury him, I've kept him somewhere safe. Please Jihad, come take a look. Tell me if I am imagining it." Lattouf's huge fingers adroitly pulled open the wrapping on the cookies. He offered the packet to Merhi who raised a hand in refusal.

"Where is he?"

"In the *mashraha.*"

"You have a mortuary?"

"We have had one for some time now. Hardly ever been used. Usually the groups, you know, take care of their own."

"And the mortuary is in the camp?" The one place where the Lebanese authorities could not go.

"*Taban.* Of course. You know it. You've been there. Used to be the butcher's shop."

Annaya, Lebanon 11:45

Back in his cell, Brother Malek pulled off his *burnus* and stepped out of his sandals. He stood there naked, his body hairy, carrying the weight of age but by no means fat. A sheen of sweat covered him, his body hairs matted where they were thickest. He should wash, it would soon be time for *salat al-Dhuhr*, noon prayer. But first there was something he must do.

Next to his mattress against the wall was the square, dark blue carrying case with his golden *argileh* inside. He knelt on the floor, flicking up the clasp of the case as he pulled it over. Gently, almost lovingly, he took out the separate pieces of the shisha, placing them carefully on the floor beside him.

But he did not assemble the pipe. Instead, when all the parts were out, he put his hand back into the case. And brought out a Sony Vaio netbook.

It was a chore using one-time-only e-mail accounts, but it was effective. And, when he needed them, he had his one-time-only *Skype* accounts too, with *Windows Messenger* as a fall-back.

One of the benefits of being in Lebanon was that the country was technology-obsessed. There were more mobile telephones in the country than there were people, there were more satellite dishes than there were houses, the social networking sites were more popular here than anywhere else in the world, every one under a certain age – and most people above it – had a computer, and, if they could, their own website. And that included the monasteries.

All the monasteries of any note had their own website, often run by one of the younger brothers of the order. And where there was a web domain there was access to the internet. WiFi.

Malek lifted the lid on the netbook and pressed the On button.

Jounieh, Lebanon 14:30

Gisele Merhi had been less than impressed when her husband had appeared at the door half an hour earlier with the huge Palestinian, but being the perfect hostess she had pretended to be pleased to see him – and so suddenly and unannounced too – enquiring after his family, his health, how was the new baby? Three already, good heavens, God's blessings upon him. Yes, she would love to visit and see him sometime.

Now she asked, "Are you sure you cannot stay for dinner, Fadi?"

Fadi looked up from the two-seater leather sofa which, with him in it, looked like it was a scaled-down chair from a kindergarten. In his hand he held his third glass of apple juice. "My dear Gisele, there is nothing I would like more. But alas, your husband and I have business. But soon, perhaps."

"Yes soon." Under her breath she added, "Perhaps."

Jihad appeared. He had changed from his uniform into casual gear: blue 'I ♥ Dubai' T-shirt (a present from his brother-in-law), light beige jeans, socks and trainers (he had wanted to wear sandals but they would not be suitable). When he had told Gisele where he was going (as if she hadn't guessed already), a classic Merhi *sotto voce* discussion had ensued in the kitchen, with Jihad winning but feeling like he'd lost ('twas ever thus). And, by the way, asked Gisele with the last word as always, just how many waifs and strays from the past was he intending to bring back to the apartment this weekend? That was two now and counting.

"Okay Fadi," Jihad said. "Let's go." Pecking Gisele on a reluctantly-offered cheek, he said "I'll text you when I'm on my way back."

Lattouf poured the remainder of his apple juice into his body and stood up, looking for somewhere to put the glass then giving it to Gisele.

As they walked towards the front door, there was the sound of a key in the lock. The door opened to reveal a small, olive skinned, black haired woman whom Lattouf instantly recognised. He gasped. "The lady! The lady from Nejmeh Square." He grabbed her hand, raising it to his lips. "My dear, how are you?"

Who said chivalry was dead? thought Jihad. "Z – Carla. Captain Fadi Lattouf. You remember him? My Palestinian cohort."

"My goodness, yes." Carla raised her other hand and discreetly stroked Lattouf's palm in the guise of turning the hand-kiss into a hand-shake. Bluff called, Lattouf let go instantly. She said, "It is good to see you again, *monsieur.*"

"Carla is staying with us," mumbled Jihad. "Come, let us go."

"And it is an honour to see you again, *madame,*" called Lattouf over his shoulder as he was dragged down the stairs.

Bourj el-Barajneh, Beirut 15:45

The Palestinian refugee camps of Lebanon are not 'camps' as such. A local politician had recently gotten into trouble for calling them 'slums', but it was an accurate description.

The Bourj el-Barajneh camp in southern Beirut is one square kilometre of basic brick and block constructions which pass as dwellings, packed so tight together that most paths between the buildings are less than half a metre wide. There are no maps, no street signs. You have to know where you are going to find your way through the tight alleyways, over the broken water pipes, under the sagging cables, past the broken windows which might at any minute open into your face, through the sewage...

Posters or drawings, nowadays mostly of Hamas leaders or martyrs, were everywhere.

The camp, and the others like it, was set up after *al-Naqba* – the catastrophe of 1948 when three hundred thousand Palestinians fled their homes in Palestine. It was built to deal with the 'temporary crisis' of the refugees. It was originally constructed to house ten thousand people, and the camp is forbidden to expand physically. By 2010, it was housing over twenty thousand human beings.

Jihad Merhi had changed out of his uniform because the camps in Lebanon are no-go areas for the Lebanese authorities. Lebanon is forbidden from interfering or intervening in the camps and from sending troops or other officials inside, including police. He was risking his job – not to mention his life - just by being here.

The place had not changed in the five years since his last visit. Still the sagging cables going from building to building, still the cracked, dripping pipes... still the smell.

He walked with Lattouf, unsure which was causing him the most discomfiture: being back in the camp or having accepted Lattouf's suggestion of popping in to visit his wife and children after they had conducted their business, which would also mean the offer of food and drink.

Five minutes in and he knew where he was, but not how they had gotten there through the complex maze of alleys. They passed the old butcher's shop, still boarded up. "We use the back way," explained Lattouf.

They turned left then left again. Lattouf could only just fit down the narrow alley between the buildings which led on to a small courtyard area.

Only one door led out into the yard, obviously the back of the butcher's shop. The other sides of the yard were blank walls with windows above, through which came sounds of habitation: talking, shouting, babies crying, radios, televisions, cooking noises. The wooden door was rotting but there was a huge for-show padlock on it which Lattouf unlocked.

As he pushed the door open, the stench dashed out to meet them like a long-lost relative. Merhi staggered backwards, hand going up to his face. "Satan's bollocks, Fadi! You've not installed climate control then."

"I told you. It is hardly ever used. *Yalla.*"

Still covering his face, Merhi followed him in. The room on the right had not changed. In the dim light Merhi could see the wide, shallow gulley in the floor with a deep hole at one end. A drain for the blood of chopped up carcasses when this used to be a butcher's, and probably the same now for its human clientele. Against the opposite wall was a table on which lay a covered shape.

Lattouf went over and pulled off the *kafan* with a flourish, like a magician's reveal. The corpse was at a slightly odd angle, corner to corner on the rectangular table. "*Allahu Akbar,*" said Lattouf softly, pulling the cloth back up to cover the genitals. Noticing Merhi had turned his head to align it with the corpse, he explained "I have tried to face him towards the *qiblah.*"

"I see." Merhi knew that Muslims should be placed with their head facing Mecca, at least when they were buried.

Lattouf seemed to read his thoughts. "I did it now because there will not be a burial." Merhi raised his eyebrows and looked a query, but did not say anything. Lattouf shrugged. "He had no family, not since the murders by the Jews. We were his only relatives. Where are we supposed to bury him here?"

Merhi glanced over to the gulley opposite, thought thoughts which he didn't want to think, and then turned back to the body. He put on his reading glasses which had been hooked over the neck of his T-shirt.

Chadi Lattouf had been just an average male in his forties, slight paunch, gentle balding, moustache, nothing out of the ordinary. His fingers showed nicotine stains. There were a few moles and other marks on the torso but nothing to indicate a violent death. The face was calm. Rigor mortis had passed but there were signs of lividity on his underside where he had been laid out.

"Look. There." Lattouf nodded towards the left shoulder.

Merhi had no intention of touching the body but he brought his head closer, squinting through his glasses. From a metre away the mark looked like any of the other moles or blemishes, but as he got nearer he could see it was different. It was about half a centimetre wide and looked like the mark that sometimes appears after a blood test. Death had stopped the spread of the bruise. And in the centre, sure enough, was a distinct puncture mark.

"I see. Hmm..." He sniffed (not the right thing to do, the body had not been perfumed) and straightened up. "You think that killed him?"

"I saw him die. It was not a natural passing. There are no other marks upon him."

"Really there should be an autopsy, you know."

"For what reason? He is dead. Dead because of that. Dead is dead. Nothing will be achieved by knowing *exactly* what killed him, only *how* he was killed. This obsession with cutting open the dead is an affront to Allah."

Merhi was surprised at the strength of his friend's opinion, and to some extent he agreed with him. He turned back for another look at the wound. After a few moments he took hold of the edge of the *kafan* and gently raised it back over the body.

"Thank you," said Lattouf. "Bless you."

"Can we go?" asked Merhi. "I guess you will be..." He made a gesture towards the body.

"Yes, I will. *Yalla.* Come."

Back out in the small yard, Lattouf refixed the padlock on the door.

"So who would murder your cousin?" asked Merhi as they walked away. "Was he involved with the groups?"

They went back down the narrow alleyway. "No, no, he was not political." Lattouf's voice was amplified by the closeness of the walls. "The family has never involved itself in such things. That is why we make good policemen! But after 2006 we came close to joining the groups. Very close. Chadi even went so far as to quit his job."

"What did he do?"

Lattouf sounded surprised. "Did I not say? He was a policeman."

"No, you didn't say."

"Well, he was. Then after his family were murdered he quit and went up to Jbeil."

Merhi trod in something and was momentarily distracted. He did not look down but he was so pleased he had not worn his sandals. There was no rising smell, for which he was grateful.

They reached the edge of the camp and turned right into Annan Street.

"And he did not work now?" asked Merhi.

Lattouf looked affronted. "Of course he worked! He was a *muhaqqiq khass*. A private dick, as they say on TV. And a damned good one."

They reached a doorway which Lattouf opened with a key. "Wife!" he called. "Nada! You will never guess who is here, who has come to see us! Our old friend Jihad! And he has come to dinner!"

Jounieh, Lebanon 23:59

Jihad Merhi sat on the edge of his bed casually stroking his wife's thigh under the cotton sheet. "They mean well, bless them, but oh my God. *Kibbeh nayeh!* The *Fattoush* was fine, but the raw meat!"

"Was it awful?" asked Gisele, leaning against the golden leather headboard.

"Actually, no. It was very nice. But it's just the thought of it. Nada prepared it especially for me, so I felt obliged to eat it. Why do people assume that if you're Lebanese you must like raw meat?"

"Well, apparently you do, you've just said so." She smiled, reaching out for her husband's hand. "How were they?"

"Fine, fine. Really it wasn't bad seeing them again. Little Mini Me is cute. Farts like his father though. The rest of the kids are getting bigger, I hardly saw them."

"So what did he want?"

Jihad looked down at their joined hands. He sighed and said, "He has a body. Again."

"What of it?"

"It's his cousin."

"And it involves you how?"

"A jurisdictional crossover thing again. Looks like murder."

"His cousin was murdered?"

"It seems so."

"That is sad. But we all know the problems in the camps, murders happen all the time."

Jihad rubbed his thumb over the back of Gisele's hand. "Not like this one. He wasn't shot, stabbed or beaten. Not even strangled."

"What then - ?"

Both their heads turned as they heard movement outside. There were footsteps on the tiled floor. A door opened and closed. Gisele said, "She's back. She has been out all evening. Left just after you and Fadi."

"Really?" Jihad stared at the bedroom door. Then turning back to his wife, he said "I don't know what she's involved in, other than this murder of her boss. This thing about – what was the name?"

"Sajida."

"This thing about Sajida I just don't understand."

"So what happened?"

"What?"

"To Fadi's cousin."

He let go of her hand and rubbed his nose. He wished he was allowed to smoke in the bedroom. "You're not going to believe this. The old poison dart."

"Ricin!"

"Maybe."

"On the streets of Beirut?"

"Seems like it, but Fadi won't allow an autopsy, so we can't be certain. Might be this new ricin-abrin compound our neighbours but two have produced. I've seen the mark." He touched his shoulder.

Gisele was shaking her head. "That's not playing fair."

"No. Not like the good old days of shootings and bombings. At least then you knew where you stood – unless your legs were blown off." He did not smile at his own macabre humour. Gisele grimaced and looked heavenward.

"So, as usual," continued Jihad, "I don't know what's going on. It's like the gods of confusion and ignorance are laughing at me again. There I was, coasting along, when suddenly two faces from the past drop back into my world, both bringing death with them. But at least this time, dear wife...." He took her hand, raised it to his lips and sucked the end of her index finger. She did not pull away.

After a moment, she asked "But at least this time, dear husband?"

He took her finger from his mouth. "At least this time they're unconnected."

12 July 2010
30 Rajab 1431

Jonblat, Beirut 09:00

"Jihad! How nice to see you again." Selim Himo was shown into Merhi's office by a young officer from downstairs. Sergeant Deeb el-Gharib, who would normally act as his captain's reception, had already been called out to a bomb scare up at Rmeil along with most of the team.

The first thing Merhi noticed was that the tall, slim man he knew as Lieutenant Himo of the Bekaa Inquiry Brigade was not dressed in the uniform of the *Gendarmerie*. Nor was he wearing the epaulettes of a lieutenant on his uniform shirt. He was dressed exactly the same as Merhi.

They shook hands. "Selim, it's nice to see you too," smiled Merhi. "What's this?" He tapped Himo's left epaulette. "Are congratulations in order?"

"Sort of."

"Coffee?"

"That's very kind, thank you."

"Sit, sit, I won't be a minute."

Out in the General Office, Merhi found the two least dirty mugs and spooned in granules as the kettle boiled. Normally he would have 'real' coffee brought in from outside but because of that damned bomb scare he had no one here to run errands.

He hoped this would not take long. Himo had obviously been promoted. Had he come here just to elicit the obligatory praise and approval? He was about fifteen years younger than Merhi and, ever since they had first met on a training course many years ago, Merhi had realised Himo was a high-flyer destined for the fast track.

Apart from any professional jealousy (which, of course, he did not have), Merhi wanted to start the wider-field enquiries regarding Carla's attacker. Not only that but today was the fourth anniversary of Operation Sincere Promise*, and celebrations were expected on the streets. The bomb scare

---

* *On 12 July 2006 Hizbullah captured two Israeli soldiers to trade them for Lebanese prisoners in Israeli jails and for the remains of resistance fighters that had been held for decades in Israel's infamous Cemetery of Numbers. In retaliation, Israel waged war on Lebanon, bombing the country for 33 days, destroying much of south Lebanon and south*

might be the beginning of the festivities.

Back in his office, coffees on his desk, Merhi said "So, you are no longer in the Bekaa?"

"I moved a few months ago."

"Promotion to...?"

"Originally a level transfer, but I've just been made up, acting at the moment."

"Not acting for long. I'm sure it's only a matter of time until it's substantive." Merhi held up his packet of cigarettes in query.

"Thank you. And *merci*." Himo shook his head.

Merhi lit up as Himo continued. "I'm now with the DGS. The guy whose role I've taken has been found dead. Murdered. That's why I'm here." He took a swig of coffee. "There's something you might be able to help me with."

Jounieh, Lebanon 09:15

Carla pressed the End icon on her mobile phone and sighed. She was disappointed but she well-understood. Money did not grow on trees. Work was work and took priority. Naturally he had not said where he was going but he said it would only take a few days. So she would have to wait for assistance, and waiting was not a strong characteristic of *djinn*. She only hoped that the other string to her bow, Captain Jihad Merhi, brought back some results quickly.

She was out on the balcony of the Merhi's apartment, dressed only in a small red cotton thong. Jihad was at work and Gisele had gone down to Kaslik to do some shopping. The sun was already hot as it crept over the mountain behind her.

Laying down on the towel she had placed on the tiles, she brought her right leg up, crossing it over the left and linking her hands under her thighs in a piriformis stretch. She changed over legs, performed the piriformis again, then lay flat on her back, feet on the floor, knees bent, thighs opening and closing in hip abductor stretches.

This was a routine he had taught her, and, as her legs parted and the sun's rays went into intimate places, she smiled at how often they had not gotten any further than this move!

Twenty minutes later she finished with a standing hamstring stretch, first

---

Beirut. At least 1300 people were killed and 1 million Lebanese displaced. The hostilities officially ceased on 12 August 2006 after the adoption of UN Security Council Resolution 1701. Two years later, on 16 July 2008, the bodies of the two captured Israeli soldiers were swapped for four captured Hizbullah fighters, one former Palestine Liberation Front member (Samir Kuntar) and the bodies of 200 Lebanese and Palestinian militants.

her right leg up on top of the balustrade, then her left. Sweat glistened on her olive skin. She had worn as little as possible but perhaps she should not even have worn that. The soaking wet thong would need to be peeled down her legs.

As she warmed-down with a few little hip movements, she looked out to sea. It was hazy out over the Mediterranean, but inland it was clear. She could see the traffic down on the coastal highway.

What she could not see, even with the eyes of a djinn, was the topless black Jeep Wrangler Ultimate with two women on board heading down into Beirut...

Jonblat, Beirut 09:15

Shit, thought Merhi. Shit, shit, piss and shit. The gods really were having a laugh, weren't they?

He decided on the naive approach. "Someone has been murdered?"

"My captain, Maroun Khoury." Himo put his mug back down on the desk. "Know him?"

"No. How was he killed?"

"Garrotted."

Merhi grimaced. "Oh dear. My condolences. You have anyone for it?"

Himo shook his head. "Not yet. That's where I hope you can help me."

"If I can help you in any way, I most certainly will. But I don't see - "

"Five days ago you asked the traffic police for CCTV recordings of a street in Ashrafieh. Why?"

Merhi took a long drag on his cigarette, staring across at the younger man. Then he said slowly, "Don't much like the tone, Selim."

Himo held the gaze. "And I don't much like having my captain murdered."

"Even if it means you step into his shoes? You always were ambitious."

"What the fuck are you implying?"

"What the fuck are *you* implying? How dare you come in here demanding that a senior officer explain his actions. I am a captain of the Internal Security Force. I can ask anyone for anything I want, and I don't have to give a reason."

Another drag on the cigarette, another swig of the coffee.

"But," continued Merhi, "if you are asking rather than demanding...?" He waited.

Ten seconds of stand-off, then Himo conceded. "I am asking."

"Then I can tell you that we are in a heightened state of alert at the moment, concerning various things that I am sure you can guess at. Have you looked at the CCTV in question?"

"Yes."

"Then you will have seen the traffic in the street, how crowded it was. We have a tip that a car bomb might be going off in the city sometime soon - our friends in the south. Even now my men are out after an alert this morning. Intelligence at the time suggested that the target was somewhere in Ashrafieh. We were trying to examine parking patterns. Comparing historical from four days previously to immediate eyes we had on the ground. To see if any cars had not been moved for a few days. Maybe there was a dud bomb sitting around."

"And was there?"

Merhi shrugged. "The CCTV was so blurred and unclear we could not undertake any useful comparison. Our eyes on the ground did not find anything."

"And if I question your team they will confirm this?"

"Don't push it, Acting Captain."

The landline telephone on Merhi's desk rang, which was perhaps just as well. He answered it with his name and listened. "*Oui... oui... d'accord... alors, j'arrive.*" He put the phone down.

Stubbing out his cigarette as he stood up, he said "I am wanted up at Rmeil. The car bomb. I take it there was nothing else?"

Himo also stood up. "For now, no. If there is anything else - "

"Send me an e-mail. Now, if you'll excuse me?" Merhi gestured towards the door, not offering a hand shake.

Rmeil, Beirut 10:15

The traffic was heavy but Merhi was surprised that it was moving at all as he drove east down Gouraud Street and took the first left after the post office. Stopping traffic in even a small section of Beirut usually had a disproportionate butterfly effect over the rest of the city.

At the end of the small street, at the junction with Pasteur Street, a police officer was standing next to the tape spread across the road, beyond which Merhi could see members of his team mingling with more of the local force. Things seem to be happening just to the right, out of his view.

He flashed his lights, the officer looked at his uniform and then pulled the tape up high on tiptoe so that the Toyota Land Cruiser V8 could pass underneath. Merhi pulled up at the top of the street, the action – or, more properly, inaction – over on the right now visible.

The local police were milling about, pretending to be important but actually doing very little. A sniffer dog was sitting chewing intently on a treat. Three members of Merhi's own team were standing near an old sports car at the fork with Berberi Street.

Sergeant Deeb el-Gharib raised his hand as he saw Merhi climbing out of the Land Cruiser.

"Standing a bit close, Sergeant?" commented Merhi as he came across.

el-Gharib shook his head. "Nothing to worry about, Captain. It's clean, at least for explosives."

Merhi spoke as he walked around the vehicle. "What is this old rust bucket?"

"A Datsun Bluebird. Not made anymore. Probably worth something, even in that state."

"An orange Bluebird. Must be some irony there somewhere. Situation report?"

"According to locals its been parked here since Friday. Was only reported this morning, by the priest from Saint Antoine's Church down there, who became a bit worried, what with the anniversary and all. The local boys called us as a matter of course."

"Of course. Keys?"

"No. Doors unlocked though. But they'll have to move it by truck, they don't have ignition keys on hand for something like this. It will be a special request. And we don't want to hot wire."

"The dog been over it?"

"Yes."

"Printing?"

"Probably not necessary."

Merhi pulled open the driver's door with his fingertips and leant in. The car smelt like a burnt-down tobacco factory. Or was that him? He sniffed his shirt.

The leather seats were worn and cracked, even split in places, stuffing hanging out like the intestines of a stab victim. The door to the glove compartment came away in his hand. "Meant to tell you about that," said el-Gharib from behind.

"You find anything in here?" asked Merhi over his shoulder as he refitted the door and then backed out.

"The usual stuff in the glove compartment. Empty cigarette packets and sweet wrappers in the driver's door, nothing in the other door. Something interesting on the passenger seat though."

"What?"

el-Gharib moved closer, speaking quieter. "A notepad. I've got it in my car."

"Informative?"

"Not particularly, but I thought you might like to have a look at it."

"Anything else?"

"Just some playing cards, a pen and a pair of sunglasses."

Merhi folded his arms, studying the Bluebird. He nodded. "Much as I appreciate being involved, Deeb, being kept in the loop, why did you call me out on this? You could have handled it, or the Lieutenant."

"We've been together a long time, Jihad," el-Gharib looked around, making sure no one else was in ear-shot. "I thought you might want to see it because there's something you should know. I haven't told the Lieutenant. I ran a registered owner's check." He paused.

"And?"

"It is registered to someone called Chadi Lattouf."

Jonblat, Beirut 11:45

Back in his office, Merhi looked at his watch, unable to believe that it was not yet even the afternoon. This day already contained more shit than the nappies in a nursery hit by an outbreak of infant diarrhoea.

On his drive back he had thought more about the upstart Selim Himo. His immediate anger after he had left for Rmeil earlier had now been moderated by the acceptance that Himo was not only investigating a murder, which he was perfectly entitled to do, but a murder of one of their own kind. Not only that but he, Jihad Merhi, had played the ignorant card – a murder? Really? – and yet truth be told he knew more about it than anybody.

Why hadn't he been open? Why hadn't he told Himo about the returned exile now known as Carla Chedid, and the fact that she had been staying with Khoury at the time of his death? Why hadn't he mentioned the fact that she had been attacked shortly afterwards? Why hadn't he shown Himo the lifelike drawing he had in his drawer of the attacker, the tall blonde woman with the white eyes?

Why? Because he should have reported the whole thing straightaway when Carla had first contacted him. He should not have let himself be beguiled into secrecy and complicity.

But he had. And when you were deep in the shit, and even if you were adding to it yourself, the last thing you wanted to do was to encourage others to dump upon you too.

Carla knew the body would be found and she knew there would be an investigation. He would tell her of Himo's involvement tonight. It would be up to her whether she contacted him or still ploughed her own furrow. Really, he had enough on his plate without this.

Opening the drawer, he brought out Carla's drawing. He would initiate enquiries with Interpol, see if anyone anywhere knew of the woman with the white eyes, and that would be the end of his involvement.

This was actually the easy part. Interpol Beirut was in this building, in a suite upstairs, he had been seconded there once himself. He knew that for a few years now they had used the Global Communications System I-24/7, so his request for 'Anything Known' would be out there in no time and results should come back quickly. Then perhaps he would have Carla out of his hair.

He placed the drawing in an envelope and left his office.

He was back within ten minutes. The great, all-powerful, all-singing, all-dancing Global Communications System I-24/7 was down. It was a problem at Interpol HQ in Lyons, France, he had been told, nothing to do with us. But if he cared to leave a copy of the picture and a note of his request, they would get round to it as soon as they were able to.

He cared to and he did.

Right, one down. How many more to go?

He needed to contact Fadi Lattouf, to tell him his cousin's car had been found. He had taken the notepad off of Sergeant el-Gharib and had told him to tell the local police that the ISF considered it to be just an abandoned vehicle but that the ISF would retain jurisdiction because of certain sensitive matters that had arisen relating to its ownership.

He frowned. Good heavens, that was the truth! At least at this time. But of course there would be more to it. Only he knew that the owner was dead.

He had already examined the notepad. Didn't seem to be any clues in it, but he would discuss it with Lattouf.

He picked up his landline phone and then put it down again. He didn't know Lattouf's number, it was plumbed into his mobile. Actually, that was the better option, what with The Listeners. He would go out, grab a bite to eat, and phone Lattouf from out in the street.

Hamra, Beirut 12:30

Although it was a Monday, Hamra Street was as busy as ever. In times past Hamra was *the* shopping district of Beirut. Many of the famous names had now moved to other locations, such as the malls and back into the rebuilt city centre, but the area still buzzed. The retail shops and the sidewalk stalls were as popular as ever, the shouts from the street-hawkers vying with the noise from the traffic to see who could be the loudest.

Merhi waited until he was in the relative calm of Hamra Square before he pulled out his mobile. It seemed to take ages to connect and then it rang for a long time. He was about to disconnect when a voice answered, "'*eeh?*"

"Fadi?"

"Who is it?" The reception was not good, Lattouf sounded as if he was deep inside a cave.

"Jihad."

There was a pause and Merhi heard the sound of metal clinking. Was Lattouf having his lunch?

"Jihad, you have caught me at a bad time. I am burying my cousin."

Merhi frowned. "But I thought you said you weren't..." His voice trailed off as realisation dawned. He did not want to think what that metallic sound had been. Lattouf was in the butcher's shop morgue, that's why the reception was bad. "Oh I see. I won't keep you."

A resigned sigh came down the phone. "No, it does not matter, my friend. Abu Yussuf is not in a hurry. In fact wherever he was going, he has arrived there already. This is just his shell."

Merhi could feel the Palestinian's sadness. "Actually, he's the reason I'm calling. We've found his car."

"You have? That was quick. Thank you for giving it priority. I always knew I could rely on you, Abu Samer."

Merhi did not have the heart to tell him that it was pure coincidence, that they had been investigating a potential car bomb and that he had forgotten about his cousin until el-Gharib had discovered the name of the owner of the vehicle. "Fadi, we need to meet. There are things to discuss."

Lattouf said something but he was drowned out by a shrieking sales pitch from a stallholder near Merhi.

Glaring at the man, Merhi said loudly "Sorry I didn't hear a word of that."

Now it was Lattouf's turn to shout. "I said, Wednesday at midday?"

Merhi drew long and hard on his cigarette, swallowing the smoke. Was that really Wednesday midday or was Lattouf using their old twenty-six hours earlier code, which meant tomorrow at ten?

"Fadi, clarify. Do you really mean Wednesday at midday?"

"No."

"Okay. My office, not the other place."

"Really?"

"Yes, this is official." And it will be good for your waistline.

"Okay then. Should I be identified?"

Knowing that the giant would be more noticeable in his ridiculous 'street clothes', Merhi answered "Yes. You can be in uniform."

"Okay. Wednesday at midday at your place. Jihad, what is all that noise? I can hardly hear you."

Without thinking, Merhi replied "I'm outside. In Hamra." As soon as he said it, he regretted it. Oh how easily a man forgets!

"Hamra!" exclaimed Lattouf, all sadness gone. "My friend, you couldn't pick me up some pickles from that stall on the square, could you?"

Ras en Nabaa, Beirut 17:00

As he left the Directorate of General Security offices that evening, Acting Captain Selim Himo was still fuming at the treatment he had received seven hours previously from Jihad Merhi. Fuming and curious. Their paths had crossed infrequently in the past but when they had the two men had seemed to get on well. Hadn't Himo helped him out with those serial killings five years ago? Okay, they might not be friends, they moved in different circles, but until that morning he had thought that they were at least close colleagues.

So why the aggression from Merhi?

Merhi had claimed ignorance of the murder of Maroun Khoury. That may or may not be true, the DGS had kept it quiet while it was being investigated. But was it really feasible that a captain of the Internal Security Force had wanted to see CCTV recordings covering the same street where the victim lived at precisely the time of the murder, the time supposedly chosen by Merhi at random for an historical check for a current sweep for a car bomb?

And had Merhi really expected him to accept it, say "Oh, okay, thanks" and clear off? Himo knew when he was being played.

He reached the parking area at the back of the building, his GMC Yukon Denali bipping as he pressed the key in his pocket. Throwing his case on the back seat, he climbed in.

So what should he do about Merhi? He did not want to go running to Merhi's boss, Major Ghanem, like a tell-tale. That would be childish. But he wasn't satisfied, he needed to look into this further. In his case he had copies of the same CCTV footage Merhi had requisitioned. He had already sped-watched it twice in the office. There was little activity in the street during the two hours in question save for one woman entering the building. She was small and dark, probably a local. Who was that? Was she the killer?

Now he was taking the discs home to watch without the everyday interruptions of a workplace. He would watch them on slow speed, to see if there was anything his initial viewing had missed.

Key in the ignition, he started the car.

He drove off, turning right into Damascus Street, pulling out in front of a Jeep Wrangler Ultimate that had just moved away from outside the French Cultural Centre next door.

Then he turned right again onto Abdallah el Yafi Avenue.

As did the Jeep.

Raousheh, Beirut 18:00

It was a straight journey to Himo's apartment just off Beirut's western corniche. At this hour the traffic was heavy as Abdallah el Yafi Avenue became Saeb Salam Avenue. The traffic moved slowly and then stopped completely when he was in the Verdun underpass. Eventually the GMC crawled out at a snail's pace, passing the three-vehicle smash at the junction with Rafic el Hariri Avenue that was causing the tailback.

Once he was heading north on General de Gaulle Avenue, the shore of the Mediterranean over on his left, he was able to pick up speed. Up the hill, by Pigeon Rocks*, he turned right then right again just west of Australia Street, pulling into the small underground parking area beneath a 1960's (1380's) apartment block.

Internal stairs led up to the ground floor where he could take the elevator to his apartment on the fifth floor.

So he did not see the Jeep Wrangler Ultimate pull up outside.

Himo's apartment was in need of some small cosmetic refurbishment and minor repairs, as could be expected in a building now fifty years old which had survived the events of 1975 to 1990, but because of its location and views it still commanded a high rent. From his small balcony he could just see the northern Pigeon Rock beyond the sea-front buildings.

Pulling open the glass door to the balcony to let in some air, he took his gun from the holster on his waistband and locked it in a drawer of his modern desk. He pressed the On button of his Hewlett Packard computer and then went into his kitchen for food.

His freezer yielded a carton of *yakhnit el samak* (fish stew), which he preferred to eat hot rather than the usual cold. He turned on his oven and then took a bottle of local lemonade from the fridge, pouring himself a large glass. Kicking off his shoes, he went out onto the balcony with his drink. The waning sun was still hot and blazed directly at him from the west, making him shield his eyes.

As he thought about Merhi and what to do, his eyes wandered down to the street below. Cars were parked on either side and he was grateful he had paid the extra for a private parking space under the building.

Deciding to shower, he walked back inside. The oven had nearly reached its temperature so he put his carton on a small baking tray and put it inside, turning the timer for twenty minutes.

He stripped, throwing his sweat-soaked shirt straight into the washing machine, together with his underwear and socks. He carried his trousers over his arm into the bedroom and hung them up.

---

* *Beirut's most famous natural landmark, two massive calcareous rocks just off the coast. The larger, southern, rock has an archway at the base made by waves and wind. The sixty metres high rocks are famous not only for their natural beauty but also for diving competitions and suicide attempts.*

As the spray of the shower hit him, first too cold then very hot, he closed his eyes, soaking his hair, feeling the water run down his body, dripping off his nose, his chin, his genitals, washing away the grime of the day.

He was not aware of the bathroom door opening, then closing again.

Jounieh, Lebanon 18:30

"Well of course it was only a matter of time until Maroun was discovered." Carla was sitting on the leather couch, bare feet curled up under her, holding a glass of orange juice. She was dressed in blue back-in-fashion leggings and a long black linen top open one button more than was necessary.

Jihad Merhi stood in front of the balcony doors with his back to her, smoking, looking out over the view down the mountain to the coast, glass of red *Massaya* wine in the same hand as his cigarette.

"What is this Lieutenant Himo like?" asked Carla.

"Acting Captain," said Merhi. "He would be the first to correct you. And that sums him up really." He turned, blowing out smoke. "Sure of himself. Knows where he's going. He probably has a - " he made bunny ears in the air, awkward because of the glass and Cedars King Size, " – Life Plan. He's as decent as a high-flyer can be, but Selim Himo is his number one priority."

Carla nodded. "I see. So you don't think he would be interested in a partnership with me?"

"Not the sort you mean."

A smile spread across Carla's face as she uncurled her legs and stood up. "What sort do I mean, Jihad?" she asked softly as she walked across and stood next to him, facing the balcony.

"The professional sort." He glanced down at the too-far-unbuttoned top and then quickly looked away, noticing mischief in her eyes.

"That would still need clarification." She looked out over the view.

Merhi coughed and drank wine, swiftly followed by a drag on the cigarette.

"Could you introduce me to him?" she asked.

"Are you sure that's wise?"

"I did not kill Maroun, I have nothing to hide."

"You haven't? What about this Sajida business that you won't tell me about?"

She put her hand on his shoulder. "It is not that I won't tell you, as I have explained. I am protecting you. Regard it as need to know. Perhaps Acting Captain Himo already knows about Sajida. If not, perhaps he is one who does need to know. Can you arrange a meeting, just between him and me?" In the reflection in the glass she noticed Gisele standing in the doorway of the room, a large chopping knife in her hand. Carla turned, letting the natural movement take her hand from Jihad's shoulder.

"The *shish tawook* is on," announced Gisele stonily. "There is *tabouleh* and *falafel* and things on the table. Whenever you two are ready." She swung round and went back into the kitchen.

Jihad sighed. "I have a feeling my own *falafel* might be on the table very soon," he said wearily. "I'll give Himo a ring later. *Yalla*, let's eat."

Raousheh, Beirut 18:30

Selim Himo wiped the water from his eyes as he stepped out of the shower cubicle, reaching for his towel.

He dried himself vigorously, leaving his head until last, his short hair sticking up in spiky style. When he was not on duty he liked his hair like this, made him feel younger, more attractive, especially in his favourite club over in Sin el Fil. He would flatten it down when he shaved in the morning.

He opened the bathroom window wide. Although the shower had washed away the grime of the day, it had done nothing to reduce his temperature. Beirut in the summer was hot, and the air conditioning in the apartment was so old that it was always destined to be fighting a losing battle. He was glad he had left the balcony door open.

Naked, he walked out into the bedroom. He could smell his stew cooking nicely out in the oven. Any moment now the timer bell would be going off.

Deciding against getting dressed, he went out into the living room.

And stopped dead.

His small table for two over against the wall had been set, cutlery, condiments, his refilled glass of lemonade, flat bread, some hummus from the fridge - and his fish stew steaming in a bowl.

He tensed, feeling totally vulnerable. He was literally completely exposed. With two leaps he was over at his desk, pulling open the drawer – to find it empty, his gun gone.

"Looking for this?"

He straightened up slowly, facing the wall. Carefully, to show he was not making any sudden moves, he turned around.

A woman was leaning against the open kitchen doorway, his gun swinging from her left index finger. She was tall, long frizzy blonde hair falling down over her shoulders, eyes a deep brown. She was wearing a white vest, combat pants and desert boots.

Himo said nothing, weighing up the situation. Was this a hit? The second External Security Unit captain within days?

As if she was reading his mind, the woman span the gun on her finger with the precision of an expert, catching it so that it pointed towards him.

"Who are you?" he asked. Although she was pointing the gun at him she had made no move to pull the trigger. "What do you want?"

The woman looked pointedly at his hairy groin, smiled, then looked back up into his face. "You."

His eyebrows raised. Who was this, the local recruiter for the Raousheh swingers society? Well, she was barking up the wrong tree with him. At the very least she would have to turn round.

Again she seemed to read his mind. "Don't be silly. I know you are not interested in the likes of us."

"Us?"

"Us," said a voice from his bedroom.

Himo jumped, looked then looked again. An identical woman was standing in his bedroom doorway. Identical except that she had green eyes. Where had she appeared from?

He looked from one woman to the other. This was spooky. And professional. He was in a total checkmate position. All his exits were covered – literally and figuratively.

Then he jumped again as the cooker timer went off.

As the woman from the bedroom walked over into the kitchen, the one with the gun said, "You should only do *yakhnit el samak* for fifteen minutes, not twenty."

The other one had turned off the timer and now stood next to the one with the gun. Identical twins. Or clones.

"What do you want?" asked Himo. "Apart from dispensing unwanted culinary advice?"

The women bent their heads to the side, one one way one the other, looking at him. Suddenly he was not hot any more. In fact he felt very cold.

Then the one with the gun straightened up, lowering the weapon. "Brother Malek sends his blessings," said Love.

"And you will show us respect, Disciple Selim," said Paradise. "Our advice was good. Come, eat your food before it gets cold."

"And don't bother to get dressed," advised Love. "We like you just the way you are."

Jounieh, Lebanon 20:30

Jihad Merhi took his mobile phone away from his ear, looked at the screen then put it back to his ear again. "No answer," he said.

The three of them were sitting out on the Merhis' wide balcony, facing the setting sun far out at sea. Humours had mellowed with the intake of wine over dinner, Jihad now augmenting his with a post-prandial *arak*. Background music was playing from inside.

"It might not be the right number," he continued. "This was the one he gave me five years ago."

"You don't have his office number?" asked Gisele.

"I have it at work." He ended the call and put his phone down on the glass coffee table in front of them. "I'll call him in the morning." He looked at Carla, sitting on the other side of his wife. "Are you sure you want to do this? Maybe his non-answer was a sign."

Carla shook her head. "I don't believe in signs. I was directly responsible for Maroun's death and I am going to find the person who did it, this woman with the white eyes. Acting Captain Himo is the only option I've got at the moment."

Jihad noted the 'at the moment' but he let it pass. Next to him, Gisele was running her fingers gently over the scar on her neck. She said, "And what about the wider picture? This Sajida?"

"Himo needs to know, I've decided."

"Won't you be putting him in danger?"

Carla shrugged. "Maybe. But at least he will be prepared. Maroun was not. We did not know that people with the knowledge were being eliminated."

"How about elimination by association?" Gisele leant forward, stubbing out her cigarette in the ashtray (only one, to be sociable, as a treat) and picking up her glass. "Something I used to instil into my students. Leave no loose ends."

"You mean...?" Jihad let the question hang.

"Us. If this assassin finds out Carla is staying here, surely we are loose ends. Even if we don't know what is going on."

Jihad looked over at Carla with raised eyebrows.

"She seems to be very meticulous," reasoned Carla. "And personal. No bombs to cause collateral damage, not even shooting. She's a hands-on killer." She smiled at her literal metaphor. "I do not think you are in danger. But be careful, of course."

Gisele gave an ironic little laugh. "Being married to a captain of the ISF, I am always careful. Comes with the job."

Jihad feigned protest. "It is a job being married to me?"

"Sometimes more than you know, *habibi*." Gisele smiled sweetly. "But I took you for better or worse."

"Till death..." Jihad knocked back the remains of his *arak*.

"But not yet," reassured Carla. "It is me she's after. She has tried twice, I am sure she will come again." She reached forward, picked up the bottle on the table and poured herself some more wine. "But she's got to find me first. And before I find her."

13 July 2010
1 Sha'ban 1431

Jonblat, Beirut 09:00

"*Bonjour* Selim. Jihad Merhi." A pause, the silence conveying an apology for yesterday which would never be spoken. "Selim, I have some information for you. We need to meet. Can I suggest this afternoon, fourteen hundred in my office...? I look forward to seeing you then. *Salaam.*"

"Hi Carla. Jihad. Still no response from Himo so I've left a message on his office phone. I've suggested we meet this afternoon at fourteen hundred here in my office, as we agreed. I'll let downstairs know you're coming and I'll come down to collect you when you arrive. Enjoy your morning."

What would the world do without voicemail? wondered Merhi. Telephones might be the invention of the devil but voicemail was a gift from God. Think of all the time saved leaving messages rather than having to keep calling back.

He was still not certain introducing Carla to Himo was the right thing to do, but she had insisted that was the way she wanted to progress. So be it. He was a mere male, he knew better than to argue.

But fourteen hundred was five hours away. Before then he had other matters to attend to. The world went on and so did his other cases.

He reached for his cigarettes which were sitting on his desk next to the three jars of pickles...

Jonblat, Beirut 10:15

Merhi knew Fadi Lattouf had arrived even before he had entered the building. The sudden cacophony of car horns outside did not disturb him at first, he was too engrossed in an intelligence report that suggested Hizbullah had invited Iranian President Ahmedinejad to visit Lebanon in three months time (surely no coincidence that right now was the anniversary of the Israeli war?), but the constant background blaring suddenly registered and he got up to look out the window.

Sure enough, down on Bank of Lebanon Street was the dented, rusting light blue police Ford Transit van with the distinctive red number plate of the Palestinian military. It was badly parked and was causing chaos as drivers tried to get round it.

It was two minutes before he heard the sound of feet in the corridor, one set thudding louder than the other. Then Sergeant el-Gharib knocked on his door, opened it and – with an Allah-help-us look – stood back to let the giant Lattouf enter.

"Morning of light, my dear Captain!" boomed Lattouf, casting an eye backwards to watch el-Gharib closing the door then doing a double-take when he saw the cracked glass. It had been like that the last time he had been in this office five years previously! He said more quietly, "How are you, my dear friend?"

"I am well, Fadi." They shook hands. "Peace be upon you."

"And upon you."

"Come, sit."

Lattouf carried his uniform jacket over his arm. His blue shirt had damp patches of sweat underneath the arms, down the centre of the back and underneath his breasts. Lebanon in the summer was not a place for man-made fibres.

"Would you like some water?" Merhi handed over a two litre bottle of *Sohat* mineral water, the outside damp with condensation, as Lattouf hung his jacket over the back of the chair. "They'll bring coffee in in a moment."

"Bless your hands." Lattouf cracked open the bottle and drank it. All of it. In one go.

Emitting a satisfied burp, he sat down, the wooden chair cracking with the strain. "Ah ha!" he exclaimed, noticing the jars of pickles. "The finest *mekhallel* this side of Gaza. Thank you. How much do I owe you?"

"We'll settle up later."

"Okay. It is good of you to give this case priority, Jihad. I thank you."

Merhi sat down behind his desk, pulling open a drawer and bringing out a large manila envelope. "We found the car up at Rmeil. Abandoned."

"What sort was it?"

"You don't know?"

"My memory."

"It is a Datsun Bluebird. Probably worth quite a bit even in its poor condition."

Lattouf was nodding. "Oh yes, I remember vaguely. Chadi liked his modern things. High-powered cars, technology. He was useless with them but he liked them."

There was a knock on the door and Sergeant el-Gharib entered carrying two steaming mugs.

"Thank you, Deeb." Merhi watched as the mugs added to the ring stains on his desk. "And the other?"

"The boy has just returned with them."

On cue there was another knock on the door and 'the boy' (a junior officer) came in and placed a bulging bag on his captain's desk. The colourful writing on the side of the bag said *Dunkin' Donuts.*

Lattouf's eyes lit up like Satan welcoming a new batch of virgins to Hades. But there was also a sadness in them.

Once the door was closed again, Merhi opened the bag. "Dive in, Fadi," he encouraged, then he frowned at the look on his friend's face.

"Alas, I wish I could Jihad. But my weight." Lattouf patted the vast, protruding expanse of his stomach. "Nada has me on this diet. I am doing well, no?"

"Positively svelte. So you will insult me by refusing my hospitality?"

"No! That I would never do." Grinning, Lattouf's hand went into the bag like a grab-a-teddybear crane at an amusement arcade and came out with three donuts. "Thank you."

"Okay." Merhi picked up the envelope from his desk and tipped out its contents, corralling the playing cards as they attempted to flee all over the place. "We found these in the car. Some cards – "

"He always liked his cards. He would do tricks for the children when he came to visit." Lattouf's beard was already sprinkled with sugar and streaked with jam.

"A pen." Merhi held it up. It had a picture of a girl in a swimsuit on the shaft.

Lattouf turned his head. "Does it...?"

Obligingly, Merhi inverted the pen, Lattouf smiling as the swimsuit came off. Merhi pushed the pen and cards across the desk. "And a notepad. Have a look." He threw the pad on top of the pen and cards.

Lattouf brushed sugar from his hands and then wiped his fingers on his trousers for good measure. He reached out and picked up the pad, flicking over the pages.

There wasn't much, but what there was was written in Arabic and French. The first sheet was headed 6/7. Underneath that on separate lines were *0930 Départ, 0950 Hallaq, 1130 Retour.* The second sheet was headed 7/7 and had a line straight across the page. The third sheet started *8/7* then *1130 Départ, 1145 Tadlik, 1415 Retour.*

The fourth sheet was headed 9/7 then *1400 Départ.* And that was it, nothing else.

Lattouf flicked through the remaining pages of the pad. Blank. He sniffed. "He was following someone."

Merhi reached out and took a donut from the bag. "But who, why, where?"

Lattouf poured the entire contents of his mug down his throat, giving a satisfied lip-smack as he put the mug back on the desk. His hand went into the bag and commandeered the last two donuts. "He specialised in marital problems and workplace pilfering."

"Specialised?"

"It was all he could get."

Merhi took a bite out of the sole survivor of the Lattouf rampage. "So it looks like he was following someone."

"Someone who didn't want to be followed?"

Both men ate, giving themselves time to think. Finishing, Merhi rubbed the sugar from his hands and said, "So tell me again how you found him."

Lattouf licked jam from the corners of his mouth. "I was coming home from work. I saw a taxi pull up near my house. Chadi staggered out. Knocked at my door. The taxi drove off. Chadi fell backwards. I reached him. He was dead. Murdered, as we now know."

"What about the taxi? Was there anyone in it?"

"Of course! The driver."

"Fadi!"

"I did not see anyone else, but I was not looking." Lattouf picked up the *Dunkin' Donuts* bag and looked inside to make sure it was empty.

"You didn't get its number?"

"Please." He screwed up the bag and launched it towards Merhi's waste bin, missing it by about two metres.

"Okay. So, as good investigators we have to ask all the questions, even those we know the answers to." Merhi reached out for his cigarettes. "Firstly, what was Chadi doing in Beirut?"

Lattouf shrugged. "He had come to see me?"

"Why? Was he in the habit of making unannounced visits?"

Lattouf shrugged again, reaching out and helping himself to a cigarette, quickly raising his other hand. "No, no, don't light it. I just want the feel of it." He rolled it about between his fingers. "No, we didn't see him that often. Two or three times a year and never unexpectedly. *Eid* would have been the next time. Talking of which, what are you and Gisele doing?"

"Secondly, why leave his car in northern Beirut and come all the way south in a taxi?"

Lattouf put the unlit cigarette in his mouth, ignoring the ignoring of his question. "Perhaps he did not want to bring his car into that area. Maybe he did not trust the locals."

"A possibility – if he had left his car in a car park. But it was abandoned at a road junction. Look." Merhi stood up and went over to a map of Beirut on the wall. With a grunt, Lattouf rose and came over. Merhi could smell his sweat as he stood next to him.

Merhi pointed at the top of the map. "It was left here at the junction of

Berberi Street and Pasteur Street."

Lattouf squinted. "I haven't got my glasses..." He could smell the stale cigarette odour from Merhi. "Okay, so let's invert the question. What was he doing *there?*"

"Yes. Good one. There is something we only found out after we'd carried the car to the pound and obtained keys. It was out of fuel."

Suddenly Lattouf leant sideways, his hand going into his trouser pocket. It came out with some car keys. "These will probably fit. I found them in his jacket."

He went to hand them over but Merhi said "You keep them. The car's yours now."

"Mine?"

"You are his only surviving relative. We can release it to you."

Lattouf nodded pensively. "Yes, I suppose I am... Okay, he runs out of fuel. Gets in a taxi to continue his journey to see me. Logical."

"And, for all intents and purposes, falls dead from the taxi on arrival. So who killed him? The taxi driver?"

"Unlikely. A murderer waiting in a taxi just in case he ran out of fuel?"

"Exactly. So he must have been mortally wounded before he got into the taxi."

Lattouf tapped the map, talking with the unlit cigarette in the side of his mouth. "Where does that road go to?"

"Which one?"

"That big one there, coming in from the right." Lattouf squinted at the writing. "The Dora Highway." He laughed. "The road for explorers! My children watch her on the television."

"Who?"

"Dora The Explorer. No? No, your boys are too old." He patted Merhi on the back.

"It goes north. Becomes the Coastal Highway. We were on it the other day, when you came to my place."

"So it heads north."

"All the way up the coast to Tripoli."

"Passing through Jbeil. Where he lived. And worked."

"Was he done there or in Beirut? If it was Beirut, his killer would have to have been waiting for him. But how would he know Chadi would be running out of fuel at that particular spot?"

"Unless he was following him," said Lattouf.

Merhi was still, looking at the map. Then he tensed. Without looking sideways, he asked "Fadi, have you farted?"

"Donuts on an empty stomach," reasoned the Palestinian. "That will do it every time."

"Unlike you to be silent. Deadly, yes. Silent, no."

"To break wind is a gift from Allah."

"If you say so." Merhi took a longer than usual drag on his cigarette. "Okay, your cousin was being followed. All the way from Jbeil?"

"That would sound more like a chase than a follow."

"And there is one other thing we have to address. Why you? What was so important? What had he discovered to make him run down from Jbeil, with someone chasing him, to see you?"

"Did he know he was dying? Did he want to say goodbye?"

"To a cousin he only saw two or three times a year? What are you, Fadi?"

"I'm sorry?"

"What are you?"

"I... I... am a Palestinian... a husband... a father... his cousin... hungry..."

Merhi put his hands on his hips. "You are a policeman. Just like Chadi used to be. You are the one person he knew he could trust. He may have been assaulted in Jbeil or it may have been in Beirut. Doesn't really matter. What you have to find out is what had he discovered that made him dash all the way down from Jbeil, with someone chasing him, to come to tell you?"

"Something that someone was willing to kill for. He tried to say something to me when he was lying on the ground, but he couldn't speak. If only."

Merhi went back to his desk. After a further moment in front of the map, Lattouf came back over, the chair cracking again as he sat down."So what do we do now?"

"We?" asked Merhi. "It is not my case. You took the body, remember. You should have reported it. My only interest was a questionable abandoned vehicle. We have since discovered it was abandoned because it ran out of fuel. We know who the owner is, unfortunately deceased. But we can release it to his next of kin, as I said."

"But I need your help."

"Fadi, I am busy. You just don't know the amount of work I've got on."

"I understand. And what is one Palestinian life, eh? What is it worth? Nothing."

"Oh no, don't you dare. Don't you dare play the Palestinian life is worthless card." Even if it was true.

"How can I investigate it on my own?" reasoned the big man. "Will you give me jurisdiction? Write me out a *laissez passer* to operate outside the camps?"

"I cannot."

"Of course you cannot." Sad eyes looked at Merhi. "My cousin has been murdered and there is nothing I can do." His bottom lip trembled. Grains of sugar fell onto his lap from his beard.

Because your friend has refused to help you, thought Merhi. Shit. Shit, shit, shit.

He sat back in his chair, wiping his hands down his face. With resignation, he asked "What do you want to do?"

Lattouf looked up, tears around his puppy-dog eyes. He sniffed and brushed a strand of comb-over back over his head. "You are truly a friend. A good friend. I thank you. Chadi thanks you. Allah thanks you." He reached out and took one of the jars of pickles off the desk. "You and me as a team, eh? Me and the best Lebanese investigator I know." He looked like a small child who had just been told that he can, after all, have that expensive toy he wanted for *Eid* (after Daddy had paid his *fitra*, of course). He popped the lid on the jar of pickles. "I think we should go to Jbeil," he said. "See what we can discover."

His hand plunged into the jar, emerging dripping with oil and holding a pepper which promptly slithered into his mouth. He held the jar out to Merhi. "Have some," he said. "The finest *mekhallel* this side of Gaza."

Jonblat, Beirut 13:45

The traffic outside cleared instantly just before midday when a light blue Ford Transit van was driven away by its keeper, back to the southern suburbs. Merhi spent an hour in a forlorn attempt to reduce the mountain of paperwork on his desk then popped down to Hamra Street for a walk, a drink, several cigarettes, and two slices of *mana'eesh* from his favourite eatery.

As he was walking back, mind elsewhere, a soft voice said from his side, "*Massah el-khair*, Captain."

His head snapped to his right to see a smiling Carla Chedid. He had not been aware of her approach. "Carla! Where did you spring from?"

"I was just looking in the shops. Then I saw you come out of the café. You did not feel me behind you?"

"No."

"Good."

Not good, thought Merhi. He was getting rusty. Or was he just getting old? He said, "*Yalla*. Himo is due at two."

Carla was dressed in a short, elegantly-patterned beige dress and co-ordinating slave sandals. The dress was button-through, her usual open one-button-more-than-necessary style at the top augmented by the same at the hem, revealing her olive inner thighs as she walked. Her dark grey Barbour messenger bag was over one shoulder. When they entered the State Security building, more than one head turned as Merhi walked her up to his office.

"Please sit down," he said once they were in his inner sanctum. "But be careful, that chair has started to creak. Coffee? Or rather, sludge?"

"Sludge would be fine, thank you. Perhaps, as a way of thanks for your help, I should donate a coffee machine to your office?"

"It would be too good for those Neanderthals. They wouldn't know the difference."

When he returned five minutes later with two mugfuls of brown liquid, she was over by the window looking out. She looked over her shoulder. "I had forgotten how busy Beirut is. Reminds me of New York."

"You like being over there?"

She shrugged. "No one likes being in exile. But better that than dead. And there are compensations." She did not elaborate but she was thinking of her man and how he was when she had left him, unconscious on the bed after twelve hours of love-making. She was missing him.

She came back over and sat down, the dress slithering off her thighs like a snake, revealing a glimpse of her white pants beneath.

He coughed. "So how do you want to play this?"

"Leave it to me. I need to find the woman that killed Maroun. But I must also remember why I came back. I have important information and, as he is now my boss, Capain Himo must be told. Whether we then involve you and the ISF will be up to him."

"If you wish to speak privately, I can make myself scarce."

"*Merci bien.*" She sipped from the mug, then said "Goodness, you are right. Sludge."

"I should have made one for him at the same time." Merhi looked at his watch. "Where is he? He's late. I hope he got my message."

Jonblat, Beirut 14:20

Now Merhi was standing by the window, smoking, impatient, irritated. He looked at his watch again. "He's not coming, is he?" Was the bastard getting his own back for yesterday? "This is a waste of time, Carla, I'm sorry."

She came over and stood next to him. "Is he usually this late?" Reaching up, she took the cigarette from Merhi's lips, took a drag, then replaced the cigarette where she had found it.

He was glad he did not have to turn round right at that moment, he was doing an impression of a drawing pin on its side. "Actually, I don't know him that well," he said to the window. "Our paths have just happened to cross once or twice. But he's a high-flyer, they're usually prompt and by the book."

There was a knock on the door.

"*Tfaddal,*" called Merhi. "Come in."

The door was opened by Sergeant el-Gharib who then stood back to let

Acting Captain Himo enter.

"Sorry I'm late," said Himo smiling, charming. "There was a hold-up caused by some Palestinian police van parked down by Hamra Square. Near the food stalls." He was dressed in an open-necked white shirt with captain's epaulettes, and the usual blue uniform trousers.

Merhi went over, glad his reaction to Carla was subsiding (Himo would probably think it was his mobile phone in his pocket), hand outstretched. As they shook, Himo looked at Carla.

"Selim, may I introduce you to... Carla - "

"Carla Chedid." She held out her hand. "*Charafna*. Delighted to meet you."

"*Heureux de vous rencontrer, mademoiselle*." He squeezed her hand as she smiled. "Have we met before?"

"No."

"You look... familiar."

"I often have that effect." She held onto his hand longer than was necessary as he laughed.

"Well it is a pleasure anyway."

"Thank you. And for me."

Merhi had pulled up another wooden chair and held it out for Carla to sit down. He nodded at the one in front of Himo. "Be careful of that one, it's beginning to creak." Merhi sat down. "Coffee, Selim?"

"Thank you, no."

"Okay." Merhi steepled his fingers in front of him. "Selim, I was not particularly forthcoming yesterday, for which I had my reasons. I do know more about the death of Captain Khoury. In fact, it might be best if I let Carla tell you. Carla?"

"*Merci*, Jihad."

She explained at length about how she was actually a member of Himo's team, the External Security Unit, albeit she had been on permanent assignment at the United Nations in New York for five years. She had found out information that had led to her returning to Lebanon to report it personally to Maroun Khoury. She was convinced this had led directly to his murder, by a tall blonde woman with white eyes.

"A tall blonde woman with white eyes?" queried Himo.

"Yes, she tried to eliminate me the next day."

"White eyes?"

"Yes."

Himo frowned. "Okay, perhaps you'd best fill me in on all of it. What was the information that made you come back?"

"Do you know who Sajida is?"

Himo tensed, controlling the sudden rush of adrenaline, hoping they did not notice his reaction. He frowned, "Sajida?"

"Sajida."

"Why don't you tell me."

Carla looked across at Merhi.

"I'll leave you two alone." Merhi stood up. "Call me when you're done. I'll be outside. Making sludge."

Jonblat, Beirut 15:30

Merhi was sitting on Sergeant el-Gharib's desk, talking football (they were both hoping Racing Beirut would improve on their eighth place in the Premier League last season) when Himo and Carla appeared in the doorway.

"We're finished, thanks Captain," nodded Himo.

Merhi pushed himself off the desk. "All done? Good." He went out into the corridor with them. "Nothing else you need me to do?"

"No, that's fine. Carla will be helping me directly now." Himo looked at Carla. "I'll be in touch. Jihad, thank you. I appreciate your help." The men shook hands. "I know my way out."

They watched him go. As they walked back to the office, Merhi asked "Everything okay?"

She nodded. "Yes. He knew about Sajida."

Well, he would, wouldn't he? thought Merhi. High-flying twat.

"Makes it easier," said Carla. "And that gets you out of it now."

"That's good news. And you?"

"He's going to let me know what, if anything, he wants me to do. I had a feeling he would like me to go back to New York and as quickly as possible. Wants all the glory for himself."

"Why am I not surprised? And will you? Go back?"

"Not until I've ripped that bitch's head from her shoulders."

"That's my girl." He tried to catch himself before he said it, but he didn't.

She grinned. "Thank you... my boy. But I'll be out of your hair soon, I can't implicate you any further. If he orders me back to New York, I'll find some other place to hole up. You can tell him I've gone if he asks."

"You're welcome to stay, you know."

"Thank you, but you and Gisele have your own lives to lead."

"My brother-in-law has an apartment up near Jamhour. He's hardly ever there. Lives in Dubai for most of the year. You could have that."

Carla did not tell him that she knew the block, that she had had an apartment there herself for a while five years ago. "Let's see what happens over the next couple of days and we'll take it from there." She picked up her bag. "Right, I've still got some shopping to do. Gisele asked me to pick her up a little something."

"She did?" He thought she was talking about food.

"Mm. You like red lace?"

Merhi sat down quickly before his mobile phone appeared in his pocket again. For God's sake, he was fifty-one years old. His wife and his lodger were going to kill him at this rate!

"What time you shooting off tonight?" she asked innocently.

He squeezed his legs together. How about right now? "F- five. Maybe six."

"Can I cadge a lift back?"

"*B- bien sûr.*"

"*Merci.* I'll see you shortly." With a swirl of the undone dress, she left the office.

Merhi sat back in his chair, thinking thoughts for which in some parts of the world he could be stoned to death. Then he reached out and opened the bottom drawer on the right side of his desk. The small digital recording machine, connected wirelessly to the pin-prick microphone disguised as a knot in the wood on the front of his desk, was still recording. He turned it off.

In the corridors of politics, power and security in Lebanon, everyone spied on everyone else, or at least tried to. Why should he be any different?

The only question was, should he now listen to what was on here? Would he be protecting himself by doing so?

Or would he be signing his own death warrant?

Bourj el-Barajneh, Beirut 20:00

"I am going to Jbeil," announced the patriarch of *La Famille Lattouf* as he sat down at the old wooden dining table. "Me and Jihad. We are joining forces to investigate Chadi's murder."

The six children seated shoulder to shoulder, three on one side of the table, three on the other, couldn't really have cared less but they knew to be quiet when Baba was seated and pontificating. The older ones even tried to look interested.

"Are you really? You are officially working with the Lebanese police?" asked Nada Lattouf as she brought in a large, steaming bowl of *lubya* (bean stew). She was nearly half a metre smaller than her husband in height but proportionately she was the same volume, a big Palestinian Mama. On the very rare occasions when she and her husband mated, the earth had no choice but literally to move for both of them. She was dressed in her usual black *jilbaab*, head uncovered as she was at home, greying hair pinned up.

"Not the police," explained her proud husband. "Better. Jihad is the Internal Security Force. When the ISF says jump, the police ask 'How high?'."

"So they are recognising you at last?"

"I knew it would be only a matter of time after I helped them solve the Hariri murder."

Five years was a long matter of time, thought Nada as she went back and retrieved the bowl of rice from the kitchen. As she came back in, she said "That is good. Your genius deserves recognition, husband." She sat down at the other end of the table, making the older children giggle as she looked heaven-ward. The children began passing their plates towards her.

"Who knows where this might lead?" pondered Fadi as he spooned a mountain of rice onto his plate then picked up the bowl of stew. "Maybe a merging of forces. Or perhaps they might want me as a consultant." He stared dreamily into the future. "Paid by the hour. When all else fails, call in Lattouf! I will be known throughout The Levant. Maybe it will get us out of here."

Nada knew better than to dampen her husband's spirits with a reality check. He would be brought down to earth soon enough, as he always was. She said, "Insh'allah" and nudged the nearest child, nodding at the bowl of stew. The nudge went down the line and Lana, the eleven year old at the end, lifted the bowl from in front of her father and passed it back down to her mother.

"Apparently we are Chadi's only known relatives." Fadi looked back down, looked at his plate of rice and then wondered where the stew had gone. "We inherit his stuff."

"Really?" Now Nada was interested. "Here, children, pass this down to your father." Back came the bowl of stew.

"Not that there will be much. The Israelis destroyed everything when they bombed his place in Bir Hassan." He slathered the stew on top of the rice, then passed the bowl back up the table on the opposite side to which it had come. "In fact, I have something already. Lana, pass me my jacket."

Lana smiled, grown up before her time. "You are leaning on it, father."

"I am? Oh yes!" Fadi turned around, rummaging in the pockets of his uniform jacket draped over the back of his chair. He brought out a pen which he quickly put back into a pocket with a sheepish look towards Nada. Then he brought out some loose playing cards, handing them over to Lana as if he was giving her the keys to the Kaaba itself.

She was less than overwhelmed, but dutifully she said "Thank you, father."

"Now you can practise those tricks Uncle Chadi used to show you," Fadi ruffled the top of her head. Then he said more quietly, "In his memory." He looked up at his wife, sadness on his face. He nodded. "We will find out who did this, Nada. And why. Me and my friend Jihad."

Jounieh, Lebanon 20:00

"I am going to Jbeil," said Jihad Merhi as he sat down at the modern glass dining table. "With the idiot Lattouf. He wants me to investigate his cousin's murder."

"Really? And you have time for this?" asked Gisele as she brought in a platter of *samak mishwi* (kebabs of monkfish, lemon and pepper).

"Well, now that Carla will be working back with her own team, that relieves me of that duty. With all respect." He looked across the table at their guest as he opened a packet of flat bread. "But do I have time? No."

Carla smiled, taking bread from the offered wrapper. "It is good that I am out of your hair. Perhaps Captain Himo can progress matters more quickly than I have been able to."

Gisele put a bowl of rice on the table and sat down. "Then why do it if you don't have time?" she asked her husband.

Jihad poured wine, a Chateau Ksara chardonnay. He shrugged. "What can I do? Refuse him?"

"Yes."

"It won't take long, we won't find anybody, I'll just be going through the motions." A picture of the butcher's shop morgue in the refugee camp flashed suddenly into his mind. "At least I can show him that the death of a Palestinian matters to at least one person in the lower echelons of authority here." He helped himself to one of the kebabs. "We'll just nip up there tomorrow, won't take long. Deeb el-Gharib is covering the office. Just one thing, though." He looked over at Gisele. "As he's up this way, I thought we could invite Fadi for dinner."

Gisele sighed, but it was not the negative reaction he was expecting. "Of course. It is only right." She sipped her wine. "You know, you are too good, my husband."

"I am?"

"Oh yes. Am I not right, Carla?"

Carla nodded as she chewed on a piece of fish. "Too good."

"One day," said Gisele, "it will be the death of you."

14 July 2010
2 Sha'ban 1431

Annaya, Lebanon 03:50

"*Subhana Rabbiyal A'ala.* Glory be to my Lord, the most high."

Brother Malek was kneeling in his cell, forehead and nose on the floor, elbows raised in the *raka'ah* posture of submission to God. The cell was in darkness save for a small tea-light candle in one corner. Malek wore nothing except a cloth around his waist.

He rose into a sitting position, saying the first of the three *takbir* that would end his *Fajr* prayer. Prostrate for the second *takbir*, back up again for the third, he then sat back on his haunches for a moment's reflection.

Reaching out, he unwound the hose of his golden *argileh* and sucked on the end. The charcoal was still alight, the water in the bowl bubbling. Two-apples flavour. He was calm.

But even at this early hour, he was warm. He ran a hand over his five-day growth of beard. He would not shave it off again, that had been a mistake and his *houri* had had to deal with the consequences. He would be bearded for his return to the Holy Land, but his followers would know him, they would know *Yawm al-Qiyamah* had come and they would rejoice.

He smoked for half an hour, in reflection and personal prayer. At 04:30 he removed the Netbook from the *argileh* case and turned it on.

He knew by heart the user name and password for the single-use e-mail and *Skype* account for today's date (it included the numbers 281431). He signed in, making friends with the similar single-use account at the other end.

It took a few moments to connect, and then he smiled as the face of his favourite disciple appeared on the screen. Malek was pleased. He never knew which of his twelve followers would be at the other end, they varied it for security and locational purposes, but this one he had the most affection for.

As the sun rose in the east they began to talk.

Bourj el-Barajneh, Beirut 07:30

As a captain of the Internal Security Force of Lebanon, it took a lot to shock

Jihad Merhi. But at that moment he sat in his grey Toyota Land Cruiser V8 and stared open-mouthed as Fadi Lattouf came out of the front door of his house.

Lattouf was dressed in a suit! Dark grey, probably polyester, off the shelf from somewhere in Bourj Hammoud as could be witnessed by the slightly too short trousers. Underneath was an open-necked white shirt. His sparse hair was plastered over his head and his beard had been trimmed to an unshaven, rather than unkempt, look. Wraparound counterfeit *Ray-Ban* sunglasses completed the ensemble. On anybody else, the outfit might look smart; on Lattouf it just looked... weird.

As the sun's early rays hit him, Lattouf immediately removed the jacket and undid another two buttons on the short sleeve shirt, his grey and black chest hairs falling out like commuters from a Tokyo subway train in the rush hour.

"Morning of light, my dear friend!" The Land Cruiser dipped to the side as Lattouf got in. "A joyous day to start our fruitful collaboration."

Merhi, who perhaps had had one too many *arak* the evening before, wondered what the hell he was doing here. Why didn't he just throw the Palestinian out and go have a normal day's work protecting the unprotectable? "Morning Fadi."

Merhi sniffed. Lattouf was wearing cologne! "You look - "

"Thank you. It is good to be out of uniform for once. To be myself."

Merhi slipped his own sunglasses on, coincidentally also *Ray-Ban* wraparounds but genuine. He hoped the two of them didn't look like The Blues Brothers. Or Laurel and Hardy.

Suddenly Lattouf leaned to the left, coming closer to Merhi, almost as if he was going to kiss him. A stentorian roar emitted from his backside.

"Left over *lubya*. That will do it every time." Lattouf was pressing buttons on the armrest, trying to open the window. Merhi was only too pleased to oblige from his side.

"The fresh air will do us good," said Lattouf as they pulled away. "How long till we get to Jbeil?"

Annaya, Lebanon 09:00

Brother Malek stood on the step in front of the altar of the Monastery Church of Saint Maron, hood up, arms outstretched, holding the hands of Paradise and Love who were kneeling in front of him. "Rise, my daughters, rise," he said deeply, gently.

Touching their lips to his hands, the women stood.

Malek locked his fingers in front of his waist and pushed his elbows out as he stepped down. The twins linked him, one either side. Slowly the three of them began to walk around the church.

"Seven weeks," said Malek. "There will be no reversion. It is as if the dates have been set by Allah himself. Satan has been defeated. The Messiah will return to the Holy Land on *Laylat al-Qadr*. The holiest night of the holiest month. The Night of Power, the Night of Destiny."

"*Sabah a Allah.*" Love squeezed his arm.

"Indeed God is good, my daughter," the hood nodded. "But so am I. Soon now we must move The Secret. We will be travelling overland, across The Levant. The journey will be as important as the arrival, it will be talked about forever. The journey that saved mankind, the true resurrection, the true renaissance. It must take forty days and forty nights to cross the desert – which means the journey must start in ten days time. The Secret will cross the desert on camel."

"On *jamal*?" queried Paradise.

Malek stopped, pulling them up sharply. "Did I not make myself clear?"

"Yes, brother," Paradise cast her eyes downward. "I am sorry. Please forgive me."

For a full thirty seconds Malek did not move. No sound came from under the hood, not even breathing. He was perfectly still. The silence of the church enwrapped them.

Then he resumed walking as if nothing had happened, their arms still linked. "The Secret will cross the desert on camel. There will be some waiting on the other side of the mountains. We must be there at the desert on twelve Sha'ban. You may chose camel also or you may travel by car. But when we reach the Holy City, The Secret will not enter it on a camel, not even on a donkey. This time it will be on a white stallion. And The Messiah will have a sword in his hand. This time there will be no turning the other cheek." Now they could hear his breathing and it was becoming heavier.

"*Yaatik al-aafieh!*" whispered Love.

"God *is* my strength, daughter." Malek's chest was rising and falling. "After all these years, the time is here. Soon the world will know that the prophesies have been fulfilled. Soon the world will know *al-Mahdi* has come to save them. Soon the world will know that The Secret..." He disengaged their arms and leant forward, his hands coming up to grasp the rim of the hood. Straightening up, he threw the hood backwards off his head, revealing the ageing mortal face and the black immortal eyes. He looked from one woman to the other. "... is me."

Mount Lebanon 09:30

"What do you think will happen?" asked Love, the wind blowing her hair as Paradise drove the open-topped Jeep Wrangler Ultimate back down the mountain. "When he returns. Will the world recognise him as *al-Mahdi*?"

"It must. Everything is as prophesied."

"And there will be peace?"

"Eventually. It is written that when he comes again it will be Armageddon, but after that there will be peace for thousands of years."

Love was quiet, contemplative, as her sister negotiated a particularly sharp hairpin bend. Then she asked, "And what about us? Do you think we will be with him as he promised? His right and left hands?"

Paradise shrugged. "Why not? He would not deceive us. Our commander has said that we are permanently assigned to him until we are instructed otherwise."

"We will truly be his companions, his *houri*."

"And his protection."

Another hairpin bend then they were on the straight run west of Hboub, heading down into Jbeil.

"Should we ride with him on the camels, sister?" asked Paradise.

"No," Love shook her head. "That must be his glory. We will follow in a car. This one. Open-topped. So we are ready to confront any non-believers."

Love stretched forward for her mobile phone as it began to ring. "I bet this is him. I knew we should have brought him more tobacco – Oh, it's not." She brought the phone to her ear. "*Bonjour mon frère... Oui?... Vraiment? Alors, c'est merveilleux... Tu es un vrai croyant... Oui... Oui...D'accord. Nous arrivons. Merci.*"

She ended the call, relaxing her head on the headrest, eyes closed. "God truly is good, sister."

"Who was that?"

A wide grin spread across Paradise's face as Love gave her details of the call. "No way! Is God on our side or what? Time to take out the lenses?"

"Maybe," said Love. "We cannot convert with them in. But there is another thought..."

By the time Love had told her sister of her idea, they had reached Jbeil. They entered on Rue Jbeil, slowing to a crawl behind a grey Toyota Land Cruiser V8 that looked like it was lost (tourists!), then overtaking it and heading down Boulevard al-Mina towards the parking area.

Their day had started early but it was far from over yet.

Jbeil, Lebanon 09:45

"See that?" Fadi Lattouf swivelled in his seat as Jihad Merhi turned in to the car park just beyond the Seven Seas Restaurant.

"What?"

"Twins! Two women. They look identical! A rare sight. I must tell Nada later. Did I ever tell you that they thought Wissam was going to be twins - ? "

"Where is your cousin's office?" Merhi applied the parking brake and turned off the engine.

Grunting, Lattouf slid out of the car, the vehicle noticeably rising on the passenger side. "Down in the souks, near the cemetery. I've only been there once, I think I can remember the way." He pulled his underwear from out of his crevice and shook his leg.

The Toyota's lights flashed as Merhi pressed the lock button on his key fob. "*Yalla* then. And we've got his house to examine after that."

"He had no house," Lattouf shook his head sadly as they began walking. "Not after his family was murdered. Had no need. He lived in a couple of rooms above his office."

"Well, that makes it easier."

They turned left onto Boulevard al-Mina.

"My friend, look!" Lattouf nodded.

A little way ahead, the twins were walking side by side. One of them carried a rucksack on her shoulder.

"Same height, same hair, same bodies, same way of walking. Even the same clothes. Amazing. Having a child is a gift from Allah, but having twins is a double-blessing."

"If you say so." Merhi lit up a cigarette and offered the packet to Lattouf, who shook his head and patted his waistline incongruously.

Beyond the Seven Seas Restaurant, the women crossed over the road, walking parallel with the medieval town wall. Lattouf eased Merhi across the road with his body.

The women turned right through the ramparts into Rue St John.

When Lattouf turned right also, Merhi exclaimed "Fadi! What the hell are you doing?"

Lattouf looked puzzled. "This is our way. The souks are down here."

"If they turn round they'll think we are two dirty old men on the pull."

Lattouf sniffed under his own arm. "Not dirty. And I am happily married, my friend. And so are you. Cannot a man simply admire one of nature's splendours?" The women turned into an alleyway by an old bookshop. "There, you see, they have gone."

They walked on and turned left at the end of the road. Tourists were already milling around outside the wax museum on their left. Lattouf pointed down the road where there was another gap in the ramparts. "The cemetery, see? I knew we were heading the right way."

"We're all heading to the cemetery, Fadi. It's only our journeys that are timed differently." Merhi drew on his cigarette without appreciating the full irony of the action.

"Yes. Very good." Lattouf suddenly seemed distracted. "Abu Samer, may

I ask you something?"

"Of course."

"Before we begin our search of Chadi's place, can we get something to eat? I'm starving."

Jounieh, Lebanon 09:45

Carla was sitting on the Merhis' balcony drinking her third coffee of the day, enjoying the sun's rays as they slid over the mountain behind her. She was dressed only in a thin white cotton T-shirt and matching pants, her bare legs stretched out in front of her, tanned and firm. Once again she was on her own, Gisele having gone out to meet some friends for a coffee morning down in Kaslik.

Her telephone rang, the opening bars of *Hey Soul Sister*, and she knew it wasn't him. It wasn't his ring tone.

"*'ehh?*"

"*Bonjour,* Carla. It's Selim Himo."

"Good morning, Captain. *Kifak?*"

"*Bien, merci.* As I hope you are."

"Sure."

"I've been thinking about things. Can you come in to discuss?"

She had been expecting it. He was going to order her back to New York. "Sure. I'll get a taxi. Give me two hours just in case, you know what the traffic's like."

"Okay, but don't come to Ras en Nabaa. I've discovered something but I don't want to put it on the Department's system, eyes and ears and all that. Can you come to my apartment in Raousheh? It's clean and uncompromised."

"*Bien sûr.*"

He gave her the address.

"Okay Captain, give me two hours. Say *muntasif an-nahar?*"

"Midday will be fine. You might be surprised at what I've discovered."

I don't think so, thought Carla. The biggest surprise was that Sajida was right. Anything else after that was insignificant. She said, "Sure."

Jbeil, Lebanon 10:15 – 11:15

"This is it," said Fadi Lattouf over a mouthful of goat *shawarma*. They were standing outside an old wooden door in the furthest part of the furthest souk in the old town. The area was quiet, not many tourists would venture down this far.

Jihad Merhi was holding Lattouf's other two *shawarmas* and his two remaining cans of Coca-Cola. He stepped back, nodding at the door.

"What?" A piece of goat bobbed on Lattouf's lower lip.

"You kick it in, you're bigger than me."

"Why should I do that?" Lattouf crammed the remaining half of the *shawarma* into his mouth and put his hand into his trouser pocket, bringing out a set of three keys on a ring with a small silver thirty-three ring *tasbih*.

Merhi raised his eyebrows at the prayer beads. "He was a religious man?"

"He was a worried man. Like we all are. These were in his jacket along with his car keys." Lattouf handed the keys to Merhi in exchange for his second *shawarma* and a can of drink.

The second key fit. The door creaked opened onto a small office. A musty smell came to embrace them.

The office contained an old desk, two chairs, a four-drawer filing cabinet and a fan in a corner. A closed door lead to another room, probably a kitchen or a lavatory, they would find out. To their immediate left a set of stairs led upwards.

A fly flew around the bare bulb hanging from the ceiling, oblivious to its several dead compatriots on the small sill below the window looking out over the cemetery.

"Well, well, look at that," Merhi nodded, impressed. On the desk sat a state-of-the-art iMac computer complete with a 27-inch monitor. "I think this is going to be easier than we expected."

But, of course, it wasn't. Lattouf was assigned the physical search while Merhi sat down at the desk.

The filing cabinet was unlocked but it was empty except for an old box of hardened baklava in the second drawer which looked like it had been there since before the French mandate. The closed door indeed revealed both a kitchen and a lavatory – in the same room. The lavatory was a hole in the floor in one corner with a shower hose coming out of the wall at waist level, the kitchen was nothing more than a water tap, a sink and a cabinet supporting a plug-in two-ring electric hob. But the room was spotlessly clean.

While Lattouf went upstairs, Merhi cracked his knuckles like a concert pianist and started on the computer. Nothing happened when he tried to turn it on, until he discovered that it was not plugged in. Situation rectified, he started again.

Lights twinkled, the monitor flickered, there was an almost-inaudible hum from the processor – and Merhi stared at the screen in disbelief. "No," he said loudly. "Shit."

Grey polyester-covered legs came halfway back down the stairs and Lattouf's voice asked, "You have found something, Abu Samer?"

"It's bloody asking me to register! This is the first time this machine has been turned on, Fadi. It's brand new! I don't believe it."

"I told you he liked his modern things. He was useless with them but he liked them."

"Shit." Merhi sat back in the chair as the legs turned around and went back up the stairs.

The floorboards above began to groan in agony as Lattouf moved about upstairs. Merhi heard drawers being opened and closed, then a door was opened, there was grunting, and the door was closed again. The legs came back down the stairs.

"Nothing." Lattouf popped the ring on the last can of Coke. The disappearance of the final *shawarma* had not been witnessed and would remain a mystery for all time. "Just one room. A bed, unmade, a small chest of drawers, only clothes, and a wardrobe, one suit and one shirt. Nothing else."

Merhi lit up a cigarette, sighing and breathing out smoke at the same time. "So that's all we have? Nothing? No papers, no records, not even any bank statements?"

Lattouf shrugged as he sat down in front of the desk. "He was Palestinian. Even now it is not easy for us to get bank accounts here. And what good would papers be to a man who does not exist? Papers can be more trouble than they are worth. Possibly the last papers he had were the death certificates of his wife and children – if they had been issued, which they probably weren't."

"So we've come all this way for nothing?"

Another shrug. "We had to check, to see for ourselves."

"He had nothing else on him when you found him, just the two sets of keys?"

"Some money, not much. Nothing else. So, where do we go from here?"

Merhi wanted to say "Straight back to Beirut to get on with our lives", but he bit his tongue. He pulled a folded sheet of paper from his back pocket. "So all we have are these notepad entries." He unfolded the paper, spreading it flat on the desk. "On 6 July someone was at the barber's at 09:50. On 8 July someone had a massage at 11:45. On 9 July someone went out at 14:00." He looked up at Lattouf. "And that's it. He has no case records, nothing. Who is this someone?"

"Can we make enquiries of barbers and health spas?"

"Where? In this street? In Jbeil? In the district? In Beirut? In the whole of the f... in the whole of Lebanon?"

Shrug number three.

"And even if we did progress this logically," continued Merhi, "say by starting with the barbers and health clubs of Jbeil, we would need resources.

We couldn't do it ourselves. I don't have time and you don't have jurisdiction. Do you really want to get the local police involved? Because that would be the only way."

Lattouf was shaking his head. "No. They wouldn't want to know, anyway."

"The death of a Palestinian private investigator would not be top of their list of priorities, no."

Lattouf looked sad but resigned. "I'll have one of your cigarettes if I may, Abu Samer." Merhi took one from his packet and threw it across.

Lattouf caught it, waited, and then said "And I'll have a light this time, please."

He leant forward over Merhi's proffered lighter and then sat back. After his second lungful of smoke he said, "We've given it our best shot, haven't we? There's no place else to go."

"Yes we have and no there isn't."

"Well at least I have a new car, and the clothes upstairs might fit my thirteen year old," Lattouf laughed humourlessly. He looked about. "I guess I will have to see about the rent on this place. A refund might be due. Or could he have owned it?"

"Unlikely and certainly not officially. But I'll look into it for you. The enquiries will be better coming from me."

"Thank you, my friend, thank you." Lattouf looked at his wrist even though there was no watch on it. "We might as well go. It must be lunchtime by now."

Raousheh, Beirut 12:15

Rather than try to negotiate its way through the centre of Beirut, the taxi had taken the coastal route over the top of the city, approaching Raousheh from the north down General de Gaulle Avenue. It had driven directly over the spot where Rafic Hariri had been assassinated five years ago and where Carla had paid homage ten days previously.

Again she had looked at the statue as they had passed by, and she had become sad. Sad and angry. She could have stopped it, she told herself, she could have. But the assassin had been so, so clever. He still was.

She smiled. And who would have thought things would turn out the way they did? With life, one never knew. Never.

Now she paid the driver and climbed out of the cab, looking up at the 1960s apartment building. She was wearing her button-through patterned beige dress, but today she had left the top and bottom one-button-too-manys done up – at least for the start of this meeting. If things did not go her way or she thought that some persuasion was needed, they would discreetly become open again. The slave sandals might be a bit exotic for a meeting with her new boss, but she had nothing else to co-ordinate with the dress. Her Barbour messenger bag added a touch of *gravitas*.

Captain Himo's apartment was on the fifth floor, one from the top. As she walked into the building, Carla wondered what awaited her. Would she be sent back into exile? Would she be reinstated, with or without honours? Would she be fired...?

The ageing elevator stopped eight centimetres above the level of the fifth floor, and she stepped out. There were four doors in the expansive foyer. Himo's was number 20, over on her left.

She pressed the front door bell, standing back so that he would be able to see it was her when he looked through the spy hole. She straightened herself, flicked her long hair over her shoulders, made sure her hair clip was in place, and put on a smile.

The door did not open.

Okay, maybe the bell was not working, she had not heard any ring or buzz when she had pressed the button. She knocked on the door – and it moved ever so slightly as she hit it.

Immediately she was alert. What was this?

Her hand went into her bag, bringing out the solid wooden Holding Cross. The down beam of the cross poked out between her first and middle finger, the cross beam held within her fist. She put the end of the down beam against the door and pushed. The door eased open silently.

She stood in the doorway, not moving. One part of her – the sane, rational part - was screaming at her to go, to leave this place, to get away. But what would that achieve? And this might be a test, who knew?

All senses alert, she entered the apartment.

The small hallway led into the living room through a doorway with no door. Tentatively, slowly, carefully, back to the wall, she stepped through the doorway, eyes scanning.

Then she smiled and relaxed.

Captain Himo was out on the balcony, sitting in the sun. No wonder he hadn't heard her knocking! And maybe this was a test, that's why he had left the door open. To see how close she could get before he knew she was there. Okay, she would show him how good she was.

Soundlessly she walked across the floor, now pleased that she had worn the slave sandals – no heels to click on the tiles.

She reached out to open the glass door. This might be tricky, this would show how good she was. He hadn't given any indication that he knew she was there, but the door might give her away.

Slipping the Holding Cross back in to her bag, she curled her fingers around the door handle. Careful now, careful... careful...

Her mobile phone rang.

Hey Soul Sister.

Dammit!

She grinned, resigned. Okay, she had gotten this far. Nine out of ten. You win this one, Captain.

Pulling the phone from its dedicated pocket on her bag, she looked at the screen. It was Gisele. *Not now, habibi.* She pressed the reject button –

And then frowned, staring out at the balcony.

Himo had not moved. In fact he was still. Far too still.

Throwing the phone back into the bag, she grabbed the door handle. Then a voice from behind her said, "Hey, Soul Sister."

Carla froze, eyes searching for a reflection in the glass.

"I wouldn't bother going out there," continued the voice. "He's been converted. He is with Allah."

Carla could see the inanimate objects of the room in the glass but there were no reflections of living objects. If the object was living.

She turned. "You."

"Me," smiled Love.

The two women were silent, sizing each other up. The woman – the killer – with the long blonde hair and crazy white eyes had her head cocked to one side. She was by far the bigger, but Carla had bested her before. This time she would need to finish it.

"Why?" asked Carla.

"Why what?" Love straightened her head.

"Why kill him? I did not tell him the secret."

"He had served his purpose. *al-Mahdi* ordered that he be rewarded with full conversion. He is with Allah in *firdaus*."

"*al-Mahdi?* You call him *al-Mahdi?*" Carla laughed, shaking her head. "He is *ad-Dajjal*, he is Satan."

"You will believe. You will be converted."

Carla nodded backwards. "And what purpose had Captain Himo served for his 'full conversion' if he did not know the secret?"

"He knew the secret," Love was speaking calmly, having a reasoned conversation. "Just because you didn't tell him doesn't mean he didn't know. All the disciples do. He was not a *kafir*. His purpose? Was to bring us you."

Carla had slipped the bag off of her shoulder, letting it drop to the floor. She so wished she had done her nails before coming out, but this bitch wouldn't know they were empty. She moved her fingers, easing the micro-needles down. "So how do you want to play this?"

Love raised her hands level with her shoulders, her fingers forming claws, her needles also showing. She smiled and turned her head a little to the side, the white eyes staring.

"Okay, a cat fight." Carla also raised her claws. "Are you sure you want to do this?" She took a step forwards. "I chased you off last time."

"But you didn't chase me off," said a voice from the kitchen doorway.

Carla looked to her left, mouth dropping with shock. There were two of them! Her eyes jumped from one woman to the other. They were the same. Absolutely and positively identical in every way. What were they, some sort of genetic mutation? Look at the eyes!

Carla's face hardened. God, if you exist, protect me now. She flicked her fingers threateningly, one hand towards one mutant, one towards the other. As she took another step forward, she reached up to her hair.

"The hairclip!" shouted Love. "Stop her!"

Then they were on her. Like a real catfight, it happened in silence, only the thumping of feet, the slapping of flesh, quick gasps as injuries happened.

A clump of Carla's hair was ripped out as the hairclip was yanked from her head. Arms moved, fingers poked, scratches were made, blood was drawn, teeth were bared.

A twin whimpered as Carla viciously striated needled fingers down her face.

Buttons flew into the air as Carla's dress was ripped open. She spat blood as she was punched in the mouth. They were all over her. Hands, knees, heads, legs everywhere. She felt flesh against her throbbing mouth and bit, hard. She heard a high-pitched yelp as the flesh came away between her teeth.

Then she was falling backwards, something was around her throat and it was getting tighter. She crashed down, grasping at her neck, scratching under her chin with her own needles. It was her bag! They were strangling her with the strap of her own bag!

She kicked out, hit someone, but she knew she was getting weaker. The pressure on her neck became heavier, tighter.

Paradise was sitting on the floor behind Carla's head, pulling and pulling on the bag. A breathless Love was now on top, moving from side to side, kicking back at the flailing feet.

Carla felt her kicks weakening, her strength failing, her life ebbing away.

Love was now astride her. Paradise had managed to grab Carla's hands above her head. Love plunged her needled fingers into Carla's exposed stomach.

As the strap bit into Carla's neck and pain flooded her gut, her sight began to blur.

Love leant forward, body to body, her face next to Carla's. She stared curiously at the dying woman. Her tongue came out and she lapped at the blood running from Carla's cut mouth. Then she kissed her full on the lips.

Love pulled her head away, not knowing if the glazed eyes below her could still see. There was blood on her face from the kiss. She put her mouth to Carla's ear, panting. *"Houri* will always triumph over *djinn.* It is written. That is the way of things. Now we want your soul, sister..."

PART FOUR
الجزء الرابع

THE SECOND COMING
المجيء الثاني

Coastal Highway, Lebanon 14:45

The black open-topped Jeep Wrangler Ultimate sped northwards, weaving in and out of the traffic. In the driver's seat, Paradise was grim-faced but satisfied. The intercession had gone as planned. The *houri* were invincible. But she was in pain, her right forearm hurt like hell. She stole a look across at her sister.

Love had her eyes closed, letting the sun's rays caress and calm her. Her right arm was held across her body, a towel from the disciple's apartment wrapped tightly over the forearm covering the bite wound. Thankfully no blood was seeping through, which was a good sign.

They had a Field Medical Kit back in Jbeil. They were both fully trained field paramedics, but neither of them had had to use their skills for a long time (not since the incident at Jebel Uweinat on the Libyan, Egyptian, Sudanese border six years before which had led directly to them being ordered to guard the body of *al-Mahdi*). Well, today Paradise would tend to her sister. The pain in her own arm might be empathetic but the pain in her sister's arm was real.

And they would both need antibiotics. Only Shaitan knew what infections the unclean djinn had been carrying...

The speed of the vehicle, the noise of the traffic, the roar of the wind over the open top, and each sister's preoccupation with their pain meant that neither of them heard the music that suddenly came from the floor in the back of the Jeep.

It was coming from the dark grey Barbour wax cotton messenger bag that they had flung there when they had left the apartment in Raousheh.

It was not *Hey Soul Sister*, it was Shakira's *Hips Don't Lie*.

A caller ID ringtone, specific to one person.

Murray Hill, New York City, USA 07:45 (local time)

The man with the long black hair falling either side of his face stood naked at the window of the 30th floor apartment on East 39th Street, looking north over Midtown. His hairless swarthy body was hard, fit, but flawed by the various scars, gouges and burns on his torso and down his legs. These marks were years old now but they would not fade, and neither would his memories of how he had received them. On the orders of a man who was once dubbed The King of Lebanon. A man who had blasted off his left ear when trying to shoot him in the head. A man now long dead.

The Damascene looked at the Nokia cell phone in his hand. He and the woman who now called herself Carla both understood that sometimes a call could not be answered. Their fail-safe procedures were that one call could be ignored, it was just a *Hi, how are you?* A second call within ten minutes meant *I want/need to talk* and should be responded to at least by text giving a time when they could speak. A non-response to the second call would mean a third call within half an hour of the first, which must be answered. If it was not, something was wrong.

He had made three calls in the last half hour and she had not responded. Something was wrong.

She had asked for his help two days ago but she had understood when he explained that he could not leave instantly, he had a job to do in Washington (as a result of which there was now a vacant seat in the Senate). Now he was back.

But where was she?

Bourj el-Barajneh, Beirut 21:00

"Well, we tried, my friend, we tried." Fadi Lattouf and Jihad Merhi were sitting in Merhi's Land Cruiser outside *chez Lattouf*.

Merhi nodded. "We did."

"Bless you for that. And thanks once again to Gisele for the *jawani*, the meal was delicious."

The chicken wings in a lemon, garlic and coriander sauce were one of the many specialities of *la cuisine de Madame Merhi* but neither she nor her husband had ever seen anyone eat the bones before.

"So, we will see you at *Eid*?" confirmed Lattouf. "We used to have such a good time, didn't we? This year it will be better than ever."

"We look forward to it," lied Merhi.

"I will make arrangements to pick up the Bluebird. Will there be any charge?"

Merhi shook his head. "I'll make sure there isn't."

"Thank you." He nodded at the back seat. "Will you give me a hand? Just to the front door."

Merhi carried the monitor, Lattouf carried the iMac processor. They put both components of the computer on the ground by the front door.

Merhi offered his hand. Lattouf took it and then yanked the Lebanese forward in a crushing bear hug. The smell of garlic encased Merhi's head like a bubble. "It was good to work with you again, my friend," said the Palestinian. The hug was maintained (unilaterally) longer than was necessary. It was as if Lattouf didn't want to let go. Then he pulled back and said, "See you in a few weeks."

Lattouf watched the Land Cruiser drive off, giving it a final wave as it disappeared north. Then he opened his front door, bent down, balanced the monitor on top of the processor and picked them both up in his huge arms.

"Children!" he called as he went through the door, kicking it closed behind him. "Come see what your Baba has bought for you!"

16 July 2010
4 Sha'ban 1431

Jounieh, Lebanon 07:00

"That's two nights now and she has not returned." Gisele was leaning against a kitchen unit in her dressing gown, eating a yoghurt. Jihad was at right angles to her, leaning against the sink, dressed in his uniform, eating his typical Lebanese breakfast (a sugared ring donut, no jam today). On the work surface next to him was a double espresso.

He shrugged with his shoulders, mouth and hands. "She is not our problem anymore. She is with Himo now, working with her own people. Perhaps she is staying with him."

"You would have thought she would have let us know. Some of her clothes are still in her room."

"Maybe she left them for you." Jihad brushed the sugar off his fingers into the sink.

Gisele raised an eyebrow. "You would like me to dress like her?"

Oh-oh. Seven a.m on a Friday morning and he could be seeing his weekend disappear before his very eyes. "I love the way you dress." Did he hesitate too long?

"Do you even notice the way I dress?"

"Of course. I am in a constant state of arousal whenever I'm with you."

"What is your favourite outfit?"

"Sorry?"

"If you know them so well, which of my clothes do you like the best?"

Well, he hadn't made any plans for Saturday or Sunday anyway. Might as well spend them in the dog house. And he had a backlog of work. "That is easy," he knocked back his coffee. "If I tell you, will you put it on for me? Right now?"

"What?"

"Will you put it on for me right now?"

She sniffed. "What is it? Which outfit do you like best?"

He put his cup down on the side. "Isn't it obvious, my little siren from Jamhour? I like your birthday suit the best!" He grabbed hold of her, his hand slipping inside the dressing gown, over her small left breast.

She squealed pushing him away. "You filthy bastard!" But her hand was around the back of his neck, and her dressing gown had opened up, and somehow they were falling onto the floor.

They fought, they kissed, they made love. Right there in the kitchen.

An untypical Lebanese breakfast.

17 July 2010
5 Sha'ban 1431

Jonblat, Lebanon 09:30

Still no word from Carla – but no word from Himo either. No doubt they were far too busy to grant Jihad Merhi even the courtesy of telling him what was going on. The External Security Unit always thought it was a cut above its colleagues in the Internal Security Force.

Well it worked both ways. He, Merhi, was also too busy. If they came knocking at his door today, he would have no time for them. Today was the tenth anniversary of Bashar al-Assad becoming President of Syria and celebrations were expected by certain factions in certain parts of the city. As usual, Merhi had been put in charge of security.

Yesterday, after a relaxed and benign Merhi had arrived at the office, his boss, Major Ghanem, had called him in to brief him on the expected celebrations and to issue orders that all his team had to be on duty that weekend. The order did not apply to Ghanem himself, of course, who only worked weekends in the direst of emergencies.

Which was why it was another two days before Jihad Merhi found out the news.

18 July 2010
6 Sha'ban 1431

Bourj el-Barajneh, Beirut 19:30

Captain Fadi Lattouf was the last to leave the conjoined cabins that acted as the camp's police station that evening. It was a regular occurrence nowadays since his team had been reduced by fifty percent over the previous two years. Recession was even having an effect in the Palestinian refugee camps!

It was 19:30 when he padlocked the door of the police station from the outside and began the ten minute walk back to *chez Lattouf*. The streets were quiet as they often were on a Sunday evening, and in these hard times fewer and fewer people were populating the nearby café.

As usual he waved at the café proprietor, shook his head at the come-inside hand signal, and helped himself to the newspaper that always seemed to be left on the table outside just as he was passing. That day's *Al-Mustaqbal*.

As soon as he opened his front door, he could hear the noise, shouting, encouragement, moaning. Time was his children would be in bed by the time he got home, but the combination of closing the police station an hour earlier because of lack of staff and the children's increasing age, meant that they were always up when he arrived home. Which, as every hard working father worldwide knew, was a mixed blessing.

Nada popped her head out of the kitchen to greet him and then went back to her – what was it? Lattouf sniffed the air. Mmm, smelt like chicken livers.

Picking up the wandering three year old Wissam in one hand, he went into the living room. Most of the noise was coming from the other three boys playing a game on the new computer. Lana, at eleven the elder of his two daughters and the image of her mother, was seated on the floor with the playing cards spread out in front of her. She leapt up when she saw her father.

"Baba, Baba! Look, I can do it!"

"Do what?" smiled Lattouf, gently placing little Wissam on the floor and wondering when his dinner would be ready.

"Uncle Chadi's trick!"

"His trick?"

"You know, the one he was always trying to do. Making the card come out of his pocket."

Lattouf nodded sadly, remembering that was the last thing his cousin had done when he lay on the pavement outside. What a man, what an uncle. Dying and his last thoughts were for the children. God bless you, Abu Yussuf.

"It's all to do with the card," enthused Lana. "You can't do it with just any one. Watch! I'll show you?"

Lattouf was tired and his lower back was aching where he was bending forward. His gut rumbled. My God, he would die of starvation in a minute!

"Come down, Baba." Lana was pulling on his arm.

"What?"

"I haven't got a jacket. It is best if you have a jacket."

There were two sonic booms as Lattouf's knees hit the floorboards, then Lana was tucking a card into the top pocket of his jacket. "This is the first card you gave me," she explained. "Before you gave me the others. It is different. Watch." She fiddled in his pocket, manoeuvring the card, getting it just so. Then she lifted her father's left arm.

Lattouf felt like an idiot, kneeling on the floor, arm out raised, on the point of wasting away through hunger.

Lana tugged his arm down. "Now as your arm comes down, squeeze it close to your body. Go on Baba!"

Hoping he was giving an avuncular smile and not looking bored, Lattouf squeezed...

And the card popped up halfway out of his pocket.

He raised his eyebrows in genuine amazement. "My darling, that is clever. So, so clever. Uncle Chadi would be proud of you." He pulled the card out of his pocket to hand it back to her. "You must learn some more - "

He frowned, looking at the card in his hand. He turned it over, looking at both sides. "This was the first card I gave you?"

"Yes, you gave me the others a few days later. They all look the same but that one is different, isn't it?"

Fadi was nodding, thinking.

Then he said, "Yes, it certainly is my darling."

19 July 2010
7 Sha'ban 1431

Jonblat, Beirut 09:30

There are days when the fan of events moves slowly and you take things leisurely. There are days when the fan of events moves quickly and you have to be on your toes. And there are days when the fan of events is moving so fucking fast that if it coincides with the biggest pile of shit mankind has ever known heading for it at the speed of light then no one, no one, escapes an ordure mud bath.

This was destined to be just such a day for Jihad Merhi.

He liked to be in by 08:00 but heavy Monday traffic on the Coastal Highway had delayed him, so he was already grumpy when he arrived at work. As he walked down the corridor past the General Office, Sergeant el-Gharib called out "*Sabah el-khair, rais.* The Major has been calling you since eight."

"The Major knows what he can do," mumbled Merhi as he walked into his office. First he needed a cup of sludge, the more awful the better. Did everyone really have to come south into Beirut at the very same time as he did? His knees were already aching from the slow drive, and the week had hardly started.

Or, he wondered as he turned on his computer, were his aching knees nothing to do with the drive? Was it just down to that one horrible, nasty, inevitable three-letter word: age?

Empty mug in hand, he was walking back towards the door when his desk telephone rang. It was the ring of an external call, so it was not the Major. Telling himself he should leave it and go get his sludge, he picked up the handset. "Merhi."

"Morning of light, Jihad my dear friend!"

No, really, this he did not need, not at 09:35 on a Monday morning. Hadn't they said their farewells five days ago until *Eid*?

"*Bonjour,* Fadi," he said flatly. "Morning of peace." Oh if only it were.

The Palestinian sounded excited. "I have found something. To do with my cousin. Maybe all is not lost after all."

Merhi sighed. "Really?"

"I think he may have left us a clue."

"A clue?"

"A clue. I had better not say too much over the phone."

"No."

"We should meet."

Now how did he know Lattouf was going to say that? Well if you start your week with the worst thing that could happen it could only get better from there. "When?"

"Tomorrow at fourteen hundred?"

"What? Can't you make it later?" Today at midday was pushing it, and he didn't yet know what new shit the Major had for him.

"No, this is important."

Merhi sighed. "My office."

"Can't we meet at the other place?"

"Just think of it as me helping your diet."

"Diet! I am wasting away. It is not good for a man to be size zero."

"That's a clothing size, Fadi, not the shape of your stomach. My office. I might be busy so you may have to wait."

"If I do I will enjoy one of your splendid coffees."

Merhi wondered whether he was being sarcastic but, knowing Lattouf, he probably wasn't. "Can you tell me what this clue is?"

"No. Later."

Merhi enjoyed two cups of sludge while carrying out a verbal autopsy on the weekend's soccer results with Deeb el-Gharib. Then, buoyed by the caffeine, he went upstairs to the office of Major Ghanem.

Ghanem was seated behind his desk, neatly trimmed greying head buried in a file in front of him. He looked up as Merhi entered, flapped a hand at a chair and returned to the file, stroking his equally neatly-trimmed moustache in concentration. Five minutes later he looked back up.

"Everything go all right with the weekend's celebrations?"

Merhi shrugged with his mouth. "As we know, there are those that support Syria's influence in Lebanon, there are those that do not. Not everyone wanted to wish Bashar al-Assad a happy anniversary. But there was nothing to worry you with."

"Good. You probably know that the Prime Minister is in Damascus meeting with President Assad today. He's expected back tonight and he might give a press conference. Keep an eye out on the streets, just in case."

In case of what? wondered Merhi. In case someone had an objection to the improving of Lebanese-Syrian relations? Ghanem was obsessed with 'trouble on the streets'. What harm was there in a little protest? Or was that a thought that had also crossed minds on the morning of 13 April 1975?*

"Sure." Merhi went to stand up.

"Just one other thing," Ghanem motioned him back down. "You had that External Security Unit Captain visit you recently."

"Selim Himo. Lieutenant. Acting captain."

"Anything I should know about?"

"He'd seen I'd requested CCTV footage of some streets in Ashrafieh, for a random parked vehicle security check. He was interested in the same streets at the same time. Just wanted to liaise."

Ghanem nodded and picked up a piece of paper from his desk. Almost as an aside he said, "He was found dead on Friday evening."

Merhi's anal sphincter tightened like the rectum of a virgin with constipation. "*What?*"

"Suicide apparently. Hung himself on his balcony." Ghanem frowned. "You all right? You look grey."

"That's... that's... It's just a shock, that's all."

"You weren't close."

"No, no. It's just the usual, you know, you're talking to the man one minute, the next he's dead. And suicide? Are they sure?"

"Why shouldn't they be? He probably couldn't hack the increased responsibilities that come with promotion, not everyone can."

"It was just him, nobody else?"

"What do you mean?"

"Well, er, his predecessor was murdered a couple of weeks ago. That's what he was investigating."

"Strange, I'll grant you. But I only know what's on this memo. Suicide."

"So they'll be looking for another new captain, three in the same month."

"I hope you're not thinking of applying?"

Merhi gave what he hoped was an ironic laugh, disguising the turmoil and confusion he was feeling inside. "Three times a charm? I don't think so."

"Good. Let the ESU sort their own house out. We have enough problems of our own."

Hamra, Beirut 11:00

Shit, thought Merhi. Shit, shit, shit. He was walking west, looking at the shops and stalls but not seeing. After Ghanem's casually-imparted news he had had to get out of the office. To think, to clear his head, to smoke at least

---

* On 13 April 1975, Palestinian guerrillas fired on a church in the Christian East Beirut suburb of Ain el Rommaneh, killing four people. Later that day a bus carrying armed Palestinians was ambushed by gunmen belonging to the Christian Maronite Phalange party; about twenty-six people were killed. The attack against the bus is regarded as the official beginning of the Lebanese Civil War.

two packets of Cedars King Size. The noise, bustle and madness of Hamra Street was the ideal place to lose himself.

Think, Jihad, think. Progress it logically.

Himo had been found dead. A death disguised as a suicide. He knew enough of the man and his high-flying confidence and arrogance to know that he was not the sort to do away with himself. So there was only one obvious answer: a death made to look like a suicide equalled murder.

By whom? Was it obvious?

His anal sphincter twitched just a little to expel a whistle of air. Nobody would notice it out here in the street.

Carla. Carla, Carla, Carla. What have you done? You come back to Liban with a cryptic message that Sajida was right, but you won't expand on it to anyone who doesn't know what it means. Your boss is murdered. You vow to track down the killer. You confide all to your new boss. You go off with him...

Your new boss is found dead.

In anyone's book you are the Prime Suspect.

But why? Why would you kill him? He didn't kill his predecessor, surely...?

Merhi drew on his cigarette and swallowed the smoke.

No, no, no. This was wrong, all wrong. The white-eyed assassin, that's who we were looking for here. The one who attacked you at the Hotel Albergo. Yes, that was logical. She had killed Himo because you had told him the secret, just as she had killed the previous guy.

But only one body had been found in Himo's apartment. Which begged the question: where was Carla now?

Or rather, where was her body?

He reached Hamra Square and, turning back the way he had come, crossing the road by the Eldorado Shopping Centre.

So what should he do? Should he go to Ghanem and tell him what he knew? Or maybe even go to the Major in charge of the External Security Unit? But that would put him right up to his neck in the shit. Two captains murdered, an exiled agent clandestinely returned and herself either a murderer or a victim. He would have to confess that he had been helping her, not to mention giving her somewhere to stay. Goodbye bollocks if not his career.

No, no. Right now he was in the clear, and he must stay that way. His reason for Himo coming to see him was neat and simple. He would repeat it to anyone who came asking. Not that they would, he realised with relief: the death was a suicide, no investigation needed.

A thought suddenly struck him, right in the middle of his forehead like a bolt shot by William Tell on an off-day. He slapped his palm on his brow as he walked along the street.

The memory card! The recording he had made of Carla and Himo in his office. It was in his drawer. Should he listen to it? Did he *want* to listen to it? Would he be signing his own death warrant? Should he just throw it away...?

Above the human and vehicle noises, he became aware of a loud beeping. There was probably a road rage fight brewing somewhere behind him. He picked up his pace. Being in uniform, he did not want to be dragged into any fray.

The beeping became louder and closer, coming from a van crawling along, now level with him. He looked to his left. It was a light blue van of the Palestinian Civil Police.

And waving across from the driver's window, two jars of pickles in his massive right hand, was a beaming Fadi Lattouf.

Jonblat, Beirut 12:00

The lid on the pickle jar opened with a satisfying pop. Contrary to expectation, Fadi Lattouf did not plunge his hand into the jar to pull out his first vegetable victim. Instead, Jihad Merhi watched from behind his desk in horror as Lattouf lifted the jar to his mouth and drank the vinegar and brine solution like a man who had just been rescued after a month in the desert.

He brought the jar back down from his mouth with a contented sigh, moustache and beard glistening. Noticing Merhi's stare, he said "This Beirut traffic is hell. Makes a man thirsty." Then his fingers went into the jar and pulled out some pepper and cauliflower. "And hungry as well."

Merhi shook his head."I don't suppose you'll be wanting any coffee then."

"Yes, please."

Five minutes later, with two cups of sludge on the desk and two empty pickle jars in the waste bin, Merhi said "So, you've found something?"

"Yes, yes!" Lattouf wiped his hands on his trousers and patted his jacket breast pocket.

"Take it off if you like," said Merhi. "The AC's not very good in here."

"No, no. I have it on for a reason," smiled the Palestinian. "Watch!"

Merhi's eyebrows disappeared into his hairline in disbelief as he watched Lattouf raise his left arm with a flourish, wave his hand in the air like a magician and then slowly bring his arm down.

"How about that?" asked Lattouf, his eyes wide, expecting praise. "Impressive, no?"

Merhi shook his head, puzzled. "Congratulations, you can raise your arm into the air. What the hell are you doing, Fadi?"

With a frown, Lattouf looked down at his pocket. Nothing had happened. "No, no, wait!" He tried it again, flapping his arm up and down, again and again, with increasing frenzy, looking like a chicken trying to take flight. "I did it at home, Lana taught me."

"Fadi!"

Lattouf stopped, looking abashed. "I am sorry. I wanted to show you. It raises up out of my pocket." He put his fingers into the pocket and pulled out a playing card.

"You came here to show me a magic trick?"

"Not just any magic trick, my cousin's magic trick."

Merhi sat back in his chair, at a loss at what to say. "Fadi... I'm sorry about your cousin's death... but... you know, I have things to do..."

"No, you don't understand. At first I thought it was just a trick too. It was the last thing Chadi did."

"Sorry?"

"As he lay dying. He couldn't speak, but he did this trick. You move your arm and the card raises from your pocket. I thought it was his farewell to the children."

Merhi was shaking his head, in sympathy, sorrow and bewilderment. For the moment, words really had failed him.

"But he was doing it for me," continued Lattouf as if it was obvious. "It was a clue. Look." He leant forward and flicked the card onto the desk.

At first Merhi did not pick it up, in case he might be affected by the madness that accompanied it. But then he saw writing on the patterned side of the card. He frowned.

"Numbers," said Lattouf.

Merhi slid the card nearer with his finger. Written across the card from corner to corner were the numbers 340715354514. He looked up.

"It matches the pack of cards you gave me from his car," Lattouf's eyes were ablaze with excitement. "But this one was in his pocket. As he died he made sure I got it." The eyes turned sad. "But I missed his intention, may Allah forgive me."

Merhi shrugged, one shoulder and mouth. "They mean something to you, these numbers?"

"No, I thought you would know what they mean."

"How the f – how should I know what they mean?"

It was Lattouf's turn to shrug. Seizing his mug, he swilled down the remains of the lukewarm sludge. "A code or something?" He wiped his mouth with his hand.

"A code? The man is dying and he gives you a code?"

"Maybe he wasn't dying when he wrote it on there."

Merhi nodded. "Point. Did you have codes between you when you were young? Boys often do."

"No, we were too busy throwing stones at the occupiers."

"Coded messages on walls, anything like that?"

Again Lattouf shook his head. "They would have shot us."

"Okay, let's have a look." Merhi opened a drawer and pulled out a notepad. He took a pencil from the caddy on his desktop. "Let's just see, try the basic." Down the paper he wrote the first seven letters of the Arabic alphabet and put numbers against them:

ا	1
ب	2
ت	3
ث	4
ج	5
ح	6
خ	7

"So, disregarding the zero, 34715354514 gives us..." He held the pad up. " ت ث خ ا ج ت ج ا ث ت. Can we make anything of it...?"

The Arabic alphabet is consonants only. Vowels are not letters, they are symbols placed on top or below consonants to create words and sounds. For ten minutes and two cigarettes, Merhi tried the code consonants with three main Arabic vowels and some vowel derivatives and combinations. Then he sat back, shaking his head. "Meaningless. Let's try Western."

a	1
b	2
c	3
d	4
e	5
f	6
g	7

"Cdgaecedead. Hm! Well, look, we have the English 'dead' at the end. Did he speak English?"

"Arabic and French. Very little English."

"So, whether he knew he was about to die or not, he wouldn't have sent you a code in English?"

"No."

Both men were quiet, reflecting on the numbers. Merhi finished his sludge and Lattouf looked into his mug and wished there was more in it.

After a while Merhi said, "Of course, there are other combinations. One and five could be fifteen, the letter o in Western. One and four could be fourteen, n in Western. That gives us..." He scribbled again. "Cdgoceden.

Great." He reached for his cigarettes, throwing one to Lattouf. The Palestinian caught it and leant forward for light. They both sat back, drawing in the smoke.

"It's the zero that bothers me," said Merhi. "Seems to indicate the numbers are, well, numbers, not coded letters."

Out of the blue Lattouf suggested, "It's a bank account! In all good mysteries there is a secret bank account! Perhaps he has left me a fortune somewhere!" He looked at Merhi's 'Yeh, right' eyes.

"Careful of those flying pigs, Fadi," advised the Lebanese. "And anyway, there's too many numbers for a bank account, too few numbers for a bank account with sort code."

Lattouf took three centimetres off his cigarette in one suck. On the exhale, he said "Telephone number?"

Merhi looked down at the pad. "Again too long... Or is it? Hold on. Let's work backwards." He wrote right to left across the paper. "Hm. Well, we have 34 071 535 4514. Or 3407 1535 4514." He showed the pad to Lattouf. "I like the first one. Could be an international number."

"Shall we try it?"

"Who has international dialling code 34?"

"Oh, um..." Lattouf put on a pensive face, giving the impression he was trying to recall something which he patently did not know.

Merhi picked up his phone and dialled four figures. "Deeb? Have you got the telephone books out there? Can you look up to see what country has dialling code 34? Thanks." He looked across the desk. "Don't worry, Fadi. He'll have it in a minute."

"Oh, okay."

Sergeant el-Gharib was back within thirty seconds. Merhi listened and nodded, said "Okay, thanks" and put the phone down. "Did your cousin know anybody in Spain?"

"Spain?" Lattouf shook his head. "Not that I know of. The family has never travelled far."

"Shall we try it? I have to leave out the zero, apparently."

Lattouf shuffled to the edge of his chair, intent and keen, as Merhi dialled.

Merhi hadn't finished dialling the full number before he put his fingers across the phone cradle, instantly lifting them off again and redialling. He did this twice more, then said "Shit. I'm getting the no-such-number tone. It won't even let me finish dialling."

Lattouf flopped back, deflated. "As you say, my friend. Shit. What can it be? What do the numbers mean?"

Merhi stole a quick look at his watch. They had been at this for an hour, a lot of time wasted in a busy day. And he still had a decision to make about a certain memory card. "Maybe it's nothing," he said. "You have jumped to the conclusion it is a clue. What if it isn't? What if it is scribble? Or random numbers that might have meant something in the past, written on the card to mark it out as the one that would come out of his pocket. Perhaps it was just a trick for the children after all."

Lattouf was grim-faced but he was nodding in reluctant acceptance. "Another lead, another dead end."

"If it was a lead in the first place. I don't see where we can go from here."

Lattouf stared into Merhi's face, his usual ebullience now flat, a look almost of anger in his eyes. Then he said, "Oh, I know where we can go from here, my friend. And you are going to go there with me. Whether you like it or not." He stood up and for a split second Merhi thought he was in danger. He had never seen this side of the Palestinian. Quickly he stood up too, his chair rolling back against the wall with a thump.

"We will go where there are no secrets," growled Lattouf. "Where all the world's problems can be discussed and solved." He stopped, stared – and then his face broke into a big grin. "Where is the nearest McDonald's?"

For a beat Merhi was shocked, then a laugh burst from his lips as he looked at the huge, grinning, stupid face. "I'd better call them and warn them," he said as he came around the desk, clapping his friend on the back. "They may have to send out for additional stock."

Jonblat, Beirut 15:00

Thank God he was gone. As much as Merhi had to admit to a reluctant, renewed and growing affection for the idiotic Palestinian giant, he had too much work on his plate right now to continue a dead-end investigation into his cousin's death.

They had gone to the McDonald's on Bliss Street in the Hamra district, and Merhi was glad they had decided to walk, otherwise he would have had to increase the tyre pressure on his Toyota on the way back such was the volume of burgers, desserts, drinks and one salad consumed by Lattouf.

They had parted downstairs, and once again Lattouf had seemed reluctant to go. They would meet again in seven weeks to celebrate *Eid* at the end of Ramadan. Yes, Merhi had confirmed, he and Gisele were really, really looking forward to once more coming down to Bourj el-Barajneh to celebrate with the Lattoufs and their six children. What could be better?

Now he was back in his office with the door closed. On the desk in front of him was the memory card from the digital recording machine in his drawer. He stared at it. Was this memory card his friend or his foe? What was on here would explain everything. It would reveal the secret knowledge that had killed who knew how many people, Himo and Carla included. But it could kill him too. Others with the knowledge had died, why should he be different?

But hold on, it was not like the knowledge was cursed, the victims had not suddenly been struck down with mortal diseases – they had been murdered. And murder meant somebody knew they knew.

Well, this time it was different: nobody knew he had this recording.

He picked up his telephone, keyed the General Office and told Sergeant Deeb el-Gharib that he was transferring his calls to him. If anybody asked, he was out of the office. He was not to be disturbed under any circumstances until further notice.

Opening his drawer, he removed the current memory card from the EM voice recorder and replaced it with the one that had been on his desk. He plugged earphones into the machine and then popped them into his ears.

Still not certain that he should be doing this, he pressed the Play key and sat back in his chair.

"Call me when you're done. I'll be outside. Making sludge." It was his own voice, picked up at the start of the recording when he pressed the button under his desk as he stood up. Six days ago. Seemed like a lifetime.

He heard the door close.

"Sajida - " began Carla.

"I know," interrupted Himo. "I was just stalling you to get him out of the way."

"You know?"

"About Sajida, yes. There's is rumoured to be an Eyes Only file at the very highest level with all the details. It is said it never goes below ministerial level. To many of us it is a myth, but you are confirming it is true?"

"I can only confirm what I learnt from my source. Sajida was right and The Second Coming is now imminent. Maroun's murder and the attempt on me seem to be confirmation of that."

"And *al-Mahdi* chose Lebanon."

"*al-Mahdi*?" queried Carla. "I hardly think so."

There was moving about. Then Himo said, "It all depends what you believe. The Saviour against Satan? There are those that have always seen it that way."

"Try telling that to the ones who died."

The voices had become muffled, as if the microphone in the desk had been covered. Merhi wondered if Carla had sat herself on his desktop and he was now listening through her bottom.

"Some will always die for the greater good," said Himo. "To spread the true word. So they say. He has many followers."

"Sounds like that includes you."

"No, no. I'm just putting the case. I am a good Muslim, that is the one true religion."

"If you say so. So if his existence is known and his presence is condoned by our leaders," there was a rustle of movement and the sound became clear again, "why kill Maroun?"

"That I don't know. We'll find out. Will you come back in? Or do you think it would be better if you went back to New York?"

"What do you want me to do?"

There was a pause. Then, "I'll let you know. Bear in mind I'm new, I don't know you. Tell me, why exactly is a member of the External Security Unit permanently based in New York?"

Carla proceeded to tell him, the story that Jihad Merhi already knew and had been a part of.

And that was it. Himo made no direct comment on the story she had to tell. They spoke more about her possible return to the ESU, about the woman with the white eyes and about where they might go from here, and then they left the room.

Merhi turned off the machine and pulled the headphones from his ears. After all that worry and consternation, that was it? He shook his head, baffled. He still didn't know who Sajida was. And what was that they were saying? *al-Mahdi*, the prophesied redeemer of Islam, had returned and was living in Lebanon? And his second coming was imminent? What was that all about?

Carla had been right – he really did not want to know about this. Religious mythology had no connection with law enforcement. He had better things to do than to indulge in legends. He should wash his hands of all of it.

Except, of course, that Himo and Carla were now dead.

But was that his problem? It might sound callous but no, it wasn't.

And, contrary to expectations and although he was disappointed, he had heard nothing on the recording to put his own life in danger.

Thank God.

al-Mahdi indeed. Whatever next?

Jonblat, Beirut 19:00

Jihad Merhi sat back in his chair, exhausted. What a day! Lots of shit had hit that fan but he was pleased that he had managed to avoid all but a peripheral splattering of the brown stuff.

First there had been his report to Ghanem on the weekend's activities followed by the casual announcement of the death of Selim Himo. And, by logical reasoning and known only by himself, the death of Carla too. Then Lattouf and his ridiculous failed card trick and the ludicrous numeric clue which was probably nothing of the sort. Then the anxiety of whether or not to listen to the recorded conversation, his fear of discovering what was on it and the disappointment that it revealed nothing other than the risible idea that in 2010 The Saviour had returned to earth. And in Lebanon!

For the last three hours he had put all the stupidity behind him and had concentrated on his real work. He had delegated Prime Minister Saad Hariri's press conference to one of the Lieutenants, and he had concentrated on finalising the security arrangements for the joint visit of Saudi King Abdullah and Syrian President Bashar al-Assad at the end of the month.

Now it was time to go home. Computer shut down, desk cleared, drawers locked, keys locked in wall safe with combination dial, he had stepped out into the corridor when he heard his desk telephone ringing. He did not even break his stride. The day was over, he was knackered, and it was probably Gisele wondering where he was.

He pulled out his mobile phone and his cigarettes. He would call her from the car, that way he could truthfully say he was en route.

He reached the stairwell and lit up a Cedars King Size as he walked down, leaving the cares and stresses of the day behind him...

Rafic el-Hariri International Airport, Beirut 19:10

The tall, hard man with the long black hair falling down the side of his face to cover his missing left ear, put down the pay phone in the airport arrivals area. No answer. Not unexpected.

He stepped away from the booth, placing his small bag between his feet and pulling a rubber band from his pocket. With two swift movements he tied his hair back in a ponytail, pulling at the sides to make sure the hole was still covered.

He was tired. For security reasons he had not taken a direct flight, instead he had gone New York – Cairo – Amman – Damascus – Beirut. That way he was a Syrian national entering Lebanon on his Syrian passport and he would not be looked at too closely at Immigration and Customs, if at all.

In fact he was not Syrian, he was originally Lebanese, although nowadays he regarded himself as nothing, not since he had been killed ten years before, right here in Lebanon at Aanjar. He had been Captain Marwan Mebarak of the Lebanese army, and records showed that he had died a hero.

Now he had no name. Dead men don't. His existence was known only to a few. But to those people who employed him as a 'problem solver', either locally or on an international level, he was known as The Damascene.

He had returned to Lebanon for the first time in five years, and this time it was personal.

He was looking for the woman he loved.

20 July 2010
8 Sha'ban 1431

Jbeil, Lebanon (time unknown)

Death was supposed to be the end of it. The merciful release, the eternal blackness, the grateful dead. Thank you and goodbye. *Finito*. Once the curtain came down there was nothing.

Or was this God-thing for real? Had all the teachings down the ages been true and not just humankind trying to make sense of a senseless moment of existence? Was there life beyond death? Was there a heaven? There must be – because she was in hell.

The pricks in her arms and legs annoyed her, the ones between the toes even more so, like the thorns of the *zaqqum* tree being pressed into her. They were an irritation, disturbing the darkness of her oblivion. But it was when her fingernails were prised out, slowly, one by one, rip rip rip, that she knew she had been sent down below. It felt like the demons of *Jahannam* were burning the tips of her fingers on the orders of Maalik, the guardian angel of the gates of Hell. Hadn't she heard his name mentioned?

Soon they would be making her eat the thorned and bitter fruit of the *zaqqum* and drink boiling water.

If you believed in such things.

Which she didn't. She was dead. Why couldn't they just leave her alone?

Hazmieh, Beirut 06:30

The Damascene woke early in his room at the Hazmieh Rotana Hotel on Boulevard Chiyah. The hotel suited his purposes for three reasons: it was just four miles from the airport; with one hundred and fifty one rooms it was big enough for him to remain anonymous; and it was on the way to Jamhour in the eastern suburbs.

As he showered, the hot water onto maximum scalding, he wondered if the old motorbike repair shop still existed near the Bejco dealership up in Jamhour.

He had need of their services again.

Annaya, Lebanon 10:00

The cowled figure sat motionless in the front pew of the small Monastery Church. He did not move when the door creaked open and the two women entered, and he gave no indication that he knew they were there as they walked silently down the central aisle and stopped in front of him.

"*Salaam*, Brother," greeted Love.

The hood rose but they could not see the face underneath.

"You are well?" asked Paradise.

The hood turned towards her. "This mortal body aches with age," said the deep voice from within. "But I am ready. Allah will give me strength for what is to come. I will not be forsaken."

"Everything is arranged?" asked Love.

The hood nodded. "I have had my final contact with the disciples in the Promised Land. The Circle of Haouch Moussa have arranged for the camels to be waiting on the other side of the mountains together with supplies for our journey. There are three members of the Circle and you will honour them with full conversions after delivery."

The twins smiled.

"I will give you further details when we are on our way. When do we leave?"

"To get you to the desert by Saturday, we will need to leave on Friday," explained Paradise. "Today is Tuesday, so we thought we would come to collect you Thursday and you can stay the night in Jbeil with us. We will look after you."

"That is acceptable."

"And we have a little surprise for you. Something you might enjoy," said Love.

Malek tensed. "I do not like surprises."

Love reached out to touch him and then thought better of it. "This one you will, Brother. I promise. You will be pleased with us."

He ignored the comment. "There are two things I want you to do. Take this." He bent forward and pulled the small blue case out from under the pew. "My *argileh*. Guard it with your lives. I will enjoy it Thursday night. Underneath it you will find the Netbook. I have deleted as much as I can. Do not turn it on. Destroy it by breaking and burning."

"Yes, Brother."

Malek stood up. He did not quite reach the height of the twins. "And buy a camcorder. A good one with plenty of memory. Hard disk with memory card option. High definition. Our journey must be recorded for history."

Jamhour, Lebanon 11:00

The old motorbike repair shop was still there and, judging by the amount of second-hand (or more) bikes outside for sale, it was still doing good business in these times of recession – at least on the buying side if not the selling. The bikes would have been bought for a fraction of their second-hand value and would be sold for full used list price.

The Damascene produced one of his Lebanese ID cards, gave a false address, handed over a huge wad of US dollars, extracted a promise that they would buy back the bike if he was not satisfied with it after a week, and drove away on a one year old 1340 cc black Suzuki Hayabusa.

Jonblat, Beirut 11:50

Jihad Merhi had just countersigned a report on street-level reaction to last week's parliamentary discussions on *tawteen** when the phone on his desk rang. An outside call.

"Merhi."

"Captain Merhi, *al-salaam 'aalaykum.*"

Merhi frowned. The voice was deep, the accent local. Slowly he said, *"'aalaykum al-salaam?"*

"Captain, I am a friend of your niece."

"My niece?"

"Carla."

Merhi said nothing.

"I am looking for her."

Another moment of silence, then Merhi said "Do you have a name?"

"No, I do not."

"I see. You work for General Security?"

"Currently I work for nobody."

"Why are you phoning me?"

"You know why."

More silence. Then Merhi said, "Call me on my mobile." He gave his number. "Do you need to write it down?"

"No."

"Give me ten minutes."

---

* *The naturalisation and resettlement of Palestinians from Lebanon's refugee camps. Parliament was debating whether to accord Palestinians three rights - unrestricted employment, social security and medical care, and ownership of property. The issue had divided opinion and had even caused a split between the previously politically-inseparable allies of Michel Aoun's Christian Free Patriotic Movement and the Shi'ite Hizbullah.*

Hamra, Beirut 12:05

"What makes you think I have a niece called Carla?" Merhi was sitting at a table in busy Hamra Square, triple espresso in front of him, third consecutive Cedars King Size between his fingers, phone to his ear.

"You do not. But did you really want her to be fully identified for The Listeners?"

Merhi sucked on his cigarette. "Who are you?"

"I am no one. Just a friend looking for a friend."

"I cannot help you."

"I would like to talk with you anyway."

"No."

"Yes."

Merhi swallowed smoke, stifling a cough.

"Let me take you to dinner," said the voice. "You and your charming wife Gisele."

"What has my wife got to do with this?"

"Gisele Merhi, née Ibrahim but known in the business as Gisele Joudeh. One time senior field operative of the Department of General Security, latterly a trainer before she resigned. Still, I am told, a very formidable ally. I would like to meet her."

"No."

"Yes. Both of you. Tonight. The Burj al-Hamam restaurant in Antelias. You know it?"

"If I wanted to I could find it."

"We have a reservation for 20:30. Please be there."

"Or...?"

"Or you don't want to know. But let me give you some advice, Captain. Enjoy your espresso, it has already been paid for. But cut down on the cigarettes, they're not good for you."

The chair clattered backwards as Merhi stood up, looking from side to side at the shoppers, phone still held to his ear. People were looking in windows, buying from the stalls, some were on their mobiles, one or two were texting, nobody was paying him any heed. He did not notice the black Suzuki Hayabusa motorbike pull away into the traffic of Hamra Street.

After two more visual sweeps of the area, he picked up the chair and sat back down, unhappy, looking at the screen of his phone to see that the call had ended. He went to put his cigarette back into his mouth and then stopped, looking at it and thinking of the advice he'd just been given.

With a curse he stubbed it out in the ashtray on the table, stood up and walked away.

Coastal Highway, Lebanon 15:00

"Are you mad?" Gisele's voice echoed around the Toyota as Jihad drove north, his mobile phone bluetoothed into the car's audio system. "Do you know who he is?"

"Someone who knows Carla. And he knows us too. Knew all about you." He dragged on the cigarette between his fingers then put his hand back on the wheel.

"I don't like it."

"What can he possibly do, in public, in a restaurant? Perhaps it's his way of reassuring us."

"Well I am not reassured."

"And there are two of us." He reached forward and turned up the fan on the air conditioning. Was it becoming hotter in the car or what it just him? *"Habibi,* he's looking for Carla. Says he's a friend. Whether he is or he isn't, he can't do her any harm now. And I know, even from the few words I've had with him, that he won't leave us alone unless we meet him as asked."

"I don't like it," she said again.

"But you'll come?"

"Of course!" she said it as if it had never been in doubt.

"I've heard it is a good restaurant."

"Even better when you are not paying, eh my husband?"

"It always makes the food taste that much nicer! We'll leave at seven-thirty. Could you get my suit out of the cupboard to air, the light one? And perhaps iron a white shirt for me?"

"Tayyib."

"And just one other thing, darling."

"What?"

He pulled out, overtook a lorry and pulled back in again.

"Make sure you choose a handbag big enough to put a gun in."

Antelias, north of Beirut 20:25

They were a respectful five minutes early, more by the grace of the god of traffic than any accurate timing. Jihad was wearing a fawn suit with an open-necked white shirt, Gisele wore a short-enough-to-be-noticed-but-not-too-short-to-be-indecent red dress with gold lamé vertical pattern and co-ordinating six centimetre heels. She carried a red shoulder bag which, to a practised eye, looked slightly on the heavy side.

The place was big with probably room for a hundred covers or more, décor of wood and cream-beige. It was busy but not full, and they had to wait in line to be greeted.

Their turn came, a black-suited *maître* greeting them as if he had known them for a long time. *"Bonsoir, m'sieur-dame.* Thank you for coming to the Burj al-Hamam. Your name please?"

"We don't have a reservation," said Jihad, "we are - "

"Ah, Captain and Madame Merhi. We have been expecting you. Please, come this way."

They were guided across the large main dining area towards the wall on the right with the impressive back-lit faux-stained-glass windows with drawn scenes of old Lebanon. Underneath a scene of the ruins at Baalbeck with Mount Lebanon in the background, a tall man stood up from a round table set for three. He wore black slacks and a loose white collarless shirt, long black hair draping the sides of his hard, tanned face, untied, no ponytail.

"Your guests, sir," the *maître* announced and then discreetly disappeared.

The man gave a half smile and held out his hand. "Captain Merhi."

Jihad paused and then, with hesitation, shook his hand, extending his left palm towards Gisele. "My wife, Gisele."

"Of course. Madame Merhi. I am pleased to meet you." He raised Gisele's hand to his lips."Please. Won't you sit down?"

There was a scraping of chairs. "And your name?" asked Jihad, sitting down, placing his cigarette packet on the table.

"I don't have one."

"Everyone has a name."

"I don't. Let us order," his hand went into the air. "Then we can talk." A waiter appeared, handing out menus. "The last time I was here the *farouj meshwi* was particularly good. I shall try it again. But please, have what you want."

Jihad was really in no mood for studying a menu, so he plumped for the first thing that sounded interesting: *kastaleta*, lamb chops with fries. Gisele took a bit more time, eventually ordering *mallifa*, a barracuda steak.

When the waiter was gone, Jihad lit up a cigarette, not offering the packet to his host. *"Alors, Monsieur No-Name.* You are Lebanese, from your accent I would say you are from the north. Tripoli?"

"If you say so."

Jihad blew smoke. "You are obviously fit. Strong. Ex-army?"

"You make a good detective."

"But what are you now?"

Water was delivered to the table and poured, sparkling for the lady, still for the men.

The Damascene sat back, arms behind his chair, smiling. "Now? I am nothing."

"That I do not for one moment believe."

"As you wish."

Pickles, raw vegetables, dips and bread were placed onto the table. Gisele handed out the bread, being Mum, letting the boys play out their pissing contest. Jihad's stream might be stronger but he was doing it into the wind and it was blowing back all over him.

"Why don't I just arrest you right now?" suggested Jihad.

"On what grounds?"

"I'll think of something."

"Very Lebanese. At least enjoy your food first." The Damascene took a lettuce leaf from underneath the pile of vegetables, dipped it in *mutabal*, aubergine dip, and took a bite. "And while you are doing so, I could reach across this table and have your head off your shoulders long before your wife even has time to get her gun from her purse." He smiled and looked at Gisele. "So, which of us has the biggest dick?"

She couldn't help but laugh as she reddened, quickly taking a sip of water. Then she said, "Okay, okay. You are both Lebanese. You know you have the biggest dicks in the world, that's why we girls love you so."

The Damascene laughed out loud, tapping his hand on the table in mirth. Jihad looked aggrieved.

"As always, the lady wins," The Damascene raised his glass. *"Touché.* Captain, I mean you no harm. I am trying to find Carla, that is all."

Jihad dipped bread into hummus. "What do you know?"

"I was with her in New York. She found out reliable information. That Sajida was right - "

"In the name of Christ!" chewed bread fell out of Jihad's mouth onto the table. "That is all I keep hearing. Who the fuck is Sajida?"

"Language, husband," scolded Gisele, still smiling about their dicks.

"You don't know?" frowned The Damascene. "Carla did not tell you?"

"Only that it was knowledge that was dangerous. She said she was protecting us."

"And so she was. If you don't know then it is best if you don't."

"Oh for God's sake! Tell me."

"No. Carla came back here to Lebanon. Looked you up. You were both kind enough to offer her somewhere to stay, for which I thank you. She said her boss had been killed after she had told him the information, and that she had been attacked."

"How do you know all this?"

"She has been in regular contact with me."

"In New York?"

"Wherever I have been. Modern technology, eh? She said she was going for the person who killed her boss. She asked me for my help, but I couldn't come right away. She told me she had met her new boss and she was hoping to work the case with him. Then – nothing. That was a week ago and I've not heard from her since. "

Jihad swallowed a piece of pepper and wiped his mouth. "You know just about everything we know. More if you count this Sajida thing..." He paused just in case an explanation was forthcoming. When it was not, he went on "There's just one bit to add. A week ago she indeed went off to work with her new boss – he was found dead two days later, hanging in his apartment."

The Damascene was still. Very still. He stared into the glass of water in front of him as Jihad and Gisele glanced at each other. It was a full minute before he looked up and said, "And?"

Jihad sighed, reluctant, knowing he was the bearer of bad news. "And Carla has not been found. No trace of another person in the apartment. It has been put down as suicide. Nobody except me - "

"And me." Gisele.

" – seems to know she was with him that day, or even that she exists."

"No notes, no record of the investigation?"

"Seems not," said Jihad. "So her disappearance means one of two things. Either she killed him and has fled..."

The Damascene shook his head.

"...or she herself is dead and her body disposed of."

Staff descended to clear away the plates in preparation for the main course. The Damascene was quiet, intent, thoughtful. Jihad did not know what to say, what else he could say.

"What are you going to do?" asked Gisele, touching The Damascene lightly on his arm. The muscles were rock solid.

"I don't know. Do you think she is dead? Either of you?"

Jihad shrugged. Gisele said, "Either that or, as Jihad said, she killed her boss and has fled."

"But no contact? With you, I can understand. All along she has not wanted to incriminate you, that is why she has not explained about Sajida. She wanted to protect you. But no contact with me? No phone call? Doesn't make sense." The Damascene turned to Jihad. "Can you get me copies of the suicide report?"

"I'm sure I could, for what good it would do."

"I cannot believe, I must not believe, that she is dead."

"If she is not," said Jihad, "that begs the question: where is she?"

"That," said The Damascene, "I do not know."

"What is she to you anyway?" asked Gisele, pulling backwards as her *mallifa* was placed in front of her.

The Damascene also pulled back to let his *farouj meshwi* be delivered. "What is she to me?" He looked from one to the other of them. "Carla is my wife."

Bourj el-Barajneh, Beirut 20:45

It had been a long, hot day, and the temperature showed no sign of dropping, even at that hour. As he locked up the police post for the evening, Captain Fadi Lattouf sniffed under the right arm of his sweat-soaked blue shirt. He was as ripe as a two-days-past-its-use-by-date gorgonzola. Thankfully *chez Lattouf* had a shower, of sorts (cold water only and the flow rate slower than a tortoise on diazepam), and he would wash immediately after dinner. It would be good to get the blood off his hands too.

He looked down at his now brown-stained fingers, dried blood encrusted down his nails. It had been hard extracting the confession from the eighteen year old, but it had been necessary. You do not, ever, steal from another person's home in the camp. Never. If you wanted to steal you went out into Beirut. The youth had admitted it eventually (they always did) and if he ever woke up from his coma he would be charged and passed on to the camp authorities for punishment.

Lattouf helped himself to the paper on the table outside the café and gave his usual wave to the proprietor, tapping his wrist to indicate his reason for not coming inside for his free coffee and shisha.

As he entered his house, a naked-from-the-waist-down Little Wissam toddled out to meet him. "Hello, young man!" Lattouf bent forward and picked up his youngest son with a blood-encrusted hand. "Why aren't you in bed yet, eh? I hope you have been a good boy for your Mama."

He carried the boy in the crook of his arm into the main living area. The two oldest boys were watching *Deal Or No Deal* on the old television (Lattouf paused as host Michel Sanan asked model Nadine to open Case 21. It was the fifty million Lebanese pounds, the last remaining high number. Tough luck). Lana was on the computer over by the kitchen and Lattouf ruffled her hair with his free hand as he went past, leaving a little flake of dried blood on her scalp which neither of them noticed.

"Evening of peace, dear wife. It is good to be home."

"*Salaam*, dear husband," greeted Nada. "Dinner is only just ready. The power."

"Thank goodness it is ready, otherwise I would have had to eat this young specimen I found in the hallway." He bounced the boy in his arm. "I need to shower but I won't have the strength until I get some food inside me..." His voice trailed off as he felt a sudden warmth against his stomach and hip. He pulled Wissam away from his body, the boy's tiny penis erect and pissing horizontally. Nada just had time to take the saucepan of rice out of the sink as Lattouf held the boy over the plug hole to finish. "Then again," he said, "perhaps I do just have enough strength left to shower first."

He passed the giggling boy to his mother and went back out of the kitchen, past Lana and into the bathroom across the hallway.

Even though the water was cold and flowed as if the house plumbing had an enlarged prostate, he turned it on to run while he stripped off his clothes, throwing his shirt into a corner but treating his trousers with a little more respect, hoping they would dry out and give him a good three months' wear yet before they needed to be cleaned. The shirt almost cringed in fear as massive Y-fronts were thrown on top of it (he'd had a good two weeks' wear out of them, time for fresh ones) and his socks walked into the corner of their own accord.

A stark naked Fadi Lattouf, the stuff of every woman's dreams (in his dreams), stepped under the shower, squealed as the water touched his skin and then let it trickle over his hairy, sweaty, blood and piss-stained body.

Five minutes later he was lathering up his groin and thinking thoughts of Nadine and Case 21, when he stopped suddenly, frowning, soap held somewhere in the crevices of his lower stomach, snugly out of sight. His face contorted in concentration, as it always did when he was thinking... What was it that he had seen...? What had occurred to him...? Something was nagging –

In the name of Allah! Could it be?

He grabbed the shower off its holder in the wall, rinsing off the soap as quickly as the water flow would allow.

Snatching his towel from the pile (Nada always insisted he use the black towels, for some reason), he quickly rubbed off the excess water and suds. Mankind had not invented a towel big enough to fit round the waist of Fadi Lattouf, but he threw it around his gut anyway, holding the ends with his hand, his right hip exposed, one of only two areas of his body that was not covered with hair (the other being his head).

Nada was just bringing the chicken and rice to the table in the living area when the damp, hairy monster, comb-over flapping away from his head, barged through the door. She shrieked, just managing to hold on to the food.

"Lana!" cried Lattouf, his eyes just a little wild. "Lana!"

The eleven year old on the computer turned around in her chair, fear in her eyes. What had she done, what had she done?

Her father dashed over to her and she flinched away. He bent forward, staring at the computer screen. "What is this?"

She could smell the warmth off him as his flesh wobbled close to her. "Un – uncle's computer," she said hesitantly, warily. "You brought it home, Baba."

"No, no. No, no. I mean what is this, this on the screen?" He poked the monitor, making the image bend inwards in the shape of his finger.

"It's... it's a geography thing. I was just looking at it."

Lattouf was staring intently at the bottom of the screen. In a calmer tone, he asked "What is it? This thing?"

"It – it's called Google Earth."

"Incredible," he was shaking his head. "Incredible. And what? It maps the earth, this thing?"

"Yes, Baba. You can see pictures of anywhere. I was just looking at New York..."

To Lana's great relief, her father ruffled her hair again as he straightened up and turned around. Nada was looking at him with raised eyebrows. "Wife," said Lattouf. "My cousin was a genius. I am a genius! God is good." He raised his arms in an expansive, theatrical gesture – and the towel fell to the floor.

The screams of his wife and children could be heard as far away as the north Beka'a.

Antelias, north of Beirut 21:10

Jihad Merhi pulled back as his *kastelata* was placed in front of him. "Carla didn't tell us she was married."

"On the other hand," smiled Gisele, looking at their dining companion, "she didn't tell us she wasn't."

"True, true." Jihad looked across the table at The Damascene. "People in her kind of work – in your kind of work – normally aren't."

"How long?" asked Gisele.

Through a mouthful of chicken, The Damascene said "We have been together five years. We married on Valentine's Day this year. It is a date that means a lot to us."

"That's nice, congratulations."

"Thank you."

Jihad busied himself cutting his chops. Valentine's Day? Five years? 14 February 2005? The day Rafic Hariri was assassinated...? He didn't want to go there. He stuffed a forkful of fries into his mouth and mumbled, "So where do we go from here?"

"You will get me a copy of the report?"

"Yes, but after that?"

The Damascene shrugged with his mouth. "You will understand that I simply cannot accept that she is dead, not without investigation."

A thought had occurred to Jihad. "There is one thing," he said, waving his fork for emphasis. "She - "

There was a sudden burst of music. Jihad frowned as the other two looked at him, wondering why he was their focus. Then he realised and said apologetically, "Excuse me." As he fumbled in his jacket for his phone, he mumbled "Never off duty." He brought it out and put it to his ear. "Merhi."

"Evening of joy, my dear friend!"

Oh Christ. Jihad turned in his seat as if the action would make him invisible to the other two. "I can't talk now. I am busy."

"But I have solved it! I know what the clue is!"

"Not now. My office. In the morning."

"Can I just tell you - "

"My office." Merhi ended the call. Turning back round he said, "Sorry about that." He picked up his fork, thinking how he would like to poke it in Lattouf's oversize gut right at that minute. "Another case."

"You were saying?" prompted The Damascene.

"I was?"

"You said there was just one thing."

"I did...?" His thoughts had been knocked sideways by Lattouf's interruption. "Oh, yes! Carla did a drawing of her assailant, the person who attacked her and who she thinks murdered her boss. It was a woman."

"A woman?" The Damascene looked at Gisele then back to Jihad. "You have the picture?"

"I have a copy of it in my office. I'll get it for you tomorrow."

Gisele had gone to the ladies' room.

"So what are you really going to do?" asked Jihad through a mouthful of mango.

The Damascene sipped his water. "You are going to get a copy of the report for me and let me see the drawing. Then I'm going to find this woman."

"Just like that?"

"I have resources."

"Who?"

"You."

"Me?"

"You. You will help me find this woman and you will help me find my wife."

"How?"

"I don't know yet. I will decide on a course of action once I've seen the report and the picture."

"I'll get them for you, but after that you'll be on your own."

"Really?"

"Really."

"No. You will help me in whatever way I want you to. Here." The Damascene held out his clenched fist, palm downwards and dropped five bullets onto the table. All five rounds of Gisele's Smith and Wesson 642 that was still in her handbag.

Jihad opened his mouth. "How the fuck did you do that?"

"It is not the first time I have had to disarm someone in this restaurant."

Jihad didn't know what he was talking about and he didn't want to know. "Bravo. A clever party trick."

The Damascene saw Gisele walking back towards them and scooped the bullets back into his hand. "Have you ever wondered what it would be like if your wife was not there?"

"No."

"Then pray you never find out."

The Damascene stood up, courteously pulling out Gisele's chair for her, and Jihad saw a whole new meaning behind his smile.

Coastal Highway, Lebanon 22:00

"That is one dangerous bastard," said Jihad as they turned right onto the coastal highway, heading north. In his rear-view mirror he saw the Suzuki Hayabusa with its unhelmeted rider disappearing into the night towards Beirut.

"I thought he was charming, in a dangerous sort of way." Gisele settled into the leather seat, resting her head, mellow. "Carla is a lucky girl."

"Really? I don't consider being dead as lucky."

"He thinks she's still alive."

"Well he would, wouldn't he?"

"Are you going to help him?"

Jihad flashed his lights at an innocuous Ford Focus before pulling out to overtake it. "I'll get him the report and the picture."

"And if he asks for anything else?"

For a moment Jihad did not respond.. He cast at glance at Gisele's bare legs stretched out next to him. Had the man threatened her or was it just his imagination, reading things into things? He said, "We'll see."

Gisele lit up a cigarette, sucked on it then leant over and put it between Jihad's lips. There was lipstick on the filter but he wouldn't mind. "I thought of asking if he wanted to stay with us."

"No!" The cigarette bounced up and down, stuck on his bottom lip. Gisele was shocked at his vehemence. "No way. You give him a wide berth, do you understand me? You must have no contact with him if I am not there."

"Oh, so it's all right for you to bring home waifs and strays, but if I make just one offer - "

"That was different."

"In what way? It would be nice for me to have two handsome men in the house for a change." Giving a provocative smile, she let her left hand finger-walk over his thigh. "It's nice for a girl to feel protected..." She poked his bulge with her index finger. "Goodness, who's an excited boy then?"

"Two things," said Jihad. "One, that is my mobile. And two, I mean it. That man is dangerous. You will leave him well alone."

She took her hand back. "He's only trying to find his wife."

"Nevertheless," said Jihad, nodding without elaborating. "Nevertheless... You will do as I say."

"Of course, dear husband. Don't I always? And who was that on the phone, one of your fancy women?"

"It was the idiot Lattouf. Thinks he's going to solve his cousin's murder. Won't leave it alone. *L'imbécile.*"

21 July 2010
9 Sha'ban 1431

Jbeil, Lebanon 07:00

With a loud gasp her body shot upright into a sitting position as the blast of adrenaline hit her system. The needle was still in her chest, pulling the skin outwards, the syringe flopping between her naked breasts like a plastic phallus.

"Lie down, lie down," said a soft female voice. There was pressure on her forehead, someone pushing her back down, and she had no strength, no will other than to obey.

She was confused. Where was she? Who was she? She couldn't remember. Wasn't she dead?

Someone was stroking her hair. Who was it? Had someone come to see her in her coffin before her final journey?

But if she was dead, she would not be having these thoughts. Or was that what death was? A cessation of the body but the continuance of the mind, the spirit?

The person stroking her hair was speaking to her softly but she couldn't understand what was being said, it was just a faraway gabble. Did the dead have their own language?

Where was the long tunnel with the light at the end? Why wasn't she floating on the ceiling, looking down at her own body? Had it all been a lie? Was life just a giant con?

There was a gentle tapping on her face, first one cheek then the other. She frowned.

Then there was a really sharp scratch in her chest and she moaned.

"There now," said a voice, and she could understand it. Something soft and damp was rubbed between her breasts. She tried to pull her arms up but they would only move a few centimetres. There was a metal on metal sound.

Slowly, warily, she opened her eyes. She expected to see nothing except the blackness of eternity, but there was a soft, very subtle, ambient light. Was this Heaven's waiting room? There were two angels with her, but they were blurred, out of focus.

Then she felt herself peeing and there was nothing she could do about it. How embarrassing, they would never let her into Heaven now. Then she defecated.

"Don't worry, don't worry," said the angel who had been stroking her head. "It happens when you come back. It's a good sign."

"We'll clean you up," said the other angel from the end of her – what was it? A bed? A cot? A mortuary slab? She tried to move her feet but again there was the metal on metal sound.

"Here, drink." Her head was lifted. "But only a little, and sip slowly."

She did as she was told, tasting the most delicious liquid she had ever experienced. Pure water. "Thank you. Thank you." She didn't know whether she had said the words or just thought them. She was put back down.

And then her system jolted again, the secondary rush of the adrenaline. Her eyes focussed, her mind cleared, and she remembered everything.

She was lying completely naked on an old bunk bed, her wrists and ankles handcuffed to the metal frame.

And this wasn't Heaven's waiting room and they weren't angels. It was more like the ante-room of hell. These were the identical murdering bitches, the *houri*.

And she was The Djinn.

And she was very much alive.

Jounieh, Lebanon 07:10

"I'm off, *habibi*!" Standing in the bathroom doorway, Jihad had to shout to be heard above the shower. Behind the glass screen he could see tantalising glimpses of Gisele as she soaped her body. The room was heavily-scented, warm and steamy, and he wished he could stay and get under the water with her.

"Okay. See you tonight."

"Remember what I said," he cautioned. "Be circumspect."

"Husband, I wrote the book on it." She had. Literally.

As he left the apartment and walked down the stairs, he wondered what the day held for him. More shit from Major Ghanem, no doubt, to add to the piles of shit sitting neatly and metaphorically on his desk already. Then Lattouf would be making an appearance at some stage with his latest crackpot theory. And, of course, there was the man without a name, who for now he would call Mr Carla.

Why, oh why, had he ever got mixed up in this? *al-Mahdi* and The Second Coming indeed. Fantasy. Madness. Murder. Why hadn't he just said no when Carla had first contacted him?

He would get the copies of Carla's picture of the assassin and the report on Himo's death, and maybe try to tap Mr Carla to reveal this Sajida business, whatever that was. No doubt he would be in touch today. But it would be nice to know exactly who he was dealing with...

With a small smile, he tapped his pocket. Maybe he would find out.

He climbed into the Land Cruiser, started up and switched on the radio underneath the unused GPS screen on the dash. He would let the music of *Voix du Liban* accompany him in to Beirut today.

During the near hour-long journey, he never once noticed that, several vehicles back, he was also accompanied by a black Suzuki Hayabusa motorbike.

Jbeil, Lebanon 07:20

"There, that's better." Love spoke sweetly, almost lovingly, caressing Carla's face gently with her right hand while her left hand held a vicious-looking stiletto to the captive's throat.

Paradise had finished cleaning her bottom, holding Carla's legs in the air like a baby while she wiped and dried. They had already removed the thin waste-covered mattress and cleaned and disinfected the floor.

"Sorry we only had one mattress," said Paradise as she reconnected the ankle cuffs to the bed frame. "Hope the springs aren't too painful."

They were more irritating than painful, little pokes, little scratches all down her back and legs. Like lying on a bed of nails. She had clenched her buttocks a couple of times but had then decided the best course was to keep still.

She moved her head, looking around. She was in a small room, musty, bare of furnishings except for the bed. Light was coming in through a small window high in one wall giving the white eyes of her captors an eerie glow.

"We'll let you up if you promise to behave," said Love. "I'll get you some food, you must be starving. We have tomatoes, *labneh*, *mana'eesh* and some *kunafi* if you're up to it, and coffee when you're ready. But be careful, your stomach will probably process it quickly." To emphasise the point she moved her hand from Carla's face and slowly ran her fingers down her naked body, stopping at her stomach and making soft, gentle circles around the belly-button with her fingertips. It felt like the gossamer caress of an angel – or the deception of a she-devil.

"I am hungry," understated Carla. She was ravenous.

"Well, here's the deal." Paradise leant over next to her sister, touching Carla's thigh. Carla looked up. The *houri* were spookily identical, it was like she was seeing double, hallucinating, the drugs not yet out of her system. "You promise to be a good girl and we'll let you up. You will remain restrained because we do not trust you, but believe us when we say we mean you no harm."

"We could have killed you," reasoned Love. "You could be dead by now."

"Why aren't I?"

Paradise ignored the question. "Will you be good?"

"Yes. Yes, I will."

The twins looked at each other, exchanging thoughts. Love nodded. She held up the stiletto in her left hand. "Remember, I have this – and these." She held up her right hand and made a small flicking movement with her thumb against the top of her index finger. The tiniest needle poked up from beneath the false nail. "You, of course, have been disarmed."

Carla tried to move her wrists, raising her head to look down at her hands. Yes, she remembered her nails being prised off. The ends of her fingers were raw and bloodied.

Paradise took keys from her cargo pants pocket and unlocked first one leg then the other, rubbing Carla's ankles as she did so. Then she stood back, as if trying to decide which wrist to unlock. "I presume, like us, you are ambidextrous, with a favour towards your left?" She stretched over and undid the right wrist.

"Now move slowly." Love was kneeling on the floor, holding Carla's legs in case of kicking and moving them around and down so that she was in a sitting position. Then she rubbed her thighs, massaging life back into them.

"May I put some clothes on?"

"No. Not yet," said Love.

"We like you like that," said Paradise. "Are you naturally smooth or do you shave? And anyway we have nothing in your size. Your clothes had blood on them, we had to throw them away."

Carla watched as Love continued massaging her legs. She asked, "Why am I alive?"

"Because we didn't want to waste you," Paradise replied, Carla raising her head upwards to look at her. "We should really have freed your spirit but we though for once that we should try a proper conversion."

"Who are you?"

"We're just soldiers of The Saviour. His trusted disciples."

"You really think he is The Saviour?"

"We know he is. He has saved his believers before and he has come to do it again. This time those who believe in him will not perish."

"And we want you to join us," said Love, stopping her hands at the top of Carla's thighs at the crease with her groin. "You are beautiful, you are talented. Become one of the chosen ones, like us. This is the time of *al-Mahdi*. Many will be called."

"But only a few will be chosen." Paradise unlocked the final handcuff as Love grabbed Carla's face, her needled nails against the skin.

"Okay," said Love, her face just centimetres away. Carla could feel her warm, sweet breath. "Now stand slowly as I raise you, as if you were newborn. Your legs will be weak, we will hold you." Hands still on her head, she pulled Carla forward and up, Paradise quickly grabbing both her wrists and pinning them behind her. Supporting her but restraining her also. "Good girl," said Love. "Good girl. Now slowly slowly let your legs take your weight. Carefully... that's good. Put one foot in front of the other... Good." She took her hands down, looking to see that Paradise maintained her grip behind. "Okay. *Yalla.* Let's get some food inside you. Then afterwards we will give you a complete pamper. You look like you've been through the wars."

Or have come back from the dead, thought The Djinn.

Jonblat, Beirut 08:15

And there indeed was today's pile of shit, awaiting him on his desk. A file and a note from Major Ghanem about the pending Gaza boats crisis*, asking for his comments on the intelligence reports that Israel was preparing to attack Lebanon once again and seeking his proposals for street-level safety.

This time it was easy. Israel had attacked Lebanon so often in the past – either by threat or actual deed – that all he needed to do was dust off some of his old situation assessments and tweak them for the current risk.

Which was good because he had other things to do.

After pouring himself a cup of sludge and exchanging banter with Deeb el-Gharib, he returned to his office, closing the door behind him. Back at his desk he retrieved his mobile phone from his jacket pocket, pressed five buttons (three of them erroneously, which meant he had to come out and go back in again) and managed to activate the phone's Bluetooth.

The Bluetooth on his desk computer was easier to turn on. His mobile and his PC sought each other out, requested permission to connect, raised a four-figure code which he typed into the PC, and then joined like old friends.

He smoked and drank his sludge as he found the images file on his phone. He chose the two pictures he wanted and sent them to his computer one by one.

The man, Mr Carla, might be clever with his party trick of removing the bullets from Gisele's gun, but he hadn't spotted the two quick snaps Merhi had taken of him as he had put his phone away after the call from Lattouf last night.

I have your face, Mister. Let see if the entire security system of Lebanon has anything on record about you...

---

* Certain factions were intending to send two ships, the Junia and the Julia, from Lebanon to the Gaza Strip in defiance of the Israeli naval blockade of Gaza. Through the United Nations, Israel was 'requesting' that Lebanon prevent the boats from departing.

He had just pressed the Enter button on the third of the three programs he was using when the telephone on his desk rang. An internal call.

He looked at his watch as he picked up the receiver. 09:00.

It was the front desk downstairs. "Captain Lattouf is on his way up to you, sir."

"Thank you," said Merhi. "Great."

Really great.

Jbeil, Lebanon 09:00

The *houri* had been right. Eating was difficult and she had wretched several times when she first tried to swallow, her stomach wondering why someone dead would need to eat and trying to reject the attempt. Thankfully she had not actually brought anything back up. She had already embarrassed herself enough in front of these two.

Over breakfast she had noticed that one of the women had a chunk missing from her right forearm. A ragged, dried but bloodied hole, a bite mark. Around the wound was a thin line of black adhesive residue, which meant it had been covered with a dressing until recently. It took Carla only seconds to remember that she had bitten the bitch's arm in the fight. What had happened to the piece of flesh...? She couldn't remember... Oh yes she could, she had swallowed it.

But at least now she had a way of telling them apart. *Houri 1* was the one with the injured arm, the one who had seemed to take great pleasure in massaging her. *Houri 2* was the one who had restrained her, the one interested in whether she shaved her body.

Now she was standing in an old, metre-wide metal bath filled with scented soapy water, her left arm raised and chained to a pipe against the wall. She looked like a perverse Venus de Milo. *Houri 1* was washing her with a sponge, every nook, every cranny, every crack. *Houri 2* was standing back, watching but also guarding.

After the final rinsing, *Houri 1* placed a pink bath towel over her glistening shoulders while *Houri 2* took her right arm, ordering "Step out of the bath." There was a small mat on the floor.

Carla stepped out, having to stretch slightly because her left arm was still cuffed to the pipe. *Houri 1* slid the bath away to the far side of the room and then came back and took hold of two corners of the towel, saying "Come, I will dry you." *Houri 2* kept hold of her right wrist.

Houri 1 was very close, her arms around Carla from the front, rubbing the towel across her back. "After this we have some scented oils which you may like, even some make-up – but you are so beautiful you don't really need any. Make-up is for mortals."

"Why are you doing this?" asked Carla.

"We told you," smiled *Houri 1*, surprised at the question. "We want you to join us."

"And what if I don't want to?"

"We have never failed in a conversion," said *Houri 2*. "It will simply mean yours takes another form."

"The other form being?"

"The freeing of your spirit."

Houri 1 rubbed the towel gently but thoroughly between Carla's legs, staring into her eyes as she did so, smiling.

"Why didn't you just kill me?" asked Carla softly.

The *houri* frowned. "We never kill anyone. We just convert them."

"Okay, why didn't you convert me then?"

Houri 1 knelt, rubbing the towel down her legs. *Houri 2* said, "Self-conversion is always more pure. We respect you as one of us. We wanted to give you a chance for redemption."

Houri 1 left the towel on the floor and stood back up, her hands running up the outside of Carla's legs, stopping on her hips. "And we are going to grant you the greatest honour anyone could ever have."

"You are?"

"Yes. Tomorrow *al-Mahdi's* journey will begin. The liberation of the believers will commence. The world will never be the same again. Tomorrow you will meet The Saviour in person. You will bow down and kiss his robes, his hands, his feet. Not because you are made to but because you will want to."

"And," said *Houri 2*, "you will do whatever he asks of you."

Jonblat, Beirut 09:05

Merhi stood in the doorway of his office and watched Fadi Lattouf rumble down the corridor like a boulder dislodged from a mountainside. He was coming closer and closer and there was nothing Merhi could do to get out of the way.

"Morning of light, my dear friend!" Lattouf was dressed in his blue police uniform, this time without a jacket to conceal the sweat-soaked shirt. He stopped abruptly at the doorway to the General Office. Looking in, he said to somebody inside "I think your Captain will need coffee, please. I'll have one too while you're about it." Then he continued on.

"Morning, Fadi." They shook hands.

As Merhi closed the door, Lattouf said proudly "I have solved it. Did I not say that you could rely on Lattouf?"

"No, you didn't."

"My cousin was a genius.."

"Sit down, Fadi, sit down."

The wooden chair disappeared under the folds of Lattouf's arse.

Merhi took his notepad out of his drawer. The numbers were still on there from two days ago together with his attempts to solve the alphabetical code. 340715354514. He wondered what hare-brained idea Lattouf had come up with now.

"We were going down completely the wrong track," enthused the Palestinian. "It wasn't a code. My cousin was a genius but he wasn't that clever. It isn't a bank account. The phone number was nearer."

"But we dialled it, there was no such number."

"Of course not. Who would my cousin know in Spain?" Lattouf spoke as if he had ridiculed the theory all along. "But it is a number!"

Merhi was bewildered. "Yes, it is a number."

There was a knock on the door and Sergeant Deeb el-Gharib entered carrying two mugs with a small cardboard carton balanced on top of them. "Your coffee, gentlemen."

"Thank you, Deeb."

"Bless your hands... Deeb," said Lattouf.

el-Gharib placed the coffee on the desk and removed the carton, placing it next to them. "Thought you might like a few baklava. Don't know how fresh they are, left over from the birthday do the other day."

"Thanks," said Merhi, knowing that the birthday do was at least two weeks ago. el-Gharib went back out, closing the door. "You have them, Fadi. I am not hungry."

"Are you sure? Look there are four. Will you not have one?"

"Thank you." Merhi shook his head. "Careful, they might be a bit stale."

All four disappeared into Lattouf's mouth in one go. "No," he mumbled, crumbs in his beard. "They taste fresh enough to me. Could have been made this morning." Swallowing, he licked his fingers one by one then wiped his hands on his trousers.

"Okay," Merhi waved his hand at his notepad. "It's not a code, it's not a bank account, it's not a Spanish telephone number. What is it?"

"What do you have on your computer?" Lattouf nodded at the PC on the desk.

"What? What do you mean?"

"What programs do you have on there?"

"What's that to do with you?"

"Do you have Google Earth?"

"Do I have...? In the name of Christ and your prophet, what are you talking about?"

"You know my cousin's computer? You helped me take it home."

"*Bien sûr.*"

"My eldest girl, Lana, was on it last night."

"Good, I'm glad it works."

"She was on Google Earth."

"I'm glad she's getting use out... of... it..." Merhi's voice trailed off as he looked down at the numbers on his pad.

340715354514.

He looked back up. Lattouf was beaming, nodding, his eyes glassy with imminent triumph. "Ah ha, there it is, yes? You can see it? Now you understand?"

Merhi looked down again. "Holy fuck." He grabbed a pencil from the caddy and wrote the numbers on the pad once again, this time in two lines of six, one above the other.

340715

354514

Then he changed it to

+ 34.07 15

- 35.45 14

He sat back in his chair. "They're bloody map co-ordinates. Thirty-four degrees, seven minutes, fifteen seconds north, thirty-five degrees, forty-five minutes, fourteen seconds east. My God."

"And mine too," nodded Lattouf. "He is good."

"Have you looked them up?"

"Ah no," Lattouf looked slightly abashed. "I don't... You know. Can we do it now? Do you have Google Earth on there?"

"Fadi, we don't need Google Earth. We have more sophisticated GPS programs. Wait."

Lattouf drank his coffee (good stuff this, just as he liked it: thick, strong... gritty) while Merhi's fingers played across the keyboard. The fingers paused, played again, paused. Then they were drumming on the desk. Then Merhi said, "Shit, not working. Okay Fadi, Google Earth it is!" More finger movement, more waiting. Then, "Okay, come round."

Lattouf came around, bringing his chair with him. He sat close, leaning forward, staring at the screen. Slightly ripe but not overpowering. He said, "I don't have my glasses."

"Okay," Merhi had the sidebar open, cursor in the *Fly to* box. "How do I do this?"

The first attempt put him in the middle of the Atlantic Ocean, the next somewhere in South America. He humphed. "On the assumption that your cousin wasn't in either of these places, I must be putting it in wrong. Let's see how they do it..." He scrolled around the screen, watching the co-ordinates changing at the bottom. "Okay, let's try this."

He typed in 34 07' 15.0"N, 35 45'14.0"E and pressed enter.

The picture on the screen raised up from South America, heading east at speed. Then it was falling. Falling, falling. Over north Africa. Over the Mediterranean. Over Lebanon.

It stopped.

"Where is it? Where is it?" Lattouf craned forward.

Merhi sat back to let him see. Then he said, "It is Annaya. Saint Charbel."

"Who? What?"

"It is a Christian monastery, Fadi. The Saint Maron Monastery, the tomb of Saint Charbel. At Annaya. Inland from Jbeil."

"Jbeil!"

"Indeed. I think this is the answer, my friend." He nodded in thought. Then he said, "But it raises more questions."

"What was my cousin doing at a Christian monastery?"

"Yes. Working, presumably? I assume he didn't restrict his clients to one religious persuasion?"

Lattouf shook his head. "Not as far as I know."

"So what we have to ask is: what was it he found at this monastery that made him dash down to see you, leaving you this clue on a playing card?" Merhi put a cigarette in his mouth and pushed the packet to Lattouf. The big man took one, bending over the flame from Merhi's lighter.

After each of them had taken a drag, Lattouf said "What had he found, what had he seen, to get himself killed?"

Jonblat, Beirut 11:00

That was a turn up for the books, thought Merhi, and an unwelcome turn up at that. He could do without this, he had too much on. The murder of Chadi Lattouf was unrecorded, a local death, the body had been disposed of, no longer any proof of foul play – why couldn't it have been left at that, what was one more dead Palestinian?

But no, it couldn't be left at that. The victim was the cousin of the local Palestinian police chief, who also happened to be a friend of his. A friend who, despite his idiotic bumbling, gluttony and unfortunate personal habits, had solved a major clue the victim had left for him.

Shit.

Merhi watched from his office window as the light blue Ford Transit van with the red number plate pulled out into the traffic with much honking of horns and flashing of lights. Lattouf had wished he could stay for lunch (Merhi hadn't offered) but he had to get back. He said something about an eighteen year old who had died in police custody. Had to take the body to the morgue. But he would see him tomorrow, around 08:30. They were going to Annaya to have a look around.

Merhi watched the van go west and then disappear south (two pedestrians crossing the road narrowly escaping with their lives), then he went back to his desk.

Right, what next? He would cut and paste his situation assessment on the Gaza boats crisis and print it out for Major Ghanem (the boss preferred not to have classified documents sent via e-mail) – but first there was something else requiring his attention.

One of the facial recognition programs he was using was flashing orange on the Taskbar on the screen. Two of the programs were still feverishly working away. The program that had reported back was the new system, the custody suite Digital Image Register with the Colossus facial image search engine inside. With anticipation, Merhi clicked on the Taskbar. Okay, Mr Carla, let's see who you really are...

Merhi's face dropped.

He was nobody.

The new system was by far quicker than the other two, but that only meant that it brought him the bad news sooner.

NO MATCH FOUND.

Shit.

That meant that Mr Carla was not in the criminal database of Lebanon, so he had never been naughty here, or at least had never been caught being naughty here.

Merhi drummed his fingers on the desk. If he was Carla's husband, it was logical that he had been living with her in New York (or was he being old-fashioned?). Should he instigate another Interpol check? No, that would be declaring his interest too publically. This one he needed to keep tightly under wraps.

Clicking that he did not want to start a new search, he came out of the program and opened *Word*, clicking on his *Security Assessments* folder.

He saved a new blank document under the title *July 2010*, opened up three old assessments and began to cut and paste.

At 11:50 his mobile phone rang as he was checking a printed copy of his Gaza boats assessment. It was a number he did not recognise.

"Merhi."

"Do you have them?"

For a nano-second he was confused, his attention being on the boats assessment. Was this Major Ghanem? Then he realised it wasn't. "Yes, I have them."

"Good. Hamra Square in half an hour. Have a coffee."

Silence. Merhi looked at the screen. The caller had gone.

Squinting at his phone, he pressed the Menu button and then the Call Logs. The app opened and he smiled. Well, well, Mr Carla, not so clever after all, are we? You've left your number. It began with code +961 which meant he was using a Lebanese SIM card.

He pressed the Call icon.

And almost immediately an automated voice told him that his call could not be connected.

He tried again. Same result.

Shit. Okay Mr Carla, you were clever, his apologies. You were using the SIM once only, it was probably destroyed by now. No call back and, importantly, no triangulation detection. He shouldn't have expected anything less.

Hamra Square in half an hour it was. He could do with a coffee anyway. It would make a change from sludge.

Merhi left his office at 12:05. Like everyone in the building, he was supposed to shut down his computer when he was going out. Like everyone in the building, he never did except at night. He simply turned the monitor off. To anyone glancing casually, it looked like the computer was turned off.

So he didn't know that, as he began to walk along the corridor, the first facial recognition program on the old facial search engine, the one used by Human Resources, reported back, followed shortly by the second program, Lebanon's national ID card database.

Hamra, Beirut 12:25

Merhi sat at the same table as he had yesterday, triple espresso, a packet of Cedars King Size and a brown A5 envelope in front of him. At midday there was no place in Hamra Square that was not caressed by the sun, so he tilted his head upwards, eyes closed, enjoying the rays.

"*Massah el-khair*, Captain," said a deep voice above his head.

Merhi jumped. Had he nodded off? There had been no one near when he closed his eyes. He straightened himself up as the man pulled out a chair and sat down.

The man was dressed in jeans and sandals and the same loose collarless white shirt as he had on the previous evening, but it looked like it had been freshly laundered overnight. His long hair was down the sides of his face then tied back in a loose pony-tail.

"This is for me?" The Damascene laid his hand on the A5 envelope.

"The report and the drawing as requested."

"Thank you. I will return them as soon as I can." The Damascene looked up as a woman from the café hovered next to him. He smiled. "A triple espresso please and a mineral water. In the bottle." The woman nodded and went back inside.

"I've got some more information for you," said Merhi.

"You have?"

"But I thought we could make a little trade."

"A trade?"

"I tell you my information, you tell me who or what Sajida is."

The Damascene sighed. "My wife did not tell you about Sajida for a reason. She was protecting you. The knowledge is dangerous."

"Shouldn't I be the judge of that?"

"In this case, no. I think we should both respect my wife's wishes."

"Okay," said Merhi.

There was silence. Merhi took a cigarette from the packet and lit up.

"Well?" nudged The Damascene.

"Well, what?"

"What information do you have to tell me?"

"Sorry, the knowledge is dangerous. I'm protecting you."

The Damascene sat back, staring hard at Merhi's face. Then he smiled again as he saw the woman coming back with his order. "*Shukran.*" She placed the cup and bottle of *Sohat* water on the table and left.

"Let me make a little trade with you, Captain." He pushed the coffee towards Merhi. "For you."

"What do you have to trade?"

The Damascene twisted open the cap and swilled water from the bottle. "The information you have for your wife's life."

"You fucking bastard."

"Thank you." He screwed the cap neatly back on. "Well?"

Merhi sighed, beaten. "Your wife first met Captain Himo, the one who supposedly killed himself," he nodded at the envelope, "in my office. I have a recording of their conversation."

The Damascene raised his eyebrows, nodding. "You have a transcript?"

"No. But I can tell you what was said, if you can believe it. Carla told Himo that Sajida was right and The Second Coming was now imminent. The Second Coming! Of The Saviour! Or *al-Mahdi* to you."

"To me? That's very presumptuous of you. Did she say it was The Saviour? Did she use those actual words?"

Merhi paused, thinking. Then he said, "No, actually, she didn't. That was Himo. Carla seemed to think otherwise."

"Himo said it was The Saviour?"

"He said *al-Mahdi* had chosen Lebanon."

A humourless laugh burst from The Damascene's mouth. "Of course he had. Had to be Lebanon, didn't it? It figures."

"It does?"

"Our country is one long mountain with a valley on one side and a coast on the other. Plenty of places to hide, in the mountains."

Merhi really didn't know what he was talking about. He stubbed out his cigarette in an ashtray and pulled over the second cup of coffee.

"I want a copy of the recording," said The Damascene.

"Why? I've told you what's on it."

"You say my wife is dead. I do not believe that." The Damascene stood up, his hand going into his pocket. Merhi tensed. "But if you are right, that is the last recording of her voice. And I want it." He pulled a fold of US dollars from his pocket, peeled off a generous quantity and threw them on the table. "I will be in touch." He picked up the envelope and his bottle of water and walked away, north towards Makdissi Street.

Jonblat, Beirut 13:30

Merhi was back in the office, staring at the voice recorder that he had pulled from his drawer. The memory card with the Carla-Himo conversation was still in the machine from the other day. He considered what he should do. It would serve that bastard right if he wiped the card, that would teach him to threaten Gisele. But what would that achieve, other than to give Merhi a spiteful triumph and perhaps to put Gisele under more threat?

There was no operational need for Mr Carla to have it, but he understood the personal need. His wife was dead. This was a recording of one of her last conversations. It might be the only record ever, anywhere, of her voice.

Telling himself not to be such a shite, Merhi fumbled in the drawer and brought out the voice recorder's USB connection lead. He plugged the smaller end into the machine and the USB into the computer. He switched on the monitor as he unwrapped, with great difficulty, the new memory stick he had bought on his way back from lunch.

The monitor opened on the ISF's official screensaver as he pushed the memory stick into a free USB port.

He then spent several minutes trying to copy the conversation from the voice recorder to the computer. He made a mental note to delete the file from the computer as soon as it had been copied to the stick. He didn't know what he was dealing with but whatever it was it was dangerous and he didn't want this incriminating evidence sitting there, implicating him.

While he was waiting for the import to complete, he noticed the other tabs on the Taskbar, the other two facial recognition programs. Well, he could take a guess at what these were going to say. Nothing. He clicked on the first tab, the national ID card database.

NO MATCH FOUND.

Well now, there was a surprise. Not. So despite Mr Carla 'not denying' that he was Lebanese from Tripoli, he had no national ID card. So he wasn't a Lebanese national at all. Just who the hell was he?

Merhi checked on the download, one minute to go, and clicked on the second tab, the Human Resources database.

And his jaw dropped.

Oh my God!

MATCH FOUND.

There, sitting side by side, was the photo he had put into the program and another black and white picture, obviously some years old. At first there seemed no similarity. The old picture was the sort of one that you would get on an identification or building entry card. Slightly blurred, showing that little care had been taken, just another photo in a long line of photos. It was of a man in his thirties, hair cropped short, strong face, staring at the camera.

Merhi's picture was in colour, had necessarily been rushed, and showed a not-quite-full-on picture of Mr Carla, long black hair down either side of his face, looking – disconcertingly – at an out-of-picture Gisele. His face was leaner, stronger, older than the face in the other picture. Was it the same?

The computer said that there was a fifty-five per cent chance of a match, and there were various graphs and charts at the side referencing point-marks on each of the faces.

Fifty-five per cent! What good was that? There was a fifty-five per cent chance Jihad Merhi looked like President Bashar Assad of Syria, less thirty centimetres in height, plus ten years in age, less the moustache, plus a few centimetres around the waist...

Fifty-five per cent was not good enough. Such a percentage would never be accepted as proof of anything in a court of law. Nevertheless, he looked at the biographical information.

```
NAME:     MARWAN MEBARAK
DOB:      01 JUNE 1967/22 SAFAR 1387
RANK:     CAPTAIN
UNIT:     COMMANDO
LOCATION: BAHJAT GHANEM NORTH
DOD:      10 JANUARY 2000/3 SHAWWAL 1420
```

And there it was. In that last line. Proof that fifty-five per cent was no good. DOD. Date of Death. This poor bastard had been a serving soldier, killed in the line of duty probably. It was just possible, Merhi supposed, that Captain Marwan Mebarak had been some sort of distant relative to Mr Carla, a cousin or something. Maybe he would drop the name in conversation, see what reaction he got.

But Mr Carla was not a Lebanese national, the databases proved it. Which begged the question: what was he? Who was he?

Realising he would probably never know, Merhi went back to the Voice screen, confirmed the import was complete, and clicked on the *Copy To F: Drive* icon.

Jbeil, Lebanon 23:59

Carla had slept well. Not the nightmare oblivion of her previous *faux* death, but real, proper sleep. But she only ever slept in three hour bursts, always had, so now she was awake.

She was on the bunk bed in her small, cell-like room, staring through the supports of the upper bunk into the blackness of the ceiling. She was no longer handcuffed to the bed frame, and a new thin mattress had appeared during the day, so she was in relative comfort for her situation. But she was still naked.

As the *houri* had promised, she had been pampered. A full, lingering body massage (the hands of *Houri 2* lingering just a little too long in certain parts, trying to ascertain whether she shaved or was naturally without body hair), a scalp massage, a hair wash and condition and blow dry. It was almost as if she was the twins' pet, a plaything. A living doll.

They had fed and watered her, gradually and carefully, throughout the day. All three of them had been pleased that there was no more bodily rejection of its intake.

But the one thing they had not touched were her hands. She couldn't have a manicure, she had no nails, just flaking scabs. When she got back to New York her nail technician, Emma at Middleton's on Madison Avenue, was going to have a fit.

Carla smiled at the subconscious positivity. *When* she got back to New York, not *if*. That was good. But how she was going to do it she did not know. She was captive, stark naked, without fingernails or her hairclip against two extremely proficient – what were they? Soldiers, like they said? Killers? Disciples?

The thought of disciples brought Selim Himo into her mind. They had admitted he was one of them, so all the stuff he had told her about there being an Eyes Only file at the highest level, about people knowing that the so-called *al-Mahdi* was in Lebanon, was a crock of shit. No one knew. She should have realised that, alarms bells should have rung when Himo said about the file, but she had no reason to distrust the guy who was her new boss. Of course there would not be a file, the secret was too dangerous. Only the chosen few would know it until the time was right. And Lebanon was incidental, chosen because of its terrain and its convenience and for no other reason. Soon it would be just a backdrop in the story. This time the Wise Men need not come from the east, their Saviour was going to them.

Their Saviour! She laughed ruefully. Well, there were many who would think he was. One man's *al-Mahdi* was another man's *ad-Dajjal*.

And tomorrow she would be meeting him...

She got up off the bed and went over and peed in the small commode in the corner.

As she lay back down, she thought of Marwan. How many days had she now been out of contact? He would have instigated their contingency procedures the third time she had failed to answer his calls. He would be looking for her. Without doubt he would be in Lebanon by now. He might even be close by.

Please find me, my husband.

Gently, she drifted off back to sleep.

22 July 2010
10 Sha'ban 1431

Jbeil, Lebanon 07:30

For breakfast, *Houri 1* prepared *baiid baladi*, fresh country eggs, fried in *awarma*, preserved meat fat, saying that they had a busy day ahead and they needed their strength. There was also yesterdays' leftover *mana'eesh* and *kunafi*.

Carla ate well, sitting naked at the table with the two fully-dressed women. She understood the reason for her continued nakedness and she had not queried it. It was standard procedure with prisoners considered dangerous. Keeping them naked was not only intended to humble and psychologically weaken them in front of others, it also ensured they had no concealed weapons (or easily-accessible weapons if they were considering internal concealment). It did not worry Carla one bit.

"Have you considered our offer?" asked *Houri 1* at the end of the meal, wiping her mouth on a tissue.

"What offer?" asked Carla, knowing only too well.

"Will you convert?"

"Or," said *Houri 2*, "will you be converted?"

Carla rubbed crumbs off her fingers onto the paper plate in front of her. "I am flattered that you consider me like you."

"You are a trained soldier, no?" *Houri 2*.

"In a manner of speaking. I am also loyal."

"As we are."

"You've killed people."

"We've converted people."

"Okay. Whatever."

"We are sure you have killed people," said *Houri 1*. "We have experienced your skill."

Carla said nothing.

Houri 2 stood up. "We have to go out today. The great journey is beginning." With a swift, unexpected movement she grabbed Carla's arms, pinning them behind her.

"And as you are not yet one of us," said *Houri 1*, also rising. "We must take precautions."

Houri 2 lifted Carla off of the chair and, before she could kick out, *Houri 1* had grabbed her feet.

"Don't worry," said *Houri 1*, "we're not going to hurt you."

"We just need you restrained till we get back."

Carla tried a token buck but she knew it would be useless. Please, she thought, no more drugs.

Houri 1 seemed to read her mind. "We want you fully alert," she said as they carried her back to her room. "But we can't have you making a noise or causing a fuss while we're not here." She dropped Carla's legs next to the bunk as *Houri 2* increased her grip, pulling her closer.

Houri 1 went over to a box in the opposite corner of the room to the commode. Carla stared, frowning. That had not been there before. The *houri* pulled out a fold of heavy textile with rope on the top. Turning back, she said "We'll be gone a few hours, no more."

"And he will be with us when we return," said *Houri 2* close to her ear. "*al-Mahdi*, Brother Malek, will wish to convert you personally."

Bourj el-Barajneh, Beirut 08:30

Jihad Merhi bipped the horn as he pulled up in his Land Cruiser outside *chez Lattouf*. Already the day was hot and the car's air conditioning was roaring dutifully in the background. No matter that he was a native, the high summers of Lebanon still roasted him alive, and at this time of year it would be only marginally cooler up in the mountains. He had dressed in a blue cotton *Lacoste* polo shirt and fawn linen trousers.

A few minutes later the Lattoufs' front door opened and, to much shouting of goodbyes and Allah's blessings, Fadi came out.

Merhi's eyes shot heavenwards. He was dressed in his grey polyester suit again! Full jacket, the works – this time including a garish tie, which might have been in fashion forty years ago – and of course the counterfeit *Ray-Ban* sunglasses. In his hand he carried a bulky package.

"A little over-dressed, aren't we?" commented Merhi as the big man slid his award-winning arse onto the passenger seat.

Lattouf stopped, his right cheek still half out of the car. Pushing his sunglasses up onto his dome, he looked Merhi up and down then looked at himself. "I thought I would dress respectfully. We are visiting one of your major religious shrines."

"Fadi, it is more of a tourist destination. Yes, it is a shrine, yes it is a monastery, but dressed like that you will stand out like... like a Muslim trying not to stand out."

"Shall I go change?"

"No, no. Damage limitation. Take off the jacket."

Lattouf stepped out, took off his jacket and threw it onto the back seat on top of a folded road map.

"Now lose the cat's vomit."

"The what?"

"That thing around your neck. It cannot be called a tie."

Lattouf yanked it off but Merhi stopped him throwing it onto the jacket. "No, no. I said lose it. You should never be seen in that, have some self-respect."

Lattouf looked around, confused. Then he simply dropped the tie in the gutter.

"Good," nodded Merhi. "Now undo a few buttons on your shirt – not too many, we don't want to scare the mountain wildlife... There, that's better. You'll feel cooler too."

Lattouf climbed back in, car dipping to the right, door slamming.

"What's in there?" Merhi nodded at the package on Lattouf's lap as he released the parking brake and checked his mirrors.

Lattouf smiled. "Our lunch. Nada made it for us – she sends Allah's blessings, by the way. Do you like goat and rice?"

"I can never think of anything else." Merhi pulled away into the traffic, the slight jerk as the car moved making Lattouf's sunglasses roll back down his sweat-soaked head and plop back onto the bridge of his nose.

Annaya, Lebanon 10:00

Paradise and Love sat in the Jeep Wrangler Ultimate, hard top on, windows open, staring at the main monastery door, one set of brown eyes, one set of green eyes (Love was now in the lead thirty-nine to thirty-seven). As soon as they saw Brother Malek emerge, they got out, bowing reverentially.

"*Salaam, oh Malek,*" they greeted in unison.

Malek was in his full-length *burnus*, hood up, feet sandaled, and he was in a no-nonsense mood as he hurried over to them. "*Salaam.* Let us go." He climbed into the back of the Jeep as Paradise held the door open. "I do not like dealing with these people," he said, referring to the fact that he had had to give the Father Superior the final farewell donation himself. "That should be your task. Why they will not let you in there I do not know. They are *kafirs*, I wish I could convert them all."

The twins exchanged looks as Paradise went round to the driver's side and Love climbed into the passenger seat. Once they were settled inside, Love said "It is over now, Brother. After all these years, your final journey has begun."

The Jeep moved off, Paradise driving slowly out of the complex, avoiding other visitors and their vehicles. Malek kept his head still in the back seat, not looking out of the window, hood up and falling forward over his face.

"You have disposed of the Netbook?" he asked.

"As you instructed," said Love. "It has been broken like the bread of the eucharist and scattered to the winds."

"And my *argileh*?"

"It is safe and waiting for you"

They reached the exit and Paradise picked up speed, braking firmly again as a car came round the first hairpin too far into the middle of the road. She negotiated the bend herself and then accelerated again.

"Do you have anything for me now?" asked Malek.

Love opened the compartment on the dashboard and held up two items of equal length: the silver tube containing a cigar and a blue and white wrapped candy bar. "Which would you like?"

Malek's hand reached forward. "I'll take both."

"And we have something else for you at base," said Paradise over her shoulder. "As promised. We think you will like it."

Without commenting, Malek unpeeled the top half of the candy bar and it disappeared up into his hood.

At the next hairpin Paradise slowed to avoid a motorbike heading up the mountain, then the three of them settled in silence for the journey down into Jbeil.

"Hell's teeth," mumbled Merhi as he swerved right to avoid the Jeep then over-compensated back again. "Bloody tourists."

Lattouf had dropped the opened, and nearly finished, packet of goat and rice onto the floor as he rolled first one way then the other, also popping out a small fart. He turned in the seat, looking back down the mountainside. "Did you see who it was?" he asked.

Merhi sniffed. "Is that you or the food?"

Lattouf turned back. "Probably both. Sorry. Are you sure you won't have some?"

Not if it smells like rotten eggs with a sulphur sauce, thought Merhi. He shook his head, "Thank you."

With great effort Lattouf strained forward between his own legs, gathered together the food that had spilled onto the car mat and rolled it back into the package. He straightened up, package in hand and once more began to eat, using his fingers.

"Who was it?" asked Merhi.

"What?"

"You asked me if I saw who it was, in the Jeep."

"Oh. It was the twins."

"What twins?"

"Do you remember? When we were in Jbeil. The two women we saw, we walked behind them along the street."

"I wouldn't know, I only saw the back of them."

"It was them. Small world, eh?"

"Indeed."

Lattouf finished the rice and screwed up the paper, looking around for somewhere to put it. They pulled in to the parking area.

"Leave it in the door," instructed Merhi as he applied the parking brake. "I'll see to it later. But - " he fiddled on his arm rest and the back window behind Lattouf popped open just a centimetre. "I think we need to let some air into the car." *I'll have a full valet and fumigation done later.*

They both got out, the car's lights flashing twice as Merhi pressed the remote locking button on his key fob. "Right," he said, admiring the view out over the mountainside and then looking to his right to Saint Charbel's church. "So, what did your cousin see here that was so shocking?"

"What did he see here that got him chased down into Beirut?" pondered Lattouf as he hitched up his too-short trousers then pulled them back out of his anal crevice.

"What did he see here that got him killed?"

"And who was it that chased him? Let us find out."

Merhi and Lattouf set off up the slope towards the church.

Jbeil, Lebanon 11:00

Paradise stopped the Jeep on Boulevard al-Mina opposite the top of Rue St John. Love got out, holding the back door open for Brother Malek. Although robed monks were not an uncommon sight in Jbeil (many were pilgrims visiting the Church of St John the Baptist and the Greek Orthodox Church, or just visitors from the mountain monasteries), one with his hood up on such a hot day might attract attention, especially if he was accompanied by two tall, blonde, young female twins. So they had decided to pull up as close to base as possible and to have only one twin accompany him. From here it was just a short walk down Rue St John to the old boarded up shop behind the Mayadoun Bookshop.

They waited for traffic to pass then Love and Brother Malek walked across the boulevard and passed through the entrance in the rampart walls.

Paradise drove off to the car park up by the Seven Seas Restaurant.

"Welcome, Malek," said Love as she unlocked the padlock and pushed open the front door.

"May Allah's blessings be upon this abode." Brother Malek entered into a large, dim room, which used to be the public area of the shop.

"We have electricity," said Love. "They never turned it off, you know what the Lebanese are like. Although it does go off when they have their daily power cuts. Mind your eyes." She flicked a switch on the wall and a bare bulb hanging from a threadbare wire in the ceiling radiated forty watts illuminating a small table containing breakfast remnants.

"You are hungry?" asked Love. "I will be preparing dinner later, but I can ask my sister to bring in *shawarma* and pastries." She took her mobile phone from her belt.

"I have eaten." The hood turned towards Love. "But thank you." He seemed calmer now he was here. Now the final journey had begun.

Love put her phone back on her belt. "You would like something to drink?"

"Water."

From a small coolbag below the table she produced a small bottle of *Sohat*, handing it over to the monk. He cracked it open and drank.

"We have a room especially for you for tonight," said Love as Malek put the bottle down. "*Yalla*, come please." She led the way down a narrow corridor to the very back of the premises, stopping by a door padlocked on the outside, key still in the lock. "Naturally we no longer need this," she said as she turned the key and removed the padlock. At that moment they heard the front door opening. Love smiled. "Perfect timing." She raised her voice. "We are back here, sister!"

Paradise appeared at the other end of the corridor, a paper carrier bag in her right hand. As she walked towards them, she said "I bought some *shawarma* and *baklava* anyway. We must all retain our strength for the journey to come."

From underneath the hood, Malek said "But she did not phone you."

"She didn't need to," said Paradise.

"Saves a fortune on phone bills," said Love. "Sister, I was just about to show Malek his present."

Paradise nodded and Love pushed open the door. The light from the corridor cast an oblong into the room. Malek gestured for Love to enter ahead of him.

"There is no light in here," explained Love. "Just a small window. But we have lanterns if you require them later."

The light from the corridor and the light from the small window cast as much light as the forty watt bulb outside. Malek stepped into the room. In front of him a small figure was standing, tied with rope by both wrists to either end of the frame of a bunk bed. The figure wore a white, hooded towelling robe, the hood up covering the face. It moved as they entered, raising its head, trying to see. The feet below were bare and obviously female.

"Our latest disciple," said Love. "She wishes to convert. We think she is worthy."

"But of course she needs your vetting," said Paradise.

Love stepped forward and put both her hands on either side of the hood. Gently, almost tenderly, she pushed it back off the head, caressing and tidying the long black hair as she lifted it out.

The captive's mouth was gagged with a tight swatch of silk, thick red lips not quite able to join together over it. Heavy mascara and dark eyeshadow enhanced the blackness of her actual eyes.

Love undid the belt, allowing the gown to fall open, revealing the naked body underneath. Her face close, she reached behind the captive's head and undid the gag. She removed a lipstick smudge from the captive's chin with her thumb and then stood back, as if she was showing off a prize pet. She said, "Let me introduce you to The Djinn. She is one of us. She is skilled. Djinn, meet Malek, your king. Our Saviour."

"Leave us," said Malek after a few moments.

"Do you wish us to untie her?" asked Love.

"No, I will do that when I am ready. Go."

Obediently the twins left the room, closing the door behind them.

Carla looked at the robed figure as she moved her jaw, loosening it after the restriction of the gag. She noticed the hood go slightly up and down as he looked at her body. Apart from that he did not move at all. After a few moments he asked, "You are like them?" He had an accent but she understood him perfectly.

"They say I am."

The hood nodded. "Good answer. Do you belong to the Colonel?"

"No."

"But my *houri* rate you."

"Apparently."

A pause, then he asked "You will join us?"

"Do I have a choice?"

"I think the choice would have been explained to you. You will join us of your own free will or an alternative conversion will take place. It really doesn't matter which. Soon the whole world will be converted."

She looked at the hood and asked softly, penitentially, "May I join you?"

Malek raised his hands, palms outstretched. "I will test your worthiness. If you pass, who knows? You may be my favourite disciple of all." He raised his hands further, grasped the edge of his hood and casually pushed it back and off.

Carla stared at his face, at the proof. All along.

That Sajida was right.

Annaya, Lebanon 12:00

"Can't you ask them?" suggested Fadi Lattouf.

"No I bloody well can't," said Jihad Merhi grumpily. Another two hours of his life wasted. They were walking back down the side of the monastery, having walked up as far as a field and then deciding to turn back. It was quiet here, visitors didn't come up this far. "What am I supposed to do? Go and knock on the head guy's door and say 'Excuse me, but do you have anything up here that will scare a man so much that he will be chased down the mountainside into Beirut and murdered?' I feel as frustrated as you do, Fadi, but short of staking out the place I don't see what further I can do. We have looked everywhere, seen nothing."

They passed the open window of a monastery washroom but neither of them thought anything of it.

"Will you do it then?" asked Lattouf.

"Do what?"

"Stake the place out."

"On what grounds? I'd need a good reason, which I don't have."

"My cousin."

"Not good enough. So he writes these map co-ordinates on a card. Might not be anything to do with his death. We might be barking up the wrong mountainside."

"I don't think so. Lattouf feels it in his gut. Something happened up here."

"Like what?"

"Who knows? A ghost? You liked that little church but I found it scary."

"That's because you're used to a mosque. Our 'idol images' as you call them frightened you."

"That museum was scary too. The saint's robes with his body secretions and stains on it, I didn't like that at all."

"No, there I know what you mean. You think Chadi was frightened by the ghost of Saint Charbel? Or, being a Muslim, just by this whole place?"

Lattouf shrugged. "I don't know, I am not Christian."

"Well, Christian saints are not normally in the habit of appearing to people and scaring the shit out of them." Actually, on reflection, maybe they were, but he wasn't going to go there.

"But isn't it one of your major concepts that the dead shall rise again?"

Merhi shook his head. "Oh God, Fadi, you are walking proof that a little knowledge is a dangerous thing. It doesn't mean that at all."

"Oh."

To avoid further theological discussion, Merhi asked "Hungry?"

"Of course."

"There's a refreshment place down here. *Yalla*. Or are you too full from the rice?"

"What rice?"

Within ten minutes the staff of the refreshment kiosk were telling customers that they had run out of food, only drinks would be served for the rest of the day.

After thirty minutes sitting near the refreshment kiosk they walked back down the slope towards the car, Lattouf finishing off the last of the kiosk's potato chips. Merhi smoked.

"So, that is it?" Chip slivers bounced around on Lattouf's beard. "We are giving up again? Another dead end... just another dead Palestinian."

"Unless you can give me any form of probable cause, any new evidence, there is nothing more I can do. This is an unreported death, remember, and you were quick to dispose of the body."

"In accordance with our teachings."

"Well, sometimes teachings and criminal investigations don't go well together. I have no body, no tangible evidence of murder - "

"You saw the wound on the body yourself!"

"My examination of a body which no longer exists is not tangible evidence. We do not even have photographs."

"But you know he was murdered."

"Me knowing is not good enough. Is there nothing else, Fadi?" *Please let there not be.* "He didn't do any other little trick? Nothing popped out of anywhere else?"

Lattouf gave him a sideways look.

They reached the Land Cruiser, the vehicle's lights flashing as Merhi pressed the key fob. Lattouf screwed up the empty chip packet and threw it over the mountainside.

"Not very respectful," scolded Merhi.

Lattouf looked chasten. "I am sorry. I just feel frustrated. Please excuse me, Abu Samer." He shook his head. "My cousin must have left that clue for some reason. Have we missed something?"

Merhi took one last drag on his cigarette, pinched the end and launched the butt over the mountainside to follow the chip packet. "Come on, Fadi. Let's go home."

They climbed in and were soon negotiating the hairpins on the downward run.

Neither of them noticed the envelope on the floor in the back behind Lattouf. The one that had been slipped through the open back window of the car.

Bourj el-Barajneh, Beirut 15:00

Much to Merhi's relief, Lattouf had not moped or kept on about his cousin on the drive back. He was more interested in why Merhi did not use the inbuilt satnav on his dashboard. "It is marvellous what these things can do," said the expert. "You witnessed Google Earth yourself. It unravelled my cousin's clue for us."

"Satnav is pointless, Fadi," argued Merhi. "Just something else that everyone's been conned into thinking they cannot live without. What's wrong with a good old map? And they always have women's voices. There is only room for one woman's voice in this car."

"Please tell Gisele I wish her Allah's blessings."

"I will. Thank you. She'll be seeing you at *Eid*." Merhi could sense that Lattouf wanted to be invited back for dinner today but that was not going to happen, he had far too much work on and he was expecting a call at any time from Mr Carla asking for the voice recording.

Merhi slowed as they cruised down Annan Street, stopping just short of Lattouf's front door. They clasped hands. "Thank you, my friend, thank you," said Lattouf, sorrow but appreciation in his voice. "Believe me, I truly know that I ask a lot of our friendship. You are very gracious."

"Fadi..."

"If I think of anything else I'll give you a call." He stepped out of the car.

"Fadi..."

"Yes?"

"Allah's blessings upon you, my friend."

Lattouf nodded. "Thank you." He opened the back door, picked up his jacket which had fallen onto the floor, then slammed the door closed.

He stood on the sidewalk, smiling, raising a hand as Merhi pulled back out into the traffic and drove away. As the Land Cruiser disappeared, the smile turned into a grin. A big, naughty grin. He draped the jacket over his arm.

As he opened his front door he let go a stentorian breaking of wind. "Surprise, my family!" he called out. "Baba's home early. Isn't that nice?"

After embracing his wife, throwing Little Wissam into the air three times and (thankfully) catching him, and being ignored by the rest of the children who were jostling around the new computer, Lattouf went into his bedroom.

He had been naughty and he knew it. But he told himself he had done it as a favour to his friend Jihad, to force him to use new technology like the Lattoufs did. Once Jihad had tried the satnav in the car he would use it forever. And now he would have to – because Fadi had swiped the map he had seen on the back seat of the car!

Cousin Chadi had not been the only member of the family that was adroit with his hands. Fadi had seen the map on the back seat earlier. It had fallen on the floor along with his jacket when they were negotiating the curves on the mountainside. When he had retrieved his jacket he had purloined the map also, draping the jacket over it so it could not be seen. A master prestidigitator!

He threw the jacket onto the bed and looked at the map in his hand.

The map and the envelope.

His eyebrows rose and his mouth opened. He had not seen an envelope in the car! How had that happened? He must have picked it up when he picked up the map. Hiding it under his jacket had concealed it not only from Jihad but from himself also!

Shaitan's scrotum!

He would have to give his friend a ring, apologise, say it was accidentally picked up with his jacket (which was true), arrange to return it. Maybe Jihad would ask him to drive up to Jounieh with it tonight. Around eight o'clock, the time when the Merhi's had their dinner...

The thought made him realise he was on the point of expiring through starvation. Nada would not have started their evening meal yet, but he wondered if he could persuade her to bring it forward. He might have wasted away by tonight. He would eat first then phone Jihad afterwards.

Leaving the jacket, map and envelope on the bed, he went back to the family room, thoughts of Little Wissam on toast with a mustard relish popping into his mind. Not seriously, of course. Well, only in extreme circumstances...

Jonblat, Beirut 15:50

Merhi had pulled into the parking area behind the State Security offices. Now he sat in his car, engine running, looking up at the building, then looking at his watch, thinking. It was nearly four o'clock. Really, after his day with Lattouf up at Annaya, he didn't feel like going in to the office. The reports on visiting heads of state, street security, parliamentary discussions, press conferences, threatened attacks by the Jews, you name it, could wait until tomorrow. And no doubt there was today's shite waiting for him on his desk upstairs.

He looked at his phone, in the well next to him behind the transmission stick, his mind going off on a different tack. Why hadn't Mr Carla phoned? The memory stick with the copied Carla and Himo conversation was burning a hole in his pocket.

He lit up a cigarette, the nicotine helping him to make the decision.

Putting the transmission into Drive, he manoeuvred back out into Bank of

Lebanon Street. Soon he was heading east. Going home.

As he had not gone up to the office, Merhi did not know that on his desk, along with today's shite, was the response from Interpol relating to the facial composite drawing he had submitted. A positive identification had been made.

Jounieh, Lebanon 17:45

He was looking forward to a shower and then maybe an hour on the balcony with Johnnie Walker, watching the sun reluctantly setting over the Mediterranean. Then he would enjoy a good bottle of wine and whatever delicious concoction Gisele was preparing for dinner. She was already in the kitchen. As he came through the front door, he could hear the voices on the radio, she liked to listen to *VDL* while she cooked.

Smiling, he crossed the hallway and went into the kitchen – but she was not there, and the radio was not on. She must be in the living room with the TV.

He walked further down the hall, opened the living room door, and stopped dead.

"Husband," Gisele looked up smiling from one of the couches, large glass of red wine in her hand. "You're home early. We have a visitor."

Sitting on the couch opposite, tumbler of mineral water in his hand, was the man Merhi called Mr Carla.

"An unexpected pleasure," said Jihad insincerely, picking up a glass from the cabinet against the wall and sitting down on the couch next to his wife. On the table between the two couches was a bottle of *Massaya* red wine, olives, nuts and savoury biscuits.

"Yes, isn't it?" said Gisele.

Jihad picked up the bottle of wine and filled his glass to the brim.

"I was passing. Thought I'd pop in," explained The Damascene. His long black hair was down, hanging loosely either side of his face. He was wearing a black T shirt, usual jeans and sandals. "Kill two birds with one stone... as it were. I spent the day up at Annaya." His eyes held Jihad's.

Jihad took a mouthful of wine. "You been following me?"

"In a manner, yes. I wanted to talk to you, to give you back the report and the picture. But you had that large gentleman with you. A friend of yours?"

"Another case. Nothing to do with you."

Gisele leant back into the corner of the couch, pulling her legs up under her. The day was hot, she was wearing denim shorts and a yellow cotton vest. "You boys getting your dicks out again?" she asked, amused.

The Damascene smiled. Jihad said, "My dick stays right here. Where it belongs." He glanced at his wife's bare thighs.

The Damascene let the moment hang while he drank some water, then he asked "Did you get the envelope? I slipped it through your car window."

"What envelope?"

"I was returning the report and picture."

"Didn't see it. Must be on the floor, maybe under one of the seats."

"The report tells me nothing. An interesting picture, though."

"You know who it is?"

"I've heard of them. Thought it was a myth. Didn't think they would operate outside of their own territory. He must be sub-contracting."

"Them? There is more than one?"

"Oh yes."

Jihad waited, expectant, feeling more enamoured with the visitor. At last he would be told something. He drank more wine. When Mr Carla remained silent, he said "Well?"

"Well?"

"Aren't you going to tell me who it is? I can find her and arrest her. Put out an ATL*, make it official."

The Damascene gave a small laugh. "You think it is that easy? You will not locate this one unless she wishes to be located."

"Who is she?"

"I have no name."

"What is she?"

"That, my friend, is a good question. A bodyguard. An assassin... A *houri*?"

"A *what*?"

"Never mind."

"Jesus Christ, this is getting too mystical for me. *al-Mahdi, ad-Dajjal, houri*. What the hell is going on?"

The Damascene frowned. "How do you know these things?"

"Here," Merhi pulled out the memory stick from his trouser pocket and threw it onto the table. "The conversation between Carla and Himo."

The Damascene leant forward and picked it up.

Unfolding her tanned legs, Gisele stood up. "I'm going to make dinner. Will you stay? I'm making *samkeh harra*. You like spiced fish?"

"Yes, I do. And I would be honoured to stay, thank you."

Gisele turned to her husband. "Jihad, why don't you let our guest listen to that on the computer?"

"I - "

---

* *Attempt To Locate*

"It's no good to him otherwise, is it?"

Jihad stared at her legs and bottom as they left the room. Then he looked back at Mr Carla and asked, "Who is Sajida?"

"It is best - "

"If I don't know. Yes, yes, yes. You're protecting me, blah, blah. Jesus!" He was shaking his head as he stood up. "Come. The computer is in my study. I'll leave you to listen to that. I have an appointment out on the balcony."

Bourj el-Barajneh, Beirut 20:30

Despite his pleading, demanding, cajoling, shouting, and whimpering, Nada Lattouf was not going to prepare the evening meal any earlier than usual. Had her husband forgotten he was on a diet? Nevertheless, the puppy dog eyes made her take pity on him and she had given him some nuts and the very last remnants of yesterday's goat and rice, which had tided him over until dinner (she never knew that by those actions she had saved Little Wissam Lattouf from a fate worse than could possibly be imagined).

After a dinner of giblets, bread and rice, Fadi announced that he was going to the bedroom as he had work to do. Nada knew that this was a euphemism for having a nap, getting some peace and quiet from the children. The day her husband brought work home was the day she would know it was time for him to quit his job.

Closing the door, Fadi sat down on the bed, the mattress collapsing its usual twenty-five centimetres as The Arse descended upon it. He lifted his jacket and threw it to one side, flicking away the map and picking up the envelope. He turned it over in his hands. It had no address or any other writing on it. The flap was unsealed.

He must phone Jihad, tell him he had it safe; he might be missing it. The Merhis would have eaten by now so it could wait until the morning.

Wonder what was in it? The open flap called to him like a siren enticing sailors onto the rocks. No, he mustn't look at another person's mail, it was private.

He put his hand inside and brought out a stapled A4 document and a loose sheet. The document looked like an official report of some kind, an investigation into a death. Well it wasn't Chadi so he didn't care.

The loose sheet was blank on the side he was looking at. He turned it over. It was a drawing of a head –

He frowned, squinting, bringing the sheet closer to his face and then holding it at arm's length.

He went over to a drawer and fumbled inside for a pair of Nada's eyeglasses. He put them on, pink horn-rims, and stared at the drawing once more.

Well, Allah be praised, what was Jihad doing with a picture of her...?

Jounieh, Lebanon 21:00

Gisele was bringing fruit to the table when they heard Jihad's mobile ringing out in the hall. Normally he would have left it, checking on the Missed Call later and ringing back if necessary. But it was a good excuse for him to leave the table. He was getting mightily pissed off with the attention Mr Carla was receiving. Sympathy only went so far. Carla might be missing, or even dead, but that did not mean that Gisele had to step into the breach.

"Excuse me," he left the room as Gisele was unpeeling a banana, laughing at something Mr Carla had said.

He lifted his phone from the hall table, looking at the screen. Oh good heavens, it was Lattouf. He looked back at the dining room, looked at the phone, and decided to answer it.

"Merhi."

"Evening of joyous discovery, my friend!"

"*Merhaba*, Fadi." *Not another meaningless clue, please.*

"I am sorry to call you at this hour, you must be having your dinner, no?"

"Just finished."

"Oh." He sounded curiously disappointed. "Good. I was going to call you in the morning, but I thought you might be wondering where it was."

"Sorry? Wondering where what was?"

"The envelope."

"What envelope?"

"I accidentally picked it up from your car when I picked up my jacket."

"Envelope...?" He remembered what Mr Carla had said. "Ah yes, never mind. You can give it to me when we meet."

"It is not urgent?"

"Just some reports that... I left there. I have copies. But thanks for ringing."

"The papers slid out of the envelope... I, er, dropped it."

"Never mind, there's no state secrets there."

"Are you sure there are no secrets, my friend?"

"What do you mean?"

"You are a sly one, you know. I think you have been kidding Lattouf."

Merhi heard laughter from the dining room. "Fadi, I have a guest for dinner. I need to get back. What are you talking about?"

"Those twins, the ones from Jbeil, who we saw in the Jeep today."

"What about them?"

"You said you have only seen them from the back."

"Yes?"

"You crafty dog, you have a drawing of their face!"

Merhi literally staggered backwards.

"I have what?"

"This is a drawing of the twins' face. I have it here in my hand right now. The eyes are a bit funny, but it's them all right. Have you been doing doodles and having naughty thoughts?"

"Have I been...?" Merhi was aware that his mouth had dropped open but there was nothing he could do about it. His muscles had frozen. *What?* "I..." He was classically confused. Reason, thought and speech were fighting a raging battle in his head with nobody winning.

"Hello? Are you there, my friend?" There was a thumping as the phone was bashed up and down at the other end.

"Y-yes... Yes, I'm here," said Merhi. He couldn't believe it. *What?* "Fadi, I'm... I'm... What are you saying? Are you sure? That is the twins from Jbeil?"

"As if you did not know, you bull. Naturally your secret is safe with me, fellow men and all that."

"My secret...?" Merhi was standing in the middle of the hallway, phone held to his right ear, his left hand held to his head. "I don't... Well, fuck me."

"You should be saying that to the picture!" raucous all-boys-together laughter boomed out of the phone.

Merhi was breathing heavily, his heart pounding. Not again, surely? Surely The Idiot Lattouf had not bungled his way into solving another case? "Fadi, listen to me. My office, nine o'clock in the morning. Bring the drawing with you."

"And the report."

"I don't care about the report. And tell no one. Don't mention it to Nada, or any one of your team. Keep it to yourself."

"Mother is the word. But there are two of them, these twins. One isn't spare, is she? Sticky seconds? Or leftovers of any kind?"

"What? Don't... don't be such a filthy bastard. I don't know how you do it but I think you've just cracked another case."

"I have?"

Merhi was shaking his head. "Nothing short of amazing."

"I am, thank you. I keep telling Nada that."

Merhi gave an ironic, sarcastic laugh. "You're a crazy man. Don't happen to know who Sajida is as well, do you?"

Lattouf gave a loud laugh, joining in the fun, co-conspirators, a crack team, him and his mate Jihad. He said, "Sajida? Of course I know who she is, doesn't everybody?"

Five minutes later an ashen-faced Jihad Merhi returned to the dining room. Gisele had the stones of two plums on the plate in front of her, and she and Mr Carla were enjoying a little humour (something about Syria and the King of Lebanon). She looked up, smiling. "Who was it?"

"Lattouf." He stared at Mr Carla, his face hard. Then he went over to the sideboard and took two bottles of Johnnie Walker whisky from underneath. Reaching further in, he brought out a packet of two hundred Cedars King Size cigarettes. He tucked the cigarettes under his arm and carried a whisky bottle in each hand.

"I'm going outside," he said. "I need some air."

Jbeil, Lebanon 23:00

Brother Malek sat cross legged on a mat in the centre of the small room he had been allocated. He still wore his *burnus*, but the hood was off of his head. Next to him his golden *argileh* bubbled as he sucked long and slow on the pipe. The room was dim, lit only by a small candle in a saucer on the windowsill.

He held the smoke, letting it trickle down his nose naturally. His eyes were closed as he rocked back and forth in contemplation.

There was a gentle tap on the door and he stopped rocking. The smoke was still trickling out of his nose. Only when it stopped did he open his eyes and say, "Come."

Love opened the door, entering and stepping to one side. Behind her Paradise guided Carla into the room by the forearm. Carla's face was heavily made-up, eyes dark, lips red and full. Her black hair was down, falling over her chest and covering her naked breasts. Below she wore red diaphanous harem pants. Her feet were bare.

"Your djinn for conversion," announced Love.

Malek took another pull on the pipe, making the women wait. Then he said, "Leave us."

The twins gave a small bow and left the room, closing the door.

Carla stayed still, feeling his eyes travelling over her, inspecting. She in turn was studying the *argileh*. Was that solid gold? The apple and mint smell of the tobacco fought with her own heavy jasmine perfume.

After two more languorous inhalations, Malek draped the hose over the plate of the *argileh* and put his hands on his knees. He asked, "Do you still wish to be converted?"

"Yes, I do."

"This is your free choice?"

"It is."

He looked at her some more. Then slowly he stood up. "You know who I am?"

"Yes."

"And you wish to be part of The Second Coming?"

"I do."

Malek undid his belt, the *burnus* falling open. "We must all appear before the seat of judgment, so that each one may receive what is due for what he has done in the body, whether good or evil. Whosoever shall deny me before men, I will also deny. Do you deny me?"

"I do not deny you."

Malek put out his hands. "True conversion starts from within. I believe you are worthy. Come to me, my child. You are welcome."

23 July 2010
11 Sha'ban 1431

Jounieh, Lebanon 02:30

Normally two large glasses of red wine and half a bottle of whisky would have him pissed out of his mind, unaware even of his very existence. But not tonight. When he craved for oblivion it would not happen. For hours he had lain on the sun lounger in the dark, slapping off the mosquitoes, willing himself into unconsciousness. But no.

Flat on his back, Merhi stared up at the diamante night sky. A few minutes ago he had watched the waxing gibbous moon setting out over the Mediterranean. In two hours the sun would be rising behind him.

His mind was a raging cascade, thoughts, ideas and memories bouncing off each other in a maelstrom of confusion. Oh Lattouf, why had you ever entered his life? One phone call and Lattouf had given him the double tap whammy, as efficient as any executioner, killing his sense of reason. Killing his sanity.

Disembodied phrases swam in his head, over and over. "Had to be Lebanon, didn't it?" – Mr Carla. "The dead shall rise again" – Lattouf. "Plenty of places to hide, in the mountains" – Mr Carla. And always the one word, the name: Sajida.

Sajida, Sajida, Sajida.

Well, he just did not believe it. He would not believe it. It was ridiculous. Preposterous. The Second Coming was a myth, a religious lie to give the gullible a reason for living, to help them make sense of the nonsense that is life.

A thought struck him and he raised himself up onto his elbows, frowning. He looked around for his phone before realising he had left it on the hall table. What time was it anyway?

Slowly he moved into a sitting position. His hips ached after the hours on the lounger. On the floor tiles next to him was a pile of cigarette butts, too numerous to count. Knees creaking, he stood up, avoiding the butts, expecting the world to spin. But it remained steady. He took a tentative step... no loss of balance.

He was pleasantly surprised. No feeling of drunkenness, no hangover symptoms – except for his mouth, which tasted like a mountain lion had crept over his balcony while he was asleep, shat down his throat and then run off. He tried to wet his lips, but his tongue felt like a desert cactus. Only one solution. He bent down, picked up the open bottle of whisky, filled his mouth and swilled the nectar around before swallowing it.

He walked over to the sliding glass door, opening it carefully, trying not to disturb the man asleep on the couch inside. He had been unable to disguise his displeasure when Gisele had suggested Mr Carla stay for the night but he had won the subsequent clenched-teeth low-growl argument in the kitchen: they would not make up a bed for him, he would sleep on the couch.

Soundlessly he opened and closed the door leading to the hall. It was dark but he did not want to risk putting on the light. His hands flap-fumbled across the top of the table until they landed on his phone. He pressed a random key and the phone lit up, sending a powerful beam straight up into his eyes.

Squinting, he found the Phonebook, scrolled halfway through the alphabet and pressed the Call key.

Bourj el-Barajneh, Beirut 02:45
Jounieh, Lebanon 02:45

Fadi Lattouf was flat on his back, mouth wide open, snoring like a Harley-Davidson doing top speed with a broken silencer. Occasionally his mouth moved and his cheeks twitched. Next to him Nada knew that this would be yet another night in her very long marriage when she slept only intermittently.

Lattouf was dreaming he was being interrogated by a set of naked blonde female triplets; he was tied down, also naked, and at their mercy. One girl was tickling his feet, one was squeezing his pineapples and the other one was tweaking his nipples. They kept asking over and over *Who killed Chadi? Who killed Chadi?* He tried to tell them he did not know but they ignored him. *Who killed Chadi? Who killed Chadi?* The one at his feet stopped tickling and opened a bag of potato chips. She placed a chip between each of his toes and then leant forward and began eating them. *Who killed Chadi? Who killed Chadi?* The one squeezing his pineapples got to work unpeeling his banana. *Who killed Chadi? Who killed Chadi?* The third one stopped tweaking his nipples and turned, backing up towards him. *Who killed Chadi? Who killed Chadi?* Her bottom was just ten centimetres away from his face, and he was sticking out his tongue trying to reach it, when music started playing. That was nice, how thoughtful - what the...?

Lattouf's eyes shot open, confused. His tongue was still poking out of his lips, prodding the air. His throat was sore. The triplets had gone but the music was still playing. Something was covering his left eye, he couldn't see out of it. Was this his punishment for impure dreams? Panic slapped him awake and he sat up in bed, his hand coming up to move his fallen comb-over away from his eye and back over his head. The music was still playing. If that was one of the children at this hour he would beat their hide raw.

Then he realised it was his mobile. In the name of Allah, who was calling him at this time of night?

He got up off the bed, causing Nada to bounce like flotsam on a stormy ocean. Retrieving his phone from next to his glass of water, he sat back down, Nada bouncing some more.

In this light and without Nada's glasses, the screen on the phone was a blur. "Yes?" he barked, thinking he was talking quietly, waking all light sleepers within a ten block radius. "Who is this?"

"Fadi, it's Jihad."

"Jihad? My friend, are you okay? Do you know what time it is?"

"Were you asleep?"

"Asleep? Me? No, no, I... I was just preparing for *Fajr* prayer." With three naked blonde triplets.

"I need to ask you something. To do with Chadi."

"You have found something? You have another clue?"

"No, but you might."

"Me?"

"The card that popped out of his pocket. The one he wrote the co-ordinates on. What was it?"

There was a puzzled pause. "It was a card. I'm sorry, I don't know what you mean."

"Yes but what card was it? You know, two of diamonds, three of clubs?"

"Oh. I don't know. Hold on, it is still in my jacket."

Lattouf got back up off the bed and went over to his old wardrobe. The door opened to much creaking and clunking. "Where the hell is it?" he mumbled to himself. "Where did she hang it...?"

He reached out and turned on the light. On the bed, Nada moaned and rolled onto her side, her hand coming up to shield her eyes.

"Ah, here it is." He pushed other clothes aside, some falling off their hangers, and stuck his fingers into the top pocket of his jacket, pulling out the card. After a moment he said, "Jihad, it is the ace of spades."

There was silence on the other end of the phone.

"Jihad, are you there? Hello?"

"Fadi, I want you to bring that card and the drawing of the twin to me right now. I'm at home."

"Now? But we are meeting in the morning."

"Not any more we're not. We have things to do. I need you to bring them to me right now."

"But I cannot."

"You can. You know where I live, you know how to get here."

"I can't."

"Don't worry about your prayer, Allah will understand. Say it on the way."

"I really can't."

"Fadi, have I ever asked you for anything? Think of all the stuff I've done for you. Really, I need you to bring the card and drawing to me now. You and I have things to do. The roads will be emptier at this hour, it will be good driving."

"I... I can't."

Merhi was angry. "Why?"

"I... I have no lights on the van. They don't work."

There was a stunned silence. Then, with a sigh that could be heard as far south as Sidon, Merhi said "It will be light in two hours. Come then. Don't let that card out of your sight. And tell no one."

"Are we going to find Chadi's murderer?"

"My friend, I think we are."

Tears welled in Lattouf's eyes. Emotionally, he said "May Allah bless you, my friend."

But Merhi had already clicked off.

Nada turned in the bed, raising her head, her eyes still screwed up against the light. "Who was that?"

Fadi was standing by the wardrobe, fallen clothes at his feet, holding the playing card in his hand, wearing just his outsize boxer shorts. Wet eyes looked across at his wife. "That... that was Jihad." He tapped the card. "He thinks he has found Chadi's killer. I am to go to him at daybreak."

She laid her head back down on the thin pillow. As she turned away from him, she said "Husband, I think it is time you quit your job. Find something better to do. Something more suited to your incredible brain power..."

She fell asleep.

Without turning around, Merhi asked "Like listening in on other people's conversations?"

"I assume the drawing you were talking about is the one done by my wife?" said the voice behind him.

The light from Merhi's phone had dimmed by fifty per cent but, as he turned round, it gave him enough light to see the shadow leaning against the living room door jamb.

"And what is this about a card?" continued The Damascene.

"Just something I've discovered."

"Who were you talking to?"

Merhi smiled, enjoying having the upper hand. "My fat friend. He is a Palestinian police chief."

The light on the phone went out completely.

"He is coming here?" said the voice from the darkness.

Merhi waited for his eyes to adjust. "Yes."

"Why?"

"To find the person who killed his cousin."

The Damascene paused, reflecting. "And what is that to do with my wife's drawing?"

Merhi did not answer, instead he said "I know who Sajida is."

Another pause. "Really? Well good for you. What has a Palestinian police chief to do with my wife's drawing?"

"He knows who the woman in the drawing is."

"So do I."

"But do you know where she is?"

The atmosphere changed palpably. Dangerously. The Damascene pushed himself up off the door jamb. "Do we need to talk?"

"Yes, we do," Merhi stood his ground. "My friend will be here in three hours. We'll talk then."

"In the meantime," said Gisele's voice from the doorway of the master bedroom, "do you boys want some coffee? Or is it dicks at dawn?"

Jounieh, Lebanon 06:00 – 07:15

Lattouf was dressed in his old jeans and pink and blue checked shirt. "Morning of joy, my friend!" he pumped Jihad's hand furiously, patting him on the back with the hand that carried the envelope. "Morning of peace, Gisele."

As Gisele reciprocated the Morning of Peace, Jihad said "Come in, Fadi. Your van worked all right?"

"Fine, fine. It's just the lights, no big deal."

"Come through, we're having breakfast." Jihad took the offered envelope and led the way into the living room.

The first thing Lattouf noticed was the table spread with meats, cheeses, labneh, tomatoes, cucumber, dates, pastries and donuts. The second thing he noticed was the man standing next to the table, plate in his hand.

"Fadi, this is..."

"An old friend of Jihad and his charming wife." The Damascene shook the fat man's hand.

"Allah's blessings upon you," said Lattouf to the man with the long hair tied back in a ponytail, noticing the scarring on the left side of his face under the hair.

"Thank you. And upon you."

"Please help yourself to food," encouraged Jihad. "We have some talking to do."

Gisele appeared with two pots, one a *rakwe* with Turkish coffee, the other a *dallah* with cardamom-flavoured Arabic coffee. Putting them on the table next to the small, handleless cups, she said "Sit down all of you. Be comfortable."

Five minutes later they were seated with their plates, Lattouf's piled perilously high, coffees on small side tables. Gisele and The Damascene sat on one couch, Lattouf and Jihad on the other.

"Right, where do I begin?" Jihad ate bread and *labneh*.

"Maybe at the beginning?" suggested The Damascene.

Gisele smiled. Lattouf ate.

Jihad spoke. "There are two separate cases here. Completely different, apparently no connection between them. But then as they go on, as they are investigated, slowly slowly they join." He pinched grease-covered fingers together. "First, yours." He nodded at The Damascene. "Case Number One. Just over two weeks ago I am contacted by your wife, Carla."

"Your wife?" said Lattouf, not yet understanding what was going on but enjoying the food enormously. "Congratulations."

The Damascene looked at him but said nothing.

Jihad went on. "I knew her in the past. Five years ago. The Hariri assassination. She was not called Carla then. But she was a member of the ESU, as she is now. That's the External Security Unit, Fadi."

"Oh."

"She asks me to help her. Her boss has been murdered and she thinks she is in danger. She has been attacked. She won't tell me why because I don't know who Sajida is. Saj–bloody–ida. She asks me to get some CCTV footage for her. And she asks if she can stay with me – us." He looked over at Gisele. "Naturally we agreed, colleague in distress and all that. I get the CCTV, she examines it, confirms the same person killed her boss as attacked her. It's a woman. A woman with white eyes. She sketches a composite," he nodded at the envelope on the floor beside him, "I run it through the system. Nothing. I refer it to Interpol. They've yet to report back, systems have been down." He paused to drink coffee. "Then I'm contacted by Carla's new boss, wanting to know why I've requested the CCTV footage. Long story short, I have to tell him about Carla, Carla asks to meet him. They meet – you've heard the conversation. She tells us she is going to work the case with her new boss. Then, while Gisele and I are both out, she disappears. Leaves. Some of her stuff is still in the wardrobe in the bedroom – you'd best take it. That was a week ago." He paused as Lattouf got up and poured himself more coffee from the *dallah*. The Palestinian looked around, holding the pot in the air. The Damascene and Gisele shook their heads, Jihad held his cup up for refilling.

"Okay," continued Jihad, watching Lattouf pile more food onto his plate. "Case Number Two. My friend Fadi here, Captain Lattouf of the Palestinian civil police." Lattouf turned and bowed. "This one I will cut very short. Fadi contacts me to tell me that his cousin has been found dead on his doorstep. We examine the body and confirm he has been murdered, something injected into him. Fadi's cousin was a private investigator operating out of Jbeil. By various methods we establish that he was up at the Annaya monastery the afternoon of his death. We deduce that he saw something up there that made him dash down to his cousin, his only relative, in Beirut. He was murdered before he had the chance to talk."

The Damascene put his empty plate down on top of Gisele's on the side table. "And what is the connection?"

"Ah, this is where Fadi comes in," Jihad looked at Lattouf who smiled, donut protruding between his teeth. "He has solved it. He doesn't even realised it but he has solved it."

Lattouf bowed again. "Thank you. You are too kind."

"When we went to Jbeil to examine his late cousin's premises, Fadi noticed two women in the street. I hardly saw them, we were walking behind them." He noticed Gisele's eyebrows raise. "But Fadi had seen them from the front. They were twins. Identical twins. We commented on how nature was wonderful, didn't we Fadi? Fadi!"

"Yes. Yes." Lattouf had dropped half a pastry on the floor. He bent down, picked it up and put it into his mouth.

"They went one way, we went the other. Thought no more about it. Now this is where it gets interesting, and a little complicated. I'll try to keep it simple. As his cousin lay dying, a card popped out from his jacket pocket."

"Popped out?" The Damascene shook his head, not understanding.

"A trick. Don't worry about it. On this card were some numbers. Twelve of them, written straight across the card, corner to corner. It took us a while to find out but we finally realised they were geographical co-ordinates. And they were pointing us to Annaya in the mountains, the Saint Charbel place. As you know, we went there yesterday. And didn't Fadi see the twins again up there, they were driving away as we got there."

"And they had somebody in the back of their car," said Lattouf.

Merhi frowned. "Did they?"

"Yes."

"You never told me that."

"Sorry. Couldn't see who it was. Didn't think it was important."

For a minute Jihad stared at the Palestinian, then he turned back and continued. "Still one might say so what?"

"I think I see where this is going," said The Damascene.

"Then last night I had that call at dinnertime, remember? It was Fadi. He had accidentally picked up that envelope you had so cleverly sneaked into the car." He leant forward and picked the envelope up off the floor. "The contents fell out and he saw this." He pulled out the drawing and held it up. "Carla's composite. Fadi recognised it. This is the face of the twins. And this..." he put his hand back into the envelope and pulled out the playing card, "is the card his cousin wrote on with the Annaya co-ordinates." He threw it across into The Damascene's lap. "Look at the suit. The ace of spades, the death card. Still I made no connections. Then Fadi told me about Sajida. And it all fell into place."

The room was silent. Jihad looked triumphantly across at The Damascene. The Damascene was looking at the card, turning it over. Gisele was looking at The Damascene's lap. Lattouf was looking at the final pastry before he put it into his mouth.

"The Second Coming and then some," said Merhi. "It wasn't some *thing* Fadi's cousin saw, it was some *one*. And it got him killed. And the twins, who you are looking for, are in Jbeil."

"And we think we know where," said Lattouf, cottoning on, the whole mystery falling into place in his head with the sudden rapidity of a building being imploded.

"If your wife is still alive, she is probably there with them," said Jihad.

The Damascene was breathing through flared nostrils. "She is still alive. I feel it. Do you have weapons?"

"Two guns."

"That will do. Come, we must go." The Damascene stood up.

"Just one thing," said Gisele, unfolding her legs and moving to the edge of the couch. She looked up at all three men now standing. "Who is Sajida?"

The full sun was already up over the mountains behind them as the three men left the apartment block. "Take my van?" suggested Lattouf.

"Yes of course we will, Fadi," said Merhi. "Not. Can you just imagine a Palestinian police van roaming the streets of Jbeil? We'll take my car, get in." He looked at the other man who was heading towards the side of the building. "Come with us," he called.

"No. I have a bike," said The Damascene over his shoulder. "I will follow you."

Merhi climbed into his Land Cruiser, Lattouf already ensconced. "He has a bike?" scoffed Lattouf. "It will need to be something to keep up with us - "

They heard a roar and then the black Suzuki Hayabusa rolled up beside them.

"Maybe not," said Lattouf.

Merhi smiled and made a mental note to get someone to ticket Mr Carla for not wearing a crash helmet. "*Yalla.*"

Gisele watched from the balcony above. She was grumpy because they had refused to tell her who Sajida was, three boys with the knowledge leaving the woman in ignorance 'for your own protection'. Ridiculous. She had more experience in covert activity than the three of them put together. Probably. Jihad and Fadi she knew, but she was unsure of Carla's husband. What was his provenance? He was tall, dark, mysterious – and he emitted an aura of danger. Not someone you would like to come across on a dark night. She grinned. Then again...

She watched Jihad's Toyota head down the mountainside, the monster of a motorbike following close behind. Touching two fingers of her right hand to her lips and then to her heart, she said softly "God speed, my heroes. I hope you know what you are doing."

Jbeil, Lebanon 07:30

Love tapped on the door.

It was a full minute before the voice from within said, "Come."

Brother Malek was sitting cross-legged on the mat, puffing on his *argileh*. His *burnus* was loosely around his body. Love glanced at the floor in front of the mat where a pair of diaphanous red harem pants were crumpled in a ball. "I expected her to be here."

Malek took the pipe from his mouth. "She was a worthy and adept convert. The process was completed quickly. You are now three."

Love nodded without comment.

Malek went on, "She has returned to her room, to pray, give thanks and to rest. I have told her of our plans and of the great journey that begins today."

Love picked up the harem pants. "My sister has prepared breakfast. It awaits you. We will leave in an hour. With the grace of Allah, we will be at Haouch Moussa by midday, where The Circle awaits us."

Malek nodded, putting the pipe back into his mouth.

Love turned, raising the pants to her nose. She went out and closed the door. Paradise was standing in the corridor."You heard?" asked Love.

"We are three. Your decision to keep her was right, sister. He is pleased with us." Paradise stroked Love's face. "But she will be on probation until we reach the Holy City."

"Forty days and forty nights. Fitting."

"Let's see how she is, he can sometimes be over zealous with his conversions, as we know."

They walked down the corridor, knocked on a door at the end and entered. Inside it was dim, just a square beam of light coming in through the high-up window. The room was heavy with the scent of jasmine.

Carla was sitting on the bed and she looked up as they came in.

"*Salaam, oh djinn,*" said Paradise.

Carla stood up, stark naked, her long black hair framing her make-up smudged face. "*Salaam,*" she replied quietly.

Love took her by the arm and guided her into the beam of light. "There is blood on your mouth. Was he brutal?"

"No, it just happened."

Gently, Love raised her hands and wiped the tears from Carla's cheeks with her thumbs.

"Do you hurt anywhere else?" asked Paradise.

Carla shook her head. "He was proper. He was divine. I am just happy. Thank you both for saving me."

Love leant forward and softly kissed her lips, tasting the blood. "He has told you of the great journey?"

"Yes."

"We leave in an hour. Clean yourself. The bathroom is free. We will bring you clothes."

"We think we've got the right size," Paradise was staring at Carla's hairless body.

"Then there is food outside," continued Love. "It will be the last time we eat until Haouch Moussa."

Carla nodded. "Thank you, sisters. You are very kind. I am not worthy of you." She knelt down on the floor, aware of four surprised white eyes looking at her. "But before I do anything, I need to pray." She held out her hands in supplication.

Love stepped back. "Of course. We will leave you."

"I'll be back with the clothes shortly," said Paradise as they went out.

As soon as the door had closed, Carla stood up. She wiped her bloodied lips with the back of her hand, grateful that the one they called *al-Mahdi* had not come in with them. He would have been astonished, because the cuts were nothing to do with him. She had done them herself, couldn't be helped, needs must.

But she was praying. Praying with all her spirit. Praying that her husband was here, that he would come to rescue her.

Otherwise she would have to kill these fucking bitches all on her own.

Jbeil, Lebanon 08:30

Merhi turned into the parking area just beyond the Seven Seas Restaurant on Boulevard al-Mina, pulling up facing the old harbour. As he turned off the engine he watched the fishing boats bobbing on the water. It had been an uneventful drive up to Jbeil. Uneventful but not quiet, because next to him Fadi Lattouf had snored like a rutting boar for most of the journey.

The Suzuki Hayabusa drove in next to the Land Cruiser.

"Fadi," Merhi shook the Palestinian's hairy arm. "Fadi!"

"Mm? What? Oh, we are here? That was quick."

"You've been asleep for the last hour."

He rubbed his hands down his face. "Lattouf never sleeps. I was just resting my eyes."

"*Yalla*, we have work to do."

Lattouf got out, nodding at The Damascene and then jumping as the Land Cruiser's lights flashed as Merhi pressed the lock key. Merhi came round, a bulky rolled up yellow and green *Spinneys* carrier bag in his hand. They wore no jackets and wearing holsters would have been too conspicuous, so the guns were simply in a carrier.

"Are you sure you can remember where the women went?" asked The Damascene.

"I have a photographic memory," said Lattouf, not mentioning that the photograph in his head was one of the twins' backsides as he followed them down the road. "Come."

They could smell the sea air as they walked out of the parking area and turned left onto Boulevard al-Mina. Merhi and Lattouf smoked.

Beyond the Seven Seas Restaurant, Lattouf led the way across the road, like a tour guide. They walked parallel with the medieval town wall then turned right through the ramparts into Rue St John.

"It was just down here, past the bookshop," explained Lattouf.

When they reached the bookshop, Lattouf nodded to the right."They went down this alley."

Merhi threw away his cigarette and began to unroll the carrier bag.

"Not yet," The Damascene raised a hand. "Wait. Let us see what is down here." He led the way, followed by Merhi. Lattouf brought up the rear, feeling at home in the confines of the narrow alley. Its width reminded him of the 'streets' in the camp – but without the broken pipes, sagging cables and crumbling buildings.

The alley was short and widened into a sunny patio area in front of a half-boarded up shop. Merhi guessed that it probably used to be a baker's, with tables outside for customers to relax in the sun. There was nothing else down here, just a dead end.

"It must be here," said Lattouf authoritatively. The Damascene put a finger to his own lips, the corners of Lattouf's mouth dropping like a scolded schoolboy. The Damascene nodded at the bag in Merhi's hand.

Spinneys carrier bags are thick and it seemed to make an unnecessary noise in the alley as Merhi unrolled it. He dipped inside and brought out Gisele's Smith and Wesson 642. The Damascene made silent gestures that Merhi and Lattouf should have the guns. Merhi passed the Smith and Wesson to the Palestinian, the small gun instantly disappearing in the folds of the large hand. Merhi brought out his own official-issue Herstal 9mm. He thought of screwing up the carrier bag and putting it in his pocket but then decided that the better and quieter option was simply to let it drift to the ground.

The front window of the shop was boarded up but the door wasn't. Standing to the side, The Damascene stretched out a hand, carefully, tentatively trying the small round doorknob. It turned...

The door creaked open twenty centimetres, and the three men flattened themselves against the wall in case of gunfire from within. There was nothing. The Damascene stretched out and shoved the door some more. More creaking. No reaction from inside.

Crouching, The Damascene pushed the door wide open, waited, then cautiously leaned inside. Slowly he straightened up. "Seems empty." He stepped inside. "But people have been here, I can smell them. The place is warm." He sniffed the air and was still and quiet. He sniffed again. Jasmine. "She was here." He could not hide the relief in his voice. "She was here and she's alive."

Merhi and Lattouf entered. Merhi screwed up his eyes, straining to see round the large, empty room. "We should have brought torches."

"Wait." Lattouf disappeared back outside. Suddenly there was a loud ripping sound as he pulled the board off the front window with his bare hands. Light flooded in. The board was discarded to much banging and clattering.

"There," beamed Lattouf, coming back in. "Light!"

There was a small table in the shop area with food detritus on it. Lattouf scooped something out of a foil container with his finger, sniffed it and put it into his mouth. He announced, "*Tahini*."

As well as the front shop area there were three rooms and a small, basic bathroom in the back. One room smelt distinctly of tobacco. The bathroom was damp, warm and heavy, recently used. Another room was empty. The final room, at the back, had an old metal-framed bunk bed against the wall.

The three men stood in the final room, Lattouf leaning against the bed, Merhi standing in the doorway, The Damascene in the centre of the room, tense, senses alert, breathing heavily. He said, "This is where they kept her. I can smell her."

Lattouf sniffed and shook his head at Merhi with a facial shrug.

"So what now?" asked Merhi. "She is alive and that's good. But where have they gone? Where have they taken her?"

The Damascene was quiet. Lost in thought, he scooped his hair up either side of his head, tightening his ponytail. For the first time Merhi and Lattouf saw the hole in the left side of his head where his ear had once been. Lattouf stepped back in shock, grabbing hold of the upright of the bed, looking at Merhi then back at The Damascene. Merhi too was gawking, but neither man said anything.

Ponytail tightened, The Damascene asked "Did your cousin leave any other clues? Anything whatsoever?"

Lattouf shook his head, still grimacing at the now covered hole. Merhi said, "Nothing. That was all. He led us to Annaya."

"And you led us here," The Damascene was nodding in contemplation. "They're on the move, aren't they? But where? To another hide out? Or is this The Second Coming? Has it begun?"

They were quiet, two men in thought, Lattouf staring at The Damascene's head.

After a minute Merhi said, "I have been an idiot." The other two looked at him. "A complete and utter fucking idiot. The Second Coming will be when Satan is cast out. I was asked to prepare a report on this recently, to see if it would have any affect on Lebanon internally. Haven't you been keeping up with the news? The Great Satan is leaving even now, with a deadline of this coming August thirty-first."

Lattouf simply looked bemused. The Damascene said, "My God, yes. It fits. Then it *is* The Second Coming. He is returning, as he said he would. His journey has started."

"But the question is, which way will he go?" pondered Merhi.

"And why does he have my wife?"

Lattouf could not understand a word they were saying, they might have just as well been speaking Slavic rather than Levantine Arabic. He could *hear* what they were saying but none of it made sense. He straightened up, his hand still gripping the bed frame – and he stopped, frowning.

His fingers moved up and down the metal frame, touching, feeling, stroking. He said, "Jihad, can I borrow your lighter?"

Merhi scowled. "Not now. Wait till we're outside."

"No, I don't want a smoke. I want your lighter."

Sighing, Merhi took his disposable *Bic* from his pocket and threw it over. It landed in the bouncy castle of Lattouf's left hand, his right hand still on the bed frame.

Lattouf flicked the lighter once, twice, three times before the flame caught. Then he brought it towards his right hand, at the same time leaning under the top bunk, screwing up his eyes as he looked at where his fingers had been. "There is something here," he said, "but I don't have my glasses. Can either of you see it?"

"What the hell are you talking about?" asked Merhi.

The Damascene stepped across, rubbing his hand on the bed frame where Lattouf indicated. Saying nothing, he took the lighter and bent under the top bunk as Lattouf had done. Then he straightened back up, a small smile on his face. A smile of triumph. A smile of love. "I knew she wouldn't let me down." He nodded at Merhi, nodded at the bed frame and held out the lighter.

Merhi came over, performing the same contortion as the other two had done. The flame flickered as he moved it back and forth, up and down. A word had been scratched into the gray bed frame, probably using a fingernail or something. The letters were shaky and bitty, as if the person who wrote them could not see what they were doing. But it was a word, definitely.

Aanjar

Coastal Highway, Lebanon 09:15

The constantly heavy traffic on the coastal highway is always more intense on Fridays and Mondays. They had been on the road for fifty minutes, sometimes moving fast, sometimes slowing to a standstill, and had just past over the Nahr el Kalb (Dog River) to the north of Beirut. But they did not need to rush, they were in no hurry. They had forty days and forty nights.

The Jeep had its hard top on. Paradise drove, Love sitting next to her. In the back, Carla sat next to the hooded Brother Malek. Carla was dressed in identical clothes to the twins: white vest top, combat cargo pants and boots, but her lustrous black hair and black eyes were in contrast to the blonde haired, white-eyed sisters.

She sat with her arms folded, scabby nail-less fingers screwed into fists and tucked under her arms. Her mouth still hurt where she had carved the word *Aanjar* on the bedpost with her teeth. One of her upper central incisors was chipped but it was too small to be noticed. And The Bitches had thought the blood on her mouth was caused by Malek!

Malek had in fact hardly touched her during the 'conversion', and she had certainly not been violated or abused. They had joined hands, he had mumbled prayers and had then breathed into her nose for five minutes, a warm and curiously sensual experience, his tobacco tainted breath strangely calming. Then he had made her kneel down and lick his feet, the posture making her more aware of her nudity.

After five minutes he had lain on the floor next to her. He was naked under the *burnus* and he pressed himself against her from behind, in the spoon position, his flesh hairy and hot. He had draped the open *burnus* over them and they had stayed that way for probably two hours. She might even have slept.

In the middle of the night he had told her to leave. As she opened the door, he said "Welcome, my disciple. You have chosen the true way."

She had not turned round but she had been aware of his eyes on her. She said, "Thank you," and went out, closing the door, suppressing a giggle and thanking the true God that Malek had not said she would be sitting on his right hand in Paradise. She might not have been able to contain herself.

Now she gave an inward ironical laugh. They called him Malek, which meant The King. The King of Kings? In his mind he was, and there were people who thought so too. Others thought he was *ad-Dajjal*, the devil who had been responsible for the death of millions in his own name.

She looked out of the window at the Mediterranean on her right and thought of her husband. Was he here? Most definitely, she knew, she could sense his presence in the country. Would he discover the disused shop in Jbeil? Would he find her etched clue? Yes, he would. But how long would it take him?

She watched the gentle lapping of the sun-dappled sea against the coastline as she sipped water from a bottle.

Tomorrow they would start the journey across the desert in another country, which would hold no fear for the man known as The Damascene. But forty days after that, when they reached the Promised Land, it would be a whole different ball game.

Come quickly, my love.

For both our sakes.

Jbeil, Lebanon 09:15

"How long ago did they leave?" wondered Merhi as the three men left the disused bakery and headed back down the alley. He could sense an air of urgency around Mr Carla.

"Not long," said The Damascene. "The bathroom was still warm. There was a residual human aura in the rooms. I'd say an hour."

They turned left into Rue St John.

"Then we can catch them," said Lattouf, slightly out of breath, trying to keep up (both physically and mentally).

"Possibly. We know they are going to Aanjar, but their route after that could be one of many. I wonder if they have changed vehicles?"

"Not here," said Merhi, "but they might be changing on route. Perhaps..."

"When they get to Aanjar," nodded The Damascene.

They walked out through the ramparts and turned left, crossing Boulevard al-Mina.

"So we must stop them." To Lattouf the answer was simple.

"Indeed, my friend," agreed The Damascene. "Obviously they are going across the desert, heading east, which figures. But there are many ways and many means. If we pick the wrong route there will be no way we can stop them."

"You really want to stop him, to change history?" Merhi lit up a cigarette, tossing one to Lattouf. The Palestinian caught it in his mighty hand, the cigarette bending in half on impact. Nevertheless he put it in his mouth, leaning forward for a light, skipping so as not to break stride.

"Or stop him changing history, perhaps," mused The Damascene. "But no. Him I don't care about. What will be, will be. That is for the authorities. For you and your kind. All I care about is my wife. We must take her back."

They entered the car park.

"So Aanjar it is then," said Merhi. "There or before. Before they leave Lebanon."

"Can't you put out an ATL?" suggested Lattouf, smoke rising upwards from the dangling half of his cigarette.

Merhi turned as they reached the Land Cruiser. "Saying what? Think about it, who would believe us?"

"Tell them Sajida was right."

"And who would believe that? And anyway, there are those that want their so-called al-Mahdi to return, we could be putting ourselves in danger. No, we're in this on our own. We will find Carla and the women who killed your cousin. The rest we will leave to fate."

The car's lights flashed as Merhi unlocked it. "Get in."

The Damascene climbed onto the Suzuki and once again tightened his ponytail. "I will be able to move quicker than you through the traffic." The bike started with a purring growl. "They will be taking the main Damascus road. If anything should happen, I will wait for you on route. Otherwise I will contact you from Aanjar." With an accelerating roar, the Suzuki drove off.

Merhi and Lattouf stood by the side of the Land Cruiser, cigarettes in mouths, trying not to look impressed.

After a few more quick silent sucks, both men stubbed their butts out under foot. As they climbed into the car, Lattouf patted his gut and asked "Can we stop off for some food on the way? I'm famished."

Mount Lebanon 11:30

Carla began to feel queasy as they drove by Bhamdoun, high up in the mountains. By the time they were passing above Qabb Elias, with the stunning eastwards view over the Bekaa Valley, she felt decidedly strange. At first she thought it could be altitude or motion sickness, but they were not things she suffered from. And she did not feel sick, just... odd.

Now as they descended to Chtaura, her head lolled and involuntarily she leant slowly, gently onto the shoulder of Brother Malek.

Paradise saw it in the rear-view mirror and smiled, nudging her sister.

Love looked round. "Just a little something we put in her water," she explained to the cowled figure. "To keep her docile until we start our journey. We always have to be careful with new converts in case they regress. Once we are out of Lebanon she will have less reason to change her mind."

For a moment Malek said nothing, the hood turned towards the woman leaning on his shoulder. Then he nodded, "As you wish. How many will be waiting for us?"

"All three of The Circle of Haouch Moussa."

"Armenians?"

"No."

"Then that is clever to hide amongst them." Malek shoved Carla back upright. Her head was forward, chin resting on her chest. She stayed up for a moment and then slowly fell the other way, her head coming to rest on the window.

"We will be meeting them at The Factory," explained Love. "Where we will be staying overnight. Then before dawn we travel to the old city and then we will set off into the hills and then the desert. We avoid Dimashq as you requested and pick up the camels at Duma."

"The old city?" asked Malek.

"For the camera," Love held up the Sony Camcorder. "For history. Your journey will start from a ruined city and end in the Holy City which you have come to save and rebuild. Good TV."

The hood turned, looking out of the window. He said no more.

Paradise increased speed as they began the straight twelve kilometre run across the valley. Love turned on the camera and began to film the lush green landscape.

Next to Malek in the back seat, Carla's head vibrated against the window...

Mount Lebanon 12:45

"Haven't we been this way before?" asked Lattouf as they passed through el-Mraijat and began the downward run to Chtaura. "Looks familiar."

Merhi spoke with a cigarette between his lips. "Five years ago. When we went to the wetlands."

"I knew it! Once Lattouf has been somewhere, he never forgets it."

"Which way did we go?"

"What?"

"Which we did we go? We made a turn here."

"Er... that way?" Lattouf pointed to the left, north-east towards Zahlé.

"No, it was that way." Merhi pointed across Lattouf to the right, south towards Qabb Elias. "But today we keep on going straight."

Lattouf finished off the last of several bars of chocolate and opened his window a few centimetres, throwing the wrapper out. He tried to close the window back up but instead it went all the way down, air blasting in noisily.

"For God's sake, Fadi." Merhi stabbed at the controls in his door and the window rose.

Lattouf looked at him. "You seem tense, my friend. I would have thought a mission such as this would be bread and butter to a Captain of the ISF."

"On a level playing field, yes. But the further south-east we go the further we get into Syrian territory. And that could add complications."

"But we are not crossing the border."

"No. But this area was the base of the Syrian *mukhabarat* in Lebanon. Aanjar, right where we're going."

"But they are no longer here. They withdrew from Lebanon after the Hariri killing."

"Maybe."

Lattouf frowned. He opened his mouth to discuss but then closed it again without saying another word. He could see his friend was not in the mood.

Five minutes later, staring ahead down the straight road, he said "Can't see the Jeep."

"No, they will be there by now. We will have to look around the town."

"Is it big?"

"No, but big enough to hide a car if they wanted to. But I don't think they will. They have no idea we're on to them. We'll just have to look around."

"Haven't seen the motorbike either."

"He's probably there now too."

Lattouf nodded. He asked, "Who is he anyway?"

"Carla's husband."

"His name?"

"He never says. He seems Lebanese but I've run him through records and nothing's come up."

Except, he thought, a dead man.

Aanjar, Lebanon 12:45

Haouch Moussa was built in the eighth century by Caliph al-Walid Ibn Abdel Malik of the Omayyads, the first great dynasty of the Arab Muslim empire. The ruins of the old walled city were discovered in the mid twentieth century and are today one of Lebanon's many tourist and academic attractions.

In 1939, France began to build the town of Aanjar on malarial marshland immediately to the south of the ruins. It was built to house Armenian refugees from Alexandretta, a Syrian province which France had ceded to Turkey that same year. The houses were built in an unaesthetic eastern European style, small and squat - but in compensation the French included wide, tree-lined avenues.

One and a half kilometres to the south of Aanjar, on an area of flat arable land, are several single-storey buildings, looking like a farm. The place was known as The Onion Factory, and, for nearly thirty years, it was Syria's main detention and interrogation centre in Lebanon.

The man who crouched on the ground in the sun, back against the wall of one of the buildings, knew that only too well. It was here that he had been killed, shot in the head by Brigadier General Ghazi Kanaan, the man who had been head of Syrian intelligence in Lebanon for twenty years until 2002, the effective ruler of the country.

Captain Marwan Mebarak of the Lebanese Commando Unit had been killed. The Damascene had taken over his body and soul, his missing left ear being the souvenir of Kanaan's bad aim. For five years he had worked for Kanaan, being his personal enforcer, persuader and, when necessary, killer. Then in 2005, at the same time as he had decided to leave Kanaan and work for himself, The Damascene had done something he had thought he would never ever do. Something that he thought he would never feel. Something that was alien to him. He had fallen in love.

And it was that love that now had him crouching on the ground in a place he thought he would never visit again. The place of blood, the place of death. The Onion Factory.

It was quiet. The sun was hot, the ground dusty.

There was farmland all around, but none of the locals would ever venture near these buildings even though Syria had ended its military presence in Lebanon over five years ago. They were too afraid of the ghosts.

He had caught up with the Jeep as they had crossed the Bekaa and had followed it at a safe distance. When he had realised where they were heading, his mood had darkened with his memories.

He had left the Suzuki behind some bushes on the main road half a kilometre back and had crouch-walked across the field parallel to the gravel track leading to the buildings.

Three cars were parked outside the next building along. One of them was the black Jeep Wrangler Ultimate.

Maintaining his crouch, The Damascene moved silently across to the back of the building, hugging the wall next to an open window. The walls were thick but he could hear voices. Carefully he looked inside.

The first thing he noticed was how different the interior was to the other building. The other one was simply an open space with stained, smelly, rotting straw on the floor and a single wooden chair in the centre of it. This one looked like it was the *mukhabarat* living quarters. It was a large room with doors leading off at the far end, probably to catering and bathroom areas. There were five beds down either wall.

In the centre of the room was a long wooden table on which sat fruit, nuts, juice and water. Around the table stood five people. The man in the hooded *burnus*, the identical female twin protectors, and two other men. They were talking, eating and drinking. One of the men was saying, "The contact will come tonight to confirm the final details..."

The Damascene leant back against the wall.

And smiled.

He had caught the faintest whiff of jasmine first and then he had strained to see in. He could just make out a figure on the bed nearest the window opening.

It was Carla, his wife.

The Damascene crouch-ran back to the other building. He sat on the ground on the farthest side, against the wall.

If the contact was coming tonight that meant that this was a Supporter Cell and not a Member Cell. Small fry. But he would take them out anyway. There was no way he could rescue his wife without killing, so they would all go. And, he acknowledged, there was no way he could rescue his wife on his own.

He pulled his mobile phone from his jeans pocket, checked there was a signal, and entered his Contacts list. He found the number he wanted and began to tap out a text message.

Bekaa Valley, Lebanon 13:00

They had just passed the turning for Barr Elias and were nearing the junction with the Rayak road when Merhi's mobile tinkled its message tune.

"Shall I get it?" Lattouf reached towards the phone in the well behind the transmission stick.

"It's probably Gisele." Merhi pulled out to overtake a fruit van.

Lattouf picked up the phone. He held it up to his face, thick fingers poking the screen. "How do you do this?" Poke.

"Just press Read."

Lattouf squinted. "I haven't got my glasses. This one? Ah, no, you don't want to go online. Hold on..." More pressing, then "Ah. There it is."

"What does she say?"

Lattouf moved the phone backwards and forwards in front of his eyes like he was playing an ocular trombone. He frowned, pouted and said, "I think she wants to meet you."

"What? Give it here." Merhi took the phone in his right hand, steering with his left. He brought hand and phone up to rest on the steering wheel.

Located. Meet at Aanjar ruins

Merhi closed the message. "It isn't Gisele, it's our friend. He's found them. Saves us a job. How's your archaeology, Fadi?"

Aanjar ruins, Lebanon 13:45

Even though it was signposted, they went sailing past the turn off for Aanjar. When they began to climb back up into the mountains again towards the Syrian border, they realised their mistake and turned back.

This time they did not miss it. On the far northern side of the town the slender columns and fragile arches of the quadrilateral Omayyad ruins contrasted proudly to the backdrop of Anti-Lebanon mountains. It was summer and there were tourists about but not as many as there would be at Lebanon's other attractions because of the easterly location.

"Keep an eye out for him." Merhi drove slowly along the northern perimeter, the entrance to the site on their right.

"I am," said Lattouf sleepily.

Beyond the entrance they turned right and cruised down the entire eastern side of the old city. At the bottom they turned west. Down here there were far fewer people. They could see the ruins of the Great Palace behind the walls on their right. Over on their left were bunkers and mess huts, not ruins but places abandoned by the Syrian army when it had left five years before.

Suddenly Lattouf nodded, alert. "There. There he is."

The man with the scarred face and ponytail was sitting astride his motorbike outside some shops a little way along. He watched the Land Cruiser as it approached but he did not respond to Lattouf's wave out of the window.

The car pulled to a stop. Merhi leant over, talking across Lattouf. "Located?"

The Damascene nodded.

"What do you want to do?" asked Merhi.

Lattouf looked surprised. "We go get her, of course!" he beamed keenly, rubbing his hands. "And get the bastards who murdered Chadi."

Merhi ignored him, waiting for the other man's response.

"Tonight," said The Damascene. "Until then, we wait. Right now what I want to do is eat. I know a restaurant. *Yalla.* Follow me." Revving the bike, he moved back onto the road and drove off towards town.

Merhi followed.

"My sort of guy," said Lattouf. "I'm liking him more and more. Reminds me of a younger me."

Aanjar, Lebanon 17:00

They ate at the Shams (Sun) Restaurant on the main road into town, enjoying superb local trout, hammour and a selection of grilled meats. The on-site bakery provided a challenge which Lattouf was happy to rise to.

The place was busy and they realised as soon as they arrived that it was no place to talk. They enjoyed their food, drank only water and juice, then nearly three hours later went back out to the Land Cruiser.

Merhi climbed in behind the wheel and The Damascene got into the back. After pausing outside for a breaking of wind that probably shook the fruit from the trees in the Bekaa Valley, Lattouf rolled into the passenger seat, giving a "What?" look to his colleagues.

As soon as the door was closed, The Damascene spoke. "There are five of them. Him and the twins and two locals. A third local is arriving tonight. It is a Supporter Cell, the lowest level of the party organisation. It is unlikely any of the cells above know what's going on and certainly not the Party Divisions or Sections."

"What party?" asked Lattouf. His question was ignored, so he tried "And your wife?"

"She is there. They seem to have her subdued, maybe drugged."

"How many in a cell?" asked Merhi.

"Three to seven. The one arriving tonight is a contact, a full member, therefore I expect there are only the three of them in this cell. You will take them out."

Merhi nodded. "And him?"

"He is mine."

Merhi opened the compartment in the dashboard and brought out both the guns. He held them up one in each hand. "Which do you want?"

The Damascene shook his head. "I do not need a gun. You two have them."

Merhi passed the Smith and Wesson to Lattouf.

The Palestinian weighed the gun in his hand. "My cousin's spirit demands revenge," he said. "I assume we do not take prisoners?

"No. But under no circumstances endanger my wife. Act only on my signal. This is what we will do..."

The discussion went on for some time. At the end, The Damascene reached back and slipped the rubber band off his ponytail. His hair fell down either side of his face like closing curtains. He asked, "Do these seats fold flat?"

"Yes."

"Then I suggest we get some sleep. We will leave here at nineteen hundred. I want you refreshed and alert for tonight. Nothing must go wrong. My wife's life is at stake."

The men in the front nodded.

And it goes without saying, thought The Damascene, that if Carla's life is lost yours will be too.

The Onion Factory, Aanjar, Lebanon 19:15

Lattouf could not keep up with the other two men as they crouch-ran across the field parallel to the gravel track. His gut wobbled on his knees and his arse seemed like it was in the thrall of gravity. He could not see his lower legs or feet and he felt like he was performing an out of breath Russian floating dance.

The sun was beginning its slow setting to the west, making his body cast a distorted oval shadow in front of him. It would be dark by twenty hundred.

He looked up to see how far he had to go. There were three single-storey buildings spread out in the middle of the field. Ahead, Jihad and the other man were heading towards the one on the right, a good way away from the middle building with the cars outside.

Merhi and The Damascene were already sitting on the ground, backs against the wall, when Lattouf finally arrived, sweating and panting. Here they could not be seen from the other building. With a grimace of pain, mouth open in silent agony, Lattouf slowly straightened up, shaking his legs, first one then the other, looking down at his limbs like long lost buddies.

He shook his head. "This is a young man's game. We're too old for this, Jihad my friend."

Merhi looked up at him. "Talk softly. You want to get Chadi's killers, don't you?"

"Of course."

"Then stop moaning." He did, however, totally agree with Lattouf. He was too old for all this. "And take the gun out of your waistband before you shoot your nuts off."

Lattouf accepted the sound advice, holding the gun pointing upwards. "Do we go now?"

"The other one hasn't arrived yet," said The Damascene. "We will wait. Take them all out."

"Will it be long?" asked Lattouf. "Only Nada will be wondering where I am."

"It will take as long as it takes. But I think he will arrive soon."

"Talking of wondering where we are, I'd best call Gisele," Merhi fumbled in his pocket for his phone. "Is it all right? I'll talk softly."

"Yes. They cannot hear us from there." The irony was not lost on The Damascene. All three men were worried about their wives; his was closest, just a hundred metres away, but in terms of contact she could be on the other side of the moon. For now.

The screen of Merhi's phone shone brightly in the fading light so he shielded it with his hand as he pressed keys, then he put it to his ear. He wondered what sort of mood Gisele would be in.

Jounieh, Lebanon 19:30

Gisele pressed the Answer key. "Where are you?"

"Hello Angel. We followed them to Aanjar."

"Aanjar! Why have they gone there? Who are they? I hope to God you know what you are doing, Jihad. I thought you were just going to Jbeil." She was concerned, not scolding.

"Needs must. But it ends tonight."

"Is Carla safe?"

"Apparently, yes."

"Will you be making arrests?"

"No."

She knew what he meant. Softly she said, "Be careful. Please."

"I will. We all will."

"The three of you are there?"

"Yes."

"That is good." Her husband was in hands she trusted, and she did not mean Fadi Lattouf. "How long will you be?"

"I don't know. But don't wait up."

"As if I am going to do anything else! For God's sake be careful," she said again. "Whatever it is you are doing."

"I will. I'll ring you when we're on our way back."

"You make sure you do. Or I will flay you alive. With my tongue."

"Promise?"

"Promise."

There was a pause, then Jihad said "See you later."

"See you then," she pressed the End key. "I love you, husband."

Gisele was sitting on the balcony, staring unseeing out over the Mediterranean, her phone grasped tightly in her hand. She was worried. Jihad was in his fifties now and physically probably not as sharp as he used to be. He was a commander or, if you wanted to be unkind, an administrator. What was he doing running halfway across the country to rescue a colleague? Field work should be left to younger men.

But there was something more behind this, she knew. He had spoken about the murder of Fadi's cousin and how it was linked to the disappearance of Carla. And then there were these twins, The Second Coming, and the mysterious Sajida who, it seemed, had been right!

And they wouldn't tell her who Sajida was, to protect her because the knowledge was dangerous. Yet Sajida seemed to be the link, the explanation as to what was going on. The clarifier.

If, heaven forbid, anything happened to Jihad tonight she might never know the answer. Imagine having to live for whatever remaining years the Good Lord had set aside for her not knowing the full reasons why her husband was never coming home again.

She frowned and turned around in the chair, staring back through the glass doors into her living room. Unless...

Could it be that easy? Was this something she should have done when all this started?

She stood up and went back inside, passing through the living room and going into what had been one of the boys' bedrooms when they had been at home. It was now their office area.

She turned on the computer, waiting a full five minutes for it to do what computers do.

Then she clicked on the Internet icon.

The Onion Factory, Aanjar, Lebanon 19:35

"Right, the sun has gone," said The Damascene. "You understand what you have to do?"

"Yes," confirmed Merhi.

"And you are happy with it?"

"Yes."

"Both of you?"

"Of course," Lattouf was solemn. "If anyone transgresses, transgress likewise. They murdered my cousin."

"We'll move over, then I'll leave you. When the final one arrives you follow my lead as we discussed." Two heads nodded. "No talking, no sound, when we are over there. *Yalla.*"

The three shadowy figures crouch-walked in ant formation away from the building. The bouncing movement made gas move in Lattouf's gut, but he knew this was neither the time nor the place even for a little pop.

They reached the next building and flattened themselves against the wall, Merhi and Lattouf one side of the open window, The Damascene the other. Light came through the window and they could hear low chatter from inside. The Damascene held up his palm indicating that they should not move. Turning his body slowly, he looked inside.

The food and drink on the table was depleted and, as always when humans had been pecking, now looked untidy. The two locals from the Supporter Cell were each resting on a bed, the twins were seated together on another bed and *al-Mahdi* was seated on the floor, his hood off, smoking from a golden *argileh*.

And Carla was sitting next to him.

The Damascene stared.

His wife and *al-Mahdi* did not have body contact but they were sitting very close, in each others' space. She was looking at one of the twins who was talking. She was smiling, attentive, her face fresh, innocent, but her eyes so, so black. It was an expression he knew well. It meant somebody was going to die tonight.

They were opposite the window but at an angle, so they would not see him looking in. Was there any way he could get Carla's attention, let her know he was here? Tell her not to do anything, to leave it to him?

He concentrated hard.

Thirty seconds later Carla stood up and went over to the table and picked up a polystyrene cup, filling it with water. When she went back to *al-Mahdi* she sat noticeably less close to him. Good girl.

The Damascene turned back away from the window. He crooked his finger at Merhi then pointed to his eyes and to the window.

Carefully Merhi turned so that he was facing the wall. Then with silent, shuffling steps he moved sideways until one eye was looking into the room.

And there he saw the proof, as if proof was needed, that Sajida was right.

In the middle of the room, sitting next to Carla, smoking on an *argileh*, dressed in a *burnus* but with the hood down, his head exposed, was Saddam Hussein.

Jounieh, Lebanon 19:35

There were 155,000 results on Google for 'Sajida'. The first and most popular one was a Wikipedia link to Sajida Talfah, the widow and cousin of former Iraqi President Saddam Hussein and mother of his two now-dead sons Uday and Qusay and his three daughters.

Where was this going? she wondered. *Sajida was right.*

Gisele read the article. Interesting, but there was no clue or indication as to what Sajida had been right about! Sajida blamed Saddam for the 1989 death of her brother Adnan, claiming the helicopter crash which killed him had not been an accident but had been a bombing ordered by Saddam because of Adnan's growing popularity – but what had that to do with anything now?

No, was this the right Sajida even? Gisele clicked through page after page of the search results. There were links to people's Facebook pages, many references to Sajidas on the Indian sub-continent, she even found out that Sajida was the 9910th most popular name in the USA! But there was nothing of relevance other than Sajida Talfah so she went back and filtered the search to just her.

Sajida was right.

Gisele clicked on many of the articles. In March 2003 just before the bombing of Baghdad began, Sajida had fled from Iraq, probably to Qatar. In July 2006 she was put sixteenth on the Iraqi government's Most Wanted list for financing Sunni insurgents under her husband's reign – but her mansion in Qatar was empty, she had disappeared.

Gisele smiled to herself. Had Sajida been Most Wanted when the invasion of Iraq had started she would have been on one of those famous playing cards with pictures of the fugitives on them –

She stopped, her finger poised on the mouse, her stomach tightening. *Oh my good God.*

What had happened in this very apartment just last night? The card on which Fadi's cousin had written the Annaya co-ordinates. Jihad had taken it from the envelope and had thrown it across to Carla's husband. The death card, the ace of spades.

On the Iraq personality identification playing cards Saddam Hussein was the ace of spades.

No, this was crazy. Crazy.

al-Mahdi? The Second Coming?

Sajida was right.

Gisele clicked again, article after article, skim-reading when she thought it was necessary. It was another five minutes before she clicked on the link to *Pravda*, the Russian newspaper.

It was an article dated 13 April 2004, two years before Sajida had been put on the Most Wanted list. It was headlined 'Saddam's wife could not recognise her husband'. It reported that the previous week Sajida Tulfah had been granted permission to visit her husband at the American military base in Qatar, his place of detention. Sajida had stormed out of the visit claiming that the person detained was not her husband but a double.

Hand shaking, Gisele now Googled 'Saddam Hussein alive' – and came up with 1,430,000 results.

1,430,000 reasons for believing Sajida was right.

The Onion Factory, Aanjar, Lebanon 20:30

Forty-five minutes after The Damascene had left them, Merhi saw a diffused glow of lights in the distance coming from the direction of the town. The glow became clearer and stronger as it got closer, morphing into headlight beams. He kicked Lattouf who was sitting on the ground sleeping peacefully – and thankfully silently – next to him.

Lattouf awoke frowning with raised eyebrows, looking up, disorientated. Merhi pointed at the lights. Lattouf looked, focussed, realised where he was and nodded his head, stiffly getting to his feet.

A car turned off the road onto the gravel track, the full beams bouncing, illuminating the central building. Merhi and Lattouf flattened themselves against the wall at the side, out of range of the light.

The car pulled to a stop. As the lights were turned off, the large wooden entrance door to the building slid open and the two other locals came out. They shook hands and kissed cheeks deferentially with the man who got out of the car.

Merhi was peeping round the corner. The Ba'ath political party had been deliberately created as a cell-based organisation with contact between cells forbidden unless it was authorised through a higher command level. This cordoned off members from each other but prevented penetrative infiltration by non-Ba'athists. A cell could be compromised but the infiltrator would be able to get no further without exposure. Carla's husband had said this was a Supporter Cell, so the two who had come out of the building would be candidate members, subservient and obedient to the full member who had now arrived. So here was one complete cell, or circle as it was also known. The local circle. The Circle of Haouch Moussa.

The men went inside and Merhi turned back. His gun was in his right hand. Lattouf was standing on the far side of the window, the Smith and Wesson just visible in his large fist. They did not speak but communicated with facial gestures.

Merhi eyebrowed *Ready?*

Lattouf nodded *Now?*

Merhi shook his head, waving the fingers holding his gun. *Wait.*

A few moments later they became aware of a very low, almost inaudible rumble. There was the subtlest of tremors in the ground, as if there had been an earthquake hundreds of miles away in Jordan or Turkey.

The rumbling got louder, the tremors increased. Merhi took a deep breath and nodded to Lattouf.

Now.

They both turned, standing in front of the open window, guns raised out in front of them.

The roar of the Suzuki Hayabusa increased as it came closer at speed. Then light pierced through the open door of the building as the bike's full beam was turned on.

Inside the three locals turned towards the light, bewildered. They began to shout and gesticulate. Then the neck of one of them exploded as shots came in through the window. Carla threw herself down, rolling sideways. Saddam Hussein looked towards the door, confused. The twins leapt across the room, pushing him to the floor.

The hip of another local burst blood and bone as a bullet struck. The Suzuki flew through the doorway, its raised front wheel acting like a circular saw severing the head of the third local, the member who had just arrived.

The Damascene leapt off the bike while it was still in motion, shouting "Carla!" as a bullet zipped past his head. He lost his footing as he landed, bouncing onto one of the beds.

Outside Merhi raised his hand across Lattouf to stop him firing as inside Carla came up in a crouch. "Get the bitches!" she screamed at the men in the window, pointing.

Paradise and Love were covering Saddam, heads raised, white eyes glaring, almost feral. Carla flung herself on top of Love but was met by a raised forearm which knocked her sideways. The twins began to drag Saddam towards the door.

The Damascene rolled off the bed, looking at his wife who was getting back up, rubbing her chest.

Merhi watched, gun raised, aiming through the window.

Carla snarled, ran forward and kicked Love in the side of the head.

Now Merhi and Lattouf witnessed the strangest sight. The woman Carla had kicked flung her head into the air as the foot made impact, unwillingly rolling away from Saddam. But so did the other woman! Identical movements as if she had been kicked too.

The Damascene threw himself on top of Saddam as Carla grabbed Love round the neck from behind.

Merhi moved his gun back and forth sideways, trying to get a clear shot.

Paradise grabbed The Damascene by the hair, lifting it upwards. She saw the exposed mess that had once been his left ear and grinned, plunging two fingers into the hole. Lashing out with his left arm, The Damascene rolled away, blood oozing out of his wound.

Love managed to stand up with Carla clinging to her back with her arm around her throat, her other hand trying to get purchase against the twin's head to snap the neck. Love swung sideways, back and forth, trying to shake off The Djinn on her back.

"It's no good," said Merhi. "I can't risk it. We'll have to go inside."

Saddam was sitting on the floor, bemused, disbelieving. What was happening? He could not fail now after all these years. America, The Great Satan, was leaving his country in forty days. He needed to be there, to reclaim the Promised Land for his people, to save them. To save the world.

Paradise grabbed hold of Carla's hair with her left hand and plunged her right hand between her legs from behind. She squeezed, feeling the cloth of The Djinn's trousers press upwards into the soft folds of her sex. Then she pinched with all her might. Carla gasped and released her hold. Snarling, Paradise raised her in the air and threw her towards the wall.

The Damascene shook his head, seeing his own blood dripping outwards. He spotted the *argileh* knocked over on the floor and he picked it up by the golden body. The heavy half-filled water bowl stayed on the end as he raised it in the air...

"Sister, come!" croaked Paradise, holding her throat in a mirror image of Love. She put her arm around her twin, guiding her towards the door.

The Damascene swung down the *argileh* with all his might. It shattered against the back of Saddam's head, the glass bowl exploding, water, glass, blood and bone bursting in a spraying halo. Hands instinctively reaching upwards, Saddam fell sideways. The follow-through blow with the pipe body smacked into the side of his head, knocking him back the other way.

Merhi and Lattouf ran together round the side of the building – just in time to see the twins stagger out. "Stop!" Merhi raised his gun, still running.

"Police!" shouted Lattouf. "You are under - "

Then he fell over.

As he fell his gun fired and there was a double scream from in front of him. He bounced onto the ground and rolled sideways – taking Merhi's legs out from under him like a tenpin. Merhi went down straight and flat, his face breaking his fall on the sharp gravel.

The Damascene stood above Saddam's body, raining blows down onto his head, into his face, again and again and again, the skull breaking, the face disintegrating, blood, bone and brain matter splashing up into his own face.

Lattouf was on his back like a beached whale, trying unsuccessfully to get up. Merhi was flat out and moaning. His forehead, nose and chin felt like they had been attacked by a sander on full speed.

They heard an engine start up.

"Stop!" said Lattouf weakly. "Police..." He looked to the side to see the tail lights of the Jeep disappearing down the gravel track. He flapped his gun against the ground, trying to get an aim.

Giving up, he turned the other way towards his friend. "Jihad? Jihad!" He moved his arm out to poke his prostrate colleague. "Are you all right? I couldn't stop them, they have gotten away." There was no reply. "Jihad?" said Lattouf helplessly, rolling like an upturned turtle. "I... I can't get up. Will you help me please?"

Merhi moved, very slowly, very carefully, very painfully. Then, face still on the ground, he said, "Fuck off, Fadi."

The Damascene knelt on his haunches on the floor next to the mess that had once been the head of Saddam Hussein. It was now just a shell, a bowl for the soup of blood, brain and bone and now-floating facial hairs within. He had last seen his wife being thrown through the air into the wall. He really didn't want to look round to find what he might find.

Across the room were the three members of The Circle of Haouch Moussa. One was headless, one was dead with his neck blown away, the other was moaning and writhing, his pelvic area a sticky mess of gore and protruding bone. It would take him a while to die. So be it.

The Damascene felt a touch on his shoulder and he looked up.

"I landed on a bed," smiled Carla. Her hair was a mess, there were bruises and scratches on her arms and shoulders, grazes on her face and a distinct cut on her lower lip. Her right collarbone looked more prominent than usual.

She caressed his bloodied face with her hands, not caring about her own pain. "You came for me," she pushed his blood-matted hair back over his head, her thumbs rubbing an ear on one side, a hole on the other.

"Did you think I would not?" He wiped his hand across his mouth, smearing his chin with blood.

"I knew you would." She bent forward and kissed him long and hard on the lips. It was a full minute before she pulled away. There was blood on her face.

"And I always will." He smiled and put out his hand for her to help him up. "You know what I fancy right now?"

Her black eyes widened. "Husband, you are insatiable! Not here, surely?"

"I fancy a coffee. And the further away from here, the better." He looked down at the body at his feet. "I would have left him, you know, had he not taken you. He was hated by many but there were an equal number who supported him. Look what Iraq was. Look what it is now. I had no feelings about him one way or the other."

"But you have feelings for me?"

"Oh yes. And that's why he had to die. Killed for love." He put his arm around her.

Stepping past the man dying in agony, The Damascene and The Djinn walked out of The Onion Factory.

The place of death.

26 July 2010
14 Sha'ban 1431

Jounieh, Lebanon 08:15

Captain Jihad Merhi had called in sick that morning, giving an upset stomach as an excuse (the Beirut Belly, the Tripoli Trots, the Sidon Shits). Something must have disagreed with him over the weekend.

Now he sat on his balcony watching the blue of the Mediterranean take on the azure of the cloudless sky in a beauty contest.

On the small table beside him were his cigarettes, lighter, a Saint Charbel souvenir ashtray, a covered *rakwe* of Turkish coffee and a small cup. On the floor underneath the table were an empty whisky bottle, a half full whisky bottle, a glass and an empty cigarette packet.

His face looked like it had been pulled through a hedge of brambles. It was slathered with emollients at Gisele's insistence but the cuts, scratches and grazes were uncovered to let the air get to them.

Out at sea he saw a plane with a distinct cedar tree on its tail climbing into the sky having just taken off from Beirut. It would be that morning's 07:55 Middle East Airlines flight to Paris with a connection to New York. He nodded to it, wishing it well.

His mobile phone rang. Ten minutes ago he had phoned Sergeant Deeb el-Gharib and asked him to have a look at his In Tray on his desk to see if anything urgent was awaiting him. This was him ringing back.

"Hi Deeb."

"Hi boss. Couple of bits from the Major. A nine year old boy was badly injured by an Israeli cluster bomb at Shaqra yesterday. Wants your comments. Also he's asked for your opinion on Blackberry phones. The Telecoms Regulatory Authority has identified security issues. Apparently Saudi and the UAE are already threatening to ban Blackberry messenger functions because of difficulties in accessing the data by law enforcement agencies."

Merhi sighed. "Oh, for Christ's sake."

"There's just one other item, in an internal envelope. From Interpol upstairs."

Merhi leant forward. "What does it say?"

There was a rustling of paper, then el-Gharib said "In response to your enquiry... Positive identification made. Two results. Paradise Grace Abu Joade and Love Maria Abu Joade. Age 34. Lebanese Army. Latterly in the *Moukafaha*, the Special Forces Counter-Sabotage Regiment, prior to that in the Republican Guard. Went to Libya on a training course in 2000, never returned. At first thought kidnapped or killed, then known to have deserted. Next heard of in 2002 as two members of Colonel Gaddafi's elite all-female protection unit. Known for their efficiency and ruthlessness. Last recorded sighting as members of Gaddafi's unit in 2004. Suspects in the elimination of various people in Iraq, Syria, Jordan and Turkey over the last five years. There's more detail, of course. Shall I fax it to you?"

"No, no, Deeb. I'm tired. I need a rest."

"Takes it out of you, doesn't it boss?"

"What does?"

"The shits."

"Yeah. Literally. Thanks Deeb, I'll probably be in later in the week."

Merhi ended the call and placed his phone on the table. He leant back and closed his eyes. Feeling the sun on the top of his head, he stood up and turned his chair around to face the mountain behind. Before he could sit back down, he heard the sound of an engine, the pop of a backfire and the complaining of brakes from down below, outside the apartment block.

He went to the side edge of the balcony and looked over. For a moment he stared, face expressionless. Then he shook his head in disbelief and resigned acceptance. Down below was an old, battered, rusting, burnt-orange Datsun Bluebird.

And next to it, looking up and waving, was Fadi Lattouf.

Gisele let the Palestinian giant into the apartment, reluctantly kissing him three times on his proffered cheeks, and then she went back to doing what she was doing in the kitchen.

"Morning of joy, my dear friend!" effused Lattouf as he squeezed through the open balcony door.

"*Salaam*, Fadi," Merhi hoped he projected more enthusiasm than he felt. "Some juice?"

"That would be kind, thank you."

From the kitchen, Gisele called "I'm getting it!"

"And perhaps a morsel to eat?" Lattouf spoke into the empty living room. "It is a long ride from Beirut."

"Of course," called Gisele again.

Lattouf waddled out onto the balcony.

"I didn't expect to see you today," said Merhi. "Here, sit." He pulled over a chair.

"Thank you, I will stand for a while. The long ride makes my bot-bot go numb." He rubbed his massive gluteals. "How are you, my friend?"

"Looks worse than it is," Merhi came and stood next to Lattouf, leaning against the rail, looking out to sea. "How's your ankle?"

"Oh fine, fine. It takes more than that to keep a Lattouf down."

Merhi went back to the table and took two cigarettes from the packet, passing one over. Lattouf took it and accepted the light. Taking a draw, he looked at the glowing end of the cigarette. "Nada would kill me if she knew I was smoking again."

"She's a good woman, she cares about you."

"She does indeed." He looked round as Gisele appeared in the doorway carrying a tray. "As does Gisele for you. What would we do without our wives, eh?"

"I've been asking him that for years," said Gisele.

Merhi smiled. "We would not be complete," he said sincerely.

Gisele gave him a small, private look.

"Nada says I am getting old," Lattouf went over and took the tray from Gisele, helping himself to some nuts from a bowl in the process. He waited while Gisele cleared Jihad's stuff from the small table then he put the tray down. As he straightened back up he said, "She says I should retire. Nada."

"Can you do that? Are you able?" asked Jihad.

"I can quit," shrugged Lattouf. "They probably won't even know I'm gone."

Jihad laughed. "I doubt that, my friend," he said affectionately. "What would you do? If you quit? What about money?"

Gisele passed glasses of mango juice to the two men.

Lattouf was quiet for a moment, savouring the full glass of juice that he had poured into his mouth. Then he said, "A business maybe?" He held his glass out for a refill as Gisele approached with a jug.

Merhi pulled a face. "It is not that easy for a Palestinian to set up a business in Lebanon. The red tape would be unbelievable."

"Who said anything about *setting up* a business?" said Lattouf. "I already have one. I am Chadi's sole heir. I have inherited his business. In Jbeil." He drank some of his replenished juice and gave a modest belch. "The thing is, it would be a very big leap for me. I don't know Lebanon that well, its nuances, its niceties. I have been too long a policeman in my own little world. Palestine it isn't. Gaza it isn't. I don't think I could handle it on my own. I would need a local partner." He smiled across at Gisele and then looked Jihad in the eyes. "How about it? Lattouf and Merhi, Private Investigators. You could be the brains and I could be the brawn. Or the other way round. Jihad Merhi, investigator first class. In partnership with Fadi Lattouf..." His face beamed and his deep voice boomed down across the mountainside as he raised his glass in a toast. "*Muhaqqiq khass extraordinaire!*"

POSTSCRIPT
حاشية

Spoiler alert! Plot machinations are discussed below.
Please do not read before reading the book.

The use of political decoys is acknowledged practice. History shows that they have been used extensively, usually to draw attention away from the real person or to take risks on their behalf. Literally to put themselves in the firing line. They are people who naturally look like the person they are impersonating or have had surgical assistance. Not all of them have undertaken their duties willingly.

In the twentieth century, the following are known to have used doubles: Joseph Stalin, Adolph Hitler, Heinrich Himmler, Winston Churchill, Field Marshal Bernard Montgomery, Harry S Truman, Indira Ghandi, Henry Kissinger, Boris Yeltsin, Michael Mouskos (Archbishop Makarios III of Cyprus), Uday Hussein, and Saddam Hussein.

Saddam Hussein was probably the most notable of them all, employing many doubles for public appearances, TV appearances and even for meetings with foreign politicians! The most obvious example of this was in the days after the invasion of Iraq in 2003 when 'Saddam' was shown on worldwide television out in the streets of Baghdad in full military uniform being mobbed by his adoring subjects. He was beaming, avuncular, benign – and never said one word.

Is Saddam alive? Did he cheat the gallows? There is a strong theory that he did. But how could that be? Unless they were in on it, surely the Iraqi authorities, if not the Americans, would have thoroughly tested the body both pre- and post-mortem to establish that it was him and to confirm his DNA? Indeed. But with so many Saddam Husseins about (there were believed to be at least eight) how could they ever be sure that they had the right DNA in the first place?

Was Brother Malek ('The King') really Saddam Hussein? Or was he just another decoy?

Perhaps Akhenaten has the answer...

Ma'ak,

David Cullen
ديفيد كولين

To Zalaya, the Man of Damascus.
Know that the king is in good health
as the sun in the heavens. His troops and
chariots are numerous... from the
Upper country until the Lower country,
from the Levant till the sunset,
all is for the best.

- from a letter written by Akhenaten (Pharaoh of Egypt 1353 – 1336 BC) to the ruler of Damascus, on a cuneiform tablet now in the National Museum of Lebanon in Beirut, originally thought to have been discovered at Byblos.

الله هو جيد

THE BEIRUT CONFESSION

DAVID CULLEN

Culpro Books

Where no counsel is, the people fall; but in the multitude of counselors there is safety
- King James Bible, Proverbs XI:I4
also the motto of Israel's Institute for Intelligence and Special Operations (Mossad)

Confessionalism - a system of governing based on the distribution of political and institutional power proportionately among communities, usually (but not solely) based on religion. For example, in Lebanon the Doha Agreement of 2008 specifies that there should be 54 Christian parliamentary deputies and 54 Muslim parliamentary deputies. Within these two groups, seats should be allocated according to the demographic weight of each community (eg Sunni Muslim, Shi'a Muslim, Druze, Maronite Christians).

In this context, a **Confession** is one of the groups (eg the Maronite Confession). It can also be used as a collective noun for any group of people sharing similar beliefs or causes, even clandestinely.

Confession is also, of course, an admission of something.

And it is good for the soul.

A Glossary of Arabic and Hebrew Words and Phrases is on pages 729 to 733

Cast in order of appearance

Ghazi Kanaan [Abu Yo'roub] – *head of Syrian security in Lebanon 1982-2002, Syrian Interior Minister 2004-2005.*

The Damascene [Marwan Mebarak] – *a mercenary, an assassin.*

Mahmoud Abdel Rauf al-Mabhouh – *co-founder and senior commander of the military wing of Hamas.*

An Israeli assassination team.

Brigadier Wissam al-Hassan – *Head of Intelligence Division, Lebanese Internal Security Force.*

Captain Jihad Merhi [Abu Samer] – *Lebanese Internal Security Force.*

Gisele Merhi – *wife of Jihad, a trainer for the Lebanese Department of General Security.*

Sergeant Deeb el-Gharib – *Lebanese Internal Security Force.*

Captain Fadi Lattouf – *chief of the Civil Police of the Palestinian Security Force in the Beirut refugee camps.*

A policeman in the Sanayeh police station, Beirut.

Major Pierre Ghanem – *Lebanese Internal Security Force.*

Violette Ghorra – *secretary to Major Ghanem.*

Larry – *doorman of an apartment building on East 39th Street, New York City, USA.*

Benjamin David – *a* sayan *in New York City, USA.*

Carla Chedid [The Djinn] – *Lebanese Department of General Security.*

Sergeant Nabil Haddad – *a spycatcher of the Lebanese Internal Security Force.*

Sergeant Claude Gerges - *a spycatcher of the Lebanese Internal Security Force.*

Sergeant Tamer Khalef - *a spycatcher of the Lebanese Internal Security Force.*

Love – *a* houri *and a mercenary.*

Paradise – *a* houri *and a mercenary.*

An old man in the Bourj el-Shimali refugee camp.

Captain Manar al-Jayouchi - *chief of the Civil Police of the Palestinian Security Force in the Bourj el-Shimali refugee camp.*

Abdul Abdulrahman – *a Palestinian Israeli spy.*

A Corporal on reception duties at the State Security Building, Jonblat, Beirut.

A mechanic on a tow truck on the Beirut River bed.

Sergeant Kanj – *Bourj Hammoud police, Beirut.*

Corporal Skaff – *Bourj Hammoud police, Beirut.*

Dr Mohammed Patel – *Medical Examiner at the* Hôtel Dieu de France *Hospital, Beirut.*

Lana Lattouf – *daughter of Fadi and Nada Lattouf.*

Sergeant Alarab - *Civil Police of the Palestinian Security Force in the Bourj el-Barajneh refugee camp.*

The owner of a boys' toys shop in Snoubra, Beirut.

A Corporal on security duties at the State Security Building, Jonblat, Beirut.

Corporal Jad Chadidi - *Lebanese Internal Security Force.*

Corporal Omar Mostafa - *Lebanese Internal Security Force.*

Corporal Michel Yammine - *Lebanese Internal Security Force.*

Corporal Peter Harrak - *Lebanese Internal Security Force.*

Corporal Emad Hmedeh - *Lebanese Internal Security Force.*

A Lieutenant of the Lebanese Internal Security Force.

A minion of the Facilities Unit, Security Services, Ras en Nabaa, Beirut.

Lieutenant Sebastien – *Lebanese General Security Unit.*

Sergeant Christof Howdra – *Lebanese General Security Unit.*

A Corporal of the Lebanese General Security Unit.

PROLOGUE
مقدمة اثنين

12 October 2005
8 Ramadan 1426

Damascus, Syria

"I didn't think it would be you."

Ghazi Kanaan, the Minister of the Interior of Syria, did not turn around from the window. He could see a translucent reflection of his visitor in the glass, standing by the closed office door, still, like a wraith. Like Nemesis. Like Death...

Kanaan had always liked this view out over the Barada River and across the northern suburbs, that was why he had commandeered this office on his appointment a year ago, rather than take on the ministerial suite of his predecessor Ali Hammoud. The formal offices were too low down. Kanaan liked it here in his eyrie.

Staring out over Damascus helped him reflect. Reflect on everything that had happened in the last year, how Syria had been thrown out of its thirty year presence in Lebanon after the murder of Rafic Hariri, how the United Nations were now investigating Hariri's death, how the UN had imposed travel restrictions and an assets freeze on all individuals suspected of involvement in the assassination. How he, Kanaan, was one of those individuals...

The irony was not lost on him. He had tried to protect Hariri, to save him from what, in hindsight, was inevitable. He had liked Hariri. Not only that, during Kanaan's twenty years as head of Syrian intelligence in Lebanon when he had effectively ruled the country, he had come to *respect* Hariri. And this was the thanks he got.

There was one other thing to reflect. The cracks in the eggshell façade of Syria's ruling al-Assad dynasty were beginning to widen, not least due to his own subtle and clandestine destabilising efforts. With a former Vice President of Syria, he was developing a challenging powerbase against President Bashar al-Assad within the Syrian Regional Branch of the Arab Socialist Ba'ath Party.

A powerbase that had been discovered. And he knew the punishment for discovery.

He turned to face Death.

Death was a tall, dark, powerful man holding a .38 Smith and Wesson. He wore jeans and a loose, collarless white shirt. His long black hair was tied back into a simple ponytail, falling down either side of his face, concealing the burns and lack of left ear. He was known as The Damascene and he was Kanaan's creation.

"Of all people," continued Kanaan, "I didn't think it would be you."

The Damascene's eyes pierced into the very soul of the man whom he hated above all others. The man who had captured Lebanese Army Captain Marwan Mebarak, who had tortured him to within a centimetre of his life and shot him in the head and, when he realised the angle of the gun had not been acute enough for the bullet to pierce the skull and instead had just shot off his left ear and severely burnt his face – and mindful of the fact that this broken husk of a man had just killed five armed Syrian *mukhabarat* with his bare hands – had taken him, brainwashed him and turned him into his own trained killer.

That had been six years ago. A lifetime.

"Life can be strange," said The Damascene. "Have you phoned the radio station?"

Kanaan nodded. "As instructed. I told them that could be the last statement I would ever make."

"How right you were."

"Do you have my body?"

"Yes."

"Where is it?"

"It is standing outside."

"Oh. Fresh then."

"Fresher than you will be."

Kanaan, the 'King of Lebanon', the butcher, the man ultimately responsible for thousands of deaths, gave a sad smile. "It is my time then. There is no other way?"

"No."

He nodded. "Better get on with it."

The Damascene walked across the room and grabbed Kanaan by the hair, pulling him down onto the chair behind his desk. Kanaan did not struggle, resigned to his fate. What had to be done, had to be done.

The Damascene yanked harder on the hair and Kanaan gasped, his mouth opening. The Damascene pushed the gun between Kanaan's teeth, deep into his mouth, the knuckle of his trigger finger pressing onto the older man's lips.

With a small movement, he tilted the gun so it was pointing up into Ghazi

Kanaan's brain...

[*Just after 10:00 on 12 October 2005, Major General Ghazi Kanaan was found dead in his office in the Interior Ministry in Damascus. He had been shot through the mouth by a .38 Smith and Wesson. The official verdict was suicide. On 9 November 2006 his brother Ali Kanaan also 'committed suicide', his dismembered body being found on railway lines near his farm in the Syrian coastal city of Jalba.*]

19 January 2010
3 Safar 1431
Dubai, United Arab Emirates

Emirates flight EK912 from Damascus landed on time at 14:35 that afternoon. By 15:20, the passenger travelling under the name of Mahmoud Abdul Raouf Mohammed had passed through immigration controls in Terminal 3 and had picked up his baggage, a single small suitcase. He did not even warrant a glance from the Customs Officer on selection duties.

He was dressed in slacks, open-necked shirt and jacket. Immediately he stepped outside the air-conditioned terminal, the desert heat wrapped itself around him like a high-tog duvet, even in January. His portly body began to sweat and he quickly removed his jacket as he waited in line for a taxi.

"Al Bustan Rotana," he said as he settled in to the back of the cab. The uniformed Indian driver nodded and they pulled out.

Mahmoud knew that it would only be a short drive, that was why he had picked this hotel, to be near the airport. Tomorrow he was leaving for Bangkok.

He was not too tired after the flight, it had only been three and a half hours, but he would need to adjust his body to the two-hours-ahead time difference here in the UAE. Perhaps a little retail therapy would help, something nice for his wife...

The cab used the overpass to turn left off of D89 Airport Road and onto the D70 Casablanca Road. Then it U-turned and bore right into the driveway of the hotel, passing the fountain on the left and pulling up as close as possible to the hotel's entrance.

Mahmoud handed over a note but did not thank the driver. Likewise he dismissed the Philippino porter who was opening the trunk, removed his case himself and walked into the hotel.

Check-in was smooth and soon he was taking a lift to the second floor, carrying his own case, no porter needed. He was in room 230.

The first thing he did on entering was to check that the room was as requested: no balcony, sealed windows. So the only way in and out of the room was through the door. That was good. Less danger.

He rarely travelled without his bodyguards, and the reason they were not with him now was mundane: there was no room for them on the flight from Damascus. Mahmoud had booked his ticket online just a few days ago and he assumed his bodyguards would also get tickets when they went online immediately after him. But he had reckoned without the annual Dubai Shopping Festival! He had bagged the last seat on today's EK912, and his bodyguards had only just managed to squeeze onto the flight tomorrow.

He would be on his own for a day in Dubai, so what? He had no business here (other than shopping and possibly a massage) and nobody knew him. He had a sealed room. He would relax. He was safe. Or so he thought.

But Mahmoud had made a mistake. Usually any bookings for any tickets he required were made by others on his behalf, using a wide selection of aliases. This time, because his trip was so secret and was made at such short notice, he had booked his air ticket and hotel reservation online himself.

Which was silly. Mahmoud had been monitored for years. Any electronic activity, any phone call, any text message, any stroke on any keypad he had ever made, had been noted, reported and stored.

For he was not Mahmoud Abdul Raouf Mohammed. He was Mahmoud Abdel Rauf al-Mabhouh, a senior Hamas military commander, one of the founders of the Izz ad-Din al-Qassam Brigade, the military wing of Hamas. He had been involved in many armed actions against Israel, including the abduction and killing of two Israeli soldiers, Avi Sasportas and Ilan Sa'adon, in 1989. He was suspected by Israel of smuggling weapons and explosives into Gaza, and recently he was known to be forging secret connections between the Hamas government in Gaza and the Al-Quds Force of the Revolutionary Guards in Iran. He was wanted by Israel, Jordan and Egypt.

And that day he was going to die.

Mahmoud had spent nearly three hours shopping in Deira City Center, and returned to his room at 20:24 (with something from *Al Masroor* jewellers for his wife and a little electronic boy toy from *Sharaf DG* for himself). His killers were waiting for him inside his room [*the VingCard Locklink electronic doorlock system used by the hotel at that time could be reprogrammed directly at the door; they had cloned Mahmoud's keycard earlier*].

Two of the assassins were in the bathroom, the third was lying on the floor by the side of the bed, against the bathroom wall and out of sight of the door.

As far as Mahmoud was concerned, his room was empty. The only thing that registered as strange, too far down in his deep subconscious even to have a thought formulated about it, was that his bed sheets had been turned all the way down to the end of the bed. Only as he put his carrier bags down on the chair was he aware of a small shape on the floor and then a sharp scratch on his left leg. *In the name of Allah, what was that - ?*

The heat roared through his body as he instinctively backed away from the shape on the floor.

Suxamethonium (colloquially referred to in medical circles as 'sux') is an almost-immediate-acting muscle relaxant. It causes instant loss of motor skills but does not induce unconsciousness. As Mahmoud swayed, awareness of his legs seeming to vanish beneath him, two men walked quickly from the bathroom and simply pushed him onto the bed. Mahmoud tried to struggle as they began to rip off his clothes, but his muscles were not working, his limbs were no longer his.

The assailants were rough but not brutal. As they threw off his clothes, the third person – the shape from the floor – picked them up and put them neatly on the chair on top of the shopping bags.

Soon Mahmoud was stripped down to his black shorts and he was laid on his back on the bed, fully conscious but now with no control over his body. It was all he could do to focus his eyes on the pillow that came down onto his face…

Murder is never clean. Humans are not a clean species. The human body is tenacious. The heart usually beats on after trauma, death only occurring after the victim has bled out or has suffered massive internal injury and shock. Pure, physical death can take a while.

The pillow was pressed onto the face of Mahmoud Abdel Rauf al-Mabhouh for ten minutes after his heart had stopped, to ensure physical death and brain death. The body had pissed itself and had expelled methane (causing one of the attackers to mutter "*Harah*, what has this *benzona* had to eat!"), but the piss was covered as the sheets were pulled up across the body and tucked cosily under his chin. His eyes were closed and he looked like he was sleeping. It would be over twelve hours before he was found by a chambermaid the next day.

By that time, his assassins were out of the country. Subsequent reports vary as to the number of the hit team, estimates ranging from nine to twenty-six. Certainly later investigations showed that eighteen people had entered the UAE on false passports in the twenty-four hours prior to the murder. Generally it is accepted that the hit team probably consisted of eleven people: lookouts, point men, distractors, transporters, technicians, killers.

CCTV from the hotel would show that just after 21:00 that evening, three people casually walked along the second floor corridor, waited in the lift lobby (smiling, chatting, not a care in the world), got into the lift, exited on the ground floor and left the hotel. Two men and one woman.

The woman, it was later determined, was travelling on an Irish passport under the name Gail Foliard – but she was neither Irish nor Gail Foliard. She was a woman of eastern Mediterranean origin, petite verging on the delicate, long black hair held at the back in a bun.

She had been the one on the floor of the bedroom, the one who had injected the sux. The shape that had been one of the last things Mahmoud Abdel Rauf al-Mabhouh ever saw…

19 October 2012
3 Dhu al-Hijja 1433

Beirut, Lebanon

Brigadier Wissam al-Hassan was the head of the Information Branch (the Intelligence Division) of the Lebanese Internal Security Force. He was also one of Lebanon's most secretive figures. Outside of the ISF, most Lebanese did not know what he looked like – which was how he liked it. He was forty-seven years of age and had been made head of the Information Branch nearly seven years previously on 19 January 2006 (19 Dhu al-Hijja 1426), tasked with leading the investigation into the 2005 assassination of former Prime Minister Rafic Hariri.

Which was ironic. Because al-Hassan used to work for Hariri as his Chief of Protocol, and as such he should have been with Hariri in that fatal motorcade on 14 February 2005 (5 Muharram 1426) – but he had taken the day off to study for a university exam [*a fact which the UN Special Tribunal for Lebanon found to be a 'weak and inconsistent' alibi. Although the Tribunal recommended that al-Hassan warranted further investigation regarding Hariri's assassination, he was not amongst those indicted in January 2011*].

al-Hassan was an enigmatic contradiction. He had ties with *Al Mukhabarat Al A'amah* (Saudi intelligence). He had close and private liaisons with Syrian President Bashar al-Assad and yet was strongly linked to the anti-Assad confessions in Lebanon (some believe he may have been a double agent). It is said he facilitated the passage through Lebanon of money and arms from the Gulf States to the Syrian opposition.

On home soil, despite some insiders claiming that he had ties to Mossad, he had uncovered and overseen the dismantling of a network of Israeli spies, leading to the arrest of over one hundred individuals suspected of collaborating with the Jews.

His division was involved in the al-Mahdi incident in 2010.

Just two months ago, in August 2012, he had led an investigation that culminated in the arrest of former Lebanese Information Minister Michel Samaha who was charged, together with Syrian National Security Bureau chief Ali Mamlouk (in absentia), with transporting explosives into Lebanon in an attempt to destabilise the country.

Every true Lebanese agreed that al-Hassan's tenure at Lebanese Intelligence had been a great success.

But there are those that do not like success...

al-Hassan had been in Paris with his wife Anna and sons Majd and Mazen three days previously when he had received the encrypted phone call. He had intended to stay in Paris over Eid al-Adha, returning next week, but the message he received was clear: he was needed back, now. An important item the Internal Security Force had been looking for for over two years had been located and apprehended. But the item would talk only to Hassan (despite the ISF's best persuasive efforts).

al-Hassan left his family in Paris and returned to Beirut on 18 October. As always, he travelled using an alternative (not fake) passport, using an alternative (not fake) name. At Beirut's Rafic Hariri International Airport he picked up a hire car. Those unused to the subtleties of Lebanese security might think this strange – surely the country's intelligence chief would travel at least in an armoured car if not in an armoured convoy? But that would be expected – and an armoured car and armoured convoy, with state-of-the-art surveillance and frequency jamming equipment, had not stopped Rafic Hariri being blown to *al-janna*. A hire car was good camouflage.

It was late and he went home, driving from the airport through the Hizbullah heartland of South Beirut without incident.

The next morning, he was in his office early. He had much to deal with, even only having been away a few days. The 'item' was being held at one of the ISF's secret offices not too far away near Sassine Square, and al-Hassan arranged an afternoon appointment.

At 14:30, al-Hassan and his driver Ahmad Suhyuni left the ISF headquarters in the Hotel Dieu area in the hired car. The drive up the narrow, winding back streets of Ashrafieh was predictably slow (where *did* Beirut's traffic come from? Where was it going?).

At 14:49 they crawled along Ibrahim Monzer Street, the secret office in sight. Nearby were the offices of the Kataeb political party. Just up the street were the headquarters of the March 14 political alliance, currently the opposition in the Lebanese parliament.

At 14:50, as al-Hassan prepared to get out of the vehicle, a nearby parked car exploded with the savage force of thirty kilograms of TNT, the blast contained and assisted by the narrow street. al-Hassan knew nothing about it. His life simply ended. He was killed instantly along with driver Ahmad Suhyuni. Two other people died and one hundred and ten people were injured, the explosion leaving a large crater in the road, tearing off the balconies of nearby buildings and blowing in windows, knocking down shelves in the ABC shopping mall two hundred and fifty metres to the north.

Ironically, Wissam al-Hassan died in an identical manner to Rafic Hariri. And, also in a manner identical to the Hariri assassination, a figure on a motorbike – no helmet, long black hair tied back in a ponytail - was seen leaving the area shortly after the explosion…

PART ONE
الجزء الأول

THE GARDENER
البستاني

21 October 2012
5 Dhu al-Hijja 1433

Jounieh, Lebanon 07:00

"Well, that's it," said Captain Jihad Merhi of the Internal Security Force. He was leaning against the worktop next to the sink in the kitchen of his spacious mountainside apartment sixteen kilometres north of Beirut. In his hands he held his breakfast: a triple espresso and his second Camel King Size cigarette of the day. At fifty-three he was still slim, reasonably fit for his age, and greying gracefully. He was also tired. So damn tired. "War has returned to Lebanon."

"Is it not an overreaction?" asked his wife Gisele, seated at the small breakfast table against the wall, a more fulfilling (and marginally more healthy) half-eaten *za'atar* croissant next to her orange juice and coffee. "Not you, dear husband," she hastened to clarify, "but..." She waved her right hand to encompass 'out there'.

Jihad shrugged with his mouth. Yesterday had been declared a national day of mourning following Friday's assassination of Brigadier Wissam al-Hassan, Jihad's ultimate boss (although twice-removed up the chain of command). Anger had erupted across the country, in Sidon in the south, in Tripoli in the north, but especially in Beirut. Opposition supporters had set up road blocks and burnt tyres, denouncing Syrian President Bashar al-Assad and his allies in the Lebanese government. There had been gunfire.

"An overreaction to the Brigadier's murder?" mused Jihad. "*Bien sûr*. But it is just another excuse, another catalyst of many catalysts - "

"Another excuse for a fight?"

"To put it succinctly, yes."

Gisele broke off a piece of croissant and put it into her mouth, her tongue coming out to receive it. Even though they had been married many years, Jihad was just a teensie bit jealous. If there was such a thing as reincarnation, he was coming back as a *za'atar* croissant.

"Did the events ever really finish?" A flake of pastry bounced on Gisele's lower lip. *['The events' is how many Lebanese refer to the 1975-1990 civil war.]*

"We both know the answer to that." Jihad stubbed out his cigarette. "And now today we have the Brigadier's funeral. The army is out in force, but God knows what is going to happen."

Gisele stood up. "I worry about you." She came across, entwining her arms around her husband's waist. She could smell the smoke and coffee off him.

Jihad bent his head and licked the crumb off of his wife's mouth. "No need," he said softly. "And since I no longer *have* to wear a uniform, things are easier on days of civil unrest."

"And you have your friend." Gisele patted the bulge on his waistband. His official-issue Browning 9mm High Power (recently changed from the Herstal 9mm because the Lebanese Finance Ministry had 'got a good deal').

One of only two friends that never let me down, thought Jihad. He said, "When are you next due in?"

"I have a class next Thursday."

"Things will have calmed down by then. *Insh'allah*."

For many years Gisele had been a member of the GSD, the Lebanese security service, firstly in the field and then latterly as a trainer. She had been involved in the Princess Diana incident in Paris in 1997, she still had the raised scar on the left side of her neck as a souvenir. Forty-something and now officially retired from field work, the slim, dark-haired 'Libanette' (as her husband sometimes referred to her) had recently been persuaded back to help train the influx of recruits into the Lebanese internal and external security services, a patriotic recruitment surge fuelled by the threat of the Syrian civil war overspill into Lebanon.

"Got your building ID?"

"Oh shit," Jihad tap-danced his hands around his jacket. He found it in his left hip pocket, the plasticised ID card with his photo; the blue lanyard with the pattern of twee little Lebanese flags was wrapped around it. It was a new thing in the State Security Building, everyone had to wear an ID around their neck. Also a metal detection system had been installed at the entrance – ironic, and more than a tad inconvenient, because each member of the Security Service carried a gun. But Management had deemed it necessary - now that the Syrian war was spilling over into Liban it was difficult to tell friend from foe.

Jihad pecked his wife on the lips. "Right, I'm off." With a lingering movement of his hand against her small breasts, he moved Gisele to one side and went out to the hallway, collecting his jacket. "I'll see you tonight."

"*Prends soin*" she said as he walked down the stairs. "Take care."

As she closed the door she said softly, "My husband."

Jonblat, Beirut 21:00

It had been worse than expected, reflected Jihad Merhi as he led his team back into their offices in the old Annexe to the State Security offices in northern Beirut, just west of downtown. Worse. Which, perversely, was exactly as expected!

Wissam al-Hassan had been laid to rest alongside the tomb of Rafic Hariri near the Mohammad Amin Mosque in Martyrs' Square. It had been a state funeral attended by thousands including significant political figures from all the confessions. During the ceremony, President Michel Suleiman had awarded al-Hassan the National Order of the Cedar in Grade of Grand Officer, one of Lebanon's highest honours (and I'm sure al-Hassan was grateful for it, mused Merhi).

Then the trouble had started. A large crowd had headed the three hundred metres down Emir Bechir Street to the Prime Minister's offices, the Grand Serail, demanding the resignation of Prime Minister Najib Mikati, calling him and the government 'Syrian puppets'. They had been pushed back by troops firing live bullets into the air and tear gas directly at the protestors. There was fighting.

Thankfully, Merhi and his much-reduced team of six (economic staff cuts) of Sergeant Deeb el-Gharib and five Corporals were not responsible for street security, that was the police and the army. It was Merhi's responsibility to assist in the discreet security of the 'significant political figures', alongside their own security teams. That had gone well.

But even now, hours after the funeral, the fighting continued in the streets. In some areas, gunmen had set up checkpoints, scrutinising the sectarian identity of passers-by. Shots had been fired. Sunni upon Shi'a, Shi'a upon Sunni. Hundreds of arrests had been made.

The occasional sound of gunfire and the constant rumble of rioting could still be heard from not too far away as Merhi entered the General Office with his team. He headed directly to the small table on which sat a kettle and a newly-acquired but before-the-ark filter coffee machine. He picked up the coffee pot, grimacing. This morning's brew of sludge had burnt and solidified. Handing the pot to a Corporal (who took it out to the gents' WC to empty it as best he could), he took out his fortieth Camel King Size of the day.

Merhi stared at the *seejaere* in one hand and the empty packet in the other, shaking his head. Why did he do this? His doctor was always on at him to quit. More importantly, so was Gisele. Carefully he aimed the cigarette at a nearby waste bin – then he changed his mind and lobbed the empty packet in instead. Lighting up, he said to el-Gharib "I'll be in my office for a few minutes and then I'm going home."

"Right, boss. You want any sludge?"

"If I'm still here."

His office was just metres down the corridor. He went in, closing the door behind him, the door with the cracked pane of opaque glass (the crack had been there for seven years, Facilities should be getting around to it soon). On his desk was a new pile of folders – which could stay there, until tomorrow or when he took a shit, whichever came first (might as well put the contents to some good use).

He stretched, yawning – and felt a tingling down his right leg. Quickly he put his arms down, fearful that the heart attack he had always feared was starting. But wasn't that supposed to be in your arms and neck?

The tingling stopped. Then started again. Then stopped. Then started again. What the...? Looking heavenward, he put his hand into his pocket and pulled out his iPhone which he had left on silent-vibrate.

He looked at the Caller ID. A local number which he did not recognise and which was not one of his Contacts.

His finger hovered between the green and red icons. It had been a long day, he should just decline the call. His finger pressed down on the red icon – and somehow brushed the green icon first.

Shit.

Tentatively he raised the phone to his ear. There was a lot of noise, background shouting, raised male voices. "Hello?" said a voice.

"Hello?"

"Abu Samer?"

It couldn't be. Not today. Not now. Lord, was there no mercy?

"Mm."

"Evening of joy, my dear, dear friend. It is Lattouf!"

Oh Christ. "Fadi, how are you?" Merhi didn't mean it, he didn't want to know, it was just how all Lebanese started their phone calls.

"I am well, my friend, well. And you and the charming Gisele?"

"As ever, Fadi."

"And your boys? Are they coming home at the new year?"

"Probably. Fadi, I can't really talk right now - "

"My friend, I am sorry for calling you at this hour. But I am in – how do you say? – a little spot of bother, and I wondered if you could help me?"

Merhi sucked a full centimetre off of his cigarette. As he swallowed the smoke, he sighed deeper than he had ever sighed before. "What is it, Fadi?"

There was a pause on the other end. Then, "Jihad, I am at Sanayeh police station."

"And what are you doing there?"

Another pause. "I have been arrested."

Sanayeh, Beirut 21:30

The Sanayeh police station was within walking distance of the State Security Building. Just across the René Moawad Public Garden and a dogleg along Mary Eddeh Street. But Merhi took his car, the official-issue decuma grey

Toyota Land Cruiser V8. He wanted to go home after he had sorted out this little matter. It would not take him long to get Lattouf out, he had the clout. Lattouf would be a free man in a matter of minutes, unless he had committed murder (and even then…).

Merhi smoked as he drove down Sanayeh Street (for medicinal purposes only, to counteract his tiredness and the stress of the day), and thought of his friend.

Fadi Lattouf. Or more precisely Captain Fadi Lattouf of the Civil Police of the Palestinian Security Force in the Bourj el-Barajneh refugee camp in southern Beirut. A giant of a man in all ways: his appetites, his oral and bodily volume, his presence, his physique. He was nearly two metres tall and measured the same around his stomach. Bearded and bald, save for the few strands of greying black hair that swept over his head from just above his left ear.

Because of his size, his rolling gait, his manner of speaking (often traditional, sometimes quite formal) and his perceived (though not necessarily actual) clumsiness, people often dismissed Fadi Lattouf as an idiot. It was a mistake they made only once. Idiots did not spend many years policing the Gaza Strip. Idiots did not become the senior police officer in charge of the Palestinian refugee camps in the Beirut area, enforcing as much discipline as was possible in the overcrowded slums while maintaining the eggshell bridge of contact with the groups that really ruled the camps: Fatah and Hamas.

Merhi and Lattouf had met many years ago. Part of Merhi's duties was to be the liaison link between the Lebanese Internal Security Force and the Palestinian Police controlling the Beirut refugee camps. Captain Fadi Lattouf was his opposite number.

Outside of the formal liaison, fate had thrown them together on other occasions, most notably during the Hariri assassination in 2005 and the al-Mahdi incident in 2010. And they had socialised with their families, despite Merhi's initial (and sometimes continuing) reluctance.

Destiny moves in mysterious and inexplicable ways, and Merhi had now accepted that his lot was to be a friend of Fadi Lattouf.

The holding cell in Sanayeh police station was compact at the best of times. With Lattouf in it it looked like a doll's house cupboard with a grizzly bear trapped inside. It was possible Lattouf's body touched all four walls at the same time.

Lattouf was at the bars, and his reaction when he saw Merhi coming down the corridor accompanied by the duty police officer was like a dog on seeing his owner.

"Jihad! Abu Samer! Evening of joy, my dear friend. Thank you, thank you."

"Evening of get out of jail free, Fadi." Merhi nodded at the policeman. "Let him out."

The policeman unlocked the door and Lattouf stepped out, giving him a disdainful look. "I told you he was my friend."

The policeman shrugged.

Lattouf was dressed in rough blue denim jeans, for which he was about thirty years too old and fifty kilos too heavy, and a loose pink and blue checked shirt – the outfit he always wore when he wanted to be casual. Merhi had known the outfit for as long as he'd known Lattouf: nine years.

"What happened?" asked Merhi as they walked back down the corridor.

"He pushed me, I pushed back." Lattouf sounded like a child called to explain himself.

"What were you doing there anyway?"

"I had come to pay my respects to your Chief. To say the *Salat al-Janazah*. It was dreadful what happened to him. Dreadful."

Merhi was touched. "Thank you, Fadi. So what happened today?"

"The crowd, it became unruly. I was swept along."

"*You* were swept along?"

"Nada has me on this diet, as you can see." (Merhi couldn't.) "I am wasting away. It's a wonder you recognised me."

Merhi raised his eyebrows. Lattouf continued. "One of the mourners pushed into me. I pushed him back…"

"Let me guess. You didn't know your own strength."

Lattouf shrugged. "It was just a gentle shove. He will be all right. If he wakes up."

They had reached Merhi's car out in Omayads Street. "Get in," said Merhi. "I'll give you a lift home."

"No, no, that is fine." Lattouf opened the passenger door. "I am parked over near Debbas Square. If you could take me there please." The Toyota dipped markedly to the right as he got in.

"Might not be a good idea," Merhi's weight made not one degree of counterbalance as he climbed in the driver's side. "They are still rioting. If they see a blue Palestinian Police van in the street - "

"What? Oh, I don't use that any more, except when I am on official business. No, it's my Bluebird."

Merhi remembered. The garish orange Datsun Bluebird rust bucket that Lattouf had inherited from his cousin Chadi. He said, "Same thing applies though. It might be dangerous downtown tonight. I'll give you a lift home. You can come back and get it tomorrow – or whenever this dies down."

Lattouf nodded. "Your advice is always good, my friend. I will take it."

Merhi offered his newly-opened packet of Camel King Size. Lattouf raised his hand. "I have given up. Nada's orders." Merhi went to pull the packet away. "But," Lattouf reached out, "I cannot refuse a man's hospitality in his own vehicle. Thank you." Merhi lit both cigarettes.

They drove off, turning left into René Moawad Street. This straight road would become Rachidine Street and then the wider Subah es Salem es Subah Avenue, leading down eventually to the area of the Bourj el-Barajneh camp.

Savouring the cigarette, Lattouf looked at his left wrist although there was no watch on it. "It is getting late but you must let me thank you."

"No, no, it is not necessary." Merhi knew what was coming and he dragged in desperation on his Camel.

"Nada would have kept my supper for me. There will be plenty."

Oh hell. "You are too kind."

"To feed you is the least I can do. And I will wake the children up. It has been a long time since they have seen their Uncle Jihad."

Oh Christ.

For something to say, Merhi asked "How old is Little Wissam now?"

Lattouf smiled, thinking of his youngest son. "He is five. He looks more like me each day. Little Fadi!" He laughed.

Merhi's mind was boggling. Distractedly, he said "I'm surprised you stopped at six. I thought Number Seven would be well on his or her way by now."

Lattouf looked out of the side window, seeing the myriad posters and pictures hanging from buildings and across the road. Some of local martyrs, some of the green arm and fist holding the Kalshnikov AK47 assault rifle on a yellow background, but most of Sayyed Hassan Nasrallah, the leader of Hizbullah. In the darkness of the night it was disconcerting.

"We all get old, my friend," he said quietly. He turned back towards Merhi. "My winkie, it is not how it used to be. For sure, it is still interested. It comes up to have a look around. But then it goes down again, too soon."

The cigarette nearly fell from Merhi's mouth and he started coughing. After a while, he said "Thank you, Fadi. That is too much information."

"You are welcome, my friend."

They drove on into south Beirut.

22 October 2012
6 Dhu al-Hijja 1433

Jounieh, Lebanon 07:00

"I am surprised you are hungry this morning, after such a late meal," said Gisele.

Her husband spoke through a mouthful of custard doughnut. "I'm not, it just counteracts the goat and rice. Lies heavy." He patted his stomach. "I had already eaten last night as well, anticipating the late evening."

"But not anticipating Lattouf."

"How can anybody anticipate that? He always turns up when you least expect him, at the most inauspicious times."

Gisele came over and, with light flicks of a finger, brushed sugar from Jihad's mouth. "How was Nada and the children?"

"The children were sleepy, but well-behaved like they always are. I gave them some money. Nada was her usual self, as big as ever and yet she has put *him* on a diet."

"Yet another one?"

"He was allowed only two plates of goat and rice instead of three."

Gisele nodded. "The weight will be falling off of him then. He will be like a catwalk model in no time."

Jihad laughed, kissing his wife and leaving her with sugary lips. He knocked back his triple espresso. "Right. let's see what horrors await me today." He pushed away from the kitchen worktop and headed out into the hallway.

"Will you be late again?"

Jihad shrugged as he shrugged into his jacket. "Who knows?"

"Ring me. Let me know."

"Sure. You going anywhere today?"

"I might go out shopping."

Jihad turned in the doorway, adjusting his jacket, making sure it covered his gun. "Well, spend wisely, and be careful if you go into town. There will still be uncertainty on the streets after the al-Hassan protests. For me the good thing is, I've had my Lattouf fix. He wanted to meet today for lunch when he goes in to pick up his car but I said no. Said I would be too busy. Wasn't a lie, we've got a section heads meeting this morning. So the next time we'll see him will probably be New Year. You take care now." He pecked her one more time on the lips and then started down the stairs.

In the world of security, 'probably' is an unacceptable adverb. 'Probably' denotes uncertainty. It is a seed of doubt.

And there was no doubt that, that day, Jihad Merhi was going to be wrong.

Jonblat, Beirut 11:30

"Abu Samer, may I have a word?"

The use of the *kunya* always grated on the Maronite Jihad Merhi, but it was one of the foibles of his boss, Major Ghanem.

"Major?"

"My office."

The section heads meeting was over and the men were dispersing. During the meeting, Major Ghanem had informed them that Colonel Imad Othman was taking over as the Head of the Intelligence Bureau. Colonel Othman had not been present, and it seemed to Merhi that he was going to be as anonymous as his predecessor, the assassinated Wissam al-Hassan (in the nearly eight years al-Hassan had been Head of the Intelligence Bureau, Merhi had not met him once).

Up on the fifth floor, Merhi nodded at Ghanem's secretary Violette Ghorra as he followed 'The Old Man' into his offices. He was rewarded with a smile.

Ghanem did not invite Merhi to sit down. From his trouser pocket he took out some keys, attached to his belt by a chain, and unlocked a drawer in his desk. "As you know, the late Brigadier had many great successes during his tenure."

"*En effet.*"

Ghanem sniffed. "Some more successful than others. One he is noted for."

"Samaha?"

"Before that."

Merhi nodded. "Ah." He knew better than to say it out loud. The Listeners were everywhere.

"Our new Colonel wants to shake things up a bit." (As they all do when they take over, thought Merhi.) "He is a great believer in delegation. He has delegated this matter. We will be in charge of it. That means you will be in charge of it." Ghanem's hand came out of his drawer holding what looked like an ATM card. It had no writing or markings on it whatsoever, just a single embedded chip towards one end. It was deep red in colour, almost maroon.

Ghanem held it out but Merhi held up his hands. "That," said Merhi, recognising the colour for Above Top Secret, "is above my pay grade."

Ghanem was quiet for a moment, still holding out the card. Then he said, "No longer, *Ra'id* Merhi."

Merhi's eyebrows rose. *Major* Merhi?

"Also as of today I am *Muqaddam*," said Ghanem. Lieutenant-Colonel. He gestured with the card. "Well?"

Merhi was at a loss of what to say. Had that just happened? Had he been promoted? He desperately needed a Camel but Ghanem was probably the only man in Lebanon who did not smoke. "Con...gratulations."

"It does not affect our jobs or location," said Ghanem, brushing away the niceties. "At least at this time. You will still report to me. You will still have your team, only now because of your rank it can be augmented as you see fit and as necessary. You are autonomous in such matters. Come on, take it." He thrust the card again.

Merhi reached out and took the card, turning it over in his hand.

"Sole systems access at ATS level," said Ghanem. "You do not need me to tell you what will happen to you if you ever lose it. You can access all the Brigadier's files and reports. Give me a report on what, if any, current action we need to take by next week. Also report on any changes you will be making to your team."

Merhi shook his head. "This... this will not fit my computer. I have no card reader ports."

"Facilities are replacing the equipment in your office as we speak. You will be required to provide scans for biometric access also. Any questions?"

Merhi thought for a moment, still looking at the card. The card that had just changed his life. Then he nodded and asked, "If Facilities are in my office, do you think that they can replace that cracked glass in my door?"

"You are a Major now," said Lieutenant-Colonel Ghanem. "Fucking arrange it yourself."

Major Merhi did not register the other staff who were using the echoing back staircase as he walked down the three flights from Ghanem's office, although he nodded to a few of them. He had his iPhone in his hand and he was trying to call Gisele. Twice the connection failed, the third time he got her voicemail.

"Hi Gigi... er, just to let you know - " He stood back, holding the landing door open for one of the female PAs. As he hovered a little too long, watching her bottom go up the stairs, he realised that his new rank now qualified him for one of those – a PA, that is. Also he realised that he shouldn't say what he was about to say on a hackable voicemail.

He went through the door and walked down the corridor. "I might be home early tonight. I've got some news. Definitely I'll be there for dinner."

"Boss!" Sergeant Deeb el-Gharib shouted from the General Office.

"Take care." Merhi took the phone from his ear, squinting at the icons, his thumb finding the red one.

He was past the General Office and from behind him el-Gharib called again, "Boss!"

"Not now, Deeb," he said over his shoulder. "I'll be in in a minute."

"Boss..."

Merhi entered his office and stopped. There were two things there that hadn't been there earlier.

First was a small, quite discreet and yet almost sinister- looking black rectangle on his desk where his old PC used to be.

The second, standing over by the window, was Fadi Lattouf.

Lattouf was dressed in his uniform trousers and light blue shirt, his police jacket draped over the back of the wooden chair in front of Merhi's desk. He turned as he heard Merhi enter, a wide grin splitting his face. Around his thick neck, the standard-length ID lanyard looked like a choker.

"Morning of happy coincidence, my dear Captain!"

For a moment Merhi said nothing. Then he frowned. "Fadi, I said I couldn't do lunch today. Even more so now."

"I understand, my friend. But I am not here for *ghadae*. It is the way these things happen. *Yadreb asfoorayn behajar*. I am killing the two stones with one bird."

Merhi raised an eyebrow.

"I had to pick up my car," continued Lattouf, "and I need to see you – officially. Something very important has happened. I received a phone call- "

"Don't!" snapped Merhi.

Lattouf was taken aback.

From the doorway, Merhi mimed an expansive room-embracing gesture with his hand and then pointed to his ear.

Lattouf continued frowning and then the metaphorical light bulb went on above his head. "Ah," he nodded.

"Was your car all right?" asked Merhi.

"What? Oh yes, yes."

"How are the streets?"

"Here it is fine, your army has done a good job, but coming up through Tariq el Jedideh things were still very tense. I think there will be trouble there later."

"How *did* you get in to town?"

"My sergeant drove me in the van. Dropped me off."

Merhi nodded, realising that he had yet to move from the doorway. He walked in and shook his friend's hand, becoming aware of a louder-than-usual commotion of bipping horns and shouting out in Bank of Lebanon

Street. He looked beyond Lattouf, out of the window, knowing, just knowing, what he was going to see.

Sure enough, down below a garish orange Datsun Bluebird rust bucket had been parked at such an angle that it was blocking one lane of the street. Vehicles were jousting to get around it.

Merhi turned back. "You know, Fadi," he said, "lunch *would* be a good idea, if you're hungry."

"I could squeeze something in."

"Let's go down to Hamra."

"Shall we walk?"

"No. We'll take your car."

As he walked back past his desk, Merhi glanced at the sinister black rectangle: a laptop. Then he looked at Lattouf. He wondered which of the two was going to cause him trouble.

As it happened, it would be both.

Hamra, Beirut 12:45

Hamra Square was busy but they had managed to secure a table, Lattouf moving with surprising speed when he saw one becoming free, cutting off an elderly couple who were also heading for it. The Bluebird was parked in a side road off Makdissi Street, and Merhi was off buying falafel, coffee and something sweet.

Lattouf loved it here. In times past Hamra was *the* shopping district of Beirut. Many of the famous names had now moved to other locations, such as the malls and back into the rebuilt city centre, but the area still buzzed. The retail shops and the sidewalk stalls were as popular as ever, the shouts from the street-hawkers vying with the noise from the traffic to see who could be the loudest. And there was a stall on the square here that did the finest *mekhallel* this side of Gaza! He had his car, he could stock up on the pickles.

He saw Merhi doing a little belly dance past the tables, carrying a large, oblong tray. This looked like more than falafel!

And indeed it was. The tray was piled with falafel, stuffed vine leaves, bread, hummus, *tabouleh*, and chicken and lamb kabobs.

Lattouf looked like he had died and gone to *janna*. "Bless your hands, my friend! Your generosity is overwhelming."

Like your stomach, thought Merhi. Out loud he said, "I've got another tray - "

"I'll get it!"

"No, no. You sort these out. And remember I'm eating too."

He was back momentarily with a tray containing a box of *baklava*, a bag with ten *ma'amoul,* a packet of four cupcakes, two king size Americano coffees and one triple espresso. "There, that should see you all right until Nada feeds you tonight."

"I might just make it," conceded Lattouf without a trace of satire. He had tucked a small paper napkin down the open neck of his shirt. It looked like, and was as effective as, a postage stamp on the outside of a tent.

Merhi noted that a lamb kabob had already disappeared. He sat down, ensuring his jacket covered the gun on his waistband. Time was he could have left the weapon in his office when he was not in uniform, but those days had gone. Beirut, indeed the whole of Lebanon, was now a jungle of refugees, radicals, extremists, fanatics, terrorists, spies, moles, agents, kidnappers, assassins, not to mention opportunist criminals. The Syrian uprising had seen to that. And in a jungle you took whatever precautions were necessary.

He chose one of each kabob, one stuffed vine leaf and two falafel.

Lattouf frowned. "No bread, my friend? *Tabouleh?*"

"No, these will do. And the chocolate cupcake's mine." He moved his espresso into his own territory, just to be on the safe side.

"You are not hungry?" Lattouf was sweeping up hummus with folded-over flatbread.

"I have other things on my mind. I didn't supersize the meal because I know you are on a diet."

"I am grateful for your consideration. Nada will thank you."

"I'm sure," Merhi pulled some chicken off the skewer with his fingers. "Fadi, I've..." He stopped and watched as Lattouf tilted his head back, lowered an entire kabob into his mouth, closed his teeth and denuded the skewer as he took it back out. "...got something to tell you."

"Andivegotsomthtellyou."

"What?"

Lattouf swallowed. "And I've got something to tell you, my friend. That's why I came to see you."

"I've - "

"You first."

Merhi watched as another lamb kebob was executed. Then he said, "I've been promoted."

Lattouf stopped chewing, staring at Merhi, his face expressionless. Then he frowned. Saying nothing, he picked up a stuffed vine leaf and popped it into his mouth whole, like posting a letter.

"Er," said Merhi, "it is usual to say congratulations?"

For a moment Lattouf was far away, then he shook his head. "Yes, yes, I am sorry, Abu Samer. *Mabruk.* Allah's blessings upon you. So you are now...?"

"Major Merhi."

"Major." Lattouf raised a greasy hand and gave a greasy salute. "Truly, my congratulations."

"*Merci mon ami.*"

"But where does it leave us?"

"Us?"

"I assume you will be moving on to other duties? Will you be replaced? Will I have to liaise with someone else?"

Ah, that explained his reaction. Merhi smiled. "It doesn't work like that, not nowadays. I take on a wider remit, in many additional matters I now become autonomous, running things myself. Everything is down to me."

"You will at last be given credit for your successes?"

"And will have to pay for my failures…"

Both men ate, each thinking back seven years to when they were within two minutes of preventing the assassination of Rafic Hariri.

But what was done, was done. Merhi shook off the thought. "I also retain all my present responsibilities. So, my dear Palestinian friend, you are still mine. And I am still yours."

Lattouf was now beaming. He picked up one of the king size cups of coffee, liquid sloshing out where he was gripping it too tight, and raised it in a toast. "To us! What a team! Lattouf and Merhi. Together forever!"

Merhi just maintained the shaky smile on his face while fighting the urge to pull out his gun and blow his own brains out. The eventual consequences of Lattouf's next remark made him subsequently wish he had followed through with it.

"Well, my dear Major, as my formal link with the Lebanese authorities, I have an official request. Last night I received a call from my counterpart at the Bourj al-Shimali camp. They have made a serious arrest down there. An Israeli spy. They wish to hand him over. As the senior officer of all the camps, they want me to come down and pick him up. But, as you know, outside of the camps I have no jurisdiction, no powers. So would you come with me, please? To Tyre."

Jounieh, Lebanon 16:45

Gisele was not in when Jihad returned home, she was probably out shopping like she had threatened or meeting with her friends, doing what girls do. He had tried ringing her again from the car on the way up from Beirut but calls were still going to voicemail. So he decided the first thing he would do, while waiting for her, was to look at this black, unbranded laptop that was now his.

Actually, no. The first thing he would do was to pour himself a large

Johnnie Walker and have a Camel, *then* he would look at the laptop.

Earlier, he had returned to the office with cakes, bottles of quality orange juice for the Muslims and champagne for the non-Muslims and had broken the news of his promotion to his team – hastily reassuring them that he was not moving anywhere except upwards in rank. Someone from IT had been waiting for him and had conducted digital and retinal biometric procedures and associated them with the laptop. Then he had been visited by someone else from IT who could have been no more than twelve years old and who gave him an introductory, very fast and very condescending run-through on the machine.

Now Merhi stood on his wide balcony in the early-evening sun, whisky in one hand, cigarette in the other, and looked out over the mountainside, across the main Coastal Highway far below and out over the Mediterranean Sea.

He had agreed to go to Tyre with Lattouf. What else could he do? He could delegate it, especially now he was a Major, but he would not foist Lattouf onto a junior (he stopped short of thinking that he would not wish Lattouf on anybody). And anyway, Fadi was a friend. Lattouf had wanted to go tomorrow but Jihad had explained that this was not possible. In his new role he had things to do, new staff to meet.

They had agreed on a trip south in three days time. The local Palestinian Civil Police Captain would look after the spy until then. They would be going in Merhi's Toyota – Merhi thought Lattouf's Bluebird was unlikely to make the 160 kilometre round-trip, despite Lattouf's protestations that he had recently given it a good service. And, reasoned Merhi, even if it did get down to Tyre its garish orange colour was too much of a target so close to the border with Occupied Palestine. Lattouf could not argue with that.

But it was bizarre. Was Lattouf a mind reader? A *sahir*, a wizard? The breaking of Israeli spy rings in Lebanon had been the other noted triumph of the late Brigadier Wissam al-Hassan. Hundreds of arrests had been made over the last two years, and overseeing the now-finishing project had been delegated to Merhi this morning. He had to report on it to Ghanem in a week, that was why he had brought the laptop home, to get up to speed.

That Lattouf had come to him with an arrested spy on the very day he had been assigned the project was, well, pure Lattouf. How he always managed to do it, Merhi did not know. Lattouf was always in the right place at the right time, bumbling about like a wayward pinball, trampling over evidence, intimidating suspects, but always getting it right in the end, even if most times he did not realise it.

Lattouf was a *marid*, a giant, powerful genie – a djinn.

Jihad took a final draw on his cigarette and flicked the butt out over the mountainside. He smiled as he finished his whisky, memories that had never gone away rolling to the forefront of his mind, exploding in Imax 3D and surround sound.

A djinn...

He had known a djinn. Twice their paths had crossed. The first time during the Hariri business, then throughout the al-Mahdi incident.

This djinn took the form of a woman, a woman who worked for the DGS, the external security service. A woman who, he had found out, was married to an unnamed Lebanese mercenary. A mercenary who had also been involved with al-Mahdi and had caught Gisele's attention as much as The Djinn had caught his.

The Djinn had even stayed with him and Gisele for a while. He remembered the small, olive-skinned body, the long dark hair, the black eyes. And the scent that followed her wherever she went and lingered wherever she had been: jasmine.

A beguiling, exotic, dangerous creature...

Murray Hill, New York City, USA 11:15 (local time)

"Thanks, Larry."

"You have a good day, Miss Chedid." The doorman touched the peak of his hat with his index finger and admired the firm, athletic legs as the olive-skinned, deep-voiced no-longer-a-babe-not-yet-a-cougar from Apartment 3030 turned left, heading west on East 39th Street. The smell of jasmine made promises to his nose which would never be kept.

Her long, black hair was down, held in place by an ornate black and gold hair clip, swaying very gently from side to side as she walked. Today she was wearing a short, loose blue dress covered by an open, padded coat, her dark grey Barbour wax cotton messenger bag over one shoulder. Larry preferred it when she wore pants or jeans and a small jacket – although there was less skin on display, he could see her ass better. And imagine.

And imagine was all he could do. Because he knew two things about her. She was a diplomat, Egyptian or Syrian or something, working over by the UN. Not an inhibitor in itself, but when combined with the fact that she was married to the tall, hard man with the long black hair and scarred face, the man who returned only occasionally, who rarely spoke and who emitted an aura of complete and utter menace, it meant that she was well off limits. She was Major League, Larry was not even Triple A – he was Saturday ball park.

Larry might have known those two things but what he did not – and never would – know was that Carla Chedid was a Gatherer, working for the Lebanese Department of General Security. Based at number 866 United Nations Plaza at The Permanent Mission of Lebanon to the United Nations, her diplomatic status was recorded officially as an Assistant Counsellor. But in reality she gathered information, facts, ideas, theories, thoughts, anything and everything that may or may not affect the security of Lebanon. She had been based in New York for seven years. Seven years since, under another name, she had been exiled from Lebanon after the Hariri assassination.

She ran a network of assets in other embassies here in Manhattan, and one or two in the UN itself. She was on her way to see one now.

She was, quite simply, a spy. A spy who would seduce when necessary. A spy who would pay when necessary. A spy who would blackmail when necessary. A spy who would kill when necessary, efficiently and without compunction.

She was also known as The Djinn.

Midtown, New York City, USA 11:30 (local time)

By the Mid-Manhattan Library, Carla turned right into Fifth Avenue heading north. Then she doglegged into East 40th Street past the side of the New York Public Library and down into Bryant Park.

It was a sunny, blue sky, late October morning and the temperatures were now dropping, so she headed for the Southwest Porch eatery and sat at a table under the pergola.

He would find her.

Fifteen minutes later, spot on time, she saw him coming in from 42nd Street. Tall, quite beefy, cropped reddish hair, rosy cheeks, dressed in a suit and tie, looking very much the all-American Manhattanite. He would have walked from the Consulate at 800 Second Avenue.

Of the four asset-control methods of seduction, payment, blackmail or threat, this one was seduction. Therefore he smiled when he saw her, her coat open, legs crossed, dress ridden far up her olive thighs. He thought of what was above them. He *remembered* what was above them…

She returned the smile and watched as he came in.

"Shalom," he leant forward and kissed her on both cheeks. "Mah Ha'Inyanim?"

"B'seder," she said. "I am fine. And you?"

"Mamash Tov. Really good. It always helps when I see you. You smell delicious as always."

She did not respond but her black eyes showed warmth – and promise.

"Can I get you anything?" he asked.

She nodded at the Americano in front of her. "This is fine, thank you."

He made gestures to an orange-shirted server that he would have the same. Carla inwardly smiled at his mirroring.

They made small-talk until his coffee was delivered. As the server left,

Carla asked "You have something for me?"

He sipped his coffee, giving the impression of thinking. Putting his cup back down he said, "Do *you* have something for *me?*"

Softly she said, "You know what I have for you."

"And I get to have it again?"

"Yes."

"When?"

"If your information is good - "

"Oh it's good."

"Then soon. Boys must learn patience." She reached across with both hands, touching his arm. Not for the first time, he saw the one flaw in this otherwise perfect creature: she had no fingernails. None at all, on either hand, just corrugated skin. It looked like the nails had been there once but had been... removed?

But he did not recoil. Her fingers were nevertheless elegant – and he remembered what she could do with them. What she could hold with them, where she could put them... He felt himself reacting under the table. He wanted her. Quickly he drank some coffee.

"Well?" she prompted.

Had he ever heard her accented voice so deep? "When?" he asked again.

"Tell me first." Her eyes were like black pools in which he wanted to drown.

He felt his temperature rise, any control that he ever imagined he had slipping away.

She reached over again and squeezed his arm. "Are you all right, *habibi?*"

He pulled at his collar. "It's hot under here, have they turned the heaters on?"

"Well it is October. Finish your coffee and let's walk. It is cooler out there."

He left money for his drink and then stood up, not caring if she saw the evidence of his desire as he moved out from the table.

Out from under the pergola, she linked her arm in his. For a while they walked in silence, the noise of Manhattan a humming, beeping background musak. Then she said "Right now if you wish."

"Right now what?"

"Good boys should be rewarded. If they deserve to be. Come, sit. Tell me what you have and you will get your reward."

They sat on a bench, passers-by paying them no heed. She held his hand, waiting.

"It's preliminary," he said eventually. "But they do not like what has been happening. They are planning on fighting back."

She sighed. "They are *what?* I thought that was all in the past. Didn't they learn their lesson in 2006? And recently?"

"That's just the point. Hands up, we have been routed. We know it, you know it. Hizbullah will never be expecting a return so soon."

Carla shook her head. "No. They must not do it."

"But we have to," he continued. "Hizbullah are in it up to their necks in Syria and now they've started foreign operations as well. Last year's attack in Istanbul, the recent one in Bulgaria. And we have hardly any eyes or ears on the ground in Lebanon, just the few they did not discover. We must get back in. Here," from a pocket of his jacket he pulled out what looked like a cigarette lighter. Quickly he took off the cover to reveal a USB memory stick, then clicked the cover back on again. "Information. Plus a list of names." He pulled down his tie and opened his shirt collar. "Do you have any water?"

She took the lighter. "No. Was there anything else?"

"Not right now. But I'll monitor. I'm really thirsty." He looked back towards the eatery.

She reached up and touched his face, leaning closer. Gently her fingers moved his head back round towards her. He could smell jasmine. "You deserve your reward," she said softly.

He felt the fingers of a djinn move down to his groin. His heart was pounding as he leant against the back of the bench, his thirst forgotten. Was she going to do it here? In public? Her slightly open lips came towards his, her warmth breath on his chin an overture to the delights of her mouth. Their lips touched...

Carla stopped and smiled, then moved backwards.

He was asleep.

She had dropped enhanced gammahydroxybuterate into his coffee when she had reached out to caress him back in the eatery. Normal GHB caused memory loss. This stuff created heightened imagination. Whatever he had been thinking would appear as real to him. She had used it on him before and he was the ideal subject for it – because she had never, ever, had sex with him although he seemed to think she had. A flirt, a kiss, a glimpse, a heavy pet – and she had let his imagination and the drug do the rest.

Now she ran her index finger over her lips, checked to ensure there was nobody in the immediate vicinity, surreptitiously undid his fly, rummaged, pulled him out (circumcised but generous even in his relaxed state) and rubbed lipstick from her finger onto the helmet. She put him back in but left the fly undone, a gentle prompt to his imagination.

She stood up and walked away.

Benjamin David, a *sayan* working as civilian support at the Israeli Consulate, would be asleep for about an hour. When he woke up he would remember forever some of the greatest oral sex he had never, in fact, had.

Jounieh, Lebanon 17:45

Jihad Merhi sat on one of the sofas in his lounge, whisky in his left hand, cigarette in his mouth, sinister black laptop open on the coffee table in front of him. He had never before officially seen an Above Top Secret report and he was impressed by its detail and thoroughness.

The Israeli spy network had covered all of Lebanon, overt and covert. The overt was down south in Occupied Palestine (which they called Israel). All along the border, from En Naqoura on the coast to the Sheeba Farms in the east, the Israelis had set up spying posts (equipped with radar stations, listening devices and other gadgets) from where they collected all types of data from Lebanon's wireless networks. Nicolas Sehnaoui, Lebanon's Minister of Telecommunications, had confirmed that the Israelis received "everything that passes through the air, from waves and vibrations to tapping of telephone cables that are above ground".

The covert was a network of spies across the entire country. Not Jews, not infiltrators, but local Lebanese recruited either by threats, blackmail or payment. They came from all backgrounds and faiths. They operated either singly or in small cells (or 'confessions' as Brigadier al-Hassan put it in his report).

But al-Hassan had routed them. Over an eighteen-month period, nearly one hundred arrests had been made across the country, all sorts from all confessions: three army colonels, a mayor, business people, school teachers, even a gas station owner who was accused of planting bugs in vehicles used by Hizbullah. Over twenty people had been indicted for the death penalty for treason.

The biggest arrest had been Adib al-Alam, a retired Brigadier General of the GSD, who was accused of running a twelve-member cell that included his wife and nephew, a GSD corporal. *[In June 2013, Brigadier General Adib al-Alam was sentenced to fifteen years hard labour and his wife, Hayat Saloumi, was sentenced to four years hard labour on charges of 'collaboration with the Israeli enemy'.]*

The most recent high-profile arrest had been a director of the Alfa telecommunications company that runs Lebanon's cellular phone network.

al-Hassan had seriously disrupted Mossad's operations inside Lebanon, much to the Israelis' embarrassment. He had poked out their eyes and cut off their ears. Not only had he discomfited Israel but Hizbullah too – the existence and national spread of the spy cells was an immense security failure by the Party of God.

Merhi drained his glass. Now this had been passed to Ghanem and himself. Their job was to oversee and monitor the project. He would introduce himself to the relevant members of al-Hassan's team tomorrow.

Mossad had been routed in Lebanon but the arrest of the Palestinian down in the Bourj al-Shimali camp proved that they must never become complacent. The weeds of espionage were pernicious – pull one up and another popped up somewhere else.

He was refilling his glass when he heard the front door opening. Moments later a pile of bags from various outlets in Beirut's ABC shopping mall rustled their way into the lounge. Gisele was somewhere amongst them.

Jihad winced inwardly but smiled outwardly. *"Ciao belle habibi,"* he didn't even realise he had spoken three languages in one three-word sentence as he stood up, helping to extract her from the bags. The contents felt soft – clothes. Something harder bashed on his leg. Shoes. "I've been trying to call you all day." They kissed on the cheeks.

"Dead battery," she rummaged in her handbag and then waived her phone in the air. "It was over fifty per cent when I went out but I left my shopping list on."

"Drink?"

"In a minute. I just have to get out of these clothes – and let you see the new ones. Fancy a fashion show?" She noticed the object on the coffee table. "What's that?"

Jihad played it nonchalant. "My new work's laptop."

"Strange-looking," she bent over it.

"It's an ATS, issued only to Majors and above."

She didn't take in his nuance. As she straightened up she said, "You've borrowed it? With permission, I hope, I know what you're like."

"No, I haven't borrowed it. It's mine."

"Well I hope you know how to work it, I was never trained on something like that..." She frowned, looking into her husband's face. "But you just said they were for Majors and above only."

"Yes, I did."

"You mean?"

"Yes, I do."

Her hand went to her mouth.

He smiled. "I hope you are going to show Major Merhi the respect he deserves."

She ran into his arms. Jihad was not the tallest of men but he was a good head above his wife. He squeezed her tightly.

Gisele kissed his lips, forgiving him the whisky and tobacco flavoured breath. *"Mabruk, habibi. Mabruk, mabruk, mabruk."* She pulled away, frowning. "But I suppose that means I will see you even less now."

"Not necessarily. We have a new regime. A new way of working. We'll have to see."

She pecked his lips again. "Bravo. That is so good. *Habibi, y*ou deserve this, it's been a long time coming."

"I never thought it would. But this new chief had other ideas."

"Will there be…" she became faux-coy, pouting. "More money?"

"Considerably more."

"Excellent." She took his hand. "You can tell me all about it after. *Yalla*."

"Where are we going?"

"Where do you think?" She pulled him out into the hallway, towards their bedroom. "Help me get out of these clothes. Come. Didn't you just ask me to show you the respect a major deserves? Let me kneel before you, my handsome hero…"

Murray Hill, New York City, USA 22:00 (local time)

Apartment 3030 of the building on East 39th Street was in darkness. In the bedroom, the blinds were open and the occupants of the bed had an unrestricted view north over the lights of Midtown and the Upper East Side, if they chose to look. But they did not. They had seen it many times before and they were too engrossed with each other.

Carla rolled off of The Damascene and snuggled in under his left arm. Neither of them was out of breath but they were both completely satisfied. The sheets were wet.

She kissed his left nipple, lightly sucking.

With his right hand he stroked her luxuriant, but now tangled, black hair. "You can trust him?" he asked, continuing their conversation which had been interrupted for the last fifteen minutes. "He is not just a *bodel* trying to make a name for himself?"

She stopped her sucking and rested her head on his lightly-damp chest. "No, he is a *sayan*, a good Jewish boy from the Bronx. A *bodel* would have no access to any information. But - " she raised herself on one elbow, her left hand resting on his stomach, fingers caressing the line of one of his scars, "I do need to check what he has given me." In one movement she leant forward, licked the scar then rolled off of the bed.

In the diffused Manhattan light coming in from outside, The Damascene watched her naked silhouette as she walked into the en suite bathroom. The picture of her superb bottom lingered in his mind as he heard sounds of wiping, peeing, wiping, washing, and drying. Shortly she came back out, moving noiselessly, not even disturbing the air. Like a djinn.

Her shadow stopped over by a small table. "Mind your eyes." She switched on a low wattage lamp. Looking back at the bed, she asked "You are satisfied, my husband?"

He opened his eyes. "With you, always."

"It does not look like it."

He gave a small laugh. "*That* is your fault." He looked at her small, lithe body, naturally totally hairless. "It does not mean I am not satisfied. But being satisfied does not mean I don't want you again."

"I will be with you in a heartbeat." She turned and opened the MacBook Pro on the table.

As the computer was powering up, Carla floated across to the other side of the room, rummaged in her Barbour bag, and floated back again. This time a waft of jasmine and natural musk caressed The Damascene's nose.

She sat on a stool, removed the USB memory stick from its camouflage cigarette lighter cover and inserted it into the computer. Momentarily, two folder icons appeared on the screen. "Jpegs," she said over her shoulder. "Too much to ask for document copies, I suppose. Still, I can zoom."

The first folder contained photographs of three typewritten pages, a report of some sort. She looked at it briefly, her eyes moving down each page like a scanner. Even though it was in Hebrew, she would be able to recall it without needing to look at the photographs again.

The second folder contained one photograph of a list of names. She looked at this one longer, nodding. Then, to herself, she said "Well, well."

"Worthwhile?" he asked from the bed.

She swivelled on the stool to face him. "Oh yes." She tapped her head. "I will read the report in detail later. After. But the list of names is very useful. I know some of them on there. So do you."

"And what does it mean?"

"It means..." She turned back round, rubbed her finger on the trackpad, clicked twice and pulled the memory stick out, putting it back into the cover. Closing the lid of the MacBook, she said "It means I need to go back." She stood up, the memory stick in her hand. "And it means you need to destroy this for me."

She turned off the lamp and glided over to the bed, the room again in silken semi-darkness. The Damascene took the stick and effortlessly snapped it in half. Then he applied crushing pressure. He opened his right palm, showing small pieces of mangled plastic. Stretching out, he put the pieces on a damp, used tissue on the bedside table and scrunched it up. He brushed slivers off his hands.

As he lay back on the bed, Carla admired his hard, muscular, equally hairless body. The many scars, almost too numerous to count, she found deliciously attractive. The long black hair, missing left ear and scarred face completed the picture of the man whom, at one time, she thought she would have to kill, even though she was in love with him. But that had not happened. Yet.

She touched his groin. "Now," she said. "Let us see what we can do about your hard drive..."

23 October 2012
7 Dhu al-Hijja 1433

Jonblat, Beirut 09:00

Major Jihad Merhi was surprised. The small office up on the fifth floor into which he had been led by Lieutenant-Colonel Ghanem contained just three men.

"We are expecting more?" he asked Ghanem.

"More what?"

Merhi gestured at the men.

"No, this is it," said Ghanem.

This was it? The team that had broken the Israeli espionage presence in Lebanon consisted of just three men? Plus their murdered leader, of course.

Merhi had seen the men about the building before but he did not know them by name. They had stood up when he and Ghanem had entered, a respect that Merhi was not accustomed to. He'd best get used to it now he was a Major.

"Please, as you were," he half-smiled, wondering if it was in fact the senior ranking officer's privilege to say that, not his. Whatever. He could do with a Camel King Size.

"As you probably know, this is Major Merhi," Ghanem spoke to the men. "Your new OIC and Directorate head. You report to him, he reports to me." He turned to Merhi. "Let me introduce you."

In fact Ghanem did not introduce anybody, the men said their own names as Merhi shook their hands.

"Nabil Haddad." Tall, slim, clean shaven, balding.

"Claude Gerges." Still tall but stouter, lighter complexion, of obviously strong French stock.

"Tamer Khalef." Short, plump, bearded.

One Muslim, one Christian and Haddad who could be either. It would be in his file. All three were sergeants.

After the handshakes, Merhi squatted on the edge of what turned out to be Haddad's desk. "Sit, please."

"I'll leave you to it," said Ghanem.

Merhi nodded. "I'll report to you in a week, as agreed."

"Good." Ghanem closed the office door behind him.

Merhi turned back to what were now his men. "Firstly, my condolences on the loss of your Chief. If you agree, let us have a quiet moment." He lowered his head.

It was a gesture that was appreciated by the men. It was a sad fact that killing was commonplace in Lebanon. At times it waxed and waned, waning particularly during the Hariri years and then waxing with his assassination and the many murders thereafter. It was now rife with the sectarian strife of Syria also being played out on Lebanon's soil. Quite frankly in the current climate, nobody was safe, especially if they were in the government, the military or law enforcement. But that did not demean or lessen the fact that a death was a death; a life lost, a life taken by people who had no business, no right, to take it; a life never to be replaced.

Merhi looked up and waited for the men to do so. Then he said, "So, only three of you? What are you, superheroes?"

Murray Hill, New York City, USA 13:00 (local time)

They kissed at the doorway to their apartment, their tongues thrusting, parrying and lunging like fencing masters. After a final flick, Carla pulled away, her height reducing by fifteen centimetres as she went back down on her heels. The Damascene bent back upwards.

Carla's cab was waiting downstairs. She was booked on the 17:00 American Airlines Flight 44 from JFK to Paris; from Paris she would travel onwards to Beirut on Middle East Airways Flight 206. The journey would take thirteen hours in all.

"*Khodi balik,*" he said as he lifted her small suitcase. They walked over to the elevator.

"I will be careful, do not worry." She pressed the Call button. "Last time was... exceptional." She looked down at her nailless fingers and for the briefest of moments thoughts flashed into her mind of the retribution she would take against the monsters who had done this to her. She said, "This time *I* will be the aggressor. I will administer penance to the confession." She took the case from him.

"I will be there soon," he said. "If you need me - "

"I always need you. Will you bring my presents?"

"One should always make offerings to a djinn."

She smiled. As the elevator doors opened, she reached up and pulled his head down, her mouth open and soft.

There were two other people in the elevator so she did not linger.

The Damascene watched as the doors closed, his face showing no emotion.

Back in the apartment, he stripped off his shirt and jeans and shook out his ponytail, pulling the hair over the hole of his missing left ear even though he was alone. Naked, he walked over to the lounge window and looked out over Midtown. Sun glistened off the Chrysler Building to the north, some rays reflecting off of the art deco tower and back across the three blocks into the apartment, onto his body.

He was not pleased. He had failed in his last assignment. Carla had known it but she had been gracious enough not to mention it. He had been very well paid to advise on the security and protection of the head of the Information Branch of the Lebanese Internal Security Force, Brigadier Wissam al-Hassan. He had succeeded for two months, since the threats had first been issued after al-Hassan's arrest of former Lebanese Information Minister Michel Samaha. It had even been The Damascene's idea that al-Hassan travel in non-descript rented vehicles. But no matter how good you were (and, without false modesty, The Damascene acknowledged that he was good), you could not legislate for the carefully placed roadside car bomb – especially in the traffic of Beirut! It was how Rafic Hariri had been murdered seven years before.

It irked him that he had failed, but 'protection' (and with it the implied *ad infinitum* – when does a threat end?) was always a tenuous undertaking, unlike the other side of the coin -   assassination – which always had a definitive outcome.

But there was a third element of his business, linked to protection but of a more finite variety: transportation. That was his next assignment. Yesterday he had received a cryptic message on one of his three cell phones. His clients were ready. Ready to go public. Ready for transportation. Like Carla, he too would be returning to the Levant.

Raising his arms in the air, he joined his hands in a static shoulder stretch. Momentarily he would begin his daily thirty minute regime of stretching exercises, but first there was something he needed to do.

He walked into the bedroom and went over to the table. The MacBook Pro came on instantly when he raised the lid.

Over at the bed he put his hand down the back, underneath the headboard, pulling out the memory stick that Carla had been given by the *sayan* – less the cover which he had crushed last night.

Sitting down on the stool, he inserted the stick into the computer. The two folder icons appeared on the screen. He opened the first one and read the report. Then he opened the second one and very carefully read the list of names...

Coastal Highway, Lebanon 18:00

The   superhero had been Wissam al-Hassan - although, from what Merhi knew of him, the late Brigadier would never have even thought of himself as that. al-Hassan's task had been massive: how do you fight one of the most sophisticated intelligence services in the world with the limited, fractured, sectarian resources that make up Lebanon's security services? In terms of sheer ability, if not size, it was like David and Goliath.

It had been al-Hassan's idea to fight the Israelis using their own methodology: don't put your own people in, use locals who are already there. al-Hassan's team (now Merhi's team) had raised a country-wide network of true Lebanese, those who would put country before confession (there were still some left). They used their eyes, they used their ears, they used their mouths: watching, listening, reporting. And, over two years, the results had been startling. No one could have ever imagined the extent of the Israeli espionage penetration in Lebanon, most of it aimed in just one direction: Hizbullah.

In 2006, Hizbullah had taken on the might of Israel. And, much to the world's surprise, had won – or at least had held them to a stalemate. At the cost of much destruction and thousands of innocent (and not so innocent) lives, the Party of God had stood firm against the satan from the south.

But the Israelis did not like to be beaten. They never would be beaten. They were coming back into Lebanon. Under the shadow of the Syrian war they had planned to make a massive, pre-emptive strike from within against Hizbullah, to annihilate them, to clear the way for – who knows what?

And Wissam al-Hassan and his team had stopped them. But Merhi knew that the Jews were persistent: they might lose battles but they refused to lose wars. Their espionage network in Lebanon had been routed, but what was now Merhi's team could not sit back on their laurels. The Israelis must never again be allowed to saturate Lebanon with spies. Any re-emerging shoots had to be nipped in the bud...

The Toyota Land Cruiser V8 powered forward as Merhi accelerated, the Coastal Highway traffic thinning beyond Nahr el Kalb, Dog River. Cigarette between his lips, left elbow on the open side window, he smiled at his simile. *Nipped in the bud...*

He was a gardener. He had to keep the Elysian Field of Lebanon free from the weeds of Israel. The garden would require constant, daily attention. Thankfully he had the right team and network to do it. Even now they knew that they had not got everyone. There was some pernicious knotweed that they had not eradicated, probably in the Beirut area. They did not know where, they did not know who, they did not know how many. A small group, a confession.

And, as every gardener knew, the smaller the weed the more difficult it was to find. Perhaps the spy they had arrested down in Bourj el-Shimali might 'volunteer' information...

The Gardener turned the Toyota off of the Coastal Highway just after Kaslik, heading for his home in the mountains.

PART TWO
الجزء الثاني

THE BOND OF SALT
الملح سندات

24 October 2012
8 Dhu al-Hijja 1433

Bahla, Oman, Arabia 15:00 – 17:30 (local time)

The small town of Bahla in the north-west of Ad Dakhiliyah province of Oman sits at the foot of Jabal Akhdar, the Green Mountain range. It is an old town, pre-Islamic, and is dominated by Bahla Fort, the largest of the estimated five hundred forts in Oman. The fort closed twenty-five years ago and visitors had long since given up coming to Bahla unless they had another reason, such as visiting the Aladawi Clay Pots Factory or any of the other pottery makers behind the souk. Nowadays the main Highway 21, linking Muscat (120 kilometres to the north-east) with the United Arab Emirates (200 kilometres to the north-west) ran nearby.

On the outskirts of Bahla, outside the ancient mudbrick town walls, well away from the fort and the highway, was a villa. Set in its own walled compound, it had a spacious inner courtyard shaded by trees, and a fountain supplied with water by the *falaj*, the underground irrigation system, of Bahla Fort. The villa had small, ornate arched windows, and large arched doors of thick studded wood - and something rarely seen in Oman: two *barjeel*, wind towers. *Barjeel* were the old Iranian form of air conditioning, capturing cool air to funnel down into the house whilst also allowing hot air to rise and escape. But here they also had another purpose: as watchtowers. Because the villa was a safe-house, purpose-built with money siphoned from Syria and the Levant by the man who had been based there for the last seven years.

A man who was dead.

The local people kept well away from the villa, and for good reason. In Omani folklore, Bahla is famous for its supernatural associations. The town is said to be the haunt of djinn, the mischievous type not the benevolent kind. Legend has it that djinn appear in the middle of the night, flying off with objects or taking possession of any human that has offended them, causing misery, pain and sometimes death. Most houses in the town contain a *nazar*, an eye-shaped amulet, or a *hamsa*, a palm-shaped amulet with an eye in the centre, to protect the house and its occupants from *ayn al hasud*, the Evil Eye and its associated demons. Many women (and some men) wear a *sumt*, a large round silver pendant said to contain an imprisoned djinn, so warning off any demon that considers attacking them.

Even the tree in the middle of Bahla souk is decorated with amulets and chains to prevent its removal by supernatural forces.

It is all pure superstition, of course, as the occupants of Bahla will tell you. Djinn have not been seen in the town for generations (although some will reason that this is because of all the precautions taken by the townsfolk). And anyway, everyone knew that there were no djinn in the villa on the edge of town.

The villa contained *houri*.

As the woman drove the black Jeep Wrangler Ultimate past the old town walls, she heard the *azan* for *asr salat*, the call to afternoon prayer, coming from the Bahla Mosque nearby.

Even though the desert temperatures were still in the thirties, the detachable top was off of the Jeep. The windrush as she drove along Highways 15 and 21 had kept her cool. She was dressed in a full, plain black *abbaya*, the voluminous overdress worn by local women in Arabia, and a plain black *shayla*, headscarf. The *abbaya* was open from the thighs down to allow her legs to move, and the *shayla* was over her head and drawn across her face as a veil. Only her eyes were visible. Rich, brown eyes. Almost an unnatural colour.

She had been shopping in Muscat. As well as buying provisions, which were now stacked in the back of the Jeep, she had been to the Mutrah Souk to buy *luban*, frankincense, both in tear form and as oil. She had bought *hojari*, silver frankincense, the best. They would use the tears in their burners and rub the oil into their bodies.

She pressed the small remote control to open the outer gates of the villa and drove in, another press on the remote closing the gates behind her. She pulled up near the tinkling fountain. She was pleased to be back, even though she had been gone only since that morning. She did not like to be alone. She felt incomplete.

She took the carrier bags of *luban* off the passenger seat and then carefully lifted the smaller purple bag that had been next to them. She smiled. As well as the provisions and *luban*, she had bought something else.

Something for Paradise.

The woman called Paradise looked at her own reflection. At the pretty face with the full red lips and pert nose, at the long wavy naturally blonde hair newly-released from the *shayla*, at the pale porcelain skin and tall, statuesque bearing. And at the eyes now that the contact lenses had been removed, at the white eyeballs and black pupils which others found so frightening, so intimidating, hence the need for lenses on journeys outside.

She kissed herself on the cheeks five times, and ended with one on the lips. Her mouth was enticingly soft, her breath pure.

She hugged herself. "My darling, you have travelled safely," she said to her identical twin sister. "Your trip was fruitful?"

The woman called Love caressed her sister's face. "I found everything, darling. They even had some new *hojari* oil in, so we can rub some into each other later. Our skin is feeling good today."

Paradise licked Love's fingers as they passed her mouth. "That is wonderful."

"Everything all right here?"

"Yes, he has been upstairs on his computer all day. He received a call this morning but he hasn't said what it was about."

"If we need to know, he will tell us."

"Indeed. So, what did you buy? It is my turn to cook today."

"In a minute. Firstly, this is for you." Love held up the small purple bag.

Paradise gave a wide, wide smile. She knew what it was, of course, because they were identical not only physically but also mentally. Conjoined twins in everything but the physical join. The moment her sister had stopped at the Amouage Perfumery on the way back, near Muscat Airport, she had known. She looked inside the bag and brought out the 100ml bottle of Amouage's signature *Gold* perfume. "You are wonderful."

"*You* are wonderful." They kissed again, on the lips, lingering. "Now," said Love, as they pulled apart, "come help me unload the Jeep. I have fruit, rice, some exquisite dates, some fresh camel and even some wild oryx which a Bedu sold me."

"Oh, he will like that."

"After which," said Love, "I will need to bathe. The sand gets everywhere. Into our hair and all sorts of other places."

"Yes, I have felt it."

"Will you help me, sister?"

"Yes, we must be clean," said Paradise. "Let us unpack the bags. After which you can relax in the *hammam* while I prepare the food. Then I will come and wash us while the oryx is roasting…"

The *hammam* was at the back of the villa, compact, ornately-tiled with a plunge pool and a domed ceiling which connected to one of the watchtowers for ventilation.

Love lay face-up between Paradise's legs as her sister finished rinsing her hair, the water running down her face, warm, perfumed, cleansing. She felt her sister's naked flesh against hers, also warm and perfumed.

"There now," Paradise kissed Love's crown. "We are clean. Come, my darling, I must check on the oryx. " Love leant forward as Paradise stood up.

"You stay here, relax, take your time. I will call you and Abu Yo'roub when the food is ready." She stepped up out of the bath, the water dropping from her body like a falling gossamer veil. Instantly she was dry but she picked up a towel anyway, gently rubbing those places from which the water could not, and did not want to, escape.

"Leave the towel," Love smiled as she watched. "I will use it, save wetting another one."

"As you wish, my sister." Paradise nodded to Love and a message went between them. She bent over from the waist, deliberately and provocatively, and placed the towel by the edge of the pool. Slowly she straightened up.

Then she turned and walked out of the room, knowing that there were two sets of eyes watching her...

Up above, through one of the supplementary air vents around the bottom of the domed ceiling, Abu Yo'roub watched.

He was naked, lying on his side, his breathing heavy, his face intense. He was old now but that did not mean he no longer appreciated the female form. And these women, these twins, these white-eyed *creatures* that had been with him for the last five months, were sublime. Bizarre but sublime.

It was eerie how similar they were, identical in every way – even down to the bullet scar they each had on their left shoulder. Abu Yo'roub could not tell them apart – except for when they were going out. Then they put in the contact lenses; one wore brown, the other wore green. But when the lenses were out it was as if it was one person occupying two bodies. One person in two places at once.

He finished what he was doing and lay on his back, his heart racing. As he waited for it to calm down, he thought about his situation. He thought about Syria.

Abu Yo'roub – Major General Ghazi Kanaan, latterly the Minister of the Interior of Syria, formerly the man who had ruled Lebanon on Syria's behalf for twenty years – had committed suicide in his offices in Damascus on 12 October 2005 (8 Ramadan 1426). At least, that was the official story. That's what it said if you Googled him.

As if he would do such a thing! What idiot would think that? But he had needed a way out. He had been developing a powerbase against President Bashar al-Assad within the Syrian Regional Branch of the Arab Socialist Ba'ath Party, a powerbase that had hoped to oust al-Assad and install a less dynasty-based leadership for the good of Syria.

But he had been found out. His arrest had been only a matter of time. He had needed to disappear. So he had called in an expert. They had set up the elaborate suicide ploy, using a 'volunteer' who had born a passing resemblance to Ghazi Kanaan (in the body, the head did not matter if the face had been blown off).

Kanaan had fled the country, to wait for the day he knew would come soon. The day the uprising came to Syria, the rebellion which some fools sweetly called The Arab Spring. It had come on 11 March 2011.

Now Syria was in turmoil, a proxy regional war being played out on its streets: the Shi'ites of Syria, Iran and Lebanon (including the ruling Alawites) against the Sunnis of Syria, Qatar, Saudi and Lebanon. The Alawites, the Ba'ath Party, were simply not giving up like the rulers of other countries had done. No matter how many of their own people they killed.

But soon they would need a new ruler. What had started out as an insurrection against the Ba'ath Party and the Alawites had turned into a singular rebellion against the rule of the al-Assads. Kanaan was an Alawite but he was not an al-Assad. He would be a good compromise, a good interim ruler.

'Interim' being a very subjective term, of course...

Naked, Kanaan walked carefully down the narrow spiral staircase from the wind tower, supporting himself with the hand rail. One floor below, there was a discreet, waist-high service door. He opened it, bent down and went through. Across a small space of two metres there was another door. Bending through this one also, he was in the wet room of his suite.

He showered, his third wash of the day, and then went out into his spacious bedroom. He had left fresh clothes on the bed earlier, and now he dressed: a white cotton *izaar* underneath a white ankle length *dishdasha*, and house shoes.

He checked himself in the full-length mirror. His iron-grey hair was now long, down to his shoulders, and his beard was full. Before he returned to Syria his hair would be cut and his beard shaved off, but for now they served as a good camouflage. A disguise for a dead man.

"Abu Yo'roub."

Kanaan jumped and nearly pulled a muscle as he twisted around. One of the women was standing there. He had not heard her come in, he had not seen her reflection in the mirror. She was dressed like a western whore in tight denim jeans and a white cotton vest, her feet bare.

"Our meal is ready," she announced. "We telephoned but you did not answer."

"I – I was washing," he said instinctively, immediately cursing himself. These women were employees, he did not have to explain himself to them.

"As is right," she held open the bedroom door. As Kanaan walked past her, she asked "You have had a... *satisfying* afternoon?"

He did not reply. Curse these women, these *creatures*, and their temptations. Until they had arrived, he had lived here in Oman in seclusion, in peace, for six years. In this house which had been built with *his* money. Just him, his two trusted assistants and a maid. Then, five months ago as the situation in Syria escalated into the all-out war against al-Assad, things had changed. His assistants and the maid had gone (they were buried out in the desert somewhere) and his expert had installed these two. Professional protectors, professional transporters. He trusted his expert, after all he had gotten him this far when really he should have died in that office in Damascus seven years ago. But why did he have to install *women*?

Behind him on the stairs, Paradise glided silently on her bare feet, smiling, as if she could hear his thoughts...

In the dressing room of the twins' suite on the ground floor, Love pulled on her jeans. Paradise had not worn underwear so neither would she. Flipping her long blonde hair out of the back of the white vest, she bent down to check herself in the dressing table mirror.

Her white eyes stared back at her. Or were they Paradise's eyes? She always thought when she looked in a mirror that she was looking at her sister, not herself. Mirror, mirror on the wall...

In their first few weeks here, they had worn their contact lenses when they were interacting with Abu Yo'roub, so as not to frighten the old man. But his attitude had not been good, he had been disdainful, querying the decision to install them, moaning that he did not need *these women*, saying he wanted back his assistants and the maid. So they had taken out their lenses and had let him see them as their true selves. And Abu Yo'roub had known what they were.

They had also explained about the conversions that had been performed on the assistants and the maid. Conversions from sentient beings to dead rotting carrion. The staff would not be coming back.

Love was content with what she saw in the mirror and she straightened up. As she did so she glanced at the large round silver pendant, the *sumt*, which was draped over one edge of the mirror. Folklore had it that a djinn was imprisoned inside each *sumt*. But there was no djinn in this one – yet. But it did contain something else.

As she often did, Love reached over and gently shook the pendant. The objects inside clicked against their prison walls. Fingernails. Ten of them. Love remembered the day in Byblos when she and Paradise had ripped them off of their captive.

The *sumt* had waited two years for the rest of The Djinn and it would wait for as long as it needed to.

One day, Love and Paradise knew, they would find her. *Houri* never left business unfinished...

25 October 2012
9 Dhu al-Hijja 1433

Bourj el-Barajneh, Beirut 08:00

Major Jihad Merhi could not believe his eyes. He was leaning against his Toyota Land Cruiser, dressed casually in trainers, jeans and grey shirt, having only his fourth Camel King Size of the day, when Fadi Lattouf stepped out of the battered front door of his small house into Annan Street.

Merhi straightened up, raised his dark glasses to confirm what he was seeing, and let them drop back down again onto his nose.

Lattouf had stopped, hand still on his doorknob, likewise staring at Merhi.

"Go and get changed," said Merhi.

"M-morning of joy, my dear friend."

"Morning of joy, Fadi. Now go and get changed."

Lattouf was dressed in his full uniform: blue trousers, blue shirt (my God, he was even wearing what passed as a tie), Captains' jacket over his arm, peaked Captain's hat balanced perilously on the back of his huge head, like a skull cap. "But we are on official business, no?"

"Yes. In the south. Near the border. You should not be wearing that. Just like your car," Merhi pointed to the glaring orange Datsun Bluebird parked nearby, one front wheel up on the kerb. "I doubt it could even get past the airport without breaking down, but if it did get to the south it would be a target for the Jews. So will your uniform. Didn't you think?"

Lattouf humphed. "We should not be intimidated in our own land."

Merhi was not even going there. You were a Palestinian, Fadi, your people were long-term guests enjoying the hospitality of Lebanon. This was not your land.

"But," nodded Lattouf, "I understand what you are saying. I will change." He pushed the front door back open, shouting "Nada! Open my wardrobe. I need clothes, quickly woman!" and disappeared back inside.

He was back fifteen minutes later, chewing on a little something he had picked up on his way out. He was now dressed in his usual casual outfit, probably the only one he had: the loose pink and blue checked shirt and rough blue denim jeans, above old trainers. His black and grey chest hair poked out of the open neck of his shirt like a 1970s porn star, and his stranded comb-over was freshly slicked down. And he was wearing sunglasses, like Merhi.

He pointed to his glasses as he came over. "Like them? Genuine Ray-Bans. I got them off a stall in Hamra the other day. Only thirty-six thousand pounds."

Merhi shook his head. "You were done, Fadi. You should have knocked them down." Thirty-six thousand Lebanese pounds. Twenty-four dollars. Nineteen euros. Fifteen pounds sterling. For genuine Ray-Bans. "*Yalla.*"

Lattouf got into the passenger side of the Land Cruiser while Merhi had to climb noticeably higher back into his side. As he stretched round to find his seatbelt, Lattouf let out an almighty burp which must have fluttered the banners across the road within a ten block radius. "Unstrained goat's yoghurt," he explained. "Excuse me."

Merhi both turned up the air conditioning and nudged the down button on his window as the sour air glided up his nostrils. Well, it was mild compared to some of the odours and noises Lattouf had emitted on previous occasions in this vehicle.

On perfect, pernicious cue, Lattouf leant to his left, raised his right butt cheek and let out a stentorian blast of gas. "Last night's giblets and rice."

Merhi just looked at him, keeping his finger on the window button so that it opened fully.

Lattouf settled down comfortably, his head almost touching the ceiling, even in this large, powerful car. He smiled. "I feel better now. Well, my friend, let us go. We have a spy to collect. *Yalla.*"

Praying to God that traffic on the southern Coastal Highway would be light, Merhi engaged Drive and pulled out.

Heading south.

Southern Coastal Highway, Lebanon 09:00-11:00

Some say southern Lebanon is the most beautiful part of the country, unspoilt, less developed than cosmopolitan Beirut and places to the north. It has coastal beaches, the beautiful blue Mediterranean, groves of bananas, oranges and lemons, and pine-forested mountains culminating in the snow-capped Mount Lebanon range in the mid-distance to the east. Druze live in the Chouf Mountains, Sunni Muslims in Sidon and Shi'a Muslims around Nabatiye. But it is a part of the country where tourists and casual visitors rarely venture – because of its recent history. Only in May 2000 was the south liberated from its twenty-two year Israeli occupation. Twice, in 1996 and 2006, the Israelis 'mistakenly' massacred hundreds of civilians in the once-pretty town of Qana on the pretext of attacking Hizbullah to stop their Katyusha rocket bombardment of northern Israel. In 2012, the extreme south below Tyre was still patrolled by the Lebanese Army and UNIFIL (the United Nations Interim Force In Lebanon), a presence which did not stop sporadic attacks from Lebanon into Israel and Israel into Lebanon. And the border area still remained full of unexploded landmines and other ordnance.

Merhi and Lattouf drove south along the highway. The further south they went, the more military and paramilitary roadblocks ('security checks') they encountered, but they passed through them unhindered, the bored guards giving them only cursory visual checks. They passed banana plantations and citrus groves, roadside traders holding up freshly-caught fish, stalls brimming with locally-grown vegetables and fruit. Eventually the temptations – and Lattouf's pleading – became too much. Just beyond el Jiye, Merhi pulled over and bought some bananas and oranges from a wizened old Druze who looked so ancient he must have been alive at the time of the Prophet (Peace Be Upon Him).

Back in the Toyota and back on the highway, orange and banana skins popped out of the passenger window at regular intervals, as if marking a trail for them to find their way back. Momentarily, a banana skin was caught on the edge of the roof, flapping like a dog's tongue in the wind before velocity whipped it off into the air.

They travelled onwards, through more security checks, through the eastern edge of the coastal town of Sidon, now the municipal capital of south Lebanon and once the northern border of Canaan. Three kilometres further, they passed a huge statue of the Virgin Mary on a hilltop to their left, marking the village of Maghdouche to where it is said Mary came after the crucifixion of Christ, to await his resurrection.

Then the road split at a roundabout dominated by statue of a hand holding a huge Soviet-style sickle, a memorial to a freedom-fighter killed in the war against Israel. The road to the left headed up into the hills to the town of Nabatiye, said to be the spiritual home of Hizbullah and the Shi'a faith. Merhi stayed to the right, continuing down the coast.

As the coastal flatland became more rugged, more desolate, so the highway petered out. 'Under Construction' signs appeared, although there was little sign of any construction going on. At Masrat el Ouastra they doglegged right onto the old, small coastal highway and drove the final ten kilometres along the edge of the Mediterranean down into Tyre.

Bourj al-Shimali, Lebanon 11:20 – 14:30

Turning left just beyond the vast al-Bass archaeological site on the landward side of ancient Tyre, they drove for three kilometres, back across the proposed highway, to the Bourj al-Shimali refugee camp.

Lattouf wiped his beard, his mood darkening noticeably as they pulled up, the Toyota attracting some curious looks. "Another shit hole," he said quietly. "May Allah have mercy on them."

Merhi had to agree. Created in 1955, the camp housed an estimated nineteen thousand people, mostly refugees from the villages of Hula and Tiberias in Palestine. Being on the edge of the UNIFIL zone, it had attracted its share of bombardments from the occupied country to the south, although it was not the nearest camp to Palestine: that dubious honour was held by Rashidiyeh, five kilometres away.

It was similar to Lattouf's camp at Barajneh, but wider, more spread out. Still the basic brick constructions which pass as dwellings, not quite as tight together as Barajneh; some paths possibly enjoying the opulence of a full three-metres width with a sewage channel running down the middle. There were the usual broken water pipes, broken windows and hanging cables. A basic refugee camp, it could have been anywhere. A displaced people of dignity stripped of their dignity.

An old man using two makeshift crutches passed by, looking into the car, rheumy eyes in a weather-beaten face beneath a black and white *keffiyeh* worn turban-style.

Lattouf nodded at him, then shook his head after the old man had hobbled on. He sighed again. "This is wrong, so wrong, after all this time."

Merhi rarely saw the serious side of his friend, and he could only wonder what thoughts were going around his head. Lattouf rarely spoke about what he had experienced as a corporal in the West Bank and then as a sergeant in Gaza, before his promotion to the relative 'luxury' of the Lebanese camps. In fact, Merhi knew very little about the backstory of his friend. He needed to rectify that.

But not now. "Do you know where the police office is?" he asked.

"Just in there, to the left. Our offices are always on the edge of the camp, for obvious reasons."

They got out, a noticeable wheeze of relief coming from the Toyota's suspension on the passenger side. Lattouf pulled his underwear out of his crevice. Merhi ensured his shirt was covering the gun in his waistband.

Before they had gone two paces, a deep subwoofer voice from behind them said, "Gentlemen welcome, *al-salaam 'aalaykum.*"

Lattouf turned. A man was walking down the road towards them. Tall, bald-headed, clean shaven, deeply tanned, dressed in a light blue shirt with dark blue cargo pants tucked into black boots. A gun bounced in a holster on his belt, next to other little pouches containing handcuffs and other law-enforcing nick-nacks. He exuded a strong presence.

"*'aalaykum al-salaam,*" Lattouf smiled and gave a small bow. "Abu Jad it is good to see you again. How are you? How is your family?"

"They are well, *alhamdulillah.* And your family, Abu Fadi?"

"*Alhamdulillah.*"

They shook hands and then embraced. Coming out of the hold, Lattouf said "May I introduce you to Cap – Major Merhi of the Internal Security Force. Major, this is Captain Manar al-Jayouchi."

"*Salaam,*" Merhi shook the proffered hand.

"*Salaam, Ra'id.* You have come for the spy," said al-Jayouchi. "He is waiting for you."

"Has he said anything?"

al-Jayouchi shrugged with his mouth, shoulders and forearms. "He is finding it difficult to talk."

Merhi could imagine. Swollen mouth, perhaps? Any of his teeth left?

"But let us not worry about the traitor for a moment," continued al-Jayouchi. "You have both come a long way. You must take refreshment." He began to lead them into the camp. "How are things in Beirut now?"

It was Merhi's turn to shrug. "Fragile."

"Indeed. These Syrians, what are they doing to themselves? How will it end, I wonder?"

"Badly," said Merhi.

They stopped outside a single-storey breezeblock building, possibly the only structure in the camp with unbroken windows. On the roof were various tall antennae and even a satellite dish; inside, electric lights were on. al-Jayouchi beckoned them in. "You must be hungry after your journey. I have coffee, dates and fish stew. We will eat together."

"You are too kind," said Merhi. "But we really - "

"Have to build up our energy for our long journey back," Lattouf patted al-Jayouchi on the shoulder. "Thank you, my friend. May Allah bless your hospitality." He went into the building, metaphorically already tucking a napkin into his neckline.

"And," al-Jayouchi turned to Merhi as Lattouf went ahead. "I have a particularly fine whisky. A malt from Scotland. From Egypt via Gaza. Excellent quality. Would you like a drink, Major? To celebrate *Eid*?"

The holding cells were not in the breezeblock building but out the back, across a rubble-strewn yard. In the one crumbling brick construction, there were two peeling solid wooden doors, with two small unglazed air slits just below the level of the combined wooden roof. Merhi thought it looked like an old outside toilet, literally the shit hole Fadi had been talking about; it certainly smelt like it.

One of the doors was ajar, the other closed with a wooden batten across it. Captain al-Jayouchi raised the batten and pulled open the door. Hot, putrid air rolled out, making Merhi snap his head to the side involuntarily.

After the initial pungent eruption had levelled off into a general all-embracing stench, Merhi squinted into the dark interior. He had been right. Towards the back was a hole in the ground where countless souls had deposited their personal waste over the years. And next to the hole sat a male with a sack over his head, his hands in front of him, tied with rope, blood-stained where it had chafed his wrists. The head in the sack moved, turning towards the door.

"Your spy," said al-Jayouchi.

Merhi's voice was mellow and slightly hoarse after three thick coffees and three whiskies (not to mention the fish stew and dates). "Get him out."

Lattouf went in and grabbed the prisoner by his arm, dragging him outside into the sun. Roughly he pulled him upright, supporting him with one giant hand when it looked like his legs would give way. Merhi ripped off the sack.

It was a boy, a teenager, probably about eighteen. Dark hair, dark skin, bum-fluff beard. His face was bruised, lips cracked and bloodied – but it looked like his teeth were intact, at least those that were left. He scrunched his eyes against the sunlight.

For a moment, Merhi studied him, taking in the sandals, worn denim jeans and dirty, blood-spotted shirt. Then he asked, *"Ma shimkha?"*

There was no reaction, the prisoner kept his head down, but Lattouf and al-Jayouchi looked surprised at Merhi speaking Hebrew.

"Chou esmak?" Merhi tried again in local Arabic. "What is your name?"

The prisoner raised his head, a glimmer of understanding in his eyes, but he did not speak.

"The cat has his tongue," Lattouf shook him roughly. "Let me loosen it."

"Later, Fadi, later." Merhi looked at al-Jayouchi. "Do you know him?"

al-Jayouchi shook his head. "No. Says he's been living here for years - "

"And you don't know him?"

al-Jayouchi raised his eyebrows. Lattouf said, "We keep the peace, we are not census registrars. Especially with the amount of people in our camps."

Merhi nodded acceptance of the point. "Why do you think he is a spy?"

al-Jayouchi opened the flap of the right pocket in his cargo pants and pulled out a small Nokia cell phone, handing it to Merhi. "He was seen to leave this beneath some stones out by the highway. An old woman was passing, thought he had dropped it. When she tried to give it back to him, he said it was not his."

"It is not mine," mumbled the prisoner. His accent was Palestinian.

"Ah, so now he talks!" Lattouf shook him again.

al-Jayouchi continued, "So she brought the phone to me. She knew the traitor, had seen him about the camp. She pointed him out."

"But why do you think he is a spy?"

"Look at it. At the photos." He saw Merhi was fumbling. "Here, give it to me."

With a few finger-presses, al-Jayouchi opened the photo app. "Look," he passed the phone back.

Merhi pulled reading glasses out of his pocket, ignoring Lattouf's comment of "Hey, I have never seen those. You look good. I must get some next time I'm in Hamra."

Merhi shielded the small screen from the sunlight. The first pictures were of a village. Normal homesteads... then destroyed homesteads. Then something which could have been an unexploded rocket. Some mortar shells. At the sight of pictures of two memorials, he began to understand where it was. He looked up. "Qana?"

al-Jayouchi nodded. "It is a ten kilometre walk. He has no explanation of why he was there."

"It is not my phone - "

"Shut up!" Lattouf slapped the prisoner round the back of the head. "You speak only when the Major speaks to you."

Then there were pictures of UN troops and UN vehicles in convoy, then some amphibious craft on the shore. Finally there were pictures of hand-held missile launchers, carried by men with their faces covered by their *keffiyeh*. Undoubtedly Hizbullah.

"Surely the Israelis are not thinking of a third strike on Qana?" mused Merhi.

al-Jayouchi sniffed. "I would put nothing past those bastards."

"Maybe that is just what the Party of God is thinking too," said Lattouf. "Where better to hide your arsenal than a place the Jews would not dare attack again?"

Merhi looked at his friend. He never ceased to be amazed at the insightful pearls that, just occasionally, came from Fadi Lattouf. Lattouf was right, of course and as always.

"Do you have anything to say?" Merhi said to the prisoner.

Silence.

"By the way, what is his name?"

"Abdul Abdulrahman," said al-Jayouchi.

Merhi did not comment. Unimaginative parents.

"Well?" said Merhi.

Abdul Abdulrahman was silent.

"Who were you leaving this for, out on the highway? Who was going to collect it? When?"

Nothing.

"Ah, the cat she is back!" Lattouf nearly ripped the prisoner's arm off with his shaking. He was close to causing minor brain damage at the very least. "We will loosen it! I will make this bastard talk. Give me something to insert into him."

"He will talk, Fadi," said Merhi. "He will talk. But not here, back in Beirut. You will be the official Palestinian observer at his interrogation."

Lattouf smiled at the honour.

Merhi put the phone into his pocket and turned to al-Jayouchi. "I think we are done here. Thank you, Captain. Excellent work."

al-Jayouchi inclined his head in gracious acceptance.

Merhi nodded at Lattouf. "Fadi, bring him."

As they were walking back across the rubble to the main building, Merhi said "There is just one thing before we go, Manar, if you would be so kind."

"Of course, Major. What can I do?"

Both men looked as the prisoner stumbled and fell to the ground in front of them after a too-hard shove from Lattouf. He was immediately yanked back up again, dust covering his jeans, Lattouf berating him and telling him he would need to brush himself down, he was not getting into the Major's car in that state.

Merhi shook his head then continued, "For the road. Perhaps just one more shot of your Egyptian Scottish whisky...?"

Southern Coastal Highway, Lebanon 14:30-16:30

Having had five whiskies, Merhi decided to let Lattouf drive the Toyota back, at least until they got to the Bourj el-Barajneh camp in southern Beirut where he would drop Lattouf off and then take the prisoner into the central lock-up in the Hotel Dieu district.

Lattouf was like a child at Eid as he familiarised himself with the controls before setting off. The weight of Merhi and Abdul Abdulrahman in the back seat provided an element of counterbalance but the fulcrum still erred in favour of the front.

Now they were on their way. They had curved into and back out of Tyre and were heading north along the old coastal road. Traffic was medium-light, most security checks were unmanned.

Abdul Abdulrahman sat on Merhi's right, so that he was not behind Lattouf. He was sullen, looking out of the window, hands still tied in front of him with the blood-stained rope. And, despite the car's air conditioning being on full blast, he stank.

Anticipating the prisoner's piquancy, Merhi had opened the back windows before they set off.

They all wore seatbelts, not only because Lattouf was driving (reason enough) but also because the car would start beeping at them if they did not.

The Toyota purred along. They could see the Mediterranean to their left and hear it breaking on the shore below the escarpment a few metres beyond the edge of the road. The warm windrush was pleasant and not too loud, a small price for the reduction in smell in the car.

"When will we start the interrogation?" asked Lattouf loudly so that he could be heard, left arm on the window edge, lightly controlling the steering wheel with his right hand.

"Tomorrow," said Merhi from behind him.

"Not today?"

"No."

"I could make him talk. The first thing I would do, Major, is to pluck out his eyes, like a sheep's head at a feast. Then I would cut off his sweetbreads one by one - "

"Yes, thank you Fadi. Enough. We have more... sophisticated techniques."

"But are they as effective?"

Merhi hmmphed. Lattouf had a point. He looked at the prisoner next to him. "You can make it easy on yourself, you know. Talk to me. Why did you take those pictures? Who were you leaving the phone for? Who was going to collect it?"

Abdul Abdulrahman continued to look out of the window, saying nothing.

Merhi shook his head. Foolhardy bravery. And the chances were that this fool did not know the answers anyway. He wasn't a Jewish spy with his raincoat collar turned up, hat pulled down over his eyes, with the theme from *The Third Man* playing in the background. He was just a skinny runt of a Palestinian, probably being paid what to him would be a fortune (but which would not buy a cup of coffee in Beirut) to take some pictures and leave the phone somewhere.

They would get the information, or lack of information, out of him, but it might cost him his life. Or at least his sanity.

"Your choice," said Merhi.

"Major," said Lattouf. "We are coming to the turning for the highway, but can we stay on this coastal road, at least to Sidon? It is very pretty, no? I have never seen it before."

"Why not?" said Merhi, staring out to sea. "There'll be much less traffic, chances are we'll make better time this way anyway."

"*Shukran!*" Uncharacteristically mindful of other traffic, Lattouf flicked on the left indicator to show he was travelling straight on and not dog-legging to the right as most of the other cars would be doing. The vehicles behind him pulled more to the right, including a motorbike.

They passed the turning. The cars turned off, the motorbike stayed on the coast road.

"Hello, what is this?" frowned Lattouf, looking across into the right side mirror. "A stupid motorbike trying to overtake on the inside. We'll see about that." The Toyota jolted as he wrenched the wheel to the right, closing off the gap for the bike.

Above the gentle roar of the windrush, Merhi heard an angry bip-bip from the bike as it was forced back behind the Toyota and out to the left.

"*Ahbal!*" shouted Lattouf. "Idiot! Learn the rules of the road!" This from a Palestinian. In Lebanon.

The bike growled loudly as it accelerated. Merhi looked to his left. It was a big, powerful machine, probably a Ducati or similar. The rider was dressed completely in black: black boots, black leather trousers and blouson, black helmet with a black visor. One black glove -

And a black Herstal FN Five-SeveN in the other hand.

"Gun!" shouted Merhi.

As always in moments of mortal danger, everything happened at once but to the protagonists it seemed like it played out in slow motion.

A flame shot out of the barrel of the gun. Merhi dived to his right, making a grab for Abdul, hindered by his seatbelt, unclipping it, fumbling for his gun. He felt the heat as the bullet missed him by five centimetres.

Lattouf swung the car to the left, nudging the bike. It wobbled, the rider fighting to keep control.

Merhi pulled Abdul forward, ordering "Stay down!" Then he raised his gun, pointing it out the window.

The bike accelerated, speeding off down the road.

"I'll get him!" screamed Lattouf, stepping on the pedal. "You fucking *kakhbah!*"

"No, Fadi, no, no!" shouted Merhi. "Pull over, pull over." He tapped Lattouf rapidly on the shoulder. "Leave him, let him go, let him go."

They were on the left side of the road and Lattouf slowed down, pulling up onto the sandy verge.

"Are you all right?" Lattouf undid his seatbelt, turning.

"I'm fine. I'm fine. Fucking felt the bullet go past though."

"What about him?"

Merhi grabbed Abdul by the shirt and pulled him back up. The boy was alive. The bullet must have passed clean through the car, in one open window, out the other.

The boy was trembling, lips quivering, bound hands shaking. A look downwards showed that he had pissed himself.

"Oh, thank you so very much," sneered Merhi.

"What?" Lattouf looked over the seat.

"He's pissed himself. Get out before it goes on the seat." He leant over and undid Abdul's seatbelt. "Go on, out, out. We should have brought your car, Fadi."

"Talking of which," Lattouf stepped out of the car, the suspension bouncing. "Funny how a brush with Allah loosens your natural functions." He walked three paces away from the car, onto the top of the escarpment. Standing with his back to the road, legs apart, he undid his fly.

With his gun still in his hand, Merhi got out to meet Abdul coming round the back of the car. "You too," he instructed. "Come on. And take your trousers and underwear off, you're not sitting in my car in those."

Abdul went up and stood near Lattouf, who had begun to urinate like an elephant.

Abdul dropped his trousers and then his grubby underwear, stepping out of them and kicking them away.

"Not too close, *merci ktir*," said Lattouf staring straight ahead.

But then Abdul took off, over the top of the ridge.

"No!" shouted Merhi. "Fadi, grab hold of him!"

But all Lattouf had hold of was something the size and colour of a salami sausage which he was pissing out of.

"I can't - !"

"Shit!" Merhi slithered down the embankment. "Abdul! Come back, you idiot!"

The boy was running across the sand about five metres ahead, naked except for his shirt.

"Abdul! Abdulrahman!" Merhi tried to keep up, sand flying up in puffs around his feet and into his shoes, the effort pulling at his calves. "Stop now! Stop, or I *will* shoot!"

But Abdul kept on running. He was hampered by his hands tied in front of him, but he was moving further away, Merhi losing ground.

"Oh hell," said Merhi, his breath going. "Oh fuck." He stopped. "Abdul!" It was almost a plea.

The boy did not turn round.

Merhi raised his gun. "Abdul..."

He fired.

A mist of red and pink sprayed upwards from Abdul Abdulrahman. His back? His head?

He did not stop running but he veered to the left, towards the sea. Then his legs began to buckle, wobbling like a new-born foal. He staggered, wobbled, reached the water, and fell face-down into the waves.

He was still, not moving, not trying to raise his head for breath.

Merhi clenched his teeth, growling first and then shouting. "Ohhhhhh BOLLOCKS!"

There was a huffing and puffing as Lattouf wheezed up beside him, still fumbling with his flies. When his zip was up he said, "Amazing shooting, my friend. Allah has guided your hand." He saw Merhi's grim, ashen face.

"He is not a martyr, he is a traitor."

"He was a boy."

"There was nothing else you could do. He was an escaping spy."

They watched as Abdul's body bobbed gently on top of a beach break wave, then a backwash took him and he was accepted by the sea.

"I should go get him," said Merhi.

"No," said Lattouf. "He will wash up. He doesn't care, Shaitan has him now."

Or Allah, thought Merhi, depending on which side you were on.

Both men heard a faint noise and they turned at the same time. Up over the escarpment, the Toyota's doors were open and it was ping-pinging a warning that somebody had taken their seatbelt off while the vehicle was still in motion.

Ping-ping-ping, ping-ping-ping, ping-ping-ping...

Coastal Highway, Lebanon 17:00-19:00

It was a subdued journey back, Lattouf shutting up after his reassurances that there was nothing else Merhi could have done had fallen on deaf ears. As he drove, he ate the remaining fruit they had bought that morning, propping the bananas between his legs while they awaited their fate. Visually unfortunate.

After the adrenalin high of the shooting, Merhi had plunged back down into a vortex of gloom. He knew Lattouf was right, there was nothing else he could have done. The prisoner had been trying to escape, and both Lattouf and Merhi were too old for a successful chase and apprehension. It was not the first time he had taken a life but he never liked doing it, especially as the target had been a scared, unarmed boy.

He was angry. Not at Captain Fadi Lattouf, not at Captain Manar al-Jayouchi, not even at himself. At Abdul Abdulrahman he was annoyed (you stupid, stupid boy) but he was angry at the Israelis. They said all was fair in love and war, but using a boy, a Palestinian whose parents they themselves had thrown out of their homeland, was low, really low.

It was interesting though that they had tried to kill Abdul after he had been captured. Firstly, how did they know? Had they been watching? Or perhaps when the phone had not been under the rock, they had put two and two together? But why try to kill him? That seemed to indicate that the boy knew something, something the Israelis did not want getting out.

Merhi dragged on his Camel King Size and snorted at his thoughts. Well, whatever it was, Abdul would not be telling them now – because Merhi had done the Israelis job for them! *Ya khorg!*

Bourj el-Barajneh, Beirut 19:10

Lattouf pulled up the Toyota with his trademark one front wheel on the kerb. Both men got out. Darkness had fallen.

"You will come in, my friend?"

"*Merci*, Fadi." Merhi shook his head.

"Nada is preparing *maqluba* tonight. She knew I would be hungry after a hard day's travelling."

"The temptation is great but no, thank you. You have my portion." Merhi slid slightly as he got into the driver's side, the leather seat had not yet adjusted back to normality after supporting Lattouf's enormous arse for four hours.

Lattouf pushed the car door closed. "You are going into the office?"

"No, it can all happen tomorrow. I thought of getting the local boys to look for the body, maybe the Coastguard. But you know what?"

"What would be the point?"

"Exactly. He is with his deity. Sorry there won't be any interrogation for you to attend."

"That is life, my friend. Or death."

Merhi lit up a cigarette, offering the packet to the Palestinian. Lattouf jumped back as if scolded, making negative hand gestures in front of his body, nodding backwards and shaking his head, eyes panicking, ending with his mouth stretched across and downwards. A human *Emoji*.

Merhi smiled, understanding. The power of wives. "Okay then." They shook hands through the car window. "New Year if not before, Fadi. And thanks for everything today."

"*Eid Mubarak*, my friend. Allah's blessing to Gisele and your family."

"And *Eid Mubarak* to you and yours. What a way to start a holiday! Give Nada a big kiss from me. *Khaetrak*." Bouncing the wheel off the kerb, Merhi drove off.

Lattouf watched the Toyota's lights disappear northwards. Then he waddled over to his doorway. He did not have a key, there was no outside lock only inside bolts, and the door was never bolted until Baba was home. As he went in he shouted, "Baba is home, children! You are safe for another night. *Eid Mubarak!* Wife, come here! I have something to give you from my good friend Jihad...!"

Jounieh, Lebanon 21:15 – 23:59

Traffic was manageable on the main Coastal Highway heading north out of Beirut (in other words, it was moving), which was just as well because Merhi's mind was not particularly on his driving. He was tired and he was grumpy. And his mood was not helped by the thoughts of the amount of paperwork he would now have to fill in because he had shot someone. Even an Israeli spy demanded reams.

He supposed he would have to get used to it now that the eradication of spies was within his remit. Thank God the late Brigadier and his team (which was now *his* team) had cleared most of them out. As far as he could tell from the meetings he had had already and the reports he had read, there was only a small caucus left, in the Beirut area. A small confession. A little group of hardy weeds which The Gardener had to eradicate.

Today had been an offshoot, a little sucker springing up way outside the main infestation. Minor, non-pernicious... But Abdul Abdulrahman was important enough for somebody to try to kill him. Who had it been? Merhi had no reason to doubt his earlier supposition that it was the person who had been sent to pick up the phone with the photographs. The border with Palestine was porous, a Jew on a motorbike could come across anywhere.

But there was something, just something, nagging at Merhi. Something about the attempted execution, something that had subliminally registered with him at the time but which he had then lost in the tumult of Abdul's forlorn escape. Something that had come and gone as quickly as his bullet had entered Abdul Abdulrahman and ended his life. What had it been?

He shrugged and threw the butt of his cigarette out of the window as he turned off the highway, reducing speed as the road narrowed and began its climb into the mountains...

It was a moonless night and the full beams of the Toyota sliced into the darkness like the heat-ray eyes of a gas-guzzling monster as it turned off the mountain road and bounced down the dirt track that led to the apartment block. The block was built into the mountain in such a way that you entered from the side in the middle, at the third floor level. The Merhis' apartment was on the fifth floor, the top.

He reversed into his usual place a little way past the main entrance in a gravelled area where the other eight residents of the building also parked, next to Gisele's older ex-official issue blue Toyota Land Cruiser LC5 (on which he had got a good deal). There were allotted parking spaces underneath the block, but as that was two stories further down the mountainside nobody ever bothered. Here was fine, by mutual tacit agreement.

Merhi switched off the AC, the headlights and the engine, and sat for a moment. He could see the lights were on in their apartment above. Gisele had been in the office giving a training course today and she would have picked up some food on the way back. He was hungry but he hoped it wasn't her speciality, *sayadieh*, fish with rice, not after the *delights* of the fish stew down in Tyre. Then again it might be good to counteract it.

He flipped the steering column wand as he stepped out of the car so that the headlights went back on to illuminate his way to the front door. They would stay on for thirty seconds after he had pressed the remote central locking button.

Halfway to the door, he held the key fob over his shoulder and pressed the button. The car did not beep but the indicator lights flashed as it locked.

"Hello Captain."

He froze, the shock of the voice from the darkness nearly making him expel the fish stew. Instinctively his right arm pressed against the gun on his waistband.

He did not move. Ahead, his own shadow from the car's lights grew and spread across the ground, losing itself in the cliff-edge bushes. Way out at sea he noticed lights on a boat. Carefully his hand unclipped the top of his holster.

He turned but his car's beams were blinding, he could see nothing. He heard the lightest of footsteps on the gravel.

Then the lights went out, plunging the area back into darkness. And still he could see nothing, just an impression of the beams seared onto his retina.

The footsteps moved closer, coming from behind the parking area. Up above, he could now see the stars sprinkled in the black night sky, his eyes adjusting.

A small shadow came towards him, between the two Toyotas. His hand remained on his holster but he had not drawn his gun – because he had recognised the voice. The deep, deep voice. A voice he thought about often.

The shadow stopped two metres in front of him.

"It – it's Major," said Merhi. "Not Captain, Major."

"Really? I'm impressed. Well, okay then *Major* Merhi. It has been a while, are you not pleased to see me?"

Carla Chedid took three paces forward, reached up and kissed Jihad Merhi full on the mouth.

Gisele Merhi had four emotions when her husband came through the door with a woman, with *this* woman. Jealousy - of course, goes without saying, she was a Lebanese wife after all. Surprise – an unexpected visitor, and this late in the evening, and after she'd had a hard day's work as well. Pleasure – she liked Carla, they had formed a close bond when they had met previously. Distress – at the fact that she was not dressed to receive a visitor, indeed she was hardly dressed at all. Okay, she and Carla had seen each other naked before when they had gone shopping and had tried on clothes and done other girlie things together, but it was hardly polite to greet a guest in just a thin red T-shirt and small yellow shorts, both of which showed that she was wearing nothing underneath. But then, Carla was hardly dressed formally either: loose white T-shirt over black leggings with black and white baseball shoes. And her T-shirt showed that she was wearing nothing underneath either.

After gasps of greeting, the women embraced with three cheek-kisses. Gisele smelt jasmine.

"I found her downstairs," explained Jihad who was only slowly recovering from the hint of tongue he had received. (Had it been deliberate, accidental, or just instinctive?)

"I found *him*," smiled Carla. "I was here first. I was halfway up the stairs when I realised I had left my phone, so I went back down to get it. And along comes your husband."

"Well come in, come in. You are always welcome to our home. Dinner is just about ready."

"Oh no, really - "

"Nonsense, there is plenty."

"You have had your haircut," said Carla. (Jihad raised his eyebrows. Girl-talk already and she was hardly through the door.) "I like it."

"I think it is too short. It does not hide my *wasm*." Gisele stroked the scar on her neck, the souvenir of Paris in 1997.

"It is beautiful." Carla reached out and lightly touched the back of Gisele's hand. "We all have our souvenirs of battle." She wiggled her fingers, drawing Gisele's attention to the lack of nails. The last time Gisele had seen Carla's fingers they had all been bandaged. "And my husband has many, many scars."

"He is not with you?"

"No, he is doing other things."

Their eyes held for a beat and then Gisele said, "Jihad, make our guest comfortable while I serve the food." She turned to her husband.

And, her look said, find out what the hell she is doing here.

"Gisele, *habibti*, that was wonderful. I have missed your cooking." Carla settled herself into one of the sofas in the lounge, placing her small, handleless cup of Turkish coffee on the side table.

"It was just *moghrabieh*," Gisele carried in the *rakwe*, the long-handled coffee pot, and put it on the table. She sat down on the same couch, at the other end.

"It is never *just* with your dishes, darling."

"You are too kind."

Jihad came in, coffee in one hand, cigarette and glass of whisky in the other. He paused when he saw the two women on the same sofa and then he sat down in the one opposite.

The room was warm, the lighting low to befit the hour.

Two subjects had dominated dinner: how things were in New York (interesting, there was never a dull moment at the UN, especially in the Security Council) and how things were in Lebanon (going to hell in a handcart and the speed was increasing). As a corollary, talk also turned to *Major* Merhi, with congratulations, respect and teasing dished out by the women in equal portions.

Now Jihad stubbed out his cigarette in a glass ashtray. "So - "

"Why am I here?" Carla had long ago taken off her shoes and she tucked her feet up under her, mirroring Gisele's naked olive legs. "Not only here in Liban, but why am I here with you?"

"There are still people who want to talk to you about the Hariri killing. The International Tribunal is due to report at any time."

"I bet it will be years yet. And when they do, it will be a fudge. Either that or civil war will return to Liban. Whenever a Sunni dies they blame the Shi'ites, and *wa'l-aks* whenever a Shi'ite dies. Sometimes there are other answers. And anyway, they want to talk to Zahia Zalloum not Carla Chedid. Zahia Zalloum disappeared on 14 February 2005… as you know."

"Hmm." Jihad drank whisky.

"Have the investigators spoken to *you*?"

Jihad paused with the glass on his lips.

"I thought not," continued Carla, "so we both have something to be grateful for."

And something to hide, thought Jihad, finishing his drink.

"I am here because I have been given some information." She heard the question before Jihad had a chance to ask it. "It is too important to transmit electronically. I must speak with someone. Tell them face to face."

"Who?"

She shrugged her shoulders and took a sip of her coffee, stretching and topping up her cup as she put it back down on the table. She raised the *rakwe* in the air. Gisele held out her cup for refilling. Jihad shook his head.

"I do not know," said Carla. "Up until a week ago it would have been Brigadier Wissam al-Hassan."

For a moment, silence. Jihad's face was stone. Then he said, "What?" The temperature in the room had plummeted like a rock thrown down the mountainside.

Carla's black eyes stared into his. "Who has taken over from him? I need to speak to him."

"Why?"

"Jihad?" Gisele had picked up the abrupt change in her husband.

"Why, Carla? We all know that the Brigadier was my ultimate boss."

"Yes, that is why I came to you."

Jihad knew he could not outstare the black eyes, but he made a valiant effort, his face hard. In eye wrestling, a djinn would always triumph over a mere mortal. As he felt her winning, he broke the hold and stood up, going over to a cabinet. He slid open a door to reveal bottles of various whiskies and *arak*, the Lebanese male's alcohols of choice. He filled his tumbler with Johnnie Walker.

"I am sorry about his death," said Carla. "But it is imperative that I speak to his successor."

Jihad was shaking his head. He walked over to the patio window which led out onto the balcony. He could see nothing in the darkness except a muted reflection of the room behind him. He spoke to the glass. "Things have changed. Already. Things have been delegated, devolved."

Carla said nothing but in the reflection Jihad could see her looking at him. Looking into him.

"If you could tell me what it is about...?" he continued. "And don't say 'Sajida was right' because I will personally throw you off this balcony, djinn or no djinn."

Carla smiled at his reference to the al-Mahdi incident. She looked from Jihad to Gisele. They were all security cleared, she by the Department of General Security, the Major by the Internal Security Force, Gisele by both. She finished her coffee and said, "I have seen a report. From Tel Aviv. About the Israeli spy cell network in Lebanon, which your Brigadier demolished."

"Almost demolished."

"More than you think. Although spies are self-replenishing and it will be an ongoing battle, for the time being he got them all."

"I am pleased to hear that. We thought we had a few still to go."

"It seems not. You have got them all. Except one."

Jihad turned from the window. "Except one?"

Carla took her feet down and leant forward. "Major, there is one left. And it is internal. You have a spy in the ISF."

26 October 2012
10 Dhu al-Hijja 1433

Jounieh, Lebanon 00:00

Spies in the security forces of Lebanon were nothing new. Retired Brigadier General Adib al-Alam and members of his family had been awaiting trial for over two years accused of spying for Israel. In the report Merhi had seen it was alleged that al-Alam had been recruited by the Jews as far back as 1992, twenty years ago. Twenty years of spying.

In a country run on confessional lines there would always be spies, each faction spying on the other even while they worked (or pretended to work) side by side. It was almost a game the confessions played, clandestinely striving to be the first to obtain intelligence on their rivals.

The confessions tolerated each other's spies. And Syrian spies were a given. But spies for Israel were not acceptable.

"You know who it is?" asked Jihad.

"No. But I have a list of names."

"Show it to me."

Carla shook her head. "It is not written down."

He took a large mouthful of whisky, rolling it between his teeth. "Tell me then."

"Tomorrow," said Gisele, leaning forward, hands on her knees. "It has been a long day, for you in particular my husband. Why don't you both continue this in the morning, with rested heads? The spy is not going anywhere."

Carla smiled, touching Gisele on the arm. "Always the good trainer." Her black eyes moved to Jihad. "You have had a hard day, Major?"

Jihad shrugged with his shoulders, down-turned mouth and raised eyebrows. He had driven to south Beirut, collected Lattouf, driven down to Tyre, eaten fish stew with Captain Manar al-Jayouchi in the Bourj al-Shimali refugee camp, picked up a prisoner, tried to interrogate him, been ambushed and shot at, had killed the prisoner - an unarmed Palestinian youth - had driven back, had deposited Lattouf, had been French kissed by a djinn, and had been informed there was an Israeli spy in the ISF. Just a normal day really.

Carla stood up. "I will go. You are right, *habibti*, fresh heads tomorrow. Shall I attend your office in the morning, Major?"

Gisele also stood up. "You have somewhere to stay?"

"I shall find an hotel. I just picked up my transport at the airport and came straight here."

"Then you will stay with us."

"Oh no no. Really I - "

"Nonsense, you cannot go back to Beirut at this hour. Tell her, Jihad."

"Well - "

"Things have changed in the last two years. It is not safe to go south in the dark. And even if it was, the hour is too late. You have eaten our food, it is our duty to look after you. And our pleasure. We have the bond of salt. Stay with us for as long as you need to."

Carla looked from one Merhi to the other, wondering how much protestation to make. She decided on very little. "You are too kind. Both of you. Thank you." She reached out and stroked Gisele's hair. "Truly you are my friends." Her fingers moved lightly over the scar on Gisele's neck, what Gisele called her *wasm*, her camel's brand. Then Carla leant forward and kissed Gisele on the lips.

Over by the window, Jihad drained his glass and felt just a little bit jealous.

But of whom...?

Jounieh, Lebanon 02:30

Darkness. No noise except for the sound of whisky-induced heavy breathing coming from the master bedroom.

Carla glided into the lounge, not even disturbing the ambient air. She was dressed only in her white T-shirt, which ended halfway down her bottom. Her feet were bare, her bed-hair fuzzy.

Normally the patio door would complain, grumble and resist when someone tried to open it, but for her it slid across noiselessly.

Outside, myriad star pinpricks in the ceiling of the sky made up for the lack of moon. Down below there were a few lights on the Coastal Highway, even at this hour. Beyond the highway there was just blackness where the sea should be.

She waited, goose-bumps popping up on her exposed flesh as a cool breeze hit from the west. Two minutes later, her left hand glowed.

She raised the phone to her ear. "*Habibi.*"

The smallest of communication pauses, then: "All is well?"

"All is good. I am in." She spoke softly, cupping her right hand over the phone.

"*Brava.* How are they?"

"They are well. He is a Major now."

"Does that help or hinder?"

"They have a new way of working, so it helps a great deal."

"Good. And the earlier matter?"

"Not as successful but it confirms the information received. *Kifak?*"

"I am fine. I'm about half an hour out."

"You will be careful?"

"Of course."

"And I will get my present?"

There was a longer pause, then: "Yes."

Carla shivered. She whispered, "The thought excites me."

"You are excited?"

"Always when I talk to you."

"Let me move your hand."

"What?"

"I am moving your right hand. Can you feel me?"

"Yes, I can feel you moving my hand. It is on my thigh…" Her nailless fingers caressed her goose-bumps.

"I am moving your hand again. To the left… upwards. You are so smooth. Can you feel what I am doing to you now?"

"Yes…"

Out over the Persian Gulf, the Qatar Airways Airbus A321 from Doha to Muscat banked to the south, heading inland, preparing for the first stages of descent.

Bahla, Oman, Arabia 06:30 (local time)

As always, Paradise and Love awoke at the same time. The daily routine was that one would shower while the other went down to prepare *ftoor*, breakfast. Then that one would come up for her shower while the other one went down and prepared the *qahwa*, coffee. They had an hour, Abu Yo'roub always got up around seven-thirty.

Today it was Love's turn to prepare *ftoor*. As a naked Paradise walked into the bathroom, Love slipped on a pair of white cotton harem pants and a white cotton sleeveless vest and tied her hair back in a ponytail. Barefooted, she went downstairs and crossed the open-plan *majlis* into the kitchen.

An iPod Touch was sitting on a small dock near the microwave. She turned on the unit and scrolled to what she wanted. Immediately, Elissa's latest album *As'ad Wahda* began playing. Love kept the volume low, but she knew Paradise would hear it up in the shower, in her head.

She began to prepare today's *ftoor*: *labneh*, strained yoghurt, with mint, olives and olive oil; pita bread with *za'atar*; dates and bananas.

Fifteen minutes later, leaving Elissa entertaining the empty kitchen, she walked back out into the *majlis*. And stopped dead.

A man was sitting on one of the low cushioned couches.

They exchanged stares, Love's head inclining to the side. Most people would be disconcerted by the white snake eyes, the blinkless gaze, the almost-white blonde hair, the white vest and pants emphasizing the pale skin. But not the man in the denim jeans and loose white collarless shirt, long black hair falling down either side of his face, hiding the missing left ear.

Their eyes were locked, like a hunter and feral prey. But which was which? Flexing her fingers, Love slowly began to move into the room. The man stood up.

Love made no sound but she bared her teeth and flicked her fingers, like a cat showing its claws, daring its opponent. You really want some?

Carefully the man took a step towards her. Love moved to the left, away from the stairs, the man turning with her.

Love stopped when she had the man at the right angle. She raised her arms in the air, her hands bent forward like cobra heads. Her nostrils were flared. Her eyes did not leave his.

Then she grinned, like a victor about to administer a *coup de grâce*.

He had heard nothing. The first thing he was aware of was a displacement of air behind him. Then something was on his back, like a *ghouleh*. Strong naked legs wrapped around his hips, bare arms seized him around the neck. A thumb (or was it a claw?) found one of his eyes.

The man bent forward, rocking his body, trying to shake off the demon.

Love laughed. Her sister was too strong for this mortal, he stood no chance.

Paradise grabbed his face with her right hand, pulling up his hair with her left. Giving the lowest of growls she moved her head around, pushing her viper's tongue into the hole where his left ear had been.

The man stopped struggling. Love stood right in front of him. Still on his back, Paradise withdrew her tongue and began to lick the scars on his face, her tongue wet, barbed but sensual.

Love placed two cobra fingers between his lips, prising his mouth open, then she leant forward and put her tongue into his mouth, kissing him ferociously, biting the inside of his lip. Making him bleed.

Paradise's legs slid off his hips and she swung around to the front. She was completely naked. Something glistened on her thighs. Her eyes closed in pleasure as she experienced her sister's kissing.

Then Love pulled her head away, breathless. Paradise too was panting.

He could feel their hot breath on his face. One woman was on his right hip, one on his left hip. The closeness of cats. Four white eyes stared at him.

Then the eyes lowered, almost in deference. Together they said, "Master."

He did not react.

Paradise looked up. "We were wondering when you would come."

"We have missed you," said Love. She moved herself against the hardness in his groin, reaching up and rubbing the blood off his lip with her thumb.

"Abu Yo'roub is not up for half an hour," said Paradise.

"We want you," said Love.

"Take us."

"Take us now."

They said in unison: "And take us hard."

Elissa was still playing as the *houri* led The Damascene up the stairs to their bedroom.

Jounieh, Lebanon 05:30

Carla, back in her white T-shirt, black leggings and baseball shoes, propped the note up against the upturned *rakwe* draining next to the sink, where the Merhis would be sure to find it.

> Gisele/Jihad,
> Thank you for receiving me, for your bond
> of salt.
> I have things to attend to. Jihad, I will be at
> your office at 9.00.
> Gigi, I need to go shopping, get some clothes.
> Are you free later today? I will ring you.
> C
> xxx xxx

Silently she left the apartment. Walking down the stairs, she smiled inwardly. The bond of salt. The old Arabic code where a visitor would receive shelter and food and the host's protection for the duration of their stay and for three days afterwards. Three days being the length of time it took for the host's food to pass through the visitor's body. If the visitor was thought to retain just one grain of salt from the host, protection would be given.

She passed through the building's lobby and went out through the main door. Outside it was a crisp late October morning, and she shivered in just her T-shirt. It would warm up later, and she genuinely looked forward to a girls-together shopping trip with Gisele. But first she had other things to do.

The vehicles outside were parked in a single line side by side. Interestingly Jihad had not queried why last night she had approached him from *behind* the cars. He had probably been too dazzled by the lights and too surprised to see her to wonder about such things. And he had had a long day.

She squeezed between one of the Merhi's Toyotas and another resident's Ford Explorer, going behind the cars to the two-metre wide area in front of the gorse bushes of the mountainside. Where she had left her motorbike...

Bahla, Oman, Arabia 08:30 (local time)

Ftoor was finished. Because they had an unexpected guest, Love had also brought out the remains of yesterday's oryx and rice to supplement the other food, so the men were full as they sat down with their coffees in the *majlis*. The Damascene, in particular, had an appetite.

The twins also sat with their coffees, but behind the men. They were both dressed in the white sleeveless vests and white harem pants.

"I have had contact from Paris," said The Damascene. "Assad is weakening."

Ghazi Kanaan rubbed his beard. "That's not what I hear. On the radio, on television, online, they all say Assad is holding fast."

"The Ba'ath Party might be holding fast, the government is still solid. But Assad is losing favour."

"They are sure?"

"The dynasty is ending. His support is waning."

"And this means...?"

"It is time for a new leader, as planned. An open, progressive leader, but someone who is still a member of the party, an Alawite. The country is ready."

"The timing must be right. I have not waited seven years for it all to go wrong now."

"Your waiting has been necessary. Remember, you should be dead. I should have killed you, but you persuaded me otherwise."

"And paid you handsomely."

The Damascene poured himself another coffee. He did not offer a refill to Kanaan. "There is that."

"I do not want them to think that I am a replacement Assad in all but name."

"I have been told that you have the support of Hizbullah and the SSNP *[the Syrian Social Nationalist Party in Lebanon]*. On the other side, the FSA *[Free Syrian Army]* and the Salafists know of the plan and they are willing to listen."

"That is all? Listen?"

"What more do you expect? You will have to prove yourself."

"They know I am alive?"

"No. They know a new leader will be installed. A leader who will negotiate, a leader who will listen to *them*. A leader who is willing to have a peaceful transition. They have not been given a name."

Kanaan was nodding slowly. "So the time nears."

"No, the time is here."

For a minute Kanaan said nothing, finishing his coffee. Then he asked, "What happens?"

"First we get you to Beirut, where you will meet with them all. If all sides agree, you will be given safe passage to Damascus. There you will be installed and you will effectively open the gates of the city to all parties. A ceasefire will be called."

"And what of Assad?"

"What of him?"

Kanaan sat forward. "I see. And do I have written guarantees of my safety, from all sides?"

The Damascene also sat forward. "Abu Yo'roub you do not even have a guarantee of your safety from *me*. Never forget that. Once we take you from this place, there is no coming back. It is a one-way street. To power... or to death. And if either side decides you are no longer to their liking, it will be my pleasure to do what history records I did seven years ago."

Anger flared across Kanaan's face. The old anger that for twenty years had been the most feared emotion in Lebanon. "You are a callous, ungrateful bastard."

The Damascene gave no indication of disagreement.

Kanaan breathed deeply, aware the women were watching him. He composed himself. "So," he continued, calmer. "I have no choice?"

"Dead men never do."

Kanaan raised his right arm in the air, clicking his fingers and then pointing at his cup which was only half a metre in front of him. "*Qahwa!*"

Love stood up and came over, picking up the *rakwe* and pouring thick coffee into Kanaan's cup. Her eyes lingered on him as she went back to sit beside her sister.

"There is one thing I ask," said Kanaan. "One thing you can do for me."

"What is that?" asked The Damascene.

Kanaan looked behind him. "Get your pet bitches to put their contact lenses in. Those white eyes are so fucking disconcerting."

Mount Lebanon 07:00

On the main Damascus road out of Beirut, before she reached Jamhour, Carla took a left off the road onto a rough cinder track. A few metres along she pulled up in front of a three-storey apartment block. She parked in the front, by the main door.

Taking off the black helmet, she shook out her hair, giving it a finger-comb, and looked up at the block. It had been new when she had first been here seven years ago, and it had not changed. The troubles of Beirut rarely reached up here to the slopes of Mount Lebanon (except when the Israelis decided to bomb the nearby electricity generating plant, which they did in 2006). The block had magnificent views out over Beirut and in her pocket she had the keys to one of the two apartments on the top floor. The keys her husband had kept when he had 'killed' the owner, Syria's Interior Minister Ghazi Kanaan. And everyone knew a dead man had no use for keys.

She wondered if the blonde Englishwoman and her Lebanese husband still lived next door with their three children, the boy and the twin girls. They were probably long gone by now.

She could have used this as her base while she was in Lebanon, she still had some clothes and other stuff up there. But she needed to keep a protective eye on the Merhis, so she would accept their bond of salt and let them think she had nowhere else to stay.

At least until she had figured out the meaning of the Israeli intelligence report she had pdf'd into her head...

Coastal Highway, Lebanon 07:30

Major Jihad Merhi drove south along the Coastal Highway, cigarette between his lips, both hands on the wheel. As always, the morning traffic heading into Beirut was heavy. On his left, the sun was making promises about the day; on his right, the Mediterranean sparkled.

So, there was an Israeli spy in the Lebanese Internal Security Force. It was interesting that Carla had been so specific: the ISF, not the security forces in general (*Brigadier General Adib al-Alam had worked in the GSD, the General Security Directorate; the CIA to Merhi's FBI*) – it narrowed the field but that still left a suspects pool of thousands.

Even though he was now autonomous, he would need to report this to Lieutenant-Colonel Ghanem. And the new Head of the Intelligence Bureau, Colonel Othman, would need to know. But it would be down to him, Major Jihad Merhi, to locate and eradicate the weed.

Where to begin? Well, with that list of names Carla had in her head. He looked at his watch. She would be with him in under two hours. Where had she gone to so early this morning? He had discussed it with Gisele but, wise trainer-head as always, Gisele had pointed out that he shouldn't worry about it, The Djinn always moved in mysterious ways – just remember everything that had happened two years ago during the al-Mahdi turbulence.

Merhi blasted the Toyota's horn at an old fruit lorry that was crawling along, and forced his way out into the second lane.

Something else had occurred to him. There was another entity who might need to know about the remaining spy: Hizbullah. All Israeli espionage activity in Lebanon was focused on the Party of God and, although it would never be admitted, Hizbullah owed the ISF big time for weeding out the incredible Israeli penetration of their activities.

That was something he did not look forward to, but at least he had his new team of superheroes. They must have liaised with Hizbullah before, they would know where to go, who to go to and, importantly, how to speak to them.

Thoughts of the murdered Brigadier Wissam al-Hassan flashed into his mind but were quickly forced out by other thoughts. Thoughts of Carla. Very special thoughts. Thoughts that a fifty-something married Major of the Internal Security Force should not be having…

Bahla, Oman, Arabia 09:30 (local time)

Both men were dressed in white dishdashas and red *keffiyehs*, the headscarves worn straight and held in place by black rope *agals*. They were followed out of the villa by two women in plain black *abbayas*, heads covered by plain black *shaylas*, faces visible. One woman had green eyes, one had brown eyes.

Each person wheeled a small, cabin-baggage style suitcase.

The woman with green eyes locked the villa's solid, ornate front door. Turning, she held up the keys.

Without speaking, The Damascene held out his hand. She dropped the keys into it.

The men climbed into the back of the Jeep Wrangler Ultimate, leaving the cases to be stacked in the back by the women. Then the women climbed into the front of the Jeep, the one with brown eyes in the driver's seat.

As if in choreographed unison the women turned to look at the men. The men said nothing. The women turned back.

The outer gates of the villa opened and the car started. They passed the now-still fountain and drove out, the gates closing after they passed through. The tyres kicked up sand on the local track as they picked up speed.

Soon they had reached Highway 21. They turned north-west, heading for Dubai.

Jonblat, Beirut 09:00

The time was eerily accurate when the telephone on Merhi's desk shrilled with the internal ringtone.

"Reception, Major. A Madame Suzi Saad to see you."

"Who?"

"Madame Suzi Saad."

"Ah, yes, yes. I will be down. Sign her in, will you?"

Suzi Saad was wearing black Cuban-heeled ankle boots, denim jeans and a green shirt with black buttons that matched the size and colour of her eyes. A dark grey Barbour wax cotton messenger bag was on one shoulder. As always, her voluminous black hair cascaded over her upper body like a waterfall, an ornate black and gold hair clip holding a scrunch of it at the back. She wore little make-up; she didn't need to.

She had passed through the metal detector and was waiting for Merhi in the small seating area. Shortly she saw him coming down the stairs (all over Beirut people avoid lifts if they can help it because of the power cuts).

"Madame Saad," Merhi gave a half-bow in greeting, right hand on his heart. He shook hands only when she offered hers, as propriety dictated.

He nodded at the Corporal behind the desk and held open the door into the stairwell, letting Madame Saad go first. She knew the way.

"You've been shopping already?" he asked as he followed her up the stairs.

"Just something I quickly picked up down the road," said Carla. "Do I look all right?" Did she actually wiggle her bottom or was he imagining it? "I've phoned Gigi and she's meeting me this evening. Will you come shopping with us?"

"Er, maybe not."

She giggled. "Wise. But afterwards how would you like to take two beautiful women to dinner?"

Reaching the second floor, he stretched forward to open the door for her, replaying her last sentence without the words 'to dinner'. "How can I resist?"

Her boots echoed down the corridor. In the General Office, the veteran Sergeant Deeb el-Gharib was tapping away at a keyboard. He looked up when Carla passed by the door, looked back down and then did a double-take.

Merhi had paused by the General Office door. "Coffee?"

She turned back. "That would be nice, thank you Major." She followed Merhi into the General Office. "Ah, I see you have a coffee machine now."

"It's still sludge."

"Sludge will be fine. Hello Sergeant. *Al-salaam 'aalaykum.*"

Deeb el-Gharib was frowning, trying to place her. She looked familiar. He stood up, right hand on his heart. "*'aalaykum al-salaam...*"

She held out her hand. "Suzi Saad, GSU. We've met before."

His memory flashed back two years. A vague recollection. Did not recall the name though. "Oh yes. How are you?"

"I am well, thank you. And yourself?"

"Overworked, underpaid..."

"Yeh, yeh, yeh," said Merhi pouring sludge.

"It *is* quiet in here," said Carla.

"Just me and five Corporals nowadays," el-Gharib swept his arm around the empty office. "They are out. The Lieutenant and the other Sergeants, *poof* gone! Staff cuts."

"We are in a transition," Merhi came over holding two mugs which might last have been washed during the French mandate. "I have another team upstairs. We will be merging soon."

Carla took the drip-striped mug that might once have been white. The very same mug she had drunk from two years ago. The Visitors' Mug.

"Nice to see you again," said el-Gharib as he sat back down.

"Ms Saad might be around for a little while," said Merhi. "Popping in and out. Don't broadcast it. Need to know. If anyone asks, tell them... she's my new temp PA."

"Okay, sir."

In the four days he had been a Major, Merhi had noticed how 'boss' was being replaced by 'sir'. Now, as he followed Carla down the corridor, something was puzzling him. Just a little niggle, a little flag that had gone up in the last ten minutes. Something he couldn't put his finger on.

"The glass in your door, it is still cracked," said Carla as she entered Merhi's office.

"Facilities are on to it."

She draped her bag over the back of the wooden chair in front of the desk. "Do you still...?" She made twirling motions with her hands next to her ears, then pointed at her eyes.

Merhi made similar motions, saying "Yes" to the ears and "No" to the eyes. Carla nodded understanding.

Merhi unlocked a drawer and brought out the black laptop, clicking it into a multi-port on his desk. "So," he said, choosing his words carefully, giving The Listeners enough so that they did not become suspicious but not enough for any adverse interest to be taken. "I will need to report the situation to my Lieutenant-Colonel, so I'm glad you're here. He wasn't in half an hour ago, but I'll try him again shortly. Meantime - "

"Meantime," Carla pulled a face as she put the mug down on the desk. "Let us go and get a proper coffee. Your sludge has not improved over the years. In fact it has got worse."

Dubai, United Arab Emirates 13:00 (local time)

During the financial crash of 2008 many ex-pat workers fled Dubai, unable to meet their commitments when their surreal bubble burst, afraid equally of their creditors and of the punishment for financial default. They left in a hurry, literally thousands of them leaving their huge, expensive 4WDs in the airport car parks, sometimes with notes of explanation and apology on the windscreen, often without.

Although the rush to depart had slowed to a trickle of miscreants and unfortunates by 2012, sand-dust covered vehicles could still be found in the airport car parks waiting forlornly for their owners who would never return, for the finance companies who could not be bothered to reclaim them or for the thieves who would eventually take them for shipment to Africa.

Such would also be the fate of the black Jeep Wrangler Ultimate. It was the sisters' vehicle of choice but, unlike men, they did not become attached to mere machines - and anyway, when working for someone as generous as their current employer, they knew that another one was already ordered and waiting for them at their destination.

The two men in the white dishdashas and the two women in the black *abbayas* left the jeep on the lower floor of the car park at Terminal 3 and, each wheeling their small cabin-baggage suitcases, made their way up to Departures, the women walking behind the men.

Their Lebanese passports showed that they were a family. The older man was Mounir Ibrahim, the younger was Joseph Ibrahim and the twins were Jenna and Jaime Ibrahim. The sisters had checked-in online during the journey from Oman and, having no bags to drop off, they went straight to Passport Control and soon were making the long walk to the world's most extensive Duty-Free Departures Lounge. Once there they went into their gender-respective washrooms, washed and made themselves comfortable, and changed from their local garments into western clothing.

Within minutes of each other they emerged from their washrooms. The bearded grey-haired older man had his long hair tied back in a simple ponytail, as did the tall black-haired younger man, only in his case the hair fell slightly over the left side of his face. Both were dressed in comfortable chinos, loafers and a shirt.

The two women, attracting the usual *oh-look-how-sweet-twins!* stares, also had their blonde hair in ponytails and were dressed in identical white blouses, slim-fit capri-style denim jeans and sandals. They both desperately wanted to remove their contact lenses which had gathered sand-dust during the journey, but they knew they could not.

Soon the Ibrahim family were sitting outside Gate 22 awaiting Emirates Flight EK953 to Beirut.

Hamra, Beirut 09:30

It was nice, reflected Jihad Merhi, to sit at a table in Hamra with just two coffees and not have the residue of the district's entire stock of cupcakes, falafel and God knows what else strewn all over the place. Carla was the very antithesis of Fadi Lattouf: neat, precise, concise, small, beautiful. And very attractive.

They were at *café Hamra* at the end of Hamra Street, just beyond the Crowne Plaza hotel. The walk down Bank of Lebanon Street and Hamra Street had been taken up with social pleasantries and the usual grumbles about work. *How were things in the ISF? How were things in the GSU? Congratulations again on the promotion. How was Merhi going to organise things in this merged team?*

Now at the table with her coffee, Carla got straight down to business. "So, I was given a copy of an internal Mossad report on the state of their cell network in Liban. In fact, it was a post mortem. The mighty Mossad could not believe it. Brigadier al-Hassan really routed them."

"He was a good man."

"He was a hero."

"And what thanks did he get? His life taken from him." Merhi proffered his packet of Camel King Size. She shook her head. As he lit up, he said "I sometimes wonder whether it is worth it. Do any good in this country and you end up getting killed. A fine reward. In Lebanon, there are more dead good people than live good people. And every one of those dead good people have been murdered. And they will be quickly forgotten."

"Not everyone is forgotten. Rafic Hariri will be a hero forever."

Merhi blew smoke down his nose. "He is a dead hero. If asked now, do you think he would chose martyrdom over life? Do you think he chose it then? He had no choice, others decided he would die. And Hariri is the exception. What about all the others that have been murdered? Can anyone except their families and friends remember their names now? You are alive for just a very short time. You are dead forever."

Carla drank her coffee. "It has always been this way. The history of Lebanon is written on the bodies of dead good men."

"It needs to fucking change."

For a moment they were quiet, sipping coffee to the backdrop of the buzz of Hamra. Then Carla said "I have that list of names."

Merhi took out his phone. "Give them to me."

"Do not write them down, not even on your phone."

"You expect me to remember them?"

"Yes. You will remember them. I can, so can you."

"I am not..."

"A djinn?"

"If you like. I was going to say 'as retentive as you'."

Carla smiled. She steepled her fingers together and closed her eyes. When she spoke, her deep voice was flat, as if she was channelling, like they were having an outdoor seance. "Deeb el-Gharib, Jad Chadidi, Omar Mostafa, Michel Yammine, Peter Harrak, Emad Hmedeh, Nabil Haddad, Claude Gerges, Tamer Khalef."

Merhi stiffened. "What?"

"The names."

"Those are the names of my men. The old team and the new team."

"Really? I did not know. They are just the names I have been given."

"Are you kidding me, Carla? Are you messing with me?"

"Do you want me to mess with you?"

"Stop it. Are you... are you saying that one of those is the Israeli spy?"

"It is the list I have been given."

"Shit." Merhi sat back, taking a full two centimetres off his cigarette in one drag. "Haddad, Gerges, Khalef are al-Hassan's team, I don't know them well. The rest are my team, some I have known for a long time. I trust them."

"Of course you do."

"al-Hassan's team were the ones who eradicated the spy cells, so it can't be one of them. So, you are telling me that one of my own team is the spy?"

"I am telling you nothing. That is just the list of names I have."

"Shit." Merhi put his hands on his head, cigarette balanced in his mouth. He looked around. "I need another coffee." He asked her the question with his raised eyebrows.

"Yes, espresso."

Still mumbling "Shit" and reaching into his jacket for money, Merhi went back inside *café Hamra*.

Carla watched him. Like a she-wolf watches a tethered goat. What was he going to do? Indeed, what was *she* going to do? For there were things that she had not told him. She had not told him it was a list of potential spies, he had just assumed that. And she had not told him the other three names on the list. Three names which took the total up to twelve.

Top of the list was Wissam al-Hassan, the assassinated Brigadier, the one her husband had been charged with protecting. Then there was Pierre Ghanem, Merhi's boss.

And then, of course, the final name, the obvious name: Jihad Merhi.

Jonblat, Beirut 11:30

"That is absolute shit," scoffed Lieutenant-Colonel Ghanem."Where did this report come from?"

"A contact in the GSU."

"Who got it from where?"

"The horse's mouth."

"The Jew's arse, more like."

Mentally, Jihad Merhi looked to heaven.

"And how do we know it is not disinformation?" continued Ghanem. "A report. What sort of report? And a list of names with no direct cross-reference to the report, just a list of names. And on this you are willing to believe that one of your team is an Israeli spy?"

"I did not say that. We have a report that the Jews have a source somewhere within the security services - "

"Tell me something we don't know."

" - and a list which names every person in my division."

"They could have gotten that from an internal telephone directory."

Merhi sighed. "I just thought you should know."

Ghanem's stare was cold. "You are at a level now where you report results, not theories. Theories stop with you. Understand?"

"Yes, sir."

"If you think you have an Israeli spy in your ranks, find them and deal with them. Then report the result to me."

And to The Listeners, thought Merhi. Twat.

"I will do that."

"Otherwise, don't bother me."

Ya khorg.

"He's not interested," said Merhi as he walked back into his office.

"You are surprised?" Carla was sitting cross-legged on the windowsill, like an imp.

"Not really, he's never been the most supportive of bosses."

"Yet you were promoted."

"Probably not on his recommendation."

Carla undid her legs and let them dangle. "So what are you going to do?"

Merhi lit up a Camel then threw the packet down onto his desk. He nodded at the ATS laptop as smoke flowed down his nose. "I'll have a detailed look at the nine names, something I should be doing with the new three anyway as they're now under my command. See if there is anything, *anything*, in the background of any of them which would indicate a susceptibility."

"And if there is?"

"They will be dealt with, commensurate with the susceptibility. But if one of them *is* a spy, it will not be that easy. Their cover will be deep. They will be the one I will not be able to find."

He watched as Carla hopped off of the windowsill. Although she wore the ankle boots, her feet now made no sound on the wooden floor as she came across to his desk, unlike earlier when she had clip-clopped down the corridor. She flicked hair back over her shoulder with her nailless left hand. For the first time, he noticed she wore no rings.

She said, "So you do not need me right now, you have no use for me?"

He bit his tongue and pushed the thoughts he was having out of his mind. Thoughts of the use he could make of her...

Instead he said, "We are certain of the provenance of the report? And of the list? It is something Ghanem asked. Could it be disinformation? A distraction?"

Carla shrugged. "It is always possible. But I got it from an Israeli source, in New York. How would they know I would do anything with it, let alone come straight to you? They are not that clever. I run them. They do not run me. Nobody does."

That was true, thought Merhi. Like you could never tame a cat, you could never tame a djinn. Unlike lapdogs. He said, "Well, I'll have a look at these personnel files, security reports, appraisals and all the rest of the crap, and let you know tonight if I find anything. Then we can discuss our next step. You will be staying with us?"

"I have nowhere else to go. Unless you think I should go to an hotel?"

Their eyes locked. The grey eyes of a Major of the Internal Security Force and the jet black eyes of a djinn. For a moment the world did not exist. The spell had been cast many years ago and it was as strong as ever. He said, "Now why should you want to do that?"

She smiled. "Thank you. You are always kind to me."

"We have been through some adventures, you and I."

"And it looks like we shall go through some more. For the sake of Lebanon."

"For the sake of Lebanon."

For a full thirty seconds they looked at each other, then, with a giggle, she broke the gaze (but not the spell, that was unbreakable). She picked up her bag from the chair. "Then I shall go shopping. I need more clothes. Even now I have no underwear."

"*Quoi?*"

"Underwear. A girl needs her pants, no? At least, some of the time." She smiled. "I phoned Gisele, we are meeting at five. And don't forget you are having us both tonight."

Merhi opened his mouth but the power of speech had suddenly deserted him.

"For dinner, Major, for dinner. Have you forgotten? You choose the location, we will meet you there."

"I... I will."

"There is one other thing," Carla was in the doorway. "Just something to think about. Probably just my suspicious djinni mind. You said you doubted Lieutenant-Colonel Ghanem recommended you for promotion. Well if he didn't, who did? Your other boss was murdered, the new Chief would not know you. So it must have been Ghanem. I grant you have a new structure, but would he really promote you if he did not want to?"

"What are you saying?"

"I am saying *why*? In hierarchical structures there comes a level where a person is no longer directly responsible. In the civilian world they call it higher management, where someone underneath you always - how do they say? - carries the can, and the shit never sticks to *you*. Ghanem has now reached that level and you are the person underneath him."

"So you think I'm being set up?"

"I think nothing, Jihad. It is you who must think. Have you been left holding the injured baboon as the lion approaches? Are you a patsy?"

She left, closing the door behind her, once again her boots clip-clopping down the corridor.

Immediately the office felt empty. The strong presence, the strong soul, had gone, leaving behind just a memory - and a waft of jasmine.

Jonblat, Beirut 13:00

Merhi knew he should not be doing it but, under the circumstances, who could blame him? It was just lunch with an old friend. God knows they had much to discuss.

The killing yesterday – was it only yesterday? – of the Palestinian boy spying for the Jews. Using the killer on the motorbike was a professional attempt at silencing, and how ironic that he had done the assassin's job for him.

Now he is told there is an Israeli spy in the ISF. Was it one of his new team? Was it one of his old team? Was he going to approach Hizbullah and tell them that, despite previous assurances, the security forces had *not* eradicated the complete Jewish spy network? Or should he keep quiet?

And what about Carla Chedid? Or Suzi Saad as she was now calling herself? Coming back into his life *again* and telling him a lot without telling him anything. And planting the seeds of doubt about the intentions of his senior officer. What was she up to? And, worst of all, was she right? And why was she so damned attractive, so hypnotic?

And what was it that was bugging him about her sudden reappearance in his life. His subconscious had picked up on something earlier but for the life of him he could not remember what it was. Like with the assassin on the motorbike yesterday: he saw something, registered it – and then forgot it.

He was getting old.

He needed to discuss things with someone he could trust, someone who had never let him down, or deceived him or kept things from him. If anybody could help him find the answers, it would be his old friend Johnnie.

Johnnie Walker.

He took out the square bottle from the lower drawer of his desk and poured the whisky into his mug until it was two-thirds full. Normally he would fill it all the way, but he had a long afternoon and evening ahead of him – and anyway he would be driving later.

He took a huge swig of whisky and looked at the ATS laptop waiting patiently on his desk. It showed the wallpaper of the ISF symbol: white shield on a light blue background, two dark blue hands on the shield, the one of the left holding a sword, the one on the right holding an upright sprig of laurel. On top of the shield was a dark blue ISF cap with a grey cedar tree above the words *Internal Security Forces* in Arabic.

And bouncing around over it was a screensaver of a Lebanese flag: sideways stripes of red, white and red, with a green cedar tree in the middle. Bounce, bounce, bounce...

Merhi ran his finger over the trackpad and the flag disappeared. One second it was there, the next it was gone. An allegory for Lebanon itself, thought Merhi, if this Syrian civil war got any worse.

Cursing the fact that he could not delegate the work, Merhi clicked onto the Human Resource system.

Right, Johnnie, where should we begin...?

Somewhere in Beirut 13:00 – 15:30

The cursor moved across the screen of the MacBook, in time with the keystrokes being made by Major Jihad Merhi on the laptop in his office in Jonblat. The Confession smiled as 'personnel files, security reports, appraisals and all the rest of the crap', as Merhi had called them earlier, popped up on the screen.

The Confession liked the Lebanese, but they could be so innocent, so naïve. Fancy even thinking that their wonderful ATS laptops were secure and impregnable. *No* computer was impregnable, even more so when you were up against the cream of Israel's cyber security black hats. Years ago they had been the first to invent the system which became known colloquially as Barking Dog, the universal hacking programme which could access any, *any*, computer system in the world. Barking Dog was effective for its age but it had needed vast amounts of equipment, memory, storage space and *time*.

Nowadays all that was needed was a portal of opportunity, either physically with a computer or online, and the black hats could not only see everything that was happening on a presumed ultra secure computer but, if they so desired, take it over completely. The Confession had taken the opportunity when it arose.

Now whatever Merhi did on his ATS was watched and replicated. Merhi was doing exactly what they wanted him to do.

Now The Confession could begin...

PART THREE
الجزء الثالث

THE RETRIBUTION
القصاص

Jonblat, Beirut 15:30

After two and a half hours of looking through personnel files, security reports, appraisals and all the rest of the crap, Merhi was punch-drunk. And frustrated. All his staff checked out. All had good histories. All were subject to annual security vetting. All had a clean bill of health.

He had known this would be a fruitless exercise, he had said so himself – a spy's cover would be deep and it would be good. What had he expected to find, a little note against somebody's name with *'This man is a spy'*? That man would have been removed from the ISF long ago, probably removed from life as well.

And this was a spy for Israel he was looking for. The Jews' clever way of using locals rather than infiltrating their own men meant that any back histories would be true not fabricated.

He was getting nowhere. This was pointless. He need another way...

There were two men in the small room on the fifth floor when Merhi entered: Nabil Haddad and Tamer Khalef, two-thirds of Brigadier al-Hassan's team of spycatchers. Both stood up when they saw their new boss.

"No need for any of that," said Merhi, "now or in the future. We are a team, sit, sit."

They sat. Merhi perched on the edge of the unoccupied desk. "Where is...?" He gestured at the desk.

"Claude," said the stocky, bearded Khalef. "Claude Gerges, sir."

"Claude, where is he?"

"Out on a recce over in Bourj Hammoud," the balding, clean-shaven Haddad had a cigarette between his lips.

"It's on his calendar." Khalef nodded at the laptop on his desk, one of the standard-issue models not an ATS.

"Which I have access to," Merhi nodded and smiled. "Thanks for the oblique reminder, Tamer. You'll have to bear with me, this is all new to me. Not only your good selves but also my promotion to God-like status. I'm told I have to have special garments whose hems you can kiss. Alternatively there is my arse."

Haddad and Khalef gave rueful laughs. The ice was broken.

"Obviously I want to get up to speed on matters, on how you operate." Merhi saw Khalef glance at his laptop. "I know, I know, it's all in your reports, which I have access to. But I wanted to talk to you all, both as individuals and as a team. I want to get to know you. I want you to know me. I want to know how you operate and I want you to know how I operate, what I expect, what I accept. And what I won't accept. I don't know how the late Brigadier operated and frankly I don't care. With his murder things have changed." He looked from one to the other, holding each gaze, making a point. He spoke while his eyes were still on Khalef. "For example, I will expect daily face to face briefings from each of you. I know it will be in your report in the system, but I want to hear it from you. I must be kept up to speed on everything. As well as that we will have team meetings at least once a week and more frequently as necessary. Do you understand?"

Haddad and Khalef exchanged glances. Both said, "Yes, sir."

For a moment, Merhi did not speak. He knew he had not only broken the ice but had pushed them through it. Then he said, "This room. You are happy here? It is secure?"

"As far as we know," said Haddad.

It was Merhi's turn to give a rueful chuckle. "Indeed."

Haddad stubbed out the butt of his cigarette on the side of a waste bin and picked up the packet on his desk, flipping the top and offering it to Merhi. They were not Camel King Size. Merhi shook his head, "*Merci.*"

As Haddad lit up, Merhi said "What you and the late Brigadier did in eradicating the Jewish spies will go down in the history of the ISF. It was remarkable. But we all know the battle with the Jews is ongoing. A new wave of spies is probably being recruited as we speak."

"But that gives us time," said Haddad. "They'll all be new."

"No more twenty year espionage veterans," said Khalef.

"Yes," said Merhi. "Good. New shoots are tender, they are easy to rub out, not like gnarled old branches which require severe chopping."

Haddad and Khalef looked puzzled at the gardening simile, but their nods confirmed they had got his drift.

"So if you need additional support I have other men downstairs. Just let me know. Eventually I intend to get all of you together, as one team. But one step at a time, eh?"

"Sir."

"Sir."

"The first step I want to take – and this is not on the system," he looked at Khalef, " – is to introduce myself to our other interested party." He pushed himself up off the desk. "How do I go about meeting Hizbullah?"

Bourj Hammoud, Beirut, 16:00

Bourj Hammoud is the Armenian district of Beirut in the north-east of the city, on the right bank of the Beirut River. Most of Lebanon's two hundred thousand Armenians live here in distinct neighbourhoods, each affiliated to a different region of Armenia. It is one of the most densely populated areas in the whole of the Middle East, save only for the refugee camps. The streets are narrow and claustrophobic but the colourful ethnic community ensures a lively, noisy atmosphere. The area is famous for its jewellery, low-priced clothing and craft shops – and that was why Sergeant Claude Gerges was there that afternoon. Next week was his twentieth wedding anniversary and he wanted to get his wife Michelle something special. Something special but not too dear.

Really he should be shopping in his own time not the firm's, but if anybody asked he would explain that he was monitoring his local informants *(Christian Armenians despised the Jews, Armenians or not, whom they blamed for the Armenian Genocide of 1915 when the Ottoman government systematically exterminated its minority Armenian subjects and drove them from their historic homeland in what is now Turkey).*

In his pocket Gerges had an amber necklace and matching earrings which he had bought in Dikran Jewellers in the Blanco Centre in Master Mall Street. Michelle would like them… he hoped. With women you could never tell, not even after twenty years.

Michelle was away at her mother's in Bhamdoun for a couple of days, due back tomorrow, so he would not have to sneak the jewellery back into the apartment, which was good – she could always tell when he was up to something.

Now he walked south down Arax Street. The roads in Bourj Hammoud were too narrow for comfortable driving so he had parked just off Bechara el Khoury Street, over near the river.

Being only about five metres wide, Arax Street, like most of the streets in the district, has become pedestrianised by default over the years. Every building has a shop on the ground floor, their wares spilling out of their shop fronts and onto the sidewalk. Cars could come down here but it would be a trek and a feat of supreme driving dexterity to avoid the pedestrians.

Difficult for cars, but someone on a motorbike could negotiate the street with little problem…

At the Karasoum Manoug, the Church of the 40 Martyrs, Gerges doglegged right then left into Marache Street, the busiest street of the neighbourhood. His nose was assailed by the heady smells of spices, meats, cheese and roasted coffee beans from Café Garo on his left and Nerses al-Halabi on his right. He half thought about stopping for a coffee and perhaps buying some *loukoum*, Turkish delight, for Michelle, but he had to get back. A text message from Tamer Khalef had tipped him the wink that the new boss was on the prowl.

He did another dogleg, past the *soujouk* (Armenian sausage) shop. Only as the streets became quieter did he become aware of a low rumbling behind him, but he dismissed it as residual noise from the bazaar-like shopping area.

He walked on, the streets still narrow but now more residential than commercial. At this time of day there were very few people about. If it wasn't for that rumbling, the place would be silent.

As he crossed the road he looked behind him. A little way back was a motorbike, coming his way. It was a big, powerful machine, hence the rumbling. The person on it was dressed all in black. Gerges' police instinct noticed that the rider was wearing a crash helmet. It was unusual to see a motorbike rider in Beirut obeying the law!

After the shadows of the narrow residential streets, Gerges emerged into sunlight by the river. Here it was more industrial. Across the river he could see the top of the electricity ministry building. He reached his car, a white Dodge Durango. The car bipped and flashed its lights as he unlocked it. Gerges turned as the motorbike pulled up nearby. Probably someone needing directions for somewhere.

The rider pushed down the kickstand and swiveled off the bike. Gerges opened the driver's door of the Dodge but did not get in. He nodded as the rider came towards him. *"Bonjour. Salaam."*

The rider said nothing.

Rafic Hariri International Airport, Beirut, 18:05

Flight EK953 from Dubai touched down at Rafic Hariri International Airport Beirut precisely on time. With only hand baggage and using Lebanese passports, the Ibrahim family were soon through the controls.

At the Information desk out on the main concourse, The Damascene produced his passport and picked up an envelope that had been left for him under the name of Joseph Ibrahim. Kanaan and the twins watched as he ripped the top off the envelope and tipped a set of car keys and a car park ticket into his hand. The Damascene looked at the tag attached to the keys, nodded and said "Our transport awaits. Not a chariot, oh King of Lebanon, but you ladies will like it. Come."

"You have trustworthy suppliers," said Kanaan as they moved off. "What would you have done if the envelope had not been there?"

"There was never any danger of that," said The Damascene. "But, to answer your question hypothetically, I would have killed someone."

Kanaan stopped, turning back to the women. "Here," he thrust the handle of his case towards them. "I am tired of wheeling this."

A set of green eyes and a set of brown eyes looked at The Damascene. He gave a subtle nod and Paradise reached forward and took the case.

"Shall I take yours?" Love asked stretching out her hand towards The Damascene's case.

"No."

They started walking again, towards the three-level car park, the men in front, the women behind. Outside, darkness was falling. As they walked, The Damascene said quietly "It is 2012 Kanaan, remember that."

"What do you mean?"

"You might have been King here once but you are no longer. The women work for me, not you. They are your protectors, not your servants."

"Pah, there are only two good places for women: either behind or underneath a man. They should know their place."

"As should a dead man."

Kanaan continued walking. After a moment's reflection he asked, "Are you threatening me?"

"Yes. We are assigned to get you here for your meetings and then into Syria. Then our contract is finished, and I for one will be pleased to see the back of you after seven years. We have been paid to transport you and keep you safe. But be aware that payments can be returned."

"What are you saying?"

"I am saying that when we get to our destination you will take your own fucking bag." Louder he said, "The car is on the third level. Are you sure you can make it up the stairs, old man?" He turned round. "Ladies, *yalla*." He reached out and took Kanaan's case from Paradise.

Two green eyes smiled at him.

Mount Lebanon 20:30

There were only two security checks on their way from the airport, one by the army and one by Hizbullah. On both occasions the armed guards were boyish and flirtatious when they saw the two identical women in the front of the new Jeep Wrangler Ultimate, and on both occasions the mood changed when they became aware of the two men in the back. For the army, a few words of greeting in Arabic by The Damascene was all it took. For Hizbullah, The Damascene handed over their passports, explaining that his sisters and father had been to the airport to meet him on his return home from working in Dubai. He gambled, correctly, that the guards would not notice that all the passports had UAE exit stamps.

Now the Jeep turned off the main Damascus road and crunched down the cinder track, its beams illuminating the entrance to the three-storey apartment block. In the back seat Kanaan gave an ironic humph. "Well, well, my apartment. It is still active."

"*Your* apartment?" said The Damascene.

"I paid for it."

"I inherited it when you died."

"Oh did you now?"

"Do you have the deeds?"

"Of course not."

"You don't have the deeds, I have the keys."

The car pulled up and they got out. Lights were on in all the apartments except the one on the top right. Kanaan began to walk towards the entrance.

"Your case," called The Damascene.

Kanaan stopped and turned, glaring at the man he knew as Captain Mebarak, the man with the long hair and one ear. In the name of Allah, thought Kanaan, was Mebarak deliberately humiliating him? He should have killed him twelve years ago when he was his prisoner in The Onion Factory in Aanjar.

The beautiful, deadly twins were standing either side of Mebarak expressionlessly staring at Kanaan, waiting. Waiting like bitches ready to attack at their master's instruction.

With a raised eyebrow of disdain, Kanaan walked to the open back of the Jeep and tugged out his case, knocking one of the other cases out and onto the cinder ground. He stepped over it as he came back round.

"Keys?" He held out his hand.

"Love, would you escort Abu Yo'roub up the stairs?" The Damascene handed the keys to the twin with the brown eyes. "Do not use the lift, a power cut is imminent at this hour. Top floor on the right. Paradise and I will bring the bags."

Love unlocked the entrance door and gestured for Kanaan to precede her. A few moments later, The Damascene and Paradise carried in the four cases. They could hear Kanaan mumbling on the stairs above them.

Love stopped outside the door on the top floor. She had overtaken Kanaan on the way up, knowing that her tightly-clad ass might give the old man incentive to manage the six flights, and she now watched him as he puffed his way up the last staircase, holding on to the handrail. So, she thought, this out of breath, wheezing, long-haired, bearded grey old man was to be the next President of Syria? Even if he succeeded, he would not last long, Allah would see to that (and if he did not, maybe she and her sister would).

The Damascene and Paradise caught up with Kanaan as he came up the last step.

"You're out of shape, old man," taunted The Damascene.

"Should have used the bloody lift," snarled Kanaan. "Look, the electricity has not gone out."

"But it will," said The Damascene, "it will. This is Beirut. Where the power cuts have their own timetable."

Love opened the front door to the apartment and stood back. The Damascene went in, turning on the light. He took enough paces so that the others could enter and then he put down the cases, looking at the place. He was not spiritual but there were memories here. Good memories. Bad memories. Haunting memories…

But he pushed the fingers of history away. He had a job to do.

The apartment was a duplex, spacious and well furnished. Tiled flooring, minimal but tasteful decoration, good quality appliances – even a flat screen smart television on the wall, a Sony. Opposite were full-length sliding windows, which led out onto the balcony. The views out over the city were enviable even in the dark, the lights of Beirut twinkling like a fairyland beyond the woodland below (subconsciously he wondered if that was the first time Beirut had ever been compared to a fairyland!). Here and there were small dark patches in the vista where the power was out. Far in the distance there were lights gliding on the blackness of the Mediterranean.

The apartment looked unused, but he knew differently. For two reasons. Firstly there was no dust on the surfaces – but his companions would not notice that, for at that moment the power went out!

Behind him there was movement from the twins and complaining grunts from Kanaan. Then two soft beams caressed the darkness – the twins had their cell phones out.

"It will be back in half an hour," said The Damascene over his shoulder. "I suggest we unpack and then go to eat somewhere."

"Somewhere where the bloody power is," mumbled Kanaan.

"My bedroom is the first upstairs," The Damascene pointed upwards with his finger. "Abu Yo'roub yours is in the middle, ladies you are at the other end. If you wish to wash, there will only be cold water for now. I will turn the hot on for when the power returns."

He turned and tried to hide the momentary jolt as he looked at the twins. Their beautiful faces were harshly illuminated from below by their phones – and they had both taken out their contact lenses. Four white eyes stared at him unblinking.

Quickly he recovered. "Please. Make yourselves at home."

"It *is* my home," said Kanaan as he picked up his case.

"Was," corrected The Damascene. "Your next home is the Presidential Palace in Damascus." Or, he thought, a coffin.

As Kanaan and the women went upstairs, The Damascene walked over to the window and looked out into the darkness. Down below, power went back on in one area of Beirut and out in another.

He thought of her. How was she progressing? Was she somewhere down there at this moment? Or was she with them up in Jounieh? He looked to his right, to the north. Wherever she was, he knew she was near. And she had been here. It was the second reason he knew the apartment had been used.

He could smell jasmine.

Sodeco, Beirut 21:30

Gisele Merhi dabbed at her mouth, leaving an impression of her MAC Relentlessly Red lips on the napkin. Opposite her, Carla Chedid rolled the final drip of ice cream back over her bottom lip, sucking her finger. At ninety degrees to both women, Gisele on his left, Carla on his right, Jihad Merhi tried not to stare at Carla. The ice cream had to be white, didn't it?

They were in *La Piazza* restaurant, by the main Damascus road down in Sodeco. It was one of Jihad's favourite eateries and he had introduced Carla to it the last time she was in Beirut. It was an amazing setting. They were inside but were sitting in an Italian town square; on the walls around them were murals of houses, some even with laundry hanging out to dry. It was quaint, charming and, unusually for a restaurant with such a strong theme, the food was excellent. Gisele and Carla had had pasta dishes, Jihad a pizza. For dessert both women had had strawberries with ice cream, Jihad chocolate cake (and ice cream).

The restaurant was busy but not full. Jihad had chosen it because, with its discreet table geography, it was an ideal situation for the unmonitored discussion of clandestine affairs (certainly more free from eavesdroppers than the ISF offices). But, as it happened, most of the discussion had been about the women's shopping evening ('discussion' being the women talking about what they had and had not bought, which they already knew, and Jihad trying to look remotely interested). The only nod to work had been a quick "Any progress?" from Carla answered by a pursed-lip shrug from Jihad.

Now Jihad finished his coffee. His eyes drifted to Carla as she and Gisele discussed the merits, the sheer orgasmic pleasure, of a pair of Louboutin booties they had both lusted after in the Beirut Souks in Fakhry Bey Street. Carla Chedid, or Suzi Saad as she was calling herself this time, with her thick long black hair, so black eyes, olive skin, elegant but nailless fingers – the most dangerous woman he had ever met. And the most attractive. Save for Gisele. And married to the most dangerous man he had ever met. An unusual, potentially volatile combination.

His mind wandered, thinking thoughts he shouldn't. He was married. *She* was married. Clandestine affairs…

"Jihad? Jihad!" Gisele was tapping him on the arm.

"Mm? Sorry, I was away somewhere."

"Away with the fairies?" asked Carla.

"Away with the Israeli spies."

Gisele put her napkin on the table. "Let us go. Get *l'addition*."

As Jihad signaled to a waitress using the universal sign, he asked, "Where are you parked, Carla?"

"Down behind your office. I left the bike there when I came to see you this morning."

Jihad's arm was still in the air. Slowly he turned his head. "Your bike?"

"Can you drop me back?"

"You have a bike? I thought you had a car."

"A motorbike. My husband turned me on to them. Much, much easier in the traffic, especially in Beirut. Something wrong, Major?"

"No, no, I'm just surprised, that's all."

"Can you drop me back? Then I'll follow you to Jounieh."

When Jihad did not respond, Gisele said "Of course we can. Jihad, what is wrong with you? And put your arm down."

Jihad obeyed. "Sorry, sorry."

"Too much thinking of Israeli spies," scolded Gisele, but warmly. "Leave work at work." Her eyes met Carla's. "Both of you."

Fifteen minutes later, and after Jihad had been left with his own thoughts for ten minutes while the women went to the toilet together upstairs, they left the restaurant.

As the Toyota Land Cruiser V8 pulled away onto Damascus Street heading north-west, a Jeep Wrangler Ultimate turned in to the restaurant's parking area from the south-east. Four people got out, two men, two women. As they walked into the restaurant, one of the men, the old one, was grumpily mumbling something about "Fucking power cuts…"

27 October 2012
11 Dhu al-Hijja 1433

Jounieh, Lebanon 02:30

Tonight it was cloudy, no star pinpricks in the ceiling of the sky to amaze her while she waited. But the cloud cover also meant that it was warmer.

Carla was naked on the balcony of the Merhis' apartment. Her hosts were asleep and she knew them well enough to know they would stay that way for several hours yet, helped in the Major's case by the copious amounts of whisky he had drunk over dinner. Gisele had been self-generous with the white wine also. Carla had not even finished half a glass.

The journey back up the Coastal Highway had been interesting. Major Merhi had driven with the exaggeration of an intoxicated driver, speeding then slowing down, speeding then slowing down. After five kilometres, Carla had overtaken the Toyota and had reached the apartment fifteen minutes ahead of them, parking up in front of the building like she had last night.

Now she performed some stretching exercises out on the dark balcony while she waited. She was touching her toes when her left hand glowed.

She straightened. *"Habibi."*

"All is well?"

"Yes. You are here?"

"You have been in the apartment."

"Yes."

"I could smell you."

"You want to smell me?"

There was a pause. Then, "You know I do."

"I left something for you. In our bedroom. In my underwear drawer. I have not had time to do any washing."

Another pause. "You are..."

"I am what, *habibi?*"

"You are a witch."

"I am a djinn. You are under my spell. As I am under yours. When will I see you?"

"You are a djinn, you can see me whenever you want."

"That is true. Are things progressing?"

"A meeting has been arranged. It will be over soon, one way or the other. How about you?"

"Things are... interesting. I need to be certain. Hands are being played very close to chests." As she spoke the simile, she looked down at the nailless fingers of her right hand. Then she asked, "My present is with you? They are here?"

"Yes."

"Good."

The Djinn smiled into the darkness of the night.

Inside the apartment, standing well back in the deepest shadows so that he could not be seen from outside, Major Jihad Merhi watched the naked woman standing on his balcony.

Mount Lebanon 02:40

On the balcony looking out over Beirut, The Damascene also smiled. His eyes were closed, imagining his wife was next to him.

"When?" said Carla into his ear.

"Soon. We will get this matter sorted and then they are yours."

"It is the best present you have ever given me. How can I thank you?"

"We will... think of something." He opened his eyes. The woodland below the block was pitch black but Beirut twinkled beyond. "I have to go."

"I am missing you, my husband."

"And me you." He took the Nokia away from his only ear and pressed the red icon.

He stood looking out over Beirut, the city that held so many memories. The city of so many deaths. He was still wearing his jeans but he was shoeless and naked from the waist up. The light breeze of the late evening caressed his hairless skin.

He became aware of a presence and turned.

Behind the glass balcony door, a pair of white eyes stared at him unblinkingly. She wore only a white thong. Her hair was down, falling over her chest, caressing but not covering her breasts. Without the contact lenses, he could not tell which twin it was. The sisters were identical, their skin porcelain, literally statuesque. This one was so still she resembled one of the living statue street performers down in Nejmeh.

The only hint of colour was the pink bullet scar on her left shoulder. But had she been shot or had it been her sister? The Damascene had been there when it had happened, over in Aanjar two years ago, but he did not know which one of them had been wounded. They had both bled.

He held the stare as the balcony door slid open. She stepped out, parts of her body reacting to the night air. Even though she was barefooted, she matched The Damascene in height.

She said, "She is here?"

"Yes."

"Good."

"When will we have our present?"

"Soon. We will get this this matter sorted and then she is yours."

She nodded. Then she said, "I wanted to thank you for today. For being so... *gallant*. For taking the suitcase." So it was Paradise.

The Damascene shrugged. "I know you are more than capable of looking after yourself – yourselves. But, even in this day and age, I cannot abide rudeness to a woman from a man. Especially *that* man."

"You were kind."

"It is a bad trait of mine."

She reached out, touching the hair on the left side of his head. "He did this to you?"

"Yes."

"And you let him live?"

"It suits my purpose. For now."

She smoothed away the hair from the scarred hole where his left ear used to be, pushing it back between her fingers, her hand grasping the back of his head, gently pulling him towards her. He could feel the heat rising from her body against his naked chest. She brushed his groin as she reached for his right hand.

Their left cheeks touched, her warm breath soothing against his sensitive scars as she whispered, "Come with me."

Twice before the twins had used him to sate their lust but this was the first time he had been taken by just one of them. On her own, Paradise was doubly energetic, as if making up for her sister's absence. Riding him, bucking, reaching her first satisfaction within three minutes, falling breathless down onto his chest.

The Damascene gave her thirty seconds and then flipped her over onto her back. As he began to take pleasure, he looked at her face below him. At the jet black hair, the black eyes, the olive skin...

He stopped and she snapped open her eyes. Her white eyes.

He was suspended inside her, hard but unmoving. He saw the scar reappear on her shoulder and her hair turn back to blonde. He pulled out of her.

"Master?"

"On your knees."

"Yes Master." She obeyed. As he slid himself back into her, she said "Master, give me more than you've ever given anybody."

As the scar disappeared and her hair turned back to black, he did.

In the third bedroom at the end of the landing, Love was on her knees on the bed, her hips bucking, lunging with every thrust that was made into her sister. She was wet. She was open. She felt Paradise begin to climax for the second time and her nostrils flared with pleasure. The women were silent lovers but they both threw their heads back, their mouths opening wide.

In their minds they both bayed liked wolves.

In the middle bedroom, the old man with the long grey hair and beard slept fitfully, sometimes snoring, sometimes grunting, sometimes snorting. He dreamt he was in a *barjeel*, a wind tower, hiding, looking down into an *hammam* that was Syria. In the *hammam* a thousand women were bathing, naked and oblivious to him and what he was doing to himself. Each woman was tall with blonde hair. They were having fun, some were washing each other, some were doing more than that.

And then suddenly they changed. The women were dressed, all in black. Their heads and faces were covered by black *niqabs* so that only their eyes were visible. They were wailing. The death ululation.

Then the women froze, their heads turning upwards. Two thousand white eyes stared at him. Two thousand white eyes of Syria.

And they shook their heads in unison.

No.

Jonblat, Beirut 08:45

A preoccupied Jihad Merhi pushed through the doors on the second floor of the State Security Building and walked down the corridor towards his office. He had not slept well and he had exchanged grumpy words with Gisele before she left for an early class down at the General Security Building in Ras en Nabaa (he would phone her at her break time and apologise).

He had been so engrossed in his thoughts on the way in he had not really been aware of the hour's drive (the traffic had been moving, the car, himself and his packet of Camel King Size had been on autopilot). Random thoughts, disparate recollections and images had flashed into and out of his mind like feral daydreams.

Drinking whisky with Captain Manar al-Jayouchi in the Bourj al-Shimali refugee camp in Tyre. The attack on the coastal road. The assassin on a motorbike. Blood shooting out from the body of Abdul Abdulrahman. Fadi Lattouf farting. His new team. The reappearance of Carla Chedid. A spy in the ISF. The list of names. The need to contact Hizbullah. Dinner with two women. Carla riding a motorbike (a coincidence, surely?).

And, above all, Carla naked on his balcony in the middle of the night, bending over, stretching. Talking to somebody on the phone…

"Sir? Sir!" Sergeant Deeb el-Gharib's voice intruded into Merhi's ponderings as he passed the General Office door. "Major!"

Merhi stopped. "What is it, Deeb?"

"Good morning, sir."

"Good morning."

"We've had an urgent phone call. From the local police up on Armenia Street in Bourj Hammoud. They've found a car in the Beirut River."

"So? Nothing unusual in that. Is the coffee on?"

"Yes. The river is low so it was visible this morning."

"Get to the point, Deeb. Jad," he called to one of the corporals, "pour me some sludge, if you would be so kind. Any biscuits?"

"The point is, sir," continued el-Gharib, "they ran number plate recognition and called us straight away."

"Why?"

"It is registered to Claude Gerges, one of your new team."

"What?"

"Sergeant Claude Gerges. His car is in the Beirut River. Over in Bourj Hammoud."

Bourj Hammoud, Beirut, 09:40

Merhi could see the car on the river bed as he drove over Yarevane Bridge and took the slip-road on the immediate left. Although the Beirut River had been turned into a canal in 1968, the water retained its natural ebb and flow. Currently it was low, the water itself metres from the crumpled once-white Dodge Durango which was lying on its side.

The graffiti-daubed canal walls were high, but here and there slip-roads led down to what would be the water's edge at high tide or the river bed at low tide.

Merhi parked at the top of the slope. As soon as he opened the Toyota's door, he was hit by the stench. This was one of the most polluted parts of the city, the river being defiled by industrial waste, sewage and refuse from the perfect storm of the factories along the bank, the nearby waste disposal and treatment centre and the city slaughterhouse just to the south in Karentina. This was the end of October. He could not begin to imagine what the stench would be like in high summer. Quickly he lit up a Camel King Size.

There were just a few people about, no crowds. The denizens of Beirut were inured to whatever the river might throw up. Cars, bodies – recently even a live crocodile. Earlier this year the river had mysteriously turned an eerie deep red for a few days. Subsequent investigations had pointed the finger at dye illegally dumped from a nearby factory – but many Beirutis suggested it was the blood of the hundreds of thousands of Lebanese murdered by internecine strife since 1985. Who was to say they were wrong?

There were two uniformed policemen standing well to one side as a civilian tow truck edged slowly backwards towards the Durango. At the back of the tow truck a man in overalls was stretching out the tow hook ready to capture the crumpled vehicle.

Merhi did not want to walk on the riverbed of silt, shingle, sand and shit but he had no choice.

"Major Merhi, ISF," he said as he crunched across, being careful to maintain his balance. He did not show any identification but his building ID was still around his neck.

"Ah, Sergeant Kanj, sir," said the plump, older man on the right wearing the sergeant's uniform (which could have been a clue). They shook hands. "You're just in time."

"Details?"

"It was called in by a local on his way to work at oh seven hundred. Saw it in the river. Didn't give a name, the usual. We ran number plate recognition. Came up as belonging to one of you ISF guys."

"How did it get there?"

Sergeant Kanj pointed up and behind to where the canal-side railing had been smashed apart. "Doesn't take much, they're nearly fifty years old, not maintained, rusted, rotted, dangerous."

Merhi thought that description could be applied to himself – except for the 'nearly'! He asked, "Anyone inside?"

Kanj shrugged.

"Was it submerged?"

The younger policeman spoke. "Partly. You can see the stains on the roof. Where the water reached. Corporal Skaff, sir." They shook hands.

As Merhi watched, the man on the back of the tow truck managed to hook the chain inside the shattered back side window. He scurried back to the base of the boom and gave it a pulse of power. The chain went taut and held. The man looked back, waiting for his command.

"Okay sir?" asked Sergeant Kanj.

Merhi nodded. "Do it."

Kanj raised his hand and the boom whirled into motion.

The Durango began to complain as slowly, slowly it was pulled upwards. Then gravitational force took over and it fell down onto its wheels with a bang, bouncing, water trickling from the bottom of its door frames.

The mechanic went to unhook the chain to place it elsewhere for towing.

"Hold on," said Merhi. "Let's just take a look."

The two policemen accompanied him over. Merhi kept his cigarette in his mouth, deliberately letting the smoke go up his nostrils to cover the ambient stench of the river. All the Durango's windows were cracked and broken, but the car looked empty.

"No one," said Sergeant Kanj.

Corporal Skaff breathed a sigh of relief. "*Alhamdulillah.*"

Merhi tried the driver's door but it was stuck. "Here give me a hand, Skaff. But be careful of the glass."

Bracing himself as best he could on the damp stony river bed, Merhi put both hands on the door handle as Skaff stood behind him and reached forward, gingerly grasping the bent door frame. Through his cigarette Merhi said, "One, two… three!"

With a sharp metallic wail, the door opened about twenty centimetres – and stagnant river water flowed out over Merhi's feet like a flushed lavatory. "Oh for fuck's sake." He looked down. Just his feet, not the Corporal's. "Pull, pull, pull."

They got the screaming door open and stood back, Merhi squelching.

"Oh dear," said Sergeant Kanj.

Corporal Skaff stared. Merhi just sighed.

There, lying in the foot well, was Claude Gerges.

With a bullet hole in the middle of his forehead.

Jonblat, Beirut 13:00

Lieutenant-Colonel Ghanem never worked Saturday afternoons and Merhi had been lucky to catch him as he was preparing to leave. The deaths of members of Lebanon's security forces was an all-too-common occurrence – it came with the job description, especially in these times – but, as the Commanding Officer of the victim, Ghanem had to show willing.

"Did you take charge?"

"The local police have been relieved of any involvement," said Merhi. "I've kept it within my team. I've got Chadidi, Mostafa and Yammine making local enquiries, see if anyone saw anything. There's no street CCTV in the area, but the factories might have something. Harrak is on to that. We've taken the body to USJ. Doctor Patel will retrieve the bullet for us. It'll be with forensics shortly. And he'll give us an approximate time of death."

'USJ' was the in-house term for the *Hôtel Dieu de France* hospital on Naccache Boulevard, a few streets away from the General Security Building down in Ras en Nabaa (the hospital being an affiliate of the *Université Saint-Joseph*, the research university, one of the top academic institutions in the Middle East, which had three campuses nearby).

Doctor Patel was, in fact, as Lebanese as Jihad Merhi. He always performed the death examinations on any murdered member of the security forces (not autopsies - the cause of death rarely needed to be established).

"Good," said Ghanem. He sniffed. "It was a professional hit?"

"One bullet," Merhi poked his index finger into the centre of his own forehead. "A professional single-tap assassination."

"What was, er, Gerges working on?"

"He was one of the Brigadier's – my – spycatchers."

"I know, I know. What specifically?" Ghanem sniffed again.

Merhi shrugged. He was about to say sarcastically "Catching spies?" but Ghanem had screwed up his face.

"Major, what *is* that smell?"

"Smell? I can't… Ah, sorry, it is me. My feet got a little wet when we were retrieving the body."

"From the Beirut River?"

"Yes."

"Hell."

"Exactly. I haven't had time to change and I have no other shoes here anyway."

"Good grief."

"Indeed. My men work autonomously, Colonel, it is how the Brigadier organised it. The other two – Haddad and Khalef – don't know specifically what Gerges was doing. They don't discuss things in the office because of the…" He made a circular motion around his ear and pointed upwards.

Ghanem raised his eyebrows. It was well known that he thought The Listeners and The Watchers were at the very least harmless, at the most urban myths.

"Their reports are in in the system, though," continued Merhi. "And they have access to each others' diaries, calendars et cetera. But when one of them decides to go out, the other two don't ask why or where."

"You need to change that."

"Maybe. It's only been four days, I've yet to decide how I'm going to take things forward with this new delegated structure."

"Perhaps you should get down to it."

"I said I would report in a week and I will. I am aware you want results not problems, you have made that clear. Now I have the new problem of Gerges' death. I will have a look at his case files when I get downstairs and I'll ask Khalef to look also and give me his analysis. It can be left with me."

Ghanem nodded and sniffed again as he looked at his watch.

"There is one thing," said Merhi. "Something that has not been delegated, it falls to the CO."

"What is that?"

"The death notification."

Ghanem's eyes shot up, his face draining.

"It's down to you... sir. His wife needs to be told. Haddad was closest to him, he is waiting to go with you. His wife has been away, she was expected back home - " it was Merhi's turn to look at his watch " – about now."

Ghanem sat back in his chair, sighing deeply. But, to his credit, he nodded. "Of course... of course. Do they have children?"

"No. They live up in Hazmieh, so it shouldn't take too long. Haddad has the address."

"I will go now." Ghanem stood up. "See, Major, we both have responsibilities in our new ranks which we have to face. This will be my first notification. It would be nice if it was the last."

And camels might fly, thought Merhi.

"I need to get some air." Ghanem went over and opened his window.

Merhi said, "One thing, sir," he put his hand into his pocket as he stood up. "Claude had these on him. Perhaps you could pass them on to his wife."

Onto Ghanem's desk he placed an amber necklace and matching earrings.

Ras en Nabaa 14:00

At the same time as Doctor Patel was removing the bullet from deep in the brain of Claude Gerges (with an unfortunate liquid suction noise), a few streets away Gisele Merhi was sitting in her car outside the General Security Building. Classes always finished early on a Saturday.

Her phone was on the passenger seat next to her. Silent, no display. She thought Jihad might have called her. He had been in a bad mood this morning and they had exchanged words before she left for her morning class. The usual procedure when this happened was for him to make a contrite call at her break time. Perhaps she should call him?

She thought also of Carla. Carla was an enigma. Was she really here just to deliver a message to Jihad about a spy in the ISF? If so, job done, she could go now, thank you very much, bye-bye. But the agent known as The Djinn never revealed her full agenda. Last time that had led to her nearly dying at the hands of those female assassins, the Abu Joade twins.

Was Carla up to something else? She needed to be careful. As she had acknowledged, there were people in Lebanon who still wanted to talk to her about the Hariri killing, people who did not have Carla's wellbeing as their priority. And, closer to home, the longer she stayed, the more doe-eyed Jihad would become. Gisele knew her husband at least had the luke-warms for Carla, if not the hots (men will always be men), but she also knew Carla was no threat. She was a flirt, a tease (and not only with men) but access to her body was reserved solely for her own husband, she had made that clear to

Gisele in one of their girl-on-girl talks. Jihad was quite safe from her.

Perhaps another girl-on-girl talk was called for, in the guise of a Saturday afternoon shopping trip. Maybe Gisele could find out how long she would be staying. And what she was really up to.

She picked up her phone.

Jonblat, Beirut 14:15

Jihad Merhi's telephone rang as he sat down behind his desk back in his own office. He picked it up, at the same time noticing that the screen of the ATS laptop was now blank. It had locked after five minutes of no use.

"Merhi."

"*Salaam* Major, it is Mohammed Patel."

"Doctor! What have you got for me?"

"I have one bullet. A fine specimen, no fragmentation or expansion, very much Hague Convention. It was a very smooth extraction. Which means that it was a very smooth entry also. It would have been quick."

"Instantaneous?"

"You know I do not believe there is such a thing as instantaneous death. Almost instantaneous. He would have been aware of a thump, a light, pain and then nothing. He would have been brain dead while he was still standing."

"Fired from close range?"

"Not too close, the bullet did not exit. One shot, from a few metres maybe."

"Any idea on size?"

"I am not an expert. Less than 9mm."

"I'll send someone over to collect it. Time of death?"

"Less than twenty-four hours, more than eighteen hours."

"Doctor, *merci ktir*. The Lieutenant-Colonel is making the notification right now, so we'll get back to you about release of the body."

"I will keep it nicely chilled until then. Now I'm off to watch some football. Chelsea are playing Man United tomorrow but the Man City – Swansea match should be good today."

Merhi smiled, said "*Ma`a as-salāma*," and hung up.

He liberated the last Camel King Size from the packet on his desk, lit up and then shouted, "Deeb!"

Momentarily the old Sergeant popped his head round the door. "Sir?" Then he frowned, sniffing, but he said nothing.

"Anyone about?" asked Merhi.

"Just Hmedeh. The others are still over at Bourj Hammoud."

"Get him over to Doctor Patel's office. There's a bullet waiting. Forensics are expecting it. Top priority."

"Is it...?"

"Yes."

Sergeant Deeb el-Gharib nodded, not needing to say anything. He and Merhi had worked together a long time, they were of the old school. And they both knew that the ISF would not rest until they had got the bastard that had killed one of their own. And had returned the compliment.

He turned to go but Merhi called him back.

"Oh, Deeb."

"Sir?"

"Any news on my door being fixed...?"

Somewhere in Beirut 14:30

"Any news on my door being fixed...?"

The Confession smiled. Major Merhi you were nothing if not human. In amongst all the spies, all the death, all the problems, you were still concerned about domestic comforts. The glass in your door had been cracked and dangerous for only seven years. Facilities would get round to it!

Maybe in your lifetime.

The Confession watched the screen of the MacBook as Merhi began accessing the open case files of the late Claude Gerges. It was interesting stuff, but nothing The Confession did not already know – except for the fact that the ISF knew it too. They were good, this team. Good enough to eliminate all the Israeli spies in Beirut. Nearly all.

And that was the reason for The Confession.

Nejmeh, Beirut 15:00

"Hi Carla, it's Gisele. I've been trying to call you but there's been no reply. I'm in Downtown, so if you're about and fancy some shopping, maybe a bite to eat, give me a call. Just us girls. Speak soon. Bye, bye, bye."

Gisele had found a space for her Toyota in the parking area in Weygand Street, opposite the Patchi department store. Saturday afternoons were always busy in Downtown so she had been lucky. Now she crossed the street through the slow-moving traffic and entered the pedestrianised area known as the Beirut Souks. The Grand Café was on her left, the Beirut Municipality block on her right.

She was dressed in denim jeans, black ankle boots, and a white T-shirt beneath a short black waxed jacket, her black DKNY bag worn across her body. She held her phone in her hand.

From further down the street, someone who had just emerged from the other parking area up by Martyrs' Square saw her and began to pick up pace.

Gisele's phone rang as she was crossing Hassan el-Kadi Street.

"Gisele. Hi. You want to meet?" said the deep voice.

Gisele liked that about Carla. Direct, to the point. No lame excuses about why she hadn't returned the earlier calls or not picked up her messages. Carla would see no necessity to explain herself.

"Hi sweetheart, you in the area?"

"I can be."

"Fancy a little retail therapy?"

"Always."

"I'm just going to have a look in Gucci. Shall I meet you there?"

Carla laughed. "I am not on a Major's salary, *habibi*! But I am hungry. I'm a little way out. I can be downtown in, say, twenty minutes."

"How about if we meet on the corner outside the Grand Café?"

"I'll see you there. Twenty minutes. Kisses."

Gisele smiled as she pressed the *End* icon.

The person further down the street turned right by the Grand Café, heading north, two minutes behind Gisele.

Jonblat, Beirut 15:15

The short, plump, bearded Tamer Khalef was the only person in the small office on the fifth floor when Jihad Merhi entered. Well he would be, Merhi reasoned to himself, Nabil Haddad was out on the death notification with Lieutenant-Colonel Ghanem and Claude Gerges was... dead.

All the drawers in Gerges's desk were open and empty, like gaping toothless mouths. A cardboard box of personal belongings sat on the desk top, pathetic items like his leave chit, his mug, a photo of his wife. Already he was being removed. The team was nothing if not efficient.

Khalef accepted a proffered Camel King Size, not least to cover the strange smell that had come in with the Major.

"Grim times, Tamer." Merhi sat in Haddad's seat, deliberately leaving Gerges's alone.

"Indeed, sir," sniffed Khalef. "First the Brigadier, now Claude."

"You think they are connected?"

"We thought we knew who did the Brigadier. Maybe we were wrong. But this is a different MO. The Party usually don't use firearms for their jobs."

"You think The Party killed the Brigadier?"

"Word is, the Brigadier was marginalising them, not keeping them in the loop. They did not like that."

"They would kill him for that?"

Khalef shrugged.

"If that is so, then it is a strange logic," reasoned Merhi. "All the spying activities were directed at them, so your eradication of the Israeli infiltration was for their benefit."

"Yes, but - "

"I know – this is Lebanon. If a plant offends you, chop it down, no matter how much it has pleased you in the past. Death is the first, not the last, resort in this damned country."

"Indeed."

"And if the murders are linked then does that mean Claude upset them in some way also?" pondered Merhi.

"I doubt it, he had no direct contact with them."

"Quite. And they usually don't kill the foot soldiers. I think we are dealing with two different things here..."

Khalef heard the unspoken conjunction. "Or...?"

"Or, if they are connected, it is nothing to do with The Party at all."

There was a contemplative silence for a moment, then Khalef said, "I've fixed up a meeting for you, as requested."

Merhi sighed, smoke flowing down his nostrils as if there was a bonfire in his brain. Hell's teeth, he did not need this now.

Khalef tore a piece of paper from a pad on his desk. "Tomorrow at 17:00. At this address. The name's on there."

Merhi took the paper. "A Sunday evening in southern Beirut. How nice. Can it be put back, considering what's happened?"

Khalef shook his head. "I wouldn't, sir."

Merhi nodded. "Sure, *je comprends*."

As he leant forward to stub out his cigarette in Khalef's ashtray, the telephone on the desk rang.

Khalef picked it up, answering with his name. "Who? Oh yes, hello. Yes, he's here... Right, I'll tell him." He put the phone down. "That was Peter Harrak, from your team - "

"Our team."

"He's on his way back. He's got something on one of the factories' CCTV."

Nejmeh, Beirut 15:20

The person following Gisele watched as she came out of the Gucci shop in Motrane Street and then followed her at a safe distance. Shopping crowds were both a help and a hindrance to a tail. They kept the tail invisible but they also meant that the subject could disappear from view easily and quickly. But this time the tail knew where the subject was going.

*

As Gisele arrived at the Grand Café corner, Carla was coming along Weygand Street from the right. Carla was dressed in her short leather biker's jacket, jeans and boots.

"Like them?" she asked, showing her right foot. The small ankle boot had double zips and a buckled strap closure going around the heel. "Giuseppe Zanotti. Sorry I did not have time to change, *habibi*, I did not bring any other clothes, I didn't think I would be going out out!" She laughed as they kissed three times on the cheeks.

"Darling, you look stunning in whatever you wear," smiled Gisele. "Or don't wear."

Carla put on an admonitory face. "You have been a naughty girl, Gigi."

Gisele frowned. "Me? What do you mean?"

Carla nodded at the Gucci bag in Gisele's hand.

"Ah, just a little something. To celebrate Jihad's promotion. Look." She took out a belt, black patent with a metal double-G as the buckle.

"Oh yes, very nice. Gucci. Gisele. Gigi. Jihad will like it."

Gisele returned the belt to the bag. "Where would you like to eat?"

"How about here?"

"Good, why not?"

"I fancy a shisha," said The Djinn. "Do you indulge in bad habits, *habibi*?"

Jonblat, Beirut 15:45

"It's not good," said small, wiry Peter Harrak. "It's distant and of course high definition it ain't. But it's something."

Harrak, Merhi, Khalef and Sergeant Deeb el-Gharib were seated around a computer in the General Office on the second floor. Harrak had just fed a disc into its side.

"Which factory did it come from?" asked Merhi, taking a mouthful of sludge while his cigarette was still in the side of his mouth with the dexterity of a true hardened smoker.

"The same one that was suspected in the red dye business earlier in the year. They were only too keen to help the authorities. As it happened, they were the only place that had anything." Khalef gave a puzzled grimace. "Sorry, sir – what's that smell?"

"It's me," confessed Merhi. "From the fucking river this morning. All over my shoes. Short of going around in my bare feet, there is nothing I can do right now."

"You could go home, sir, have a nice early Saturday," smiled el-Gharib.

"There is that, Deeb, yes. I could use your health and safety as a reason!"

The men laughed.

The computer had decided it liked the disc and agreed to play it. After a few jumps, a grainy scene appeared on the screen.

It was a black and white northward view with the river on the left, shot from a height of about ten metres, the camera probably half way up the factory wall. In the top left of the screen the date read --/--/--. In the top right the time read 00:00:00.

"No time, no date," said Merhi. "Not very security conscious then?"

"I don't think they ever look at it," said Harrak. "Only if they ever had any break-in. And that place is so rank nobody would ever willingly go near it."

"Sure we're looking at the right time?"

"Wait, sir."

In the foreground were the factory's outside warehouses, obviously the original subjects of the CCTV, but beyond them at the top of the screen the riverside road headed northwards. Faraway a light-coloured car was parked on the road. Indistinct but it was big enough to be a Dodge Durango.

Nothing was happening. If it had not been for a bird flying past they could have been looking at a still photograph.

Then a figure walked casually into the top corner of the screen. As it did so, a motorbike pulled up on the far side of the road. The rider pushed down the kickstand and got off. The rider was wearing what were probably motorbike leathers; the head was covered by a dark helmet with the visor down.

The first figure reached the car and opened the door, turning to look back at the motorbike rider. Walking towards the car, the rider's left arm came up.

And the first figure fell backwards into the Dodge.

"Wahw!" It was Khalef who gasped but all four men sat backwards, a subconscious reaction of shock and avoidance. Deeb el-Gharib blew out his cheeks, shaking his head. Merhi frowned.

Harrak was nodding. "There's more."

On the screen the motorbike rider went round to the other side of the car, out of sight of the camera. Moments later the legs of the victim slid backwards and upwards, into the car. The rider came back round and climbed into the driver's seat, closing the door. Moments later, the car reverse-turned, backing out of the screen.

"Is that it?" asked Merhi. Harrak raised his hand.

Suddenly the Durango came back into view, moving forward, heading directly towards the river. It did not decrease speed but in one fluid motion crashed through the riverside railings and fell down into the river, out of sight of the camera.

"Holy shit!" said Khalef. "You bastard."

The rider ran into the screen from the top right and stopped by the smashed railing, looking over into the river. Five seconds later, the rider calmly walked back across the road to the bike, got on, pushed forward off the kickstand and drove away.

Harrak clicked the mouse. "That's it."

The four men were quiet, contemplative, reflecting on the murder of their colleague.

After a full minute, Khalef said "Well, we know how but we don't know who. Can't identify anything from that."

"At least it's something," said Harrak defensively.

"Yes," said Merhi. "Well done Peter. It might have told us more than we realise, Tamer. Upload that onto the system and send me the link. I need to think." Merhi stood up. The other three men also stood.

"I'll make some more sludge," said Deeb el-Gharib.

"Good idea," nodded Merhi. "You men take what you want and then bring the pot into me, Deeb. I'll be in my office. I will not be disturbed."

Merhi watched the murder of Claude Gerges, over and over. His office door (with the cracked glass) was closed and, as he had instructed, nobody disturbed him.

After the seventeenth viewing he froze the picture at the point where the rider was walking towards the still-living Gerges. Then he advanced the video frame by frame, watching as the rider's left arm rose. Even frame by frame it was quick and efficient. There was no hesitation about the killing, no last second doubt – one of the frames, just one, even had a flash coming out of the end of the rider's arm.

Merhi sat back in his chair. There was something about the rider... The biker's leathers hid a lot, and the helmet and visor certainly obscured the face, but the rider was slim and quite small. The Lebanese were not a tall race, the average male height was 176.2 centimetres, 5 feet 8 inches. Lebanese women were a good 12 centimetres, 5 inches, smaller. Merhi did not have any cross-reference on the screen to judge accurately but, even allowing for a possible boost by the riding boots, the rider looked below average height.

For a man.

Merhi's face was stone. Oh shit.

An assassin on a motorbike. He thought back to the attempt on Abdul Abdulrahman on the way back from Bourj al-Shimali. An assassin on a motorbike...

The incident played again in his head. The bike drawing level with the car. Lattouf trying to take evasive action. The rider firing... and he remembered the things that had registered with him at the time but which had then been lost in the brainfreeze of age: the gun had been in the rider's left hand... the left hand was ungloved revealing a thin wrist... delicate enough to be a woman's wrist...

Like a four-reel slot machine in the Casino du Liban, the recollections clunked home. One, two, three...

A female assassin on a motorbike shooting at Abdulrahman. The very same evening Carla Chedid turns up at his apartment – using, as he discovered only subsequently, a motorbike. A coincidence surely? She was a conundrum, The Djinn, a Lebanese agent exiled from Lebanon, married to a man who was one of the most lethal, cold-blooded mercenaries currently operating, a man she had once been hunting... But she had come back for a reason and Merhi knew it was not simply to warn him there was an Israeli spy in the ISF. Was it to hunt the spy herself? Was Claude Gerges the spy? Merhi rubbed his chin. Now, that would make sense. Shooting at Abdulrahman, the Israeli spy. Assassinating Claude Gerges, an Israeli spy...

Without warning, the fourth reel of the slot machine clunked into place. Carla again. Going up the stairs in this building... She had arrived two days ago (seemed like two weeks) and had gone to the Merhis', with no place to stay. Conceivably she could have hired a motorbike at the airport (did they do that?). But she had no suitcase, so anything she had would have to fit in the sidebox on the bike. It was a small sidebox. When she had appeared outside his apartment two days ago, she had been wearing a T-shirt, leggings and baseball shoes. They would fit in the sidebox, together with her large shoulder bag. If she had brought biker leathers with her, they would interchange in the sidebox with the other clothes. But what would not fit in the sidebox was another pair of boots. When she had walked up the stairs in this building yesterday in the elysian pool of Merhi's admiring gaze, something had niggled him. He now knew what it was. The boots. She said she had been shopping that morning so her clothes were new – but the boots were used, the heels worn and scuffed. Unless she had been to a charity sale (and The Djinn would never do that), where did the boots come from? Did she have another base in Beirut? Was she lying to the Merhis? And if so, why?

The fourth reel on the slots had fallen into place. But did he have a line of golden bells or even a line of cherries? Or was he, in fact, a loser?

What the hell was going on?

He picked up his telephone.

Nejmeh, Beirut 16:40

"What's going on, Carla?"

The two women were sitting outside the Grand Café at a table for two. Carla's leather biker's jacket was draped over the back of her seat and her thin white T-shirt showed once again that she wore nothing underneath it.

Most of the other tables around them were taken but nobody was paying them any attention. Beautiful Lebanese women were plentiful in downtown Beirut on a warm Saturday afternoon, many exposing much more than The Djinn.

They had eaten a mezzé of *tabouleh*, *labneh*, *kebbeh* and *falafel* with flatbread, and Carla had had some *knefeh* to satisfy her sweet tooth (Gisele had declined). Now they relaxed with coffee and Carla smoked a mint-flavoured shisha.

Carla smiled. It was a question she had been expecting. She put it back. "What do you think is going on, *habibi?*"

"You have come to tell us there is a spy in the ISF."

"Yes."

"And... much as I love your company, my darling..." Gisele let it hang.

"Why am I still here?"

Gisele agreed with a shrug.

Carla took a final draw on the shisha pipe, wound the hose round the body of the *argileh* and carefully placed the pipe across the plate. "Yes, you deserve an explanation. No Sajida moments this time." She smiled briefly. "I think there is something more going on. The report I received was in Hebrew – which did not help, I can't exactly Google a translation service for a stolen secret document. I have a knowledge of the language but not the nuances. The spy situation might - *might* – have resolved itself. We will see very shortly. Then the other matter will come to a head."

"What is the other matter?"

Carla looked Gisele in the eyes, deciding how much to say. "It would be wrong to speculate. I might be completely wrong."

"That I very much doubt."

"I was wrong in the Hariri killing."

At that moment Gisele's phone rang. She picked it up from the table, looked at the screen and pressed the green icon. "*Habibi.*"

From across the table, Carla could hear a voice on the other end but the words were indistinct. It was a deep voice, male, and presumably Jihad (unless there was something Gisele wanted to confess). The caller spoke at length, Gisele unusually not saying a word. At one point, although she did not want to, Gisele's eyes looked towards Carla. It was just for a nanosecond, but The Djinn caught it. And at that instant she knew what the phone call was about.

"Yes," said Gisele. "Yes, yes *d'accord*. Okay *habibi*. I'll see you later." She pressed the red icon.

Across the table, Carla appeared uninterested, sitting back in her seat, relaxing.

"That was Jihad," said Gisele. "He's going home. He got wet earlier in the

Beirut River and he's stinking the building out." She smiled but not with her eyes.

"*Merde alors!*" laughed Carla. "No threesome for us then. Here, I mean."

"No. I have to pee." Gisele stood up. "Do you want to?"

"No. I'm fine."

Carla watched Gisele go into the restaurant, then she signalled a waiter for *l'addition*.

As she went upstairs, following the stick-figure signs for the lavatories, Gisele felt the *wasm*, the scar, on her neck throb. A sure sign of stress. Jihad had been brief to the point of curt but basically he had said – heaven help us – that Carla was a killer on a motorbike? And that she was killing Jewish spies? *What?* That was not correct, simply not correct. How many whiskies had her husband had?

Jihad had told her not to say anything if she was with Carla, and by her silence he had known she was there. He had asked her to 'be normal' (yeah, right), stay with Carla, there was nothing to worry about (the Merhis weren't Jewish!) and that, at the end of the day, she might be doing the ISF a favour. He had to work it out. She was not, of course, to say anything to Carla directly.

The women's lavatory was empty and she went into the first cubicle (checking there was paper) and sat down.

She did what she had to do and stood up, wiping herself. Outside, the door to the lavatory opened.

And the lights went out.

"Shit!" she said, her curse in keeping with the location. "Hello? Hello? Is anyone in here?" Perhaps the person had gone out again as soon as the power went off. She finished wiping, hopefully threw the paper into the bowl and fumbled for the flush button, finding it after a couple of slaps against the wall.

There is nothing darker than a windowless indoor lavatory when the lights are out. It was black, totally pitch black, as if she had suddenly been struck blind.

Or was dead.

What a time for a bloody power cut! Lebanon you would try the patience of the apostles.

She flapped her way out of the cubicle, her arms in front of her. She found the sinks, wondered what the hell she was doing (hygiene and cleanliness were not the first priority when you had just lost your sight) and flapped her way to the left, along the wall, over pipes, over the light switch and to the door.

She slapped her hands down the door and found the handle, turned it, pulled – and was nearly blinded by the light from outside as the door opened.

"Shit!" she shouted again, bending over, screwing up her eyes. "What the fuck!" With a growl she straightened up, slowly, slowly opening her eyes, getting used to the light again. Her hand was on the doorframe, her fingers still against the light switch. She felt the switch. It was up. She pushed it down – and the lights came on in the lavatory.

It wasn't a powercut, somebody had turned the lights off. Some stupid fucking idiot. Hadn't they realised someone was in there?

Still shaking her head and breathing heavily, her scar pulsing, she went back down the stairs. No point in complaining to the management, if it was a member of staff they would not admit to it.

Outside, the table where they had been sitting was being reset.

Carla was nowhere to be seen.

Coastal Highway, Lebanon 17:00

On a Saturday evening, traffic was going *into* Beirut so the journey northwards was relatively light. Jihad laughed through the cigarette smoke and mentally gave two fingers to the lanes of crawling vehicles on his left. They might reach the capital in time for midnight at the Sky Bar.

He drove with the air conditioning full on and all the windows open. Not until he had been in the Toyota for ten minutes in the crawl of Beirut had he realised just how much his feet and lower legs stank of the shit of the river. The stench was so thick you could almost taste it. No wonder his staff had encouraged him to go home early! As it was, he had had things to do – but five in the evening was still an early departure compared to other times of manhunt. Or womanhunt.

He had come to his own conclusion about the motorbike killer, and he was happy with his reasoning. But, for the next part of this affair, he needed his friend again. There were some things he could not do on his own.

He glanced down at the lightly clinking carrier bag in the passenger's foot well which held four hundred Camel King Size and three one-litre bottles of Johnnie Walker. You were a good friend, Johnnie, and he would be seeing you soon (and tending to the welfare of the Camels).

But this time it was another friend he needed.

Bourj el-Barajneh, Beirut 17:15

With a bang that could be heard as far away as Cyprus, the front door of *chez Lattouf* in Annan Street crashed open into the ever-suffering wall and stood trembling like a guard caught sleeping on sentry duty. "Family, I am home!"

boomed the voice of Captain Fadi Lattouf of the Palestinian Civil Police. "Baba is here!"

As always, he was ignored. The sounds of gunfire and explosions came from the iMac computer in the far corner (Lattouf had inherited the machine from his cousin Chadi). Four of his children were gathered around it. In another corner his youngest, five year old Little Wissam (or Fadi Mk II), was sitting in front of an old black and white portable television (yes it still worked) watching loud and horrific violence – a *Tom and Jerry* cartoon. That left one unaccounted for.

"Wife!" shouted Lattouf as he threw down yesterday's *Al-Mustaqbal* newspaper which was left for him each night on the solitary table outside the café down the road.

"Your dinner will be ready in ten minutes!" called Nada Lattouf from the kitchen.

"Where is Lana?"

"Upstairs. On the iPad."

Lana was their eldest daughter, thirteen now and growing up fast. And, like all fathers, Lattouf was not and would never be equipped to deal with a teenage female. He had given her the iPad two years ago to thank her for the way she had helped him solve the al-Mahdi case (it would be best not to dwell on the dubious provenance of the iPad – in fact, it was their second one: Lattouf had put his finger through the first one on the night he brought it home).

Lattouf sniffed the air. Chicken livers! Sniff. Beans... flageolet! Sniff. Rice!

Nada popped her head round the kitchen door, smiling. "You go and have your shower, get changed into your comfortable clothes, relax."

"I will." It never occurred to Fadi that each night his dinner was always *almost* ready, just giving him enough time to shower away the sweat and smells of the Bourj el-Barajneh refugee camp. He thought it was always perfect timing on *his* part.

Upstairs in the family bathroom, he sang his own versions of selections from *The Sound of Music* ("Ford every mountain, climb every stream-ah!") as he stood under the less than enthusiastic shower spray and soaped himself with *X-Men* shower gel (*The Pirates of The Caribbean* had run out yesterday. Didn't last long this stuff, three palms-full and the bottle was empty).

He was walking naked back along the corridor, still damp in the parts of his body that neither he nor the towel could reach, humming "High on a hill stood a pile of goat's turd, lay odelay odelay he hoo!", when he heard music coming from his bedroom. It was the universal theme tune to Sky News.

He stopped. Was Lana in there on the iPad? If so, he was busted. Nada had told him not to walk around naked anymore, now that the children were getting older. Frantically he looked around for something to cover himself, grabbing a small teddy bear from the floor and ramming it over his private parts.

Then he realised. Lattouf, you are an imbecile! It was his cell phone ring tone! He had been mighty pleased with himself to get the Sky music as an illegal download recently (the police office in the camp was now equipped with a broadband connection).

Still defiling the teddy bear, he walked into the bedroom. His phone was in his jacket which he had thrown onto the bed. He fumbled with one hand, realised he didn't need the bear's protection anymore and slung it, then retrieved his phone. He did not have his reading glasses to hand so he could not see who was calling.

He answered in time-honoured fashion, shouting "Yes?"

"Fadi, it's Jihad Merhi."

"Cap – Major! Evening of pure unadulterated joy, my dear friend! How are you?"

"Good, good."

"And your good lady?"

"Fine, fine. Fadi, I need you to repay a compliment."

"You are the most handsome man I have ever seen."

"No, no, no. Are you fay oom aft...?"

"Hold on, my friend, this is a bad connection."

"I undring fee cud..."

"Hold." Lattouf took his phone away from his ear and slapped it up and down in his palm. "Is that better?" He listened and then frowned. Did Jihad just say "Bollocks"?

"Wait, I will take you downstairs. I am just out of my shower. I will just slip my comfortable clothes on. Can you hear me?" Without waiting for an answer, Lattouf threw the phone on the bed and put on his comfortable clothes: a sleeveless vest and baggy Y-front underpants, both of which might have been white at one time.

He walked down the stairs, trusting in Allah because his gut completely blocked the staircase from his view. He was shouting down the phone but Jihad was still saying strange things. There was only one thing for it.

He opened the front door and walked out into Annan Street. Immediately the reception improved.

"Can you hear me now?" asked Merhi.

"Indeed, my friend, indeed. That is better."

"Fadi, are you free tomorrow afternoon?"

"For you always."

"Like I accompanied you to Tyre, I would like you to accompany me somewhere."

"Anywhere, my friend, anywhere."

"It's nearby to you. I have a meeting and I don't think it's good that I go alone."

"Who with?"

"Hizbullah."

Lattouf was quiet. Then he said lowly, "You have some interesting bedfellows, my friend."

"Don't I just? Will you come?"

"Of course, for you."

"*Merci ktir*, Fadi. I'll pick you up just after three."

"I will get Nada to cook us a feast for afterwards. I saw some magnificent sheep's testicles in the butcher's today."

"You are... too kind."

"Tomorrow then, my friend."

"Tomorrow."

"Allah's blessings upon you."

Wondering why passers-by were giving him strange looks and a wide berth, Lattouf scratched his bottom, turned and walked regally back into his house, his underpants wedged firmly up his butt crack.

Jounieh, Lebanon 18:45

"So you think she is doing your job for you, killing the remaining Israeli spies?" Gisele was standing in the doorway of the Merhis' steamy en-suite bathroom. Her husband had just stepped out of the shower, the hairs on his body flat against his skin and dripping. He was still relatively slim at fifty-three, almost lithe, and he was greying gracefully. Even 'down there'. At one time of playful lust, Gisele had likened his greying pudenda to Mount Lebanon with snow on the peaks (or his *falafel* and *kibbeh* with a dusting of icing sugar).

"It fits," Jihad rubbed the towel over his head, under his arms, down his chest. "You know what she's like. I'll do a complete, in-depth analysis of Gerges and his work tomorrow, see if anything comes up. I'll go in early then go to meet Lattouf. I won't say a word to Ghanem until I'm sure."

"But she'll never eradicate all the Israeli spies in Lebanon. The Jewish espionage machine is like the Lernaean Hydra. Cut one head off, another two appear."

"So says the trainer." Jihad had reached his *falafel* and *kibbeh*. "You're right, of course. It will be an ongoing battle. But getting rid of the old school is a triumph."

Gisele came over, took the towel from him and began to rub it down his back. "And what if you are wrong?"

Jihad closed his eyes and tilted his head back, enjoying the all-too-rare sensation of having someone else dry him. "I will face that if I come to it. Perhaps I should ask her." He turned. Gisele kept the towel on his back so that her husband was now in her arms. Captured. His *falafel* had turned into a *makanek* (a Lebanese sausage).

"You think she will turn up?" she asked.

"You know how she appears and disappears at will, causing mischief and leaving mayhem in her wake. Truly a djinn."

"If you say so." Gisele could smell whisky on his breath. "But it is unlike her to disappear quite so suddenly, and just after your phone call to me."

"You think she has been taken? Again?"

"Who would take her? If your theory is correct all the spies have been eradicated. Or maybe she is on the run."

"From what?"

"A good question, my husband. You can ask her if you find her."

"You never find a djinn, the djinn finds you. But there is one thing I know," he felt the towel on his bottom and grinned wickedly. "You won't find her up there!"

Gisele pushed him away in mock disgust, thwacking him with the towel. Jihad laughed and turned his back to her in offerance. "But look by all means!"

Ashrafieh, Beirut 20:00

She had been in two minds whether to return, but it was central and it was convenient. Her husband had taken over the apartment so she couldn't go there. There were hundreds of other hotels in Beirut but she knew the Hotel Albergo on Abdel el Wahab el Inglizi Street well – she had nearly died the last time she had been here. She was on the fourth floor, same as before, but her room this time was at the other end of the corridor, facing out back.

Carla stood at the window, wearing just her T-shirt, thinking back two years to the attack by the *houri*. A *houri* who, it had turned out, was one of an identical pair. Even now she could feel the rope around her throat, feel her life force leaving, her soul screaming for release…

Breathless, she snapped herself back to the present. She held her hands up against the window, looking at her fingertips. Her nailless fingertips. And, as she did often, she went back again, back to Byblos, feeling the pain as her nails were prised off one by one…

A tear formed in the corner of her left eye but it did not fall. She would not allow it to. She had shed enough tears over the murdering antics of those bitches. But she would have her revenge. Soon now. They were here, in Beirut. Her husband had brought them for her. It had been a masterful tactic by Marwan, employing the bitches. The twins had seen him only briefly at the climax of the al-Mahdi affair, and they thought he had come for al-Mahdi not to rescue his wife. Subsequently he had found them again, mercenary to mercenary, employing them to bodyguard the next President of Syria – at the end of which he was giving them to his wife.

Their missions were running parallel. When they were both finished, the bitches would be hers. She looked forward to what she was going to do to them.

But first she had the matter of the Israeli spies to finalise.

Mount Lebanon 20:10

Two statues stood on the balcony, their eyes fixed on the horizon, watching darkness fall over Beirut. Statues with long blonde hair, porcelain skin and white, white eyes. They were barefooted and both wore denim-look jeggings. One wore a green shirt, the other a brown shirt. This had been at the insistence of the older man who was inside discussing things with the younger man.

Nothing moved except their shirts which flapped lightly in the warm breeze slithering up from the city below.

Then the statue on the left, the one in the green shirt, spoke, only her lips moving. "She is here."

There was a five second pause

"I can feel it," said the other statue.

Another pause.

"Can you smell her?"

Pause.

"I can smell her blood."

Pause.

"The blood from her rancid, evil womb."

Pause.

"We will make her watch as we convert her."

Pause.

"I will kiss her as you eat her entrails."

Pause.

"The whore will become one of us, we will consume her."

Both statues began to breath heavily. Slowly, their eyes closed. "We are becoming excited," said the statue in the green shirt. "We will need The Master again tonight. Do you think he will drink us?"

"He will not resist."

They were silent, both sharing the one thought of what would happen. Erotic waterboarding.

Two minutes later, four white eyes snapped open. Their heads turned.

The rigor of the statues left them.

"Let's go inside," said Love. "It looks like they've finished their discussion. Tomorrow they will have their meeting with The Party and then we will get the old fool to Damascus."

"Then after that..." said Paradise.

"Then after that..." agreed Love.

28 October 2012
12 Dhu al-Hijja 1433

Jonblat, Beirut 08:45

Although the Internal Security Force of Lebanon was not a five-days-a-week nine-to-five job, the building was always quieter on a Sunday morning. Same with the roads, Merhi had done the journey from Jounieh in almost record time.

A check of the rosters had revealed that Corporals Jad Chadidi and Omar Mostafa were on duty, the rest of his team (his *old* team) were off. Of the two remaining superheroes (his *new* team), Tamer Khalef was due in, Nabil Haddad was off - this was a pity as he had wanted to ask Haddad how things went with Ghanem and the death notification yesterday.

Merhi was first in so he had brewed a pot of sludge while his computer did what computers do when you turned them on. Now he sat at his desk, a full mug of sludge to hand, the computer waiting in anticipation like a whore on hourly rates (obedient, compliant, willing, open to suggestions, but always in command).

Merhi was content with his conclusion that Gerges had been the Israeli spy. His assassination fitted perfectly with the attempt on Abdul Abdulrahman. So was the biker killer Carla? Had to be, it was too much of a coincidence to think otherwise. She arrives back in Lebanon, the killings start. But why hadn't she told him? If she had said she was here to eliminate the Israeli spies, he would have helped her, given her access to their system, even gone with her on the hunt. Whatever she wanted.

But that was the nature of The Djinn. She played things her way, to her own rules. Sometimes reticent, often dangerous, usually mysterious, and always, always so damned attractive.

His thoughts wandered, but not to the appeal of The Djinn, that had been just a window. He thought about his wife Gisele and how she had taken him up on his offer to search for Carla last night. He laughed. Then they had played their 'Kiss and Tell' game (where they talked about their past lovers) and things had got steamy. For once, the smoke in the Merhis' apartment had not been caused by Camel King Size!

The screensaver on the laptop kicked in and brought him back to the present. Right, time to access all case reports, staff appraisals, security vetting reports and other HR files, anything and everything in the system which contained the word 'Gerges'. He would find something, anything that he could take to Ghanem. "Results not problems."

After which he might have to find The Djinn. Ghanem would not like it but she deserved a medal. Because of her questionable status and the fact that certain parties still wished to talk to her about the Hariri killing, he could not identify her to the Lieutenant-Colonel by her real name (which was what? Carla Chedid? Zahia Zalloum?). He would use her current *nom de guerre* Suzi Saad...

Somewhere in Beirut 09:00

The Confession watched the MacBook as the reports that Jihad Merhi was accessing came up on the screen, tab after tab. The Confession sat back, watching. All very interesting, Major, and probably of no use to you whatsoever.

Next to the MacBook were two sheets of paper. The Confession leant forward and picked them up. The Israeli report in Hebrew and the list of names. After a brief glance, the report was flipped back down onto the vanity unit. The list of names was retained.

The list of twelve names with two crossed through.

Mansourieh, Lebanon 11:30

The village of Mansourieh, ten kilometres east of Beirut, sits on top of a ridge and is bordered to the south and southwest by the Beirut River. The river here is a real river, wider with steep natural banks of shrubs and trees, not the artificial, heavily polluted canal it becomes in Beirut.

During the French mandate, the river was dammed at Mansourieh to divert water for the irrigation of the Hadath and Kfarshima coastal plains to the south of the capital. On top of the dam is a narrow, picturesque bridge known locally as 'Jisr es-Sid', quite simply the Bridge of the Dam.

It was a place Sergeant Nabil Haddad always liked to go, even more so since his wife had left him twelve months ago (she had blamed the pressures of his job, he had blamed the local baker with whom she was a mite too friendly). He still lived in their house in the village (his wife and two children (and the baker) had moved north to Broummana) and on Sundays he liked to attend the Maronite church of Saint Thérèse just down the road in Mkalles.

That Sunday was pleasant and sunny. He enjoyed the walk down to Mkalles but a persistent neighbour (coincidentally a female and coincidentally a widow) had insisted on giving him a lift back up after Mass. Obligingly she had dropped him at the top of the small road, hardly more than a pedestrian pathway, that led down to the dam.

Nobody was about, the dam was off the tourist trail and the locals didn't care about it. Birds twittered and chirped. He felt like the only human around, a complete contrast to the maelstrom of Beirut.

As it neared the bridge, the road dropped steeply and the birdsong was drowned out by the roar of the water flowing over the dam.

Haddad walked to the centre of the bridge. Leaning against the rail, he lit up a cigarette and closed his eyes, enjoying the hit, enjoying the sun. Because of the booming of the water he did not hear the motorbike approaching from the main road, the way he had come. And even if he had heard it, it would have meant nothing to him – he had not seen the CCTV of the motorbike killer yesterday, he had been out on the death notification with the Lieutenant-Colonel and had then gone straight home.

Aware of a rumbling in the air, Haddad opened his eyes as the bike touched the bridge and drove to within eight metres of him. The rider was dressed in classic biking gear, all leather (including some rather snazzy boots), black helmet and black visor. Incongruous for the weather and the tranquil location but necessary for the highways of Lebanon. Haddad's natural police instinct mused that it must be the only biker in the country to obey the law and wear a crash helmet...

The rider dismounted and flipped open the lid of the hardshell side box.

Haddad was a little irked that his solitude was to be interrupted but he accepted this was a public place and he couldn't always have it all to himself, so he nodded his head in acknowledgement and greeting as the rider turned. It was the last voluntary movement he ever made.

The bullet went through his right eye, this time not stopping but taking out the back of his head in an explosion of white bone and pink brain matter. Nabil Haddad knew nothing about it. One moment he was alive, smoking, enjoying the sun and the sounds of the water, next he had ceased to exist. Blackness, oblivion.

The force of the bullet bent the body backwards against the rail, swaying. The rider ran forward, placed the gun on the ground and with both hands grabbed Haddad by the knees. Using the body's own momentum, the rider lifted the knees upwards and pushed.

The body tipped back and over the edge of the bridge, coins and keys flying from its pockets, arms outwards as if it was attempting flight. It hit the top edge of the dam with a thud and then span the last twenty metres into the cascading river.

The rider looked over the edge as the body was swept downstream, face down, arms out. Turning to go, the rider noticed something on the ground and bent down. It was Haddad's cigarette. A casual flick of the fingers and the cigarette flew through the air, falling, over and over. It was grabbed greedily by the water and pushed on its way, chasing the body. Another piece of unwanted garbage in the Beirut River.

The rider put the gun back into the side box, started the engine, pushed off the kickstand and drove away off the Bridge of the Dam.

Or the Bridge of the Damned.

Jonblat, Beirut 12:00

Jihad Merhi sat back in his chair, took off his reading glasses and rubbed his eyes. Three hours. Three hours of nothing. He lit up his twelfth cigarette of the morning.

Well, not nothing. He had come right up to speed on all Gerges's cases, both current and historic, and he had read the encrypted files on Gerges's informants and what he had on each of them. And he had gotten to know Gerges intimately, both professionally and privately, through his staff appraisals and annual security vetting reports. He had even accessed his finance and credit records. Married, no children, with leanings towards Maronite Christianity, the wife more than Claude. But what Merhi did not have was anything, anywhere which gave even the slightest indication that Gerges was anything other than a loyal Lebanese. He had been responsible for the arrest or elimination of around thirty of the hundred-plus spies dealt with over the last two years.

But of course, as Merhi had reasoned before, if Gerges was a deep-cover for the Israelis his cover would be... deep. It was bizarre that the more nothing showed the more possible it was that he was an agent. Damned if you do, damned if you don't, Claude.

Merhi thought of requisitioning his cell phone records but he knew that would tell him nothing. Any phone Gerges used to contact his controllers would be a one-use disposable, his own phone would be pure.

So he had nothing to take to Lieutenant-Colonel 'Bring me results not problems' Ghanem.

He couldn't be wrong about Claude Gerges. Could he? He needed to talk to Carla. Where was she?

Merhi pulled open the bottom drawer of his desk and looked at his friend Johnnie. He moved to shake hands but then pulled his arm back. Best not. Not today. Not with whom he had to meet this afternoon.

And he was not thinking of Fadi Lattouf.

Mount Lebanon 12:30

"Ladies, I will not need you. There are some places you cannot go."

Paradise and Love turned towards The Damascene as he came down the stairs. They were dressed in combat cargo pants tucked in to heavy black boots, white sleeveless vests with *keffiyeh* scarves tied around their necks. Their contact lenses were in.

They inclined their heads, one to the left, one to the right. "Master?" said Paradise.

"This is a very delicate time. They will not take kindly to you. They will not want women there." The Damascene explained, out of courtesy not out of necessity.

"We are not women," said Love simply.

"You know what I mean. To them, you are."

The twins looked at each other, turned back to The Damascene, then looked at each other again.

"As you wish," said Paradise turning back once more. They knew better than to argue. While he was subservient in the bedroom last night (he had survived the waterboarding), he was their controller for this mission, their master, their *pay*master. And they knew from experience he was a dangerous man.

"Right, ready?" came a gruff voice from above.

Two brown and two green eyes moved upwards as Ghazi Kanaan came down the stairs. He was dressed in a plain grey suit and a white shirt done up to the neck, no tie. His hair was still long and his beard remained, on The Damascene's instructions. The twins bowed their heads as he reached the bottom step.

Kanaan raised a sardonic eyebrow. "What is this, humility at last?"

"They will not accompany us today," said The Damascene.

"Really? Why not?"

"Because I said so."

Kanaan opened his mouth to argue but then jumped as the women's heads came back up. They had removed their contact lenses. "In the name of Allah!" he growled. "I have told you not to do that."

"Come," said The Damascene. "You do not want to be late for your... sponsors."

With one more withering look at the twins, Kanaan followed The Damascene out of the apartment. Four white eyes watched him go.

Downstairs, the local man and his English wife from the apartment opposite were entering the building. The Damascene held the door open for them, but Kanaan swept regally through. The couple acknowledged The Damascene's nod of greeting and head-shake of apology.

Kanaan went over to the Jeep, tugging at the passenger door. "Well, open it."

"Not that," said The Damascene. "We're not taking it."

"What do you mean?"

The Damascene walked over to a Suzuki 1500 VL Intruder motorbike parked on the gravel a little way away.

"You have got to be joking!" said Ghazi Kanaan.

The Damascene climbed aboard the bike, starting it with one turn of the ignition. Kicking off the stand, he rolled over to Kanaan. "Get on."

"I'm not getting on that!"

"You are."

"Fuck off."

The Damascene sighed – and grabbed Kanaan by the balls with his left hand. Kanaan stiffened, instinctively going up on his tiptoe. "Get on," repeated The Damascene.

"I – I am paying you," gasped Kanaan. "Show me respect – ah!"

"You paid me to protect you and to get you to Damascus, old man." The Damascene spoke softly. "All the money in the world could not buy my respect for you."

"I - " A tug on the balls shut Kanaan up.

"I have gotten you this far, haven't I? And I will get you to Damascus. Where we are going today, this is a better mode of transport. We will take the back ways, avoiding the roadblocks. A car is a very big target. A bike is not. It is faster in the city. And if things go date-shaped it will provide us with a very quick means of escape. Now get on." He unclenched his left hand.

Kanaan was pale and sweating. Meekly he said, "Helmet?"

"Man-up, Abu Yo'roub, this is Beirut."

Without another word, Kanaan climbed onto the bike.

"Hold me," instructed The Damascene. "Lean in."

Reluctantly Kanaan did so.

"You've been on my back for seven years," said The Damascene. "Another hour on this bike will do you no harm... Mr President."

The Suzuki crunched up the gravel to the main road, turned right and zoomed off. On the back, Ghazi Kanaan prayed to Allah that his balls were the only things that would go date-shaped today.

As the Suzuki zoomed off north-west on Damascus Street, another motorbike, sitting discreetly at the side of a parade of shops on the other side of the wide road, started up. It was difficult performing a straight traverse across the busy highway, but the rider managed it. As soon as the bike was off the road, the engine was turned off again and it was allowed to roll down the cinder track. It stopped at the beginning of the parking area in front of the apartment block.

Ten metres away, three cars were parked. Kicking down the stand, the rider dismounted and went over to the car on the left. The black Jeep

Wrangler Ultimate.

A black leather glove was pulled off and four nailless fingers were stroked down the side of the Jeep, caressing, sensual, almost tender.

Lifting the visor, the helmeted head looked up at the apartment on the top right. There was no movement, no one looking out.

Her instinct was screaming at her to do it now, use the element of surprise. Kill the bitches, kill, kill. But it was not yet time. There were other things to do yet. She would wait. As would the pair of professional gardening secateurs she had in her pocket.

Pushing the visor down, she climbed back onto the bike, kicked off the stand, started the engine, scrunched up the gravel track and turned right onto the main road.

Bourj el-Barajneh, Beirut 15:30

Jihad Merhi knocked on the rotting wooden door of the small house in Annan Street. Really, he thought, the Chief of the Civil Police of the Palestinian Security Force in the Bourj el-Barajneh refugee camp, who was also the senior officer of all the Palestinian camps in Lebanon, deserved better accommodation than this. But, of course, this small, ramshackle 'villa' in amongst the terrace of equally small and ramshackle shops was like a palace compared to the conditions in the camps. And the official line would be that he was Palestinian and Lebanon was doing him and his countrymen a favour anyway.

Before Merhi could think any more seditious thoughts, the door was flung open, a thick-screwed hinge flopping out of the doorframe and back in again. Fadi Lattouf stood there in his vest and underpants.

Merhi frowned and looked at his watch. "Fadi, we mustn't be late."

"Afternoon of cautious optimism, my dear Major! What should I wear? I forgot to ask."

"Not your uniform. Something respectful."

Lattouf looked Merhi up and down. The Major was wearing dark slacks, a grey jacket and a blue open-necked shirt. He nodded. "I'll take your lead. Come in, my friend, come in."

"I'll wait in the car." If he went into the house he might not get out this side of the Prophet's birthday (peace be upon him).

"Nada has made some cakes with leftover rice, filled with jam – and just a trace of chicken livers. I think there might be one left. That woman is the Delia Lawson of Palestine, the Gianna Garten of the kitchen!"

"Later, Fadi, later. You have the cake, top up your energy for the journey. I'll be in the car."

Fifteen minutes later, the front door reopened and Lattouf stepped out.

He was wearing scruffy trainers, his rough blue denim jeans and the pink and blue checked shirt which was older than most of his children and which he always wore when not in uniform. Above it was a well-lived-in black leather bomber jacket which almost fit him. And wrap-around dark glasses.

"Lose the glasses," advised Merhi as the Palestinian pulled open the Toyota door.

Without argument, Lattouf pulled off the glasses and threw them over his shoulder. "In matters of fashion, I bow to you my friend."

"I like the jacket," Merhi was raised twenty centimetres into the air as Lattouf climbed into the car. "Haven't seen that before."

"It is new," which it palpably wasn't. "At least, for me. I was given it."

"A very generous gift, second-hand leather sells for a good price up in Hamra."

"The previous owner... will not be needing it anymore."

Deciding it was better not to pursue the matter, Merhi started the engine. Before he could pull out, Lattouf touched him on the arm. "My friend, can we go indirectly?"

"What do you mean?"

Lattouf looked uncomfortable. "I cannot be seen to go where we're going. You know, the groups," he nodded in the direction of the camp.

Merhi understood. Fatah and Hamas might not take kindly to the camp police chief meeting with Hizbullah. And, after all, Fadi was doing him a favour. "*Je comprends.* Tell you what," he looked at his watch. "We have time, traffic won't be too bad on a Sunday. I'll head back into town, then we'll loop over and come down the back streets."

"Thank you, my friend. Allah has caressed your brain with wisdom."

Merhi doubted that, but he didn't argue. Going to meet Hizbullah was one of the most foolhardy things he had ever done. But he had no choice, it came with the new job.

Annan Street was light of traffic so he pulled out and did an immediate U-turn, then took a left, heading west towards the coast.

South Beirut 16:45

Jihad Merhi never liked coming into southern Beirut. Driving *through* it was tolerable, you kept to Camille Chamoun Avenue, but driving *into* it was like entering a different world. Which, in fact, it was.

Haret Hreik, their destination in the Dahieh suburbs, was to the north of Bourj el-Barajneh, so they had driven west to the coast, north along Rafic Hariri Avenue, east along Saeb Salam Avenue and then south again.

It was the heartland of Hizbullah. Restoration after 'the events' (the civil war) had not proceeded at the same pace as the rest of the city, and, over twenty years later, many buildings here still carried the reminder of war, pockmarked with shell scars and myriad bullet holes. Some buildings still remained simply destroyed shells. There was even a rusted old car still on its side as if it had taken root, in the same place as it was thirty years ago when people hid behind it from the sniper-fire. And died behind it. A *de facto* monument to futility.

And, of course, there was evidence of more recent conflict. Dahieh ('the southern suburb') had been carpet-bombed to rubble by the Israelis in July 2006. Eight years of rebuilding had not eradicated the visual scars. And there was newer bomb damage caused by the current and continuing Sunni and Shi'a internecine strife, the Syrian civil war being played out in the theatre of Lebanon.

The yellow and green Hizbullah flag was everywhere, in windows, draped between buildings, even painted onto walls, sometimes just abbreviated to the raised straight arm holding the Kalashnikov. It was matched in quantity and locations by images of the Hizbullah leader, Sayyed Hassan Nasrallah.

Merhi had got used to the political decoration on his visits to Lattouf in Bourj el-Barajneh but here, in streets unknown to him, he could feel the intimidation, not helped by the roadblock as they entered the area. Merhi told the serious, unsmiling paramilitaries who he was, where he was going, who he was going to see, and the Toyota was allowed on its way.

"So I am Sergeant Deeb el-Gharib?" grinned Lattouf as they drove not too fast not too slow.

"For these purposes, yes," nodded Merhi. He was scanning the buildings.

"I am your deputy. Like in a cowboy movie!"

"If you like."

"I ride shotgun."

Merhi was preoccupied. "I think it's this way."

They turned a corner. The streets seemed busier because they were narrower. A motorbike with two men on board came from the opposite direction, weaving in and out of the traffic.

"See that!" Lattouf turned in his seat, looking out the back window.

"No, what?"

"Two gay boys on a Suzuki! The old one on the back looks terrified! Look at the way he's holding on to his boyfriend!" He laughed. "Probably going over to Sin el Fil for an evening of ass-splitting!" He turned back and then frowned. One of the gay boys looked familiar. He looked into the wing mirror but the motorbike had already disappeared. He shook his head. No, Lattouf did not know any gays.

"Ah, here it is, of course," said Merhi. Up ahead was a walled and gated compound, heavily guarded by armed militia, no pretence of discretion. He pulled over in front of a recently rebuilt shisha café. "Ready, Fadi?"

Major Jihad Merhi and Sergeant Deeb el-Gharib stepped out of the car and headed across the road for their meeting with the Commander of the Hizbullah Intelligence Division.

Mount Lebanon 17:30

Love and Paradise were sipping sparkling mineral water on the balcony when they heard the key in the apartment door. By the time the door had opened they were inside, one on one side of the room, one on the other, hands in the claw position. They stood down when The Damascene and Ghazi Kanaan entered.

The Damascene's hair was in its usual neat ponytail, Kanaan was windswept and grumpy.

The twins did not ask the question but they inclined their heads.

"It is a go," said The Damascene. "They have agreed. In three days we will take Abu Yo'roub into Syria where we will be met by the Syrian Army. We will accompany them on to Damascus where Abu Yo'roub will be kept safe until Assad is removed."

"How will that happen?" asked Love.

"They have asked me to do it. I have said no. At this time..." He looked at Kanaan. "I might change my mind when I'm there."

"It is dangerous."

"So am I."

Paradise asked, "And the opposition?"

"They are intrigued by the proposal. Replace Assad, open the gates of the city to all parties, call a ceasefire. The Free Syrian Army, the Al-Nusra Front and the Islamic Front have all said they will not stand in the way."

"And the others?"

"They will be handled. So, ladies, Abu Yo'roub, let us mark this occasion. Let us eat."

"First I need a shower," Kanaan growled as he went up the stairs. "I still don't see why we couldn't have taken the car."

"Cheer up, Abu Yo'roub, your destiny is about to be fulfilled," called The Damascene as Kanaan walked into the bathroom and slammed the door. He turned to the *houri*. "Maybe more than he knows. Right, we should prepare too. We will go to Antelias, to the Bourj al-Hamam restaurant. We will celebrate. Then when we return..." He watched as the twins walked up the stairs.

Paradise said over her shoulder, "Perhaps we can celebrate some more."

Ashrafieh, Beirut 17:40

In her room in the Hotel Albergo, Carla pulled the headphones out of her ears and thought about what she had just heard.

Three days... Three days and the end of the Syrian war might begin. Or the beginning might end. With the irony of history, it might be that Ghazi Kanaan, The Butcher, the erstwhile King of Lebanon, was the catalyst for peace in the country. Or would they be just changing one dictatorship for another? The problem with the Middle Eastern culture was that fighting was ingrained, like a drug. If they had nothing to fight over, they would find something. Witness her own Lebanon.

But that was not her problem. Her problem was a list of names and a report in Hebrew which she had at last managed to understand.

Gently she laid her iPhone down on the vanity unit. Her other problem was the murdering twins, the *houri*. Again her husband would be with them tonight. But was it infidelity when you screwed creatures that were not human?

She looked at herself in the mirror, at her luxuriant long black hair, at her dark skin, at her black eyes. She undid the black and gold hairclip holding her scrunch and shook her head, her hair falling over her face. She stared into her one visible eye.

Was it time for her to confess...?

Bourj el-Barajneh, Beirut 18:30

"Well, I think that went better than you expected, my friend." As they drove over a pothole in the road, Lattouf raised a hand too late to stifle a dislodged, sour, bi-directional burp that shot out either side of the cigarette in his mouth. Bekaa Valley olives were the best in the world – must be their proximity to the cannabis and opium crops. The nuts had been good too, and the fruit juice.

"Indeed." Merhi was relieved but he was under no illusion. The meeting with the Commander and two Lieutenants had retained a formality and a pleasantness. They had welcomed Merhi as the ISF's new spycatcher-in-chief and had expressed polite remorse over the assassination of Brigadier al-Hassan. But they were still in denial over the extent of the Israeli penetration into their activities, inferring that the hundred-plus arrests over the last two years had been massive overkill by the security services (in some instances literally). But it was a face-saving denial. They knew, Merhi knew, and they each knew the other knew that the spycatchers had done Hizbullah a huge favour. When Merhi told them that there was one suspected deep-cover agent left, operating from inside the Internal Security Force, they had expressed confidence that Merhi would find the man. Quickly. Merhi had resisted the urge to tell them he might already have been found, and by a rogue outside agency.

Now they were out. The direct journey back to Bourj el-Barajneh had taken only ten minutes. "It is done," said Merhi through his cigarette. "Formal introductions made. My man Khalef can talk to them in the future, he's their usual link."

Suddenly Lattouf sat bolt upright, slamming his hand on the door, pressing buttons. The passenger window went down, up, down, up and then all the way down. As they turned into Annan Street he threw his cigarette out into the road, waving a hand, attempting to expel the smoke.

"Tell her it was me," said Merhi sympathetically. "Tell her it was me."

At that moment, Merhi's phone rang. It was in the well between the front seats, next to the packet of Camel King Size and bottle of Sohat water.

Merhi was pulling into a space near Lattouf's house, so he said "Get that for me, would you Fadi?"

Leaving the window open, Lattouf leant to his left and picked up the iPhone. "I cannot see who it is, I haven't got my glasses."

"Just answer it then."

Lattouf proded in the general direction of the green icon. "Hello?" he shouted. "What? Yes, this is Sergeant Deeb el-Gharib. What? Oh, *you* are Sergeant Deeb el-Gharib." He took the phone from his ear and said, "It is Sergeant Deeb el-Gharib."

Merhi put on the parking brake. "Give it to me... Deeb? Yes, *bon soir*... Oh good, what do they say?... Right, fine. You in tomorrow?... Right, I'll see you then." He pressed the red icon with his thumb. Turning the engine off, he said "Ballistics have got back on the bullet that killed Claude Gerges."

"The spy?"

Merhi nodded. "A small bullet. 5.7mm. They've run it through the system but there's no match on file."

Lattouf nodded, pressing the button to close the window. He said casually, "A Herstal FN Five-seveN as I thought. That supports your theory, Abu Samer."

"I'm sorry?"

"The 5.7mm bullet, designed and made specifically by Herstal of Belgium to fit their FN Five-seveN pistol and F90 personal defence weapon. You were right."

Merhi tried not to look gob-smacked. "Right?"

"It's the same person who shot at – what was his name? The Palestinian child?"

"Abdul Abdulrahman."

"Abdul Rahman, yes. That was an FN Five-seveN. Did you not notice?"

"I had other things on my mind, Fadi."

"Lattouf does not miss these things. It was an FN Five-seveN. Same gun. So, same perpetrator. So, you are right. Somebody has killed the spies for you. Your case is over. You could have told Hizbullah."

Merhi's eyebrows were raised.

Lattouf opened the car door. "How do you like your testicles, Major? Well done, medium, rare or blue?"

Jounieh, Lebanon 22:00

"How was it?" asked Gisele after they had embraced.

Jihad took off his jacket. "I feel ill. No man should be forced to eat testicles, it is against nature."

Gisele grinned as she went over to the cabinet. "I meant your meeting." She began to pour him a whisky.

"Successful. Nerve-wracking but successful." He patted his right hip. "I felt naked without my gun. It's surprising the reassurance it gives you." He took the full tumbler.

"But with them it was the wisest move."

"Yes, we were thoroughly searched. Even Fadi's arse did not escape scrutiny."

"Please!"

"Talking of reassurance, I think Lattouf has done it again. Did you know he was an expert on firearms?" He flopped down on the couch, being careful not to spill a drop of his nectar.

"Er, no?"

"Well he is, apparently."

"What happened?" Gisele sat down next to him.

"The Party were not too happy that we still have a spy left but they were content to leave it with me to get results."

"Like a football manager."

"Sure."

"And we know what happens to unsuccessful football managers."

Jihad breathed out heavily, his eyebrows acknowledging the point. Then he said, "Lattouf has scored a last-minute winner. The lab phoned. The bullet removed from Claude Gerges was a 5.7. Lattouf tells me it is made specifically for the Herstal F90 and FN Five-seveN. He says that it was a Five-seveN that Carla used to try to kill the Palestinian boy on the way back from Tyre. He saw it."

"So that confirms it?"

"As far as I am concerned, yes. She has killed Gerges the spy. She has done it for me."

"That is typical of her. But why has she disappeared?"

"Well, she has killed a member of the ISF. There are those that would have her arrested even though the victim was an Israeli spy. Ghanem, for example."

"Will you tell him?"

"I will have to. But I need to speak to Carla. Has she been in touch?"

"No."

"If she's still in the country I will give her time to leave. I don't have her number, can you give it to me?"

Antelias, north of Beirut 22:15

She sat on the motorbike outside the Bourj al-Hamam restaurant knowing they could not see her. Out here it was dark and moonless, inside the place was bright. They were sitting towards the front of the restaurant over on the side beneath one of the impressive back-lit faux-stained-glass windows of drawn scenes of old Lebanon. Her husband's back was against the wall so that he had a view of everyone in the place and anyone who entered. The bitches were either side of him, Kanaan opposite.

Should she do it now? She could just walk in, pop the bitches in the head, kiss her husband and leave without breaking stride. But no, that would be too easy, that would be too quick. They were not Israeli spies. She wanted the bitches to feel it, to know they were dying, to know who was killing them, to know they were dead. She wanted to witness their souls screaming for life as they were dragged down to hell.

And she wanted to cut their fingers off one by one. The human body has nine orifices. She wanted to insert a finger into each one and keep one for herself as a souvenir.

She watched as her husband settled the bill and they all stood up. Her husband said something and the older man nodded and went off, probably to the toilet.

Silently she wheeled the motorbike further into the shadows. Her husband and the bitches came out. They were talking but they were not touching, not arm in arm, not holding hands. Which was reassuring. The bitches laughed at something her husband said.

Momentarily, Kanaan appeared and they walked over to the Jeep Wrangler, the men getting in the front, the bitches in the back. Then the bitch on this side stopped by the open car door. Slowly she turned, staring into the shadows.

Carla knew she could not be seen, and yet the bitch seemed to sense something.

Then the Jeep started up and the bitch turned back, rubbed her eyes and slid into the car, closing the door. As the Jeep pulled away, a face with two white eyes stared out of the back-side window.

Looking straight at The Djinn.

As she threw her leg over the motorbike, her right breast tingled. Of all the times! She pushed off the stand, started the bike and drove off, her headlight piercing the darkness like a tracking laser. Touching the Bluetooth button on the outside of her helmet, she said "Yes?"

"Carla, Jihad Merhi."

"I cannot talk right now, Major."

"Where are you? I need to see you." When she did not respond he continued, "I want to thank you."

"What for?"

"You know." Again no response. "Can we meet?"

"We will, but not yet."

"When?"

"Soon now Major, soon. Things will be resolved."

"You need to leave Lebanon."

Nothing. Then she said: "Things are not finished."

"What do you mean?"

"I will be in touch."

She pressed the side of her helmet as she reached the Coastal Highway and turned south for Beirut. The Jeep Wrangler was about five hundred metres ahead.

Jounieh, Lebanon 22:20

Merhi frowned, the phone in one hand, his whisky in the other.

"What did she say?" Gisele had her hand on his thigh.

"She seemed preoccupied. Said... said things are not finished."

"There are more spies?"

Jihad shrugged as he put the phone down on a side table. "I don't see how there could be. She was the one who told me about 'a spy' in the first place. I don't know what she's up to. But..." he lit up a cigarette. "She said she'd be in touch."

"When?"

He shrugged again as he blew out smoke.

Patting his thigh, Gisele stood up. "I'm going to bed. You could do with a good night's sleep too, my husband. Things might seem clearer in the morning." She stretched and yawned. "You coming?"

Jihad smiled. Even after all these years of marriage, he got a thrill looking at his wife's body, especially when she wore those shorts and vest. It aroused and calmed him at the same time. "Always the trainer, always the good advice," he nodded. "I'll be along in a minute, I'll just finish my chat with Johnnie and bed the Camels down for the night."

"Don't be too long," she said from the doorway. "I might need help getting to sleep."

29 October 2012
13 Dhu al-Hijja 1433

Jounieh, Lebanon 06:15

Well, the trainer was not always right. Things seemed no clearer in the morning.

Jihad leant against the kitchen counter drinking espresso and eating a jam-filled donut. He was dressed for work: dark blue suit trousers, open-necked white shirt, gun on his hip. The traffic on the Coastal Highway was always heaviest on a Monday morning so he was leaving early to arrive at his normal time. Gisele would not be too far behind him, she had a new course (Interrogation Techniques Level 2 Part 1) starting at 10:00 down in Ras en Nabaa.

She came in, dressed in her first-day-of-new-course outfit of knee-length black skirt and blue shirt. "Will you ever stop eating those things?" she scolded, taking an orange from the fruit bowl and loading a capsule into the Nespresso machine.

"Your course started already?" smiled Jihad. "Spousal Interrogation Basic?" He was tempted to dab a speck of jam on her nose but he didn't want the course to change into Spousal Abuse Post Graduate (F to M).

"You smoke too much, you drink too much and you eat those things. You must look after yourself more. Think of what you are putting into your body." She ignored his lecherous leer. "They will be the death of you."

He tapped her bottom as she walked past, her coffee in one hand, orange in the other. "No, *you* will be the death of me, after what you did to me last night." He rinsed his cup in the sink. "Two nights running! And me an old clapped-out incapable fifty-three year old!"

"You are not incapable, I'll give you that. About the rest, you are right." She squealed as splashes of water flew in her direction. Then she asked, "You going in now?"

"*Oui.*"

"I'll leave round about seven. Is your head any clearer this morning?"

"Frankly, no. I don't know what Carla is up to, but it seems she'll tell me in her own good time. Need to know, as always. I'm going to go through the files of Haddad and Khalef today, to get myself up to speed and also to see if there is anything else. But we can't have more than one spy, surely? The spycatchers can't be the spies!"

"You know what the Israelis are like. What better cover?"

"But that cannot work, eliminating your own spies defeats your own objectives."

"Maybe. But remember Security Induction Course Day 1 Module 1: suspect everyone, trust no one, question everything, check everything. Then do it all over again."

"I remember when there were enough hours in the day to do that. Right, I've got to go." He pecked Gisele on the cheek (he knew better than to mess up her lipstick on a work day) and went out into the hallway, pulling on his jacket. "I'll see you tonight."

"Shall I cook?"

"No, I'll get something out. Don't know what time I'll be back."

She would cook anyway, they both knew it. "Take care, husband."

"Another day, another dollar."

Jihad closed the front door behind him, unaware that to that maxim could be added 'another death'.

Mount Lebanon 06:30

Paradise and Love awoke simultaneously, as they always did. They were lying in the wide double bed like inverted bookends, their bodies mirror-imaging. White eyes looked at each other and they smiled and kissed.

"*Sabah el-khair, habibi,*" said Love. "We slept well."

"As we always do when satisfied."

They touched the space in between them. The Master never stayed the night. He was always there when the sisters went to sleep but never when they woke up. He would be back in his own bedroom.

Paradise got up, slipped on her pants and a vest, and went out (it was her turn to prepare breakfast while Love showered). Behind the closed door of the next bedroom, Abu Yo'roub was snoring as if he was in the finals of a lumberjack competition. Further along, The Master's bedroom door was open. Paradise looked in, wondering if it was a signal that The Master required more pleasure. But the room was empty. His bed was made but she knew that when he was alone he always slept on the floor. He was not on the floor.

He was not downstairs either, not even out on the balcony performing his daily stretching exercises. He was gone, up and out early.

Paradise knew it was not her place to concern herself with The Master's activities. If his absence impacted on her and Love's duties, they would be informed as necessary.

She began to prepare *ftoor*.

South Beirut 06:35

The Suzuki 1500 VL Intruder weaved through the back streets. Beirut was a late-to-bed early-to-rise city and already the streets were busy but at this hour the daily gridlock had not yet taken hold. The Damascene drove fast but kept within the speed limit.

Half an hour ago he had received a call.

He was needed urgently.

Somewhere in Beirut 07:30

The Confession looked at the list of twelve names. Twelve names with three crossed through. Three was good but this was taking too long, the rate of reckoning needed to be increased.

The open MacBook showed the calendar entries for today for all the sinners. Like there were mass weddings and, sometimes in this country of death, mass funerals too, perhaps there should be mass penance? Communal retribution.

The Confession put down the coffee cup and looked out of the window. It was a bright, sunny day. Nine names left out of twelve.

Or was it ten out of thirteen?

Ashrafieh, Beirut 09:00

Carla left the Hotel Albergo and turned right on Abdel el Wahab el Inglizi Street. She was wearing a short green cotton dress and a white jacket, her Barbour messenger bag over her shoulder, her Prada sunglasses hiding her eyes from the low sun of the autumn morning. As always, her black hair cascaded down her back, bouncing as she walked, with a scrunch held by the black and gold hairclip.

Her biker's leathers were in the panniers on her Honda VFR1200FD which had overnighted in the secure indoor Parking next to the ABC shopping mall eight hundred metres down the road (one did not turn up at the exclusive Hotel Albergo on a motorbike!).

Bikes were becoming fashionable in Beirut. As she crossed over to the north side of the narrow, busy street, she saw more than one motorbike manoeuvring in between the slow-moving vehicles. One of the bikers even wore a helmet!

She reached the Parking and made her way down to the lower level. It was quiet down here, some cars, just two bikes in the motorcycle area, no people. But she knew there were cameras. There were always cameras. She could hear echoing brake squeals from higher levels as drivers negotiated the always-too-tight turns of this typical parking area. As with any indoor car park in the world, the place smelled of petrol and piss.

Retrieving her leathers from the panniers, she walked up into the mall, found the nearest rest room and changed.

Back at the bike, she took her helmet from the top box (there would be at least two bikers wearing helmets on the streets of Beirut today, something of a record!), started the bike and set off up the slope to the exit.

She was at the barrier when she noticed something and held back. Over the other side of the street a bike was waiting by the kerb, a big bike, possibly a Ducati. The rider, like her, was clad in leather, with a helmet and black visor. Was it the one she had noticed coming down the street on her way in? If not, make that *three* bikers wearing helmets on the streets of Beirut today.

An SUV came up the exit slope, a GMC Yukon, and she waved it ahead of her, patting her pockets as if looking for her ticket. The driver of the Yukon fed his ticket into the slot, there was a momentary pause while the machine thought about it, and then the barrier raised.

As the Yukon drove out, Carla side piggy-backed it, keeping level with the vehicle, hidden from the view of the biker opposite. She resisted the urge to gun her engine and speed away, that would only draw attention, so she kept level with the Yukon for a few metres and then whipped the bike left into the narrow Madrassat es Salam Street. Quickly she pulled over by the road leading to the back of the Empire cinema, looking round, waiting for the other bike to appear at the top of the road.

Nothing happened, no bike appeared. Beneath the visor she smiled. She set off again, taking an immediate left into Mariam Jahchan Street. At the end of the street she stopped, looking left across the road. The Ducati was still there, opposite the parking exit.

Carla settled back in her seat. She had a good idea who it was. Someone who had recognised her in the street, someone who knew she favoured the Hotel Albergo. Someone who had come looking for her and had found her. Someone who wanted her dead?

Well, two people could play the waiting game…

Bourj el-Barajneh, Beirut 09:30

It was a fine day but the sun's rays did not find their way down into the Bourj el-Barajneh Palestinian refugee camp. The one square kilometre of basic brick constructions which pass as dwellings are packed so tight together that the sun stops at the top of the buildings, not daring to venture down. Most paths between the buildings are less than half a metre wide, some alleyways even tighter.

Normally Captain Fadi Lattouf would not attend a call-out in the camp, that was the responsibility of Sergeant Alarab who himself would delegate it to one of the Corporals. But this crime, if true, was different. It was the most heinous crime of all, and it demanded the presence of the police chief. It was a crime greater even than rape (of which there was very little), murder (some), violence (plenty) and robbery (hardly any – what did these poor souls have that was worth stealing?). The crime needed to be dealt with expeditiously and the results erased before the groups found out: someone had daubed a Star of David on one of the walls in the north of the camp. What was worse (if anything could be worse), it was over a wall-stencil of the smiling face of Abu Ammar (Mohammed Abdel Rahman Abdel Raouf Arafat al-Qudwa al-Husseini, popularly known as Yasser Arafat).

Lattouf stepped gingerly over broken water pipes and around liquid puddles (which might not be water), ducking as necessary beneath overhanging electricity cables. Next to him Sergeant Alarab was equally cautious, even more so because he carried a tin of paint.

The crime would not be solved, of course. In a camp of thirty-thousand inhabitants pressed into one square kilometre of hell, very few crimes were solved, very few miscreants brought to justice – at least by the police. The groups had their own justice system and meted out their own punishments.

Even with their knowledge of the camp, it took Lattouf and Alarab half an hour to find the defiled wall and another twenty minutes for Alarab to paint over the abomination. Unfortunately it meant that the face of Yasser Arafat was obliterated as well, but that could not be helped. And now there was a nice blank piece of black brick that would be daubed upon by nightfall, hopefully this time with something patriotic.

As Lattouf ambled back to the police offices out near Annan Street, he saw a group of five boys playing football in a small, rubble-strewn open area. When the loose ball rolled over towards him, he kicked it back with glee, smiling and nodding as he walked on. He was past the boys when, with a dinging thud, the ball hit him on the back of the head.

Suddenly, all was quiet. Even the ball had not bounced away, it had fallen at his feet in shame. Lattouf turned. Five pale faces looked at him. None of them could have been older than ten. Lattouf looked down at the ball then back to the boys.

A snot-nosed urchin put his right arm across his heart. "S-sorry, *ustaz*." *Ustaz!* Cheeky little sod. "I – I was aiming at him." He pointed at one of his pals.

Lattouf bent down and picked up the ball in one hand, the plastic distorting in the agonising grip. His eyes went from the ball to the boys. Then he said, "No harm done. But be careful. Don't go breaking any windows." A daft thing to say, he realised. Were there any windows in the camp that were not broken? He threw the ball back and, without so much as a thank you, the boys continued playing as if the incident had never happened.

Lattouf walked on, wondering if it was lunchtime yet (Nada had given him a package of finely sliced leftover testicle with a white sauce and couscous). Then he stopped. Slowly he turned back to the boys who were once again oblivious to his presence. He watched them, passing the ball, trying to tackle each other, kicking the ball towards the one goal marked out with stones. Sometimes scoring, sometimes shooting and missing.

Lattouf frowned in thought.

Shooting and missing...

Snoubra, Beirut 10:00

Sergeant Tamer Khalef, short, plump, bearded, spycatcher, sat at a table outside *Pain d'Or* beneath the Itani Building. Snoubra means pine tree in Arabic, and local legend says that a pine tree covering over forty square metres once stood at this spot. Imported Egyptian watermelons were sold under the canopy of the tree. Khalef did not have watermelon, he had a sweet flaky pastry and his second espresso.

On the table was a folded copy of that morning's *L'Orient-Le Jour* newspaper. The paper was folded because inside it was an envelope. And inside the envelope was five hundred US dollars.

Khalef looked at his watch. 10:00. He finished his coffee, stood up, brushed pastry flakes from his jacket, tucked the paper under his arm and began walking in the direction of the Hotel Bristol. He stopped outside a boys' toys shop, admiring the televisions, cameras and computers in the window.

"Can I help you, sir?" A small, wiry, not-too-clean man had come out of the shop. "You are interested in something? I give you good price."

"No, no," said Khalef. "Just looking. How much is that?" He tapped the newspaper on the window in the general direction of a Canon SLR camera.

"For you? Five hundred dollars." The small man smiled, showing a gap either side of his two brown front teeth.

"Too much," said Khalef and walked away.

"Thank you, sir!" called the small man who somehow now had the newspaper under his arm. "May Allah's blessings be upon you!"

"Whatever," mumbled Khalef. Five hundred dollars was steep but the small man's information had proved useful. A similar shop down in Dahieh – who just happened to be the small man's business rival – was suspected of including malware in the computers, smart TVs and even cameras it was supplying to certain local residents. Malware which enabled a third party not only to listen to but also to see everything that was going on in the vicinity of the device. That third party may or may not be Mossad.

Khalef had blocked off the entire morning in his calendar for this visit, it was a nice sunny day, so he decided to walk back to the office. He headed north-east up Dunant Street. He would cut through to the Sanayeh Public Garden, enjoy a smoke, maybe watch some old men playing cards, backgammon or chess...

Sanayeh, Beirut 10:15 – 11:00

The Sanayeh Public Garden has never actually been called that. When it was created in 1907 it was called the Hamidi Public Garden, then over eighty years later it was renamed the René Moawad Public Garden in honour of the 13th President of Lebanon who was assassinated nearby by a 250 kilogram car bomb on 22 November 1989 after just seventeen days in office. But to locals the place has always been simply the Sanayeh Public Garden.

It was early yet, a few old men were shuffling about or sitting down with groans but no games had started. Further out near Sanayeh Street, two artists were setting up their work for exhibit.

Tamer Khalef found a bench near the centre of the park and lit up a Cedars cigarette. The sound of Beirut was a constant three-sixty degree hum but the further you went into the gardens the more muted it became, so here it was just a background purr. No sound could be distinguished separately.

So he was not aware of the sound of the motorbike engine as it circled the perimeter of the gardens...

With a sigh and an exhaled lungful of smoke, Tamer Khalef stood up, stretching his back. Time to return. He had just received a phone call from Sergeant Deeb el-Gharib asking him if he knew where Nabil Haddad was, his colleague's calendar was blank which meant he should be in. Khalef had a good idea where Haddad might be but he didn't say so – the good Christian Haddad went to church on a Sunday, where there was a widow that was always pestering him. Maybe this week he had succumbed to her charms and was having a lie-in after a day of ravagement! He looked forward to hearing a blow by blow account.

As he walked nearer to the edge of the gardens, the sound of Beirut increased. By the time he was at the Rue Spears exit, the city had engulfed him again. Now there was too much noise for him to distinguish one sound from another. So he was not aware of the Ducati motorbike approaching.

He crossed the road, turning left at the Faculty of Law Administration and Political Science Building into Halwani Street. It was a straight five minutes' walk north to the State Security Building. Cars passed by, people walked on the sidewalk.

The motorbike drove at a reduced speed a little way back, the rider leaning forward, steering with the right hand, something metallic and black in the left. Gradually the bike drew level with Khalef. The left hand raised.

Suddenly there was a thunder of acceleration and another bike roared into the street, heading fast for the Ducati. The second bike clipped the Ducati's back wheel and then roared on, not stopping. The Ducati wobbled and tipped. Instinctively, the Ducati rider jumped out and away, like a pilot ejecting from a crashing warplane, avoiding the bike as it fell, expertly rolling on impact with the ground to minimise injury.

Lithely the rider stood back up, avoiding a hooting car and quickly hiding the gun in the half-open leather blouson. One or two people were looking but most seemed not to care. Not removing the helmet or raising the visor, the rider ran back over to the Ducati. The machine had cut out and was half under a parked Mitsubishi Outlander. The rider dragged it out. With a superhuman effort, and after four attempts, the rider managed to pull the bike back upright. It was scraped but there seemed to be no serious damage, no fluid leakage. It started after the second turn of the key.

By now, Tamer Khalef had reached the intersection with Bank of Lebanon Street. He had heard the sound of a mild impact, which was an every day every minute occurrence in Beirut. He looked back to see a motorbike rider walking across the road to an overturned bike. He shrugged. At least the rider was wearing a helmet!

He crossed Bank of Lebanon Street and entered the State Security Building.

The Ducati reached Bank of Lebanon Street, turned right and drove away.

Somewhere in Beirut 11:00

The Confession slammed a gloved hand down onto the fuel tank of the bike as it wove in and out of the traffic as Bank of Lebanon Street became Michel Chiha Street, heading into central Beirut. By the British Embassy, the bike nearly took out two tourists heading for the nearby Grand Serail, the Prime Minister's offices. Fists were shaken. Choice words were shouted in return but they were confined within the reflective visor.

As it entered downtown, the bike was forced to slow by the narrowness of the streets and the amount of traffic. In Martyr's Square, in between The Tomb of the Martyr Rafic Hariri and the Virgin Megastore, The Confession pulled over.

The visor was raised. The chin strap was unclipped and the helmet was pulled off. Hair was shaken out. Two leather gloves were pulled off and slapped against the fuel tank. The Confession sat back in the saddle in contemplation, breathing heavily, bringing emotions under control.

That should have been another name crossed off the list. It would have been had it not been for that meddling bitch. How had she managed to turn the tables so that the hunter became the hunted? But the interference had been inevitable. The Confession had been too kind, too understanding. Too friendly.

The Confession had failed. The Confession did not like failure. It was not, as they say, an option.

And it was only temporary.

It was time to end it.

Jonblat, Beirut 11:00

"Have you found him?"

"Nothing yet, sir," said Sergeant Deeb el-Gharib from the doorway. "He's not answering his mobile and I've tried his home. I've phoned Khalef but he doesn't know where he is."

"Okay, keep trying, will you?"

"Sir. Oh by the way, Facilities have been on. The door will be done this week."

"Thank you, Deeb."

Merhi did not like the management side of the work, rankers (somebody who had come up through the ranks) never did, unlike the college-educated twats that came straight in at senior level and were good for nothing else. But it would be his pleasure to tear Nabil Haddad's bollocks off when he turned up.

First thing this morning, Merhi had gone up to what he had taken to calling The Spycatchers' Office on the fifth floor, only to find it empty. A check of calendars revealed that Khalef was out with a source in Snoubra but Haddad's calendar was blank, which meant he was due in. He had not turned up, no phone call, no text message, not even an e-mail. From a reading of the HR files, he had found out that Haddad lived alone so maybe, giving him every benefit of the doubt, he was lying in bed too ill to even reach his phone. Merhi would have to send somebody up to Mansourieh later if needs be.

Haddad's non-appearance had prompted him to call a team meeting for this afternoon. The spycatchers were too remote up there, too autonomous in their little eyrie on the fifth floor. He would announce at the meeting that both his teams would be situated together here on the second floor, that would enable cross-working also, thereby enhancing the resources of both his teams without any actual increase in staff. That would please Lieutenant-Colonel Ghanem. Results not problems. Deeb el-Gharib had sent out the e-mail moments ago. Team Meeting, General Office, 16:00 today, Monday 29

October.

"So you think – what was his name? - *Gerges* was the spy?" said Lieutenant-Colonel Pierre Ghanem in a tone that said he didn't believe a word of it.

"I am satisfied," said Jihad Merhi. "You said to bring you results not problems. I am bringing you the result."

"What about his wife? I felt nothing untoward when I made the death notification."

"You wouldn't. She probably knows nothing about it. But I'll have her brought in for interrogation."

"Go easy. She took it badly."

"Of course, but what better time? I doubt she knew a thing, but we'll find out." Merhi reached into his pocket for his cigarettes and then remembered where he was. Ghanem's office was a smoke-free zone.

"And he was killed by a member of the GSU?"

"Yes."

"After receiving intelligence from abroad?"

"Yes."

"Fortuitous. It's a pity we didn't expose him ourselves."

"In the war with the Jews we must utilise all resources whether they are at our direct disposal or not."

Ghanem nodded. Then he said, "I am not happy that a member of the GSU takes it upon himself to kill a member of the ISF though." He raised his hand as Merhi was about to interject. "But I can understand in this instance. Needs must. But it should not happen again. So it's a 'Well done', Major."

"I would like to honour the GSU operative."

"No."

"As you wish. On other matters, I have done a brief report for you on the future of the team, as requested. It should be in your in-tray," he nodded at Ghanem's laptop. "I'm bringing them all together, I have room on the second floor. They will cross-work as one unit. So saving resources and, indeed, freeing a room up here."

"Good, Major, good. We'll make a manager of you yet."

Please don't. "I'm having a team meeting this afternoon at sixteen hundred. Will you come to it?" He knew Ghanem was usually on his way home by that hour.

But the Lieutenant-Colonel surprised him. "Actually, yes, I think I will. We can show them what a good management command you and I make. Send me the agenda, will you?"

Sergeant Deeb el-Gharib intercepted Merhi as he passed by the General Office door. "Boss – sir. Two things. Khalef is back. And Captain Lattouf has been trying to get hold of you."

Merhi wondered if his groan was out loud or just in his head. "Why the hell didn't Lattouf ring my mobile?" He pulled the iPhone from his pocket. It was dead. "Shit. Battery. Okay Deeb, thanks. Did he say what it was about?"

"Not as far as I could make out, sir. You know how he shouts."

"I'll call him later. Any sludge on?"

"Just brewed a fresh pot."

Back in his office with his coffee, Merhi took his lightning charger from a drawer, plugged it into a wall socket, plugged his phone into the charger, inserted the systems access card into the ATS laptop then stuck his right index finger on the laptop's biometric pad. The screens on the laptop and the phone illuminated simultaneously. He lit up a cigarette as he waited for the Desktop screen to appear on the computer.

Suddenly his floor started buzzing. His iPhone was glowing. The charging wire was not long enough to stretch up to the desk so he had to bend over in his chair, stretching the wire as he quickly raised the phone to his ear. He had seen who it was, he needed this call.

"Ms Saad."

"Major, we need to meet."

"Are you all right?"

"Yes but there is something you need to know. I cannot tell you over the phone."

"Of course not. When and where?"

"The Palestinian Code, tomorrow at 16:00."

"The what?"

"Think, Major, we have used it before. Your friend."

"My...? Oh! Yes, yes. I'll be there. Thank you for sorting out our little problem. With the... interloper."

"That *is* the problem. I have sorted nothing."

"You are being modest - "

"You are in great danger. *Tomorrow. Sixteen hundred.* You understand what I am saying?"

"Yes - "

She was gone.

Merhi looked at the screen showing just his wallpaper of the Jeita Grotto and placed his phone back down on the floor.

Now what was that all about? He stayed bent over, cigarette in his mouth, looking like he was hiding behind the desk. Carla had used The Palestinian Code before – it was named after Fadi Lattouf. Originally it was the code he and Merhi used when they met for clandestine liaison between the ISF and the Palestinian Civil Police in the dark days (as if the days were any brighter now!). The named time less twenty-six hours. So tomorrow at sixteen hundred would be today at fourteen hundred. He looked at his watch. Under two hours' time. The location would always be the same: the Food Court on the second floor of The Dunes Shopping Mall over in Verdun.

Fourteen hundred was cutting it fine. If she wanted to see him straightaway why didn't she just come here to the office? And what did she mean, he was in great danger? And she had sorted nothing? Killing Gerges the spy had sorted everything. Unless she was going to confirm his speculation that there was more than one spy...?

Slowly, slowly he straightened up, his back stiff and on the verge of a spasm, coming up from behind his desk like a dragon rising from its rest, exhaling smoke. Then he jumped and the cigarette almost fell from his mouth, ash cascading onto his lap. A giant creature was standing in his office doorway.

"Lunchtime of bounteous ideas, my friend," smiled Fadi Lattouf. "*Al-salaam 'aalaykum.*"

Somewhere in Beirut 12:15

"You are in great danger. *Tomorrow. Sixteen hundred.* You understand what I am saying?"

"Yes - "

The Confession pulled out the ear buds and placed the iPhone down on the table. *Tomorrow, sixteen hundred* meant *Today, fourteen hundred.* And the location, always the Food Court in the Dunes Shopping Mall. Hopefully Merhi remembered The Palestinian Code.

The MacBook was on the table with the Team Meeting notification and small Agenda on the screen. There was now an additional e-mail above it. The Confession filled in the time, so that the e-mail read:

Subject: Team Meeting Notification amendment

The Meeting will now start at 14:00 in the General Office. Attendance is mandatory.

JM

The Confession pressed the Send button and the e-mail went on its way, forwarded to all.

Finishing the black Americano coffee, The Confession nodded thanks at the barista behind the counter and left the café.

The bike was parked two streets away, but that was no problem. The Confession no longer needed to rush.

Jonblat, Beirut 12:15

"Shaitan's bollocks, Fadi, how did you get in?"

Lattouf was in his uniform trousers and open-necked blue shirt under the black leather bomber jacket. The 'Visitor' ID was around his neck. "My twin brother signed me in. Your Sergeant, Deeb el-Gharib, my fellow shotgun." He laughed. "Fadi and Deeb, the el-Gharib brothers!"

"I'm busy right now, Fadi, I have an urgent appointment in Ver - " Oh shit.

"Verdun? Are you going to Verdun? The Dunes?"

"No, I - "

"Perfect. I've hardly eaten all day, I am starving." It must have been a full half hour since he had finished yesterday's leftover testicles and couscous together with a side helping of scrapings from the children's plates. "I'll give you a lift."

On cue, car horns started blaring from the street below. Merhi refused to go over to the window, knowing what he would see. "Your car or your official van?"

"My car, of course. It is less conspicuous."

Verdun, Beirut 12:30

Fifteen minutes later (after pausing at the lavatory to let Lattouf open his bladder and send alarm bells ringing in the flood defences of Beirut) they were in the less conspicuous bright orange Datsun Bluebird coughing and growling down Dunant Street. In between making derogatory remarks about the local drivers, Lattouf was waxing lyrical about the plethora of masticatory delights that awaited them in the Food Court of the Dunes Shopping Mall: *McDonald's*, *DipnCrunch*, *Doodle Doo*, *Haagen Dazs* and their mutual favourite *Cup Cake*. Such was his enthusiasm that Merhi was unable to ask him the reason for his appearance in the ISF offices until they were driving into the mall's parking area.

"What did you want, Fadi?"

"Thank you, my friend. A supersized Big Mac Meal with Coke, two apple pies, a Smarties McFlurry and a cup cake and coffee for dessert."

"No, why did you call? Why did you come to see me?"

Lattouf found a free bay and pulled up sharply, glaring at a Ford Mustang coming towards him with equal intentions for the space. "No way, flash boy!" He gave dismissive flicks of his hand out of the window and then crunched the Bluebird's manual gear shift into reverse. Merhi closed his eyes and trusted in God.

Actually Lattouf parked with the dexterity of an expert. As he switched off the engine and Merhi opened his eyes, Lattouf said "Football statistics."

"I'm sorry?"

"I will explain upstairs. It is something for you to consider. Let us go before I expire from starvation. *Yalla.*"

As they got off the escalator at the second floor, Lattouf's face fell. *Cup Cake* was no longer there! And *Doodle Doo* was just history. But his face rose again when he saw that there was now a *Zaatar w Zeit* selling *manousheh* (filled flat bread) and an *Urbanista* ('Food, coffee and people'). And thank Allah for *McDonald's!*

Merhi instructed Lattouf to find a table, and he went over to order, thanking God that he had been to an ATM this morning.

It took him ten minutes, by which time Lattouf had not only found a table but, by a combination of unfortunate bodily sounds and his sheer physical presence, had cleared all the tables around also, as if that corner of the Food Court was a crime scene – which it would become as soon as Lattouf started murdering his food.

The tray held the pre-requested items from *McDonald's* plus three grease-wrapped *manousheh* and two double espresso.

Merhi sat down opposite, taking one of the coffees and a *manousheh.* "I got you one *zaatar* and one *jibneh.*"

"Bless your hands, my friend, you are too kind. But you are a bad influence, you know. Nada has me on a diet."

Merhi reached out to take the other two *manousheh* but Lattouf snatched them faster than a hand-grabbing money box. "But I am not ill mannered. As always, you are generous." Lattouf opened a *manousheh* wrapper, tore the twenty centimetre long folded over flatbread in half, put both halves together on top of each other, bent them over into a semi-tube shape and slid the entire construction into his mouth.

Merhi had known the Palestinian giant for too long to be even remotely fazed. He looked at his watch, then glanced around the Food Court and over to the escalator. It was 13:00. One hour to his meeting with Carla. One hour to feed and get rid of Lattouf. "So," he said, "what is it about football statistics that brings you all the way into town to see me?"

"You were not answering your phone." Had the *manousheh* been chewed at all or simply swallowed whole?

"It was dead."

"Ah." Lattouf flipped open the lid of the Big Mac box with the gleaming eyes of an explorer opening a chest of treasure. "It is just something that occurred to me in the camp today. Something to consider. Regarding your internal spy."

"That is done with."

"It probably is, as we said. Have you told The Party yet?"

"About the conclusion? No."

"Good. Just in case." Half the Big Mac disappeared.

"What in the name of Christ are you trying to say, Fadi?"

"Isa and all the prophets. I might be just crossing my eyes and dotting my tees here. You know how when you watch football on TV, especially those English matches, they have statistics coming up, number of fouls, number of corners, number of shots, number of shots on target, number of shots off target."

"And?"

"The gun, the FN Five-seveN. Same gun, same perpetrator, we know, right? The attempt on – what was his name, the Palestinian child?"

"Abdul Abdulrahman."

"Him. Yes. A shot but off target."

"Yes, I was the one that shot him."

Lattouf finished off the Big Mac. "So how can we be certain that Abdul Rahman was the target?"

Merhi sat back in his chair, frowning. What was Lattouf going on about? "Because he was spying for the Israelis."

"And your man – what was his name?" A handful of fries followed the Big Mac.

"Gerges. Claude Gerges."

"How do you know he was a spy? Do you have proof?"

"Because Ca – because he was shot too. Two Israeli spies. Eliminated. Perfect goals, to use your analogy."

"What if the goals were disallowed for offside?"

Merhi said nothing.

"What if the gun was not aimed at Abdul Rahman at all?"

The incident was playing in Merhi's mind. Lattouf driving along the coastal road, their windows open. The motorbike behind drawing level. The gun. *The bullet missing him by five centimetres...* And Carla's recent phone call. *"You are in great danger..."*

No, it could not be. That would mean everything he had thought, everything he had assumed, was wrong. It would mean that Claude Gerges was not a spy.

"What if the gun was aimed at you?"

Jonblat, Beirut 13:15

The Confession walked into the State Security Building and nodded at the Corporal on security duty, taking the MacBook out of the shoulder bag and laying it on top of the bag on the inspection table. The Corporal picked up the MacBook and gave it a cursory visual check, then he checked the empty bag and nodded. The Confession walked through the metal detector. No alarm went off.

Gathering up the MacBook and the bag, The Confession walked over to the Reception desk, greeted the Corporal on duty there, and signed in.

Verdun, Beirut 13:20

"It is just a theory," said Fadi Lattouf, Smartie McFlurry caught in his beard like fairy lights on a Christmas tree. "An alternative scenario."

It had taken Merhi several minutes of contemplation to even entertain what had been suggested but reason and cold logic told him that Lattouf had a point. Nothing about this matter had sat easily with him. Carla had said there was a spy in the ISF – she had not said anything else. He had formulated his own hypothesis and had run with it, but Lattouf had now turned that on its head. That was not to say Lattouf was right but it was worth considering (suspect everyone, trust no one, question everything, check everything: Security Induction Course Day 1 Module 1).

"So in your alternative scenario, I was the target."

"Yes."

"Why?"

Lattouf finished his ice cream (the apple pies were but a memory) and frowned at the tray. "That I do not know," he said distractedly. He lifted several wrappers and the Big Mac box, looking underneath.

Merhi sighed. He was in desperate need of his psychoactive chemical but the Food Court was non-smoking. "*Cup Cake* has gone, Fadi, remember? But I'll get you a coffee."

"I couldn't eat any more anyway, I am full." Lattouf couldn't keep the disappointment from his voice as he patted his rotund gut. "I think Nada's diet is shrinking my insides. But I'll enjoy a coffee, thank you. A triple espresso and an Americano please."

Merhi stood and walked towards *Urbanista*.

"Oh Abu Samer," called Lattouf. "Maybe I can squeeze in a New York cheesecake?"

Merhi nodded, "Two triple espressos, one Americano and one slice of cheesecake," and continued on.

"No," shouted Lattouf. "One cheesecake."

Jonblat, Beirut 13:20

The Confession walked up the stairs, the visitor's ID tag bouncing, the lanyard with the continuous pattern of twee Lebanese flags outside of the hair at the back.

As The Confession reached the landing of the second floor, the door swung open and Sergeant Deeb el-Gharib came through with a folder in his hand. He smiled when he saw The Confession and reached back to hold the door open. "*Ah, bonjour*, nice to see you again."

"*Bonjour* Deeb, is he in?"

"No, he's out at the moment but he'll be back soon. Have you come for the meeting?"

"Yes. I am a surprise Agenda item. Any other business."

el-Gharib smiled. "There's some sludge, if you want it."

"Thank you."

"You know where it is. Make yourself at home." He looked at the computer in The Confession's hand. "Use his office if you want some peace and quiet."

"Thank you, I'll just prepare for this afternoon."

The Confession went through the doors, Sergeant Deeb el-Gharib went up the stairs.

Verdun, Beirut 13:35

Merhi watched as the last of the whole cheesecake (and his US $40) said goodbye to the world. Lattouf burped out of politeness (and necessity) and picked up his Americano.

Merhi had had a quick Camel in the lavatory while Lattouf was snuffling his cheesecake, and he now felt calmer. "So, what does it mean if the assassin was aiming at me?" It was a half-question half-rumination.

"Have you upset anybody?"

"In this job? Well now, let me see..."

"You have been a good boy? No upset husbands?"

"Fadi!"

"I joke, my friend." Lattouf wiped his beard clean with his hands. "There is a problem you Lebanese have, I have noticed it before."

"Just the one?"

"The Lebanese have many problems. One day we might discuss them. Right now I am thinking of one problem in particular."

Merhi didn't really want to hear it. Problems? Lebanese?

Lattouf continued. "You always take things personally."

"I what?"

"As a race. You Lebanese always think it's all about you. On a personal level. You think you are the wasp's ankles whereas in reality you are ostriches."

"What are you saying?" Merhi could not keep the pique from his voice.

He did not need to be lectured on the Lebanese psyche by a bloody Palestinian!

Lattouf swilled Americano. "Perhaps the assassin was not aiming at Jihad Merhi."

"But just a few minutes ago you said I was the bloody target!"

"The Major of the ISF was the target. Not Jihad Merhi. It was not personal."

The empty Americano cup was put upside down on the other detritus on the tray. Merhi was staring at Lattouf. Lattouf gave a sympathetic, almost regretful, smile. "It is worth considering."

"But Gerges was shot..."

"Yes. And if he was not your Israeli spy, why was he? What would he have been?"

"What?"

"If they had managed to shoot you and then shoot him, what would he have been?"

"The second victim?"

"No."

"No?"

"The third victim."

"The third...?"

Lattouf held up four massive fingers, like a butcher holding up four meaty sausages. "Your Brigadier was the first." He bent one finger down. "Then it would have been you." Another finger. "Then Gerges." Third finger down.

Merhi knew his mouth was open slightly but he made no effort to close it.

Lattouf still had one finger in the air, unfortunately the middle finger. "Are the ISF spycatchers being killed off one by one?"

Merhi moved his mouth but nothing came out.

"And if so," Lattouf wiggled his finger. "Who is the next one?"

Jonblat, Beirut 13:40

Jacket and bag left in Major Merhi's office, sludge finished (it wasn't too bad, it had the same consistency as Turkish coffee only with grit), The Confession walked up the stairs to the fifth floor carrying the MacBook. People passed on the stairs, one or two nodded.

Lieutenant-Colonel Ghanem's PA, Violette, was behind her desk. She looked up and smiled in recognition. "Hello! How are you? It's been a while since *you've* been up to the rarified atmosphere of the fifth floor!"

"I like to confine myself to the troops," said The Confession. "Keep my feet on the ground. But I have to discuss something with the Chief, is he in?"

"He might be having his nap. Wait there."

Violette went over to Ghanem's door, tapped lightly, gently opened it and peeked in. Then she straightened up and announced the visitor. There was a deep response and then Violette turned, deftly pushing the door open behind her. "He'll see you."

"*Merci ktir*, Violette." The MacBook was placed on the corner of Violette's desk. "Could you look after this for me?"

"*Bien sûr.*"

The Confession went in, lifting the ID tag and pulling off the lanyard over the dark hair. Violette closed the door.

Ghanem stood up, hand outstretched. "How are you? Nice to see you again, I hear you have been having great success."

"Oh, one tries, sir." The Confession shook the outstretched hand.

Ghanem was expecting the light Arabic handshake (in the Middle East a firm handshake indicates aggression) but instead his fingers were grabbed and he was pulled forward, as if the visitor wished to embrace. He jolted, knocking over a mug of tea on his desk, and his first instinctive reaction was to smile at the stupid accident.

But then the lanyard was whipped around his neck. "Wha - "

Two steps and The Confession was behind Ghanem, expertly pulling the lanyard across Ghanem's windpipe, using the plasticised ID tag as a garrote, twisting it sharply.

Ghanem's hands went to his throat but the lanyard was already too tight. The Confession kicked him behind the knees and he went down, the movement tightening the lanyard even more. He was gasping.

The Confession pulled backwards, hearing Ghanem's ageing knees cracking, his gasps turning into gruff wheezes. The Confession twisted the garrote even more, using forearm strength, shaking Ghanem's head from side to side, seeing thick spittle flying from his mouth as his swollen tongue tried to move to let air in.

Ghanem's nails were clawing at his own neck, drawing blood, his white shirt collar becoming light red. His mouth was moving but no air could go in or out. His body was jerking as he tried to breathe. The Confession pushed his head backwards and forwards, side to side, the lanyard with the twee little Lebanese flags cutting, choking, strangling...

Ghanem tried to reach backwards to grab The Confession but his weak hands just flapped in the air. The Confession banged Ghanem's head on the desk. Once, twice... The lanyard was merciless. Strength left Ghanem, his hands dropped. Eternal darkness descended. Spilt tea dripped onto the floor...

The Confession maintained the garrote for five minutes after Ghanem died to ensure his spirit had left his body. It was five minutes shorter than the time given to Mahmoud Abdel Rauf al-Mabhouh in Dubai in January 2010 because al-Mabhouh was suffocated not strangled.

Gently The Confession lowered Ghanem's body to the floor behind his desk. The lanyard with the Lebanese flags was embedded deep into the bloody neck, like a patriotic necklace. Or a choker. It would be too messy to remove it, so The Confession left it where it was, unclipping the Visitor ID tag from the back.

Opening the office door by just fifteen centimetres, The Confession said "Violette, I left my laptop on your desk, could you bring it in please...?"

Verdun, Beirut 13:55

Merhi looked at his watch. Five minutes to go, and Lattouf was still there, eating an éclair to help his fourth mug of coffee go down. The cream on Lattouf's beard made him look like he was foaming at the mouth. Which was what Merhi should be doing after the insulting comments Lattouf had made about the Lebanese. Comments which made Merhi all the more angry because they were true.

And Lattouf's postulation about the spycatchers being killed off became more and more plausible with each second, with each thought. He had forgotten about the very public slaying of Brigadier Wissam al-Hassan. Had that only been ten days ago? It was the Brigadier's assassination that had brought Merhi into the realm of spycatching.

And Lattouf's theory cast a sinister shadow over the absence of Sergeant Nabil Haddad this morning. Had the fourth victim already been claimed?

He needed to talk to Carla. Maybe that's what she wanted to tell him, that the spycatchers were being killed, confirming Lattouf's premise. On reflection it was good that Lattouf was still here, he should hear what Carla had to say.

He looked at his watch again. Two minutes.

Opposite, Lattouf sighed contentedly, licking cream from his fingers and mouth in such a lascivious manner that Merhi felt personally violated. Lattouf leant sideways and, with a gratified smile, farted like a bull elephant on heat.

Jonblat, Beirut 13:59

Violette didn't know she had died. One moment she was bringing in the laptop as requested, the next nothing. It was all over, blackness, as if her life had never happened in the first place. Her neck broke easily with one expert jerk of The Confession's arms.

The Confession caught the MacBook with one hand and lowered Violette to the floor with the other, flopping her body face down on top of Lieutenant-Colonel Ghanem behind the desk, Violette's arms either side of the dead man, her legs apart. Violette's skirt had raised making the scene look like a necrophilial sexual defilement. Considerately, The Confession pulled the dead woman's skirt down and kicked her legs together.

Crouching, The Confession flipped open Ghanem's jacket and removed his gun from his waistband holster, the standard-issue Browning 9mm. Drool rolled from Violette's half-open mouth onto Ghanem's swollen purple lips.

The Confession stood up and took one look around the room. Fingerprints did not matter, a false gossamer skin was being worn on the hands. Any residual DNA traces did not matter, they would match up with the fingerprints which would lead to the data of a person who had died years ago.

The Confession left the office and closed the door, taking a small, metallic object, like a matchbox, from a pocket. It was cutely named a 'Treble Clef' by its inventors in the south. Putting it by the lock, The Confession wiggled the box in place, pressed the On button, pushed it, turned it – and heard the lock click. Then a similar maneouvre slid the internal security bolt across. The door was now locked and bolted from the inside, just like the room in the Al Bustan Hotel in Dubai two years ago.

Putting the Treble Clef back in a pocket, The Confession took out a phone and looked at the time.

14:00.

Verdun, Beirut 14:01

Jihad Merhi looked at his watch for the thousandth time. Across the table, Fadi Lattouf sat back like a satisfied Buddha, hands resting on the plateau of his stomach.

Merhi's phone rang. He took it from his inside jacket pocket, looked at the screen and then banged his finger against the green icon.

"Where are you?" as he said it he looked around the Food Court and then out into the shopping area.

"I am here."

"I cannot see you."

Watching Merhi's eyes dashing from one side of the Food Court to the other, Lattouf joined in even though he did not know what he was expected to see.

"Of course not. The Palestinian is with you."

"Yes, we had… other business."

"I cannot appear if he is there."

"Well, he is," Merhi looked across the table. "And he has an interesting theory."

"That the spycatchers are in trouble? Your team is being killed?"

"How did you know?"

There was silence.

"Carla...?"

"Because it is true."

"What?"

"I finally figured out the cryptic report. It is simple. The list of names is a hit list. You put paid to the total Israeli espionage operation in Beirut. Now they are putting paid to you."

"Revenge?"

"The Israelis are good at that. And with your team removed they can initiate new operations, new people, get their activities back up to speed. They cannot be in a position of disadvantage, especially with what is happening in Syria. We have said before, Major, that battles might be won but the war is never over."

"But you said there was a spy in the ISF."

"There is."

Merhi frowned. "What are you saying? They are getting help from the inside?"

"Perhaps more than that."

"I cannot believe that one of my men would be responsible for – Just a minute, we have the CCTV. It shows you killing Claude Gerges."

Lattouf was staring at Merhi, fascinated at the one side of the conversation he could hear, eyebrows raised.

The voice on the phone said, "Shut up you idiot."

"Don't you fucking tell me to – "

"It was not me!"

Merhi span around in his seat again. "Show yourself."

"And have you and your fat friend arrest me? Believe me when I say I have only Lebanon's interests at heart. Only your interests."

"Are you sure they're not Israel's interests?"

Silence again. Then, softly, she said "You do not understand, do you?"

"What?"

"For the majority to live, some have to die."

Merhi shook his head. "No, they do not. That is a myth. Show yourself now, come in and we will sort this out together."

"No. It is better that I stay outside."

"Then consider yourself wanted."

"I have been wanted for seven years."

"Our business is not finished. I will find you."

"*I* will find *you*. In the meantime, Major…"

"What?"

"Get back to your office as quick as you can. Your team is in danger."

"Carla, what have you done?"

"I will find you, Major."

"You little bitch, I'll… Hello?…Hello?" Merhi threw the phone down onto the table. It landed on the tray, its fall broken by the empty Big Mac box. Greasy papers flew onto the floor. "Fucking bollocking arseholes!"

People from the non-evacuated tables were beginning to look. Merhi's eyes searched the area again. He was fuming, face red with anger. Then he pulled his Camel King Size from his pocket, lit one up and swallowed the burning smoke like a dehydrated man in the desert gulps water. He glared at Lattouf as if it was all his fault.

While Merhi still breathed heavily, Lattouf's fingers walked daintily across the table and took a cigarette from the packet. "My friend," he said as he leant further forward and picked up the lighter. "Can you smell jasmine?"

Jonblat, Beirut 14:05

"Hi, sorry I'm late." The Confession walked into the General Office, jacket over forearm, bag on shoulder.

"Don't worry," said Sergeant Deeb el-Gharib, pouring himself some sludge. "The boss isn't here yet."

A makeshift conference table had been set up by pushing three desks together. "Where's he gone?" The Confession found an empty place at the end nearest the door and put the bag on the seat.

"Don't know. His calendar is blank."

"He'd have our bollocks if it was one of us," grunted Sergeant Tamer Khalef who was smoking over by the window.

The rest of the team laughed ruefully. The five Corporals were already seated around the makeshift table: Jad Chadidi, Omar Mostafa, Michel Yammine, Peter Harrak and Emad Hmedeh.

The Confession threw the jacket over the back of the chair, opening the bag and taking out the MacBook.

"Where's your…?" asked Khalef, making motions at his own ID tag around his neck. "We all have to wear them nowadays. If you haven't got one on we must 'confront' you. Mwah-ha-haah!"

The Confession held up the ID tag. "The neck-thing broke, fell off and got wedged somewhere."

"Cheap crap," Khalef blew smoke out of the half-open window.

"I'll have a word with Facilities," said el-Gharib. "They're coming up sometime this week to fix the boss's door. Right, I'm just going for a leak. If the Major turns up, don't start without me."

Jad Chadidi looked at his watch. "Don't know why he had to change it to two o'clock anyway if he's going to be late."

"Ours not to reason why, Corporal, ours not to reason why." el-Gharib went out.

"So, to what do we owe this honour?" Michel Yammine asked The Confession. "Or is it a secret?"

"New procedures," explained The Confession. "New ways of working. I've been asked to talk about them. I'll tell you more later."

"No handouts, I hope," said Peter Harrak. "There's nothing worse than fucking handouts at a meeting."

The Confession smiled at the faux-complaint. "Actually I do have something you can have now." The Confession flipped open the top of the bag, rummaged inside with a screwing action of the right hand – and brought out Ghanem's Browning 9mm, now with an AAC Spider 2 suppressor on the end.

It was over in five seconds, less than one second for each of the six men in the room.

Peter Harrak went first, on the left next to The Confession, the right side of his head taken off. Then the gun swung over to the right, a bullet into the forehead of Emad Hmedeh. Still on the right, the left eye of Michel Yammine. Left, the top of the head of Omar Mostafa. Left, the entire face of Jad Chadidi.

Sergeant Tamer Khalef had actually begun to move away from the window, but he had been distracted by Yammine's blood splashing into his face. His right hand was at his waistband when a bullet slammed into his heart, sending him sprawling backwards on top of the sludge table, mugs and pot flying, breaking, dark coffee splattering over an area disproportionate to the amount spilled.

It was done.

The Confession looked around, satisfied, then put the jacket back on, put the MacBook into the bag, the bag over a shoulder and walked out into the corridor, closing the door. Once again, the Treble Clef was used and the door was locked from the inside. The Confession walked off, gun in hand.

On the coffee table back in the General Office, blood oozed out of the chest of Tamer Khalef, mingling and mixing with the spilt coffee.

Adding body to the sludge.

The lavatories were out on the stairwell, male and female on alternate floors. On this floor it was the *Femmes*. The Confession did not have time to wait, an informed guess needed to be made. It is easier to carry a full bladder downwards than upwards, so The Confession went down.

The *Hommes* lavatories on the first floor smelled, as *Hommes* lavatories do everywhere (tomcats will be tomcats). The three urinals were empty, one out of the three cubicles was in use. The Confession entered the cubicle next to the occupied one. Standing on the bowl, The Confession looked carefully over the wooden partition into the next cubicle.

Deeb el-Gharib was squatting, trousers around his ankles. He was reaching for paper when The Confession shot him in the top of the head from above. Because of the downward trajectory, there was no blood spatter, no outwards shards of bone, a maroon hole just appeared in the top of his head and the body slumped but remained in the sitting position. The bullet would later be found amongst the excreta in the bowl, having passed straight through what was once Deeb el-Gharib.

The Confession gingerly unscrewed the hot suppressor, placed it and the gun in the shoulder bag, and left the cubicle, giving a little shove on the occupied cubicle's door. No need for the Treble Clef this time, the subject had locked the door himself.

Over by the outside door, The Confession turned. Of all the deaths that had been ordered, that of the long-serving Sergeant Deeb el-Gharib was the saddest. He had been like a permanent fixture of the Internal Security Force, the wise, experienced *maître d'* of the second floor. If only the spycatchers had not come his way...

With respect, The Confession said "Ours but to do and die, Deeb, ours but to do and die," and left the lavatory.

Jonblat, Beirut 14:50

Traffic had been busy on Rachid Karame Street down in Verdun and by the time the same street became Dunant Street in Snoubra it was crawling at less than walking pace. The occupants of the bright orange Datsun Bluebird did not know that the cause of the inordinate delay (rather than the usual ordinate delay that was expected) was the butterfly-wing effect of an altercation between two motorbikes in next door Sanayeh earlier that day.

The traffic started moving freer again as they turned into Spears Street by the Sanayeh Public Garden. Lattouf crunched the Datsun into third gear and sped up, squealing left into Halwani Street. Immediately they could see the flashing lights up ahead. Tape was festooned across Justinien Street which ran down the side of the State Security Building. It looked like a carnival was in progress, but there weren't any cheering crowds. Army vehicles intermingled with police vehicles and fire service vehicles. Traffic was being moved on on the crossways Bank of Lebanon Street, uniformed policemen banging on the hoods of any gawking ghouls, shouting at them to keep moving.

Lattouf kept his hand on the horn and Merhi held his shield up to the window as Lattouf forced, forced, forced his way across the traffic. A policeman frowned at them, gesticulating wildly and shouting, then saw the shield and waved them on. With a final stab of acceleration, the Datsun broke through one of the tapes across Justinien Street as if it was the winner of a marathon. It screamed to a stop by the Aresco Palace Theatre.

Merhi leapt out, Lattouf following after two failed attempts to lift himself out of the driver's side.

"What happened?" Merhi was shouting. "What happened?"

There was chaos all around. The quantity of flashing lights was blinding. Nobody seemed to know what they were doing, nobody seemed to be in charge. There was too much tape, the default position of law enforcement when they felt helpless: tape it off. It was similar to the headless chicken pandemonium when one of the city's daily car bombs went off, except here there was no explosion damage.

Merhi ran closer to the building, grabbing a young Lieutenant he recognized. "What happened?"

The Lieutenant looked confused, desolate. Afraid. "They – they've killed them."

"Who? Who's killed who?"

"The second floor. All of them."

"What are you saying?" Merhi shook the Lieutenant by the shoulders. "Speak to me."

"They're dead. The spycatchers."

"All of them?"

The Lieutenant nodded.

"How?"

"Shot."

Lattouf ran up, puffing.

"How could they all have been shot?" snarled Merhi. "*All* of them?"

The Lieutenant nodded again.

"I don't understand – Will somebody please turn those fucking sirens off!"

The chaos continued, one or two sirens were muted but not all of them.

"Where is *Muqaddam* Ghanem?"

"Don't know, sir."

Merhi looked up at the building. He could see his offices on the second floor, one of the windows was half-open. Lights were flashing inside, people taking pictures. His eyes travelled up to the fifth floor. Behind one of the windows, lights flashed there too. Ghanem's suite.

In the name of God.

He patted the Lieutenant's shoulder in thanks then said, "Fadi, I'm going in. Come."

"Me?"

"Yes, come. I'm going to need you." Merhi looked around once more, frowning at the noise and chaos.

Lattouf snarled and took a deep breath. "TURN THE FUCKING SIRENS OFF!" His shout swept over the street louder than bomb percussion. Windows rattled as far away as Beirut Port. An earth tremor was felt in Jordan. But it had the desired effect. The place went suddenly and eerily silent. All eyes looked towards Merhi and the giant.

Then a sweet little tune played from somewhere. It might have been playing for some time, but they could not have heard it above the din. Merhi frowned at Lattouf. Lattouf frowned at Merhi. "It's not mine," said the Palestinian.

"Shit, it's me," Merhi reached into his jacket and pulled out his iPhone. He tapped the screen, read what was on it and froze. Did his face go a little greyer?

"What is it, Abu Samer?" asked Lattouf.

Merhi still stared at the screen. Then he passed the phone to Lattouf. The Palestinian frowned and pulled a face, trying to focus. Holding the phone at the longest arms-length he could manage, he finally made it out. It was a message from Carla. Only four words.

RUN FOR YOUR LIFE

PART FOUR
الجزء الرابع

THE CONFESSION
اعتراف

Mount Lebanon 15:30

There was no music playing when The Damascene entered the apartment, but Paradise and Love were in the living area dancing. One was wearing ear buds connected to an iPod on her waist, the other was not and yet she danced in time with her sister, as if she could hear the music also. They were wearing pink vests and white denim shorts. Their contact lenses were in, in deference to their guest. When they saw The Damascene they stopped dancing, Love (with the green eyes) turning off the iPod and removing the ear buds.

"Where is he?" asked The Damascene, walking into the kitchen area.

"Upstairs, at prayer," said Paradise.

The Damascene nodded, taking a flatbread from a packet, tearing it and scooping up some hummus from a bowl left over from lunch.

"May I get you something?" Love came into the kitchen area.

"You look tired," said Paradise.

"This will be fine. Thank you." He poured himself some orange juice. He looked into the green eyes then into the brown eyes. "It has been a busy morning. Our friends asked me to come back. They were all there today even those that weren't yesterday."

"And they have all agreed?" asked Paradise as her sister poured fresh coffee.

"Eventually, yes. It was fraught. At one point I thought they would come to blows, which of course would be nothing new. They were so fractious, it was like a meeting of the Lebanese parliament."

"Perhaps it was, some would say they are the true parliament of this country not the powerless ineffectual puppets in Nejmeh Square."

"There is that. *Merci.*" He took the tiny cup of Turkish coffee from Love. He leant on the breakfast bar, the sisters in front of him. "There has been a change of plan..."

Jonblat, Beirut 15:35 – 17:00

Merhi and Lattouf stood behind the tape looking into the General Office. This was one of the few tapes Merhi had not ripped away in anger as he walked through the building. *This* was the crime scene – at least, one of the three crime scenes. The door was ripped off having been kicked in, locked from the inside the Scene of Crime Officers said.

At the insistence of the SOCOs they had put on white forensic suits and overshoes, hoods up. Merhi's fitted perfectly and was done up at the front. Lattouf's suit stopped halfway down his limbs and would only do up at the front if another three metres of fabric had been added. His hood reached to the back of his head only, his overshoes surprisingly fitted perfectly until he realised they had split across the soles.

Silently they looked in at the scene. They did not have facemasks and the smell of hour-old death touched their noses. The smell of blood, the rank internal smell of human beings, the dry-sour smell of piss, the rich smell of shit. And coffee.

Six bodies. Cadavers that just an hour or so ago had been living, breathing beings. Merhi's team. Each had died quickly, of that there was no doubt, but Merhi was of the school of thought that humans do not die instantly. Each of them probably had at least ten seconds of sentience after they had been shot to realise they were dead. Tamer Khalef possibly had more because he was shot in the heart not the head.

Then he thought of Deeb el-Gharib whom he had already seen downstairs. The most undignified death, trousers and pants down, arse unwiped. He hoped it had been quick.

Next to Merhi, Lattouf was still, saying nothing.

Merhi sighed a deep, deep sigh. A sigh of emptiness. "Fadi, let us go upstairs, we should see it all. Will you be okay with the stairs?"

Lattouf nodded. "Better that than get stuck in the lift in this place of death."

On the fifth floor, secretary Violette's room looked normal although there were SOCO minions dusting, measuring, photographing. The door to Lieutenant-Colonel Ghanem's room had also been kicked in, but it seemed to have been done more carefully, the door was still on its hinges only the frame broken, unlike the door to the General Office which had been shattered. Perhaps rank was respected even in death – or maybe the door was simply newer.

This locking the door from the inside was becoming an Israeli calling-card. They probably had some new toy that did it.

Inside, behind the desk, Violette was on top of Ghanem, her lips resting on his poking tongue. They were staring into each others' eyes. Merhi wanted to feel sick but he couldn't. He did not feel anything.

Behind him, Lattouf said lowly "Whoever has done all this will die, my friend."

"That is for certain, Fadi. I only hope it is soon and it is at my hands."

"Allah will be merciless. Trust in him."

Merhi turned away from the bodies. "I do, by whatever name he is known. But I am sure, sometimes, he would not mind a little help." There was a sincerity in his eyes as he said, "Thank you for coming in with me, Fadi."

"My friend, we are a team. Lattouf and Merhi, remember?"

Merhi placed a tender hand on the huge round shoulder of the

Palestinian. With a small, deep, sad laugh he countered, "Merhi and Lattouf. Need a smoke?"

"More than I ever have."

"*Yalla*, there is nothing we can do here."

As they were walking down the stairs, Merhi's mobile rang, a phone call not a text. It was a number he did not recognise. Surely this was not that murdering bitch Carla ringing to taunt him?

"Merhi."

"Ah, hello, Major Merhi? Sorry to ring you on your mobile, switchboard gave it to me as you were not answering your phone and this is urgent. It's Facilities here over in Ras en Nabaa. When would be a convenient time for us to come and fix your door?"

Outside even the weather had turned sombre. The sky had clouded over as if showing a mark of respect to the deceased – or maybe just as a prelude to the Beirut winter which would arrive soon, two months of cold and rain before the sun returned in February.

Merhi and Lattouf sat on the metre-high wall at the side of the steps leading to the entrance to the building. Official vehicles were still parked everywhere, some lights still flashed, but there were no sirens (and possibly there never would be again after Lattouf's admonishment) and no more headless chickens. Order had descended. As had something else: news crews, TV vans and reporters.

Merhi and Lattouf had kept their forensic suits on, hoods still up (well, in Merhi's case), so that they looked like two tired SOCOs having a break, a good camouflage against any media intrusion. If they knew a Major was out here, and the sole surviving person of the murdered team at that, they would be swarming like hornets.

Down at the end of the street, the road had been re-taped, a policeman lifting it as necessary to let people and vehicles in and out. The traffic was still heavy on Bank of Lebanon Street but it was moving. Any incident in Beirut was old to the public after two hours, done, dusted, how many dead? Whatever, move on.

Merhi drew hard on his cigarette and swallowed smoke. Lattouf sat with his cigarette between his lips, smoking without hands. They watched the comings and goings, people in uniforms, people in forensic suits like theirs, people in civilian clothes. The media kept on the other side of the road. Down near the Aresco Palace Theatre, TV crews had set up so their on-the-spot reporters could broadcast with the State Security Building in the background.

Lattouf took the cigarette from his mouth. "You think it was this djinn, this Carla?" he said contemplatively.

Merhi was quiet for a while before he replied. "I don't want it to be but it must be. The problem is she never says what's going on. Always cryptic. A hint here, a piece of information there. Always need to know. Well, I'll tell you what, Fadi, I fucking well need to know now."

"I always thought you and her... You know, when she stays with you..."

"No chance. Not for the want of thinking. But do you really think I would risk losing Gigi? For a... a..."

"For a djinn?"

"And anyway you have seen her husband. Not somebody I would want to cross."

"And you think she has now turned assassin?"

"The Israelis are wiping out the spycatchers. You said it. She said it. Maybe she has turned, maybe she is freelancing like her husband."

"Maybe," Lattouf shrugged, his eyes fixing on a pretty female TV reporter who was eating a sandwich. "She said there was a spy in the ISF."

"Disinformation, distraction."

"Maybe." The TV reporter finished her sandwich and Lattouf lost interest. "Have you written up your reports on this case?"

"Well, not today obviously. But up until yesterday. Ghanem is... *was*... very strict about it."

"So your report states that there is a suspected Israeli spy in the ISF?"

"Yes."

"And you suspected that spy to be – what was his name?"

"Claude Gerges."

"Yes."

"And he was killed by an agent of your sister GSU."

"Yes. Where is this going?"

"But now all your team is dead. Killed *after* Gerges."

"Yes."

"So it could not have been him."

"No, I will be amending my report."

"But you have not amended it yet. Your report still says there is a spy in the ISF. All your team is dead."

"Yes."

"Except one."

Merhi was about to flick his cigarette butt into nearby bushes but he stopped with his hand in the air, his head turning to Lattouf.

Lattouf gave a shrug with a downturn of his mouth. "Just thinking of it from the point of view of an investigator coming in cold. To me, the one survivor would be a great person of interest."

Merhi let the cigarette butt take flight.

"Even if he was the leader of the team," said Lattouf.

*

Down on Bank of Lebanon street, a motorbike pulled up to the Police Do Not Cross tape. The leather-clad rider wore a helmet, unusual for Beirut. Lifting the visor, the rider looked up Justinien Street. In amongst all the media, all the official vehicles, all the people, the rider noticed two men in white forensic suits sitting on the wall outside the State Security Building. The smaller man could have been anybody, from this distance it was hard to tell. But the larger man, who seemed to be bursting out of the forensic suit like an over-inflated balloon, could only be one person. And that meant the rider knew who the smaller man was too.

The final target.

Still in the forensic suit with the hood up, Merhi pushed past other people dressed in a similar manner and went into his office. He needed his laptop, he needed to amend and augment his report. He couldn't do it here but neither could he remove the machine from the crime scene – at least, not openly.

Lattouf had made a good point. The sole survivor of the murdered team would come under great suspicion, the prime suspect – especially as his own report said there was an Israeli spy in his squad. He did not want to sit in a room for hours, maybe even days, while some high-flying twat from the GSU grilled him as to what was going on - because he couldn't tell them, he did not know himself. Not yet. If he made himself scarce and updated his report, that might keep them at bay for a while. Give him time to figure out what was really happening. And, if necessary and as advised, run for his life.

Turning his back to the cracked, frosted glass of his office door, he slipped the laptop inside his forensic suit and zipped it back up to the neck. It looked like he had a hard, square groin (a cyber hard-on!) but he might get away with it, people outside were too busy to even notice one more person in a white suit.

He went out into the corridor, closing the office door behind him. Cameras still flashed, white suits still went here and there. Incongruously, as he walked away he wondered if Facilities would fix the General Office door as well as his own. Or would that take another seven years?

Downstairs, Lattouf was standing over the other side of the road by his Datsun. Merhi knew he would not be able to retrieve his Toyota from the building's car park, the place would be in lockdown, so Lattouf was going to get them out of there. He and Lattouf had decided to keep their forensic suits on. Should anyone query why the Datsun was being removed they could say they were taking it away for analysis.

As it turned out, no one stopped them. They had to crawl away slowly so as not to take out several esteemed members of the Lebanese media (the *Al Jazeera* bimbo came within one centimetre of having her ass poked by a Datsun Bluebird wing mirror) and down at Bank of Lebanon Street the policeman proudly and conscientiously in charge of the tape took one look at their forensic suits and held the tape high for them to slip under, Merhi giving a thumbs-up of thanks.

As they turned left, the street becoming Michel Chiha Street, Merhi's phone rang. He looked at the caller ID and answered. "Hi *habibi*."

"Jihad," said Gisele. "I am hearing things. What is going on? Are you all right?"

Coastal Highway, Lebanon 17:10

It took ten minutes to explain, not helped by Gisele's constant interruptions as to his health and well-being. His team were dead – yes, every one of them. Shot. He could be a prime suspect. Ridiculous yes but that was the way these things worked, she was the trainer she would know that. Guilty until proven innocent. He would sort the matter out but he couldn't do it at the office, too much uproar. He was on his way home. What? Fadi Lattouf was driving him, in his car yes – it was a long story. His Toyota was in lockdown. If she was asked, she did not know where he was. Was she on her way home? One hour to prepare for tomorrow's Interrogation Techniques Level 2 Part 1 Day 2 and then she would be leaving. Yes, he would take care. By the time she arrived home he might have got it all sorted. Love you too. Bye, bye, bye.

He had not told her about Carla's text message.

As he hung up he noticed the little red dot with a 1 in it by the phone icon. He had a voicemail. He accessed it on the third attempt.

"Ah, Major Merhi, this is Lieutenant Sebastien, GSU. I have been assigned today's assassinations. I wonder if you could contact me please, as a matter of urgency. My number is..."

Mount Lebanon 17:20

On his prayer mat in the bedroom, Ghazi Kanaan sat back on his haunches, wincing at the pain in his old bones. *Maghrib salat* was completed. Normally he would not observe all five prayers of the day (often he would not observe any) but these were different times, he needed all the help and blessings of the Almighty that he could get.

In two days he would enter Syria. By the end of the week, his country could have a new President. The al-Assad dynasty would be over. He knew his sponsors regarded him as a temporary dressing on the open wound that Syria had become, an interim catalyst to draw the many factions around the conference table, but he had different ideas. Arabs could not be governed by egalitarian means, history had shown that. Democracy was not within their cultural psyche – witness Iraq and Libya and what was happening in Egypt, and the constant pathetic violent stalemate that was Lebanon. Arabs needed to be told how they were to be governed, not be allowed to choose – witness Saudi and even Oman, the UAE and the other Gulf States. Syria did not need democracy, it needed a new dynasty. And he would supply it.

He stood up. Through his half-open bedroom door he could hear the sounds of cooking coming from downstairs. And the sounds of a male and female voice coming from the bathroom along the landing.

The Damascene leant forward as Love rinsed his hair. Gently but effectively her fingers massaged his scalp. It was weird, even for this mistress of the eerie, to feel an ear in one of her hands and nothing in the other.

"Stand please." Although she used the adverb, it was not a request.

The Damascene rose, water rolling down his tanned body.

Love stayed on her knees by the side of the bath. She could see by his reaction that her washing had pleased him. "You will need us again tonight?" she asked.

"Our mission reaches its climax," he said, without a hint of innuendo. "Our minds must be clear, not preoccupied with stress or corporal needs. The best way to deal with these things is to confront them. So yes, you will be required."

She smiled, the green contact lenses illuminated from behind.

"Tell your sister," he instructed.

"She knows. She has heard you. So, soon now we will have our bonus?"

"The bonus will be yours."

She leant forward and kissed his reaction. Then she stood up, undoing the cord from around her waist and letting the thin cotton robe fall to the floor. "I must wash for dinner also," she said as she stepped into the bath next to him. "Will you help me?"

Coastal Highway, Lebanon 17:20

"I think we may have company," said Fadi Lattouf as they drove over Nahr el Kalb (Dog River). His eyes were switching between the road ahead, the rear view mirror and the wing mirrors.

Jihad Merhi had been preoccupied, his dual core train of thought composing the amendments and augmentations he would make to his report and wondering whether or not he should phone this Lieutenant Sebastien, whoever he was. "Mm, what?"

"Way back, there is a motorbike."

"Fadi, there are loads of motorbikes, all around us. This is evening on the Coastal Highway."

Lattouf squinted in the rear view mirror. "In black leathers, helmet, visor down."

Merhi leant forward to look into the right wing mirror and then turned around to look out of the back window. About six vehicles back was the motorbike, as Lattouf had said. It was gaining on them. "Shit."

"Is it him?" asked Lattouf.

"Her," corrected Merhi. "It is a her. It's Carla." He took his Browning from his waistband. "Okay, if this is what she wants."

"You want me to lose her?"

Merhi laughed mirthlessly. "You'll never outrun her in this rust bucket!"

Lattouf took his hands off the wheel, shaking them in supplication, then quickly putting them back on again as the Datsun veered. "My friend, I have not had Donna for two years without making some little, er, modifications to her!"

Donna? He called his car Donna?

"What is it to be?" asked Donna the Datsun's Dad. "Fight or flight?"

Merhi looked back once more. Carla knew where he lived but he might have a better chance in a gunfight in the mountains and there would be less chance of collateral damage. A shootout here on the Highway could cause utter carnage. He said, "Flight."

Lattouf wrenched the gear stick down and hard to the right.

Suddenly Merhi was pressed back in his seat, like an astronaut at the point of take-off. He expected his face to gurn with centrifugal force at any moment. With a beep, beep, beeeep on the horn, Lattouf swerved out into the left lane, 60 to 200 in 15 seconds.

Briefly, the bike disappeared way back. Then the rider realised what was going on and the bike began to move forward again, but it was not approaching at even half the rate it was before. At this pace they could race all the way up the Highway and still be well in front at Byblos.

Merhi remained turned in his seat, gun in hand, not only because he wanted to keep an eye on the bike but also because he would rather not see what was happening in front of the vehicle. The noise of the horn was deafening. He would put his trust in God – and Fadi Lattouf.

"Bravo, Fadi," he said. "Bravo. *Yalla, yalla, yalla.* We'll get her in the mountains."

"That is the problem with taking in waifs and strays," Lattouf had taken his hand off the horn but he still had to shout over the screeching of the engine. "They always then know where you live."

Merhi turned to him, frowning. "But how did she know I was in this car?"

"Might have seen us, might have been following since your offices."

"And we didn't spot her?"

"They can appear and disappear at will."

"Who can?"

"Djinn."

Merhi looked back. "That apply to their motorbikes as well?"

They were coming up to the Kaslik turn off. The bike was still four cars back, at a level distance, not gaining.

"We turn off here, Fadi."

"Yes, my friend."

"Don't you think you better slow dow - "

Merhi banged his head on the window as Lattouf wrenched the car to the right. "No need, Donna can handle bends at speed."

But the Datsun did now have to slow. The road was narrower, climbing, bending its way up the mountain, but Lattouf still took it like a man who had complete trust in Allah. Merhi remained on point, but the road was so twisted that he could not see further than half a kilometre back.

"Sometimes I read your Bible," said Lattouf, one hand on the wheel, one hand on the gear stick, feet moving up and down as if he was playing a pipe organ.

Merhi didn't really think it was the time to have a theological argument. If you want to call God Allah, Fadi, then Allah He is – at least until we get out of this alive. "Really?"

"As I am sure you read the Koran."

"Of course." What was a lie when you were facing imminent eternity?

"Your Saint Matthew said it."

Merhi seriously thought of turning the gun on the Palestinian. "Said what?"

"The first will be last and the last first."

"Well good for him."

"Saving for the Brigadier, you were supposed to be the first of your team to be killed, down in Tyre. But now you are the last. Funny, eh?"

"My sides are splitting."

"The first will be last…"

Merhi banged against the door again, this time with his back, as the Datsun skidded to the right at ninety degrees and shuddered to a stop, gravel dust rising like a smokescreen. He looked out of the window. Somehow they were at his apartment block.

"Right, out!" He unclipped his seatbelt, pushing open the car door. He was used to the height of his Toyota and he jarred his knee painfully when the ground met him half a metre earlier than it usually did.

Lattouf emerged through the gravel dust from around the front of the

Datsun like a genie appearing out of smoke. "Do you have another gun?"

"No."

"I will pretend."

They leant against the shield of the car, Merhi resting his arms on the roof, pointing the Browning down the mountain road, Lattouf resting his arms on the roof, his hand shaped like a gun, his barrel fingers pointing down the mountain road.

Jounieh, Lebanon 18:30

It was getting dark, getting cooler, and the mist on the mountains above was becoming lower by the minute. Soon they might literally have their heads in the clouds.

It had been fifteen minutes and Merhi and Lattouf had not moved from their positions. Lattouf in particular held his arm rigid in readiness, ready to go "Peew, peew, peew" at any bad guy who came up the mountain road. But nobody had, nobody did.

"Don't understand it," Merhi pushed himself up off the Datsun. "She hasn't come. Where is she?"

Lattouf took the signal and relaxed. The Datsun groaned as he pushed himself up off of it. "Maybe she does not fancy taking on two strong men on her own."

Merhi looked around, wondering where the two strong men were, but the gesture was lost on Lattouf. "If she can take on the might of the Lebanese Internal Security Force I don't think we would be any problem for her." He stared down the mountain road which was now covered in mist. "Is she playing with us? What is her game?"

"A game that only one side can win. There can be no stalemate now. Your pieces have been taken and it is just you and your Queen. And your loyal pawn." Lattouf shivered. "It is coming, you know. Winter. I hate Lebanese winters."

"I suppose Palestinian winters are better?"

"We are further south, we have a meteorological superiority."

"Of course you do, by all of eighty kilometres. Come, let us go upstairs." Merhi stopped. "Gisele. She will be here in maybe half an hour. I must warn her." He reached for his phone.

"I don't think this djinn is interested in your wife, Abu Samer. It is you she wants. When your Queen arrives perhaps you should take the advice you have been given."

"Shit, no signal." Merhi held the iPhone in the air, doing the universal little circular dance of a human being without a cell phone connection. "Dammit. Must be the clouds. I'll use the landline. What are you saying,

Fadi? That I should run?"

"Tactically retreat and regroup."

"Let's discuss it upstairs."

"I will just move Donna."

Merhi looked over at the outside parking area. Most other residents were home. "You can squeeze in there, that's where I would normally go, but leave room for Gisele. Or there is an actual sheltered car park down under the building if you would prefer."

"Here will be fine," said Lattouf. "Donna is used to spending her nights out under the... clouds."

He parked expertly, man and machine as one, leaving plenty of room for Gisele's Toyota. Merhi was no longer surprised at his dexterity.

"Gisele will be fine," said Lattouf as he ambled towards the building's entrance.

"Aren't you going to lock it?" Merhi nodded at the Datsun.

"Doesn't lock. If Carla was coming she would have been here by now. Perhaps she is retreating and regrouping also."

"True." Merhi held the door open for the Palestinian to squeeze through.

"But we must be on our guard now, until this is finished," counselled Lattouf.

"We?"

"We. You ate my testicles. We have the bond of salt. I am in this with you. We will triumph. But we must be careful, the djinn, like God, moves in mysterious ways."

"The Bible again," said Merhi as he watched Lattouf ascend the stairs with remarkable lightness considering his massive frame.

"Not at all," said Lattouf over his shoulder, his voice echoing in the stairwell. "That is a common misconception by you Christians. And no, it is not the Koran either. Nor is it Winston Shakespeare. It is the first line of a hymn by Englishman William Cowper, 1731 to 1800. *'God moves in a mysterious way, His wonders to perform, He plants His footsteps in the sea and rides upon the storm.'* Marvelous what you can learn on the game show channel." He reached the landing and stood outside Merhi's front door. "Do you have any food, Abu Samer? A morsel of cheese perhaps? A piece of bread? A whole cooked chicken? All this exercise is making me hungry. I think I have shed ten kilos since we left Beirut."

Mount Lebanon 19:00

Ghazi Kanaan finished the last spoonful of *ashta* (clotted cream with rose water with a fresh strawberry decoration) and put down his spoon. He picked up his coffee, leaning back in the chair. They were seated around the dining table, Kanaan at one end, The Damascene at the other, Love and Paradise on either side. Their main course, a spiced lamb and apricot tagine prepared by Paradise, was long gone, lingering only in the air and their memory. Kanaan would never admit it openly but these bitches could cook.

"Of course Syria has chemical weapons," said Kanaan in response to a question from The Damascene. "We first obtained them from Egypt back in 1973 as a deterrent against the Jews. Later we developed our own capability, with the help of... certain friends."

"But it has never been admitted."

Kanaan sighed, shaking his head like a parent tolerating the ignorance of a child. "They know we have them. We know they know we have them. What is there to admit? It is, if you like, an open secret."

"Does Syria have them or does the regime have them?"

"The regime is Syria. Syria is the regime. And always will be."

The Damascene finished his coffee. "I need to get some air. Abu Yo'roub, will you join me?"

"No, it is too cold out there."

"There is something we must discuss." The Damascene's eyes quickly looked from Paradise to Love then back to Kanaan.

The old man received the message. "If we must."

They went out on to the balcony, The Damascene sliding the door closed behind them. Inside, the twins began to clear away the table.

It was dark outside. The sky was occluded by cloud, the lights of Beirut twinkling like stars way down beyond the wooded mountainside, giving the unnerving impression of the world being upside down. The earth above, the stars below.

"What is it, Mebarak? I am freezing," grumbled Kanaan. "Why don't you just tell those bitches to fuck off? We should not have to come out here."

"What happened in Aleppo in August?"

The question surprised Kanaan. "What? What are you talking about? Aleppo? How should I know? I haven't been to Syria for seven years, as well you know."

"But you have contacts, you must have heard something."

Kanaan looked out over Beirut, over Lebanon, over the country where he had been King for twenty years. He thought about it for a long time before answering. "I have heard that there have been tests – only tests mind – of certain chemical weapons."

"But it has always been the stated position of the Syrian leadership that these weapons – which anyway they don't have – have been made to be used only in the event of external aggression against Syria. They have said they would never be used against the Syrian people."

"And they have not been!" snapped Kanaan. "It *is* external aggression.

Those bastards who are against the regime are not true Syrians."

"You are condoning it?"

"No, I am explaining it."

For a minute neither of them said anything else. Then The Damascene asked, "What will the next regime do?"

Kanaan thought before answering. "There will be no 'next regime', you know that is not what's going to happen. Assad will be removed, I will take over. The regime will stay the same. It is for the good of Syria."

Looking out over Beirut, Kanaan had not heard the balcony door slide back open because it had done so silently. He was not aware of the twins stepping out onto the balcony, no longer wearing their contacts lenses. He saw the man next to him turn and give a short nod, but he thought he was agreeing with his last comment.

Literally his last comment.

Paradise and Love took three steps across the balcony, grabbed one of Kanaan's legs each and threw him over the side of the building.

People do not shout and scream when they are falling to their death, that is only in television and movies. People are too busy wondering what is happening to them or, if they have their wits about them, trying to grab hold of something, to worry about screaming. All Kanaan was aware of was that suddenly he was flying. A not unpleasant sensation but not one that was expected. As he fell he tasted strawberry-flavoured spiced lamb tagine. And just before his head was impaled on a vertical branch of one of the pine trees in the wood below he realised that the last word he ever said was 'Syria'.

The Damascene looked over the edge of the balcony, the *houri* standing next to him. He could see nothing in the darkness below but he knew nobody could survive that fall. He was sad. Not because Kanaan was dead but because he had not had the pleasure of actually physically killing him himself.

The meeting in southern Beirut that morning had been extraordinary, not only for the fact that most known and relevant factions involved in the Syrian civil war had been present by representation (Hizbullah, the al-Abbas Brigade, the PFLP (Popular Front for the Liberation of Palestine), the FSA (Free Syrian Army), the Islamic Front, the al-Nusra Front, the Ahfad al-Rasul Brigade, the Syria Revolutionaries Front, the Army of Mujahedeen, and the Kurdish units) but that they had all agreed on one thing: chemical weapons must not be deployed in the war. The news had come through overnight about the chemical weapons 'testing' by the Syrian regime in Aleppo two months ago. Something that the Opposition factions had thought would never happen, would never be allowed to happen, had happened. This instantly changed the dynamics, the course and the intentions of the war.

Anyone who supported Bashar al-Assad or the Alawite regime must, by default, be considered an apologist for the use of chemical weapons. And as such could no longer feature in the Opposition's plans.

The *houri* moved so that they were standing either side of The Damascene. Their arms came up, one left arm, one right arm, hands resting on his shoulders.

"So do we now get our reward?" asked Love.

Slowly, The Damascene turned. He looked at the glinting white eyes, the flared nostrils, the cheeks just flicked with a hint of pink after the satisfaction of the kill.

"Yes," he said. "The reward is yours. You have earned it."

"And you have earned us," said Paradise as the three of them went back into the apartment, the balcony door sliding closed behind them.

[In November 2013, skeletal remains were found in the wood underneath the apartment building on the Damascus road on the slopes of Mount Lebanon. The body had not been discovered before because it had been wedged high up in the mass of pine trees, invisible from above and invisible from below. It was discovered after a human tibia bone fell out of the trees and nearly hit a local hunter on his way home.

The skeleton has never been identified. There is absolutely no reason to connect it to Major General Ghazi Kanaan, Syrian Interior Minister and erstwhile 'King of Lebanon', who of course was found dead in his office in the Interior Ministry in Damascus on 12 October 2005 having been shot through the mouth by a .38 Smith & Wesson.]

Jounieh, Lebanon 19:05

Gisele Merhi opened the front door of the apartment and froze. A gun was pointing straight into her face. For the briefest of seconds she thought that her life was over, but then she relaxed when she saw that it was her husband who was holding it.

"Gigi, thank God." Jihad embraced his wife. Behind him Fadi Lattouf put down the chef's knife which he had been holding in the air as if he was re-enacting the shower scene from *Psycho*.

"Jihad, what the hell is going on?" Gisele looped her bag over one of the hooks on the wall and pulled off her black jacket. "Your team is dead?"

"Every one of them. And she's after me."

"Who is?"

"Carla."

"*What?* I don't understand."

Jihad explained as he followed his wife into the kitchen, Lattouf ambling along behind. "It's simple really. She is working for the Israelis. They are annihilating all the ISF spycatchers, not only in revenge for our success but also to leave the way clear for a new wave of spies to emerge in Beirut."

"But Carla? She was here with us, she said there was a spy in the ISF."

"Disinformation. And she has told me to run for my life."

"She has told you to run for your life and yet she wants to kill you?" She opened the fridge door.

"I think she's playing a game, enjoying the hunt. You know what she's like. The mysterious Djinn!"

"Where's the chicken gone?" Gisele frowned into the fridge.

Both men looked guilty. Lattouf smiled wanly like a fox caught with feathers in his mouth.

"I see. You have fed our guest."

"Just an *hors d'oeuvre*," said Lattouf. "We had a stressful journey."

Jihad explained about the motorbike on the Coastal Highway, their evasion and then their attempt at confrontation. "But she didn't follow us up here."

"But she knows where we live."

"Yes, Fadi made that point too."

"There is another point I would like to make," said Lattouf. The Merhis looked at him. "That is a mighty fine sea bass you have there," he nodded at the fridge. "Your cooking is divine, Umm Samer. Will you be...?"

She sighed. "Gisele, please. Or Gigi. Not Umm Samer. I can make it stretch to three."

"Yes, particularly if you add vegetables and rice. Often I advise Nada on her cooking."

"And I am sure she appreciates that. I'm going to get out of these work clothes, have a shower and then I will prepare it."

"I'm going to access the system," said Jihad. "Update my report. See if I can get an ATL out on Carla. We've got to get her."

"Is it too much to hope that she has changed her mind?" wondered Lattouf. "She has got everyone else, maybe she will leave you alone. Because of your friendship. The two of you. You two, I mean." He flapped his hand between Jihad and Gisele.

"Then what was all that down on the Highway?"

"A good point, my friend. I am just talking out loud."

"Come Fadi, my woman needs her space."

In the lounge, Lattouf said softly "Not Umm Samer?"

"The boys are mine, not hers."

"I did not know that."

"Rita, my first wife, died many, many years ago. Gigi adopted the boys, but she is not their biological mother."

"If I have caused offence I must apologise to her."

"No, no, don't worry."

"How are the boys? I have not asked."

"Fine, fine. Samer is a pharmacist in Rome, Sary plays for Inter Milan Under 21s. They say he has a good future."

Lattouf nodded. "We must socialise more often, Abu Samer. After we've got this little matter out of the way."

Jihad said, "She is stressed, you know. Gisele."

"As I hope Nada would be if I had been threatened."

"She has been touching her *wasm*."

"I beg your pardon?"

Merhi touched his neck. "The scar. She calls it her *wasm*, her camel's brand. She always touches it when she is stressed or nervous."

"I like camels, supreme creatures."

"Talking of which," Merhi offered his cigarette pack.

Lattouf helped himself. "Purely for medicinal purposes. To relieve the stress of the day."

Merhi went over to the drinks cabinet. "Would you like a Coke?"

"You are the most genial host."

"I'm having a little whisky in mine." He held up a bottle of Chivas Regal. "But you Muslims don't drink, do you?"

"Alcohol, no. So I will just have a small one," Lattouf held up three fingers as Merhi poured the Chivas into two glasses. "Purely for medicinal purposes."

"To relieve the stress of the day?"

"What a good idea."

Ashrafieh, Beirut 19:20

Carla sat on the easy chair in her room in the Hotel Albergo, her legs in the lotus position. She was in her T-shirt and pants, her biker's leathers over the chair in front of the vanity unit. Her eyes were closed, the headphones still in her ears, her iPhone on the chair in the warm canyon created by her legs.

She had not only heard them at dinner, she had watched them as well. She could see the entire lounge area via the camera in the Sony smart TV on the wall of the apartment, even when the television was not on. She had seen and heard her husband and Ghazi Kanaan discussing the chemical weapons capability of the Syrian regime. Then they had, literally, taken it outside and she had lost access to them. But she had seen the bitch *houri* tidy up the table then walk calmly back into the room and, seemingly, bow their heads to each other. She knew what that meant. They were taking out their contact lenses. And she knew what that meant also. They did not like to kill with their lenses in.

She saw them glide across the lounge. It was probably an optical illusion, a deception of the camera angle, but it looked like the balcony door slid open without either of them touching it. They went outside.

Five minutes later they were back. With Marwan, her husband. But without Ghazi Kanaan.

What had happened? Well, it didn't take a genius (or a djinnius) to work it out. The lenses had been removed for a purpose. Kanaan had been, in *houri* parlance, converted. But why? After seven years? Something must have gone terribly wrong. Someone must have changed their mind big time.

As her husband and the bitches had re-entered the lounge, one of the bitches was speaking. " – earned us." The three of them walked across to the stairs on the right of the television, out of view.

"She is ours." (It might have been the other bitch talking, Carla couldn't tell, their voices were identical.) "I will suck her essence from her putrid carcass."

Marwan did not respond, but Carla heard his footsteps on the stairs (the *houri* would be soundless) and she knew where they were going. She had microphones in the bedrooms but no cameras, but she did not change the phone App to follow them. She did not need aural confirmation of what was about to happen.

She took out the earphones, wondering what her husband would do when she made her confession. What would they *all* do? For she had the matter of Major Jihad Merhi to finalise also. Nobody would like what was going to happen, but things needed to be finished.

Once and for all.

Jounieh, Lebanon 19:30

"First things first," said Jihad Merhi, exhaling smoke. "I'll amend my report and then put the ATL out on Carla – pity we don't have any pictures of her." He was sitting at the table in the lounge, the ATS laptop open and humming in front of him.

Lattouf was lounging on one of the leather couches, enjoying his second Chivas and Coke. Purely for medicinal purposes. "Is there not one in her staff records?"

"She is GSU, not ISF. I doubt I'll be able to access them, even on this. But I'll try – oh fuck."

"My friend? What is it?"

"Fadi, look at this."

With a crackle of leather, Lattouf arose from the couch. He frowned over Merhi's shoulder. "I don't have my glasses."

Merhi ripped the ones from his own face and passed them over.

Lattouf frowned at the screen. "Ah."

Merhi's report was on the screen in the background but a banner had flashed up over it. It was an ATL, an Attempt To Locate. Priority: Immediate. On the screen was a picture of Major Jihad Merhi of the Internal Security Force. Wanted for questioning in connection with the shootings in Jonblat this afternoon. Immediate apprehension required but approach with caution, considered dangerous.

"Shit and fuck!" Merhi grabbed his phone from the table, his thumb moving like someone in the final stages of Parkinson's, tapping and scrolling to his Missed Calls log. He pressed more icons then put the phone to his ear.

After a few moments, he said "Lieutenant Sebastien, Major Jihad Merhi... No, I have been busy. Avoiding the assassin. Just got your message. What's this fucking ATL?... I told you, I just got your message... No, I'm not at home. Somebody is trying to kill me... My team was not safe in our own fucking building, what good would protective custody do me?... I don't know, maybe tomorrow. I've got to sort this out... No, I told you, I'm not at home... Right, okay." He tapped the red icon. *"Con."*

"What did he say?" asked Lattouf.

"Wants to speak to me immediately. Suggests *if what I am saying is true* that I should come into protective custody. Jesus -"

"Isa and all the saints."

" – that's straight out of Securing Custody Techniques Basic Day 1. But he said he'll take the ATL down."

"That is good. And Carla?"

"This has got to end, Fadi, this has got to end. Let's put the ATL out on her." Merhi paused, fingers hovering over the keyboard like a concert pianist awaiting the fall of the baton. Then he said, "What the hell do I say?"

"Just describe her and why she is wanted."

"What? Name: Zahia Zalloum, Carla Chedid, Suzi Saad? Known as The Djinn? Member of the General Security Unit, at least was. Sent into exile. Wanted for questioning over the assassination of Rafic Hariri. Known involvement in the al-Mahdi incident. Now thought responsible for the extermination of the entire ISF spycatcher division – except me?"

"Just name, description and current reason for interest." Lattouf was pouring more whisky into Merhi's glass, and taking a top-up for himself also. "It is a pity we do not have a photograph but that is the position in which we find ourselves."

"I'm going to look like a fool."

"A fool who is under arrest for multiple counts of murder if we don't sort this out."

"You're right." Merhi's fingers began to move over the keyboard.

Lattouf went over to the patio doors, looking out into the darkness. He couldn't see much outside, mostly the reflection of the room behind him, but it looked like the mist had cleared although the sky was still black. The winter's rain would not be too far away.

"How about this?" said Merhi after a few minutes. Lattouf turned around, staying by the glass door.

"Carla Chedid also known as Zahia Zalloum. Maybe using the name Suzi Saad. AKA: The Djinn. Female. Age: 30+. Nationality: Lebanese – I assume. Height 1.4 metres approx. Build: Petite."

"What about her...?" Lattouf nodded to his own chest and made an 'arthritis' gesture with the hand that was not holding the glass.

"Stop it. Hair: Black, long, thick. Eyes: Black. Skin: Type 4. Wanted for questioning in connection with the murder of ISF officers. Known to use a motorbike as method of transportation. Last known location: Beirut. Immediate apprehension required. OIC: Me... What do you think?"

"Better than nothing, but without a photograph..."

"I know, I know. I'll try it and see." Merhi's fingers moved over the keyboard again, accessing programs, copying, pasting, confirming his Authority To Issue, Are you sure you wish to proceed? Yes. "There, it's gone."

"So all we do now is wait?"

From the kitchen there came the sound of sizzling. "And eat," said Merhi, turning in his chair.

"I am famished," said Lattouf. "And talking of eating, we should consider a tethered goat."

"A what?"

"A tethered goat. To supplement your ATL. You. If Carla wants to kill you, if she is coming for you, we should stake you out in plain sight. Lure her. And when she comes, pounce!"

Merhi was not going to let on that he had thought the same thing, but he needed more than Fadi Lattouf to do the pouncing. "Thank you, Fadi, we 'll cross that *jisr* when we come to it."

From the kitchen, Gisele called "Dinner in two minutes!"

"That's our cue to wash and freshen up," Merhi turned back to the laptop. "I'll close this down for now - " He paused. "Hold on..." He moved his finger over the track pad, clicking and refreshing. He gazed intently at the screen and then said, "You fucker."

"What is it?"

"Sebastien. He has not removed the ATL on me."

"Not only that," said Lattouf. "Look." He pointed out into the darkness.

Merhi came over. He tried to see but the internal reflection was too strong. "What?"

"Down there."

Merhi strained to see. "Turn the lights out, Fadi."

Lattouf waddled over to the light switch on the wall. The room was plunged into darkness save for the rectangular beam from the screen of the laptop.

Now Merhi could make it out. The immediate mountainside could not be seen from the apartment because of the wide balcony, but beyond the edge there was a good view of the Coastal Highway way down below and the first half kilometre or so of the mountain road.

And on that mountain road was a convoy of vehicles with flashing lights.

"But I told him I wasn't here! The bastard. How did he - ?"

Lattouf took two steps over to the table, picked up Merhi's iPhone and slammed it onto the floor, stamping on it once, twice, three times. Merhi looked on aghast.

"Your GPS," explained Lattouf.

Merhi's mouth moved then his voice came out afterwards, almost out of sync. "What the fuck? Couldn't you have just removed the battery and the SIM?"

"No time to worry about that now. Anyway it was a 4, you need an upgrade to the 5. I have done you a favour."

"What is going on?" Gisele was standing in the doorway, illuminated from behind. "What was that banging?"

"Gigi, we need to go. They're coming for me." Jihad nodded backwards to the balcony.

"How far?"

"Ten minutes."

Gisele left the doorway, moving fast, first to the kitchen to turn off the food then to the bedroom.

"But how can we get past them?" Lattouf quickly finished his drink.

Jihad was busy closing down programs on the laptop, signing out, pressing buttons. "Upwards. There is a back way, over the top, around Harissa. We'll take my – er, we'll take Gisele's car."

"But what about Donna?"

"Don - ?"

"If we are running, she is quicker than any Toyota."

"Ready?" Gisele was back in the doorway, bag over her shoulder.

Merhi pulled out the systems access card from the side of the laptop. "We're taking Donna."

"What?"

"Fadi's car."

"We are?"

"It is faster," said Lattouf.

Gisele gave her husband the raised eyebrows.

"It is, believe me," confirmed Jihad as he slipped his Browning into the holster on his waistband and pulled on his jacket. "You are in for... an experience - "

"I will drive," announced Lattouf.

" - in more ways than one." He kissed Gisele on the forehead. "*Yalla,* let's go."

They dashed down the stairs, the Merhis in front, Lattouf a little way behind balancing a platter of pan-fried sea bass in his right hand.

Jounieh, Lebanon 20:45

The three cars pulled up outside the apartment block, their flashing red, white and blue lights illuminating the area, looking like a mobile disco had come to town. Already other residents of the building were looking out of their windows.

Lieutenant Jacques Sebastien, young, wet behind the ears, out to make a name for himself, got out of the first car, followed by his Sergeant Christof Howdra. From the other cars, assorted crime scene and anti-terrorist officers appeared, the latter carrying a frightening array of weapons.

Sebastien looked up at the building. "Which one is it?"

"Top floor, sir. All of it," said Howdra.

"Someone's there, the lights are on."

"Shall I clear the building?"

"No time." Sebastien nodded at the assembled men behind him. "We're going in now."

The Lebanese Mountains 21:00

Donna the Datsun Bluebird complained like a newborn baby as it headed up into the mountains but it kept it's speed, putting the Merhis' apartment building out of sight way behind them. Inside, Donna smelt of petrol, sweat, old leather, perfume, farts and pan-fried sea bass.

They reached the top, up by the village of Ghosta, and there were three sighs of relief as they joined the road which would take them round to Harissa and onwards.

"Right," said Lattouf relaxing, his sweat betraying the effort of the drive up the mountain. "Where exactly are we going?"

"Friends are out of the question," said Merhi, watching the beams bounce in the darkness on the marginally better road. "I could simply go and face Sebastien and co, but in the office, on my terms. But would that be a good idea right now? I didn't manage to amend my report, so officially I'm still saying there is a spy in the ISF. And I'm the only one left."

"What does our trainer say?" Lattouf glanced in the rear view mirror. Gisele was in the back seat with a platter of cooling pan-fried sea bass on her lap.

"I don't think going in to confront them at this time is the best idea." The fish bounced as the marginally better road became marginally worse again. "We need to take stock, regroup, plan. Somewhere safe where we will not be found – by anybody."

"My place it is then," nodded Lattouf. "Good choice, that's what I would have done."

Jihad protested. "But Fadi, we can't endanger you and your family."

"My friend, I am in this now almost as much as you. I am glad I'm not the target but I am involved. It is my duty to protect you. The bond of salt. Nada will not mind, in fact she will insist, and the children would love to see you. And, let's face it, who would think of looking for a fugitive Major of the Lebanese Internal Security Force in the Bourj el-Barajneh Palestinian refugee camp!" He was the only one in the car to laugh. "That is a brilliant idea, Umm – Gisele."

Gisele frowned at the back of Lattouf's head. "But what about the roadblocks? The ATL on Jihad is an Immediate Apprehension, they will be checking vehicles."

"I know where they will be," said Jihad. "We'll drive around them."

"And I know the streets of south Beirut," said Lattouf. "We'll drive around them too!"

They had rounded Harissa and were now descending again, the road no less treacherous because of the downward inclination. They would hit the Coastal Highway at Nahr el Kalb. Literally, thought Jihad Merhi, if the brakes on this rust bucket failed.

They were the only ones on the winding, twisting road at this hour. Outside it was dark, lonely and sinister. Inside, Fadi Lattouf sniffed and once again looked in his rearview mirror. He asked, "I don't suppose anybody thought of bringing a fork or a spoon, did they? Or a piece of bread?"

Mount Lebanon 21:30

Love and Paradise lay naked, face down on the wide bed in The Damascene's room, heads turned towards each other, smiling. They did not sweat, never had never would, despite the exertions. But their activities had left them with pink scratches on their bottoms and thighs, the whiteness of their skin emphasising the scars of the sexual battle, making the marks look worse than they were. By the morning they would have disappeared.

The Damascene stood by the side of the bed, looking at the women, the creatures that it had taken him two hours to subdue and even then only temporarily. His dark hairless body was glistening, his face and groin wet. They always paid particular attention to the hole in the left side of his head and their bodily fluid was still oozing out of it, like syrup. The teeth marks on his shoulders and upper arms would still be there in the morning and for some days to come.

One of the twins purred. The other one leant over and licked her back, like a cat washing a kitten.

The Damascene pulled open a drawer. Two items were inside. One was a cell phone. The other was a Holding Cross, a ten centimetre long piece of solid olive wood carved into the shape of a cross with the cross beam uneven to fit comfortably between a person's fingers, made exclusively in Beit Sahour, near Bethlehem in Palestine. It was his weapon of preference, he had killed many with it.

He touched the phone and the cross. Suddenly he was aware that the air had changed behind him. He turned. The twins were standing a metre away, their white eyes glistening. He could feel the heat emanating from their bodies.

"You are superb," said the one on the left. "Truly you give us more than anybody ever has."

"You are Shaitan's acolyte," said the other one.

"I am simply human," said The Damascene. "Unlike you."

"There is one thing more that you have to give us."

He stared into the white eyes on the right. "She is yours."

"Now?"

"Now."

The two faces smiled, eyes half closing in ecstasy. The one on the left said, "Then we will clean ourselves and prepare." She noticed something on her sister's left breast, touched it with her finger and put the finger in her mouth.

"We shall make a clean conversion," said the one on the right as they walked out of the bedroom.

The Damascene stared at the doorway for a few moments, the image of their identical bodies imprinted on his mind. Then he turned back to the drawer and picked up one of the objects.

Ashrafieh, Beirut 21:45

In her room in the Hotel Albergo, Carla looked at the item on her iPhone, spreading her fingers, zooming in, shaking her head in sadness. Oh Jihad, you stupid, stupid man. Why had you put out the ATL on her? You had no picture but it was a good description, especially the bit about the motorbike. Now she would have to be careful. But at least you were running. Running for your life, that was good. But if only you knew. Now she really would have to find you. Your GPS had stopped two hours ago, last location Jounieh. Very good, you had realised they were tracking you. You might be able to avoid your law enforcement colleagues but you could never outrun a djinn.

Especially a djinn that had not only cloned your phone but your wife's as well.

She looked at the ATL again. Would they be stopping all bikers in Beirut? She would be covered by her leathers and the helmet and visor – but what if they asked her to take the helmet off? Female. Age: 30+. Nationality: Lebanese. Height 1.4 metres approx. Build: Petite. Hair: Black, long, thick. Eyes: Black. Skin: Type 4. They would have her.

So, it was time for the confession. For something no one knew, not even her husband. She had no choice.

She stood up and removed the black and gold hairclip from the scrunch at the back of her head. She leant forward, shaking her hair, letting it cascade down around her face. Then she reached up, massaging her head where the scrunch had been. Rubbing, maneuvering, shaking, pulling, gently, carefully, painfully, ripping…

Her hair came off in one piece. She straightened up, looking at herself in the mirror, at the close-cropped white stubble on her head. She peeled off her dark eyebrows. Then she leant forward, rubbing her eyes. And straightened up again, the black contact lenses in her hands, her white eyes staring back at her from the mirror.

The mirror of her true soul.

Jounieh, Lebanon 21:45

Lieutenant Jacques Sebastien was not happy as he pushed through the main door of the apartment building and went back outside into the night. In fact his young, wet behind the ears face looked like it might burst into tears at any moment, his pout making him look like a duck.

Merhi was not there. And neither was his wife. But the smell of cooking and the warmth of the hob told Sebastien he had missed them only by minutes. They must have seen them coming. Their apartment was like a watchtower up there, they had a good view down the mountainside. He should have thought of that.

His men had searched the other apartments in the block, just in case some kindly misguided neighbour was giving the Jewish spy sanctuary, but they had come away empty-handed. Neighbours said how nice the Merhis were and hadn't the Captain recently been celebrating a promotion?

To make his presence felt, and out of sheer spite, Sebastien had ordered that the Merhis' apartment be ransacked. His men had been reluctant but they had complied, no drawer unturned, no cupboard unemptied, no mattress or chair unripped, no skirting board unprised, no power source unscrewed. And all they had at the end of the carnage was what they had found on first entering the apartment: a smashed iPhone and an official ATS laptop, which was useless without the machine- and person-specific systems access card, which was nowhere to be found.

Sebastien stood with his hands on his hips looking up at the dark sky. So where had Merhi gone? No vehicle had passed the convoy on the road so he must have gone up the mountain. There must be a way out up and over. But what had they used? Merhi's official Toyota was in lockdown at the State Security Building, Madame Merhi's ex-official Toyota was here, right in front of him. Surely they weren't fleeing on foot across the mountains, like a Levantine version of *The Sound of Music*?

Sebastien stared at Madame Merhi's car. They would take that away. He did not expect to find anything but they would examine it until it was a write-off, just for the sake of it. He turned and then turned back again. There was an empty space next to the Toyota... Had they had help? Was someone else with them? Perhaps he should have ordered his team to dust the apartment for fingerprints, but it was too late now, they had been all over it. It had not been that type of search.

"Sir?" Sergeant Howdra walked out of the darkness by the side of the building.

"Yes Christof, what is it?"

"There's another parking area under the building, sir. It's a bit of a slope to get down there, it's hardly ever used, so the neighbours tell me. It's empty now."

"So?"

"Empty except for one thing." Howdra nodded over his shoulder as one of the Corporals came round the corner wheeling something up the slope.

Beirut 22:30

There are many ATLs on the security systems of Lebanon, some going back as far as the events (the civil war) and one even to the French mandate. ATLs are usually read by law enforcement officers on the day they are issued and are then left on file in the system until the subject is later apprehended for some other reason. There is one exception: ATLs flagged 'Immediate Apprehension'. They appear on the system in red and demand a proactive response for 48 hours: enquiries, searches, road blocks (after 48 hours their colour is changed to black and white and they join the thousands of other ATLs waiting like *yatama* for the attention that will never be paid to them).

The Djinn had seen that the ATL on Carla Chedid was for Immediate

Apprehension. The Last Known Location was Beirut. Therefore there would be checks on various main arteries going out of the city and some in town also. But she would be allowed to proceed – she looked nothing like the description given.

She left the Hotel Albergo dressed in her leathers, nodding at the Concierge desk as she crossed the foyer. Nobody knew who the woman with the cropped white hair and white eyes was but she walked purposefully as if she was a guest, as if she belonged. She must have been checked in on the previous shift.

The roads of Ashrafieh were busy and she attracted no attention other than the occasional stud smile (a woman in leather, wow!) as she walked the eight hundred metres to the indoor Parking next to the ABC shopping mall. She picked up her Honda VFR1200FD. This time there was no one waiting for her as she left. She drove down Ashrafieh Street, touched Elias Sarkis Avenue and crossed Damascus Street.

Damascus Street. The Green Line of Beirut during the events of 1975 to 1990, the division between the Muslims to the west and the Christians to the east. Called the Green Line because of the foliage that grew in the uninhabited space. Nowadays there was no trace of the foliage, no evidence of the Green Line – except in people's memories.

And further down that long, long street, in the apartment on the slopes of Mount Lebanon, were the *houri*, the bitches that two years ago had taken her, tortured her, raped her, killed her and brought her back to life – but never, not even during the most debased moments when they had done things to her that only a female would know how to do to another female, had the *houri* discovered the true djinn. They had said that they thought she was like them, but they had not known how right they were.

Well, tonight they would find out.

And they would die.

The Djinn drove down Bechara el Khoury Avenue then took a right into the backstreets of southern Beirut.

Mount Lebanon 22:30

The *houri* were dressed in denim-look jeggings, baseball boots, black T-shirts and black cotton jackets which gave a sharp monochromatic contrast to their blonde/white hair and white eyes.

The Damascene handed over the phone he had taken from the drawer in the bedroom. "The tracker app is open. The blip is her."

Love took the phone, checked the battery (full) and studied the screen. A small red dot was moving over a map of Beirut.

"What if she ditches her phone?" asked Paradise looking over her sister's shoulder. "Or has ditched it already? How can we be certain this is her?"

"She can ditch as many phones as she likes," said The Damascene. "The signal is not coming from her phone."

"The bug is on her bike?" asked Love.

"Her clothes?" Paradise.

"No."

The *houri* smiled. "She is the bug," said Love.

"It is inside her," said Paradise.

The Damascene said nothing.

"Has it been there long?" asked Love. "We didn't find it when we were inside her."

"We didn't have eyes on our fingers," said Paradise.

Love smiled at the memories.

"It was a wedding present," said The Damascene. "I always like to know where my property is. She knows nothing about it."

"You are a bad, bad man." Paradise kissed him on the mouth, her tongue – barbed like a cat's – licking the inside of his upper lip.

"Very bad." Love's rough tongue scratched the hole of his left ear.

"The money has been transferred," said The Damascene. "When you are finished, you may return here to collect your things and leave that phone."

"We will leave pictures on it for you - "

" – of her empty shell."

"The door will be open. Latch it when you leave. I will not see you again."

"Until the next assignment?" wondered Paradise.

The Damascene did not respond to the suggestion. As the *houri* went out the door, he said "May ad-Dajjal go with you."

"Our father always does," said Love as they went down the stairs.

Bourj el-Barajneh, Beirut 23:00

"Wife, you have saved my life," said Fadi Lattouf in earnest gratitude, putting the spoon down after his third bowl of *shorbat adas* (lentil soup). "And it went particularly well with the cold sea bass. Abu Samer, you are not hungry?"

Jihad and Gisele Merhi sat awkwardly at the table in the room which served as the sole living area in the small two-storey abode that was *Villa Lattouf*.

Jihad said. "Fadi, you are too kind. And Nada, I mean no disrespect, but two bowls is enough, *merci*."

"Nada, this bread is wonderful," said Gisele. "Did you make it yourself?"

"Nothing more than any wife would do," smiled Nada Lattouf modestly.

If she had minded her husband turning up late at night with unexpected guests, and these two unexpected guests at that, she had not shown it. When Fadi had slammed through the front door with a bang loud enough to awaken the dead as far away as Tripoli (but not the six Lattouf children who were all asleep in their bedroom upstairs), shouting "Woman, we need sanctuary!", she had greeted the Merhis warmly, her only concession to their arrival being to retire momentarily to put an *hijab* over her head. Now she stood up. "I shall make coffee. Or is it too late?"

"It is never too late for *qahwa*!" Fadi spoke for them all. After the journey they had had, after the day they had had, after the life they had had, they needed coffee. Now.

After Nada had gone into the kitchen, carrying an armful of plates, Fadi asked, "So, what are we going to do?"

"*I* am going to rip the tiny bollocks off Lieutenant Sebastien and feed them to him like grapes, that's what I'm going to do," growled Jihad.

"After you've cleared your name," said Gisele with the calm and reason of a trainer. "Priorities, Jihad."

Jihad sighed. He was desperate for a cigarette but he knew smoking was banned by the woman of the house. "I shall go in tomorrow. Confront them on *my* terms. There was no way I was going to be led off in handcuffs in the middle of the night from my own home. Sebastien will have some explaining to do, I can tell you."

Gisele nodded. "Pity you didn't bring the laptop with you."

"Yes, I could have amended my report here and now. Do you have Wifi, Fadi?"

"In the office, in the camp. It sometimes stretches this far."

"But you know what? At the end of the day - "

"Which this is," agreed Fadi logically.

" – I'm the innocent party here. I'm not the fucking Israeli spy!" He looked towards the kitchen and then gave a silent mouth-shrug of apology for the swearing. "Is it my fault I'm still alive and all the others are dead?" Gisele touched his right hand with hers, subconsciously raising her left hand to touch the scar on her neck. Jihad noticed the movement and gave her hand a squeeze. Then he asked, "Can we go outside, Fadi? I'm dying for a Camel. Angel, do you want one?"

Gisele shook her head.

"We will go out the back," Fadi got up, remembering not to lean on the table for support (what had happened last time did not bear thinking about). "It is not good to be out in the street at this hour."

While the women washed up, the men were in the little two square metre walled yard at the back of the house. Fadi had received special dispensation to have one cigarette, just the one mind, Nada was not having him slip back into old habits.

For half a cigarette (which was just two drags in Fadi's case) they said nothing. Then a sigh by Jihad broke the silence, so Fadi said "You will sleep in our room tonight, you and your good lady."

"Not at all, Fadi, not at all. We will sleep downstairs on the chairs. That is your room."

"You are our guests."

"And you..." Jihad looked at the Palestinian giant, the mountain of a man with the scruffy salt and pepper beard, the ridiculous comb over, the concerned face, and the explosive stomach which would have western doctors prescribing him statins like M&Ms. The man who had put himself and his family at risk. "You are a true friend." Jihad extended his hand. "Thank you. I will not forget this."

"What are friends for?" Fadi took the hand and then pulled Jihad towards him, crushing him in a bear hug.

When the hug was released (which was entirely at Fadi's caprice, Jihad did not have the ability to move while in hold), was there a wetness in the corner of a Lattouf eye?

"I have never had friends, you know. Not real friends." Fadi looked everywhere but at Jihad. "In my job and..." he gestured at himself. "How could I? I am so pleased that I can help you."

Jihad did not know what to say.

Fadi's hands were clasped together, his head bowed. "When you told me about your first wife I was, you know, proud. Proud that you would entrust me with such knowledge. Only a true friend would do that. You do not judge me, Abu Samer. You accept me for what I am."

Jihad felt the guilt of the world descend on his shoulders. He had not judged him? Like shit. Only not to his face. Coward. Now he felt like pulling out his gun and blowing his own brains out. He reached up and kissed the Palestinian three times on the cheeks. "I *am* your friend, Fadi." He tried his own hug but all he succeeded in doing was to put his head on the giant's chest as if he was a medic listening for a heartbeat. "But that doesn't mean I'm sleeping in your room tonight! We'll stay down here."

Fadi laughed as the sadness evaporated from his eyes. "If you can convince Nada, I will agree!"

"I'll put Gisele onto that!" He clapped Fadi on the shoulder. "Any more of this open emotion and we'll be comparing willie size!"

"That would put you at an unfair disadvantage. And I will not be giving you a head start!"

"Come, it's going to rain at any minute. You'll probably feel it up there before I do, you big lump."

Laughing, the two men went back inside.

In the kitchen, the plates had been washed up and were draining on the side. The smell of coffee came from the living area.

Fadi and Jihad walked in. And stopped dead, the smiles falling from their faces.

Nada was sitting on one of the battered old couches, pale, her eyes desperate.

Gisele was standing against the far wall.

Pointing a Herstal FN Five-SeveN at the men, the new BFFs.

Jonblat, Beirut 23:15

There were plenty of empty spaces around Major Merhi's decuma grey Toyota Land Cruiser V8 in the car park of the State Security building. Most other vehicles had been allowed to leave once the Toyota had been checked by the bomb unit and found to be clear. The fact that nothing suspicious had been found would not stop the Toyota being stripped down to its chassis, thought Lieutenant Jacques Sebastien as he parked Gisele's blue Land Cruiser LC5 two spaces away. He left the dipped beams on for illumination and stepped out, beckoning Sergeant Howdra who had been following him in one of the official vehicles.

"Chris, give me a hand, would you?"

Howdra came over as Sebastien raised the back of the LC5.

"It'll be easier getting it out," assured Sebastien.

They leant in, grunting, groaning, pulling.

"It's spilt some oil," said Howdra.

"Who cares? This car will never see the Coastal Highway again, not after I've finished with it."

Howdra humphed and braced his arms, steadying himself. With a few scrapes and a final bounce, they managed to get the item from the back of the car, both of them frantically steadying it as it hit the floor. It was the item Sergeant Howdra had found in the never-used parking area underneath the Merhis' building.

The Ducati Multistrada 1200 motorbike.

Bourj el-Barajneh, Beirut 23:30

The Confession looked at the three people in front of her: the idiot Lattouf, his stupid fat wife and... her own husband.

"Gigi?" Jihad gave the puzzled half laugh of disbelieving bewilderment that humans give when they are confused. He made to come towards her but she stopped him with a flick of the gun.

"Draw your gun, Jihad."

"What?"

"Draw your gun and pass it to me. Don't try any heroics because I will shoot you."

"What's going on?" He asked the question as he pulled his Browning from the holster by his fingertips, holding it out.

She took it with her right hand. "Sit down." She motioned to the couch.

Jihad shook his head, still not comprehending.

"Now."

Staring at his wife, he went over and sat next to Nada Lattouf.

"And you." She moved the gun towards Fadi.

Knowing he would not fit on the couch with Nada and Jihad, Fadi went to sit down on the opposite couch, also knowing that by doing so he would be widening the range over which Gisele would have to aim.

"Not there!" snapped The Confession. "Do you think I am stupid?"

"Anyone who uses a SWR Spectre 2 suppressor on a Five-SeveN is not stupid," said Lattouf. "You must have an EFK threaded barrel as well then."

"Well now, you're not as thick as you look, are you?"

"No."

"Sit on the floor. At your wife's feet. Where you belong."

Fadi did as he was told, dropping arse-first onto the floor like a hundred and seventy kilo sack of potatoes falling off a lorry in the Beirut Vegetable Market in El Chiah.

"Gigi?" said Jihad. "What the hell - ?"

"Shut up, Jihad."

"Please," said Nada. "I do not know what this is about but please - my children."

"Your children will be safe." Just for a moment there was a flicker of woman-to-woman compassion in The Confession's eyes. Then she said, "Unless they come down stairs."

Nada sniffed.

"Start that bloody wailing and I will shoot you," said The Confession. "And your damn children."

Nada looked up with red-rimmed eyes but she did not wail.

"What is going on, Gigi?" Jihad's face was stone. "Is there something I do not know?"

The Confession laughed mirthlessly. "Something you do not know? You know nothing, you pathetic man. For fourteen years you have known nothing. Fourteen years of your smoking, your drinking, your fucking, your damned family with whom I had to pretend to get along, even to *like*, when all I wanted to do was scream, to put a gun to their heads."

"*You* married me."

"On orders."

There was silence. On the floor, Fadi popped out a sharp little fart but he was ignored. "Excuse me, the fish."

"On orders?" said Jihad.

"Sorry *husband*, this isn't a movie. No expatiation, no explanation."

Jihad rubbed his hands down his face. "*'There is a spy in the ISF.'* Carla was right, wasn't she? And it *was* me..."

"Only you didn't know it."

"The one remaining Israeli deep-cover operative in Beirut. My wife."

The Confession touched the *wasm* on her neck. "But now the spy has to go."

"You are leaving?"

"No, you are. As far as everyone is concerned you are the spy, remember?"

"Why did you miss me at Tyre?"

"The speed, the angle..."

"No. I know you. If that was you then you deliberately missed. Couldn't you bring yourself to kill me? And why haven't you popped me off in the last four days? It would have been so easy. When we were sleeping, even when we were fucking - "

"Shut up. And you shut up too!" A whimper had come from Nada causing Fadi to put a comforting hand on her foot.

"You were saved by the God you do not believe in," continued The Confession. "At the very moment I was aiming into your window, word came through that I was to hold off. My controllers had just read my report that the new head of the spycatchers was my own husband, they needed time to consider, to see if that changed things."

"And did it?"

"It would have done if it had not been for that interfering bitch Carla. I could have slipped back into my cover, played the dutiful wife for fourteen more years, feeding them information from the head of the spycatchers. But she had to tell you there was a spy, didn't she? You had to start investigating. So I was ordered to continue with my mission."

"Who are your controllers?"

"Well now, who do you think?"

"Mossad," said Fadi Lattouf.

"Give the fat guy a cigar. Oh no, that would mean you would have to go outside and smoke it behind your wife's back, wouldn't it?"

"You abuse me, you abuse my family's hospitality - "

The Herstal spat.

Nada gave a stifled scream, she couldn't help herself. Fadi looked at the hole in the linoleum between his legs. Two more centimetres and Abu Samer would have won the willie contest.

Jihad had jumped as the gun went off. Now he was shaking his head. "This isn't you, Gigi - "

"This *is* me. The clues have been there, you have just been too blind to see them."

"Or too trusting - of my own wife. A fourteen year secret, a fourteen year lie..." Jihad sighed deeply and then looked up. "You bitch." His whole body, his demeanour, his very aura, was suddenly different. He had changed. Each of the people in the room could feel it. As if the sigh had expelled his *qarin*, the *djinni* who is the constant companion of each human being, always whispering negative, bad, evil or disobedient thoughts. "Right, let's do this. But leave Fadi and Nada alone. You will have to run now anyway."

"Oh, he's laying down terms, is he? And who says I will have to run? Only you three know my secret." She held the Herstal in her left hand, the Browning in her right. She nodded at the room. "The problem with these old cardboard boxes they put you Palestinians in. They're like tinderboxes. They can go up with just the smallest spark - "

"You fucking - " Jihad leapt to his feet.

The guns twitched in his direction.

There was a thumping on the front door.

"Who is that?" asked The Confession.

"I am the Chief of Police of the camp," said Fadi from the floor. "It could be anybody. Maybe one of the tinderboxes has gone up."

"Get up. Answer it." She moved around the edge of the room, Jihad's eyes following her, his body shifting, always keeping her in front. She stopped by the far wall, outside the kitchen, so that she now had a view back into the room, the door to the small hallway at one o'clock. "Try anything and I will put a bullet in your fat wife's brain. Jihad, why don't you sit down?"

"I will stand." His eyes were cold.

"As you wish, whatever."

With some huffing, puffing and one more little accidental fart, Fadi rolled up onto his knees then stood up. He walked across the room, opened the door to the hallway and went out.

"Remember," warned The Confession. Fadi said nothing.

The three people in the room heard the front door grinding open. But there was silence, no voices, no muffled unintelligible conversation like the sound on a prime time television programme, not even any grunts. Nothing. Except the door being closed again.

Fadi came back in, shaking his head. "There was no one there."

The Confession raised the Browning in her right hand pointing it at the giant. "A bit late for the children to be playing Knock Down Yasser, isn't it?"

"But never too late for Djinns and Ladders," said a deep voice from the kitchen doorway as a gun was pressed hard against The Confession's head.

Everyone in the room froze. Nada on the couch, Fadi over by the hall doorway, Jihad in the centre, The Confession where she was, looking straight ahead at her husband but staring right through him.

Fadi's mouth dropped. Jihad frowned. Who on earth was this? *What* on earth was this? It was probably female, there were curves even though the body was hidden in biker's leathers. The hair was close-cropped and white. The eyes... the irises were white almost translucent, nearly blending with the sclera, the pupils also white but with the thinnest black ring.

Nada gasped and her hands began to shake as her lips moved, whispering softly *"'A'oothu billaahi minash-Shaytaanir-rajeem. Allaahu laa 'ilaaha 'illaa..."* I seek refuge in Allah from Satan the outcast - Allah! There is none worthy of worship but He... A *dua'a*, a prayer of supplication to protect against evil.

"I am sorry you had to see me like this," said the deep voice. "But it was your fault, Major, you put the ATL out on me."

"Carla?"

Fadi had not managed to close his mouth up. "W-... w-...?"

"Captain Lattouf, please tell your wife she has nothing to fear from me. Unlike you." She bumped the gun, a small Beretta 82, against The Confession's head. She reached with her right hand to take the Browning. "Let it go, let it go. There's a good little Jew."

"I am not - "

"Give the other one to your husband. Jihad take it." She nodded at the Herstal in The Confession's left hand.

But before Jihad could move, two things happened.

A voice from behind Fadi Lattouf said, "Daddy what is happening, who is that strange lady?"

And the lights went out.

Power cut.

In the darkness, there was a gunshot, a smash, a child screamed, an adult gasped.

For a moment there was the absence of sound which always happens after something monumental has happened, as if the world is coming to terms with the unexpected. Then: "Wait, wait!" said the voice of The Djinn. "Nobody move. Wait."

A bright beam pierced the room like a light-sabre. It was the torch on The Djinn's iPhone. It moved from person to person. Nada was still sitting in the chair, her eyes staring, possibly in total catatonia. Jihad was standing where he had been; he looked down at his body to ensure he had not been shot. Fadi was on his knees on the floor, arms outstretched, protecting the person behind him. Thirteen year old Lana Lattouf was standing shocked in the hall doorway, a quarter of her iPad in her hand, the rest of it scattered into glass and plastic crumbs on the lino. A bullet was embedded in the wall just inches from her chest.

The Confession was nowhere.

"She's gone," said Jihad.

"Not past me," said Fadi.

"Past me," said The Djinn. "I smelled her. She's gone the same way I came in. Over the back wall. I'm going after her." The beam whipped round into the kitchen and then disappeared with The Djinn.

In the renewed darkness, Fadi groaned to his feet. "Quickly, we can get her. She has to come out into Annan Street at some time. We call it Rome."

"What?" said Merhi.

"All roads lead here." Lattouf turned and bumped straight into his daughter. "Lana look after your mother. Abu Samer! *Yalla!*" The front door slammed open.

Jihad Merhi turned his head to the kitchen then turned towards the front door. "Lana," he murmured. "Do what your father says. We won't be long." He followed in Fadi's wake, realising he had no weapon, he had not had the chance to take the Herstal of off Gisele, and Carla had kept the Browning.

But he had his hands. "Fadi, wait!" he called in a loud whisper. "Where are you?"

Back in the house, Lana Lattouf walked carefully over to her mother. Her feet had been scratched by the exploding iPad but she felt no pain.

"Mama? Mama?" she shook Nada Lattouf and felt for her face in the dark. "It will be all right, Mama, it will be all right. Baba will sort it out. Allah is with him."

Even at thirteen, she did not know if she believed the words she was saying. But what she did believe in was the God of her age: the power that was social media. As she had walked silently down the stairs she had been recording all the sounds and talking that had been going on. She had come into the room and had recorded two seconds of the strange leather-clad creature that was over by the kitchen. If only her iPad had not been smashed, think of the sensation that would have caused on YouTube.

She would have gone viral.

30 October 2012
14 Dhu al-Hijja 1433

Bourj el-Barajneh, Beirut 00:05

The Djinn jumped over the back wall as if it did not exist, landing in a crouched position on the other side. She had never been to the Bourj el-Barajneh refugee camp so she had no way of orientating herself save for her internal body compass. North was straight ahead. It was dark but she turned the beam off on her iPhone, letting her eyes adjust naturally. Still in the crouching position, she raised her head and sniffed. Gisele had turned right. She would be looking for the quickest way out of the camp.

Tucking the small Beretta 82 into her leathers and keeping the Browning in her hand, The Djinn set off after The Confession.

"Fadi? Fadi!"

As Jihad Merhi walked cautiously down Annan Street, he noticed a massive oval shape at the side of the road. In the darkness everything was shadow, but this shade was panting for breath, leaning against a car.

"Do not worry, my friend," came Lattouf's voice from the shape. "I am always like this, it's the same when I go to the gym. Good cardio-vascular exercise."

The gym? "Where are we?"

Lattouf got his breath back. "The entrance to the camp is just down here on the left. This is my commute to work every day."

"Three minutes?"

"I know. I am a martyr. I am always exhausted by the time I get in."

"So we just wait?"

"She will come out this way."

"There *is* only one way in and out of the camp?"

"There is only one *road* in and out of the camp."

"So she could get out other ways?"

"Of course. This is not a prison. There are no high walls with barbed wire, no sentry towers. We are displaced Palestinians."

"Maybe we should go in. You can be my eyes, you'll know her likely route if she doesn't come out this way."

"If you think we should. But this exit needs to be guarded, her passage needs to be blocked."

As only a man can, Merhi thought that he would never again be doing that to Gisele. Whether or not he got out of this alive.

Lattouf pushed himself up off the car. As they walked warily towards the entrance to the camp, Merhi held out his hand. "It is starting to rain."

"Yes, it has been raining up here for a few minutes."

Merhi looked up at his friend and smiled.

Even if they had realised it, the knowledge would not have helped them as they were unaware of the significance, but they did not know and never would: the car Lattouf had been leaning on was a Jeep Wrangler Ultimate...

The Confession could not run as fast as she would have liked. Too much rubble on the ground, too many dangerously low cables hanging between the buildings (which she saw only at the last second as they bobbed down out of the darkness), too many broken half-open windows which could never be closed. It was like being on a Ghost Train at a fairground.

It was not meant to end like this. Her cover had been deep, her cover had been good. She could have stayed where she was, playing the bereft widow (with a sizeable Major's widow's pension), retaining her position as one of Lebanese State Security's top trainers, while all the while spying for Tel Aviv. Maybe she would have married again, in-house, to somebody in the security services (of a rank no lower than Captain, of course, the information quality would not be sufficient lower down).

Had it not been for one person. Damn you, Carla Chedid, damn you. She should have killed you at the ABC centre. She had intended to, because she had realised you were getting close, but somehow you had evaded her.

The Confession splashed into something wet on the floor, nearly turning her ankle. She ran on, feeling the rain starting.

She reached the road colloquially known as the Champs Elysée because it was the widest road in the camp: just over one metre across. She stopped. If she turned right, it must lead out of the camp. But if she turned left...?

Was it too late? Could she still salvage this? The only people who knew about her were here in this camp tonight. If they were all gone she could still save this operation...

The Djinn ran through the darkness, overhanging cables trying to capture her neck, the shadows of the permanently open windows grinning at her, the silhouettes of doorways gaping at her like the shocked, toothless open mouths of harridans.

She stopped at a corner, an intersection of three alleys. Once again she raised her head and sniffed. The camp was notorious for its smells but, like a tracker dog, once she was tuned in to a scent it stuck with her (well, she had been called a bitch enough times). Gisele was ahead and to the left.

Something dripped on her head from a cracked pipe above. She did not have the protection of her Carla-hair now and she could feel the wetness on her scalp instantly. She also felt it beginning to rain.

In the darkness to her left she could see four tiny pinpricks of light. Were there some residents out with torches? At this hour she would expect everybody to be inside. Who would be out in a power cut in the rain?

But they were not torches, they were not throwing any beams. They were just tiny lights, like LEDs. They were moving very subtly, like stringed fairy lights in a gentle breeze.

The rain became heavier, soaking the rubble and mud at her feet. There was a far-off rumble of thunder.

The Djinn remained completely still, not even breathing…

"Do you have any guns?"

Lattouf and Merhi were standing across the entrance to the camp in a not very enthusiastic they-shall-not-pass formation. Merhi spoke softly, almost whispering, not only in respect to the hour but also not to betray their presence in the darkness should Gisele come this way.

"The Palestinian police are strictly forbidden to carry arms," Lattouf's whisper was like a shout from a normal man. "It is one of the Conditions of Tolerance laid down by your government."

"You have not answered my question."

"Of course I do! I have two in my office. A Lee-Enfield No. 5 carbine and a Heckler & Koch HK 416."

"How far is your office?"

"One minute down there. Don't you remember? Near the old butcher's shop."

Merhi had been inside the camp once before but he had tried to blot it out of his mind. "Oh yes. Let's get them."

"But what if she goes past?"

"What can we seriously do if we're unarmed? She has the Herstal."

"But if we lose her…?"

"Okay, look, you go. I'll hide in the shadows, I might be able to break her neck."

Lattouf did a double-take but realised Merhi was not joking. "I will be right back."

The big oval shadow disappeared into the dark as Merhi stepped into a doorway out of the rain.

The Djinn pressed herself into the lee of the wall, feeling the crumbling, uneven breezeblocks on her back. The lights were still bobbing in the air, but were they coming towards her? They were so tiny it was hard to tell.

The rain became harder, turning from a shower into a substantial downpour. This would be in for the night. She sniffed the air again but the force of the rain was now masking any scent.

The lights were definitely coming her way. Somehow she had found herself against a black piece of wall which seemed recently painted. This would serve as a good camouflage for her leathers but it would enhance her white hair, her head would stand out. And so would her eyes...

She straightened up, holding the Browning out in front of her with both hands. Her eyes...

The four pinpricks of light stopped about five metres away. Then two of them moved forward to the left, the other two to the right.

"Hello sister," said a familiar voice, the voice of her nightmares.

"We have waited for this moment for so long," said the other voice, identical to the first.

"We have been patient."

"Now we have our reward."

There was a flash of lightning and Love and Paradise were illuminated in front of her.

Fadi Lattouf raced like an Olympic Champion towards the portakabin that served as the Bourj el-Barajneh police office. At least, he did in his mind. In reality he wobbled little faster than walking pace, gasping like a drowning man just pulled from the sea, a simile given extra credence because his hair and face were now soaking wet from the rain. As he reached the door, fumbling for his keys, finding the right one for the padlock, the electricity came back on in the camp. Not that it made much difference, there were no suddenly-blinding streetlights, no swathes of light to disorientate him, just a few diffused reflections coming from some of the windows in the dwellings. A radio began to play again, somewhere a dog barked.

He fumbled with the padlock then wrenched it off, the lock plate ripping out of the wood. Pulling open the door, he stumbled inside.

One light in one of the windows above showed that the electricity had come back on. The *houri* were still in shadow but The Djinn could now see them clearly.

"I am not your sister."

"Oh yes, truly you are," said Love.

"You became as one with us when we converted you," agreed Paradise.

"You never converted me, you bitches. You defiled me, you killed me, but you never, ever, converted me."

"Really? Look into your mirror."

"What mirror?" The Djinn still held the Browning in both hands.

"Look at us. We are your mirror. You are one of us. You are our sister."

The Djinn raised the gun and fired at the *houri* on the right, Paradise. The striker came down on the spring of the gun but nothing happened. The Djinn pulled the trigger again, pointing the gun at Love, then again, back to Paradise.

The twins giggled. "*Really?*" said Love. "Come, come, don't be silly."

The Djinn pushed her left hand into a pocket, pulling out the small Beretta 82 and slipping off the safety, firing towards Love. The hammer came down and hit the primer but nothing happened.

"Put them down," instructed Paradise tolerantly. "Put them down."

"I would like to say we don't want to hurt you," said Love. "But we do." Both *houri* put their hands up to their left shoulders where they had been shot two years ago.

The Djinn relaxed, bending her knees, dropping the guns the last twenty centimetres to the ground. Slowly she straightened back up, raising her hands in the air.

"Tonight we complete your total conversion," said Paradise. "You will reach ecstasy, like you did before."

"With us inside you," said Love. "You will die in rapture."

"Right here?" said The Djinn, clasping her fingers behind her head.

"No, on an altar of sacrifice." Love placed her hand on The Djinn's left shoulder, Paradise did the same on her right shoulder. The Djinn could feel the burning even through the leather.

"We have the perfect place," said Paradise. "*Yalla.*"

The Confession held the Herstal FN Five-SeveN in front of her as she walked down the Champs Elysée. Here and there a few lights were back on which helped her to see but it was still, basically and literally, as dark as night. Somewhere a baby cried. The rain was easing but her hair was plastered to her head, water dripping off her nose.

As much as she would have liked to continue in post, playing the widow, she realised she could not. Killing the head of the spycatchers was one thing – she would still do that if she was able – and killing the idiot Lattouf and his fat wife would be a relief for the world. Carla could be a problem but not an insurmountable one. But one thing she would have to do, and one thing she could not do, was to eliminate the Lattouf children. All six of them. She was not some sort of weird bitch machine like Carla, she was a woman – a Lebanese Israeli Intelligence Agent maybe, but a woman still. She might have shot the Lattouf girl, that was a collateral of war, but she could not cold-bloodedly kill the other five. So she would have to go. Get away. Live to fight another day?

She could see a few more lights on in Annan Street, about fifty metres away. Lattouf's car would be out on the street, she would hot wire it (Pursuit Evasion Techniques Level 4 Day 5) and be on her way. There were safe houses all over the country. She would head south.

Then a voice from behind her said, "Hello Gigi."

The alleys were so narrow they could not walk three abreast, so while Paradise held The Djinn's hands at the back of her head Love walked on, sufficiently in front to be out of kicking distance. At one point The Djinn stumbled, going down on one knee in a puddle that might have been water, but she was instantly dragged back up again by Paradise. They seemed to be heading towards the front of the camp.

They squeezed down an alley so tight that The Djinn's raised elbows almost touched both walls. It led to a small courtyard area. Three sides were blank walls with windows above. In the fourth wall there was an old door, broken and open. The Djinn could smell blood. Ancient blood and lots of it.

"The camp morgue," explained Love as if she was a tour guide. "Used to be a butcher's shop. A fittingly good use, don't you think?" She brushed rain off of her brow.

"The altar is inside," said Paradise.

"There is also a disposal gulley. You will meet al-Mahdi in pure, hollow form. No blood, no entrails. You will be a virgin again. See, are we not considerate?" Love's eyes shone just a little brighter in anticipation. "We will keep you alive as long as possible. You will enjoy this. Your rapture. Come."

As Love pushed the door open, Paradise shoved The Djinn forward. And that was the mistake.

The shove meant that Paradise let go of The Djinn's hands. Instantly The Djinn jumped forward, kicking Love in the back, sending her tumbling through the doorway. The Djinn turned to Paradise – and held up her left hand.

Paradise had her hands in the raised claw position, but what she saw stopped her from moving. In The Djinn's left palm was a tattoo of *ayn al hasud*, the evil eye. And it was glowing, the eye white, the sclera a deep blue.

Paradise's distraction was only momentary, but it was enough. The Djinn put her right hand back up behind her head and from inside the neckline of her leather jacket pulled out her husband's gift: a Holding Cross. As she leapt through the air, she twisted the cross in her palm so that the down beam poked out between her first and middle finger, the cross beam held within her fist.

The solid olive wood landed with a horrible cracking thud above Paradise's left eye. A scream came from inside beyond the doorway. Paradise gasped, her claws trying to raise to her head. The second strike split her skin. The third cracked her skull and she fell.

The Djinn was on top of her like a feral demon, banging the Holding Cross into the same place on her head, hearing the skull crack more, feeling it open. Something splashed up into her face but she kept thumping the cross against the skull, feeling hot, soft substance on her fingers.

Only when there was a seven centimetre hole in Paradise's head and the light had gone out of the open white eyes did The Djinn stop. Paradise was staring up into the rain. Her face was smiling.

The door behind banged and The Djinn whipped around. Love staggered out into the yard, holding her head above the left eye, blood and light pink matter oozing between her fingers. She looked at The Djinn, opened her mouth, and fell to her knees.

The Djinn stepped over, raised her fist with the Holding Cross – and then watched as the light switched off in Love's eyes and she fell sideways onto the wet, muddy ground. Her left leg twitched violently as the soul left her body, following her sister from the earth. Then she was still for eternity.

Slowly, The Djinn lowered her arm. She looked from one body to the other.

"*Ila jaheem ma'ik,*" she said.

Go to hell.

"What is happening?" Jihad Merhi stepped out of the doorway into the rain. "Is this a nightmare? Am I asleep?"

The Confession raised the Herstal Five-seveN. "You have been asleep for fourteen years."

"When...? How...?"

"Before I met you. Paris 1997, when that mad bitch shot me." Her left hand went up to her neck. "I was saved by the Israelis. Not by my own country but the Israelis. Without them I would have been dead. A woman called Melanie Nathanson recruited me. She remains my controller to this day."

"So everything has been a lie?"

"You were my target, I was to seduce you, marry you, even adopt your sons. And wait."

"Did you kill Rita?"

"We are not that callous. It was a genuine car accident. That was when we chose you, when she died. You were a rising *Molazim,* a Lieutenant with a good future. And a widower. You had a vacancy, we filled it."

"When were you activated?"

"Five years ago."

"Five years? When you started going back to work?"

"Having brought up your sons."

"Our sons."

"Your sons."

Jihad brushed water from his hair. He was grateful that the rain was falling onto his face. She wouldn't be able to see his tears.

"How did you become a killer?"

"I always have been. Even in Paris. That stupid bitch shot me but I killed her. And recently I have done things that you cannot even imagine. The nights I have been away – do you really think I have been giving classes somewhere else, in Tripoli, in Jbeil, up in Baalbeck for an overnight stay?"

"I had no idea."

"Husbands never do. They take everything for granted and they always become complacent. That is why I was ordered to marry you. To be the picture of domestic bliss."

Jihad sighed. Water dripped off of his chin, only some of it was rain. "So what now?"

"Now I have to complete my mission."

"You are going to shoot me?"

"Then the confession will be over. Job done. Thank you, Jihad, it has been fun."

She pulled the trigger and the Herstal spat flame.

The force of the bullet sent Jihad Merhi flying backwards, feet off the ground, slamming into the doorway he had stepped out of, his head banging against the door like a fugitive seeking sanctuary. A sanctuary that would be too late. Wordlessly his body sank to the ground.

And was still.

The Confession heard the bullet zip past her ear like a giant hornet before she heard the gun blast. She leant to her left, firing five rapid shots into the darkness. There was a thump, then a blinding pain in her right wrist as the Herstal exploded out of her hand.

As she saw the idiot Lattouf emerge from the night, a gun in his hand, firing, she turned and ran, zig-zagging over the rubble, crouching, not stopping, not looking back (Pursuit Evasion Techniques Level 2 Day 1). Bullets thudded into the ground near her feet, flew over her head, hit the walls, shards of breezeblock scratching her head, cutting her face.

Then the bullets stopped, but she kept running, down the wet, stinking path, out into Annan Street, putting the camp of death behind her.

"Abu Samer? Jihad? JIHAD!" Fadi Lattouf dropped the empty Heckler & Koch HK 416, dashing over to the body in the doorway. "In the name of Allah the most merciful, no, no!"

The giant fell to his knees, reaching out, touching a foot, shaking the leg. "Jihad... Jihad... No."

Gently, tenderly, he put an arm under the flopping head and pulled the body up into his arms, like a father cradles a child. He began to rock back and forth. With a sob, he began to recite *"Inna lillahi wa inna ilayhi raji'un..."* Surely we belong to Allah and to Him shall we return...

"Can I help?"

Lattouf's head snapped round. The woman in leather with the short cropped white hair and spooky white eyes was standing out on the path, the woman who used to be Zahia Zalloum then Carla Chedid then Suzi Saad. Something dark had been splashed across her face, giving her a strange freckled look. She did not have a gun, just an old carrier bag in her hand containing what looked like small sausages. Freshly made sausages because blood was dripping from the bag.

"What are you?" said Lattouf.

"I am what you see."

"You can do things, can't you?"

The Djinn shrugged.

With watery eyes, Lattouf asked "Can you raise people from the dead?"

The Confession ran out into Annan Street. It was quiet as befitted the hour. Very few lights were on in windows but as the street was of normal width, not tight and intimidating like the camp, it was easier to see out here. She was holding her right hand. Her wrist felt broken, but she could drive one-handed, at least to get away out of this area. She wondered if her Ducati had been discovered underneath the apartment block in Jounieh. She could sorely do with it now. She flipped her wet hair away from her face. The Lattouf house was only a minute or two up the road, the car was outside.

She maintained her run. There was nobody about but the Palestinian might be stupid enough to follow her. Mind you, she would hear him from kilometres away, like you hear a freight train in the distance long before it reaches you.

She saw the Datsun Bluebird up ahead. Outside the house. Just for a second her *qarin* whispered in her ear that she still had the opportunity to go inside and rid the world of Lattoufs forever. She could stay in Lebanon, play the grieving widow...

She dismissed the thought. Only because it was impractical, for no other reason.

She was grateful that the car did not lock. She had the door open when she became aware of a presence behind her. Keeping her injured right hand against her body, she turned.

A tall man was standing there. A man she knew. A man she liked. They had a history, especially in her fantasies. He was dressed in a leather jacket above a collarless white shirt. His hair was long, tied back into a simple ponytail, the left side pulled down to ensure it covered the hole where his left ear used to be.

"H- hello," she smiled. "I didn't expect to see you here." Was this her rescuer? Her knight in shining armour? Across the street she saw a motorbike, probably a Suzuki, she remembered he liked them.

"My mission is completed," he said.

"Really? So is mine. What say we get out of here?"

He shook his head. "That will not be possible. I have spent a long time on this mission. It started in 2010."

"Before we met?"

"Yes, when we met I did not know."

"Know what?"

"That you were one of them. Now you are the only one left, the last of the confession."

"What confession?"

"The group of Jews that killed Mahmoud al-Mabhouh in Dubai. You were in the room, weren't you? You were the one that injected him."

She stared at him in shock. How the hell did he know that?

"Hamas send their regards," said The Damascene. His hand came up, the Holding Cross protruding between his index and middle fingers. It rammed into the head of The Confession. She fell back into the car, The Damascene on top of her.

He did not stop punching until her head was unrecognisable, by which time she had been dead for three minutes.

He folded her feet into the car, then pushed the body over onto the passenger seat. There was blood and gore on the driver's seat but it could not be helped. It would wipe off his leather jacket and he could buy new jeans. He got in the car, closed the door and fiddled beneath the dashboard for a few moments. The Datsun roared into life.

The Damascene drove off, taking the last of The Confession with him.

Fadi Lattouf carried the body of Jihad Merhi in his arms. He was solemn, sad, still mumbling the verse from the Qur'an, the verse for the dead and those who had experienced tragedy in their life. His trousers were wet but he was oblivious to the rain.

The Djinn walked next to him. Despite the grief, one part of Lattouf wondered about the sausages the woman was carrying. He had never seen sausages with nails before...

He saw a car drive off up ahead, but he thought nothing of it. At his house he kicked the front door open, being careful not to bang the body as he carried it in.

Nada was inside, pale but back in the world. Lana was with her. Lattouf could hear his other children awake upstairs. Nada gasped when she saw her husband carrying his friend, and she flinched away just a little when she saw The Djinn, especially with her bloodied hands and gore-splattered face.

Lattouf laid the body down on the couch. "Bring water, woman, he must be washed."

As Nada and Lana went into the kitchen, The Djinn knelt on the floor beside the couch, stroking the still, pale face of Jihad Merhi.

Lattouf still mumbled his prayers, his eyes dull with sorrow and pain.

Pain…?

Nada and Lana carried in a brimming basin, but Nada stopped as she saw her husband, now no longer shielded by the body of his friend. "Fadi? The blood!"

"I know, it is Jihad's."

Why was the pain getting worse?

"No, Baba, look, look!" Lana pointed at her father's stomach.

Lattouf looked down. There were three bullet holes in his shirt, holes that were pumping blood. His trousers were already saturated, but not with the rain as he had thought

Fire shot through his belly like the skewers of Shaitan.

"Well, in the name of Allah…" said Fadi Lattouf. His eyes rolled into his head and he crashed onto the floor with the force and finality of a giant sequoia tree falling to earth.

EPILOGUE
خاتمة

FIVE MONTHS LATER
أشهر خمسة وبعد

23 March 2013
12 Jamada 1 1434

Jbeil, Lebanon 10:30

He sat at one of the tables outside the Bab el-Mina (Harbour's Gate) Restaurant looking out over the ancient Old Port of the Byblos of history. A few small boats were moored at the harbour side, bobbing contentedly, awaiting their masters on this warm, sunny Saturday. Over by the surviving but crumbling fortified Crusader tower at the harbour's entrance, a boat full of tourists set off for a short – and very expensive – trip along the coast.

The restaurant was not yet open so he had bought himself a coffee and a hummus wrap at the Citadelle Café up near the souk. It was his local, they knew him there. In fact he had bought two coffees and two wraps because he was expecting a guest.

He had asked his guest to come to his offices in the souk but his guest had asked to meet here first of all. There was nowhere more private than out in public.

It took him five minutes to eat the wrap (his appetite was not what it was) and he was casting lustful eyes at the second one when he saw his guest walking along the harbour side. He stood up, a grin creasing his face, huge hand raised into the air. "My friend, my friend!"

The guest stopped about three metres away, looking at the giant and shaking his head, smiling. There was a wetness in his eyes. He said simply, "Fadi."

Fadi Lattouf said simply, "Jihad."

They embraced with three cheek-kisses. Jihad went to step away but Lattouf pulled him back for three more kisses. "It is good to see you, Abu Samer."

"And it is good to see you, you great lump."

"Lump! Look at me! I am half the man I used to be!"

It was true he had lost a quarter of his bodyweight. In a normal person that would have been dangerous. In Fadi Lattouf it made no visual difference whatsoever. "Nada is trying to build me up, she says I am too skinny. She likes her men more... rotund."

Jihad laughed. They both knew that had it not been for Lattouf's rotundity, his massive gut, he would have died from his wounds in Bourj el-Barajneh five months ago.

"Sit, sit, my friend," urged Lattouf. "I have bought you breakfast."

They sat. Jihad took the lid off the coffee and reached for the wrap. Then he stopped, looking at Lattouf's doe-eyes, and pushed the wrap over. "You have it. I'm not hungry."

"It would be a shame to waste it," agreed Lattouf, and the wrap began its final journey.

Jihad Merhi let the warm sun caress his face as the Palestinian ate. After a moment he said, "Who would have thought, eh Fadi?"

Lattouf looked at his friend, his much-changed friend, unrecognisable from the man who used to be a Major in the Internal Security Force. His hair was now completely grey but he had let it grow and it was now a tight, if thinning, mop of curls. His five-day-old stubble still held reluctant flecks of brown. He had never been fat, but he had lost the layer of middle age, he was trim, fit.

"No regrets?" asked Lattouf.

"Total regret," said Merhi.

"About us?"

"No, no, we had always talked about it. It makes sense. But about everything else? Well, you know how I feel."

Lattouf shook his head. Allah had looked after Jihad, He had bestowed His blessings. Five months ago the bullet had past clean through Jihad's body, in the chest out the back, just nicking his spinal cord. He had spent weeks in hospital and, thanks to Allah, the cord damage was non-consequential and he had made a complete physical recovery. He had been thoroughly investigated by his erstwhile colleagues in the ISF and GSU (the one called Lieutenant Sebastien had been a particular little *ilishael*, he was a turd, he would go far), the eventual findings being that while Major Jihad Merhi had not known what was going on and had committed no crime, he *should* have known what was going on and should have stopped the crimes that *were* committed. Ignorance and trust were crimes in themselves. He was requested to fall on his sword. Jihad Merhi had been retired on a Major's pension, no lump sum.

What had happened to Merhi's wife might never be known. Was it her that had driven off in Lattouf's Datsun Bluebird on that fateful night? Who knew? Neither she nor the Bluebird had ever been seen again (although in early February the burnt-out shell of a vehicle had been found in a ravine near Birket el Bouhairi, on the border with Syria, the closest point of the border to Damascus. It was thought the vehicle had been obliterated by insurgent or regime rockets. Rumour had it that one, just one, flake of orange paint was found on the metallic skeleton).

Merhi finished his coffee and looked at his friend. His true friend. God had looked after Fadi, He had bestowed His blessings. Fadi had spent a month in hospital, undergoing three operations to remove the bullets from his gut and repair the internal damage (anaesthetising the giant had been difficult and additional supplies of desflurane had had to be flown in from Saudi Arabia). The doctors had agreed that the bullets would have killed a normal person but the sheer size of the Lattouf gut had prevented any mortal damage (which nevertheless did not stop the doctors advising him to lose weight 'for the sake of his health').

The groups had asked Lattouf and his family to leave Bourj el-Barajneh (outside agencies could not be permitted to wreak havoc in a Palestinian refugee camp, that was the preserve of the groups). A new police chief had been sought and Captain Manar al-Jayouchi from down in Bourj el-Shimali had moved up two months ago. Fadi Lattouf had retired – with nothing.

Nothing, that is, except the property he had inherited from his cousin Chadi two years ago. The property in the Jbeil souk, up near the Roman road and backing onto the cemetery, a two-storey building with enough room upstairs to house a family of seven and with spacious (by souk standards) offices downstairs.

"I have something for you." Lattouf picked up a carrier bag from the seat next to him and took out a large rectangular object wrapped in tissue paper. "Now it is for real." He smiled as he handed the object to Merhi.

It was heavy, making a scraping sound like there were two items inside. Merhi laid it down on the table and opened the tissue paper to reveal a golden metallic rectangle about twenty-five centimetres by fifty, with pre-drilled holes in the corners. A business wall-plate.

Lattouf & Merhi

Muhaqqiq Khass
Détectives Privés
Private Enquiry Agents

"Lattouf and Merhi?"

"Look at the other one."

Merhi raised the plate and removed another piece of tissue paper to reveal an almost identical plate underneath – except this one read '**Merhi & Lattouf**'.

"Why worry?" said Lattouf. "We put one one side of the door the other the other! Palestine and Lebanon, working side by side as always!"

Merhi smiled, nodding. "I don't know how you do it, Fadi, but you always come up with the solution."

Lattouf spread out his hands in self-deprecation. "Allah guides me."

"You know, my friend, I believe he does." Merhi looked out over the harbour. "A new beginning, eh? Do you know what today is Fadi?"

"Saturday?"

"In the Christian calendar, tomorrow is Palm Sunday." (Lattouf looked at his hands.) "In the Eastern Orthodox and Byzantine churches, the day before Palm Sunday is known as Lazarus Saturday. He was the friend who Jesus – Isa – raised from the dead. Fitting, eh?"

"We rise like the *anka'oo*, the phoenix. No one can keep Lattouf and Merhi down!"

"Merhi and Lattouf."

"Now, *yalla*," Lattouf stood up. "Nada is expecting us. We are having a little celebration, to mark the start of our new career, our new life. She is cooking camel tongue and pigeon livers, with garlic couscous."

"And a little salad?"

"Of course! We must have our five a day!"

The men laughed. As they walked away along the harbour's edge, Fadi reached round and pulled his pants from his backside, releasing a loud, rumbling fart. "Excuse me, the hummus." The water of Byblos Harbour trembled and Jihad Merhi wondered if Cyprus should be warned to expect a tsunami later that day.

Midtown, New York City, USA 09:30 (local time)

The woman in the black leathers lay on the roof of the New York Public Library and looked down the telescopic sight of the Accuracy International AWSM Sniper Rifle. It was a fine, windless day – always preferable. Down below, Manhattan's commuters were crossing Bryant Park, some picking up their morning coffee, some stopping for a quick breakfast at the Southwest Porch eatery. She could have picked off any of them should she have wished but she was a professional. She had just one target.

She thought back. Was it only six months ago when she had met Benjamin David down there? The civilian support at the Israeli Consulate who had given her the information that led to those events in Lebanon? Seemed like a lifetime ago.

She no longer worked for the Lebanese Department of General Security, she had quit after the carnage in Bourj el-Barajneh (quite frankly, her masters had been pleased to see her go, too much of a liability being exiled from Lebanon but still working for the country at the United Nations). She was now freelance. Like her husband. She had decided it was time for a new life. Literally.

She moved onto her right hip to ease the pressure on her belly. She was just beginning to show. Yesterday she had felt the first flutter. The doctors had said it might be twins – but they always said that, didn't they?

Twins... No way, she had had enough of twins, she was not going to be the catalyst for them to be born again. Her baby was going to be singular and normal. Well, as normal as the child of a djinn could be.

She threw back her jet black hair, her black left eye focusing down the scope. It was 09:30 and, like all good freelance mercenaries, she had done her research, she knew her target well. He would be on time.

Over the far side of the park she could see a man sitting on a bench. A dark haired bearded man from the Syrian Consulate over on Second Avenue. She saw him look at his watch and then he noticed somebody coming towards him from the south eastern side of the park, underneath her. She made a final adjustment to the recticle, the crosshairs, in her scope and waited.

Her target walked into her view. She would have one shot only and she would be merciful. He would not even know he was dead. She followed his back across the park and waited until he stopped in front of the Syrian.

She focused on the head of her target. The man in the denim jeans, leather jacket and collarless white shirt, long hair pushed back in a ponytail but pulled down the side of his face to cover his missing left ear.

Her nailless finger tightened on the trigger...

You have made The Confession.

You are absolved.

GLOSSARY OF ARABIC AND HEBREW WORDS AND PHRASES
والعبارات الكلمات والعبرية العربية للغة معجم

Arabic

'aalaykum al-salaam	[and] upon you peace
Aasif	sorry
Abbaya	voluminous black overdress worn by local women in Arabia
Abu	a *kunya*, a name honourably given to the father of an Arabic child, Abu (father) plus the name of the first son, as in Abu Yo'roub
ad-Dajjal	in Islam: the Great Deceiver, the devil
Agal	rope (usually two circles) worn on the head, holding a *keffiyeh* in place
Ahbal	idiot
Ahlan	hello
Alhamdulillah	praise be to God/Thank God
al-Janna	paradise/heaven
Allahu Akbar	God is great
Al-salaam 'aalaykum	peace upon you
Anka'oo	phoenix
Arak	aniseed-based drink, a relative of absinthe, ouzo and similar
Argileh	Lebanese word for shisha pipe or *nargileh*
Arnab	rabbit
Ashta	clotted cream with rose water
Asr salat (salat al-Asr)	afternoon prayer
Awarma	preserved meat fat
Ayn al hasud	The Evil Eye
Azan	Islamic call to prayer
Baiid baladi	fresh country eggs
Baklava	layers of filo pastry filled with chopped nuts and sweetened with syrup or honey
Barjeel	windtower
Batatis	potatoes
Beyti beytak	'My house is your house'
Burnus	a long, hooded cloak, usually of coarse fabric
Charafna	delighted to meet you
Chou esmak	what is your name? [to a man]
Dallah	traditional Arabic coffee pot, curved shape with spout, lid and handle, often ornate
Dishdasha	the standard Arabic male outer garment, ankle length long sleeves, like a robe; also called a *thawb* and a *kandura*
Djinn	origin of the English word 'genie'. In Arabic folklore and Islamic teachings, djinn, humans and angels make up the three sentient creations of God. Djinn can be good, evil, or neutrally benevolent. in modern usage it can also mean a seductive, beguiling female
Dua'a	a prayer of supplication
'eeh	yes

Eid	a festival or holiday, notably *Eid al-Fitr* (the Festival of the Breaking of the Fast) at the end of Ramadan, and *Eid al-Adha* (the Festival of the Sacrifice) which always falls on 10 Dhu al-Hijja in the Islamic calendar
Eid Mubarak	'Blessed *Eid*', a greeting used at *Eid*
Falafel	deep fried ball or patty made from ground chickpeas and/or fava beans
Falaj	irrigation system of underground channels supplying water from mother wells dug into the water table
Fajr salat (salat al-Fajr)	dawn prayer
Farouj meshwi	grilled chiken
Fattoush	bread salad
Firdaus	the highest level of Paradise
Fitra	alms given at the end of Ramadan
Ftoor	breakfast
Ghadae	lunch
Ghouleh	a female *ghūl* (ghoul), a demon
Habibi	darling (said to a male but now often used for females also)
Habibti	darling (said to a female but *habibi* usually used)
Hammam	bath/bath house
Hamsa	a palm-shaped amulet with an eye in the centre
Hajj	the annual pilgrimage to Mecca
Hijab	scarf or veil covering the female head and chest, with the face exposed (sartorial)
Hojari	silver frankincense, the best quality
Hon	here
Houri	in Islam, houri are the companions of humans and djinn who enter paradise. They have great beauty and are noted for their white eyeballs and black pupils. They can be male and female. In European usage, houri are voluptuous, beautiful, alluring women
Ibneh	a soft, white cheese similar to feta
Ila jaheem ma'ik	go to hell
Ilishael	shit
Insh'allah	God willing
Izaar	a male garment like a sarong which can be worn under a *dishdasha* or as a lower outer garment.
Jahannam	hell
Jamal	camel
Jawani	chicken wings in a lemon, garlic and coriander sauce
Jilbaab	traditional long, loose-fitting garment worn by some Muslim women
Jisr	bridge
Kaaba	the most sacred site in Islam, the cube-shaped building surrounded by the *Masjid al-Haram* mosque in Mecca, Saudi Arabia
Kafan	cloth to cover a corpse
Kafirs	non-believers (in Islam)
Kakhbah	swear word: equivalent to 'son of a bitch'
Kebbeh	meatballs stuffed with pine nuts and minced meat
Keffiyeh	Middle Eastern headdress
Khaetrak	goodbye (to a man)[Levantine Arabic]
Khiyar	cucumber

Khobz	Arabic flat bread
Khodi balik	be careful (said to a woman)
Kibbeh nayeh	minced lamb or beef, served raw
Kifak?	How are you? (To a man)
Knefeh	a baked dessert of semolina pastry and cheese served with a sweet syrup
Kunafi	pastry stuffed with sweet white cheese, nuts and syrup
Kunya	a name honourably given to the mother or father of an Arabic child. Abu (father) or Umm (mother) plus the name of their first son, as in Abu Yussuf or Umm Samer
Labneh	strained yoghurt, very soft cheese made from strained yoghurt
Loukoum	Turkish delight (confectionary)
Luban	frankincense
Lubya	bean stew
Maa?	What?
Ma`a as-salāma	Goodbye ('Go in peace')
Ma'amoul	small, decorated shortbread pastries with nut filling
Ma'asel	tobacco for *argileh* or shisha
Mabruk	congratulations; good luck
Madrassa	place of learning
Maghrib salat (salat al-Maghrib)	sunset prayer
Majlis	meeting room, sitting room, lounge
Makanek	a spicy Lebanese sausage
Mana'eesh	Lebanese pizza, a circle of cooked dough topped with a mixture of thyme and sesame seeds
Manousheh	filled flat bread (with cheese, zaatar and similar)
Maqluba	meat, rice and fried vegetables placed in a pot, which is then flipped upside down when served, hence the name, which translates literally as "upside-down"
Marid	a large and powerful wish-granting djinni, a giant
Ma sha'allah	God has willed it (literal)
Mashraha	mortuary
Massah el-khair	Good afternoon/good evening
Mekhallel	pickled vegetables
Merci ktir	thank you very much (mixture of French and Arabic)
Merhaba	Hello
Moghrabieh	semolina cooked with meat and spices
Molazim	Lieutenant
Moukafaha	Lebanese Special Forces Counter-Sabotage (Terrorism) regiment
Muhaqqiq khass	Private investigator
Mukhabarat	the Intelligence/Security Service
Muntasif an-nahar	midday
Mutabal	aubergine dip
Muqaddam	Lieutenant-Colonel (military rank)
Nazar	eye-shaped amulet to ward of the Evil Eye
Niqab	veil or mask covering the female face (sartorial)
Qahwa	coffee
Qarin	a *djinni* who is the constant companion of each human being, always whispering negative, bad, evil or disobedient thoughts
Qiblah	the direction that should be faced when a Muslim prays, towards the *Kaaba* in Mecca
Ra'id	Major (military rank)
Rais	leader, chief, boss

Raka'ah	cycle or unit of prayer
Rakwe	long-handled coffee pot used for serving Turkish coffee
Raqs sharqi	belly-dance (literally: 'Oriental dance')
Sabah a Allah	God is good
Sabah el-khair	Good morning
Salaam	Peace (greeting)
Sahir	a wizard
Sahira	a witch
Sahtik!	Cheers!
Samak mishwa	kebabs of monkfish, lemon and pepper
Samkeh harra	spiced fish
Sayadieh	fish with rice
Seejaere	cigarette
Shahada	The Islamic Creed
Shaitan	Satan
Shawarma	food: an Arabic wrap
Shayla	headscarf
Shorbat adas	lentil soup
Shou	What?
Shukran	Thank you
Subhana rabbiyal a'ala	Glory be to my Lord, the most high
Taban	of course!
Tabouleh	a salad traditionally made of bulgur, tomatoes, cucumbers, parsley, mint, onion and garlic, and seasoned with olive oil, lemon juice, and salt
Takbir	The Arabic name for the phrase *Allahu Akbar*
Tasbih	prayer beads
Tayyib	okay
Tfaddal	Come in (To a man)
Uhktee	sister
Umm	a *kunya*, a name honourably given to the mother of an Arabic child, Umm (mother) plus the name of the first son, as in Umm Samer
Ustaz	'Uncle', a term of respect for elderly males
Wa'l-aks	vice-versa
Wasm	the owner's brand on a camel
Yaatik al-aafieh	May God give you strength
Yadreb asfoorayn behajar	'Kill two birds with one stone'
Ya khorg	asshole
Yalla	let's go (or 'come' in the same context)
Yatama	orphans
Yawm al-Qiyamah	Judgment Day
Zaqqum tree	a thorned tree that Muslims believe grows in hell. Its fruit is spiked and bitter; those in hell are forced to eat it to add to their discomfort
Za'atar	a popular Middle eastern herb mixture (ground dried thyme, oregano, marjoram, mixed with toasted sesame seed, and salt)

Hebrew

Benzona	son of a bitch
Bodel	a young person, usually Jewish, running errands and performing chores for Mossad agents
B'seder	okay
Harah	shit
Mah Ha'Inyanim?	how are things?
Mamash Tov	really good
Ma shimkha	what is your name?
Sayan	an 'assistant', an operative recruited locally to help with Mossad operations in their own country
Shalom	hello/peace

Also available

DAVID CULLEN

THE EUROPEAN COLLECTION

THE EYE OF MAKARIOS
THE MESRINE CONCLUSION
THE WINDSOR SECRET

DAVID CULLEN
THE EUROPEAN COLLECTION

Three full-length novels

THE EYE OF MAKARIOS

1974. From the USA to Russia, from the Middle East to Europe,
the chase is on to find THE EYE OF MAKARIOS
- before the world explodes into chaos.

THE MESRINE CONCLUSION

1978. Can French Public Enemy Number One Jacques Mesrine
retrieve the stolen dark secret of the British Royal House of
Windsor before his hunters track him down?

THE WINDSOR SECRET

1997. The dark secret of the British Royal House of Windsor
leads to the death of Princess Diana in Paris.

plus bonus short story

SHADE
There are no such things as ghosts

ISBN 978-0-9559911-7-2

DAVID CULLEN

KNOCK ON MY DOOR

ONE LOVE, ONE LIFE - A THOUSAND DEATHS

"They say a lady should always have some secrets, layers which she allows to be peeled away only by the intimate few, a striptease that goes beyond the physical… The hard part is when the layers of your mind are stripped away also, level by level, until the very core of your being is exposed. And if that is attacked too, if the very essence of who you are is taken away, what are you left with? Nothing. So how far shall I strip for you? How far should I go? All the way?"

Based on true events, David Cullen tells the story of Carly, a woman who thought she had met The One to take her to heaven – and found herself in the depravity of hell itself.

**She thought he was the love of her life.
He thought he was the end of it.**

KNOCK ON MY DOOR
ISBN 978-0-9559911-3-4

also available as a eBook and on Amazon Kindle

David Cullen